The Hermit of 69th Street is the most ambitious of Jerzy Kosinski's fictional works—which include his world-renowned novel *The Painted Bird*—and is his most commanding novel to date. Dubbed an "autofiction" by the author, it is at once suspenseful and funny, savage and tender, sexual and pious. It is a compulsive adventure in which Kosinski explores the complex universe of one Norbert Kosky, a survivor of the Holocaust, immigrant to America from the only slightly mythical country of Ruthenia, and successful but tortured writer in search of spiritual order and freedom, especially the freedom to be himself in the ultimate sense. Kosky is a born storyteller whose rise to fame, as well as his downfall, stem from both his sadistically realistic fiction and his buoyant self, no less than from his well-publicized ability to levitate publicly in water.

A roller coaster, *The Hermit of 69th Street* takes the reader on a wild ride through extravagant, often untrodden psychological landscapes. It fuses and, says the author, willingly confuses footprints and footnotes, alchemy and spiritually, sex and cabala. It is Jerzy Kosinski at his narrative best.

BOOKS BY JERZY KOSINSKI

NOVELS
The Painted Bird
Steps
Being There
The Devil Tree
Cockpit
Blind Date
Passion Play
Pinball
The Hermit of 69th Street

ESSAYS
Notes of the Author
The Art of the Self

NONFICTION
(under the pen name of Joseph Novak)
The Future Is Ours, Comrade
No Third Path

THE
HERMIT OF
69th STREET

THE WORKING PAPERS OF NORBERT KOSKY

JERZY KOSINSKI

ZEBRA BOOKS
KENSINGTON PUBLISHING CORP.

For Katherina,

Although I conquer all the earth,
yet for me there is only one city.
In that city there is for me only one house;
And in that house, one room only;
and in that room, a bed.
And one woman sleeps there,
The shining joy and jewel of all my kingdom.

(Sanskrit)

Those who read this book,
we beg them to correct anything
they may see which is amiss.
For they who wish
to understand such things,
know well
how hard the matter is.

(Willem van Hildegaersberch, late 14th century)

Preface

Norbert Kosky left this English-language *brudnopis* (Ruthenian for working papers) on *Nostromo,* an unassuming fishing junk he leased from the Manhattan Marina shortly before his untimely disappearance.

These Working Papers first came into my possession when, some few years ago, I was entrusted by the trustees of Norbert Kosky's Fund with the task of bringing them to the attention of his reading public.

A painful experience in childhood, a disappointing love, a cruel father, and numberless facts of personal biography may be a window on the work of the author, but notebooks such as these stand closer to the work than does any event.

writes Edward Wasiolek[1] and what he writes fully applies to Norbert Kosky, the Hermit of 69th Street, as he was commonly known among his friends.

—Jerzy Kosinski

---

[1]From the Introduction to *The Notebooks for Crime and Punishment:* Fyodor Dostoevsky Edited and Translated by Edward Wasiolek (The University of Chicago Press, Chicago and London, 1967).

1

The present book is intended, as far as possible, to give an exact insight into the theory of relativity. . . . The author has spared himself no pains in his endeavor to present the main ideas in the simplest and most intelligible form, and on the whole, in the sequence and connection in which they actually originated. . . . May the book bring someone a few happy hours of suggestive thought. (Albert Einstein, Preface, 1916)[1]

At the Manfred, the turn-of-the-Century brownstone, its stone no longer brown, on Manhattan's seamy West 69th Street, all the lights have gone out — but one. Appropriately, the single sixty-watt bulb shines in a two-room apartment above the head of one Norbert Kosky, a latter-day esoteric hermit[2] who, pencil in hand, frenetically scribbles one word

------

[1]Albert Einstein, *General Theory of Relativity*, 1915. Einstein, the German-Jew, was lucky because already in 1919, "observation of the total eclipse of the sun bears out Einstein's theory of relativity" (Bernard Grun, 1975). Meanwhile, in storytelling, no matter how far it is carried away, no novelist can count upon to have his or her view of narrative relativity visibly borne away.

[2]*Shall we again bring up the subject of whether a work such as The Hermit Saints Triptych, a piece of modest dimensions, was conceived as an object of worship and stood upon an altar? The Hermit Saints Triptych:* in Hieronymus Bosch, The Complete Works, Antwerp, 1987 "the best Bosch book ever" (Jay Kay, 1988).

after another on yellow white six-by-nine-inch index cards spread out on his desk.

Kosky is a frenetic man. His frenzy stems primarily from his four-decades long preoccupation with words and letters no less than it does with breathing. Even numbers—even as well as uneven—are figures of speech to him. And speech—speech meaning expression as free as breathing—means, a world to him. No wonder: an aspiring master of the Ruthenian-Jewish oral tradition and an adept of Tantric Yoga,[3] he has been since 1965 a naturalized American. Besides, the year 1966 saw the publication of the unexpurgated edition of his first fictional narrative tale, about a little Gypsy or Jewish toddler during World War II. In order to render his tale as fictional as he feasibly could (by then he himself was a monstrous basket case), he refused to affix to his novel any biographical note—other than his name, first and last, and the name of Jerome (or Hieronymous) Bosch, (d.1516) the painter whose Monster with a Basket, a fragment from his triptych "Last Judgement", was reproduced on the reader-alerting book's cover. This is the very Bosch who once portrayed Christ as a little naked toddler entirely in *grisaille*, i.e. in black and white.[4]

SS

Writes Kosky on the margin: according to every numerologist's indispensable *The Timetables of History: A Horizontal Linkage of People and Events* (by Bernard Grun, based on

---

[3]Yogatantra—Yoga; the yoke; tantra; the loom; also the power to harness; also a manuscript of a book. See *Tantric Yoga: The Art of Primal Concentration,* by George Niskisko (Los Angeles, 1982).

[4]Defending Bosch almost 400 years ago, Fra Siguenza wrote, "If there are any absurdities here, they are ours, not his." Bosch described terrible, unbearable holocausts crushing mankind for its sins. In a century of turmoil and strife, it is hard not to feel that the absurdities pictured before us may, after all, be our own. (Stanley Meisler, *The World of Bosch,* Smithsonian, March 1988).

Werner Stein's *Kulturfahrplan,* 1975), in 1965 the Nobel Prize for Literature went to M. A. Sholokov. That's unfair, considering that it did not go, say, to Dostoyevsky or Conrad! In that very year six former Auschwitz prison officials were sentenced to life imprisonment in a normal prison instead of say, being condemned to death in a Nazi-built oven. Just as well, since the penalty of death has already been imposed on all of us (and *accident, that master nihilist* [Karol Irzykowski] can carry out this penalty at any time, I oppose arbitrary imposition of it for a second time!

In addition, the year 1965 saw such spiritually sensational headlines as PRESIDENT JOHNSON APPOINTS ABE FORTAS TO THE SUPREME COURT. FELIX FRANKFURTER DIES. MARTIN BUBER, THE FELIX FRANKFURTER OF JEWISH PHILOSOPHERS, DIES. POPE PAUL VI VISITS NEW YORK. RALPH NADER DECLARES DRIVING A U.S.-MADE CAR UNSAFE AT ANY SPEED.

Nothing blunts and destroys taste so much as endless journeying; the poetic spirit is not the wandering Jew. (Sainte-Beuve, 1869)[5]

Sainte-Beuve might be wrong; nothing typifies poetic spirit more faithfully than the spirit of a wandering Jew. Particularly if the wandering Ahasuerus[6] happens to be wandering into his self by means of writing (defined here as writing on one's inner wall as well as an omen. PRINTER: omen not amen), fully aware that "Death and Life are in the power of the tongue." (Proverbs 18:21)

Lost in writing, (lost, but also found), Kosky hears Hear O Israel! The phrase resounds resolutely in the lobe of his ear — the ear being Kosky's euphemism for his heart as well as his mind.

---

[5]Charles Augustin Sainte-Beuve (d. 1869): An inspired literary critic who, daring enough to ask *What is a classic?,* was wisely inspired not to answer such a daring question.

[6]"We have not yet encountered this syndrome in those of Jewish origin," write in a footnote on page 77 M. David Enoch and W. H. Trethowan in The Munchausen Syndrome, chapter six of Uncommon Psychiatric Syndromes, London, 1979.

"The sound sounds only for as long as it is heard by your sublime inner lobby." Kosky now hears his inner monk tell him. **Whatever is manifested as sound in the heart or in the ear is a power of nature. The state of decomposition of conceptual thought is beyond all form. It is divine. (Hatha Yoga Pradipika, No. 100)**[7]

No terrestrial being can disregard the sound of life — certainly not at a time when firing of even one wrong SS [surface to surface] — no matter how small — "can turn into a world-beheading headline or behead the world," in the words of WHM World Headline Making Channel 6 TV.

RISK OF WAR. **Thanks to the addition of many of the latest SS missiles to the multinational arsenal, the world is now on the brink of a new era — the age of strategic serfdom.** *(New Speak Magazine).*

Extinguishing the lights in his flat here flatly defined as a 2 1/2 rms. with 1 1/2 bathrooms $669/month flat, our literary numerologist[8] goes out to scan the urban marshland for signs of life.

SS

Out on the street, walking back and forth and back again between Sixth and Ninth avenues, in front of the infamous

---

[7]Hatha Yoga does not distinguish between the inner light and the inner sound. To a Tantric, words emanate images which talk to the eye and images are heard by the soul (as transcribed by Hans Urich Rieker, op cit.). For the most apt rendering of such spiritual "meeting of the eyes" (Rawson), the reader is henceforth most urgently referred to the color plate No. 66 ("the twist which affects the pattern of energies in the spinal column," Nepal, eighteenth century) and the black-and-white plate No. 69 ("Couple from 'Heaven Bands'") in *The Art of Tantra,* by Philip Rawson, 1978.

[8]Numerology: a time-tested spiritual system of predicting one's fate, based on the numerical value concealed in the alphabet, and hence in one's name (as first practiced by the ancient Hebrews and codified by Alessandro di Cagliostro).

Chamisso Towers for the Homeless "who barely living in the street gutters as human litter, literally menace our collective mind and our very soul." (Jay Kay).

Suddenly, the phone rings in the nearby glass-encased empty telephone booth. The phone rings twice, three times, four. A wrong number, no doubt, but to a numerologist no number is wrong. Should Kosky answer the call?

Why shouldn't he? **The only part of the conduct of anyone, for which he is amenable to society, is that which concerns others. In the part which merely concerns himself, his independence is, of right, absolute. Over himself, over his own body and mind, the individual is sovereign. (John Stuart Mill, 1859)**[9]

A good Samaritan who believes in R.S.V.P., as much as he does in the calling of life—a calling so often made by a fundamental caller—Kosky rushes to the booth—and he rushes into it with the speed of John Stuart Mill bodily rushing into Mrs. Harriet Taylor on their first physical love-filled meeting of the minds. He picks up the receiver on the sixth ring.[10]

"Sorry! Wrong number." He whispers into the receiver the public domain's most public cliché.

"Don't be sorry," answers a man's voice. "It's the right number. You're my number now!"

---

[9]*On Liberty,* (1982 ed.), page 60.

[10]As every numerologist trained in the hieroglyphical interpretation of the Hebrew alphabet knows, number six stands for the letter W or *waw,* the sixth letter of the Hebrew alphabet, which signifies, according to *The Mysteries of the Quabalah* (1922), "the eye of man as well as the ear is the emblem of water. According to the same by-now-well-tested theory, standing for *T* or for *teth,* the ninth letter of the Hebrew alphabet, the number nine stands for a refuge, resistance and shelter." Finally there is *yod,* the tenth letter, which stands for all manifested power. See also "Kabbalah" (Chapter 10) in *The Earth Is the Lord's: The World of the Jew in Eastern Europe,* by Abraham Joshua Heschel (1949–1977), pp. 69ff. (A spiritual must written initially in Yiddish by my all-time spiritual guru! Norbert Kosky, 1981).

"How did you find me?" asks the always curious Kosky.

"Through my infrared field glasses my friend. The infrared makes you look yellow, but I don't mind. I like what I see!" says the far-out urban ranger bent on his Binocular Sport/Utility Pickup™, the newest far out big-town adventure.

This colossal centralization, this agglomeration of three and a half million people on a single spot has multiplied the strength of these three and a half million inhabitants a hundredfold . . . But the price that has been paid is not discovered until later. (Engels)

Dumbfounded, Kosky looks up at the block upon block of hotels, hospitals, apartment houses and office buildings and subway entrance which scraping the moonlit sky, block the moonlight like a multifloored domino. The Voice-Over could be watching over him, as well as looking him over, from just about anywhere above, next door or below. Kosky suddenly crouches down in the phone booth as if it were a flat-bottomed canoe, thus disappearing from sight.

"Now you see me, now you won't." Kosky turns into a Jewish *waterchilde* hiding from the German-Nazi SS in the Pripet marshland during the war![11]

"Hey! Where are you?" the Voice screams.

"Here!" Kosky says, getting up.

---

[11]Mare Herodotis, now known as Pripet (pron. P*ree*pet) Marshes in Polesie with its fisherfolk and fishes were until 1945 the most inpenetrable "unique corner of Europe" (Louise A. Boyd, 1937) its maze of swamps, slough, and waterways forming in pre-war Poland a swampland, as large as Holland and Belgium combined. (J. K.)

"Polesie is a geographic entity in Eastern Europe extending along the Pripet River . . . The Pripet has a number of tributaries which form an excellent communication network for the region . . . Polesie can be generally characterized as a region of marshlands and forest . . . Only a small amount of the total land area was cultivated or in meadowland. . . . Isolated both geographically and culturally, Polesie thus attracted the attention of Slavic ethnographers who viewed it as an archaic region, a territory of conservative folk culture. Throughout its history Polesie (and all of Pripet, J. K.) had

"Good! Tell me, why are you out so late—?"

And when he had worked for hours at a stretch, forgetting food and sleep and everything, he would rise from his desk at last and stagger forth into the nighttime streets, reeling like a drunkard with his weariness. (Thomas Wolfe)

"I'm out looking for my opposite number."

"By the by," the Voice intones. "Where does your accent come from?"

"Ruthenia. Ruthenia used to be part of the Polish Commonwealth until 1939."[12] You see—accept this is something even you can't see—I'm *Rusin*. In English Rusin means Ruthenian. "The word is derived from both, Ruth, the idyllic Moabite widow in the eighth book of the Old Testament and ruthenium, the silver-grey metallic chemical element No. 44 used as hardener in jewelry, pen nibs and pivots of musical instruments."

"Tell me, my ruthless friend, I can't quite make it out from here—are your pants made of leather?"

"Wool."

"What about your jacket?"

"Pure cotton."

"How do you stay so trim?"

"Easy. I'm an all-around Yale stoic."[13]

---

been one of the most economically and culturally backward areas in the Slavic world." *"About Polesie"* by Oksana Irena Grabowicz in *The Changing Peasantry of Eastern Europe* by Joseph Obrebski, 1976.

[12]"Those Ruthenians incorporated into the Crown in 1569 obtained all the privileges already enjoyed by the Polish nobility as well as by the Ruthenian nobility on the lands earlier incorporated into the Crown by Kazimierz the Great." (*Ruthenia, Cossackdom, the Ukraine, and the Commonwealth of Two Nations,* by Andrzej Sulima Kaminski, *The Polish Review,* 1987).

[13]The philosophy of Stoicism was most convincingly professed by Lucius Annaeus Seneca (died A.D. 65), a Roman Spaniard, in a collection of his public essays disguised as private letters. (Imperative: read again *The Stoic Philosophy of Seneca:* Essays and Letters of

"Is your widow's peak black or white? I don't mean your widow. I mean: your skin color. I can't quite make it out from here."

"Why do you ask?"

"Because it looks kind of grey. Is it a tan or skin?"

"It's a VSOP—the Very Superior Old Pale."

"Good. And your height?"

"Five ten. Plus my heels," says Kosky.

"Good. And your weight?"

"About 69 kilos. You figure it out in pounds."

"I like that!" the Voice drawls. "And your health, my friend? I bet you go through a VDOL[14] ordeal as often as you can!"

"I certainly do. It's the only blood ordeal I won't refuse to go through."

"So what else do you do?"

"I write!" Kosky gives himself a Star of David.

"Write?" What do you mean: *write?* I mean what do you *really* do?"

"I write. Really, I do. I mean is there anything mean in writing—or in being a writer?"

"It depends for whom you write. For whom—not upon what. Do you write for movies or for TV?"

"I write books."

"Books! No kidding! What kind of books?"

"Novels. And not for kids."

"Good. I go for adult novelties," says the Voice. "What are your books about?"

"The usual spicy surface-to-surface sex," says Kosky.

Seneca, translated with an Introduction by Moses Hadas, 1958). It helps to cope. Doubleday Anchor Orig. Yale: in Hebrew, a mountain goat (*ya'el*). See also *Yale: a Pictorial History* by Reuben A. Holden, 1967. Also Yale Trivia by Christopher Harding, 1986.

[14]VDOL: A little-known abbreviation for only too well-known international and interracial blood ordeal.

"Hit me with your spicy titles!"

Prompted, Kosky recites one title after another.

Don't think I can go on. Heart, head — everything. Lolita, Lolita, Lolita, Lolita, Lolita. Repeat till the page is full, printer. (Nabokov)

"Those titles are dry!" The Voice voices concern. "You need wet titles. Wet and hot. Don't ever confuse heat with being dry. True heat is always wet. So how many novels have you written altogether?"

"Eight. I'm well into my ninth now. Nine is one of my sacred numbers."

"How long did it take you to write them?"

"Over thirty years."

"You averaged four dry years on a single novel? A *novel* — not even an encyclopedia?"

"That's right," says Kosky. "But these years were not dry to me." **Words are like water. (Bernard Malamud)** "Besides, what the general public does not know is that writers need a lot of time to write since most of them write by rewriting. Ask Balzac. Ask F. Scott Fitzgerald. Ask Leo Rosten. They also need a liberal dose of libertine sex. Did you know that John Stuart Mill would never have written *On Liberty* without the liberties he took all the time with Harriet Taylor?"

"Speaking of time, how old are you, my libertine?"

"Over fifty-five."

"Over fifty-five? Are you pulling my leg?"

"Your leg is too far," says Kosky. "Of course I'm over fifty-five. So what?" **At fifty — yesterday — I feel I have just begun to write. These are the best years. I spit on the grave of my awful forties. (James Thurber, 1944)** Seneca wrote his *Letters from a Stoic* at sixty-nine. **Do you know the worst of all vices? It is being over fifty-five (Trotsky quoting Lenin quoting Turgenev)**[15] "What's so unusual about being over fifty-five?"

---

[15]PROOFREADER TO AUTHOR: Please provide text for footnote.

AUTHOR TO PROOF-READER: Can't find it at this time.

"Nothing unusual," says the Voice. "But in my book over fifty-five means a port of old age. I don't go for old port — or for an old sport." The Voice hangs up on Kosky.

SS

His spell for adventitious adventure — misspelled, spell-bound by the prospect of starting with it a brand new literary spell, Kosky returns home and, following Balzac, the mentor of his *cuisine litteraire* (Balzac) instantly goes to work.

You don't know what it is to stay a whole day with your head in your hands, trying to squeeze your unfortunate brain to find a word. With you, ideas come very easily, incessantly, like a stream. With me it's a tiny thread of water. (Flaubert to George Sand)

At his desk, our broken literary broker now alerts the usually absent-minded inner reader to one finer, hence less visible, thread of his narrative tapestry: the importance of certain consecutive words as long as they begin with the letter S to be noted in his forthcoming spiritual satyricon (SS), and this in order to undo in his head damage done to it by the order of SS — the German-Austrian Nazi elite killers. Since Kosky grew up in the Nazi-occupied Ruthenia during World War II, the letters SS stand here, by the way, as a pointer to *Anatomy of the SS State* (an anthology of articles), Walter Verlag 1965, English translation 1968, the key to all his forthcoming literary *Mors Osculi*.[16] Hence, in his new book, the letters SS

Besides, in a novel such as this one, certain quotes, like certain high-proof vodkas, automatically evoke spiritual proof No. 96.

[16]*Mors Osculi* (death of the kiss, as opposed to *Murs Justi*, kiss of death — the ultimate state of carnal ecstasy and spinal exaltation): **One of the Hasidic texts reads: Our sages declare that there is a kind of death which is as difficult as drawing a rope through a ring set on a tall mast, and there is a death as easy as drawing a hair out of milk, and this is called the death of the kiss. (See** *Encyclopedia of Esoteric Man,* **by Benjamin Walker, 1977.)**

will first and above always refer to Sabbatai Sevi,[17] the spiritually sacred Jewish mystic who, once considered a Jewish messiah, died in 1676 at the age of fifty. At the same time the letters SS might stand for the sensuous sensations, (SS) or words which either stand for all that is soulfully straightforward (SS) or for all that is spiritually sterile (SS).

Spiritual is his favorite word and for a reason: it contains the word spirit, as well as ritual. Just think of the scribe who first invented this word! And speaking of inventive words, how about the word sexton? Imagine having, in one bell-ringing word, sex, sexto (a book—and at that one formed by folding sheets into his favorite number six!) and a bon-ton of professions too: a warden, a caretaker and a janitor! A bell ringing word which, for him also evokes *sexta hora,* that is a *siesta;* a well deserved nap in the afternoon, adapted from Latin sp. for 6th hour. (Origins, *A Short Etymological Dictionary of Modern English,* by Eric Partridge, 1958).

There is a sequence about the creative process, and a work of genius is a synthesis of its individual features from which nothing can be subtracted without disaster. (Seneca)

By first putting all these paired letters SS in parentheses (to him, each parenthesis, no matter how closed, is a form of linguistic prison cell opened for additional scrutiny) Kosky gives himself and the reader a chance to interrogate each SS at will and to decide, in the light of the available evidence, where they came from, what they stand for and whether they belong in his spiritual Storyville No. 9.[18]

---

[17]Sabbataism was the largest and most momentous messianic movement in Jewish history, . . ." writes Gershon Sholem in his *Kabbalah.* "The figure of the man (Sabbatai Sevi) who occupied the center of the movement is one of the *most completely documented* of any Jew who played an important role in Jewish history."

[18]Storyville, an area in New Orleans so named not in order to honor a storyteller, but in order to honor a censor of public morals:

In his own storyville, our literary alertman defends narrative art and with it his entire inner thesaurus, against the onslaught of the bestial[19] as well as sterile with SS-1, SS-69 and SS-96, his three most potent multi-headed and inward-heading SAM narrative missiles—the word SAM standing for the Ruthenian *sam*, meaning *alone*, and not for SAM, the Satellite Antiballistic Missile. For instance, in Kosky's arsenal, the SS-1 stands for Survival of the Strongest, its No. 1 ranking always as the spiritually most inferior rank of number. By containing in it sixty-nine, a euphemism for love making, the SS-69 defends the survival of the species while SS-96, his spiritual narrative top of his narrative line, protects the safety of his spiritual survival—and the survival of those who, like him, see humans as the only spiritual species (SS) known to exist in nature because number nine leads to number 10, which, by linking number one with zero, leads to the Grand Beyond.

SS

One way to explain why he, our selfish fish, is compelled to stay home for at least the first half of each day practically every day of the week and write his *brudnopis* (Ruth. for working paper, lit.: dirty text) instead of going out, say, to the beach, or to any other outing, is to refer the reader to one

---

Mr. Sydney Story. Sydney Story, or SS as he was familiarly called, was the city's morally least alerted alertman, who, alerted to the existence of the French practice of *soixante-neuf*, also known as the English vice, so popular in the bilingual, French-English New Orleans, restricted its performance to the town's multi-tongued as well as bilingual red-light district coded by the town's police as precinct 69.

[19]See *Anatomy of the SS State* by Helmut Krausnick, Hans Buchheim, Martin Broszat, and Hans-Adolf Jacobsen. Appendix (6) compiled by Brian Melland. German-language edition, 1965; English-language edition, New York, 1968.

of our sopher's 1939 memory slides. On it, talking to the six-year-old Norbert, his father, Israel, points his index finger at a daily-newspaper photograph of William James Sidis, portraying him first at the age of six as "America's Greatest Child Prodigy," then at another photograph, showing Sidis, in the words of the headline printed in large yellow letters as FAT AND FORTY AND DOING NOTHING WORTH DOING.

"Too bad Boris Sidis, Billy's father, didn't explain in time to *his seed* where Billy could find happiness," says Israel Kosky.

"Where could he?" asks Norbert.

"There. In one's own head. Only there," says his father, touching his head with his forefinger.

"And how is one supposed to look for happiness without getting a *kapdoloro?*" Norbert proudly flashes. Esperanto word for headache.[20]

---

[20]Esperanto (the word means "one who has hope"): the auxiliary language which, consisting of only sixteen rules and equally easy to learn vocabulary, was invented by a Polish-Jewish eye doctor, Dr. Ludwig L. Zamenhof (1859–1917) and meant for those who learned enough in their own language to know "that we must *first* find some solution to the 'language problem.' Not until we have settled this comparatively minor matter can we begin to understand one another across the frontiers and then to discuss the grave social and economic problems that face us." (*Esperanto,* by John Ceswell and John Harley, M. A., 1957, 1968, 1984, p. 9). Born in Bialystok, Poland, Dr. Zamenhof saw the first Esperanto textbook published in Warsaw in July, 1887.

In July 1987 the International Language Esperanto celebrated its Centennial in Warsaw with some 6,000 people from 70 countries. Around the world, some 10 to 16 million people speak and write Esperanto at no extra cost to their respective native tongues. (Swiss Radio International carry its programs also in Esperanto). By now, most literary classics of all nations have been translated into Esperanto. Just think of being able to find oneself at home in any country simply by carrying in your head Esperanto, the address book of local Esperanto-speaking folk and the text of Universalia De Klaracio de Homaj Rajtoj, (Esperento for Universal Declaration of Human Rights. Universal Esperanto Association is located

"By reading and writing while sitting on your ass. You were born Loewinkopf. Remember that it's all in the name and in your name *Loew* stands for Judah Loew ben Bezalel,[21] a great Jewish lion born in 1609, and *kopf* stands for head ever since 1069 when, escaping the first crusading Crusaders, the first large groups of Jews settled in Poland, a country they soon called Polin from the Hebrew *poh lin* meaning: *Here Shalt Thou Lodge.* These are your traditional relations, with the word *relations* meaning a traditional narrative as well as narrative tradition. One day, if you're lucky, you might even be invited to visit the Bezalel Academy in Jerusalem!" says his father, whose image disappears just when our literary engrosser passes by Lion's Head, a restaurant and a literary hangout in lower Manhattan.

Speaking for the Romanians in Paris and, more generally, for all those who have decided to remain in the West, I said that we weren't émigrés but that we were in exile. I thought that an exiled writer should imitate Dante, not Ovid . . . For Dante, exile was more than a stimulus; it was the very wellspring of his inspiration. (Mircea Eliade)[22]

---

at the UN Liaison office, at the United Nations Plaza in New York City. J. K.)

[21]Kosky is Kosky's second given name, adopted by his parents at the outset of World War II in order to replace, as well as supplement, Loewinkopf, his initial Jewish family name. **For Rabbi Loew, as for his rabbinic predecessors, the evil inclination is not evil in itself. It only becomes evil when it is misused. Paradoxically the aspect of the soul most related to privation and matter—the evil inclination—provides man with the possibility of transcending privation and matter. The aspect of man which may lead to sin and to the enslavement of the body may free man from sin and from the corrupting influence of the body. From *Mystical Theory and Social Dissent: The Life and Works of Judah Loew of Prague*, by Byron L. Sherwin, published at 69 Fleet Street, in London, in 1982.**

[22]Translated from the French by Derek Coltman (1982).

One way to break out of exile left to our *homo Judens* without exiting from his hermitage is to revert to the use of his phone cum-fax, but this particular gadget poses a clear threat to his inner him, our Sidis Billy.[23] After all, SPEAKING ON THE PHONE HAS ALREADY REPLACED SPEAKING FACE TO FACE AS NO. I MEANS OF INTIMATE COMMUNICATION, says an advertisement placed in every sixth issue of the *U.S. Phone Industry Views.* And look at what the fax is doing to replace the old good literary, hand-written facsimile?

The recent sex communication cleverly confuse the ding-a-ling fusion of numbers and words via phone, fax and one's TV. Thus among its newest sex ads, the seven character cryptogram USA-GIRL is, in fact 872-4475 while the innocent looking 825-5739 can mean ISS-SINS and JKJ-KISS turns into 955-5477. All this, of course, makes as a matter of course full use of easy to remember, mnemonic sexual customization of digits and letters. Scattered throughout this nation's printed pages, they selflessly advertise many mouth-to-ear sex-phone activities such Total Digital Conferencing as HOOKERS' PHONE SEX while proclaiming JACKING OFF IS A CRIME AND PUNISHMENT (DOSTOYEVSKY) ON THE PHONE. MISTRESS KARA. ALL MAJOR CREDIT CARDS ACCEPTED.

However, to Kosky, to our Tantric neophyte, **the merging of mind is achieved by listening to inner sound (Hatha Yoga Pradipika),** not by listening to a lustless, invisible woman throwing up on the phone a stream of usually carelessly chosen and poorly rehearsed sexually ritualistic innuendos.

There is bound to be a way for our master oralist to be able at the same time to remain bound to his narrative tradition, yet become free of it—free only in order to dive deeper into the hidden nature of his bondage. There's bound to be such a way, and there is.

---

[23]See *The Prodigy: A Biography of William James Sidis, America's Greatest Child Prodigy,* by Amy Wallace (1986).

Our inventive paraphrast finds such moral *No Exit* in his use of the services of another fellow-oralist, preferably a woman who as an expert of literary *gamahucher*, has been professionally trained in the art of mechanical keyboarding as opposed to being spontaneously creative. Her sole purpose (other than tempting him with her soles) is to correct typos, strike-outs useless hyphens, and check punctuation and spelling in his text, while staying clear of touching idiosyncratically his idiom and syntax.

"She is a privately hired, part-time professional literary vulvar cleft, be it a typist, a proofreader, a line editor or even a licensed full-time galley printer — an indispensable tax deductible literary ghost every writer must employ at one time or another" in the words of Norbert Kosky, as he was quoted, for once verbatim, by *Writer's Tax*, a tax-deductible magazine. She is the sociolinguist to be imagined from her Editing offered ad appearing in publishing industry magazines. Hence, she is the opposite of the young videomate, a hot, blond and bitchy cunnilinguist who, if you call her over ordinary phone lines with the right telephonic cryptogram will promptly appear on your TV set. The advertisement says it all: SEE OUR GORGEOUS VIDEOMATES ANXIOUS TO GIVE YOU HARDCORE READOUT LIVE WHILE YOU SPEAK TO THEM RIGHT ON YOUR OWN TV. DON'T JUST FANTASIZE; VISUALIZE!

As every writer knows, good writing ghosts (don't confuse them with ghost writers. J. K.) are hard to find. Already at the turn of the century — on August 9, 1900, to be exact — the august Henry James, a man who knew a great deal about the perils of being a public figure,[24] wrote to William Dean

---

[24]In *The Reverberator* (1888), a novel by Henry James, George P. Flack, a corrupt newspaper reporter who writes flack and nothing but flack, is reported to be one of the two literary ghosts said to have influenced the *Right to Privacy* by Warren and Brandeis (1890). The other ghost was Steadfast Dodge, the corrupt newspaper editor,

Howells, "It is not easy to concoct a ghost of any freshness."[25]

Now, writes Jay Kay on the margin of his own manuscript, why in the era when, at a press of a button, the whole Gutenberg Bible can be faxed (i.e. mailed by phone, with the speed of sound). I cannot start a brand new type of synthetic story—no less novel than is, say, a new synthetic material such as Lumber TM or Formica?

SS

Kosky's preoccupation with number sixty-nine as a figure of speech as well as a figure from life stems from many spiritual stems.

As everyone knows, of all numbers, only numbers six and nine when written down can be looked upon as images of human figures. Thus, ortographic number six often comes out of its creative closet disguised as number nine, by simply walking with its head up, while just as often number nine goes out disguised as number six—by simply walking on its own head—its preferred disguise. Inordinately fond of each other, the two numbers often meet and, by joining their opposite ends in a tight embrace, they become number sixty-nine or ninety-six, which for Kosky signifies the very best in human intercourse.[26]

---

who, steadfastly dodging truth, can be found in J. Fenimore Cooper's *Home as Found* (1838).

[25]Even those who are not into numerology must pause here to think what a chance James—that all-time literary master of ceremonies—took by writing about *concocting a ghost* and, of all things, by writing about this to another writer! If dear Dean Howells were jealous of James, he could have easily turned things around and claimed that James was capable of writing about such a ghost only because the ghost possessed him first. "For Henry James a ghostly narrative could be neither clinical nor analytic; it had to have all the richness of life and all the terror, wonder, excitement, curiosity, the mind is capable of evoking." Leon Edel in his Introduction to *The Ghostly Tales of Henry James*, (1948).

[26]Joining the initials of spiritually suggestive (SS) words is one

Hence anything to do with the numbers nine and six—particularly when joined together in sixty-nine—is for him a top SS.

His preoccupation also stems from his coming of sexual age when, at eight, back in 1941 in his native Ruthenia, he first saw the figure sixty-nine acted by Ewunia and Adam, the two consenting Ruthenian minors of his age, who acted it for the first time and in one short act only on a bed of grass. Equally stimulating is a vision of himself as a child, "a *vision*, not an examination, or a revisitation of a childhood" (Jay Kay, 1965); reenacting at the age of nine the esthetically complex head-to-muff ritual with a girl of fourteen appropriately named Mufka.[27] After the war, after learning French and English sufficiently well, our Ruthenian Nabatean[28] also learned the obvious life-and-breath-giving benefits of *sixty-nine*, also known to him, one who already in his Ruthenian high school was an Anglophile at Frenching and being

---

way through which our literary Tantrist alerts the reader's own *spiritus* (Sanskrit: prana; Greek: pneuma).

"Among some of the best known SS," wrote Norbert Kosky on the margin, "is *Sesame Street*, a National Education Television program presented daily except Sunday, to an estimated audience of 6,699 preschool children and childlike adults."

[27]In 1948 Professor Stefan Szuman, a foremost Polish-Jewish child psychologist and educator (see his *In Praise of the Dilettantes*, 1947 and 1962), collected some 2,388 drawings in which Polish children in 1946–1947 answered such questions as "What happened in your family and among your kin during the War and Nazi Occupation (1939–45)." Almost half of those who answered drew what during the War they saw most often and now remembered most vividly: "murders and execution." (From *Ohne Mitleid: The Child in the Hitlerite System*, by Kiryl Sosnkowski [1962], page 169.)

[28]First incorporated as a sect in Mesopotamia, the Nabateans believe that only a most natural practice of unnatural acts (unnatural defined as what comes to most of us naturally and not as being contrary to one's innermost nature) invariably leads to the development of unnatural spells of one's speculative psychic powers.

Frenched à la *soixante-neuf*. This was the time when, with TB rampant in the big cities as well as in the countryside, the Ruthenian health authorities mindful of the poisonous power of bad breath, and the dangers of catching TB via an innocent first-date first lips-to-lips kiss, warned against the dangers of face-to-face sexual cohabitation. Their warning indirectly contributed to the popularity in Ruthenia of head-to-toe love number 69.

Asanas (postures), various Kumbhakas, and other divine means, all should be practiced in the practice of Hatha Yoga, till the fruit — Raja Yoga is obtained.[69]

End of chapter 1st, on the method of forming Asanas. (The Hatha Yoga Pradipika, op. cit.)

His preoccupation with self-disclosure also originates from more recent American-made history. On the evening of August 9, 1969 (8-9-1-9-6-9), a lovely hamlet of Hollywood's Prince Hamlet in Destiny City, California, was invaded in the prince's absence by a Doomsday Daddy gang, composed of three American Desert Foxes disguised as passion flower holymen.

The stimulus-starved gang cut open Ophelia's silken throat with a straight razor, "and they danced on her belly until the baby she expected in a week was no longer kicking" *(The Los Angeles Transit)*. They cut down the laughing Rosencrantz by knifing him many times with an army knife and they killed the slovenly Guildenstern by shooting him in the groin again and again with an American-made 6.9 caliber gun. Then, and only then, did they kill Mrs. Guildenstern. Call her Mrs. even though she and Guildenstern were not married.[29]

---

[29]See *Black Medicine: The Dark Art of Death,* by N. Mashiro, Ph.D. (The vital points of the Human Body in close combat) (1978).

2

Restless, though full of happy narrative autobenediction,[1] still glancing through the Hot Personals—the personal ad pages of the *Hot Air Corsair,* Manhattan's notorious libertarian weekly—our autofictionist catches sight of Moving Finger. The Moving Finger happens to be the advertisement for Madame Wharton's Cumpany ("Cumpany, printer, cumpany!") whose motto is: "If you can't come, then call." The Moving Finger offers "outcall touch-typing," and placing Mme. Wharton's reputation on the line, the ad guarantees "type-free *expurt* services, (expurt, printer!) having anything your Hard (hard, not heart. J. K.) desires typed by one of our black or white female x-spurts."

SS

With *pneuma* in mind, our literary mover telephones the Moving Finger (their telephomnemonic GDY TYPO translates to ordinary numerical telephone numbers) and talks to Madame Wharton ("Call me Edith—but call"), who then transfers his call to one Maule Hawthorne, who introduces

---

[1] See "The Taxonomy of Benediction and Malediction" by Rudi Schmid, in *Maledicta*, Vol. X 1990.

herself to him as "a white part-time touch typist." With a touch of sexual *prix-fixe* (prefix No. 69) Mademoiselle Hawthorne offers her heavenly body's go-go services at "half rate after midnight."

Not a bit touchy, Maule assures him she can touch'n'type "as well as touch anybody who is or is not my type" and assures him that, in her previous job, she specialized in "writing birthday bellygrams as well as delivering and getting turned on by playing them person-to-person particularly, if that other person was getting turned on by the sight of my belly." Soon after she says it, Kosky asks her to come to his flat right away — as long as right away means after midnight.

While impatiently waiting to be mauled by this tax-deductible Maule, our impatient sex patient talks back and forth to Sadhaka,[2] his inner Hatha Yoga Mole, and he talks to him about his need for biological drama for "a prerequisite to being able to see oneself as insatiably procreative."

"Fucking this girl will undoubtedly give you momentary exaltation — but how long will such memoryless exaltation last?" Sadhaka speaks in a soothing whisper.

"It will not last long," our outer Sadhaka agrees reluctantly. "But then nothing does."

"Aren't you wasting the flame of the everlasting Self?"

"Body is a candle and Self a flame," replies our sexual spider all inflamed. "Can the flame live apart from the candle?"

The role of individuality in the struggle against evil becomes particularly conspicuous when we consider the fact that the essence of evil lies in suffering and when we recall what has been said about the role of individuality in the struggle against suffering. If evil is suffering, it is not fully communicable. (Jan Szczepanski)[3]

---

[2]Sadhaka: a yogi aspirant who follows certain heat-generating Tantric disciplines.

[3]Jan Szczepanski, one of Poland's most versatile sociologists, was during Kosky's university studies one of his intellectual mentors. (J. K.)

Midnight strikes. Soon after, Maule Hawthorne arrives at Kosky's door, telling him she had entered the Manfred through one of six supplementary entrances that allow a visitor to bypass the main entrance and avoid the face-to-face encounter with Señor Santos, an ex-Cuban marine who's now the building's night doorman.

Our Sadhaka takes one look at her. She is a natural being. Looking natural is one thing; being natural is quite another. As natural as Formica. Formica, not wood. As natural as, given American ability to look natural, is Lynn Shaver, a nonnaturalized American being.[4] He takes one more look at her. This time he does it mindful of the Bill of Rights as well as of the portrait of Thomas Jefferson at 55 as he was painted by the fifty-three-year-old Pole Tadeusz Kosciuszko at Monticello, Jefferson's residence. Jefferson, himself a champion of Polish liberty seeking champions, called Kosciuszko "the purest son of liberty of all."[5] (Read Jefferson Views Poland, by Janina Hoskins *Quarterly Journal of the Library of Congress*, Washington, D.C. 1976). Now, he takes another look at her. Her cheeks are naturally rosy. She is full of *Ros*, of *liquor vitae*, life's subtle inner dew. No wonder. She is young. Awfully young. How young is she?

To sustain a conviction of rape under California rule, the evidence must authorize a conclusion either that pros-

---

[4]Profiled by *Cavalier* magazine, the nineteen-year-old Lynn Shaver "shaved her body because the G-string she wore in one of the routines was so small that she had no alternative."

[5]In 1810, in recognition of Jefferson's constant commitment to the cause of free Poland, he was elected a member of the Scientific Society of Warsaw. Tadeusz Kosciuszko (d.1817), great Polish humanist and military man, (and at one time Jefferson's business partner, J. K.) in 1794 issued the Manifesto of Polaniec which freed Polish peasantry from servitude. (See: *God's Playground:* A History of Poland in two volumes, by Norman Davies, Columbia University Press, 1982).

ecutrix resisted and her resistance was overcome by force
or that she was prevented from resisting by threats of
great and immediate bodily harm accompanied by apparent power of execution. (*People vs. Lay* (1944) 66 C. A. 2d
889)

. She is old enough, she tells him with the conviction of an
old convict. How old? he persists with the fear of an old
convict-to-be. Well over eighteen, she says speaking to him
from the well of experience not to be ever confused with the
inner well.[6] She is, also, she adds quickly, a Quick Touch™
typist—sixty-nine words per minute—a typist, not a mind
decipher, and not a hieroglypher. But she qualifies as a proofreader since she can proofread elementary texts written for
elementary schools, but only when they are already set by the
printer. Other than that, he asks himself, possibly instead of
asking her, is she still a virginal flower child or a child still
ahead of menstrual flow? In other words, is she a hawthorn,
a sweet *madeline* never touched by either Childe Roland, that
brave knight,[7] or Childe Waters, that heartless lover?[8] **I was
immensely touched; her youth, her ignorance, her pretty
beauty, which had the simple charm and the delicate
vigour of a wild flower. (Conrad)**

---

[6]MINORS: 1. Definition. We have achieved a new definition of
"minor" which will apply nationally. The term "minor," as used
herein, means any performer under the age of eighteen years,
except that it shall not include any such performer if: (1) the
performer has satisfied the compulsory-education laws of the state
governing the performer's employment; (2) the performer is married; (3) the performer is a member of the armed forces; or (4) the
performer is legally emancipated. (Screen Actors Guild [SAG] and
American Federation of Television and Radio Arts [AFTRA], August 1986).

[7]"Childe Roland to the Dark Rower Came," a poem by R. Browning published in his *Men and Women* in 1855.

[8]"Childe Waters": an Old English ballad about Submissive Ellen,
who serves as a page to Childe Waters, her cruel lover.

Dressed in messy-looking though clean'nd starched pajamas—his favorite working costume, made by MittleEuropa Ltd. in Ruthenia—Kosky takes her straight to his desk where, in order to find out *Is She or Isn't She* over Twenty One, a bit absentmindedly, (though still breathing only through his nose: a yogi prerequisite) he shows her the working papers of one chapter of his novel—which, mauled by corrections, is desperately in need of healing, i.e., of prompt retyping. It all must be retyped—in his favorite pica[9] before it can be read by Dustin Beach Bradley Borell, his editor—who is also the editor-in-chief of Eidolon Books, Kosky's prime-time publishers who have published him since the days of his writing prime. Maule takes one look at him, then at the messy *brudnopis* of his chapter and calling his text graffilthy (not graffiti, printer!) asks with a smirk if there is anything else she could do for him in the field of quick touch?

She certainly could, he says, and he tells her what it is that he has on his mind and what he wouldn't mind transferring elsewhere. **The male sexual function is performed in a single act: in coitus. (Franz Alexander)**[10] She quotes him her cut rate—cut in half after midnight, to say sixty-nine minutes of saliva sterile 69.[11]

"Tell me again, how old are you?" he asks almost involuntarily. Are you one of those love struck and sex-awed teens

---

[9]Pica: a unit of linear measurement for type. Also one suffering from a craving for unnatural food, such as black chalk or yellow paint, etc.

[10]Franz Alexander: eminent American-Hungarian Jewish psychoanalyst, author of *Buddhistic Training as an Artificial Catatonia, The Don Quixote of America, Zest and Carbohydrate,* and many other works. See a tribute to Franz Alexander, M.D. 1891–1964, by Institute for Psychoanalysis, April 24, 1964.

[11]In saliva sterile 69 safe sex, body fluids are allowed to escape each lover's body only under the strict supervision of both lovers who make certain that while their bodies do mix, their bodily fluids do not.

who write *Letters to Alyssa* in *Teen Beat* magazine? **With the passage of the Children and Young Person Act in 1933, the term "girl-child" is defined as a "girl who is over eight but under fourteen years"** . . . This is all very interesting, but I daresay you see me already frothing at the mouth in a fit; but no, I am not; I am just winking happy thoughts into a little tiddle cup." (Nabokov)

"My age doesn't matter. My time does," she says, glancing at him and at the room's only clock.

"Is it likely that, say, in California, you would be still considered a child by law? In California, where — so I hear — the old vice squads and the new movie censors tend to easily confuse copulation with coupling and circumstances with surroundings?"

Each case involving a lustful advance upon a child must be decided by the evidence introduced and is not necessarily controlled by a previous decision. (109 C.A. 2d 189)

"I wouldn't worry if I were you," she says. "We're in New York, not California. This is the place where long before Safe Sex, booby-sniffing tit-vibrations, flicking nip, and boob-lubing first started."

The body is an instrument of life; a pinnacle of being. Don't hold it a prisoner. (Tantra)

"Why aren't you in the phone sex business?" he asks while introducing her gently into the art of *kaula*.[12]

" 'Cause I'm not verbal, I'm into nouns, not verbs. Some guys like to do their own thing — and some like to be told

---

[12]The practice of *kaula* path is even more difficult than walking on blades of swords, holding the neck of a tiger or a snake in the hand . . . This peculiar form of worship was prescribed only at a very advanced stage of spiritual development when the extreme type of self-control has been achieved, when the things that normally cause distraction could create no mental disturbance." (O. P. Jaggi, op. cit.)

what things to do. Giving head is one thing, and being a talking head is quite another. Things are nouns. All I want is to suck-seed." (SS) The daddy's girl gives our daddy a lesson of how to SS.

Only now, with the first stage of *kaula* completed, he lets the baby quail undress and, naked, fall back onto his monastic bed. **It has been observed that in girls the occurrence of puberty is earlier in brunettes than in blondes. (J. H. Kellog, 1888)** Unwilling to beat around the bush, wanton and taut, draping one leg over the edge of the bed, she opens her thighs, offering him the sight of her flesh, then, with her fingers, stretches its delicate membranes.

Where life becomes a Spasm, And History a Whiz: If that is not Sensation, I don't know what it is. (Lewis Carroll)

To postpone a decision, (a decision about what *not* to do) our literary cat chooses to notice the girl's oversize silver ring and bracelet, the center of each a replica of the pupil and iris of an astonishingly real-looking eye — which stares at him without so much as a blink.

"A lovely set," says Kosky, staring at her with a stare he borrowed from his favorite photograph of Baudelaire.[13] "These eyes look awfully real!"

"The set is called Peeping Tom and the eyes in it — they are real, and by real I mean raw. As raw as raw talent," says Maule. "Ante, my jeweler, uses only real eyes. Ante wouldn't touch a glass eye." She glances at her ring and bracelet.

"He uses what?"

"Real eyes only." She pouts, then goes on. "Owls' eyes, catfish's eyes, dogs' eyes — he likes German shepherds — as well as good-quality human eyes. The human eyes are the easiest to frame, but they are most costly. **When he spoke I gazed at a wicker basket on the Poglavnik's desk. The lid**

---

[13]"Baudelaire chose a symbolic suicide; he killed himself gradually," writes Sartre about his metaphysical arch-enemy Baudelaire.

was raised and the basket seemed to be filled with mussels, or shelled oysters — as they are occasionally displayed in the windows of Fortnum and Mason in Picadilly in London.

"Are they Dalmatian oysters?" I asked the Poglavnik.

Ante Pavelic removed the lid from the basket and revealed the mussels, that slimy and jelly-like mass, and he said smiling, with that tired good-natured smile of his, "It is a present from my loyal ustashis. Forty pounds of human eyes." (*Kaputt* by Curzio Malaparte, 1946) "All Ante said was that an eye is a work of art. Even an evil eye. Period." The female flasher holds out her hand. "Didn't you really know that this set comes fitted with original carefully preserved human eyes?" she says giggling sweetly.

"I certainly did not." Kosky backs away from the evil eye as he would from the soap made from Jewish fat) the civilized-German nation's contribution — yet another — to the history of racial hygiene. "NAZIS USED HUMAN BODIES IN SOAP. Warsaw, Dec. 8 (AP). — Colonel Edward J. York of San Antonio, Tex., described here today a German concentration camp he saw in the center of Gdansk (Danzig) where the Nazis made soap out of human bodies. York said that in a group of buildings behind five-foot-high brick walls were long rows of aluminum vats which held 400 gallons of liquid under steam pressure. He said that alongside each cooker were recipes in German on the walls describing how long parts of human flesh should be cooked and how to extract fats for soap making. He asserted some vats still contained torsos and arms and legs. *New York Herald Tribune*, December 9, 1945.

"Where does your Ante get these eyes?" Kosky hangs onto his literary optic nerve.

"He buys them from his customers and pays for them ahead of time. Too bad you can't lease eyes just for a year or so," says the Rhine maiden, U.S.A. "That's why he believes in an eye for an eye. He pays good money for them and he always pays in cash."

"I didn't know people sell their eyes ahead of Final Blindness," says Kosky, the spiritual child of the Final Solution.

"Why not?" The body-seller is affronted. "People sell hair and blood, don't they? They sell their kidneys and their rare parts and organs—such as, for instance, their foreskins, and they often sell it ahead of time. They even accept early reservations. I read this with my very own eyes in *The Uncut Men's Magazine.*"

She breathes at the ring, then polishes the lens of its eye with a finger. "When I bought my Peeping Tom set, the jeweler gave me a certificate that the eyes in it are real gems," she says. "I mean, that they came out of a living body—seconds after that body was no longer living in order to preserve their natural shine."

"Was the living body a man or a woman? American-born or foreign? Was he or she cross-eyed?" asks Kosky, peeping at her Peeping Tom. While coiling his arm around her child-like waist.

"That's my secret," says Maule, coyly coiling and uncoiling her girlish frame. Fondly, she removes the ring, then the bracelet, and places them on the night table.

Quickly, she slips out of her immaculately white shirt and baring her bare and slim shoulders steps out of her skirt, abandons her white brassiere and her even whiter bloomers, kicks off her high-heeled shoes and rolls down her immaculately white stockings, writes Kosky for the second time, this time a bit more specifically ("he lets the baby quail undress") but still as a part of his yet-to-be rewritten narrative.

Watching the spotless frame of his Childe of Elle,[14] our *cherubim* Childe Harold[15] notices a stream of most natural-

---

[14]Childe of Elle: the subject of an Old English ballad.

[15]*Childe Harold's Pilgrimage:* a poetic composite Byron began in Albania in 1809. "The multi-segment poem purports to describe the outer as well as inner travels of a pilgrim who, sated and disgusted with a life of pleasure and revelry, seeks spiritual distraction in

looking blood seeping onto him from her center spread.

"Is the blood real?" he asks mindful of the creative mind of Ante Pavelic. "And if it is why are you *already* bleeding?" Our *childe* molester becomes *flebile*.

Once I shaved my pubic hair and found out how comfortable and cool it was, and how neat it looked, I just decided to keep it shaved. . . . I wear small bikinis when I'm on the beach and I don't have to worry about pubic hair showing . . . even though I know that's a turn-on for some guys. (Lynn Shaver, 1984)

"It's only my period," she proclaims with a satanic smile.

"Your period? You didn't tell me you had your period."

"Yes I did," she retorts sweetly. "When you called, I told you I was coming at cut-rate because I was 'wet.' Wet meaning a period," she says, tracing with her fingers the spokes of invisible wheels on his creatively menstruating body.

"I thought you said, 'I'm coming at cut-rate because I'm wet. Wet meaning excited but not a menstrual *monsoonal*. Wet meaning fresh. Wet meaning anything, even W. E. T., the association of Writers, Editors and Translators once ruled over by that Ataman Kosinski."[16] He goes on. "I'm a writer and period means a lot to me. First, it means a natural inner flow to which Jews have devoted, a tractate Niddah. But the menstrual flow matters to me also because I am also a Kosher Nostra Tantric. *Only in this way can the sādhaka reach what is called Rasa (juice-joy) or Mahārāga (the great emotion). Mere mechanical performance is no less absurd than mere undirected indulgence. For certain rituals it is also important that the woman's own vital energies should be at their peak, and that she should be menstruating. (The Art*

---

foreign lands. In the fourth canto Byron gives up the unconvincing persona of his pilgrim and continues the narrative in yet another voice disguised as his own." (Norbert Kosky, 1981).

[16]Ataman Kosinski, a Polish nobleman, triggered massive peasant disturbances during 1591–3 in Podole. Another Kosinski, a robber appears as one of the robbers in *Die Rauber*, (1781), one of the plays of Friedrich von Schiller.

of *Tantra,* op cit. Illustration No. 65; Nepal, c. 1699. "Two, for the importance of the period read Chapter One in *The Well-Tempered Sentence: A Punctuation Handbook for the Innocent, the Eager, and the Doomed* (by Karen Elizabeth Gordon, published in New Haven and in New York," he tells the girl ogling her like the biblical Daniel who in 605 B.C., carried himself off into captivity:[17] **In the adult, novelty always constitutes the condition for orgasm. (Freud)**

She lies on the bed, drawing him closer with the expression of her face no less than with the position assumed by various parts of her body. Then, with her hand, she guides one part of him, her captive, toward her body, then presses it against her own. Under her touch, he opens up; he grows rigid; he softens again.

"I thought you weren't supposed to bleed on the job," he says firmly. "Isn't a period a curse—to a working girl, I mean?"

The consciousness that superhuman strain was no longer required had put a period to her power to continue it. (Hardy)

"It isn't. Touch typing is a curse. What's wrong with you?" she growls. "A lot of *foumarts* like you go bananas peeping at a girl who's riding her red pony. Haven't you heard of *The Second Sex?*"[18]

Looking up at the wall, Kosky catches sight of his father, who gazes down at him from a black-and-white photograph

---

[17]See page 9, *From Torah to Kabbalah: A Basic Introduction to the Writings of Judaism,* by R. G. Musaph-Andriesse New York: Oxford University Press, 1982.

[18]Writes Simone de Beauvoir in *The Second Sex:* ". . . It is during her periods that she feels her body most painfully as an obscure, alien thing; it is, indeed, the prey of stubborn and foreign life that each month constructs and then tears down a cradle within it; each month all things are made ready for a child and then aborted in the crimson flow." (As quoted in *Waters of Eden: the Mystery of the Mikvah,* by Rabbi Aryeh Kaplan.)

Norbert took of him in Ruthenia. His father's lips smile, but his expression is tenderly grave, as grave as the one probably worn by Isaac Troki. (Troki, printer, not Trocki!)[19]

"Please be careful," says his father. "This is the time when, as perfect a creation as woman is, she is momentarily less perfect to touch and be touched by her, than she is most of her regular time imperfect. Don't touch her, or anything that is hers. Don't let her touch you or anything that is bodily yours." Sadly his father looks his seed in the eye. "When with her, use your senses—four of them if you must, but not the fifth. Do what Sabbatai Sevi would do under such circumstances."

"C'mon, father—please! May I at least express my true Self through her?" asks our Nathan of Troki.[20]

The patriarchs came into the world to restore the senses and this they did to four of them. Then came Sabbatai Sevi and restored the fifth, the sense of touch, which according to Aristotle and Maimonides is a source of shame to us, but which now has been raised by him to a place of honor and glory. (Jacob Emden, 1877)

Without a word, Israel Kosky nods as if in disbelief and turns away from his seed, who is about to be carried away by a wind of concupiscence.[21]

---

[19]Isaac Ben Abraham Troki (b. ? d. 1596) a Polish-Jewish Karaite scholar from Troki in Lithuania (where he is buried) who wrote in Polish, Latin and Yiddish and whose *Hizzuk Emunah* (published as *Satan's Arrows of Fire*), Voltaire considered a "masterpiece of one kind."

[20]In circa 1629, Zerah, born Nathan of Troki, first offered the book of Troki, Sr., for publication in Amsterdam where (it was turned down not unlike Kosky's first work of fiction) by several publishers.

[21]"But this all-embracing meaning of 'concupiscence' has often been reduced to a rather special meaning, namely, the striving for sexual pleasure," writes Paul Tillich, who then elaborates elsewhere: "Only a perverted life follows the pain-pleasure principle. Unper-

Free of spiritual supervision, a formidable SS, Kosky slides his hand between her thighs, stroking her flesh. As she slides lower, he bends and licks her breasts and now, she wraps her lips around his living flesh, then surfaces for breath. **This whole world, from Brahma to a worm, is held together by the union of male and female. There is nothing to be ashamed of this when God Shiva himself was constrained by passion for a young girl to assume four faces in order to keep on looking at her. (Varahmira)[22]**

Sliding from side to side, she glides over him, a fish wiggling up and down the stream, her shoulders, breasts, belly, thighs, hands and feet pounding, sliding, pressing. She brushes the toes of his feet against her nipples; she strokes her arms, hands, elbows, knees, ankles and heels. Her thumb and forefinger twist, grasp, and pull his toes, but no matter what she does our Tantric seed won't lose his seed or his self-control while remaining slightly left of center of his sexual plateau while always centered on his spiritual history. **As a semen I dwell in the female. (Hevajra)**

---

verted life strives for that of which it is in want, it strives for union with that which is separated from it, though it belongs to it. This analysis should remove the prejudice toward libido, and it can give criteria for the partial acceptance, partial rejection of Freud's libido theory." *(Love, Power and Justice.* Ontological Analyses and ethical applications, by Paul Tillich, London, New York.) (Timeless: Norbert Kosky).

[22]Keep on looking at her? But what if, as Kosky found out when he last played polo in a land he calls Arabia, "Whenever a lady leaves the house, she wears . . . a large loose, gown whose sleeves are nearly equal in width to the whole length of the gown. Next, she puts on the burka or face veil, which is a long strip of white muslin, concealing the whole of the face except the eyes, and reaching nearly to the feat." . . . Members of the Hebrew faith also cloak themselves in sackcloth as noted in the following quotes: Genesis 37:34, Samuel 3:31, Esther 4:1–4. Quoted from Why do Muslim Women Wear The Face Covering the Weil? by As Sayyid Isa Al Haadi Al Mahdi, 6th Edition, 1989.

True, our Ruthenian tells himself, but as my learned father's only seed, I grow out no less from the thousand-year-old Polish-Jewish history.

Our Prince Krak (Krak, printer, not crack!) perceives this so thoroughly shaved'nd polished American-made Krakowianka (Polish for a female from the city of Krakow or Cracow, J. K.) first in terms of self-immolation by sinful offerings dwelt long before Kosky's own close shave with the Nazi-SS by Rabbi Moses Isserles Remuh (note SS in his name!) from Krakow.[23]

With his own smoothly shaved face buried in her smooth centerfold, ("the one coming to him no doubt straight from *Close Shave* magazine, a bimonthly published by Leisure Plus Publication," acidly adds Jay Kay), our Krak carries his Krakowianka beyond the lines of the City of Niddah to total immersion in the tub. There, in the Waters of Eden her sodden silk (SS) body covered lavishly with Remuh Bubble

---

[23]Founded by legendary Prince Krak, the town of Krakow (Cracow) is first mentioned by Ibrahim ibn Yagub from Cordova in the year 965. Ever since a spiritual and cultural capital of Poland, featuring the largest medieval city square (automobile free. J. K.) in the world, Krakow is today one of "ten most valuable cities of the world" (UNESCO) and the seat of Jagelonian University, the world's foremost, (where, among others, Kopernicus studied.) Kazimierz, Krakow's Jewish municipality, has been for centuries (like Lwow and Wilno, J. K.) a fortress of Jewish learning, as testified to by great number of most accomplished scholars, scientists and artists who came from it. Today, the remnants of the oldest Jewish sacral architecture in Poland still tower there, final victors over the crematoria of Auschwitz-Birkenau—ironically within an hour's drive from Krakow's Kazimierz. Moses Isserles (known as Remuh) a foremost Jewish philosopher, author of Torath Chatath (Sinful Offering) and Torath ha-Olah (On Sacrificial Immolation), lived, taught and in 1572 died in Kazimierz where he is buried at the Remuh cemetery next to the Remuh house of prayer built by his father, the top banker for King Sigismund Augustus.

Bath Foam, the two of them bounce soap and splash, (SS) beat about, sway, giggle, "getting ready to shave one another with the sharpest straight (SS) razor yet," adds the always sexually sarcastic (SS) (Jay Kay.)

She came safe out of his arms, without a struggle, not even having felt afraid. (Conrad)

3

The pen is the tongue of the soul, says Cervantes, and while writing implies the most unrestricted freedom of inner movement and a license to go out, mentally and otherwise, it also implies enclosure as well as stillness **in posture and breath. (Swami Rama)**

Mobilizing all his psychic powers by first modifying his Breath Power, as if on cue our Raja Yogi becomes the resident of the little-known State of Total Concentration, a state otherwise inhabited by writers, artists, scientists and other monks of creative Self.

My thoughts drip from my brow like water from a fountain. The process is entirely unconscious. (Balzac)

In such moments of creative calm our Muzak (Muzak, not muzhik, printer!) man sees himself as a composer of his narrative opus Number 9. "If one is to absorb this music," says Karlheinz Stockhausen, "one must take one's time: it does not carry one along with it, but leaves one in peace; most of its changes occur very discreetly in the intimacy of its notes *for things that happen must have someone to happen to, someone must stop them.*'" Add to this what Valéry, the French poet, says in his *Aesthetic Invention* (page 66): "In so far as 'creation' is defined by 'order,' disorder is essential to it. Once the universe of sound is thus defined the musician's mind is situated, as it were, in a single system of possibilities," a single system Valéry called the Musical State.[1]

Here, in his private mental concentration camp, he is free to first "give head to some mindless thoughts," then, in the words of Jay Kay, compose them on paper, in order to have his head examined, preferably by an erudite (and erotic: J. K.) proofreader who is not afraid to step out of line on her way to becoming a full-blossomed line editor.

As Balzac, Tolstoy and Thomas Wolfe confirm (these writers wrote out of inspiration (fused with perspiration, J. K.) by means of rewriting their mss. many times — the need for reliable and exact transcription of "The Harmony of Prose" (F. L. Lucas) posed difficulties already in the nineteenth century when manual labor was readily available, and "since the mere mechanical labor of a dozen rewritings is enormous" (F. L. Lucas), if transcription by hand is not manual labor, what is?

The very thought of a woman typist manually laboring over his book, his veritable child of labor, excites him as long as she is not a child or in labor. Whether she is black, yellow, or white; whether she is nice or nasty, petty or pretty, stubbornly fat or weakened by anorexia nervosa or by typing novels written in Esperanto, he cares not. At this particular

---

[1]This is, believe it or not, the same poet Valéry who, "in the closing stages of the second world war, had an inkling of the forces that would drive Europe towards project 1992 40 years later.

History will never record anything more stupid than European competition in politics and economics, compared and contrasted as it is with European unity in matters of science. The poet went on:

Just think what will happen to Europe when as a result of its labours, there will exist in Asia a couple of dozen Creusots or Essens, Manchesters, or Roubaix, in which steel, silk, paper, chemicals, textiles, ceramics and the rest are produced in staggering quantities and at unbeatable prices by a population which is the most frugal and numerous in the world. (*The Economist*, 1989).

novels written in Esperanto, he cares not. At this particular creative junction, our Dr. Faustus thinks of MALE AND FEMALE CREATED S(HE) THEM (Chapter 9, p. 96, in *Women, Sex and Pornography,* by Beatrice Faust, 1980).

All monks,[2] as is well known, are unmarried, and hermits more unmarried than the rest of them. Not that I have anything against women. I see no reason why a man can't love God and a woman at the same time. . . . There is a lot of talk about a married clergy. Interesting. So far there has not been a great deal said about married hermits. Well, anyway, I have the place full of ikons of the Holy Virgin. (Thomas Merton)[3]

Getting out of his camp in order to secure, as well as procure, literary associations excites him the way anything to do with *Style* (1955, 1962) or *Tragedy* (1957, 1962) excited that most literary fellow F. L. Lucas. There is something quite daring in sharing his *brudnopis,* his secretly sweating manuscript with the impeccably dehydrated literary world of uptown. After all, written in the present tense, his manuscript carries the secret of a writer's manu—manu, not menu—his innermost script, and this for a reason. The reason is that words, whether verbs or nouns, adverbs, adjectives or even small verbal particles, are neither monks nor hermits. Words don't like living alone. Like people, whether male characters,

---

[2]A monk's actual possessions are very few, and any other objects around him should be regarded by him as on loan from the Order. He has only eight Requisites: An outer double-thick "cloak," an upper-robe, an under-robe, a bowl to collect food, a needle and thread to repair his robes, a waistband for his under-robe, a razor, and a water-strainer to exclude small creatures from his drinking water so that neither they, nor himself, are harmed. (Bhikkhu Khantipālo).

[3]From *Day of a Stranger,* by Thomas Merton (1981). (Library of Congress Number: 81-9153. "Among the highest spiritual span ratings!" says Jay Kay.)

or female, transsexual she-males and he-males,[4] or even sexual neuters, they like to pair and stay together; like people they often marry most unlikely partners and no less than people the words too part company with one another with those they have shared some phrase — or even cliché — for years or decades.[5]

Once married to each other by a writer — or even, with or without his knowledge, by his typist, proofreader or editor — the words either stay together or dash away from one another on a dash, a dot, a colon or semicolon. In Kosky's manuscript words are usually and often unusually tied together — tied as in bondage. Once paired by him — paired as well as pared — his words seldom divorce; they cohabit, if often uneasily, either in a bracket or inside a parenthesis, living there in a state of constant fear of being crossed out by a politically cross-eyed — or esthetically crooked (or not constant enough: J. K.) — editor or publisher.

When the novel can no longer tell a simple tale, it becomes the mode that notes the indifference of its reader and finds the new dimensions of its fiction in the relation of that reader to the author through the object between them. (*Limits of the Novel*, David Grossvogel)[6] The above quote starts a chain of reactions. First (hence, the least important), it makes him think of himself: a storyteller no longer capable of "concocting a plot of any freshness," to

---

[4]See, *The Transsexual Phenomenon*, by Henry Benjamin, M.D. 1966 (Ch. 9 pp. 166–177) "Legal Aspects in Transvestism and Transsexualism." Also in *Jewish War, IV*, 559–567 by Josephus describing their militarily innovating conduct during the Roman siege of Jerusalem circa 69 A.D. "all wearing makeup, and all dressed as women, under history's first neon-lights," (Jay Kay).

[5]See *Word Origins: The Romance of Language*, by Cecil Hunt (1949). Also "Methods of Writing" (Chapter 11), pp. 266–99 in *Style*, by F. L. Lucas (1962).

[6]As quoted by Charles Newman in II. "The Anxiety of Noninfluence," (*Salmagundi*).

paraphrase Henry James' phrase. As a result, his novel No. 9 can "no longer tell a simple tale." Then David Grossvogel makes him recall Deborah Vogel who *sexpired* Bruno Schulz the way one Cathy Young shamelessly shamed (SS) Kosky when she worked as his assistant at the University of Beulah School of Drama.

A book in progress brings to his mind a swimming pool still under construction: only the constructor himself must decide when the pool is worthy of water, not only of swimmers. To a Jew, the words *pool* and *water* might signify *mikvah* — a gathering of water, gathered in a **special pool in a non-moving status, for the purpose of tvilah is ritual purification of objects and persons** as defined by Shmuel Rubenstein on page one of his *Mikvah Anthology*[7] is synonymous with storytelling. "Water, being the prototype fluid . . . Genesis, 49:4 (The "gathering of water" consisted of the "water under the heavens" which are the "female waters" mentioned earlier. *The Mystery of the Mikvah,* Op. cit., page 65.) Particularly so since, "In order to understand how and why a mikvah makes something ritually pure we must first know how objects or persons become 'impure' as it were." (Shmuel Rubenstein) "Is that why one of the first Nazi laws prevented the Jews from using German public swimming pools?" asks Jay Kay, who believes that while most of the old Nazis died, most of their notion of the Jew as the demon as reflected in the Nazi philosophy, law and regulations unfortunately have not died with them. It must be noted, notes Jay Kay, that when the Nazi anti-Jewish policies first took off in mobilizing the German-Austrian masses in their anti-Jewish campaign by effectively tapping into the latent or manifest reservoir anti-Jewish sentiment, they were never counteracted en masse by Jews themselves and their enlightened

---

[7]An illustrated analysis of the construction and use of the *mikvah*. *The Mikvah Anthology* ("The Bris Milah"), by Shmuel Rubenstein, Bronx, N.Y. (5728).

Christian allies, who failed to inform the German-Austrian masses so ignorant about Jews, about the very scope of Jewish contribution to Christian society, in education, science, medicine, technology, public service, arts and crafts—all the way to film, drama and music.

Given the importance of a writer's creative *mikvah*, or gathering of his narrative waters, it is only just that the writer—and only the writer who longs for a state of Inner Justice—is to be judged as the prime conveyor of his tale and hence the prime architect and constructor of his narrative pool, even if his tale contains too much water; even if the pool's narrative concrete was at one time or another used to reinforce someone else's swimming pool—or another writer's creative port. "Even if the writer is Ibsen or Hardy, Zola or Proust, Andrzejewski, Rilke or Joyce—all those who, by not receiving the Nobel Prize, have ever since caused great anguish to the transmigrating soul of that explosively soulful'nd sorrowful fellow Alfred Nobel," writes Kosky on the margin.

I am distinctly conscious of the contents of my head. My story is there in fluid—in an evading shape. . . . It is all there—to bursting, yet I can't get hold of it no more than you can grasp a handful of water. (Joseph Conrad)

There you have it: only the omnipresent writer must judge how much water he must draw from rain, wells, natural ice and artificial ice: the four permissible sources of *mikvah*. Only he must ask: Is my inner swimming pool Kosher for my reader's total Immersion?

The idea of spending several additional years of his *Life-Yet-to-Be* (Israel Kosky) on writing another novel, *another*, not necessarily *new* and not even a necessary one, excites him the way the very thought of a cat excites a catfish and catching a catfish excites a cat.

"What's the next novel about?" he asks Jay Kay knowing that novels are not "about" anything. Novels just are. They are to be read. That's all.

"Anything or anyone that you find particularly exciting or excitable," says Jay Kay. **But, lay the stress "on the inci-**

dents in the development of a soul: little else is worth study." (Browning)

"Could I perhaps write a novel about the making of the Nouveau Roman? About freezing of the frames of the literary text rather than about letting them go at sixty-nine frames per minute? ("A novel as different from an ordinary kind as the sport of chess, the royal game, is from polo, the king of sport? Read *The Chess Reader:* The Royal Game in World Literature, compiled by Jerome Salzmann, 1949). Now why couldn't I write a novel like that?"

"You could," comes the answer. "But who would want to read it?"

When the Jewish scribe — the sofer — sets out to copy the Torah, he must, according to religious law, take a ritual bath in order to purify himself of all uncleanness and impurity. This scribe takes up his pen with a trembling heart, because the smallest mistake in transcription means the destruction of the whole work. (Emmanuel Ringleblum, 1944)

After six hours of concentration, he steps out of his concentration camp. What a Terezin! he exclaims, when he is instantly stopped by his narrative Jewish Soul. "You're a Jew! Your Inner State must be determined by *hitlahawuth* — the Hebrew for joy — a joy of life not to be spoiled by the four letters HITL reminding you of Hitler. Then," the Soul goes on, remember that Theresienstadt (called Terezin) was one of the most perfidious Nazi-Final Solution Concentration Camps.[8] It housed primarily Jews over sixty-five — among them the German Jewish World War I veterans who had earned the Iron Cross First Class. As well as children and teenagers under sixteen. Some four thousand drawings, and bits of story telling, poems and songs in verse or in prose executed by these youngsters between 1942–1944 were left behind

---

[8]See *The Destruction of the European Jews,* by Raul Hilberg (1961).

after their young authors themselves went to their death to be executed by the purposefully most dehumanizing technology or asphyxiation by Zyklon gas, or plain starvation.

Their fate matched the fate of, among others, some four and half million Soviet prisoners of war similarly exterminated in German hands, who, after the war, left behind one soldier, as "sole spokesman for five million muted tongues" (Gerald Reitlinger, 1960) to testify on their behalf at the Nuremberg Trials.[9] These kiddy drawings gave Stefan Szuman[10] the idea of first asking the children who survived the war about what *The War Meant to Them*. **"Through the original Holocaust Survivors Film Project deposit, our own videotaping, and that of our seventeen affiliates, we are now the curator of one thousand registered testimonies. We have initiated the new phrase of 'creative frame' taping to describe the experiences of special groups, such as the deaf, to explore the interaction of survivors and their children, to follow up themes from previous testimonies and to clarify the effect of time on memory." (Geoffrey H. Hartman, 1987.)**

Writes Kosky on the margin: I am a writer; a wordsmith who works with words, and who loves playing with them, as much as playing with women. But while creative women still

----

[9]Chapter Three: The Prisoners of War in *The House Built on Sand: The Conflicts of German Policy in Russia 1939–1945* by Gerald Reitlinger, London, 1960.

[10]Stefan Szuman, a noted psychologist of aesthetics, whose theories of creative dilletantism influenced Kosky, had similar impact on Bruno Schulz who in 1932 attended one of Szuman's public lectures, and later corresponded with Szuman, who became his learned idol. See, as a must, *Letters and Drawings of Bruno Schulz*, with Selected Prose, ed. by Jerzy Ficowski, New York, 1988).

"Ptaki" (Birds) was the very first story Schulz published in a Polish literary magazine in 1933 (the year of Kosky's birth) as well as the year when John Mansfield published in the U.S.A. a novel entitled *The Bird of Dawning*.

threaten me as much as, say, the noncreative ones threatened August Strindberg, words do not. They do not, except one. Each time I write the word *burn*, I feel burned. Burned—not burned out. Burned not by anyone in particular, but by the entire Western Civilization. Keep in mind that, greedy as the Nazi leaders were, they did not eliminte Jews so mercilessly only because they intended to use Jews as slave labor, and gain income, in the words of one Nazi concentration camp financial report, "from Jewish gold teeth, valuables, clothes, money, and efficient utilization of Jewish bones and ashes—less the cost of burning the corpses." In fact, they extermi-nated Jews solely for their being Jewish. Jewish, that is, shared in Jewish ancestry, or communal history, literature, in inherently Jewish tongues (Hebrew, Yiddish or Ladino), in Jewish folklore, ethics and traditions, since this is more or less what being Jewish means in the Jewish ethos, remarks Jay Kay. Please read "What Is A Jew?" by Rabbi Morris N. Kertzer, (1978). The modern civilization literally burned in the gas ovens so many of my people and so many others who, spiritually akin, were only indirectly mine Kosky continues. *With a view to freeing the German people of Poles, Russians, Jews and Gypsies and with a view to making the eastern territories which have been incorporated into the Reich available for settlement by Ger-man nationals, I intend to turn over criminal jurisdiction over Poles, Russians, Jews and Gypsies to the **Reichsfuhrer-SS** (Himmler). In so doing I stand on the principle that the administration of justice can make only a small contribution to the extermination of these peoples.* (Otto Thierack, the German minister of justice, on October 13, 1942.)[11] Yet, while I feel burned by the Holocaust, I also feel torched by it: torched not scorched. With the word *torch* signifying light and inner luminosity. **In the words of my guru, "civilization is not our religion, nor is it the reli-**

---

[11]As quoted by Hilberg in *The Cunning of History:* The Holocaust and the American Future, by Richard L. Rubenstein, Introduction by William Styron, 1975.

gion of our problem. **Judaism is the art of surpassing civilization.**" (Heschel)

His writing time over, our Inner Camp Commander turns to matters of his literary property, which to our writing male means, simply, reading his mail. Kosky hates mail as much as he hates the phone (or such a phrase as a final solution: J. K.). They all enter your life uninvited — and when *they* want it. "They are our life's totalitarian agents who spoil man's spiritual soil," he writes on a spare mental index card.

The management of literary property is more than the economic stewardship of a limited and wasting monopoly conferred upon an author under the copyright laws. How such literary property is exploited affects not only economic aspects of the author's works, but the esteem in which the author is held. As such, management of a literary work requires a delicate balance between economic enhancement and cultural nurture. *(New York Law Journal,* **1987)**

Number six on his list is a fat envelope from Eidolon Press in New York. The envelope contains a paperback version of his latest novel first published in hardcover two years earlier. Fresh from the printer it is anything but fresh: it is a cheap pocket-size printed in gray ink and on poor paper.

The *Art Populis* cover of the book portrays an uncovered nymphette — call her Lollipop — her upper thighs show, and how! — the image of whom would make Nabokov flush. (Flush, printer, not blush!) On top of this, this little skinny girlie is shown sitting astride a polo saddle placed on top of a wooden practice horse. This is not a cover: it is a cover-up — an affront to graphic art.

Affronted, Kosky calls Joe Kempner at Eidolon's art department and is about to start a fight over Lollipop on the Hermes saddle, when Joe disarms him by simply saying, "Don't judge publishers by their covers. Don't compare that clean-cut cover girl with your sixteen-year-old slut inside the book." "This is substitution of textile for text," (adds all incensed Jay Kay.)

The law of the narrative "which has no law" (Mark Twain) is one thing; a writer's ego is quite another.

His ego now checks the title page of the paperback. It contains no errors in the spelling of his first and last name. His ego sighs with relief. But then he goes into vanity shock: two of his books are not listed among the titles of his past novels! Imagine such an affront! As if this is not bad enough, at the end of the book he finds "ABOUT KOSKY," a four-page italicized, unsigned appendix.

Trotsky credits me with the authorship of the publicity copy accompanying the distribution of his booklet to the press. On this matter, too, much to my own vexation, I must reply to him a categoric denial. I am not the author of this prospectus; I have had no part, direct or indirect, in composing it; I have no idea who the author is; and I do not care either. Is that clear enough? (Victor Serge, 1939)

This inflames his literary vermiform appendix to the point of appendicitis. Our monster dampens the heat of his momentarily monstrous ego by dumping the ego-offensive paperback on a book shelf. Only then starts to *monstruate*. (Monstruate — careful printer . . .)

He calls John Spellbound, Jr., Eidolon's publicity director. He gets him, (him, who keeps on advertising in Leg Show magazine "slim, 38, seeks to meet extra tall ladies wearing textured leg-wear") but then Marion Spitfire, John's assistant, also gets on the line and she is the one whose hobby is to receive hot'nd nasty sex memos from prison incarcerated men.

"What's up, Norbert?" says John.

"It's down, not up," says Kosky. "On the title page of my last novel you've listed only six titles of my eight novels. I wrote eight novels, not six."

"So what?"

"C'mon John! It took me as much time to write these eight novels as Balzac needed to write seventy-four. To write them word for word, in my own hand, mind you, not to dictate, like Stendhal or Henry James."

"So what?" says Marion.

"By missing my two titles, you've wiped out on paper two-eighths of my past mental being—of my spiritual total state of my Self-history." Kosky fails to score a spiritual point.

The writer, at the point when he can be judged "successful," has served a grueling apprenticeship that can't be determined in credit hours or degrees. Willingly or unwillingly, he is a student of contemporary history and a compassionate observer of whatever struggles intrude upon society. This provides the gravity of conscience. (Roy Newquist, 1964)

"But what 'About Kosky'? I hope you like it," says John.

"What? This appendix must be excised before it will make too many readers sick!" A true yogi, Kosky can't bring himself to raise his voice. **The line of demarcation between mental health and mental illness, between saneness and unsaneness, is unclear and often defined by environmental circumstances. (JAMA)**[12] (Unsaneness, printer, not insaneness!) By claiming I had suffered from Malic disease[13] it makes me potentially crazy." **No longer a great man, the Author was now a nobody.**[69] **(Bentham, 1822, as quoted by F. L. Lucas, 1962)**

" 'About Kosky' is a come-on to reading," says John.

"It's a mere composite, not an original composition," says Marion.

"It's an on-the-spot compost, not a composite," advertises Marion.

---

[12]JAMA: Journal of the American Medical Association.

[13]Malic Malaise, the name of which is derived from the French words *mal* for evil and *malheur* for misfortune, is a prolonged manic condition characterized by hypothyroidism (the impaired function of the thyroid gland), due to the excessive presence or deficiency of malic acid commonly found in man. Malic acid ($C_4H_6O_5$) is derived from the apple and contained in apple cider. (*Acta Paramedica*, 1966).

"It's a poisonous compost, not even a compot," hisses Kosky.

"It's bio-fiction. A kind of biodegrading literary leg wear," pleads John.

"It degrades biography no less than fiction. Call it friction." Kosky gives it a final grade.

Already unsettled by his publishers, Kosky attempts to find solace in a handwritten letter forwarded by them from a woman reader in Brooklyn, she writes:

Norbert: I've just finished reading your evil horse novel. And, by the way, kiddoo, have you taken lately, a look at that mini-barrel chest of yours? Or that maxi-hooter of a nose the Jew-hunting Nazis must have been blind not to grab you by it during W.W. II? Judging by what you did to the Fat Girl on page 169 — simply because she was stupid enough to fall for a man like you — you must be one of the meanest heteros on earth. Yours, Patricia Peggotty. (My friends call me Fat Pat.)

Her letter unsettles him even further. And why not? After all, one of his latest proofreaders was "as fit as a base fiddle" (Buf Magazine) and he has never made a secret of being a devotee of Buf, a magazine devoted to "a bevy of mountainous babes, as well as of Gem, "a Queen of the Female Jumbos," a publication containing a Fat Fantasy Corner. Besides, it was his polo playing proto-onanistic protagonist not him, the Author, who did this or that to that Fat Bimbo on page 169 of Kosky's novel. Just listen to this: "As an actor playing Hamlet is neither Hamlet nor merely an actor, but, rather, an actor as Hamlet, so is a fictive event not totally a created fiction with no base in experience; *it is an event as fiction.*" (He quotes from J. K.'s *Notes of the Author,* Chapter One, page 9, 1965.) Does her hostility and resentment stem from him, from the esthetic weight of his work, or from her weight?

There's an all-out war going on right now. An all-out

war declared by "Large Busted" women against gravity. Gravity pulls everything down. Gravity is the worst enemy of big tits, creating anything from bad back to sagging balloons. Large-breasted women must unite and fight this evil force. . . . (Juggs)

Quickly, he consults that old and wise *Guide for the Perplexed*, a magnum opus said to have been written by Moses Maimonides, "in ten years of hard work by day and by night" in order to "save him in advanced age the trouble and necessity of consulting the Talmud on every occasion." (M. Friedlander, 1904)

The *Guide* leaves Kosky even more doubtful. "The bird in its flight is sometimes visible, sometimes withdrawn from our sight," writes Maimonides on page 66. What he does not say is that in their flight such birds often become withdrawn into their own selves—that is, perplexed by the issue of their own flight, their own visibility. Would Fat Pat have written him such a hostile letter had Kosky listened to the advice of his father and kept on, throughout his life, reading books rather than writing them? Still unsettled, he turns for advice to Marcus Aurelius:[14] 69. *To live each day as though one's last,* and this depresses his creative Self even more.

His *brudnopis,* his working manuscript, his *forza* and *froda,* both *picaresque* and *picturesque* (Warwick Wadlington),[15] happens to also be fat, and it gains narrative yin-and-yang by the day. "What a madness & anguish it is," Melville wrote to Evert Duyckinck, "that an author can never—under no conceivable circumstances—be at all frank with his readers."[16]

---

[14]Marcus Aurelius, who died at sixty-nine, was an educated Stoic turned Roman emperor. "To refrain from imitation is the best revenge," he wrote in maxim six of Book Six of his *Meditations.*

[15]See *The Confidence Game in American Literature,* by Warwick Wadlington (Princeton and London: Princeton University Press, 1975).

[16]See *The Letters of Herman Melville,* ed. Merrell R. Davis and William H. Gilman, Yale University Press, 1960, p. 96, New Haven, Conn.

Americans love fat, his publishers assure him, and the majority of his readers are middle-aged midwesterners — after all, the Midwest is America's fat middle — most of whom are women over thirty. "And most of whom, when it comes to sex, are eerie enough to boat freely on Lake Erie," says Jay Kay.

My cheek blanches white while I write, I start at the scratch of my pen, my own brood of eagles devours me, fain would I unsay this audacity, but an iron-mailed hand clenches mine in a vise and prints down every letter in my spite. Fain would I hurl off this Dionysius that rides me. . . . (Melville)[17]

And, speaking of his own love of flesh, our skinny narrator of skin-flick fiction has for years been an avid peruser of such flesh-pot magazines as D-Cupper, and DDoubles and, to be mentioned for the first time, the Playtboy (Playtboy, printer, not Playboy; from *playta:* Polish for downfall. J. K.) sexually all-out-Polish language adults only magazine published — you guessed it! — for the first time in 1990 in Poland — resurrected to be free for the first time since 1939.

There is a valid reason for Kosky's preoccupation with fat: a fat woman — one truly devoted to the pleasure of eating and growing flesh (despite what others say about it and despite what she thinks they undoubtedly think of her) — could become in his hands, precisely because of her lack of concern, an ideal *dombi* — a perfect sexual Princess *Fat*ima, turned by her fat into *dombi fat*ale. " — and a perfect companion for our American Paul Célan."[18]

----

[17]Ibid., p. 69.

[18]Paul Célan, a Jew born in Romania, educated in Romanian and Yiddish, wrote his poems in German while spending most of his time in Paris. Like many other writers (Virginia Woolf, Hart Crane, and Johnny Berryman) Célan killed himself in an act of suffocation by water, i.e., drowning.

$$4$$

Set according to the numerical guidelines of his inner calendar, first put to use circa 966 years ago (just when the duchy of Polonia had officially joined Christendom) Kosky's inner alarm clock wakes him up as it has done without fail over the years — at six minutes to nine. A bright Manhattan morning! Since in the Jewish calendar the day begins at sunset — and at sunset it ends — he likes to think he wakes up at the Jewish midday.

AUGUST 23

1349 The Black Death Persecutions reach Cologne, Germany, and the mob attacks the Jewish population. Although the Jews defend themselves, most of the Jewish community perishes when a fire breaks out. Among the dead is Rabbi Israel Thann.

1648 The Jewish population of Koric, Ukraine, is massacred by the Cossack hordes of Chmielnick . . .

1940 The Nazis single out 1,000 young Jewish men between 18 and 25 in Czestochova, Poland, who are sent to a forced labor camp in Ciechanov, Poland. None of them will survive. . . .

1942 The largest deportation of the 40,000 people in the Jewish quarter of Lvov, Poland (today Ukrainian S.S.R.), to the Belzec extermination camp — where they all are murdered by the SS—ends. (Simon Wiesenthal)[1]

As he looks back at such nothing-but-Disasters entry he wonders: why must he, like so many Jews today, let himself be defined by the presence of persecution and death (call them the Jewish Yellow Star Wars) and not by Creativity and Life, by his formidable biblical and post biblical most Self-enlightening presence in history's every life enchancing endeavor? Defined by Jewish constant Tree of Life, mind you, not by physical absence so cruelly forced upon the Jews from time to time by the combined forces of occasionally mindless History, pointedly points out Jay Kay.[2]

Manhattan might be ready to be decoded, but our not yet extinct mastodon is not ready to decode Manhattan. He is too unsteadied by such relentless doses of Self-martyrdom. Not yet. Not for another six hours. Engaged in decoding himself, he won't even see Manhattan today. Or tomorrow. Or even after tomorrow. He is a free man: free to see or not to see anything he chooses, remember? He is a wordsmith: a self-employed writer.[3]

Writing is like Prostitution. First you do it for the love of it, Then you do it for a few friends, And finally you do it for money. (Moliere)

Such vocational identity brings to his mind one dreaded word: taxes. Is it because "the purse strings tie us to our kind"

-----

[1] *Every Day Remembrance Day: A Chronicle of Jewish Martyrdom* by Simon Wiesenthal, 1987, p. 189. Forget the steady dose of martyrdom. Enough of this canonization of the anti-Jewish cannons! How about the yet-to-be-written Hour-by-Hour Chronicle of Jewish Invention? How about the day by day record of the Jewish presence in History? Presence, not absence!

[2] Here Kosky refers the reader to the "Unique" Intentionality of the Holocaust, in *Post Holocaust Dialogues:* Critical Studies in Modern Jewish Thought by Steven T. Katz, New York University Press, 1985.

[3] See *The Wordsmith's Rights,* the Basic Zohar Foundation Guide to the spiritual rights of poets, playwrights, essayists, editors and novelists, by Carolina Wordsworth, Ph.D., and Jerry Swinburn, M.A., Eidolon Books, 1969.

(Walter Bagehot, 1879)? No, it is not. It is because "Money makes a man laugh." (John Selden, circa 1669) To Kosky "money is a mindless text: what is imprinted on it makes no sense even to a numerologist. Just empty numbers! Yet, look how many different things even an idiot will see in it! You see, in the eyes of the law, Kosky is a U.S. citizen first, and only then a self-employed literary masker. This means that however mobile he is as a person, his mental whereabouts are considered by the U.S. government to be American—as American as the Statue of Liberty. Hence all his creative earnings which originate in the State of Mind, are considered by the Federal State as having first originated in his U.S. home. Home, mind you, not mind, even if his mind is still two-thirds Jewish-Ruthenian—even if during the last nineteen years, he has spent, on an average, at least two months a year in Valpina, a superior ski village in the Swiss Valais.

In spite of the role played by the Word both in the creation of the world and the State of the Union, Kosky's anything-but-royal writer's royalties are brutally taxed to the fullest and indeed the foulest by the federal, state and city governments. In addition, because of the "royal," inside "royalties," the anti-royalist, the democratic yet greedy U.S. government has recently introduced VAT (the Valor-Added Tax—valor, not value)—which, defining a writer's royalties as luxury, taxes them by an average of 6.9 percent each year. And, if all this wasn't humiliating enough, unlike an average U.S. business, as a writer Kosky, "our foremost literary meat cutter" (*American Writer* magazine), is not allowed to depreciate from year to year his naturally diminishing mental faculties the way, say, is his neighborhood butcher who from year to year depreciates his diminishing meat cutting business.[4]

---

[4]See *The Writer's Tax and Recording Handbook, Including Everything You Can Legally Deduct,* by William Atkinson, Chicago, 1983.

"Freelance writers are a strange lot as far as the IRS is concerned. We are 'professions without an occupation.' Few, if any, of the examples cited in tax manuals for purposes of explaining tax law

Won't these federal folks ever learn that **the voice is a second face. (Gerard Bauer, b. 1888)** And, above all, that **the accent of one's birthplace persists in the mind and heart as much as in speech,** in the crystally clear words of *Maxims* written in 1665 by the one and only maximist maximus, La Rochefoucauld. Worse, were he a criminal, and one already sentenced by the Law for his crimes, who would write a book, either *sam* (alone, in Polish. J. K.) or one coauthored with, say the Son of Sam (SS), who killed six people circa 1977, the Law would have confiscated all his royalties from such a book in accordance with the Son of Sam Statutes. (SSS) Now why? True, Crime Must Not Pay, but why should the just cause of confessional literature be so unjustly punished—particularly, when the criminal already was punished by being justly beaten, often to death, by the Law? Beats me! confesses Jay Kay.[5]

Tracy Pickwick Tupman, Kosky's ardent tax accountant, who sensibly sensitive, tends to fall in love with any handsome IRS tax inspector simply because, as a girl, she fell in love with Gogol's Inspector General, tells the following story each time she and Kosky get together to look for another tax loophole, another hidden tax-deductible category. There she is, Tracy says, in the office of the Infernal Revenue Service (PRINTER: Infernal, not Internal) when this handsome IRS guy tells Tracy this; some half a million people in this country write for publication. Call them American literary surplus. Most of them write nonfiction. Only a handful of people make a living from income derived solely from writing novels. A handful!

"How full is the hand?" Tracy asks him.

"Sixty-six people," says the IRS person to Tracy. "Sixty-six

---

ever refer to freelance writers." ibidem, (p. 9)

See also *The Jewish Aspect of Levying Taxes During the French Revolution of 1789,* by Zosa Szajkowska, in *The Journal of Jewish Studies,* 1960.

[5]"Criminals, Authors and Criminal Authors." by Sam Roberts, NY Times Book Review, 1987.

people in a nation of 260 million. Yep. Sixty-six. That's all. And among them there are some child prodigies who write full-time, six days a week, take no vacations and, in order to be protected from child molesters, write under pen names."

"What? Parents allow children to be employed as full-time writers?" Tracy condemns exploitation of children.

"They are self-employed! They are employees of their own Self." Kosky defends creativity at early age.

Stirred, our hermit reluctantly lifts his fatigued frame from his cot. He is fatigued by the essence of life, not by its fat. Writing is a self-propelled mission, as well as a most selfish emission, and this makes a writer a missionary, a revivalist and a Healer.

I have just spent a good week, alone like a hermit, and as calm as a god. I abandoned myself to a frenzy of literature; I got up at midday, I went to bed at four in the morning. I have written eight pages! (Gustave Flaubert)

Promptly, he slides into his mental slide projector several slides showing his mother at the piano. There she is, "a piano player too bosomy to play a piano" as Israel Kosky jokingly called her, the one and only daughter of Maximilian Weinreich[6] (the famous chess player born in Łodz,[7] a town

---

[6]See also: *Dr. Max Weinreich's History of the Yiddish Language*, papers read by Dr. Edward Stankiewicz and Dr. Shlomo Noble at the Yivo Institute for Jewish Research, New York, 1974.

[7]The ghetto of Łodz was the first urban concentration of Jews established by the Nazis, which thanks to the most thought-out (if irksome, at times) leadership of Rumkowski, endured longer than any other wartime ghetto: 1,296 days. Its history is carefully recounted by the fifteen authors of *The Chronicle of the Łodz Ghetto* (Op. cit.). "My ghetto is a small kingdom: no Germans will ever dare touch my prerogatives, and I will never let any" (Rumkowski in Warsaw, May 15, 1941.) "My mottos for the year 1942:

1. Work.
2. Bread.
3. Care for the sick.
4. Care for the child.
5. Calm in the ghetto. (Rumkowski's 1942 Calendar). Reading this

which, with no river to speak of or any other natural water of its own, allowed itself to be called Łodz—and, in Polish, Łodz stands for boat as well as for being one of the largest textile centers in the world). There she is, with a figure straight from the pages of *Double D* magazine, insert in *Vogue* magazine and his piano-playing mother's intimate bottom reminds him of Lotta Top—the Oklahoma-born queen of *Big'nd Busty* magazine. "Don't I look like a Gypsy?" his mother asks him, her three- or four-year old suitor, as she raises and lowers her vibrant wrist above the *klaviatura* and the vibratory octaves giving him *The Sense of Beauty:* being the outline of Aesthetic Theory. (George Santayana, 1896). "My piano books tell me I must not throw my hand too far back for the hammerblow octaves, since, Yod forbid, stiffness could set in, and, there's no place in art for stiffness except at an early stage of stage fright or in a man fully engrossed in the art of making love," she instructs her son already stiffened by "one of the dangers to which a modern artist is exposed: the seduction of his predecessors." (ibidem p. 96.)

Enough digressing. He looks at his *brudnopis* novel's most tentative narrative master-plan. The plan calls for no less than, as Matthew Arnold called it, "to extract" himself.

(I am on trial and) I will tell everything. I will write everything down. I am writing this for myself, but let others and all judges read it (if they want to). This is a confession (a full confession). I am writing for myself, for my own needs and therefore I will not keep anything a secret. *(Dostoyevsky, Notebooks)*

Kosky's *brudnopis*, his dirty slave scroll, also called *brulion* in Polish, brings to his mind *Novele i bruliony* (Short Stories and Brulions, 1985 by Maria Kuncewicz, a foremost Polish prose writer. *Tristan 1946,* her novel starring two Tristan and Isolde-like lovers whose once ever-lasting passion could not

---

do keep in mind that the first Annihilation Camp (Vernichtungslager) began full operation on December 8, 1941 at Chelmno, a small town some twenty-some miles from Lodz. J. K.

outlast their first full-time job assignments, made Kosky fear such assignments and dream of becoming self-employed, ever since as a young man he read it soon after the war. Time for another digression. CONFESS ABOUT LILITH PIZNAI. Lilith Piznai, also known in the hardcover book business as Lililu Ardat, is his current tax-deductible manuscript-page proof-reader, and one who gives good *manu* to his script. As skillful as she is, Lilith likes to be used as a roughie—a euphemism for a proofreader who proofs only the author's first rough draft. "I give great hand. Hand, not head," she admits. In these reminiscences, should he write about her first from memory, i.e., invent her altogether, or must he first call her, or better yet, call upon her?

It doesn't matter because by now Lilith is proverbially bad. Just think of the *Odds Against Piznai* (as the *New Worker* maga-zine had in June 1986); they intimated that, it was thanks to her that "Adam" (every one in New York knows who "Adam" is, just as everybody knows "Eden") parted from his initial wife.[8] As a result, even her name is bad, so full of moral decomposition that even the straightforward New York So-cial Scripture (NYSS) devotes to her name no more than just one line, and yet our literary conspirator likes to be with her a lot! What he likes most is to momentarily share with her a system of reciprocal breathing maintained between two people of the opposite sex or, better yet, **same-sexers (Gore Vidal)** who, sufficiently drawn to each other, are able to establish a mental rapport by synchronizing their breathing rhythm.[9] C'mon, in your fiction, even more than in your life, you are your own boss, aren't you? he asks himself. Show the

---

[8] He was encountered by a Lilith named Piznai, who taken by his beauty . . . (PRINTER: Rumor Self Censorship Order No. 6699. DELETE FROM HERE ON—)

[9] This mental resonance was called "arch-natural respiration" by T. L. Harris (d. 1906) and its intimate aspects were perfected by Laurence Oliphant (d. 1888) through the method of sexual *sympneumata*.

reader what it means. **Razumikhin has a very strong nature, and as often happens with such strong natures he submits completely to Dunia. (N. B.: This trait, too, is often met among people, who though most noble and generous, are rough carousers and have seen much dirt: he, for example sort of humbles himself before a woman, especially if that woman is refined, proud and beautiful. (Dostoyevsky)** Why don't you call Lilith now? Let her give you a hand! What you pay her for her honest-to-badness service is honest-to-goodness tax deductible. She gives him a sales slip for proofreading of each successive draft and besides, there's a lot of proofreading to be done on some sixty-odd raw manuscript pages retyped the other night by one Lola Gazonga, his latest part-time typist who, calling herself his Naughty Neighbor, keeps on, as her hobby, collect (and wear) all kinds of silky satin slips (SSS) and coarse corsets (CC) not always kindly looked upon by community censors. Shouldn't these pages be now checked, word for word, by Lilith, before they can be eventually verified line by line by one of his also privately procured out-of-line sexual line editors?

Meanwhile, Lilith is the one who, paid by him by the hour and asked to come to work at 9:06 in the morning, often comes to see him already at 6:09 A.M. and starts working on him long before she actually begins to work with him. This she does *not* in a room he calls his office of his two-room flat and *not* in his bedroom but rather in his bathroom, the most intimate center of his two-room *garçonière*. Call it his Black Box.

To a modern, big town Tantric, such as himself, one deprived of his temple, his bathroom becomes his Gym Med, a meditational gymnasium, a minireplica of what *Walden: Life in the Woods* was for Thoreau. There, in the bathroom, it is Lilith, and only she, who assists him during his L-5, and S-1, S-2, S-3, spine-stretching (SS) exercises. Steamily stripping (SS) him of what she calls his "sexual status symbol," she aims at the zones of irritation of the sacrum and the pelvis. Working solely with her soles initially formed by walking the beaches of the sunshine state of Florida where she grew up, she relieves the cause of but also causes, various metaphysical as well as medical and physical pressures which originate in the sacred sacroiliac joint, the address of which in the subtle body only the Tantric Buddhist knows for sure.[10]

Besides, shouldn't Lilith now check whether Lola Garonga, that slippery silky Buf Plumper of the month, missed by chance a word or a paragraph or a page while typing, then retyping, his manuscript pages? Was Lola able to follow to the letter his most intricate system of letters, numbers, footnotes—all marked by many different, and differently colored, transposition marks? For instance, did Lola notice the paragraph torn out of its rightful context on page 36, which was then flung by him all the way back to page 16—but then moved again to page 38? Did she see the single wrong word which, initially speared, was then spared and reinserted back to where it was? Here, our Author refers Lilith to the following words of William E. Buckler who edited and Introduced *Passages from the Prose Writing of Matthew Arnold Selected by the Author,* (1963) "A literature chiefly of exposition and argument, non-fictional prose depends for its continuing vitality upon the apt expression of apt ideas rather than upon the grandeur of its architecture." (ibidem, p.x) While, relieving his stress with her soles, the sole she stresses is that **The act of commerce with woman lies in refraining from ejaculation, and causing sperm to return and nourish the brain. (Cacravarti, 1963. p. 89)**[11]

---

[10]See also "Manual Medicine" (op. cit., 1984), Chapter 6, fig. 66 and fig. 69, both demonstrating the zones of spinal as well as spiral imitation.

[11]Also known as *acclivity* ("The direction of sexual energy upward toward the brain for the purpose of enlightenment and power." See page 1: *Encyclopedia of Esoteric Man,* by Benjamin Walker, op. cit.).

Since our Friar Kerouac[12] still writes from the top of his head, rather than from life, spinning out stories on TV talk shows no less than in the TV-less bars and spelunks of sexual downtown, how is he to start his next chapter? "Start with your last night's dream. Latest, not midsummer's," his narrative voice tells him. Was Kosky's latest dream an esoterica—a simple illumination—such as his once recalling during his routine sleep that the wipers of his car didn't wipe? "Is your dream wet or dry?" asks an editorial in *The Astral Guide to Good Writing*. It was a wet dream. Here he was, all wet, standing alone on the all-wet deck of a nameless trawler cutting across a nameless bay but, somehow, our literary fisherman was not there on it, for the thrill of fishing.

If words are indeed supposed to flow like water, and he is a floater, is water—or word—his true element? How is he to know? He, to whom, when he was a boy of six, water was first synonymous with being sparkling clean, a source of life, only to become, when he was nine, a symbol of the sudden absence of air, of drowning and death by suffocation. Words are also said to be pregnant with meaning and the word *pregnant* signifies life at its most wondrous. No wonder Webster's devotes almost eighteen of its page-long columns to the word *water*,[13] and only nine columns to the word *air*.

---

[12]**Typically praised for their naturalness, for the ostensibly unmediated access to experience, in fact, Kerouac's texts were routinely engendered by other texts (these, however, spoken rather than written). Kerouac encouraged the misunderstanding of his transformative enterprise by publicly eschewing rewriting and editing, which he evidently regarded as impediments to getting at the nontext of raw reality. That the reworking of his material in the form of verbal anecdotes was itself already a textualization of reality appears never to have occurred to him. (David Packman, 1984).**

[13]Water: "Let the waters under the heavens be gathered together to one place, and let the dry land appear" (Genesis 1:9); Ruthenian: *woda;* Esperanto: *akvo;* Latin: *unda,* water defined only as a wave. 1. The liquid which descends from the clouds in rain, and which

There is no word in Hebrew for fiction—I boycott that word. It means the opposite of truth. Prose, yes, but not fiction. I write prose. I aim at truth, not facts, and I am old enough to know the difference between facts and truth. (Amos Oz, 1985)

Is his dream a memory oppressed by memory of World War II, or is it only a long-repressed memory? But what was he—he, a land-locked scribe—doing in a boat? Above all, why in his dream is he wearing a bright yellow foul-weather jacket?

Yellow denotes his inner foul weather. But NOT, repeat NOT his Yellow Pages, the most useful supplementary Manhattan Telephone Directory. Yellow stands for "jealousy, inconstancy, and adultery." (*Brewster's*) Yellow denotes yellowish bile. Yellow speaks of gall. Yellow was the robe worn by Diego Alonso, one of Kosky's favorite historical, real-life figures charged with heresy on the order of the Spanish Inquisition. Heresy defined by the Inquisition as crime of spiritual decomposition. Since in matters of faith decomposition means treason, the guilt of the accused must be established by his own statement obtained, if need be, by the application of torture, that is torture by water, by pouring water into him—liter upon liter of, if need be yellow water also called urine—and by making the aforesaid prisoner go through the inner flood, and if he or she won't confess, by being so drowned.[14] One understands the gall of the vile Nazi

---

forms rivers, lakes, seas, etc. 6. Hence, a specified degree of excellence, or thoroughness; as, artists of *all waters* were represented in the exhibitions, a scoundrel *of the purest water*. 9. Finance: An addition to the shares or other securities issued by a stock company not representing a corresponding increase in assets, the effect being to increase the par value of the shares, but to diminish the actual value per share. 10. Roofing (*Webster's Second International*). "To the gathering (Mikvah) of waters, he called seas." [Genesis 1:10]

[14]Read, by all means, "The Case of Diego Alonso: Hypocrisy and the Spanish Inquisition," by Stephan Gilman, in *Daedalus: Journal of the American Academy of Arts and Sciences* (Hypocrisy, Illusion and

SS who forced their captive Jews to wear on their clothes a striking, visible, spiritually humiliating, Yellow Star on Jews yellow, even though the Jewish Star of David is sky blue.[15]

Finally, the yellow signifies the Yellow Books, the official documents called in England Blue as well as Yellow Press.[16]

In last night's wet dream, then, what was he fishing for? It seems that he was fishing for catfish — a fish called *sum* in Ruthenian.[17] Quickly he checks the content of his dream in *Ten Thousand Dreams, or What's a Dream?* (1931) and learns that dreaming of catching a catfish — or worse yet, catching one — means that "you will be embarrassed by evil designs of enemies, but your luck and presence of mind will tide you safely over the trouble."

Evasion), Summer 1979. "How far should we take the language into historical description and analysis? It is language that serves the ends of policy and ideology as much as it may serve the ends of history," writes Edward Peters in *Inquisition*, p. 9, 1989. Also, *From Spanish Court to Italian Ghetto:* Isaac Cardozo: A Study in Seventeenth-Century Marranism and Jewish Apologetics, by Yosef Hayim Yerushalmi, 1981, the author of absolutely quintessential Zakhor: Jewish History and Jewish Memory, 1982.

[15]In its final form the decree — dated September 1, 1941 — provided that Jews six years or over were to appear in public only when wearing the Jewish star. (Raul Hilberg, 1961).

[16]Yellow Press: the name arose in the United States about 1898 as a result of the scary Higher Truth Campaign, i.e., grossly misleading articles published in certain American newspapers about the Yellow Peril — the supposedly already then forthcoming conquest of the world by China and Japan.

[17]*Sum* (Ruth.): An impressively large freshwater killer sheatfish the Ruthenian miniversion of *Orcinus Orca* — the American killer whale) which, sporting six large catlike whiskers is commonly found in the Pripet Marshes as well as in the Polish river San and the Polish until 1939 river Bug.

From a literary point of view, the dream seems a waste: it offers no useful narrative drama. What William E. Buckler says about Matthew Arnold fully extends to Jay Kay, comments Kosky about his protagonist's narrative *sculptorids*:[18] "It is curious to see such a man at the very height of his career, confidently cutting himself down to size. To see him do it in prose is even more interesting. After all, poems are individually distinctive and complete: their form protects them . . . Prose on the other hand, is never really complete: it maybe an aphorism, an essay, or a volume . . . Thus it is the most open-ended of all forms of writing." (op. cit. p. ix) Reluctantly, our wordsmith stares at the pages he wrote and, staring him in the face, the pages ask: Do we belong in a novel, or in a *tractate soferim*, a writer's tract?

The Jewish nation is the nation of time in a sense which cannot be said of any other nation. It represents the permanent struggle between time and space going through all times. It can exist in spite of the loss of its space again and again, from the time of the great prophets, up to our days. It has a tragic fate when considered as a nation of time, it is beyond tragedy. It is beyond tragedy because it is beyond the circle of life and death. Time and Judaism (in *Theology of Culture*) by Paul Tillich, 1959.

---

[18]*Sculptorid,* a word first coined for bronzes "radiating space and time, proximity and distance, like Constellation Sculptoris" a Forward to the Exhibition Catalogue of Ambiguous Figures/New Bronze Works, at Wildenstein Gallery, 1990. (J. K. 1990).

5

There are three rules for writing the novel. Unfortunately, no one knows what they are. (Somerset Maugham) I'd like to know whether what happens to me happens also to others; whether others are as I am. (Pablo Neruda)

While correcting his text by pencil our literary yogi keeps on amusing himself by playing his favorite inner Self-O-Tronic Path Man game. Each time our sole word-player runs in his text into double-joined letters, each one starting with spiritually sedulous a letter *S,* he either scores or loses six hundred spiritual points.

Whenever in Kosky's text, the letters *SS* stand as the initials of life-enhancing words—both happily married to each other—he scores high and his creative spirit carries him closer to the throne of spiritual safety occupied by the one and only Sabbatai Sevi.

SS

Chasing the double-jointed SS and either spiritually joining them or shooting them down, "from hero to zero" (Eddie Rickenbacker) in his text, a well as in life, is one of our literary Captain Eddie's favorite spiritual sports, and part of his deeply felt soft-sell spiritual style—and here with two harmless double SS in a row, he scores twelve hundred points!

Keep in mind, dear reader (here Kosky addresses his entire readership), that, as I've already stated elsewhere, but would like to restate again and again in the face of such films as *Shoah* (Claude Lanzmann, 1985)[1] of all the occupying countries, including the Third Reich itself and its Nazi satellites, only in Poland (and Ruthenian, then part of Poland. J. K.) the Germans enacted the penalty of death for anyone and his or her entire family for sheltering a Jew, no matter for how long, whether for an hour or for a year. That, deportation to a concentration camp (where life seldom exceeded nine months. J. K.) legally threatened any non-Jewish Pole, and, again, his or her entire family, no matter how old, for failure to denounce (i.e., mention to the SS even in one word or a whisper) the Ruthenian who had dared to hide a single Jew or Jewess. That, therefore, in order for a Jew like me to survive the net of SS (like Poland, Ruthenia was the most densely covered by SS: J. K.) a network of many dozens of most-selfless non-Jews was needed, in order to hide a Jew, not just once, or twice, but day after day, year after year? And yet, in spite of such dangers, thousands upon thousands of Jews like me survived the Holocaust thanks to their fellow Ruthenians.

PRINTER TO AUTHOR: I didn't know that!

PROOFREADER TO AUTHOR: Neither did I.

LINE EDITOR TO AUTHOR: I didn't know that either, and I bet you anything that neither did anyone who lives where I live near Jefferson's *Monticello* by William Howard Adams, New

---

[1]*Shoah*, an Oral History of the Holocaust, the complete Text of the Film by Claude Lanzmann, preface by Simone de Beauvoir, Pantheon Books, N.Y. 1985.

York, 1983 (Illustrated. A must! J. K.) Why don't you come and visit me for a non-fluid exchange visit sometime?

EDITOR TO AUTHOR: Once upon a time, weren't the Polish Gentiles known to be from time to time hostile to Polish-Ruthenian Jews (their historical tenants for a thousand years. J. K.)

AUTHOR TO EDITOR: They were, and why shouldn't they be? Life is often hostile, and speaking of life: Jews lived in Poland longer than anywhere else except ancient Israel, and for almost a thousand years, in Poland, numerically speaking, in the largest numbers in the entire Jewish history until 1939, they mixed freely with their non-Jewish fellow Poles. The hostility they often felt for one another stemmed from a spiritually sticky situation — from proximity, not distance, from "occasional cursing or baiting," even a cursory beating of Jews but certainly it stemmed *not* from the mostly Nazi-made stick'nd shtick of *racial* hate and *racial prejudice.* From the way the word *Wy* (you, in Polish.) opposes the word *My* (we, in Polish) that is, the letter *M* opposes the letter *W* — its opposite. Opposite, as yet a mere reversal! Enough said. Here, enraged by ignorance, Kosky asks J. K. to send the following cable to Jay Kay's readers: HOW COULD YOU NOT ZAKHOR (Remember J. K.) THE DIFFERENCE BETWEEN ANTI-SEMITISM AND ANTI-JUDAISM? WHILE ANTI-SEMITISM IS ALWAYS RACIST CALL-ING FOR UTTER CASTRATION OF A JEW OF JUDA-ISM AS TYPIFIED BY THE GERMAN AUSTRIAN NAZIS AND THEIR ULTIMATE EXTERMINATION OF JEWS. ANTI-JUDAISM OFTEN XENOPHOBIC (as was the case in Ruthenia. J. K.) SIMPLY OPPOSES JEWS AND JUDAISM THE WAY TRADITIONALLY THE CHURCH OPPOSES THE SYNAGOGUE AND THE SYNAGOGUE THE CHURCH. (Opposes, a Jew and, at times, even politically or culturally dispossesses Jews, but not of life, unless a mob, as in Kielce in 1946, is prompted to progromize a Jewish community by among other, freely distributing alcohol, politically inspired, professional pogram instigators.[2]

Not enough said, rebels Kosky's Inner Ethnic. **To be a Jew in the twentieth century/ Is to be offered a gift. If you refuse,/ Wishing to be invisible, you choose/ Death of the spirit, the stone insanity./ Accepting, take full life, full agonies:/ The gift is torment. (Muriel Rukeyser)**

Staring at the words around him through his SS-tainted glasses, under heavy inner PreSSure (thank you, printer) our street smart savvy spectator keeps on playing, whenever he can, his wordy stop'nd shop SS game.

And, as he plays it to the fullest, so does one of the still unnamed characters who, driven crazy, tries to incorporate spontaneously in his text (for the sake of scoring many SS's) such diverse and often spiritually sterile concepts as solid state, silk stockings, and even the start-spangled space-shuttle. Wow! look at so many SS: Long live Sabbatai Sevi!

A character who, like Kosky, in order to entertain himself with the memory of various SS's must, from time to time, screen-service such diverse delicacies as shrimp-scampi on the way to a steamy swap-session with sautéed sea scallops all listed on Sans Souci restaurant's famous 3-S menu (please, not a word here about spinach salad, à la plus ordinaire, or the steak sandwich Lumpenproletarien!).

Finally, think how happy he is (happy, meaning impressed with his power of his SS-driven Self) when, in an inner space station, he lets Jay Kay, that spiritually shipshaped salesman

---

[2]For the assessment of how in different countries, among them, Germany, Austria, The Netherlands and France, Jews were picked up one by one in order to be exterminated in toto by the German-Austrian Nazis. The reader is directed to *One By One: Facing the Holocaust,* by Judith Miller, 1990.

of his soft-sell scrimshawing, come across the Scared Skinny Technique: an article starting on page 96 of the shipshape *Shape Magazine!* All this gamesmanship, he hopes (and so does Jay Kay), brings him closer to a spiritually shipshaped narrative ship named Kevala Kumbhaka.

Let it be said that in order to concentrate more fully on what constitutes purposeful writing, he locks himself in his bathroom, the bathroom's fluorescent lights turned off, his inner self illuminated to the fullest. This is the closest he, an urban dweller who dwells in thoughts and whose sole tools are Jewish oral tradition, breathing and concentration, can come to the *mikvah*, a word which, in English translation approved by the Learned Rabbis, means, among many other learned meanings, a gathering of water contained, for the purposes of *tvilah*, one's supreme spiritual immersion: "When kevala kumbhaka without inhalation and exhalation has been mastered (this must follow rule No. 69 of plavin kumbhaka— "floating upon the water like a lotus leaf") there is nothing in the inner world that is unattainable for the yogi. (Attention: this is already the state of a post-ordinary Royal yogi. J. K.) Through this kumbhaka he can liberate the breath for as long as he likes," says the next in line rule of Hatha Yoga Pradipika—the yoga of Light.[3]

After an hour of intense concentration our Royal yogi rejoins his politbureau with pol standing for Polin, lit for literary and bureau for his Polish-made wooden desk.

At his publisher's request, he is to write one more advance blurb of his forthcoming novel to be listed in their next year's

-----

[3]See *The Yoga of Light*, a classic esoteric handbook of Kundalini Yoga by Hans-Ulrich Ricker, op cit., page 96, no. 69. Hatha Yoga Pradipika, by Svātmārana-Svāmin, from the fourteenth century (circa 1369), is the oldest Tantric text "based on the lost Hatha Yoga" (Mircea Eliade).

catalogue. "This is the story of a writer gripped by an inner terror. Call it a novel of arch-natural writing. Of mind's own liturgy. Of homegrown garden for the perplexed. Call it *The Book of Concealment* or *Noli me Tangere* or *The Greater Assembly,* even *Office of the Hours* but, please, don't call my office during my work upon my next work of fiction coded Instruments of Passion. Behold the Man!" He declares his creative intentions, as well as inventions.

Finally, our Ruthenian pen slave stops working at his fatalistic thirteenth hour. With ample time before his 6:00 P.M.–9 P.M. obligatory nap, he shaves, he dresses, he grabs a sandwich—eating is no big deal to him—and as breathless as an arch-natural sentence, he rushes to his apartment building's underground parking garage. Within minutes, our Tibetan mystic drives out into the daylight in his Crabriolet (with him for a crab, and cabriolet for his "motor car with fixed sides and folding top"), as COD calls his two-door 1969 Decapitado convertible—one of the last great ozone polluters in automobile history but at 469 hp also one of the most authentically flashy American horseless carriages *ever*—made by the now extinct Freud Motor Company. (PRINTER: Freud, not Ford.)

Today, Kosky floats on his flashy super-sport[4] all over

---

[4]In each case you missed it—here Kosky addresses his car-conscious reader—back in 1926 the words *super sport* meant the only American-made automobile made to the order of Captain Eddie Rickenbacker by his Rickenbacker Motor Company. This particular sports car was capable of doing ninety miles per hour at a time when most cars could not make it to sixty-nine. As for Captain Eddie, he was, in case you forgot, until then, a famous flier, a flier not a famous driver, or a carmaker. He was the all-time Ace of Aces, the truest American war hero who, *Fighting the Flying Circus* (the title of his 1919 best-selling book) single-handedly shot down twenty-six

Manhattan's flashy gilded toe of Wall Street, up and down, and down and up from the Trenchtown Townhouses (Impasse Row in the East Village), practically facing King Petaud's Court and the Bowery Terrace Hill Apartments. He then reluctantly passes by the Hooverville Condos, and the garbage-littered Parson Abraham Adams Plaza (next to Jefferson Park, yet so far from Jefferson!) then, in need of a quick change of social scene, he makes his way through the congested downtown to the West Side Highway, pausing for a quick look at theEffie Deans Youth Hostel at Hylas and Jukes Street.

Now why is he so happy driving aimlessly through this cement countryside "where traffic accidents alone cause ten times more loss of health and property than all the other crimes and violence combined" (Kosky, 1982)? **The first Portland cement concrete was used to pave a small stretch of public road from Detroit to the Wayne County State Fairgrounds in 1909. . . . There are 3,600,000 square miles of land in the United States and over 3,600,000 miles of road; that's one mile of road for every square mile of land. . . . Today, 60 percent of the total air pollution in most U.S. cities is caused by auto exhaust. (Entropy, op cit., 1980)** say 69 percent, printer![5]

German World War I flying machines. But with the word *back* in his name, how could he succeed as a businessman? The year 1926 saw the fall of Captain Eddie's motor car company when most of his backers ran out.

[5]Buicking around his various innermost personae, our literary Buick feels the way J. Frank Duryea (the Polish-American. J. K.) must have felt when he built the first automobile in this country, and in 1895 won the first car race in the United States!

Passing by the 96 year old this year (1986) Carnegie Hall, the history of which brings so much Jewish music performed there to

Such motoring has represented to our Ruthenian cosmopolitan ever since his arrival in America in 1957 his neverending pro-tem liberation. Liberation from his *politbureau*, from his writing, from his morally spinal task, hence, as is the case with man's spine, prone to back pain, as well as from his desk, and even from his privately hired female typing pool. Motoring around in his *berlinette*, Kosky is singing to himself Izzy Baline's "God Bless America." Indeed, he feels like Izzy Baline, that Ruthenian-Jew also known as Irving Berlin. The name resulted from a printer's error! Turning Baline to Berlin is like turning Kosky into Kosinski by simply dropping *sin* from the middle of the word! Do you hear me clear, printer? In case you missed the point, Irving Berlin, who drove around in his favorite U.S.-made Buick, was also the author of "White Christmas," the biggest song-seller since "Salomon Psalms" as well as "There's No Business Like Show Business" meaning, clearly, the business of music! It also has represented to him, what wandering, say, represents to such representational novelists as Washington Irving wandering, mind you, not to Washington, D.C., but abroad "over the scenes of renowned achievement . . . to loiter about the ruined castle, to meditate on the falling tower, to escape, in short, from the commonplace realities of the present and lose myself among the shadowy grandeurs of the past."[6]

---

his narrative ear, he feels the way Max Grabowsky (Polish-American. J. K.) must have felt when, he first designed and built the horseless truck named The Rapid in his Grabowsky Power Wagon Company (1908–1913). "A true first ever sport/utility vehicle, made with a 22 hp two-cylinder engine The Rapid was fastest best one-tonner of the period." (Jay Kay).

[6]"The overwhelming motivation of Irving's literary life, in relation to the patterns discussed, was *romance.* . . . (Cosmopolitanism in American Literature before 1800," by Stanley T. Williams, in *The American Writer and the European Tradition,* ed. by Margaret Denny and William H. Gilman, 1964).

At the Yantra Hotel, his prime destination, Kosky parks his convertible in a vacant lot behind a burned-out tenement and, mindful of car-wreckers, covers his super-chromed toy from top to toe with an ordinary yellow plastic car cover. ATTENTION: $C_{23}H_{30}O_7$ TOXIN! EXTREME CAUTION — AUTHORIZED PERSONAE ONLY, says the sign printed on it in striking purple letters. The personae is not a printing error. It is poetic license issued by the city of literature to any aspiring writer.

Next, our depressed occultist stops briefly in Matahari, the hotel bar known for the variety of its pinball machines. (This is where Patrick Domostry, the composer, back in 1978-9 composed his Cantata Automobile in preparation for 1990, the Centenary year of the Invention of the automobile. (1985 saw the Motorcycle Centennial. J. K.) Of Polish origin, Domostroy mentioned in his Cantata, the Polish-American brothers Duryea whose, 20 hp. two-cylinder, 1903 Winton Touring Car some seven years before, made the first horseless-carriage journey from San Francisco to New York and who accomplished "the first ever sale of an American motorcar" (Smithsonian, 1990). (And then, of course, Domostroy eulogized the Moon River vehicle, the invention of a Polish-American Mieczyslaw Bekker, this first motor vehicle in history traversing the moon after the Apollo 15 arrival there in July 1971.)

With his inner heat, his Kundàlini at the lowest, Kosky needs a drink of heat-generating testosterone — and at this time he can get it only from Murena Livingstone Moor, a spectacular creature whom he had first met by answering her ad in the *Uptown Crier.* ("Big Busted Blk Lactating Mama Seeks Wht Male Big boob banger. I've got nothing to bust but my bust!"

A few words about Murena. She is the twin sister of Rachelle, the famous black model who displayed her aSSets in *The Best of Big Boobs* magazine, under the head-turning headline: SEE THE MOST AWESOME MEGABOOBS IN THE WORLD. "And what about our TV being called the Boob Tube." (Jay Kay). Now Murena enters his fictive world with a bit of her own history. Busting off male chauvinist breast exploitation, she was the first black to burn her bra on a public burner. Luckily for Kosky, whose passion she inflames, she did not burn her breasts.[7]

Murena is his black bosom buddy. Her titanic jungle jugs measure sixty-nine inches at midday,[8] filling him with joy felt by those deep-sea divers who, diving deep, discover the sunken body of the *Titanic*.

While Murena Livingstone Moore is not exactly as leggy as Josephine Baker, (so thoughtfully photographed by Man Ray, the artist who obsessed by both, saw women and chessboards, (saw and, obsessively, photographed both as "Objects of my Affection," [Man Ray, 1945] in terms of her extra-breasted beauty-tonnage she comes within a hair of the mouth-watering super stacked Mary Waters.[9]

---

[7]"An excellent exercise for conditioning the muscles around the breast . . . is this, stand tall and straight, the end of your spine tucked in, your shoulders back, chest high, chin in. Pick up a heavy book—a dictionary or encyclopedia volume would be best." From *The Health Finder*, Rodale Books, 1957.

[8]Depending on whether the woman is right- or left-handed, a woman's breasts and nipples vary in size. They also vary in the morning, at midday, and in the evening, as well as when her breasts are strained, exercised, fatigued or relaxed, before, during and after her period. **I didn't know that! (Printer)**

[9]MARY WATERS — STILL A FAVORITE AFTER ALL THESE YEARS: I am a guy who likes breasts that hang down a bit and I think Mary is one with some of the best "droopers" I have ever seen. (*Gent* magazine "a typical example of its CC) Carnal Concupiscence. (CC).

In addition, as a tribute to both the concept of carnal concupiscence (CC), Candid Camera (cc), and the antidictatorial antics of Charlie Chaplin (CC) in his mental casual contact corner (CCC),

Attention, all literary crew! We are about to enter the spiritually suspicious pages 60–69 of this ms. Kosky issues a warning to his entire "literary production-line writing machine." Here, most adamantly Kosky quotes Pierre Macherey who, writing in *A Theory of Literary Production,* first published in France in the seminal year 1966, sees The Author as a producer of a collectively played literary slot machine) and is "equally hostile to the idea of the author as 'creator.' " (Terry Eagleton)

The image of Murena's cataclysmic cleavage and the steadily jiggling mass of her fleshy orbs takes along a bra-busting orbit our whopper worshipper all the way to the Big 'Uns of his own straight laced mother, linguistic conditions, referred to as being *well hung.*

What is important for Dostoyevsky is not what his hero is in the world but above all what the world is for the hero and what he is for himself! (Mikhail Bahtian, *Problems of the Poetics of Dostoyevsky,* Moscow, 1929) There he is, our future literary sailor, barely six years old, resting with his mother and father on a beach in Sopoty, a Baltic sea resort, on a sunny August day a mere few days before the German invasion of Ruthlandia. He is there to tend to his thyroid balancing act. "Thyroid is a gland which secretly secretes a sacred substance which permeates all creation," in his father's learned words.

As he listens to his father and keeps on inhaling the yonder-inducing Yod nicknamed iodine, from the heap of seaweed deposited by the foaming Baltic, Norbert examines once again the body of his mother, whom he now sees so tanned in fact, that if it weren't for the white patches of flesh

---

Kosky systematically notes that in English the letters CC are pronounced *see see,* and this evokes in him the sound of the spiritually saturated letters SS.

showing from under the edges of her swimsuit, she could be golden black—as black as Murena.

His mother catches his look. "You might say you've got yourself a well-mammarized mama! These super stacked DDoubles *bazooms* were shaped to perfection by nature, Norbert! By nature, and naturally, thanks to their most natural up-and-down-and-up again movement, not by some Aryan-made Jug-gernaut juggs exerciser! You might as well take a good look at them and test their firmness with your own touch." Here, with Norbert's father looking the other way, into his boundlessly Talmudic Self, his mother lowers her swimsuit, letting out for the briefest of moments her pendulously perfect breasts. This is how mother-son inner tit'nd touch conspiracy began.

"I know what you're thinking, you dirty old boober!" canceling out his flashback. Murena gushes him to an oozing oral orgasm (printer to J. K. Another tripple O!) "You're thinking about my two slaves." Murena goes on, her whisper wetting his thoughts. "Don't believe it when they tell you dangling dollops are fun to play with. They're not. They get hurt by their own weight; by being squeezed and rubbed and pinched by a bra.

"My tits made me who I am not today," she says fondly. **Hope springs eternal in the human breast; Man never Is, but always To be blest. Alexander Pope (d. 1744).**

"If until today I still can't get employment as a dental assistant, it's 'cause my tits got in my way of seeing the patient's teeth. *Tits for teeth!* A gal stacked like me needs a well-stacked bar, to rest my creamin' juggs on." She gives him a look first given him in Miami, Florida, by Miss Big Boob of the Year 1969, and, no longer logical or teleological, he leans forward over the bar animated by the sight of her pillows of brown flesh. By what her sight does to his self. *Sight for Self?* rebels his inner Jew. *"Next thing you know you'll be in love with Arabesque!"*

86

"I'm an animal who won't touch animal fat. All I eat is organics," says Murena, knocking his elbow off the bar "with the overly ripe nipple of one of her knockers," (Jay Kay). "Milk is good for me, but only my own milk. Did you know I lactate nonstop? That I lap my own milk? That, as I lie down on my bathroom floor I can squeeze my paps so hard they squirt milk right into my own big mouth, both at the same time?" She goes on and her words drown his Self in his bone dry thyroid. "Here, go ahead. Go down on them with your writing hand."[10] She slides her boob-a-rama from side to side, when, momentarily, he dips his hand between her two milk boobs which trap him the way a booby-trap traps a tank.

"See what I mean?" she asks, then hisses when instead of mouth-holing her lips, he kisses her own tit-affected hand.

"I've been thinking about your skin-dipping in that swimming pool the other day, you black-head Grosbeak." Murena casts a downcast glance at our sexual outcast. "About your sticking your skinny body—body but not your Jewish head, all the way down in the deep. Most guys I give breast to go under in a minute. They've got no staying power." She whispers, then full of chesty charms, she sexily straddles the bartender's stool while he promises himself to buy the widest-angle lens for his old 69mm camera and photograph her glistening milkers *au naturel* the first chance he gets. Promptly, in order to look deeper into her bursting cleavage, her mammoth mammary milk-making pool, Kosky slips off his stool and leans over the bar. "One day, at the right time, I'm going to answer the wrong ad from the right man, and

---

[10]BREAST see MAMMARY GLAND see CHILDHOOD see ADOLESCENCE see SPEECH see SEX ORGANS see Encyclopedia of Medical Self-Help by Max M. Rosenberg, M.D., Books, Inc. New York 1950, dedicated to "Remembering my Father and Mother".

not the other way around, as it was when I met you," says this African-American milkmaid deluxe, touching his head with a forefinger armed with a superbly long naturally grown purple nail. From under her brassiere she pulls out a worn-out personal ad typed on a six-by-nine weatherproof Lithoid® index card, removed by her, no doubt, from the hotel's bulletin board, where hotel guests, and the staff, are free to advertise their search of either the fulfillment or getting rid of their most pressing carnal needs. She hands the card to Kosky. Sniffing the ad for her body perfume, but getting instead the scent of the bar, Kosky pretends to read it as if he did not know it by his head of heads.

JOHN KEVALA KUMBHAKA, A WRITER WHO BOMBED, OVER FIFTY, 5'11", 139 LBS., SEEKS BLACK FEMALE TBF-I AVENGER[11] FOR MAITHUNA[12] EXERCISES IN MYSTICAL PHYSIOLOGY,[13] BOX 666, LATA-SADHANA MAGAZINE, VERBAL ICON PRESS, NEW YORK CITY.

Time to go. Time to stress pure action and forget about SS-1 or even SS-69. It's time to fire SS-96. Reluctantly our hardened boner parts company with Murena and takes the elevator to the Narcissus spa on the hotel's ninth-floor roof-top. There, all alone, our Grosbeak undresses, leaves his plumage in a locker and, wearing a bikini small enough to

---

[11]TBF-1 AVENGER: A famous Navy heavy-duty bomber plane which joined the fleet in 1941.

[12]Maithuna: in Tantra, either a symbolic or actual act of carnal coition.

[13]Like Kosky, Mircea Eliade, his guru, specialized in certain psychophysical, as well as physiological, exercise he named *mystical physiology.* For an inner portrait of the man see his *Ordeal by Labyrinth,* conversation with Claude-Henri Rocquet (French version, 1978; American, 1982). (When I initially read this book in 1980 I rated it 69 96 66 on SIN with the word *sin* signifying my Spiritual Index Scale: Norbert Kosky).

enhance his procreative apparatus, walks to the pool. There are three characteristics of an earthenware vessel: it absorbs, it does not excude, and it does not taint what is in it. (Tractate Soferim)

Shaped like an eye, its lids painted black, its retina blue, the pool takes up most of the hotel's roof, offering a wide-angle view of Harlem and a telephoto view of Wall Street. **The old dualistic world-concept which envisages the ego in opposition to the universe is rapidly losing ground. (W. Gropius in *Bauhaus*).**

To this particular Jew, the economic view of Harlem as contrasted with the view of Wall Street does present a problem. (Call this problem a study in social contrast. Contrast, printer, not contract!) Please don't confuse letter S with letter C. In Polish, for instance, the word *Siebie* means Myself, while *Ciebie*, means Yourself. Think what a difference one letter makes! "Pliant as a reed, not hard as a cedar," (Soferim), our Sopher must think of it in purely spiritual terms, not only in terms of gallons of spiritually thermal water and of his Self's immersion in such water for the purpose of purification of one's thoughts until the soul shines through. **This is the period of my ambition. (Shakespeare)** The laws of *taharah* — one's purity — and of *tumah* — one's impurity — are in his literary mind perceived as narrative devices, narrative mind you, not ritualistically religious, and they are closely linked with life's potential, with one's becoming either fertile or sterile — an egg or an egghead — Period.[14] Third, he must pause, and answer a simple question: IS THIS SWIMMING POOL KOSHER FOR IMMERSION?

---

[14] The twelve-volume *Oxford English Dictionary* devotes over one page to the period.

Standing at the pool's edge, Kosky stares at the pool's smooth surface as if it were a blank page. He stares at it the way F. Scott Fitzgerald stared at a blank page as he was photographed in 1929 by Nikolas Muray, the famous Hungarian-American portrait photographer. The pool stares back. It's a skoal between his Self which by itself, a writer's self is always semi-conscious collage and his mind, which as a writer's mind, is always conscious montage. "Isn't it nice," his Mind now addresses his Self in full view of the Harlem River, "to be Jewish? Jewish meaning free and spiritually universal enough to know to enter and to float in just about any narrative swimming pool?"

"No wonder knowing how historically important the very notion of free access to water is to Jews, the first thing Nazis did was to forbid Jews access to swimming pools!" says Kosky's inner sensuous Sartre and, as an old sensualist, Sartre knows such existential details better than any other non-Jewish writer. "It seemed to these foul Nazis," Sartre goes on, "that if the body of an Israelite were to plunge into that confined body of water, the Jew would be no longer befouled." *Anti-Semite and Jew* (1965). means enough said.[15]

Slowly, hanging on to the pool's edge by his hands, our Master Shallow lowers himself into the deep end. He breaks the calm surface, first with his toes, then feet, calves and thighs. "There are three kinds of sweat which are beneficial to the body: sweat caused by sickness, by a bath and by work. The sweat caused by sickness brings healing, and the sweat caused by a bath has no equal as a cure." [Tractate Soferim]. He lets the water claim his belly, but then he takes his hands

---

[15]See *Sartre: A Life,* by Ronald Hayman (1987).

off the edge. With his arms at his sides, his feet together, he submerges vertically, but once the water reaches his neck, he wills his body not to sink any lower.

Through their art, they diminish the daily number of their expirations of breath. They can inflate another's body by their own breath. In the hills, on the borders of Kashmir, there are many such people. (Amir Khosru). How can we transform the organization as destroyer into the organization as contructive experience? (from The Spirit of Transformation in Corporate Life by Murray Stein, in *Psychological Perspectives*, Los Angeles, 1990).

His body obeys, and so does the water. It is a stalemate. Our Beast 666[16] and water hold on to each other. He won't sink any deeper; the water won't rise any higher. No wonder: A zealot of the Bizarre Self Floating, he keeps contemplating The Jewish War by Josephus, which, mentioned earlier in this narrative, tells of the Roman siege of Jerusalem when all of Judea rose in the organized revolt against Rome. Keep in mind that Rome was then the most powerful empire on earth say, today's United States, "and Jews merely a small swarthy tribe," (Jay Kay). This is when certain units of the Jewish forces were composed of the sub-sect (SS) of bizzare She-Males who ". . . from mere satiety unscrupulously indulged in effeminate practices, plaiting their hair and attiring themselves in women's apparel, drenching themselves with perfumes and painting their eyelids to enhance their beauty. And not only did they imitate the dress, but also the passions of women, devising in their excess of lasciviousness unlawful pleasures and wallowing as in a brothel in the city, which they

---

[16]The Beast 666, the creative disguise of Edward Alexander (Aleister) Crowley, the British novelist of Sexual Sanctum Sanctorum, (SSS).

polluted from end to end with their foul deeds . . ." **My self being, my consciousness feeling of myself, that taste of myself, of I and me above and in all things, which is more distinctive than the taste of ale and alum, more distinctive than the smell of walnut leaf or camphor, and is incommunicable by any means to another man . . . this unspeakable stress of pitch, distinctiveness, and selving, this self being of my own. (Gerard Manley Hopkins)**

Sniffing the pool as if it were filled with sex-giving yod rather than chlorine, our yodler begins to meditate. He does it first by focusing on words and numbers. Today, he starts with Yod, "the tenth letter of the Hebrew alphabet equivalent to English Y as in *yeti;* as number 10" (in the Webster's New 1953 International Dictionary the word Yod is immediately followed by the word Yoga. J. K.)

Meditating, he lets his inner Yod practically put him into a trance-like sleep.

Held up by an invisible net of his arch-natural respiration, our *waterchilde* remains afloat, his head above water, his feet together, his hands along his thighs, his shoulders rotated back, his chest expanded, his muscles at ease.[17] In his innermost CenterState, a constitutional republic with him elected President-for-Life, the President instructs the tower-of-strength operator to hold all incoming calls for as long as he is submerged, and he shuts off most of his inner communication system, leaving open only the Self Alert. Just as well: the self cannot be shut at will. He remembers Corneille's: "What is left you?" "Myself!"

---

[17]The "arch-natural respiration" was first publicly demonstrated in the United States by Thomas Lake Harris (d. 1906)

Now, our Yorde Merkabah[18] further separates himself from the outer intrusions by freeing his mind from any further responsibilities for his body. Promptly freed, his mind dons a monk's cloak and starts floating freely on its own. *One must break it all up; the dogmas must clean themselves up and the patterns take on new excitement.* Federico Garcia Lorca, 1940.

Now floating peacefully, Kosky dreams of a new narrative compound, (N.K. TO READER: PLEASE DON'T CONFUSE NEW WITH PURE.)—as new as was the compound, the alchemical gold—Cagliostro assured his fellow Poles he was about to create alchemically but merely in order to supplement with it the mineral gold—to create a commercially valid supplement, not a valuable replacement for real gold.[19]

A pure metal is that which, when melted in a crucible, does not give off sparks nor bubbles, nor spurts, nor emit

---

[18]Yorde Merkabah: a Jewish mystic who, descending to the depths, ascends to heaven and sneaks up to the Divine Throne through a path of his own; "whom the Talmud describes as sunk in prayer."[68] "The posture is one of self-oblivion, suitable for the induction of the prehypnotic auto-suggestion. It has been described in another context as follows: she sits down on a low chair and bends forward so that her head rests on her knees. Then in a deep, measured voice she repeats three times an exorcism, whereupon a certain change appears to come over her." See "Death and Rebirth in the Buddhist and Jewish Traditions, in *Judaism and the Gentile Faiths, (Comparative Studies in Religion,* by Joseph P. Schultz). op. cit.

[19]Nothing could have been more flattering to Cagliostro than the welcome he received on his arrival in Warsaw in May 1780. Poland, like Courland, was one of the strongholds of Freemasonry and occultism. Within a month of his arrival he had established at Warsaw a Masonic lodge in which the Egyptian Rite was observed. (Trowbridge).

any sounds, nor show any lines on the surface, but, tranquil like a gem, shows signs of tranquil fusion. (Rasarnava)

Kosky's writing compound—one which, like Cagliostro's gold, is to merely extend existing narrative, never to replace it—must accommodate to the letter his own inner camera obscura as well as an outer Camera Lucida (Roland Barthes: *Reflections on Photography*, 1981). It must include the French notion of composition,[20]; the lead, copper, and zinc of the Jewish joke; the healing precepts of Ruthenian folklore; and the yellow brass[21] and pewter of American journalism—old as well as new. "Three things returned to their original place: Israel, Egypt's wealth, and the heavenly writing. [Tractate Soferim]

A spiritual alchemist, Kosky must now decide what literary hue he should give his brand of narrative, the spirit of which must also incorporate to the letter the essence of beletrystyka. (Ruthenian for *belles lettres*. J. K.) Should this hue be gold?

The *Oxford English Dictionary* devotes to *gold* some six columns of foot-high small print. Now, that's a presence! Chemically inactive—not affected by water, air, or ordinary acids—gold has had innumerable alchemical imitations particularly because, as a color, gold is only one shade removed from yellow.[22] How ironic that so impure the color yellow

---

[20]"The first clear manifestation of his (Matisse's) new style appeared in 1908 when he painted a large composition which he called *Harmony in Green;* a subsequent repainting turned it into a *Harmony in Blue* . . . in 1909 (Sergei) Shchukin received the painting transformed, this time into a *Harmony in Red* ." (*Great French Paintings in the Hermitage*. Text by Charles Sterling. New York, 1958, p. 169.)

[21]Yellow brass: an alloy of copper and zinc, with traces of lead and iron.

[22]This corresponds to the notion of "mystical physiology" (Eliade)

misses being as pure as gold only by a small difference in taint!

Yellow. 1. Of the colour of gold, butter, the yolk of an egg, various flowers, and other objects; constituting one (the most luminous) of the primary colours, occurring in the spectrum between green and orange. (*OED*)

The *OED* devotes to *yellow* almost nine of its columns. That's three more than it gave to *gold*. Why? Is it because for centuries yellow has been the color of decomposition: of the diseased complexion, of "old discoloured paper" (*OED*); of jealousy ("yellow hose" [OED] — of yellow fever and of a yellow cross to bear for any admiral of the literary rear?)[23]

Should he, an egg-laying literary egghead, abandon the idea of creating a new alchemical formula for his egg No. 9? After all, the yolk alone of an egg contains some fifty percent water; the rest is fat, protein and ash. **Writing is liberation. (Sainte-Beuve)**[24]

He is awakened from his alchemical reverie by the sound of English speech. The American Trio: a dad, a mom, and a kid, all blond, blue-eyed and peachy, have arrived at the pool in their Taiwan-made American Rio swimming gear.

The **Rash Southerners** (Berry Fliming, 1943) settle into lounge chairs at the pool's edge, from where they occasionally glance at Kosky.

He glances at this pure American family unit who are, no

----

where the "noblest and most precious" is hidden in the "basest and most common" (Tantra), a thought the Western alchemists transferred from sex to science.

[23]A yellow admiral is a navy captain, retired as a rear admiral in Her Majesty's Fleet and not attached to any particular Red, White and Blue squadron.

[24]Rephrased by Heinrich Böll as **"Writing is freedom,"** and by Kosky (1969) as "Freedom means writing."

doubt, visiting Harlem, this urban heart of darkness, on a tourist fact-finding money saving vacation plan. Unfortunately, the looks of the two barefoot babes, and the look of their boobs, carry no spiritual fascination for him at this moment of his life in the fast lust lane. At this moment our heel would rather be confronted by a couple of naked, yes, but also WILD, WICKED HIGH-HEELED SULTRIEST SEPIA SEX SLUTS (*Leg Show Magazine*) or even two or three pictorials of black madonnas dressed in nothing but black and white stockings'nd sneakers coming to him straight from the one-and-only *Black Pictorials* magazine.

"I'm Natty Bumppo Effingham. We're all Effinghams." The dad introduces his family to Kosky. "We came to Manhattan from Mobile, Alabama. How are you, Mr. Lotus Floatus?" says the "handsome Mr. Effingham" (Cooper),[25] waving at Kosky with his yellow underwater camera.

"Couldn't be better," says our alchemist, waving at them with both hands momentarily taken out of the water while, thanks to his all-body breathing rhythm, our Archimedes does not sink any deeper.

"How's the water?" asks the mom.

"Couldn't be more fluid," says Kosky. **I must claim the**

---

[25]Edward Effingham: a hero of J. Fenimore Cooper's *Homeward Bound* and *Home as Found* whose creation enraged the American critics and led to the subsequent burning of Cooper effigies in his native Cooperstown as well as in New York and London. Then came Fenimore Cooper's Literary Offenses by the one-and-only Mark Twain (Jay Kay) ridiculing Cooper's *Leatherstocking Tales* and his preoccupation with Indian women, leather and stockings. This, in turn, led some critics to seek restless restifism in Cooper's fiction. (Restifism — from Restif de la Bretonne, a French novelist who established his foothold in literature by celebrating female shapely beauty starting from the shape of her foot up. J. K.)

virtue of absolute novelty. (Samuel Goldwyn, 1919)

"Why don't you dive all the way down to the bottom?" asks the Templeton teen.[26]

" 'Cause I am not a sea robin," says our Talmudist.[27]

"Then why don't you at least splash like Donald the Duck?" she investigates further.

"I keep my splashing inside," he says in keynoted phrase No. 6. "Just as well: two thirds of man is water. Two-thirds — not counting tears," he briefs her. *The main vehicle for this is the Torah, which, as our sages teach us, is also a spiritual counter part of water.* (Aryeh Kaplan)

"Is what you do the dead man's float!" The kid goes after him.

"How could I? I'm alive. . . . **some unscrupulous so-called yogis are trying to profit out of the current popularity of Yoga. They make unimaginable claims ranging from squatting on water to the cure of all types of diseases including cancer. (O. P. Jaggi)**[28]

"Is this pool a Red Sea?" she says, laughing.

"It is to the Jew in me," he answers her.

The earth was empty and desolate, with darkness on the face of the deep, and god's spirit fluttering on the face of the water. (Torah)

"You don't look Jewish," says the Mom. "With a tan that

------

[26]Templeton, the fictitious setting of Cooper's novels *Homeward Bound* and *Home as Found* — a supposedly fictional setting "which fooled nobody in Cooperstown." (Niskisko).

[27]Talmud, body of original Jewish oral wisdom, was completed whether in its Babylonian or Jerusalem version, almost 1600 years ago, and was named after these two places of its origin. Ed.

[28]See *History of Science and Technology in India,* by O. P. Jaggi (1966–1969).

deep you could be black deep inside."

"I like wearing disguises," says Kosky. "Besides, I've got *A Choice of Masks*." (Oscar Pinkus) **Go from yourself. (Stanislavsky)** "Jewgreek is greekjew. Extremes meet." (Joyce in *UlySSes*)

"He could be from Cooper's *Leatherstocking Tales*, yes, Indian, but not a Negro. Not in a thousand years!" says the man, taking a Polaroid picture of Kosky.

"Why not, Natty?" asks his Honey Queen.

"Because Mr. Floatus floats like a green toad, and blacks can't float. It's a fact!" says Natty. "Have you ever seen a black playing water polo at the Olympics?" he asks his Honey Bee.

"I don't think I have but how many private water pools do blacks have in Mobile, Alabama? What's wrong with water polo?"

"Nothing wrong. But blacks have natural trouble with floating. Their bones are too dense — and that's a scientific fact. Naturally, their bones are just too heavy. That's what's wrong. Blacks have too many minerals in their bones and not enough air. That's all."[29]

"A bone is a bone, not a brain. I thought the bones of all people were the same inside," says Queen Bee defending the immobile honor of Mobile, Alabama, with an expression which says to him, *I'm your sweetest taboo* yet.

"Only among us whites," says Natty. "Black bones come in all densities. And I don't mean only the whites or blacks of Alabama."

---

[29]Here, Mr. Effingham probably refers to the abstract of *The Density of the Lean Body Mass Is Greater in Blacks than In Whites,*" by E. J. Townsend, J. E. Schutte, J. Hugg, R. Schoup, R. Manina and C. G. Blomquuist, University of Texas, Austin, and U. T. Health Science Center, Dallas; American Journal of Physical Anthropology, Vol. 60, 1983. (Ed).

"He must carry a cork in his trunks." Honey Queen smooths her metallic swimsuit as she ogles Kosky, who now rests stretched like a frog on top of the water.

"What I carry in my trunks couldn't possibly keep me up for that long, madam!" says our literary producer turned into Master Mariner with a modest expression on his face.[30]

[69]For we all know, regardless of how deeply we inhale, we will hardly float along like a lotus leaf, no more easily, in any case, than we are used to in swimming. (Hans-Ulrich Rieker)

---

[30]The writer *embodies, expresses, translates, reflects, renders;* all of these terms of equal inadequacy, constitute our problem. (Pierre Macherey, *A Theory of Literary Production*, translated from the French by Geoffrey Wall [1978], op. cit, p. 119) See also Joseph Conrad, "Master Mariner, 1857–1924" in *Perspectives*, a Polish-American Educational and Cultural bimonthly, Washington, D.C. 1987.

$$\boxed{6}$$

"Why don't you call your book *Hermes?*" Dustin's words are to be counted carefully. He is, after all, "the nation's supreme literary accountant, who, according to *Writers'nd Editing*, others edited C. G. Jung's 3 volumes of *Alchemicals*," as well as being the editor-in-chief of Eidolon Books Unlimited, "the nation's sixth largest iconographic book company," in the words of *Spiritual Market Place*, the nation's only book and publishing rating journal.

"Why *Hermes?*"

"Hermes. The mixed-up master of creation. The son of mighty Zeus and his flowering Maia after whom we named the month of May."

"Hermes? As the prototype of the pony-riding shepherd, didn't he steal some of Apollo's cattle?" asks our literary child Herod (Herod, not Herolde printer!).

"He certainly did!" Dustin agrees.

"Wasn't his mercurial rise to fame damaged by stories of his childish tricks told by him or about him? Wasn't that why, in spite of his obvious accomplishments, no temples were erected to celebrate Hermes, but only herms? These pathetic oedipal busts set atop phallus-shaped street pillars and road posts, signaling to weary travelers where they could find phallus-worshipping hitchhikers or be ambushed by hordes of highway hookers?"

"So what? Don't you yourself favor in your fiction **The Golden Ass (Apuleius),** hairy mounts, feetal attractions—I mean feet not fetus—and whores and an occasional red scare?" Dustin asks pointedly.[1] "Besides, the name Hermes also refers your reader to Hermes Trismegistus, the founder of alchemy, the science of Hermetic art known today as philosophy."

"But what about his reputation tarnished by these stories told about him?"

"So what if it was? Doesn't a storyteller's reputation depend on stories? The taller the stories, the higher the teller," Dustin counterattacks with certainty, of Florian Znaniecki.[2] "Some forty-two books are said to have been fabled by this Hermes, all written under his dictation—an art he invented and Stendhal perfected. Or was it Henry James? Besides, like your character, Hermes was a classic hydrocephalic who, suffering from hydrocephaly saw the world as made of fluid—and at the same time believed matter is undestructible, as long as it doesn't move!"

"Let me meditate about this seed," says Kosky, mindful of his literary SuCCeSS story (thanks, printer, for such multiple SS!)[3] **"Remember that imagination is the quality that enables one to see things and people in their real as in their ideal relations. If you cannot realize it by yourself,**

---

[1]See *Red Scare: A Study in National Hysteria, 1919–1920,* by Robert K. Murray (Minneapolis: University of Minnesota Press, 1955).

[2]Florian Znaniecki: (b. 1882) Polish born, Polish-educated sociologist who, writing in English, develops the concept of "humanistic coefficient" and defines human action as being *always* a form of conscious conduct (CC).

[3]**You should meditate in a time and place where you will not be interrupted or disturbed by people, phone calls, or noise. Rabbi Nachman said that it was best to have a special room for meditation if possible.** *(Jewish Meditation* by Aryeh Kaplan, 1985).

talk to others on the subject. I have had to look at my past face to face. Look at your past face to face. Sit down quietly and consider it. The supreme vice is shallowness. Whatever is realized is right." (Oscar Wilde, *De Profundis*.)

Kosky trusts Dustin's intuition. It is purely American since, as his name indicates, Dustin comes from a very pure Boston family. Propelled by an inner wind, Reverend Dan Beach Bradley Borell,[4] Dustin's most revered ancestor, bravely sailed from Massachusetts all the way to Bangkok, where he — a typical Boston Brahmin! — hoped to introduce the Gospel to Siamese Brahmans — the all-time champs of what is latest in the art of meditation — to start a new Meditational Church in Siam.

"Speaking of a *herm*, of a footnote, of leaving your footprint in the text," Dustin's secretary tells Kosky on the phone the instant Dustin signs off, "Mr. Beach Borell would like you to describe your presently untitled novel for our next year catalogue. Please describe it in one word."

"Confessional," says Kosky.

"And your family background? In two words, if possible."

"Jewish Ruthenian."

The kind of Russian family to which I belonged — a kind now extinct — had, among other virtues, a traditional leaning toward the comfortable products of Anglo-Saxon civilization. . . . I learned to read English before I could read Russian. (Nabokov)

"And for our writers' questionnaire catalogue, could you answer this question? 'What is the single feature that at this

---

[4]The Reverend Dan Beach Bradley, M.D., author of *Medical Missionary in Siam, 1836–1873*, op cit., was "one of the many proper Boston Brahmins fascinated by the Orient and by its rigorous — almost puritanical — physical and mental discipline." (Kosky, *A Floating Lotus Lecture*, 1986).

creative junction you—you speaking only as a novelist, only as one who while courting reality, would never as much as curtsy to life, (she knows from Dustin how to address him)—most admire in woman?' "

"Abandonment," says Kosky.

"And in literature? Also, if possible, in one word."

"Decontrol. Never mind the politics, style a tangled tangle or **The Dynamics of Literary Response (Norman N. Holland, 1968. Dedicated 'For my mothers and fathers'.)"** On this thought Kosky ends one more manuscript chapter.

7

Suddenly an ordinary day turns into extraordinary. After he had washed his hair under the faucet with Miller's Muff Shampoo recommended for the abnormally aging, say, drying out, male with a rapidly dry, as well as drying-out, scalp, on the bottom of his bathtub's bottom, Kosky comes across an ugly apparition: a clump of human hair clogging his bathtub's drain.

Someone is losing a lot of hair — and this someone must have lost it in his bathtub relatively recently. Now, who? He examines the clump. The hair is black. It must have belonged to glorious Gloria, his latest proofreader in transit, who because he won't share his bed with anyone when asleep, slept in his bathtub last night. But wait! Gloria is black and her hair is snaking, while this greasy clump of hair covered with dead skin is composed of straight hair — one half of which turns out, under closer examination, to be greasy gray. He examines the clump again, this time under the light and through the magnifier: THE HAIR LOSS CAUSES PSYCHIC SHOCK, says his inner mordant examiner. He goes over it with a fine tooth comb. The hair is his. Sic transit Gloria mundi. Enough said.

Our *Jude the Obscure* (Thomas Hardy, 1894)[1] is losing hair

---

[1]Since every novel, no matter how ahistorical, has at least a five-year-long history: *"The history of this novel* (italics: J.K.) is briefly as

and he is losing it fast. Too bad: just think of the miracle of hair! Think of the two full pages of adjectives hair attracts in the Sotto Synonym'nd Word Finder Guide to Larger Vocabulary (1969). Hair is at the same time shaggy'nd sheeny, stiff'nd soft, straight yet flowing in the wind; solid yet floating in water. A head of hair makes him—him, a homo sapiens—a member of the hairy kingdom of the ape. Growing out of his body faster than just about anything else, including nails, hair is at the same time dead: it feels nothing. And speaking of feeling nothing, of death: by being alive and dead at the same time and, mark this, able to grow out of a man's dead body, doesn't hair connect man's present world with the one next-in-line? So much, then, for losing hair. "But what about turning bald? What about it? Isn't he our literary monk? And aren't monks supposed to be bald?" **Is it not true, rather, that nothing really matters in life but states of mind? (F. L. Lucas)** asks Jay Kay.

Jay Kay misses a point. Losing hair is not unlike losing reputation: you can replace it, but you can never grow it back. You can replace it with a real-life spiritual *halo* (a halo, not one more creative hello!); you can even carry this halo

---

follows. The scheme was jotted down in 1890 from notes made in 1887 and onwards, some of the circumstances being suggested by the death of a woman in the former year. The scenes were *revised* (italics: J. K.) in October 1892; the narrative was written *in outline* (italics: Novak) in 1892 and the spring of 1893 onwards into the next year; the whole, *with the exception of a few chapters* (italics: Ed.), being in the hands of the publisher by the end of 1894. . . . Like former *productions of his pen* (italics: Kosky), *Jude the Obscure* is simply an endeavour to give shape and coherence to a series of *seemings* (italics: Kosinski) or *personal impressions* (italics: Jay Kay), the question of their consistency or their discordance, of their permanence or their transitoriness (not transistoriness, printer!) being regarded as not of the first moment." (Thomas Hardy, Preface to the First Edition).

with you nonstop all the way to your grave—but, halo or hello, the fact is that a head of one's own hair means a head out of which out of which a fertile something might still grow.

Time for a visit to his own spiritual shaman, Dr. Christian Salvarsan, M.D. The good doctor sees Kosky in his office located in the basement of the Hotel Loisada, 666 East Ninth Street, an inexpensive Lower East Village establishment the maintenance of which allows Dr. Salvarsan to charge most of his minicare patients half price, if only after midnight.

At one time or another every respectable M.D. writes a respectable medical book, and Dr. Salvarsan is no exception. His widely known books, *The Teeth of Your Skin*, *Skin Dipping* and *Skin Deep*, tell all there is to know about the limitless self's most outer limits.

A mirror and a comb in hand, Kosky describes his condition to the doctor. In fact, there's nothing to describe; the good doctor can see a widower's peak for himself. A veritable horseshoe. "It's an emergency," says Kosky pointedly. "Could the fallout be stopped?" Doctor Salvarsan takes one look at Kosky's peak, then lowers his eyes. The verdict is clear.

"Losing hair is what frightens primitive men most," he says. "Here you are, supposedly at the peak of your growth, and your hair starts falling out of your peak. How sad!"

"But wait, Doctor!" says Kosky. "I'm barely under sixty. That's no reason to be bare." He won't say bald. "Can't this however scanty fallout wait at least until I'm over fifty-five, when, according to Turgenev and Lenin—both were *writers*—one's creative life—one's growth, so to speak—must end anyhow?"

"Now, now, control yourself. Be wise. Begin living like a grown-up man who remains productive no matter what his outer growth."

"Too bad wisdom can't be seen, while baldness can," says Kosky. "Besides, hair means virility. Am I losing virility as well?"

"The loss of hair as well as virility could be a result of Malic disease. Still, we need a blood test to confirm what I suspect is the case. Bad blood is one thing — sick blood is another!" The doctor prepares a syringe while Kosky boldly rolls up his sleeve in anticipation of his voluntary blood ordeal.

Any strange girl who lets a man use her has let other men use her also. If she has done this very often, she's a natural to have caught a disease. The army can protect you from many diseases, but you'll have to protect yourself from V.D. The only sure way is to stay away from women. There's no substitute for morals. (U.S. War Department, 1942)

"Don't be afraid of the needle. I won't let it escape into your vein. Don't panic at the sight of your blood. I won't let you bleed to death," says the doctor routinely.

In vain, the doctor attempts to pierce Kosky's blue and swollen vein with the tip of the needle. Is the needle too thick or is it his patient's vein? He tries again. This time he hits the flesh next to the vein, but not the vein. He withdraws the needle dripping onto the floor a priceless drop of pure Jewish blood,[2] and tries again.

---

[2] A propos of "pure Jewish blood": Jewish writers viewed sexuality in a remarkably positive light. When appropriately expressed within the framework of marriage, sexual activity required no apologies, transferences of meaning, or obligatory links with procreation. . . . Stress was placed on the achievement of sexual balance and mutality, not the prevention of sin and the avoidance of the promptings of the devil. . . . The universal need of both men and women for sexual release was unconditionally accepted. Sexual activity was also considered necessary to keep men's minds from wandering during study. writes Kenneth R. Stow in *The Jewish Family in the Rhineland in the High Middle Ages: Form and Function* (The American Historical Review, 1987). Read also *The Pariah*

In order to wipe this bloody experience out, Kosky reverts to storytelling, crossing once more the illusory border between *The Red and the Black* (Stendhal).

"Did you know," our Literary Bluff begins, "that from the time I was six until I was nine I routinely used leeches for various bloodlettings?"

"How were they used?" asks Dr. Salvarsan, while slowly detaching the vial from the needle and leaving the needle stuck deep in the vein, then attaching to it another vial — one of the six he intends to fill with Kosky's blood. In the process, another drop of Kosky's blood spills onto the floor.

"At one time during my World War II days when, like any other Gypsy I too suffered from *The Pariah Syndrome* (Ian Hancock)," Kosky goes on, "I saw leeches being used to first excite a woman — excite her to no limit." He pauses, slowed down by both his true-life emotion as much as by his by now well-tested overly narrative stage skill. "But then I also saw her being punished for being an overly excitable woman! by these crude, stupid, simple men. Punished by them — and by the leeches they brought for the occasion."

"How was she excited? How was she punished — how?" The good doctor becomes overly excited.

"First, pinned by these men — pinned down by their natural pins she was forced to watch men remove the leeches from a jar. Then they placed the leeches, one after another, on her *lower lips* to suck on her until the men decided the leeches had sucked her off enough."

"Go on," says the doctor. "I can take it!"

"Oddly enough, peeping under a door in another village, I saw leeches used exactly in the same manner on another

----

Syndrome: An Account of Gypsy Slavery and Persecution, by Ian Hancock (1987).

woman. This time, however, they were used not to punish her, but to cure her."

"What was she suffering from?" asks Salvarsan, attaching vial No. 3 to the needle sticking out from Kosky's trembling arm.

"She was lovesick," says Kosky. "She was in love with the wrong man. Her love for him made her so sick that she could not feel love for her rightful husband. Leeches were used to make her more sensitive."

"No wonder you turn out to be such a blood-sucking leech in your books," says Dr. Salvarsan. "With experiences like this, how could you miss?" Unknowingly he paraphrases an American book critic.

Expertly the doctor detaches vial No. 6 and throws away the needle — now a useless harpoon.

"As a writer I could miss either when I use emotion — or let myself be used by it," says Kosky, relieved that, given the doctor's nasty comment, the storytelling drama is finally over.

Whatever he may do — close his ears, swear that he hears nothing — the words "I Am That I Am" remain imprinted on his soul. He has received a message. He can do what he likes with it. But he is a Jew by virtue of that message and of what he intends to do with it. (François Fejtö)

While our vice conscious Avicebron[3] ponders next drama

----

[3] *The Fountain of Life,* the twelfth century Spanish classic, ever since particularly popular with Christian readers, and assumed to have been penned by Avicebron, whose life and vices nothing was known, in the nineteenth century was pronounced by Solomon Munk, the French-Jewish scholar, to have been the work of no one else but Ibn Gabirol (died in 1069) the foremost, and the best known poet of Spanish Jewry. "This eight centuries old pen-name

of *The Fountain of Life* (Ibn Gabirol) the now-indifferent doctor carefully seals the vials and then, on the enclosed label, most legibly writes Kosky's last name first, and first name last, followed by the initial N of Kosky's middle name.

SS

The next day Kosky visits the Whiskerandos Hair Harem Salon, known "to service some of the most visible people in the publishing industry" in the words of the prospectus.

The walls and the ceiling of the salon are covered with glass mirrors. Here, nothing obstructs the view of a balding head, and every mirror tells you what a difference hair makes.[4]

Here he is politely accosted by the hirsute redhead, whose sexy six inch high-heel spikes leave instant foot prints in his mind and offer a brand new sole-full (sole, not soul) narrative experience. She is an employee assigned to him, who, after asking him for his name "and preferably an I.D.," then asks him to call her simply Hairlet.

In her early thirties, Hairlet sports a "perfect munchable itty bitty chest" (Jay Kay) 33AA-33-33 frame, a double hare-lip,[5] a bouncy butt straight from an adult Butt magazine, and, in keeping with the salon's policy, leaves her legs and underarms unshaved, a welcome reminder of his fleeting

---

was the longest kept secret in literary history." comments wryly Jay Kay.

[4]The *OED* assigns almost ten columns to the word *hair*. That is about two columns more than it assigns to *gold* and about six more than it does to *man*.

[5]Harelip: a congenitally divided lip, commonly an upper one, like that of a hare.

furry, as well as fleecy and furious, wartime lovemaking days in the Pripet Marshes.

"Ever since Sir Harry Hairster started this business based upon his 9 relative degrees of Male Baldness Misery," says Hairlet, "the name Whiskerandos has been antinomous with hair — or is it synonymous, I forget! you might say." Dressed to the last hairpin, her simple, rough haircloth shirt is in lovely contrast to her red hair.

Eager to incorporate her Haironymous self into his life — that is, in writing fiction — he does to her butt in fantasy what doing in reality in half the states of this supposedly so-free country the Law puts you behind the heaviest bars. (For six to nine years or is it 69 years? J. K.)

"You can comb what's left of your hair over the horseshoe. A lot of junior execs do that. Or you can swirl your sideburns all the way up. You can also grow a beard long enough momentarily to cover your bald spot. In other words, you can make quite a macho show of yourself," says Hairlet as they pass the hall of mirrors, the sight in one of which brings to the sick mind of our Dirty Old Man her own High Heel Appeal.[6]

"What else?

"You can get a convertible — a toupee top, but take it off before you put down the top of your convertible — or you'll blow your top off," she hisses with a hairy smile. "Above all, don't wear it when you're screwing in bed. Like a bad condom, the toupee comes off faster than you do!"

A hairum-scarum prospect. "What else can I do?" asks our literary Hairoglodyte, feasting his feisty eyes on "The Color of Her Hair" (pop song and a hair commercial. J. K.)

---

[6]See *Eros and Thanatos:* Or, The Mythic Aetiology of the Dirty Old Man, by Leslie A. Fiedler, *Salmagundi*, 1977.

Time for a consultation about the inevitable male-pattern baldness. Inevitably, this process takes our progressively balding Hair Monger® to the fully mirrored private room, where Hairlet places him in front of a triptych mirror, then runs her fingers through his hair. In the mirror he catches sight of her ring finger and her hair ring — a lock of hair cast in diamonds. This sight casts in him a brand-new image of her caught by him in his mental Sex Act club. There she is, a weary French *midinette,* undressing wearily — then leaving nothing but her hair flowing round about her.

"Technically, you're thinning out. Your hairy years are definitely over. Your hair follicles seem to be genetically predisposed to be shut down by your own male hormones. From now on, your looks suggest spiritual exhaustion — and the art of dying," declares the hairy oracle.[7]

"How about the dying art of giving head? Giving it say, when I'm sunk in prayer No. 69 on my knees and all bent down?" asks our fatigued sexual combatant, fatigued already by the very thought of dress, nodress and undress.

"You can, sir, start wearing a hat. Wearing it nonstop. Even when doing the 69," she says wearily. "Or you can wait for our invention of a magic Formula One hair tonic which will grow new hair all over your bald spots with the speed of a Formula One racing car. Meanwhile you can also do nothing."

"What technical options do I have?" he asks hairily.

"You can, my dear sir, get hair waves, made of hair-grass woven across your scalp. Unfortunately, each time the wind sends a wave through your hair, everybody can see the weave — and leave."

———————

[7]Hairy oracle: Brit. slang, circa 1799 — synonymous with pie, hairy-ring, hair court and hairburger; American slang, circa 1899 — hairy organs of a hairy-bit woman. See *Americanisms,* by John S. Farmer (1889).

"What comes next?"

"Sutures." The Up-the Skirt Teaser pinches his scalp a bit painfully. "First, surgical threads are threaded into your scalp, then phony hair is threaded into the thread."

"Any problems with that?" He edits out his own terror of surgery.

"Periodic inflammation, followed by rejection by the body. This can be prevented by multiple checkups."

"How multiple?"

"At least three to four times a month. And multiplying."

"That's a way of life which for sure would kill my creative concentration!" cries out our Jan Sobieski.[8]

"Consider then, the transscalp method of Dr. Mohican. Dr. Mohican plucks out hair from the remaining few fertile follicles of your barely fertile body, or from the body of a fertile young and virile hair donor, and plugs them into your scalp's infertile hair-brain temples," she says, humiliating him all too openly.

"That's too Mohican for me," says Kosky. "What's left?"

Her fingers move over his scalp like a hair-streak butterfly. "There's the Whiskerandos Hairlet-by-Hairlet method." She lets a lock of her hair fall over his face, which makes him think again of a woman's hair as being a form of her most natural dress.

"Think of your current hairline as a bare story and the bald patches as what's missing in that story." She customizes her language, to suit her customer. "We can fill these bald

---

[8]Jan Sobieski, the Polish king who died in 1696 was known for his military infatuation with Heavy Hussars as well as with his Queen Marysiènka, a well-known expert 69 to whom he wrote his famous "sexually obsessed" *Letters to Marysiènka* his sex-stricken wife.

Read also *God's Playground: A History of Poland*. Vol. 1 The Origins to 1795; Vol. 2 1795 to the present by Norman Davies, 1982.

patches — these lapses in your story, so to speak — by editing in new hair to your barely existing narrative hairline. The process doesn't really end there," she says. "Once our hair — your new hair — is in place, it must be, like your natural one, shampooed at least thrice a week. It must be trimmed and groomed since, unfortunately, your old gray and ugly hair still grows. Our highly trained assistants — men or women, or couples if you so desire and can afford to pay for them — take care of all this attention — will pay utmost attention to your fear of being a no-longer-desirable man and do it at a slight extra cost." She keeps on stroking his neck with her ring, while he watches her lips. "With your hairpiece in mind, we also offer other useful services. We can invest your money for you. And, to spare you the embarrassment of dating someone who doesn't know the truth about you, about your hair, we even run our own Hairline dating Fail-Safe Sex service," she smiles at him offering our heel a déjà vu but still Kundalini-generating a hare-lipped smile.

SS

TIME FOR A FLASHBACK.

Instantly, a memory slide slides between him and his so caressingly narrative Village of Pieszczyce. He sees Pripet Marshes. Old Ruthlandia.[9] It is a hot Sunday in the unusually hot August, 1942. A friendly old fisherman smokes half of his hemp-filled pipe, then falls asleep next to his plywood boat at Lake Pripet. Next to it, not in it.

Is this the time Kosky must leave the village? He must —

---

[9]On October 23, 1905 in West Rutland, Vermont (U.S.A.) *The Rutland Herald* announced the blessing of the cornerstone of the Stanislau Kostka Church which was to serve Ruthenian immigrants employed in the local marble quarries. (American History).

this time his Self speaks to him in the third person—rather than ought to. He must before he is noticed. Already too many village people look at him as if he were a Jewish or a Gypsy stray. As if he were made by the Germans. Made to be a purveyor of disaster. It is a miracle no one has given up on him and given him to the Germans. **Live your life unnoticed. (Israel Kosky)** I'm sorry father. I'm about to be noticed again. Time to go. Good-bye Pieszczyce! (In Ruthenian, pieszczota means a caress. J. K.)

With the fisherman safely asleep on the marshy shore, Kosky takes off in his boat and starts rowing toward the next village. This is the fertile time of the year. Anywhere he looks, hand-hewn, flat-bottomed canoes and fishing boats ply the calm, sunny waterlands, as these marshes are called by their inhabitants who, locked in by landlords, have for millennia lived in these landlocked waters.[10]

Propelled by a breeze, he arrives in the next-in-line village by midday. This is Sunday—with everybody in church, this is a good time to make one's arrival unnoticed. GLINISZCZE is the name of the village carved on a wooden plaque hanging on a wooden cross, half-sunken in a marsh grave. Good omen. Before the war, his father had read to him a poem called "The Marshes of Glynn." How far could it be from Glynn to Gliniszcze if both places—one existing only in his head, and one in life—are located on marshland, a stagnant water?

Our journeyman leaves the boat on the shore and, sneaking behind the rows of fishing nets drying on their poles planted along the bank spots a small house safely hidden

---

[10]See, *The Changing Peasantry of Eastern Europe*, by Joseph Obrebski, 1976. Obrebski, (1905–1967) a distinguished Polish sociologist, studied the utterly non-homogenous peasants of Pripet Marshes.

behind the granaries. Molested by no one, not even by the tied-up and sleepy dog, Norbert enters the house. Inside he first kicks the bench in the entranceway. Since he can't speak (this is one of his mute years), this is his way of saying, "Hi, I'm here." (At the time, Norbert Kosky suffered from a case of aphasia, a temporary loss of speech following a mental affliction. — Estate Editors). Nobody answers. In the kitchen, he pounds on the metal stove with his *comet* — a portable stove made of an empty preserve can. Nobody answers.

He walks out of the house, crosses the courtyard, and walks into a barn, its wall, and slabs of stone — coldplates built over the fireplace of a steam bath *cum* sauna. He is about to leave the barn when he is stopped — arrested! — by the view. The view of a naked woman. She is lying on a platform made of slabs of wood covering slabs of stone, and she still hasn't seen him. She seems to be dozing, but is she? There is only one way left to find out before leaving this creepy barn. Creepy, yet so tempting. Now — why? Is it because of this sleeping woman? Bosomy *and* sleeping? Let's sneak up on her. Safety is one thing, curiosity another. Careful, though, like most people he too often speaks to himself in the third person: You're a stray — she is local. Besides, you're a Jew, she's a Gentile. **Also in Poland the Nazis imposed the penalty of *instant deportation* to the concentration camp for failure by a Pole — no matter how old, be it an adult or a child — to report the whereabouts of a single Jew, or his non-Jewish keepers, no matter how old the Jew was, or who was his keeper. (Kosky, 1987)** There is a price put on your head by the SS in the nearby town of Pinsk, on the head of every Jew who might hide or be hidden by the townfolk. If this so lovely-to-look-at naked local woman, or anybody else in the village, chooses to deliver you to them you will die by being burned in Treblinka. But if she, or somebody else, chooses to keep you, if only for her or their amusement, and the Germans find out, they will burn the

117

entire village, as the German soldiers and SS and the village elders keep reminding everybody. Not to mention a large in size wall posters WARNING: DELIVER ALL JEWS TO US OR ELSE! which, distributed by the SS to every village, no matter how small, depict graphically—in caricature-like drawings—a prototypical Jewish man and woman—old, middle-aged, teenager or child. Too bad that, these so threatening posters, show a Jewish boy who looks amazingly like Norbert Kosky—**Reflect upon it, don't speculate. Life comes only moment by moment. Moment means reflection. (Israel Kosky)** His father is right: the Germans are not here and this woman is. In order to reflect on what he sees, he must see her again. He tiptoes toward her, passing her Sunday dress hanging the best way it can on a broken tree branch tucked in between the stones of the wall. She is of his mother's stature. She is flabby where his mother was firm, and albino blond where his mother was Gypsy brown, but so what? Will she love him like a stepmother? Enough to save his life? Her breasts are full—as full as, during that last prewar August, were the breasts of his mother. His mother who once told him that a man loves a woman with his *tip* (meaning *also* the tip of his tongue. J. K.) and a woman loves a man with her heart, ("which, no doubt, meant giving his father's other tip a most welcomed trip between her bountiful jumbo tipsters," tips the reader never sexually satiated Jay Kay.) **The fact is, next to her clitoris, a woman's nipples are just about the most sensitive part of her body—or at least they *can* be, if she takes the time to develop their erotic potential. Each tit is supplied with nerve endings that connect to the uterus, which is why nipple sucking can make a woman come.** Lana Davies, (Gent magazine).

He tiptoes closer, and closer still. He closes his spiritual ranks around her. He is now three feet away from her. Just look at those milk-filled udders, life's miraculous jugs. Could he drink milk straight from these female udders the way he drinks a cow's warm milk each time he milks a cow, when there is no one other than other cows around?

The woman wakes up. She looks at him without fear; she does not even cover herself. He looks her in the eye.

Breast Symphony is what your father likes me to play for him most. (Elisabeth Kosky to Norbert, circa 1938)

"Call this symphony a Boob Bop BeBob." adds Jay Kay.

"Where are you from?" she asks.

He nods his head in the direction of the lake—not in the direction of Pieszczyce. This could mean that he is a water-baby, a helpful little earthling who, the down-to-earth peasants believe inhabits their quaggy fernland.

He steps closer still. He is now the knight errant, a man he had read so much about before the war. He is also Simplex, the German boy called Simplicius Simplicissimus, his early childhood first SS hero. "You don't necessarily have to follow the complex and silly Sidis Billy," his mother says to him again and again on his memory slides. "You can follow the sexy boy simply called Simplex." Sneaking up on her like that he is also Emil—from *Emil and the Detectives*—once his favorite fictional hero. He steps closer—closer still. He does it because he already likes her. She first raises herself on her elbows and, cutting her armpits from his view lets one of her bombers dive at his face. Then she sits up, yawns, stretches like a cat after a long nap and runs her hands through her hair—then, just like that, in front of him, through her flat-bush hair. Enough said.

"What's your name?" she asks him.

Our Simplex averts his gaze. He now sees this woman wearing nothing but a very purple *areolae*. *Areolae, printer, not Aureole Aureola* which means *halo* in Ruthenian. Halo, not hello!

"C'mon, you're not a plant! Can't you talk? What's your name?" she prompts him, our nameless Boy from Kosky's first novel.

In reply, he opens his mouth, then soundlessly closes it. He hears his mother say, **your father likes to suckle them my nipples and oreolae like a baby.**

"Are you mute, or also deaf?" She tests his hearing. "How old are you?"

Our Bell Boy shows the Busty Belle all but one of his fingers.

"Nine? Really? You look six." She reaches out to him and, with her large hands placed on his bony shoulders, draws him to her as if he were a little calf and she a cow to be suckled by her baby.

"Do you want to stay here, to work?" she asks, and, burning with kundalini, our little Jewish piglet nods in an unqualified "yes." **O breast, whereat some suckling sorrow clings. (Swinburne, 1866)**

Now what is this woman going to do? Will she tell her neighbors that she decided to harbor a Jewish flotsam? What if her neighbors will report it to the nearest local police station? Or worse yet, will this lovely Gentile — so gentle that no wonder she must be called Gentile — keep him, but only for a while? and only because she hopes to be paid for keeping him — and why wouldn't she hope? Greed is human and so is poverty. And is not there a price to be paid for taking a risk. For risking one's life — the life of this strange-looking Other? You see, what you do not see is her entire family, her many children, who with their father are this very minute in church where they pray to their Father Almighty, and not to Moses. What if one of her children, be it a little boy, or a little girl, squeals on him to one of the village elders?

Next thing you know a German plainclothesman, or even a unit of SS or plain Wehrmacht soldiers might unexpectedly show up at her doorstep and, pistols in hand, ask her to show them the way to that illegally harbored Jewish *pistolero* — that *kleine Jude.*

He remembers the lesson of the Talmud his father gave him many a time: "Your life is more important than your neighbor's." End of quote. "Now, ponder this," his father would say here. "If this is what we Jews think of saving the life of another,—even another Jew—why should we expect anyone—be it another Jew or even the nicest Gentile—to sacrifice his or her life to save the life of another person, particularly if that person wasn't even their kin, and, as is your case, Norbert, does not even remotely look like a Gentile?"[11]

Suddenly, mindless of his safety, his peeing Tom begins to misbehave again. It begins to grow, threatening to be noticed. This threatens his safety; after all he is a Jew whose "peeing Tom must never be seen by any Gentile—particularly when he and you are both peeing together, even when peeing into the same Shibboleth, into the same river," says his mother to him on one memory slide after another. "Man's race is written not on man's face but, most unfortunately for some Jews, on man's member," his mother then says to his father and she says it as if Norbert could not hear. "You can change a family name, but you can never undo the circumcision. Never ever." In spite of such warning, his peeing Tom keeps on growing like that magic stalk growing out of a magician's transparent glass pot seconds after being planted there by the magician's voluptuously beautiful woman assist-

---

[11]Kosky's father combined the knowledge of the Buddha's Four Noble Truth and his Eightfold Path with the intimate sense of *Duties of the Heart* by that Jewish Buddhist Bahya Ibn Pakuda, conceived, or written, circa 1069, and the equally Buddhist *The Way of the Upright*, by Moses Hayyim Luzzatto (that eighteenth-century Jewish mystic.—Ed.). From the Author: And as for saving the Jews, the reader is referred to *The Abandonment of the Jews: America and the Holocaust, 1941-1945*, by David S. Wyman, New York 1984. Introduction by Elie Wiesel, 1985.

ant—a nightclub act Norbert particularly admired as a boy of five, when he saw it first accompanying his mother in a real, adult nightclub, mind you, not in some overly obvious children's circus.[12]

The woman notices his magic act, but either it does not surprise her, or she doesn't show her surprise.

"Drop your pants," she says. "Let's peek at your peeing Tom." He obeys, and drops them promptly.

The buxom lady peeps at his divination rod. ("What luck she was not a German fraulein," adds historically minded Jay Kay).

"My, my, I've never seen a skinned snake like that. Who cut you so horribly?" she exclaims, watching our Cagliostro, Jr., put on his overly tight pants with some difficulty. "What happened to you, my poor child?" she exclaims with tears in her eyes.

"Evoking real tears whether of sorrow or laughter in an audience is a good artist's ultimate goal," Kosky hears his mother address him just before the War. "Any artist, not just a good pianist," he corrects himself. "Anybody who, for this reason or that, must play upon, or speak up from The Big Stage"—Big Stage being his mother's euphemism for life.

SS

Good health is as relative as happiness; as phony as magic," Dr. Salvarsan says ominously during Kosky's return

---

[12]Because of her breasts, which she called "overly obvious," Elisabeth Kosky (nee Weinreich: J.K.) never performed on a legitimate pianists' stage. Hence, she was drawn to any nightclub act which, in her words, "enhanced an independently rhythmic performance of the strippers' breasts."

visit to his office. "You should know: aren't you the plot maker who conjures up illusion? Only the other day I saw you healthily demonstrating your sick literary wares on a talk show *Who's For or Against the Khazar Theory*[13] on my Cable TV."

" 'Why boys, I'm no magician. I do not do tricks. You have me all wrong. I'm just an actor!' " Kosky quotes Frederic Tilden[14] as quoted by Harlan Tarbell.[15] "Never mind my magic. How is my health?"

"You're not exactly healthy. Nobody is, and that's why we all need doctors," says the doctor. "Just as well: Remember that, to Cioran: A man of good health is always a creative disappointment to a writer himself as well as to others, particularly to his physician. In substance I regret to say there's nothing wrong with you." He glances offhandedly at the blood test. He smacks his lips, then says, "In reality, however, there's only one minor mental problem and this might rekindle your lost sense of life's never-ending drama."

"How minor?" Kosky asks, his lips suddenly dry. **Life doesn't pose problems. Man does. (Israel Kosky, 1945)**

"You've got the beginning of the Ganser Syndrome. Ganser was the first to describe its symptoms, and described it as

---

[13]See "Six Arguments Against the Khazar Theory of the Origin of Eastern European Jewry" in *The Book of Jewish Lists*, by Ron Landau, 1984, p. 96. (While some of these arguments make some minor sense, the others are wholly unconvincing: J.K.) Here, as is often the case in the rest of this MS., these initials indicate Jay Kay, the protagonist of Kosky's never-quite-polished and yet to be published novel: J.K.)

[14]Frederic Tilden, a great stage magician, played the leading role of Alessandro di Cagliostro in *The Charlatan*.

[15]Harlan Tarbell, "one of the greatest conjurers of the 20th century." *(Magic and Showmanship, a Handbook for Conjurers,* by Henning Nelms, 1969.)

colorfully as if he were a novelist, and the syndrome was invented by him. Today, this condition, 'the pseudodementia caused by the overproduction of Malic acid' is primarily known as Malic disease. Malic, not Ganser, in order to make medical science more objective we now drop out the names of those doctors who often make up classy sounding names of mental illnesses. Don't confuse Malic disease with the spiritually fatal Malison illness," says the good doctor. "Both conditions differ from each other as much as do such words as worship and warship, malic and malignancy — or, say, Svahili and Svengali."

"Malic disease?" our Svengali lisps.

"Yes. For some reason, your Adam's apple started to heavily overproduce Malic acid. Overproduce and for an unknown reason." He peeks into his file. "You've always had too much of it — for your age, the average norm is four to five — but it was still within the norm. Now it's over six! And nine tops the chart. To be exact, it is six point nine."

"What does Malic acid cause?"

"In most cases, it causes *vorbeireden*, a condition defined by *Materia Medica* as an occasional need to be vague, or giving an approximate — even phony — answer rather than a yes or no — in order to improve one's image of oneself, or one's act, and by so doing forcing the spectators to believe they are witnessing an act of inspiration, not simple magic. *Vorbeireden* is commonly found among professional conjurers and artists, such as novelists, who, in their act, depend on inner magic."

"Be brave, Doctor. Anything else?"

"Well, yes. In certain patients, this malaise is said to affect the working of the brain's *insula* — the peninsula of free speech, so to speak — as well as the area between the parietal and temporal lobes, the junction of The Minimal Self (Christopher Lasch),[16] as we, the niggly medical psychics, call it."

---

[16]See The Minimal Self: Psychic Survival in Troubled Times, by

"Anything else?"

"Malic disease can easily be considered a minor mental aberration, one which might or might not lead to Malison illness,[17] an illness which has nothing to do with either Malic acid or apples. 'Their malison was almost as terrible as the curse of a priest,' says G. Smith already in 1861, and he's right. Malison illness is a result of deficiency of creative estrogen which affects a person's entire being. Like anxiety, it is an illness of the spirit," the doctor goes on.

"Well?" Kosky paces the room. "How minimalist is my condition?"

"He, (Pasqualino, from Wertmuller's "Seven Beauties", J. K.) is a sexually dependent worm at the start and a pitiable abused worm at the end, and his metaphorphosis is entirely superficial. [Kosinski, 1976]).

"It depends on how seriously the sick man reacts to a healthy environment — or a sick environment to the healthy man. Both Jeanne d'Arc and Sabbatai Sevi suffered from it, and so did our own Commodore Perry and Captain Elliott, at least according to what J. Fenimore Cooper had to say about them both in his outrageous *Naval History of the United States*. (Cooper himself suffered from it: J. K.) President Andrew Johnson[18] was known to have contracted it. And, at

---

Christopher Lasch (author of *The Culture of Narcissism*) New York, 1984. See also *The Minimalist Aesthetic:* Art and Literature in an Age of Extremity. *ibidem.*

[17]First described circa 1320 in Sir Beaues 3969 as a malediction and curse. (*OED*)

[18]Andrew Jackson the 17th president served from 1865 to 1869. "These dates alone tell you all about his problems with his public image," (Norbert Kosky).

125

the time of the Dreyfus Affair, most of Dreyfus's family, though, ironically, not Dreyfus himself." The very Dreyfus who, unimaginatively stolid, stolid, not just stoic, for a French Jew, until the end, still did not understand why he was hit. Did you already see "The Dreyful Affair" at the Jewish Museum?[19]

"Have any novelists other than J. Fenimore Cooper suffered from it?" Kosky paces the room while Dr. Salvarsan watches him calmly.

"Answer for yourself," says Dr. Salvarsan.

Self-Centered Risk:
HEART ATTACK FROM THE PRONOUN "I"

Whether you focus more on yourself or upon the world outside could affect the health of your heart. Drs. Larry Scherwitz and Lewis Graham, of the UC San Francisco Medical Center, looked at the frequency with which people use self-references like "I," "me," and "my." Their findings: The less you use the first-person singular — the less self-involved you are — the lower your risk of coronary heart disease.

— *American Health*

---

[19]"The Dreyfus Affair: Art, Truth and Justice," The Jewish Museum, New York, 1987. From the program: "The exhibition offers a view of the tempestuous history of the false accusation and conviction for treason of Captain Alfred Dreyfus, a French Army officer and a Jew. In 1894 Dreyfus was charged, on false evidence, of spying. He was solemnly degraded of his rank and condemned to perpetual imprisonment on Devil's Island. Four years later he was retried by appeal in Rennes, but still found guilty, this time with extenuating circumstances. Although the illegality of the first trial and insufficient evidence against him became widely known through public debate, *it was not until 1906* that Dreyfus was exonerated and subsequently reinstated in the Army with high honors."

"At this time there are no legally approved drugs for use in the diagnosis, cure, mitigation, treatment or prevention of Malic disease." Dr. Salvarsan closes Kosky's dossier. "Therefore the market is flooded with the spiritually spurious Tantric preparations." He pauses thoughtfully. "Don't be upset. You will live with this condition until you die—though die not necessarily from it."

The doctor gets up and, taking Kosky by the arm, walks him to the door. Speaking about death, or even about **sex and character (Otto Weininger),** about Eros dating Thanatos, is his way of showing Kosky that, like life, the consultation must also eventually end, and that **A successful author is equally in danger of the diminution of his fame whether he continues or ceases to write. (Dr. Johnson).**

┌─────────────┐
│   │
│   *8*   │
│   │
└─────────────┘

Complete originality is rare. The most ingenious conjurer can spend a lifetime without hitting on a wholly
new device or an entirely novel effect. Fresh illusions are
another matter. (Henning Nelms) How true. Try, if you are
a storyteller to devise a wholly new literary vice or a device,
be it in a work of fiction or nonfiction; tough ticky — unless
you're Dostoyevsky, Stefan Zweig, the love-obsessed Stendhal, or even Yehudah Halevi — "the greatest narrative master of them all." (Niskisko, 1982)[1] **If through some**

---

[1]Judah (or Yehudah) Halevi (or ha-Levi or Halevy, c. 1069 [or
1075]-1141): Jewish poet and philosopher born in Tedula, Spain.
He is the author of the *Book of the Khazars* (or Kuzari), translated by
Hartwig Hirschfield, 1964. **"The conversion of the King of the
Khazars to Judaism is supposed to have taken place about the
year 740, some four hundred years prior to the composition of
Halevi's work (1130-1140). In Cordova, where the author lived
and worked, the tale of the Khazars was a vivid reality, since a
number of Jewish families in that city claimed descent from the
Khazars. It was, therefore, quite natural for Halevi to relate his
philosophy to the reputed triumph of the Jewish religion in the
debate held at the court of Bulan, King of the Khazars."** *(The*

cataclysmic catastrophe all Jewish books, from the Bible to the last Yiddish daily, were lost and only the *Book of the Kazari* remained, it would still be possible for the historian to faithfully reconstruct the diverse strands of thought and sentiment which enter into the making of the traditional Jewish mentality. (Jacob B. Agus) Tonight, wearing the hat of the Haunted Conjurer, haunted by the Obeah Man's curse,[2] Kosky will experiment with switching literary routine. Tonight, right at 9:00 P.M. in one of his neighborhood's largest and fanciest mass-feeding restaurants, he will test whether an old magic disappearing act can be first adapted by him, then adopted as a literary trick.

Wearing a blond wig, a false nose and thick bifocal glasses, he chooses for the stage of his Self-test the brightly lit center table at the Elsie Venner Viennese-American restaurant located in tourist-infested central Manhattan.

All alone, he then waits for a waiter, building within himself a veritable wall of creative tension made of magic. To him, to a "first-rate second-rate novelist," (Kosky on *David Mailman TV Show*, 1984, also in *Polityka*, 1987) such elementary, and, granted, often silly outings, are as necessary as the suspension of disbelief.

This is his walking along *The Street of Crocodiles* (Bruno Schulz, also known as *Cinnamon Shops* [1934, 1963, 1985]). This is, in short, his short-cut from fiction to life and back to fiction — a strange zigzagging between Manhattan's own folklore and East European fictional lore. **The whole forest seemed to be illuminated by thousands of lights and by the stars falling in profusion from the December sky. The air pulsated with a secret spring, with the matchless**

Evolution of Jewish Thought from Biblical Times to the Opening of the Modern Era, by Jacob B. Agus, London, New York 1959).

[2]The Obeah Man: a creature who, while inhabiting us, con-

purity of snow and violets. We entered a hilly landscape. The lines of hills, bristling with the bare spikes of trees, rose like sighs of bliss. I saw on these happy slopes groups of wanderers, gathering among the moss and the bushes the fallen stars which now were damp from snow. (Bruno Schulz, 1985 edition)

Keep in mind also that such a bout with reality represents to Kosky what *A Stroll with William James* (Jacques Barzun) could be William James, brother of Henry, worked with Boris Sidis, the period's best known child psychologist and on *How To Make Your Child a Genius,* (Sarah Sidis). Born on April 1st, the Fool's Day, in 1898, Bill Sidis, son of Boris and Sarah (she was a well-known medical doctor) was no fool. Disraeli-like at the age of eighteen months, he was already able to read and understand *The New York Times*.

It was, after all, not an accident that Billy Sidis was named Billy after William James, who, when Billy was born, was the best-selling and most renowned psychologist in the world. James was a close friend of Boris Sidis and sponsored the various experiments Sidis conducted on various humanoids, including Billy. **It is impossible to conjecture what kind of psychology James would have developed if he had been an atheist like Freud, but it is certain — and I am devoting the rest of this book to demonstrating this argument — that if Freud had been a believer like James, he would not have developed psychoanalysis. (Peter Gay, 1987)**[3]

The waiter shows up. He is an American wise guy. Don't ever confuse wisdom with being wise.

------

stantly attempts to make us look foolish by forcing us to lose our temper. (J.K.) —

[3] *A Godless Jew:* Freud, Atheism, and the Making of Psychoanalysis, by Peter Gay 1987.

"Call me Smike," the wise guy says to Kosky. "What's your fancy tonight?" From some three feet away he tosses to Kosky a menu as if it were the antigravity hat.[4] This is Smike's magic act.

Our Mr. Wisdom takes a look at the menu. "Nothing on it attracts me," he says and he says it as one who has just lost his spiritual banner. "Can I have just a plate of thickly sliced North American raw onions mixed and covered with a few chunks of preferably Israeli-grown lemon?"

"Raw onions mixed with lemons? Are you nuts? That's pure acid rain! What are you going to do with all this shit?"

"It's my scurvy special," says Kosky. "I'm going to eat it! Eat it 'cause it's good for my gums." He pauses. "You see, what you can't see is that my gums were fatigued by the lack of food during World War II."

Smike takes a long look at him. The look says, "Have it your way, nut! Nobody *I know* cares about the threat of war!"

The instant Smike leaves the table, Kosky bends down, as if searching for something, maybe a coin, maybe a comb, he's just dropped next to his table, the magician's purposefully audience-distracting routine. Then, when he's convinced nobody is paying any attention, to him or to his forthcoming action, our artful dodger drops out of sight — that's his act — by literally dipping under the table, the tablecloth opening for him, then closing behind, like a parenthesis. Our smoothie does it fast. Our speedy does it smoothly. No wonder! This is, do note, not a selfish act of a

---

[4]The antigravity hat: "A boy pours a cupful of liquid into a hat. This should be timed so that the magician almost catches him at it. The magician now does a number in which he wears his hat. But when he puts it on, the boy is disappointed — no water runs out." (Henning Nelms, *Magic and Showmanship: A Handbook for Conjurers,* op cit., p. 69)

selfish man. Self is a hunter. Call this a spiritual hunting exercise. He does it the way he used to do it as a kid, except that then, doing it in the Pripet, at the sudden sight of a stranger or of anyone who was unfriendly, or an outright enemy, he would drop out of sight, like a straw thrown into a nearby haystack, or nature-made gazebo. Doing his disappearing act, then, he was full of fear—fear of being caught by the Germans while now, testing himself against an unsuspecting, (here, unsuspecting means a well-meaning audience) he's merely full of himself: of his acting, reacting and over-acting Self.

Shielded from view by the tablecloth and the chairs, our literary magician-turned-into-a-W.W.II-rare-beast-called-survivor,[5] remains there, all scrunched up, watching and waiting for a psychic shock—a syncopal kick, Nabokov called it—a shock as much his own as Smike's.

In the "search for oneself," in the search for "sincere self-expression," one gropes, one finds some seeming verity. One says "I am" this, that, or the other, and with the words scarcely uttered one ceases to be that thing. I began

---

[5]Himmler had declared that it was the mission of the German people to destroy the Polish people (in what he termed a "delayed genocide": J.K.) He predicted the "disappearance of the Poles from the world." To a significant degree, Himmler's prediction came true. Besides the massive hardships endured by the Polish people under Nazi occupation, about 5,000,000 non-Jewish Poles were forced into slave labor by the Nazis. Furthermore, about 2,200,000 non-Jewish Poles were systematically murdered.

The number of Poles—Jews and non-Jews—in German-occupied Poland was about 22,000,000. Of these, about 3,000,000 Jewish Poles and 2,200,000 non-Jewish Poles were murdered. Almost one of every two Poles (i.e. Polish subjects: J.K.) in Nazi-occupied Poland was either enslaved or murdered by the Nazis. (*Encountering the Holocaust,* by Byron Sherwin and David Weinberg, op. cit.)

this search for the real in a book called *Personae,* casting off, as it were, complete masks of the self in each poem. (Ezra Pound)

From under the table, our minimalist[6] Aesthetic Ascetic Boy sees Smike's feet as the waiter returns to the table.

"Have you seen this blond onion freak who ordered this crap from me?" Smike asks someone as, scarcely two feet from Kosky's feet-sniffing nose, Smike's feet perform another step-balancing act.

"We didn't see anyone there," says a woman at a neighboring table and you can hear the all-American sincerity in her Texas-made voice.

"I think the guy got up and left," says a man from behind and he too says the truth as he has seen it—or has not but doesn't know it.

"Oh, fuck that onionhead," Kosky hears Smike moan while the waiter's feet carry him and the onion platter away from Kosky's table.

If I were to reduce all my feelings and their painful conflicts to a single name, I can think of no other word but: dread. It was dread, dread and uncertainty, that I felt in all those hours of shattered childhood felicity: dread of punishment, dread of my own conscience, dread of stirrings in my soul which I considered forbidden and criminal. (Hermann Hesse, *A Child's Heart*)[7] Just when Smike is about six feet away, our Hermann the Great[8]

---

[6]See Chapter Two, "The Survival Mentality," which appropriately for our numerological hero begins on page 60 and ends on page 99, in *The Minimal Self: Psychic Survival in Troubled Times,* by Christopher Lasch (op. cit.).

[7]As quoted in *Prisoners of Childhood: The Drama of the Gifted Child and the Search for the True Self,* by Alice Miller (1981), p. 96.

[8]Hermann the Great (died 1896) adopted the Inexhaustible Bot-

emerges from under the table as fast as a live pigeon miraculously flying out of the Magic Cauldron filled to the brim with steaming water boiling over a pigeon dummy.

"What's wrong, Smike?" Kosky calls to the waiter, and he does it sitting at his table as calmly as if he had never left it. Hearing him, Smike stops midway, then turns his head, a polo pony stopped in full gallop on a mere dime. For Kosky, this is The Ball and the Polo-Stick, also called The Book of Ecstasy (Arifiti of Herat).[9]

A strong experience in the present awakens in the creative writer a memory of an earlier experience (usually belonging to his childhood) from which there now proceeds a wish which finds its fulfillment in the creative work. The work itself exhibits elements of the recent provoking occasion as well as of the old memory. (Freud)

"Where were you?" Crying his eyes out over the platter, the waiter walks back to the table.

"What do you mean where *was* I?" asks our literary Sword Swallower. **When acting, play your point of view of the character, not the character. (Vakhtangov)**

"You weren't here!" Smike puts the plate on the table. Is it

---

tle as well as Divination or Second Sight, both magical stage routines invented by Robert Houdin.

[9]"It is related with what veracity we do not really know, that fifteenth-century scholars in the Middle East, having heard of the great mystic Arifiti and his system of spiritual development, refused to read the *Book of Ecstasy*, on the grounds that "there could be no serious value in a book about the game of polo." Some recount this reaction as evidence of the foolishness of the scholars: others maintain that Arifiti, wishing in traditional Sufi style to protect his work from the interference of mere litterateurs and theorists, employed the aversion technique by styling his work *The Ball and the Polo-Stick*." Writes Al Fagir, in the opening to the book's Introduction. [*The Ball and the Polo Stick: Book of Ecstasy*, by Arifiti of Herat, (1980)]

the onion or anger that makes his eyes water?

"Of course I was here," says Kosky. "How did you know it was my *onion con limone* unless I was here to order it?"

"You were not! You know what I mean," says Smike warily. He watches Kosky cut a lemon, then an onion, and when Kosky eats both pieces without any change of expression, the waiter's face contorts. "How can you eat it like that?" he says, sitting down at Kosky's table, salivating like a breast-sucking infant.

"Why not? It's a great onion. Compliments to the chef."

The waiter keeps swallowing fast the rush of saliva. "That's some food! Are you into some new safe-sex food-magic?"

"How did you know?" says our idyllist, swallowing another round of round onion ring, juicily dipped in the freshly squeezed lemon. **The man is either crazy or he is a poet. (Horace)**

"The disappearing act. Not bad! Not bad at all."

"Disappearing is easy. Reappearing can be a bad lemon indeed," says Kosky. **I must run away. I must hide. (William James Sidis)**

"Where did you learn the trick?" asks Smike.

"I learned it as a kid, running away from the Nazi SS."

"Could I learn it, too?"

"You might not want to learn it. People don't like to be fooled," says Kosky.

"Unless they know that they are," says Smike. "Then they like it."

"Quite so," says Kosky. Testing himself even further, he says pointedly to the waiter, "Each time I take off my toupee in the presence of a woman I have just met, she screams as if she was being scalped alive." Here, quite noticeably, he pats himself with both hands on his head, as if checking whether his wig is still in place. In spite of this, Smike fails even to look at Kosky's hair.

"Once upon a time" — Kosky keeps on testing his narrative

136

SAM missiles for his newest, yet to be completed, Ruthenian-Jewish tale, "I was invited with some other guests to the Industran Embassy in Washington, D.C., for a bash given there by the Imperator and Empress of Industran for the Israeli Ambassador Sevi-Effendi and his missus. A big bash. A lot of secret service, too. Israeli, American, and Industran's own PERSAUD not to mention many others too secret to be seen or mentioned. Now, imagine the very tense moment: everybody awaits the arrival of their Royal Highnesses. No cameras or TV allowed—only tension. Suddenly, when they arrive—when the Imperator and the Empress enter the room—when everybody, even Secret Service men, turns to look at them, at this splendidly so feudal pair, I quickly slide along the backrest and under the pillows of a huge sofa. I pull the pillows over my body and there I wait, lying on my back like an overturned lizard. I learned this trick during the Big War when I was a green toad."

6: "To refrain from imitation is the best revenge." (Marcus Aurelius, *Meditations*, Book Six, #6)

"Nobody sees you?" Smike no longer minds the sight and smell of Kosky's onions. "Nobody. Not even the PERSAUD's Secret Service?"

"Nobody. I know my timing better than does PERSAUD," says Kosky, ending on this phrase his spiritually spiral page 96.

"I'm surprised. I really am. With all that Secret Service all around I still kind of can't suspend my disbelief, if you know what I mean by this."

"I do. I used to teach drama," Kosky winks at him. "But, you see, in my act, I'm pretty secret myself." What you don't see, buddy, is that **On such a night, unique in the year, one has happy thoughts and inspirations, one feels touched by the divine finger of poetry. Full of ideas and projects, I wanted to walk toward my home, but met some school friends with books under their arms. They were on their**

137

way to school already, having been wakened by the brightness of that night that would not end. (Bruno Schulz, 1934, 1985, 1990)

"I see what you mean. Tell me what happened next." Smike swallows the narrative hook, while Kosky keeps on chewing on his Haifa-grown Israeli lemon.

"Well, then, first the Imperator sits down on the sofa; then the Empress, then the Ambassador and his wife. All these excellencies and highnesses sit propped against my body!"

"Propped against you? Against this bony bird body?" Smike chokes on the story. "I don't believe a word of this, but go on. It's too good not to be true. Tell me what happens next." He is hooked on this so perilously close to Kosky's real-life Sufi tale.[10]

"At first, nothing," says Kosky. "At first they all sit and talk—in French and in English—and have their drinks brought to them by Secret Service waiters and their photographs taken by Secret Service photographers. Then . . ."

Smike falls into a narrative trap. "Then—what?"

"Then, from behind the cushions—and through them—I start to nudge them. Ever so gently. First, I nudge His Excellency Ambassador Sevi-Effendi. After all, he is the guest of honor!"

"Nudge him? How?"

"By kicking him with my foot from behind the pillow," says Kosky. "By kicking his ass once, then twice. Then three times. Nothing! He won't even budge."

"Maybe he didn't feel the kick," says Smike, who, by saying *didn't* shifts his question, into past tense. "What if he was sitting on some Moving Pillow?"

---

[10]See *Hasidic Tales of the Holocaust*, by Yaffa Eliach (New York, 1982).

"The Ambassador feels it, all right," says Kosky, who keeps on testing his first-person-present-tense narration. "From under the pillow, seeing nothing and barely hearing their talk, with my mind's eye I can almost *see him feeling it*. I feel him fidgeting. He moves a bit too earnestly to the left for a rather liberal Israeli, then for an Israeli, by far too far to the conservative right, but he won't look to find out who in the center is kicking! In moments like these, being an Israeli is not enough. In moments like these you've got to be as imaginative as was that smartass of a novelist turned British prime minister, so appropriately named Disraeli.[11] He is, in short, a typical diplomat trained by Sri Swami Rama."[12]

"I wonder why?" says the waiter. "Maybe he thought you were a secret agent assigned to protect his ass. Still, why didn't he do something? For instance, why do you suppose he didn't scream?" Smike keeps on hanging onto the past tense.

"Because he's wise enough to know how to ignore a mere kick in the ass, as long as the kick does not soil the couch." Kosky hangs on to the present.

"I bet he did nothing, not because he was diplomatic, but because he thought he was being tested," volunteers Smike. "In any case, you were lucky. If he so much as screamed or yelled or jumped up at the sight of you, all three secret services would have pumped so many bullets into those cushions that you'd have become a cushion yourself. So tell me what happens next?" He now asks by adopting Kosky's narrative present tense.

---

[11]Benjamin Disraeli's father, Isaac D'Israeli, was an English critic and historian (who clearly architected his son's unprecedented march to spiritual victory: J.K.) His best-known work is *Curiosities of Literature* (6 Vol).

[12]See *Exercise Without Movement,* manual one, as taught by Sri Swami Rama of the Himalayas, 1984.

"Well, when the Ambassador does nothing, I start to nudge—to kick, if you will—the next person in line."

"Don't tell me you kicked the Imperator himself," says Smike. "Because if you do, I won't believe one word of it."

"This is exactly the next thing I do," says Kosky. "But just for the sake of my inner public opinion poll, tell me why won't you believe me?"

"Because he doesn't call himself the almighty for nothing."

"Almighty or not, I do kick him, once twice, and when he does nothing I kick him again. He still doesn't respond. Only then do I decide to kick the lovely Empress—right in her behind. Mind you, at this time in my most personal Book of Lists she was listed as one of the world's six most beautiful women." **I should have been born, your Imperial Majesty, not in Russia, but somewhere in the forests of America, among the Western colonists, there where civilization has scarcely dawned and where all life is a ceaseless struggle against wildmen, wild nature, and not in an organized civil society. Also, had fate wished to make me a sailor from my youth, I would now probably be a very respectable man; I would not have thought of politics and would have sought no other adventures and storms than those of the sea. But fate did not will either the one or the other, and my need for movement and activity remained unsatisfied. (Mikhail Bakunin to Tsar Nicholas I, 1851)**

"She sure is a beauty. What a piece of ass! So what's next?"

"Well, next I kick her through the pillow once. Kick her most graciously—but, since a kick is a kick, a bit horsely. (A bit, printer, not a bet!) **In writing one doesn't bet on a word; one chooses it. (J. K., 1982).** Well, after the kick I wait for a while, and when she doesn't respond I kick her again. Once, then twice. Nothing. Finally, after a third and most final kick—by now I'm all sweat, slowly suffocating under these pillows, and under the weight of the sitters, I feel her twitch! Twitch ethereally, but twitch." Like most Ruthenians who cannot pronounce the Anglo-Saxon *th*, Kosky strains when pronouncing the word *ether*, but then, a realist by nature, he has no trouble with the word *really*.

"You felt her ethereal ass twitch, not her," Smike corrects him, inadvertently becoming one of some 669 of Kosky's unacknowledged privately hired secretaries, proofreaders and in-line book editors.

"I feel her ass twitch," Kosky gladly incorporates the correction. "And, if this isn't enough, I feel her warmth."

"You feel her heat. Heat, not warmth. Heat from her ass, you worm!" Smike corrects him again.

"I feel her heat." A pedantic character, Kosky, our literary correction officer, loves mss. correcting. "I keep feeling it spread all through the pillow. As a result I'm in heat, too."

"Maybe she thinks she's being goosed by the Israeli ambassador," Smike says. "Maybe she thinks he is making a pass at her."

"I doubt that, since she is a spiritually perfect lady. Anyway, I wait a minute and just as she is saying, 'We find America to be so full of surprises,' I kick the pillow she leans against really hard and right in the middle of the sentence!" Kosky pauses. "Only then, only after she completes her thought, do I feel a response. I feel something creeping under the pillow."

"Oh, no! Oh, no!" Smike moans.

"Oh, yes!" says Kosky. "It is her hand, no doubt about it. Her perfectly narrow royal hand. I feel her royal fingers creep along my shoe, then moving upward along my trouser-leg—higher and higher."

"I bet she grabs you by—" Smike can't wait.

"She grabs me by my cuff." Here, our conjurer willingly lifts the suspension of disbelief.

"By your calf? Or by your cuff? I don't get your accent." Smike strains.

"By my calf. Right by my ankle!" says Kosky. "And—I

promise you—she digs inch-long nails into my flesh. All the way. Now I'm in pain—but I won't budge!"

"You were lucky the Empress didn't try to move her sweet little hand any higher. And root you out by your root," says Smike. "But go on—what's next?"

"Next I start to fidget. Next, I put my hand out and very gently tap the Ambassador's back. At first, he is startled. He thinks he's being patted by the Emperor and this is my chance to survive all this little drama without being killed like the biggest fool that ever was. Just when the Ambassador starts sliding his body off the pillow that presses against my head, I squeeze my body out and crawl from under the pillow head first—crawl out, breathless, my tuxedo all messed-up and no black tie, which I lost under the pillows. The second I hit fresh air I hold up my hands in the universal sign of surrender and scream, all smiles, of course, 'SHALOM! I'M A JEW. DON'T SHOOT.' " **It is difficult to find a single definition of a Jew. A Jew is one who accepts the faith of Judaism. That is the *religious* definition. A Jew is one who, without formal religious affiliation, regards the teachings of Juadiasm—its ethics, its folkways, its literature—as his own. That is the *cultural* definition. A Jew is one who considers himself a Jew or is so regarded by his community. That is the *practical* definition. (Rabbi Morris N. Kertzer)** Of course now they all jump—the Imperator, the Imperatrice, the Ambassador, and the Ambassador's wife, not to mention the PERSAUD men descending on me, their guns drawn! Thank Yod that, just then, everybody starts laughing. Laughing 'cause they know me. Laughing 'cause they have seen my number before. And so I get a salvo of laughter—instead of that other salvo!"

"And so the Secret Service men all laugh, now, and they all love you all the way to dinner, right?" Smike begs for a happy ending.

"I wouldn't say love, and certainly not all the way," our

Ruthenian **outcast of the islands (Conrad, 1896)** ends, cryptic at best, his manuscript page 101.[13]

---

[13]See "In the Kingdom of Conrad," in *American Nights Entertainment*, by Grant Overton (New York, 1923). See also Conrad's photograph on page 65 and how "out of that uncouth time and those bizarre experiences the man Conrad has got back certain pages in *The Mirror of the Sea*, pages that we all remember" (p. 69).

9

"Helena Powska arrives in New York," reads a short one-line item in the *Daily Ruthenian,* a copy of which Kosky finds on Times Square. Her name rings an instant bell. **Slowa sa bez poreczy: Words have no banisters. (Jerzy Peterkiewicz)**[1]

Helena Powska is a Polish poet, and when it comes to poetry Kosky is a Ruthenian at heart; **poets are born, not paid. (Wilson Mizner)** No bad man can be a good poet, said Boris Pasternak, and he was partly right. Partly because neither can a bad woman.

How can I calm myself—
full of fear are these eyes of mine,
full of terror these thoughts of mine,
full of shudders these lungs of mine,
full of panic this heart of mine—
How can I calm myself?
(Stanslaw Wyspiański)

---

[1]In *Five Centuries of Polish Poetry 1450-1970:* Second Edition, compiled by Jerzy Peterkiewicz and Burns Singer with new translations by Jerzy Peterkiewicz and Jon Stallworthy (1971). See also *Monumenta Polonica:* The First Four Centuries of Polish Poetry: A Bilingual Anthology by Bogdana Carpenter, Ann Arbor 1989.

Kosky remembers a large photograph of Powska he first saw published on the cover of *Today's Ruthenia*, the official English-language publication published by the Ruthenian Ministry of Culture and distributed freely in the free West.

In the picture Powska posed next to a snow-capped Ruthenian *dacha* wearing a Zakopane[2] fur hat and a black leather sleeveless tunic which reveals the outline of her breasts, and low-heeled leather boots. "Take her poetry away from her, and—judging by her looks alone, she could be the Slavic Slut, a Russian model who recently posed in various stages of sexual undress of the bimonthly Leg Show magazine under these *sextalitarian* words: "Maybe because I am a Russian I need to dominate my men. I want them to feel like worms, like filthy disgusting dogs. I want them to feel totally worthless. And all this because I love them so."

He knows her poetry only too well—he once tried to translate it into English but failed: only a poet who knows the value of silence can translate a poet.[3] **Perfect lyric poetry should be like a cast in plaster: the slashes where form**

---

[2]Zakopane, a Polish ski resort, is to Poland what Aspen is to the United States: nature's grand design and a meeting place for the world designers of art and thought. **During the whole stay at Zakopane (1914) Conrad was in an exceptionally relaxed and agreeable mood. "His wife remarked on this several times, adding that this was only natural," meaning tht he felt thoroughly at home in the Polish countryside.** (*The Polish Shades and Ghosts of Joseph Conrad,* by Gustav Morf. op. cit.)

[3]"A contemporary translator may look back upon an old and praiseworthy tradition. Among his most remote predecessors are the Greek translators of the *Old Testament,* the so-called Septuagint, and Livius Andronicus, whose Latin translation of the *Odyssey* is regarded as the beginning of original Latin literature. Translators were in many epochs the first creators of national literary languages," writes Jan Parandowski in "On the Significance and the Dignity of the Translator," 1955.

passes form, leaving crevices, must be preserved and not smoothed out with the knife. Only the barbarian takes all this off from the plaster with his knife and destroys the whole. (Norwid)[4] He gets her phone number, and calls her. He introduces himself to her in Ruthenian. "It's the language of my sexual prime," he tells her. "Your Ruthenian poems talk to me with the voice of my beloved Pripet," our phoney keeps whispering seductively into the phone. **Man acts as if he were the shaper and master of language, while it is language which remains mistress of man. When this relation of dominance is inverted, man succumbs to strange contrivances. (George Steiner, 1975)**

He invites Helena to join him for either a "casually relaxed" lunch — or a stately, though not "totalitarian," dinner — at the American Relax — the downtown literary café, where, allegedly, in 1860, Emerson wrote his *Illusions.*

> Know the stars yonder,
> The stars everlasting,
> Are fugitive also. . . .
> Flow, flow the waves hated,
> Accursed, adored,
> The waves of mutation;
> No anchorage is.
>
> (Emerson)

Calmly, Helena turns him down. "Not today," she says with a touch of aversion. "Maybe some other time." He calls again, and is again turned down. "I'm running out of time. I can't waste my time. Not today." One more call: "Would she like to go with him to the Audubon Society Birds' Calls Exhibition at the Academy of Spiritual Art at the Leo Baeck

---

[4]As quoted by Jerzy Peterkiewicz, op. cit., p. 69.

world-famous New York art gallery owned by the Super-rich Ribnitzer family. Ribnitzers initially came to America from Rybnice in Ruthenia and they *all* descend from Ribnitzer Rebbe who was born in 1369," our humming bird hums like a Bird of Passion.

"I'm not into visual art," she tells him. "And, I'm neither a bird nor a Ribnitzer watcher."

"Don't you like bluebirds?" asks our *Barbe Bleue*.

"I don't like bluebirds like you," she tells him straight into his ear. "Particularly, when they turn yellow."

"Is it 'cause I'm Jewish?" He does the unfair trick of implying the presence of a yellow star when there is none.

"Not at all," she snaps back. "After reading Tuwim, Wittlin, Wat, Gillon, Slonimski and Leśmian (the names of some of the greatest poets who happened to be Polish-Jewish: J. K.) at least half of my poetic blood is Jewish and it flows with the speed of Julian Tuwim's *Lokomotywa*, which I memorized as a kid, like every Jewish and non-Jewish kid in Ruthenia. Simply, I won't go on a blind date with you."

"Why not?"

"Because, in my private dictionary the name Norbert Kosky is synonymous with Ruthenian renegade," she says and then hangs up on him with a smash, on him, the most smashing literary cavalier.

Renegade—a harsh word even for a Ruthenian Kos[5]—a migrating bird of linguistic prey. **If writing—which consists in allowing a fluid to flow out from a tube upon a piece of white paper—has acquired the symbolic meaning of coitus, or if walking has become a symbolic substitute for stamping upon the body of Mother Earth, then both**

---

[5]In Ruthenian, while *kos* means *minos polyglottos*—a mockingbird—*kosa* means a scythe. Also Kos, a Greek island, which, until the end of W.W. II, sheltered Jews who spoke Ladino.

writing and walking will be abstained from, because it is as though forbidden sexual behavior were thereby being indulged in. (Freud in *The Problem of Anxiety*)

In Ruthenia, where the saber is the country's national symbol (as it is in neighboring Poland, as any Sarmatian painting will testify)[6] a poet is a spiritual fencer. Poetic language is Helena's saber.

Does Helena call him a Ruthenian renegade because, to her, he abandoned Ruthenia, the country of his dominant language and its 969-year-old culture and tradition? Or is he to her a renegade as a writer, because, *kos* that he is, he has migrated from Ruthlandia,[7] leaving behind the Ruthenian language, the idiom of his adolescent past, and leaving it for the sake of English, the idiom of his exile?

There, in Eastern Europe, the Jewish people came into its own. It did not live like a guest in somebody else's house, who must constantly keep in mind the ways and customs of the host. There Jews lived without reservation and without disguise, outside their homes no less than within them. (Abraham Joshua Heschel)

Disguised as a Hasidic Don Quixote, with his toupee, beard, mustache and sunglasses firmly in place, Kosky waits for Helena outside her hotel. Finally she emerges and goes for a walk. He follows her for a moment. Again and again, the Gospels resemble a palimpsest: new things have, as it

---

[6]For the origins of Sarmatian paintings, see *The Polish Way: A Thousand-Year History of the Poles and their Culture*, by Adam Zamoyski, 1987, p. 196. See also *Sarmatism and the Ottoman Empire*, (ibidem).

[7]Throughout the text Norbert Kosky willingly confuses Ruthlandia (the official name of the Ruthenian Republic) with Ruthenia, which until the War, was an integral part of Polish Commonwealth. [Estate Editors].

were, been written over the old tidings. But on the whole it is nevertheless possible to get back to the original tradition. (Leo Baeck, *Judaism and Christianity,* 1958) He finds her *faultless* is the word, but how could he describe her? He often asks himself such questions. Yes, he could. He could, but only if he could find an English alchemical word compound which would fuse the genius of Cyprian Kamil Norwid, his favorite Polish-language poet, with the French flavor of flawed flowers of evil found only in the "obscenely gifted."[8]

"You look so lovely," he says to her in his most personal version of Swiss-English which allows him to disguise his Ruthenian accent by modifying his voice's volume, bass and treble. Finally, our mini-Baudelaire blocks her path like a persistent human semicolon found on the steps of a colonnade. "As lovely as fall. Fall in Lake Tear of the Clouds on Mount Mercy. That's in the Adirondacks — not far from New York!" A foreigner himself, he enunciates like a foreigner who speaks with a French accent. **Heart — a trembling gauge so shoddily made. (Halina Poświatowska, 1966)**

"Sorry?" she replies. "Please have mercy! Don't laugh at my crooked English. When Conrad arrived in England at twenty, he knew English only barely, and look what he did with it a few bare years later! Now that's what I call concen-

---

[8] ". . . It is along such a path that some investigators find similarities between Norwid and Baudelaire, or even with the French philosopher P. S. Ballanche, as well as with some others among Norwid's French and English contemporaries. We ourselves would be much more inclined to look at Norwid's models among the Italian writers of Christian Humanism beginning with Dante, to Manzoni and Mazzini. Italy was for Norwid a second homeland which was, it seems to us, a constant source of his artist inspiration," writes Olga Nedelkovic in *The Polish Review* (1986).

tration![9] For me, English still has too many clouds. In English, I can't swim—not even in the lake of my own tears," she stammers. "But I am not so cloudy in French!"

"French? You speak French? Hey, that's great! *Quelle chance!*" Our Hasidic cowboy bows gallantly, then introduces himself in French as Monsieur Georges Flotsam "from Valpina, a ski'nd golf high-mountain town in Valais, in French-speaking Switzerland," he says, then goes on. "I come from *in between*. Between the medieval ruins of Sion and the medieval church in Raron, perhaps the two most famous sights in all the Alps." **The Acropolis does not overhang Athens in a more kingly style than these rocks frown upon the humbler town of Sion, nor do I believe that the architecture of the former, however pure and classical, is half as picturesque. [James Fenimore Cooper][10]**

"Flotsam?" she repeats.

"Yes. Flotsam," he nods, while catching sight of himself in

---

[9]"During his whole life, Conrad involuntarily retained a strong Polish accent, as strong as his typically Polish accent on universal principles of justice (which to him, a Briton yet a Pole of 96 percent, was feasibly synonymous with the sound of free falling water and why not: "let justice roll down like waters, and righteousness like a mighty stream," [Amos 5:24]). His manners also remained quite Polish . . . Everyone noticed Conrad's Polish manners [polished—as well as Polish.—Jay Kay] writes Gustav Morf in "The English Shock," Chapter 10 of his *The Polish Shades and Ghosts of Joseph Conrad* (op. cit). What nobody noticed was the creative role of his wife (a British *lassie* who spiritually—(spiritually, not sexually) prompted creativity of that mildly asexual Polish literary mole.

[10]See also "Rainer Maria Rilke's Valaisan years," and "The Beginnings of Christianity in Sion," both in *Zermatt and the Valais,* by Sir Arnold Lunn, 1955. (Since William the Conqueror's coronation in 1066 was marred by most destructive riots, Ermefroy, Bishop of Sion, visited England in 1069, in order to crown the Conqueror again in 1070.

a shop window. Is his South Korean toupee in place? Will the Hong Kong mustache and his goatee made in Thailand peel off in the heat of the day?

"In Ruthenian, *sam* means solo and *flotsa* means a fleet," she says in French. "But isn't Flotsam an unusual name for a Swiss, a man of mountains—not of water?" **Now only he began to feel, rather than see, the unequaled formation of her brow, gleaming with the whiteness of snow or of a block of Carrara marble, a brow which housed unknown thoughts, unfamiliar, subtle, beautiful, like music coming out of the darkness of night, and young as the billows of a wellspring. (Stefan Żeromski)**

"Oh, *mon dieu!*" she exclaims. "Here you tell me so much about your Swiss universal self and I forget to share with you even my name."

Her name is Helena Powska, she introduces herself. And she is a published poet, she admits with pride.

She is also a member of Ruthenian PEN—an ultimate honor. The letters PEN, in case he wouldn't know, she explains, stand for Poets, Essayists and Novelists. No wonder she writes poetry about love and dieing, one's penultimate fall, she says, stressing in the world penultimate the word *pen*, so ultimate to every writer.[11] Only Rilke would know what she means. **We writers are in some sort trustees for human nature; if we are narrow and prejudiced we harm the human race. And the better we know each other . . . the greater the chance of human happiness in a world not, as yet, too happy. (Galsworthy)**

---

[11]An intended pen pun. PEN stands for Poets, Playwrights, Essayists, Editors and Novelists: an international association of penultimate writers. Initially started in England by Mrs. Dawson Scott and John Galsworthy, the American Center was founded in 1922 by Robert Frost, Marc Connelly, Walter Lippmann and Eugene O'Neill. ("Booth" Tarkington was the first president of the American PEN.)

"Rilke died in Switzerland," says Kosky. "He is buried at Raron, not far from Valpina, where I reside. His grave has been a veritable tourist attraction. Writers in all languages come to it and seem to meditate at its side."

Without instinct of migratory birds, we are not whole. Featherless and tardy, coercing winds, we sparkle at lagoons, without welcome. (Rilke)

"Did you know that Rilke suffered from incurable TB that made him feverish?" says Helena in English, then, catching Kosky's stare, she returns to speaking French. "That each time he looked at a woman's breast or thigh or any other part, his sexual excitement would cause his fever to shoot up—and, suddenly mute—mute either in German or French, the two languages his soul loved most—he would start talking in body language.[12] Do you know"—she changes *did* to *do* in English, then goes on in French—"that in order to avoid breathing TB germs at each other, Rilke and his lovers (and he had many of them, very many) made love to one another not face to face, but side by side—or upside down—facing one another only in the mirror? The mirror placed in front of them, above or next to their bed or sofa or separate chairs? Do you know that in the lingo of those healthy men and women who prey on making love to the victims of terminal illness the terminally ill," she assures him forcefully, "are called hyenas? Can you imagine"—she now shifts to speaking English again as if afraid to reveal too much in her

---

[12]"Sexual activity consists in speaking what we might call 'body language.' It has its own grammar, delineated by the body, and its own phonetics of touch and movement. Its unit of meaningfulness, the bodily equivalent of a sentence, is the *gesture* . . . body language is essentially expressive, and its content is limited to interpersonal attitudes and feelings." (Robert Solomon in *Sexual Paradigms*, as quoted by Janice Moulton in *Sexual Behavior: Another Position in The Philosophy of Sex:* Contemporary Readings, edited by Alan Soble, 1980)

more fluent French—"That each time Rilke loved a woman—each time he *physically* made love to her," she corrects herself—"he knew he was, *physically* speeding up his death, his Book of Hours?"

They have walked for over an hour. She is pale, she is tired. But she wants to keep on walking. She wants to "know all of Manhattan before it is too late, before I'll be able to transfer what I know into words," she says and as she says it, she sweats while trembling from cold. Cold in the heat? Trying to distract herself she starts reciting to him a poem by Rilke and she does it in a Ruthenian translation. As one who doesn't know Ruthenian, can he guess by its sound which poem it is? she asks.

He listens watchful, watching every move of her lips. He pretends not to know. Then he asks her to recite it for him again.

"It was 'L'Étranger'—the Stranger. My favorite Rilke poem," she says.[13] "Because while so universally true it also makes me feel true to my Self. But tell me about your universe, about your universal you?" For the first time she takes him by the hand, but then, too soon, she lets his hand go.

They walk again. Each time he touches her a Tantric shiver of desire runs along his spine, and so touched by her,

---

[13]"To translate is to betray. Translations are like women: if they are beautiful, they are not faithful; if they are faithful, they are not beautiful," says a French saying, and readers are encouraged to seek confirmation of the above contained in *Themes Modeles:* French Renderings of English Passages set in Modern Language Scholarship Examinations at Oxford and Cambridge compiled by S. W. Segger, M.A., Cambridge, 1964.

The "themes modeles" have been selected from literary models, among them, Joseph Conrad (No. 1), Author Unknown (No. 66), Anthony Trollope (No. 69), H. E. Neale (No. 6), A. G. Street (No. 9) and V. Sackville-West (No. 60).

he touches her with his hands, or elbows, or even with his hip, but such touch won't do. He must touch her with words. The well chosen words. So well chosen she would cling to them and through them cling to him. It is Kosky's turn. He recites, in his Swiss-French, a few lines of Rilke's poem "Eros."

Here our hipster scores — and how! Helena listens with her eyes closed. She listens to him as engrossed as he is when listening to Patrick Domostroy, the Ruthenian-American pianist, playing Chopin's great A-flat Polonaise. Then, looking at Kosky attentively, she wonders aloud how good this French translation of Rilke is. After all, Rilke, the greatest German poet wrote this poem "Eros," like all his poetry, in German.

She is wrong, Kosky tells her. "Eros" happens to be one of several poems Rilke wrote in French. By writing in French, and, of all things, about Eros, a subject which affected his erotically feverish nature more than most, Rilke proved that, *had he wanted to*, he could have been a German-French poet. In fact, he could have been recognized as the greatest French-language poet who had ever lived. French, not German! Recognized as such at least by French-speaking Valais. [After Manhattan and Beulah University in Waterbury, Connecticut, the Swiss-French speaking Valais was Norbert Kosky's favorite. Ed.] No wonder, Rilke spent the last years of his life in French-speaking Valais which, to him, was the most wonder-evoking place of all. Her mind is tired by recalling again and again something else. Something, not someone. Something which resides within her with a finality she can express only in writing. But never mind. **The only true exile is the writer who lives in his own country. (Julio Cortazar)**

Helena is surprised. She didn't know all this, or did she? She can't remember. Not now, anyhow. He says, Let's talk more. This time, talk of prose, she pleads with him. While poetry sings to the heart, prose is serious. It's all a matter of heart, you know.

"My life has been twisted. It feels unnatural from within. By within I mean my mechanical body," she says, waving her hand aimlessly. "Ever since I was a child, my heart has threatened to stop. *To stop dead.* It has misfired ever since it first fired. Do you know that in order to appease my misbehaving heart, I've never climbed hills? Never skied? Never swam? Never played volleyball or tennis?"

She looks at him starry-eyed. Her eyes are large and oval. Her expression is veiled. The veil comes from within. It could belong to the face of an Arab woman.

"I know what you mean. I too have a chronic problem," A disbeliever at first, (but since first is for him always a wrong number), he dismisses her terminal story with a supposedly terminal story of his own and shows her his Medicus Medallion, his cardiac trophy, hanging from his chest.

"Anything serious?" She voices concern as if he too were condemned to instant death.

"Serious enough." Our false face displays his Hasidic act of sadness. **Tradition is not the monopoly of an elite. Each Jew is obliged to say: "Into my hands has been given the future of the entire people." Just as every person is a microcosm, so is every Jew a miniature Jewish people. He carries within him the soul of the entire people. (Abraham Joshua Heschel in *The Individual Jew and His Obligations*)**

"It's final. Final, but not terminal," he says humming Frank Sinatra's song *Young at Heart* (1964). He then says with a face of one who will not go on. "It's final in a sense that, like every other being, at any given time I too am condemned to a sudden death. Meanwhile, I learned to live with my PAT (Paroxymsmal Atrial Tachycardia. J. K.) or CAD (Coronary Artery Disease. J. K.)"

As they pass a large newSStand, she notices the look he gives a young woman shown naked on the cover of *Wild 'nd Wide Open* adult man's magazine who look at them from a newsstand.

"My mother would *never* let me unbutton my shirt or wear a tight sweater, high heels, or Ruthless panties. Never! Never! Never! I always had to keep my skirt pulled down! I was not allowed to shave my underarms. Or my legs. She kept saying, 'You don't want any man to get excited over your nakedness. In turn, his excitement over you might then excite you. Excitement can stop your sick heart forever.' "

She and Kosky sit down on a park bench. The sun beats down on them. She breathes with effort. To let her heart calm down, she takes off her jacket. Is this an act acted out in order to keep him sexually at bay? Is she acting, reacting or overreacting? Or is she really seriously sick? Kosky keeps calling his Zones of Irritation at the Sacrum."[14] She unbuttons her short-sleeved blouse. Her underarms are shaved, and, speaking in English, in some remote fashion, he recalls aloud for her how, as a boy of nine or older, he used to like watching "the *hairy armpits* of the peasant women." The phrase "hairy armpits" makes her laugh when he translates it for her into French.

They are sitting at an old dock overlooking the Hudson. Above, a Carolina wren hovers restlessly. An exile from the predictably warm Carolinas, the bird is not certain of the so changeable climate of Manhattan. A Canadian warbler enviously watches American egrets having fun in the shallows. Ducking its head in the water, a pintail duck majestically floats off the docks. In the river, two schools of fish swim up and down, passing each other, one above, the other below,

---

[14]See fig. 66: Zones of Irritation at the Sacrum, and fig. 69: Position of the supraspinous ligament and schematic representation of the interspinal muscles, among them Kosky's most painful L-5 and his most irritative SS-1 as well as SS-2 and SS-3. See Chapter Six, *Manual Medicine*, by Jiri Dvorak and Vaclav Dvorak (Stuttgart—New York, 1984).

without as much as saying hello to each other. No wonder. Hudson is an affluent river. As affluent as was VOC, the Dutch-owned United East India Company which, awarded the long-term trade monopoly on all trade and shipping east of the Cape of Good Hope. One day in 1602, VOC hired an Englishman Henry Hudson, and his Dutch vessel *The Half Moon* to look for a shorter route to the East than the one around the Cape. Instead, blocked by the icebergs of the Arctic Sea, Henry Hudson wisely headed for North America. Finally, in 1609, as the first European ever, he set foot on the island that would in time be called New Amsterdam, then New York, and — *voila!* — Manhattan.[15] The salty and heavier water from the Atlantic flows below, near the bottom while the fresh and lighter water from the Adirondacks flows above it. Call this a cohabitation of river with the sea.

Helena and Norbert keep on walking. The reach Riverside Park. Here they run into a crooked-looking small bird. "Look at this poor little thing! This bird is called *kos* in Ruthenian!" she says. They stop to watch it and *kos* watches them intently from the lowest branch of the tree.

"Because it mimics the chirpings of other birds, *Kos* is called mockingbird here," says our Kos, with trepidation. "Actually, it should be called a mimicbird, since, apparently, no animal possesses a notion of mockery. While mockery supposes a sense of irony and ridicule, mimicry does not." **In**

---

[15]VOC, or United East India Company was the first company in history which raised capital by means of issuance of stock, of the very first stock in history. (J. K.) Not a bad record! In fact, as good, as the opening in 1989 of the First United States Bank of America (FUSBA) in Poland, the first foreign (and entirely American. J. K.) majority-owned bank in Poland opened there since 1939 and the Nazi invasion of Poland. Like Ruthenia, Poland, remained Communist dominated until it became a democracy in 1990. (Jay Kay)

our area the mockingbird has apparently always been rare and erratic north of Central New Jersey. (Stone, 1908) Until its recent comeback in the mid-1950s. (John Bull)

They keep on walking without a word for a while, they let nature talk, but in time, they talk back to it.

"Look there: a bird called a Hermit Thrush. My spiritual fellow," says Kosky, pointing at the most unfriendly creature thrashing under the solitary bush. "This is a most peculiar bird, you know! I know him and he knows me too," he says pointedly. "The Hermit Thrush knows more about wearing disguises than any other bird of its kind, whether it's a painted bird or merely a tainted one. This bird proves that one could change disguises even after death."

"You mean to say that the bird is not the Hermit Thrush? That it is only disguised as one?" She is a natural word'nd nature lover.

"It's a Hermit Thrush but only for as long as it lives. The instant this bird dies the color of his plumage changes so much and so unpredictably, that nobody, not even his closest kin, knows who he was in life. Now how's that for leaving no traces — not even a trace of your own life?"

They stand next to each other and, an old hand in such matters (at his age not only his hand aged), he begins to sexually close in on her. Such closing-in used to be, in his good old days, a spiritually rewarding process which, if explained with sexual directness of the libertine sixties could evoke a guilty conscience in the reader of today, so fearful of sexually transmitted diseases. She does not mind his transgression. Far from it. She responds to him with the ease of one brought up in the century-old tradition of Ruthenian-Polish freedom and tolerance, a tradition which, mixing the romantic and the pragmatic, became a heaven for the Jews and Protestants alike during the Reformation, then gave mankind the concept of — and the cultural prototype of — an incurable revolutionary romantic welded to unrealistic positivist pragmatic. But it is Kosky who now pulls away from her. He is not afraid of her tolerance; he fears violating her heart, her unnaturally restricted sexual self. (SS).

And so walking, sitting down, and nature watching dominate his mental frame now. They walk along the docks. They sit down. They watch the river. A big yellow bladder fish passes by in the water. "A man-of-war genus Fair Medusa; his bladder happens to be his sail," comments Kosky. "On certain days Fair Medusa sails with it under full sail and on an empty bladder, and on other less fair days it is the other way around. On some days the Medusa drifts forth, up the river; on others, it drifts back, down the river, as if lost in the mainstream of Manhattan. Follow it for some twenty-four hours and you will see it drift some 6.9 of a mile down the river, then 9.6 of a mile back. Is the Fair Medusa an all-washed-up drifter? Is it going up the river—or down the drain? Life isn't fair. The Fair Medusa is not a drifter: the Hudson River is," he concludes as if speaking about himself.

From the riverside grove Helena and Kosky watch the *Halakah,* an impressively large Israeli aircraft carrier of the Midrash class, as she inches her way into New York harbor under the gaze of the battalions of migrating jays flying overhead in tight formation. The massive bulk of the floating Red Sea fortress looms over the *Witchcraft,* an impressive sailing ship of the Manhattan Golf and Tennis Club, circling around the aircraft carrier next to the Staten Island Ferry. The humming and buzzing of damsel flies, bumblebees and wasps drown in the sound of sirens and high-pitched whistles coming from the flotilla of welcoming tugs and motor boats.

Time to go back. At the hotel, Helena invites him to her room which offers, she tells him in addition to the maritime view of the entire harbor a Conradian view: black Harlem to the left, white Wall Street to the right.

What absorbs him in her room is not the view of the impressive Israeli-owned American-built aircraft carrier and not even the sound of her taking a shower in the bathroom but the Heartfelt 009—a portable electronic heart monitor placed on its own mobile stand next to her bed. She returns to the room. Casually, he assesses her frame as being overly girlish, a far distance from Isabel Miraflores, his current sexual favorite adorning the pages of La Ultima Vampiresa, a Mexican adult magazine. Helena is long-legged, with finely sculpted feet. She wears only a Taboo bra and Sexy Salsa strawberry green (SSS) panties—both clearly acquired in New York. Surprised by his unintentionally obvious lack of interest in her body, she tells him that the electrocardiograph was installed in her room by her American doctors. She pauses for a long beat, then says she is visiting the U.S. in order to undergo a complex heart surgery. So technologically complex that, since technology means progress, and Ruthenia is still so much poorer than America, such surgery has not yet been performed there. The machine records her heartbeat when she is resting or sleeping—a record her doctors need to know.

> . . .*mieszka we mnie chwiejny chronometr*
> A shaky chronometer inhabits me
> *serce*
> heart
> *O wadliwej konstrukcji*
> Of faulty construction
> (Halina Póswiatowska)

"But this is a place my heart paces tranquilly." She points at a volume of her poetry on the bureau. "And here it rebels!"—she clutches her chest—"though it could be the other way around," she pauses. He asks her for how long will her inner rebel stay?"

"Another ventricular fibrillation. Nothing serious." She catches his anxious stare. "The American surgeons will soon edit it out of my heart!" She looks at him. "Your face is like a bilingual test: the original and a translation—all mixed up," she says. "You look like Yankiel, that Hasid from Conrad, that renegade Pole, imposed over Jankiel created by the Polish *numero uno* poet Adam Mickiewicz." She stares at him. **I can immediately tell he is a Jew: his beard is black and curly, his nose is slightly hooked, his ears stick out, he wears steel-rimmed glasses, a hat pulled down over his eyes, black clothes, his gestures are quick and nervous. (Sartre)**

"It's strange," she says. "We've just met, but I feel I've known you longer. You shape your thoughts in your brand of French the way I do mine in Ruthenian. Come to think, both of us think in a very awkward way, awkward by non-Ruthenian standards, I mean. We seem to share secrets (SS) the way Conrad did in *the Secret Sharer* (SS).[16] There's something we have in common, but I don't know what it is." She moves closer to him. She is pale; her eyes darken. The coming of fall. She draws him to her. "Kiss me," she says stepping one step closer to him.

He evades her embrace by discreet Body English. "Why did you choose this hotel?" our Secret Sharer asks, anxious to distract her. **I can't say that I've fallen in love with you. In any case you're not a part of the background, but a separate complex of very intricate combinations. As such you exist in my consciousness. That's a great deal. (Witkacy)**

"Jan Lechón, the Polish poet of Love and Death, once

---

[16]Conrad wrote his psychological masterpiece (*The Secret Sharer*, 1909) almost a dozen years after his Congo stories. It was one of the rare works he was satisfied with. "Every word fits and there is not a single uncertain note," he wrote to E. Garnett . . . Like the *Nigger* and the Congo stories, it is a story of an all-male world, "no damn tricks with girls there." (*The Polish Shades and Ghosts of Joseph Conrad*, by Gustav Morf, op. cit.)

lived across the street," she says.

"Do you know how Lechón died?" asks Kosky cautiously.

Halina Póswiatowska is understandably human and, understand-
ably, must die as many people died before her

Halina Póswiatowska just now busies herself With her own dying.
Halina Póswiatowska, (in Polish) Philadelphia, 1958.

JAN LECHÓN DIES IN FALL FROM HOTEL. Poet Jan Le-
chón (pen name of Leszek Serafinowicz) was killed in a
fall from the roof of a hotel overlooking the Hudson
River. He was fifty-seven years old. (*American Exile*)[17]

She is surprised that he, an American-Swiss, had heard of
Lechón. "Well, yes! Lechón fell from the roof of his hotel to
the street," she says. "Does it really matter whether he fell, or
jumped, or was pushed down by a sex'nd dope-pushing male
lover? What does matter is that he died instantly. Can you
see Lechón dying slowly and in pain? Lechón, that most
Catholic Polish poet, whose best friend was Julian Tuwim,
another great poet, who was a Jew?"

"And you picked this hotel in spite of Lechón's death?"

"I picked this hotel because of that. 'How else but through
a broken heart may Lord Christ enter in?' asked Oscar
Wilde. I too might die of a broken heart," she muses somberly.

"Do you know what broke Lechón's heart?" **Equally tragic**
is the case of the poet. Walled up in his own language, he
writes for his friends — for ten, for twenty persons at the

---

[17]Says E. M. Cioran, that exile par excellence, "In whatever form
it happens to take, and whatever its cause, exile — at its start — is an
academy of intoxication. And it is not given to everyone to be
intoxicated. It is a limit-situation and resembles the extremity of the
poetic state. . . ."

See also *Exile,* a literary quarterly (Exile Editions, Ltd., Toronto,
Ont., Canada):

most. His longing to be read is no less imperious than that of the improvised novelist. . . . Let us say such a man becomes—transforms himself—into an editor of such a review; to keep his publication alive he risks hunger, abstains from women, buries himself in a windowless room, imposes privations which confound and appall. Tuberculosis and masturbation, that is his fate. (E.M. Cioran) "Do you know," he goes on, "what made him jump from the roof, him, who in Polish poetry stood on the very top of Polish poetry?" Kosky paces the room.

"Jump? The official papers wrote that his fall was an accident," she says a bit uncertain. "Wasn't it? Was there any reason for suicide?"

"There was. Slander," says Kosky. "His various enemies both in Poland, and those in exile, piled sickening slime upon his reputation. Eventually Lechón couldn't take such debasement anymore. The roof of the hotel was his way out of that moral basement."

"How come you know so much about Lechón, a poet known only to well-read Poles?"

"Poetry belongs to everyone," says Kosky.

"And how!" She comes to life as if reinvented again. (PRINTER: Reinvented, not reborn. *Bardzo dziekuje*. Thanks a lot. J. K.) "Too bad that most American people don't know they've got some of the greatest pen-hood of The Melting Pot!"

"And how!" he reverberates with the joy of Robin Hood. "The Melting Pot gives American writers a new spiritual dimension. Thanks to the First Amendment, the freedom of self-expression, they live in a spiritually Superior Situation, if not necessarily a Spiritually Superior State." He provides his text with an additional series of SSs.

"So what else interested you about Lechón? Was it his—" Now she hesitates. "Overly abundant carnal concupiscence?" She borrows his CC, and so he eliminates it from his newest literary inventions.

"What else? Not much. Just that Lechón was born late on June 13, and so was I," he says with a grave expression. He takes her by her hand, then by her wrist. Here our actor does it in order to take her pulse, as well as in order to touch her. "It is erratic but O.K., it oscillates between 69 and 96 beats per minute," he tells her and what he says reassures him, more than it does her, his voluntary poet patient. Slowly, from the top of the console he picks up the volume of Julian Tuwim's poetry. Slowly, for maximum effect, he opens it to his all-time favorite poem, and, at random, still slowly and still even greater effect, he starts reading the poem. Now he reads it quickly (with a speed of rhythm he first learned, as did she, from reading Tuwim's *Lokomotywa* [locomotive. J. K.]), just as quickly reclaiming the cadence of his mother's tongue and no longer acting or acting-out — while submerged in the poem's at first unhurried, then progressively more and more hurried rhythm, the movement of the poem matching — in an ideal onomatopeic fashion — the motion of a *Lokomotywa,* moving at first slowly, then faster and faster.

"I am a Pole because from infancy I was nourished there on the Polish language; because my mother taught me Polish poetry and songs; . . .

A Pole — because it was in Polish that I confessed the turmoil of first love and in Polish that I stammered about its happiness and storms.

A Pole, too, because the birch and the willow are nearer to me than the palm and the citrus, because Mickiewicz and Chopin are dearer than Shakespeare and Beethoven. Dearer for reasons which, again, I cannot justify by any logic." Julian Tuwim: We, the Polish Jews in *Lamentations,* 1944.

From across the room, she listens to him, transfixed.

"Only one foreordained by his native language can read in it like that. Why didn't you tell me you were born Polish? That's not fair *Monsieur Flotsam!*" She is about to cry.

He rushed to her. "Wait — please! I'm not entirely Polish.

I'm Jewish-Ruthenian American. Ruthlandia was once part and parcel of Poland and so was I. But this was years ago. So long ago, in fact, that I forgot not only my country, but also, with it, the meaning of Polish poetry. Dig it?" Sitting down, he draws her close.

Suddenly he lets her go. Quickly, in front of her, he lifts off his wig. He peels off the mustache and beard. Pensive, she watches his sudden metamorphosis.

"Strange!" she marvels, sitting on his lap like a doll and examining his features. "It's like seeing some freaky original emerge from a perfectly decent translation." Her eyes rest on him. "Funny," she says. "You look familiar. I have a feeling I have seen you before we first met. Besides, it seems I saw you before my arrival in New York and under some rather pleasant circumstances. For me, *pleasant* means literary." She closes in on him with all the poetic zeal and skill and samovar-made passion and tries to ridicule the scene.

She gets up and smooths out what's left of his own hair.

"Tell me: have I seen you somewhere before?" she asks in earnest.

"I doubt it. Not in person, anyhow." THOMAS WOLFE DENIES HAVING PORTRAYED ASHEVILLE. (Asheville *Times*, 1929)

"If not in person, then—how?" She ogles him as if from within.

"Perhaps in a photograph—a newspaper photograph," he says guardedly. "Or on a foreign book jacket," he says while ogling her, and already hoping for a 69 kiss. **For instance, there can be kisses exchanged merely in intense glances. A sort of "spiritual" kiss can pass between the adoring eyes of a pair of lovers. The hotblooded Latin races know the power of such kisses. (Hugh Morris, 1977)[18]**

"Which newspaper? What book?" Terrified, as if speaking

---

[18]*The Art of Kissing* by Hugh Morris, New York, 1977, page 69.

about some foreign totalitarian terror, she is hissing at him, and dare she disregard his para-literary (literary, not military, printer!) The Art of Kissing.

"All kinds of newspapers: The Asheville *Times,* the Asheville *Citizen,* the Asheville *Daily Mail.* . . . You name it, but none of it matters even though they all have named me." He tries to laugh it off, but can't. It means *the painted veil which those who live call life.* (*The Painted Veil* by W. Somerset Maugham, 1928).

"I think I know who you are," she says. "You're Norbert Kosky—the émigré writer. You're the one who sold out to English-language. Tuwim called 'poetic creation—unthinkable in any other language, no matter how fluently I might speak it, other than in the language of my own.' "

Prostitute n. 2. a person, as a writer, artist, etc., who sells his services for low or unworthy purposes. (*Webster's New Twentieth Century Dictionary*). "I'm no less perfect and no more than so many other writers," he recoils. "While in his writing, Anatole France embraced France, I embraced English tongue and through it the United States of my innermost self. What's wrong with that?"

"Twice if not thrice I told you on the phone that I didn't want to see you Mr. Kosky." She raises her voice. "I think you should leave me now—and please don't come back." She seems fatigued. Emotions fatigue.

"Haven't you heard of motion illness? Well how about emotion? Can't you give the original the same chance you gave its bilingual edition?" he pleads with her.

Of Mr. Cooper we desire to say but little. At all times and on all suitable occasions since the appearance of his *Home as Found,* we have described that work as grossly libelous upon our people, their manners and their customs; and of its author, as the most wholesale slanderer of our people of any man living. This is our deliberate opinion at this time; and this opinion we now repeat, in the well-grounded conviction, that there cannot be found in

the United States twelve honest men who will not agree with, and justify us, in holding up to the merited scorn and contempt of his countrymen, one who has thus wantonly and recklessly traduced them. (*Courier and Enquirer,* 1843)

"Please let me stay with you—and read with you the rest of Tuwim," he pleads with the book of Tuwim in hand. This does the trick, even though it is no longer a sexual trick he is after. Oh no! he's falling in love with her as fast as he once did with the poetry of Tuwim—as if she were one of his most beloved Polish Flowers, a poetic epic by Julian Tuwim, which our Diaspora Jew now reads to her. Coerced by poetry as only a poet can be, the poetess lets him stay with her—and in her permission vests a poetic promise as much as poetic license.

"This Ruthenian-made *karafka* (carafe) contains pure 69° proof Lechistan Vodka." (Lechistan means Poland in Turkish. J. K.) she pours him, and herself, a glass and—typical *inteligent* that she is—proposes that the two of them drink a *Brüderschaft.* They drink it, with their arms intertwined as the custom requires. A form of skoal carried to its logical conclusion *Brüderschaft* allow them to abandon the customary form of addressing him as *Pan* and her as *Pani.* First *Pan* Kosky, then *Pan* Norbert, finally *Pan* Bert, even though Bert is already a familiar diminutive, under such ambiguous circumstances it is and it still must be accompanied by the formal *Pan.* The *Brüderschaft* lets him call her simply Helena and the more familiar the language, the faster it leads to a state of mental, then physical intimacy. This means that from now on they must call each other by an intimate *you*—such as the French *tu* (or *ty* in Polish or Russian or Ruthenian)—As they talk they both complain that so intimate *Ty,* (*Ty* as opposed to You) does not exist in English. The very English in which You, (the collective *Ty,*) is employed as a form of address, regardless whether one addresses one's lover, or people in general—"or an Army, Navy, and Air Force general." (Jay Kay.)

She dims the light, a fact significant enough to italicize mentally, if not in print. **He senses that she senses that he senses her. This is still another level of arousal, for he becomes conscious of his sexuality through his awareness of its effect on her and of her awareness that this effect is due to him. Once she takes the same step and senses that he senses her sensing him, it becomes difficult to state, let alone imagine, further iterations, though they may be logically distinct. If both are alone, they will presumably turn to look at each other directly, and the proceedings will continue on another plane.** (Thomas Nagel)[19] It is hot in the room, "so breathlessly hot," she complains, she could use some rest, "but please, don't leave me now. I'm not dead. Not yet," she asks him. Would he mind if she undressed entirely? He wouldn't. Go ahead. Your poetry undresses you the way my prose undresses me. She undresses and, wordlessly, so does he, piling his clothes on the floor next to hers. They are both naked. Now the naked king and the naked queen lie in the same American king-size bed, next to one another. Their elbows touch, and so do their feet and hands.

---

[19]As quoted by the already quoted Janice Moulton, who writes: "Flirtation, seduction, and traditional courtship involve sexual feelings that are quite independent of physical contact. These feelings are increased by anticipation of success, winning, or conquest. Because what is anticipated is the opportunity for sexual intimacy and satisfaction, the feelings of sexual satisfaction are usually not distinguished from those of sexual anticipation. Sexual satisfaction involves sexual feelings which are increased by the other person's knowledge of one's preferences and sensitivities, the familiarity of their touch or smell or way of moving, and not by the novelty of their sexual interest." (op. cit. p. 111).

Nothing else. How is she? How is her heart? he asks her. Having suffered, like his father before him, from MAT (Multifocal Atrial Tachycardia. J. K.) he knows that cardiac arrest is often caused by emotions.[20] She had opened for him a whole and wholesome universe of love which arrests. A universe penetrated only once before—when he was twelve and in love with a girl called Bożena, and at thirteen became a sex-offender. She moves closer. "Hear my heart for yourself, doctor!" she says. He lays his head face down on her breast, listens and counts the sound of her heartbeat. Her heart is racing wildly. Does her excitement originate in her heart or in her mind? In reply, she stretches sinuously, brushing his question away. He looks at her breast; he sees her heart.

"Dotknij mnie prosze. Touch me, please. Touch with your Self, not just with your eyes," she prompts him. "Touch me with your hand. Even with your index finger. Please!"

He won't touch her. He is afraid, can't you see? Afraid of his own panging heart. He is still a World War II kid gripped by some inexplicable, and not yet described or diagnosed, "enhanced automacity" (*The Merck Manual,* 1987)

"Touch me," she prompts, leaning against him with her hip. "Touch *cialo poetki*—poet's flesh. I read somewhere you are a Tantric yogi.[21] Are you? Don't yogis believe in six sexual organs? Is that why the ideal Lotus grows six petals?" She watches him as if he were a petal-growing lotus.

---

[20]Read *Heart Rhythms:* Breakthrough Treatments for Cardiac Arrhythmia—the Silent Killer of 400,000 Americans Each Year, by Jeffrey Rothfeder, 1989.

[21]"There is small wonder that the 'Tantric Age,' which followed the lifting of the puritan tendencies of Orthodox Buddhism, became the age of abandon, in which erotic poetry . . . and frank references to sexual practices of great finesse began to flourish in literature and other forms of art." ("Sex and Religious Art," in *The Art of Nepal,* by Lydia Aran, op. cit.)

"Fuck me, you stupid fuck," she laughs him in the face when he does or says nothing. "Fuck *poetka*, a poetess, who devoted two-thirds of her poetry to her own falling in love and less than one-third to her failing heart. One who speaks of sex as *miłość*, as love, but also as *zmysły*, the senses. One who writes of sex as a love of procreation, and of creation, sure, but also sex as love, as fucking, as *kochanie sie* but also as—forgive me, sir, for *saying this in your face—pierdolenie.*" (fucking): the most elementary word.

She examines his dormant face, as dormant as his flesh. He examines his Sexual Self (SS) as until now he himself has never examined this particular SS before. Why is he put off by the word *pierdolenie?* Is it because, for some inner reason, the native word sounds perhaps dirtier to him than the Anglo-Saxon *fucking?* Is the word *pierdolenie* harsher to him because he heard it for the first time as a boy of six from a crude Ruthenian peasant girl who, clearly afraid of his menacing looks, said, *"Odpierdol sie!,"* meaning "Fuck off!" which could also mean she could squeal on him to the Germans (though obviously she did not: J. K.). Is this why the word *pierdolenie* sounds to him more vulgar hence, like any common phrase, eminently more accessible than the domestic *fuck off?* Or is he more or less (or differently, J. K.) excited by its Ruthenian associations?

A compromise is reached: our sexual con man makes her sign a sex concordat. According to it, they will make love under certain conditions. They will make love to one another not with one another.

He reminds the Good Great Anglo-American poet W. H. Auden said of the poet as one "encased in talent like a uniform," while a novelist was, to him, the one who ". . . in his own weak person, if he can, must suffer dully at the wrongs of Man." [W. H. Auden]

Time then, for *kochanie sie,* for Ars Amandi, even though she hates the English phrase *making love.* "Making love sounds like a manufacturing process," she says. "I prefer the simple

171

pierdolenie."

Expertly, (as if she were an expert of sexual bondage) she attaches one after another the monitor's leads to her limbs and torso, their straps coiling around her like water snakes, their suction caps sucking into her skin like leeches. Briefly, most briefly, their form, their sight and feel make him think of—even see—various neck-to-waist and waist-to-wrist restraints he used to use, first himself, (use, not abuse) then in some of his past fiction. The leads make contact with the oscillograph. The transmission begins. **"I wish I could hold you," she continued bitterly, "till we were both dead! I shouldn't care what you suffered. I care nothing for your sufferings. Why shouldn't you suffer. I do! Will you forget me. . . ?"** (Emily Brontë)

On the monitor the black electric heart waves rush across the pastoral ECG screen. They rush from left to right. No wonder that, when writing in Hebrew characters, the language of their heart, the Jews write from right to left whether in Ladino, Hebrew or Yiddish, the mother tongues of Jewish soul.

Helena draws him closer. He crawls under and in between the electrodes. He kisses her breasts; he watches the monitor. **All female orgasms are clitoral, of course; but there's something very special about coming solely through nipple stimulation.** Lana Davis (Gent magazine). Hearts flutter is individual—as individual as one's handwriting. As individual as love. Heart is no longer to him another metaphor for the same manuscript of life—for him, it is now an instrument of love. To Kosky this is a brand new manuscript. He reads it carefully.

Glued to Helena, he monitors the monitor. On the ECG screen her heart waves come fast—too fast—a sign that the heart's own natural pacemaker cannot conduct them all. Is she going through a heart blockage? Will it be **Death: the shatterer of worlds? (Tantra)**

"I'm not anymore excited by your bodily curve," he tells

her in English, knowing that the English word curve evokes *kurwa*, Polish for whore." he says, and pulls away.

"You're heartless," Helena recoils. The unnatural shape of her *P* wave becomes natural. Her heart's tunnel is no longer blocked. They both lie back, elbows touching. "Kosky is a Ruthenian name," she reflects. "Were you born as Kosky — with that Semitic face? With that Jewish nose?" she asks skeptically.

"It's an ethnic pen name. My father followed the example of Israel Bael Shem Tov, a Polish-Jewish storyteller, who believed in the power of the name," says Kosky. "At the war's outset, to distract the Nazis from the shape of our Jewish past, we took the name of Kosky. After the war we kept the name as an amulet of good luck: after all, thanks to it — and thanks to countless Ruthenians who sheltered and saved us again and again — we survived the war."

Helena cuddles next to him. Her eyes downcast, she pinches with her fingers the bulb of his *szczypior*.[22] Her lips are moist, her eyes watery.

"Leave the onion alone. Obey your doctors," he tells her, no longer strong enough to tell her she must obey him, the macho trick he used to perform — perform, not act out — with so many other women.

"I obey life. Like it or not, the sex instinct is the *lokomotoywa* of my life and of my poetry. Get on the train!" she tells him point blank. She likes the onion and particularly its tip with which she plays most inventive games of press'nd squeeze. She strokes it. She tastes it, slowly first, with her lips, then with her mouth and tongue. She takes her time. She has not tasted it for a very long time, she tells him, and at first she finds its taste too raw, though not as hard as she first thought. She is wasting a lot of her priceless energy on trying to turn

---

[22]*szczypior* (Ruth, n.): a small onion without a bulb.

173

his steam-emitting stem into an empty stalk and in order to slow her down he allows himself the rare luxury of losing a drop of his spiritual spleen disguised as Hasidic-Dionysian seminal fluid. She keeps tasting it and stroking it until the bitter nectar bursts out of the hard core and the core turns soft and pliant. But even then she won't let go. She keeps on kneading it in her hands and then, to her amusement, attempts to peel its skin off.

"Our newspapers wrote that in your first novel you did your native country harm." She squeezes him painfully, as if testing his resistance to pain. Now, she manipulates him verbally, even though, in Polish-language, where adverb and adjective hold court of impressions, the verb is much less powerful.

"The same was said about Cooper and Wolfe; about Conrad and Tolstoy. About Ibsen and Pasternak," says Kosky. **"When it comes to books, I must say that this gentleman who writes novels in English nearly gave me a nervous fit. I felt, when reading about him, something slippery and disgusting coming up in my throat."** (Eliza Orzeszkowa about Conrad, 1899)

· Fond of the memories,[23] Kosky fondles his *brit*. The *brit* responds to his touch.

She presses him hard. "You've got so much Gentile slack in you; so much loose skin."

"Maybe loosened, never loose. Please—this whole thing is hard enough. Don't make it any harder than it already is. I'm told that, in Hebrew, *milah* means both word and circumcision." He defends his faith in himself. "I am a Jew," he says. "I was born in Ruthenia as so many of my precious ancestors were born and I was born to Jewish parents and in the strict

---

[23]Circumcision does not interrupt any vital function. It simply counteracts excessive lust. In addition, it gives all Jewish people a common bodily sign. (Maimonides)

observance of Jewish customs always respected by our non-Jewish neighbors, I set forth to leave my mother's *mikvah* and at six minutes to nine P.M. my forehead emerged, which, once the child's head is safely out of water, in the Jewish faith is considered as the actual moment of one's birth. Accordingly, I was circumcised eight days later. It was, I'm sure, a very proper Jewish ceremony attended, I have been told, by all sixty-six (SS) members of my family. Every Weinreich, Loewenkopf and Lenkowski was there in full strength. Just to think that by 1945, all but three of them: my parents and I, were left to attend the 1946 concert to life. The *baal brit*, the master of the circumcision ceremony, kept me on his lap in his function of *sandek*—as my godfather. I've been told, that, as customary, an unoccupied chair was left in the room for Prophet Elijah who, in one form or another, in order to protect the newly born, is said to attend every *brit*. I assure you I'm circumcised to the fullest. My picture could never be published in *Uncut: The Magazine of the Natural Man.*"[24]

"Then there's only one way to find out. Grow inside me," she says. "Grow like a living plant. I hate dead plants—they are always soft." She goes on. "Forget my heart. Be hard. Until you, until this moment, the only man I have seen naked all the way down was my boyfriend?" She most carefully studies, then kneads his *szczpior* again.

"Still, is it possible that in spite of your circumcision, you might not be Jewish? That, say, you were circumcised, by nature—born without a prepuce or a membrane?" she seems concerned.

---

[24]"A high-quality, bimonthly magazine, *Uncut* explores every facet of the uncircumcised man with articles, features and the most lavish photo layouts of uncut men ever to appear . . . the most beautiful magazine in history devoted to foreskin," in the words of its own ad. (See also *Foreskin Quarterly* and Other publications of the Uncircumcised Society of America.: U.S.A.)

"Being born circumcised would make me the only *nolad mahul*—'one born circumcised'—found since the sacred commandment of circumcision was given to Abraham, almost four thousand years ago! Now that would make me truly unique!" **There are things, moments, that are not to be tossed to the public's incomprehension, for journalists to gloat over. No, it was not an experience to be exhibited "in the street."** (Joseph Conrad)

"Is it true that being truncated, without a foreskin to protect him, makes every man whether he is a *Żyd*[25] or not, end up being less sensitive as a lover? That as a result, every circumcised man is, by nature of the circumcision, always torn between guilt for not feeling enough and lust for feeling more?" She squeezes his flesh in yet another test by pain.

"Can one determine what is lust and what is feeling? What, when it comes to feeling or lust, is less or more?" asks Kosky.

"Only a poet can determine that," she declares.

Her eyes glow. Her lips are red. "Love me. Me, not my heart. Love me the way nature intends man to love a woman. Love yourself in me. Make me love myself in you. Let's do it at least once. 'I must be allowed to start life everywhere,' says Rilke. And so must I."

"What about your heart?" he asks. **What for I washed my breasts/and combed each hair in the narrow mirror?/my hands are empty/and so is my bed.** (Halina Poświatowska in *Wiersze Wybrane* [Selected Poetry] in Polish, Cracow, 1987.)

"What does the heart know!" She kisses him on the mouth, her tongue probing. With her hands, she opens her flesh to him. "My heart, my heart," she sighs. "Fuck me, not my

---

[25]*Żyd*—in Ruthenian Jew, pron. *Gide*. (André Gide was the French Nobel Prize-winning controversial novelist who "might have been, as his name alone indicated, a *Żyd*." (Jay Kay)

heart!" She draws him to her.

Exiled from the Image-repertoire *exil*/exile **Deciding to give up the amorous condition, the subject sadly discovers himself exiled from his image-repertoire.** (Roland Barthes, *A Lover's Discourse: Fragments,* trans. by Richard Howard, 1978.)

SS

The State of the Arts Hospital in Manhattan, New York State. Escorted by nurses, Helena disappears behind a steel door. Surgery. Recovery. No visitors. Is it because the electrocardiograph says it or because her doctors don't like the sight of her — her, *their* patient, kissing Kosky in their presence? How can he know?

From afar, Kosky watches her enter the plane of Samoflot, the Ruthenian airlines. From afar, she sees him. She raises her hand. She is gone.

Jealousies, anxieties, possessions, discourses, appetites, signs, once again amorous desire was burning everywhere. It was as if I were trying to embrace one last time, hysterically, someone about to die — someone for whom I was about to die: I was performing a denial of separation. (Roland Barthes, ibidem, p. 109)

SS

A few weeks later, from Ruthenia, he receives her letter. She writes:

Recently, I wrote "The Blue Bird" — a short story — published this week in *Litlife,* our foremost literary review. The story is autofiction, neither truth nor lie. It revolves around an event — neither fiction nor fact — about my affair with one Norbert K, Ruthenian exile, whom I met in New York while waiting for my open-

177

heart surgery. If for whatever reason his portrait hurts you, please remember that it is how I wrote about him that is my gift to you. How, not what. It is a gift of poetic prose, of all the waves which flowed from my Soul and not from my American-repaired semimechanical heart. Who knows such things better than you — the mini Bruno Schulz of the American literary prairie. As for the rest? Not even the *Party Organ* can stop my heart from telling me with every beat that I love my memory of you though I am no longer in love with your organ.

Helena.

He reads "The Blue Bird," then rereads it. The story is painful to read. It is vicious. It is manipulative. But it is also written with malice, that marvelously creative force which propelled Swift and Pope. Where would PEN people — poets and novelists, essayists, editors and translators — be without malice? rhetorically, he asks himself. The Yellow Pages are written without malice. But would you ever read them for fun? For a while, to recover from the impact of her yellow pen, Kosky does not write or call her, and he returns all her letters to him unopened. Is he cruel or is he hurt? "As a novelist, he is both." (Jay Kay). But then, he misses her. She is his Lady Fall, his gossamer, his swan. By now she might be fully recovered, her heart ready to love and be loved without Thanatos for a witness. **To love is to escape from doubt and live in the self-evidence of the heart. (Gaston Bachelard)** One fall night he telephones the sanatorium in Poland. The chief nurse is on the line. Excited, he tells her he wants to talk to *Pani* Helena Powska — and he says it in his best, most festive Polish. A long pause. "Citizen Helena Powska died months ago," says citizen chief nurse, who on orders from someone official was asked to substitute citizen, the relatively new word for the centuries-old form of *Pan, Panna* or *Pani*.

Citizen Kosky's heart misfires. "What? Are you sure, citizen nurse?"

Without the Other I apprehend fully and nakedly this terrible necessity of being free which is my lot: that is, the fact that I cannot put the responsibility for making-myself-be off onto anyone but myself even though I have not chosen to be and although I have been born. (Sartre)

"As sure as I am of the fall outside," says the nurse.

"But—her American surgery was a success! Why would she die?" he cried.

"Because her heart got broken. That's why," says the nurse.

Powska is dead. Think of her as if she had never gone. The telephone connection goes dead. Think of her as if she were Veronica, a woman from "The Bearing of the Cross," (circa 1505) a painting by Bosch.

Yet there is One who holds all this falling in his head, gently and without end. (Rilke) No call, no letter, no apology can bring her back. But her story is here—and so he rereads it. As a character, the Blue Bird is a dreadful man. As a story, "The Blue Bird" is as lovely as any man's fall.[26]

If I had to make a choice among the people I would like to address today, I would chose as a priority, even if this comes as a surprise, two types of women and men. The first ones are those who are tempted to commit suicide, whatever the reason or the means be: moral, psychic, or physical (you can destroy yourself in many ways and not only physically). To those people I would say: Your life is more than what you think. Accept this life not because it

---

[26]"The cadence of the sentences, which differs from the usual speech melody or sentence melody, and the peculiar rhythms that appear also alert the reader to the fact that the language is not being used for normal communication, nor does it aim at the common real world." Rainer Maria Rilke's *Lay of the Love and Death of Cornet Christopher Rilke* (Roman Ingarden, 1937).

is such, but accept it to receive life; it comes from farther away than you do; it is more beautiful than you think; believe in the life you received and accept its trials. (Jean-Marie Cardinal Lustiger, 1983).[27]

---

[27]From Our Jewish Roots, in *Dare to Believe* by Jean-Marie Cardinal Lustiger, The Crossroad Publishing Company, New York.

Jean-Marie Lustiger was born of Polish-Jewish parents in Paris in 1926 and converted to Catholicism as a youth. He studied literature, philosophy, and theology at the Sorbonne. He was appointed bishop of Orleans in 1979, archbishop of Paris in 1981, and elevated to the rank of cardinal in 1983.

10

THE FIRST DIFFICULTY WE MEET is posed by the question: among what kind of objects is the literary work to be included—the real or the ideal? (Roman Ingarden, *The Literary Work of Art*, 1973.)[1]

"An ordinary suicide note is the least understood genre of undistinguished penmanship (as distinguished from distinguished literary creation), and we hope, my dear Mr. Kosky, to understand its nature better by asking you—as well as some other six hundred distinguished American fictional pen-masters, to write for us, *pro bono publico*, one quasicide: a simulated suicide note—such as you would write if one of your fictional protagonists was suicide-bound, and for yourself were you ever to voluntarily dispose of your physical Self by means of suicide," writes Dr. Sam Hill, Jr., the author of *The Self Execution* (Felodese Press, 1986) who heads up

---

[1] Roman Ingarden, *The Literary Work of Art:* An Investigation on the Borderlines of Ontology, Logic and Theory of Literature, with an Appendix on the "Functions of Language in the Theater." Translated from Polish with an Introduction by George C. Grabowicz, 1973. See also: *The Cognition of the Literary Work of Art* (1973) by Roman Ingarden, translated from Polish by Ruth Ann Crowley and Kenneth R. Olson, 1973.

Thanatos Institute in Yama, California, and he writes his letter to Kosky on the most beautifully engraved a bit old-fashioned white stationery most appropriately framed by a black margin.

To any serious writer, death and dying are most familiar. Death as The Grim Reaper. Death as skull'nd crossbones, the deadly spiritual symbol of the Nazi SS and human extinction and extermination they stood and fought for. Death as passing (though no longer trespassing); as ceSSation and diSSolution. (Thanks, printer, for these extra SS's!) Death as the fires of Sheol or the ashes of Shoah. But also death from the Primary SS — the medicalese for Sjogren's Syndrome, i.e. from extreme drying out of the body's mucous membranes i.e. from absence of life-providing moisture. ("If you're prone to dryness of the eyes or mouth, and if you're traveling often by airplane — the most dehydrating experience — do consult the latest Sjogren's Syndrome Symposium (SSS) Newsletter," promptly advises the always moisture-minded Jay Kay).

As much as the Holocaust transcends my understanding, even greater is my inability to understand the regenerating and the recreation of Jewish life, culture, religion and creativity that has emerged since the Holocaust. The demonic and the miraculous appear at last equally vexing. (Byron Sherwin, 1986)[2]

Death as quick as Black Horse and as silent as Quietus. Death the Great Adventure and the Grand Release. Who doesn't remember the classic scene of Nero's suicide ending *Quo Vadis*, the novel by Henryk Sienkiewicz?[3] Or Farewell, my love, farewell/Don't be upset, don't furrow your brow.

---

[2]"Conceptions, Misconceptions and Implications of the Holocaust: A Jewish Perspective," by Byron L. Sherwin, *Shofar*, Summer 1980. Also, in order to keep the Holocaust in focus, consult: Special Focus: A Distance From the Holocaust, *Tikkun Magazine*, 1989.

[3]Henryk Sienkiewicz, a Polish Nobel Prize winner in Literature (1905) who gave us *Quo Vadis?* (1896). His trilogy, *With Fire and*

Dying isn't anything new in this life/And, of course, life isn't any newer," lines written by the sad Russian poet Esenin in his own hand, and with his pen dipped in his own blood, only a day before hanging himself in an anonymous room of a Leningrad hotel.

Voracious time devours everything, moves all things from their places, allows nothing to endure for long, Rivers Fail, the land encroaches on the receding sea. Mountains subside and lofty peaks collapse. Why do I speak of such petty matters? The whole most beauteous structure of the heavens will suddenly burn away in its own flames. Death commands all things. It is a law, not a penalty, to perish. A time will come when there will be no world here, says Petronius, the elegant Roman writer forced by Nero in the year 66 to die at forty-six.

Besides the already-quoted *Book of Jewish Lists,* what about *American Epitaphs:* Grave and Humorous by Charles L. Wallis (New York, 1973).

Strange Creek, West Virginia, was named for William Strange, who was lost from his companions during a surveying trip in 1795. His bones were found several years later near a tree against which his gun still rested. On the bark Strange had carved this epitaph before he perished of hunger and exposure:

Strange is my name and I'm on strange ground
And Strange it is I can't be found.

(*Stories on Stone,* ibidem.)

Sword (New York, 1991), a Polish all time national epic, translated in time for its hundredth anniversary for the first time from Polish into English during six years of non stop literary-love labor by W. S. Kuniczak, the noted Polish-American, who wrote, among others, *Valedictory, The Sempinski Affair, The March* and *The Thousand Hour Day,* (J. K.)

Like all other fictional notes collected by Thanatos from the other professional writers, Kosky's quasicide note (note, as opposed to a notebook, a diary, short story, a play or a novel), he is informed by Dr. Hill, "will later be scientifically matched, in terms of scientifically defined motivation," unsigned, against notes (notes, as opposed to a verse, an idyll, a love letter, etc.), each one written to the best of our knowledge by one suicidee; notes written by a hired suicide expert or ghostwriter were not considered. "As far as we were able to ascertain," Dr. Hill's letter goes on, "none of the suicidee notes (often ink-stained prosody or villanelle written with blood drawn from one's own vein) were written by a person aspiring to be a professional knight of the quill — be it a verse, librettist or a ballad-monger, though a great number of them, it must be noted, seemed to stem from physiological reactions induced by either an overdose or underproduction of one form or another of existential despair.[4]" continues Dr. Hill, who then goes on to say that, what will ultimately distinguish the suicide notes used in our study from the quasicide notes written by writers known to be masters of creative usurpation, and against which these notes will be rated, is that none of the authors of the suicide notes is still among the living. Acting promptly upon their notes, every one of these suicidees has killed himself or herself (though it could be assumed that they might still be living in some other

---

[4]See: "Choice of Method for Suicide and Personality: A Study of Suicide Notes," by David Lester in *Omega*, vol. 1, 1971. For years Kosky mourned the suicide at the age of 58 of John Berryman, the American poet, (whose *The Dream songs*, [1969] Robert Lowell ranked as the greatest American poetic expression since W.W. II. J. K.:) Both Berryman and Kosky won the 1969 National Book Awards at a ceremony at New York's Lincoln Center during which Berrymen noted that while he "perspired outside, Kosky was perspiring on the inside," (Estate Editors).

invisible and even unforeseeable reincarnatory form). Subsequently, their suicide notes were retrieved by the Institute from the records of medical examiners and homicide bureaus all over the country."

In him, too, as in the unthinking animal, there prevails a sense of security as a permanent state, a security which springs from the innermost conscious—that man is nature, that he himself is the world. Because of this security no man is noticeably bothered by the thought of a certain and never distant death; but everyone continues to live as if he were to live eternally. This goes so far, that one could say that no one actually has a living conviction about the certainty of his death. Otherwise there could not be such a great difference between his mood and that of the convicted criminal. (Schopenhauer)

So muses our Tantric muse.

"A Tantric ritual; during the initiation ceremony, you are given a mirror in which you see your own image. Contemplating it, you realize you are nothing but that, i.e., nothing. To what end, so many pretenses, so many airs and graces, when it is so easy to comprehend one's insignificance?" writes the incomparable Cioran,[5] one of the most *delicate* minds of real power writing today. Nuance, irony, and refinement are the essence of his thinking. Yet he declares in the essay "On a Winded Civilization": *"Men's minds need a simple truth, an answer which delivers them from their questions, a gospel, a tomb. The moments of refinement conceal a death-principle; nothing is more fragile than subtlety,"* writes Susan Sontag.

Every one of those six hundred suicide notes came from

---

[5]See Susan Sontag's introduction to *The Temptation to Exist* (1968), by E. M. Cioran. Read also "The Tree of Life" and "On Sickness" in his *The Fall into Time* with an Introduction by Charles Newman, 1970.

under the writing hand of one who, in life's fatal, as well as final, moment, even though not a writer, reached for a pen, a pencil, or any other writing instrument, to write words with it — words, mind you, not drawings or arabesques. ". . . for a mighty pen connects one directly with the Almighty." (Israel Kosky) Second, remember that these real-suicide notes were written for us, for the living, by hundreds of women, and men who, whether young or old, fragile or strong, sexually subtle or living without sex at all, literally finished themselves off (effectively ending their life as writers: J. K.). Finally, mark that those who wrote these notes, killed themselves by — let us be purposefully vague here — passive means, such as inhaling gas, swallowing poison, or drowning in a hot bath — as well as by active means. These suicide notes were written by those most diversely universal kind of people. Among them, no doubt, were some ordinary American Tantrics who, eager, say, to die fast, rather than to fast endlessly, died by (let us spare us details) injecting themselves with poison, either directly, into their arteries with a hypodermic needle, or indirectly, via swallowing poisonous pills; by those who, sportspersons to the end, jumped without a chute from a plane or drowned after a jump from a bridge or balcony. Among them, there was a stripper called Joanna who, after stripping, locked herself from inside in a giant factory meat freezer — then . . . (description deleted. Proofreader No. 68 to author: I can't take all this suicide anymore! I'm quitting now. Bye-bye. — Rita Maria.) **There's nothing bad about death except the fear of it.** Someone must have said it, but who? Was it Seneca? Or was it Megan Leigh, one of Kosky's favorite adult film'nd video actress and exotic dance circuit most talented star.

Bye-Bye Megan: IT WASN'T PORN THAT KILLED ME-GAN LEIGH. IT WASN'T EVEN SEX. AS FAR AS PO-LICE INVESTIGATORS COULD DETERMINE FROM AN EIGHT-PAGE LETTER SHE LEFT BEHIND, IT

WAS THE EMOTIONAL STRESS OF NEVER BEING ABLE TO TRULY PLEASE SOMEONE NEAR AND DEAR TO HER. . . . SHE WAS DRESSED IN A NIGHTGOWN AND WEARING FULL MAKEUP, AS IF EXPECTING A VISITOR. THE BULLET THAT KILLED HER CAME FROM A SMALL HANDGUN SHE CARRIED WITH HER ON HER DANCING TOURS FOR PROTECTION. (*Hustler* magazine). See cheek-peek: MEGAN LEIGH CARESSES HER OWN RAUNCHY BUMS! (Rear Action magazine, 1990), and MEGAN IN MEMORIA, (Adam magazine, 1990).

"Science tells us that those who are about to kill themselves organize their thoughts pretty much the way professional, i.e., creatively bound, writers do, because a disorganized mind could never execute suicide—an act of rational self-execution," note the scientists at Thanatos. Hence, they say, the purpose of this experiment is to predict, on a blind basis, and with the help of advanced psycholinguistic methods,[6] which of the "final notes" are real, i.e., written by those who killed themselves, who meant what they had scribbled down, and which were written by writers such as who, like Kosky, contemplated suicide, but committed it only on a written page, and only as an act of creative usurpation.

(Writes Isaac Watts in *Divine Songs Attempted in Easy Language for the Use of Children* (1773, 1956, 1971)

---

[6]"These methods use the following parameters: Age. Sex. Marital status. Words per note. The use of self-centered as well as other-centered pronouns and possessives. Verbs of explicit thought or too explicit action. The ratio of rational to irrational, or "I want to *die*" as opposed to "I want to *kill* myself" or "I wish to be killed." The use of dread-inhibitors or courage-prompters." (Thanatos)

Let me improve the hours I have,
Before the day of grace is fled;
There's no repentance in the grave,
Nor pardons offer'd to the dead.
Just as a tree cut down that fell
To north, or southward, there it lies;
So Man departs to heaven or hell,
Fixt in state wherein he dies.

And what Watts so cheerfully writes about applies to everyone on this earth, whether one is cheerful or not. ("Let's then be positivist about it," writes Kosky, "and rather than romantically kill oneself by an overdose of, say, a hot bath à la Seneca, I would prefer to live and work for the laying of a foundation for the spiritual reconstruction of my Ruthenian-Jewish origins disguised by the Second Holocaust (**Abraham Joshua Heschel**) as remnants. To let these "remnants" die pulverized by "time, their indifferent jailer." (Kosky, 1990) die is to accord the Nazis—the Nazis who planned the final annihilation of everything Jewish, the Nazis, not just annihilation by indifferent time—a final salute of Victory! And, WILL FELLOW AMERICAN-CANADIAN JEWS PASSIVELY STAND BY *AGAIN*? screams from Kosky's imaginary grandstand his rebellious Jay Kay.

Whether skilled writer—or perhaps a person who had himself experienced the suicidal state without actually taking his own life—would be able to intuit the suicidal state more completely, and thereby encode the style more faithfully, we do not know. (Charles E. Osgood, 1960)

Besides, the *pseudocide* test requires of Kosky, first, to imagine himself as being someone else—someone utterly different from himself. It forces him to become, if only in fantasy, fed up with life or with himself or with both that, for the first time in his life, he must feel desperate enough to kill himself. Kill himself? Voluntarily? When? *Soon*. By tomorrow.

Maybe, the day after tomorrow. **All is Number. Number is the individual. Ecstasy is a Number. (Charles Baudelaire)**

In order to facilitate such mental operation he imagines himself first as one whose number is literally up whether he likes it or not, as one, say, whose number was written for him on his skin somewhere between his wrist and elbow, written there not by merciful nature, but by unmerciful man. In his imagination, he is a World War II concentration camp inmate sentenced to die gassed to death in a Holocaust oven. No longer one of those "literary soldiers of fortune who can take the count of nine — and get up when ten is heard" (Vincent Lopez, *Numerology,* 1961), he is now, say, one of some 4,500,000 Soviet prisoners of war who were also gassed by the Germans, or starved.

This imaginary concentration camp number gives him a **case** of pain that he feels in his ethical tennis elbow. It is the **pain** of slow suffocation by gas. Slow and purposefully painful. It was suffered for the first time in history, when the Nazis exterminated their own mentally ill (euthanasia program), the barbaric compulsory eugenic sterilization law (first used against the mentally ill German Jews. Read *Hitler's Professors: The Part of Scholarship in Germany's Crimes Against the Jewish People,* by Max Weinreich, New York, 146. Apropos: Kosky's mother was born Elisabeth Weinreich. Ed.) When those "certifiably insane" were gassed in gas chambers disguised as showers, **a dry run for the extermination (David Weinberg and Byron L. Sherwin, op. cit.)** of Jehovah's Witnesses. Of homosexuals. Of Gypsies. Of Jews. And of Catholic Poles, millions of whom perished together with millions of other Slavs in the Nazi-induced specifically anti-Slavic and just as barbaric clamor.[7]

---

[7]"In 1939 the world Jewish population stood at about 18 million, and in 1945 at about 12 million. One in every three Jews was

Having found being gassed as a proper way to go, Kosky now must decide HOW MUCH YOUR LIFE IS ACTUALLY WORTH TO YOU, SINCE WHEN YOU DIE YOU ARE WORTH NOTHING.

This is easy. Now once again he imagines himself dropping dead, not as a result of suffocation caused by gas, but invaded by the most common cardiac arrythmia which kills silently some half million of Americans every year. What then? *Nothing.* "There is no doubt in my mind that in my case such death would resolve all the unresolved." (Norbert Kosky, 1982)

What else could he now do to make the task of writing his last note more convincing (i.e., most realistic and life-resembling) and yet, at the same time, make it as narrative art requires, more original, (i.e., entirely invented — imagined, not copied from reality)?

THE FINAL DAYS

I concluded my remarks to the medical professions with these words: If there is anything I can leave with you in terms of the treatment of patients with a terminal illness it is this: we are all terminal — we all must die sometime — so why should a terminal illness be different from terminal life? There is no difference. (Jacob K. Javits, 1984)

A professional literary villain, he could describe, say, in the form of a villanelle or even a villanette, the very act of killing himself in the greatest detail — then, following the

---

murdered, two of every three in Europe. Four of every five Jewish scholars, schools, synagogues, and libraries were destroyed.

"Of the Poles, it is estimated that about 2.2 million were systematically murdered and about 5.2 million were enslaved. Neither the experiences nor the memory of the six to eight million non-Jewish victims of Nazi-designed and implemented systematic murder can be obscured, forgotten or minimized. Such revisionist history, in my view, should not be tolerated, especially by Jews or from Jews. Recognizing the victimization of others in no way mitigates the victimization suffered by Jews during the Holocaust," writes Byron L. Sherwin in *Shofar,* op cit. (1986).

description, actually kill himself. Now, how does that grab you for mixing fact with fiction, and turning a literary pseudocide from his newly invented autofiction into an act of nonfiction? — into a Self propelled Auto-da-Fe.

But depression, even a hopeless one, is one thing, suicide is quite another. Kosky believes that in his life until now he had considered suicide twice: first at the age of six (at six he was still, to himself, a child), then at nine, when, after a sudden loss of speech (as much as of willingness to talk), muted from within as well as from without, he no longer wanted to continue as a man.

Now, our post-modern literary retrogradist must try to kill himself if only on paper. Looking into the fictional mirror, he must see another being in it, not himself. A ghost? A ghost of whom? Since none of his fictional characters who inhabit Fictlandia, his private fictive Center State, has ever committed suicide, Kosky, our literary ghost supreme, must look for one in Gravelandia — a land of graves in the public domain. After several telephone inquiries about the topic, as well as about who could be an ideal typist for his suicidal hype, he is clearly not, by chance, invited to be a keynote speaker on the subject Intellectual vs. Suicide, one of the heavier topics of the already heavy convention appropriately named "The Ultimately Suicidal State?" He accepts on the condition that, speaking as an apolitical novelist, he sees the subject matter of his talk the way he regards suicide: as being both *either too serious — or too funny for words*.

ROMAIN GARY SHOT IN HEAD: APPARENT VICTIM OF SUICIDE

Romain Gary, the controversial novelist, died of an apparently self-inflicted gunshot wound. *Roots of Heaven*, one of Mr. Gary's best-known works, takes place in a German concentration camp, where its hero finds mystical comfort thinking about wildlife.

Mr. Gary used World War II as the theme of other

novels. *His Dance of Genghis Cohn* tells the story of a German-Jewish nightclub comic who becomes a dybbuk of Auschwitz.

Equally fluent in French, English and Polish — he was born in Lithuanian Poland as Kacew Gary, his mother's stage name and spent his early boyhood there. **It is also a form of the Russian verb to burn. (*The New York Times*, July 1, 1981)** Mr. Gary wrote some of his novels in English (which he then translated into French) and some in French (which he then translated into English) at the rate of one every year.[8]

(*Times Square Record*)

Then, of course, our literary *pseudocidee* recalls his friends, the Koestlers. In case, my dear reader, you don't know, the Koestlers were found dead in their London flat, a bottle of barbiturates and a glass of brandy in Arthur's hand, a glass of whiskey next to Cynthia and plastic bags neatly wrapped over each one's head: their brand of Socrates' hemlock. **The closest I could get to writing would be to work for a writer. (Cynthia Koestler)**

He examines his face in the mirror: this is the face about to be defaced by the quasicide, by his own writing something quasi, i.e. artificial; by, for once, writing it on orders from someone else, from the Thanatos, and writing it in order to imitate real life. Imitate, not re-create — yet, not imitation, but creation. After all, creation is his business. "Call his story-telling, his creation, by its real name: recreation," (concludes Jay Kay.)

---

[8]See also "Jean Seberg and the Media Myth Makers," by Jeffrey Hart in *The Saturday Evening Post*, 1981, and "Death of a Friend," by François Bondy, in *Encounter*, 1981, and "Romain Gary's Double," by François Bondy, *ibidem*, 1981.

Suddenly, one got an image of his own death . . . of a shameful death that went out softly, dully in anesthetized oblivion, with the fading smell of chemicals on man's final breath. And the image of that death was hateful. (Thomas Wolfe)

Now, his ghost says to him: pull yourself closer to your writing desk, and Norbert, pull yourself together. You are about to become your own ghostwriter. Got it? Every writer has at least one living within one's self. Ask Henry James. Or O'Henry. Ask Thomas Wolfe. Or Virginia Woolf. Ask Turgenev or Thomas Mann. Ask Sylvia Plath or Anne Frank. Ask any writer who has lived in a Secret Annex. **In the meantime, I must uphold my ideals, for perhaps the time will come when I shall be able to carry them out. Yours, Ann. (1944)[9]** Ask Simone Weil.[10]

Above all, for your current spiritual serial number consult Conrad, Célan, and Cioran, Jay Kay's favorite bilingual literary three C threesome. (Author to Editor: Since I am a literary floater, I'll say little about Paul Célan, who killed himself by drowning. Better yet, writing about writer's *inwardness* rather than suicide consult Bruno Schulz, on the subject of his narrative *foot-age*.)[11]

I am leaving life. I am lowering my head, before a

---

[9]Anne Frank's *Diary* ends there. Soon after, the Gestapo raided the Secret Annex. Anne Frank died in the Bergen-Belsen concentration camp. See *Antisemitism:* A History Portrayed. Anne Frank Foundation, Amsterdam, 1989.

[10]Born in 1909, the essayist Simone Weil (*Waiting for God*) died in England (after her arrest and torture by the Gestapo in Marseilles) "as a result of voluntary starvation, for she refused any food beyond the rations allowed the French in the occupied zone." *The Essential Prose,* op cit.

[11]In 1992, the Jewish Presence Foundation will be celebrating worldwide the 100th anniversary of the birth (1892) and death (1942) of Bruno Schulz. Schulz, an archtypical Polish-Jewish novelist (Polish Kafka: J. K.) and graphic artist, taught art in a Polish

hellish machine, before which I am helpless and which, has acquired gigantic power, fabricates organized slander, acts boldly and confidently. (Bukharin, 1938)[12]

Now, must he start rewriting Bukharin's note as he would rewrite his own? There are so many directions in which he could go in rewriting it. But would a man who is about to kill himself bother to rewrite his—or even somebody else's—suicide note?

It depends on who such a man is. But if Kosky is to write his quasicide note as a writer, and one who is himself now

---

high school in Drohobycz (then in Poland; today in the U.S.S.R.). Having the option to write in Yiddish or German, the languages he mastered as a child, he wrote instead in Polish, considering Polish to be his mother tongue as did many Polish-Jewish poets and novelists in Poland (e.g., Aleksander Wat, Boleslaw Lesmian, Antoni Slonimski, Mieczyslaw Jastrun, Jozef Wittlin, Marian Hemar, Janusz Korczak, Benedykt Hertz, Roman Karst, and many others: J. K.). The author of *Sanatorium Under the Sign of the Hourglass* and *The Street of the Crocodiles*, Schulz died in 1942, murdered by the Nazis at the age of fifty.

A superb graphic artist in his own right, in his drawings Schulz was "a classic *restifist, female idolator*," (Jay Kay) See *The Drawings of Bruno Schulz*, Northwestern University Press, 1990; also his *Book of Idolatry*, Interpress, 1990, an act of adoration of a female foot, usually performed by a "man seen as a 'pokraka'" (a misshapen creep), in the words of Witkacy. (St. I. Witkiewicz) See also *Bad Girls of the Silver Screen* by Lottie Da and Jan Alexander, 1989.

[12]One day some nine hours before his execution on Stalin's orders in 1938, Bukharin asked his young wife, Anna Larina, during her only, and last, visit to his cell, to memorize his suicide note as he told it to her.

"Bukharin married his third wife in 1934 when he was fifty-four; she was Anna Mikhaylovna Larina: a beautiful young woman of nineteen. In 1935 she moved in with him and they began living together, though without registering the marriage. Anna came from a family of professional revolutionaries." (Roy A. Medvedev, *Nikolai Bukharin, The Last Years*, 1980)

writing a novel about a suicidal writer called Jay Kay, must he impersonate this other hypothetically real-life writer and write his suicide note as if he were Jay Kay or should he consider at this time of his life writing one as himself and leasing it, as it were, to the main character of his novel? What sort of writer must Jay Kay be? For instance, must this writer be a he or she? A mixture of Mayakovsky with Tadeusz Borowski or a Slut Scrabble (SS) with the Serpent of the Slums — an all-American bad girl of the sexually suspect (SS) cinema?[13] **Seriously — there was nothing else I could do. Greetings. (Mayakovsky, 1930)**[14]

Finally, Kosky brings himself to his writing desk and sharpens his "twice the pleasure, half the speed" Blackbird 669 pencil. A moment of concentration. Must his note open on a romantic Good-bye, Cathy! and end on a neo-realistic phrase: "Death, I'm ready!"[15]

---

[13]Tadeusz Borowski (who killed himself, J. K.) wrote *Good-bye, Maria*, entitled in English, *This Way to the Gas Chamber, Ladies and Gentlemen.* "One of the most memorable spiritual imprints to emerge from W.W. II." (Jay Kay).

[14]From Mayakovsky's real-life suicide note he addressed "To all." Vladimir Mayakovsky, the Russian Poet-Reverberator of the post-revolutionary period, killed himself because, as he said at a writer's meeting shortly before his death, **so much abuse is being flung at me and I'm being accused of so many sins (real and unreal) that I sometimes think that I should go away somewhere for a year or two so as not to listen to so much invective.**

[15]"Suicide was for several decades the favorite hunting ground of sociologists; but literary suicide, while not reducible to statistical methods of inquiry, would be a curious subject for study. Our contemporary novelists have to resort to automobile accidents and to stoical and inordinate absorption of whiskey to replace the former means of dismissal of fictional characters, which were suicide, consumption, and general paralysis exacting the wages of sin." Henri Peyre in "The Personal Novel," in *Literature and Sincerity*, 1969, Chapter 6.

The reports of my death are greatly exaggerated. (Mark Twain)

After he had written, rewritten and written and rewritten again, his quasicide note, (and after it was retyped two or three, or even four or five times by a different and, most often, indifferent woman proofreader, Kosky puts the final text (final indeed!) into an envelope and, instead of mailing it in the Institute's SAE, sends it to Thanatos by his privately hired most-reliable messenger. Such confidentiality, and expense are justified. Just think what yellow-press hoods could do with Kosky's note or self-styled suicide (SSS). They could for one, take it literally and publish it, say, first as a literary death warrant. (WRITER SAID HE WANTED TO KILL HIS SELF.) Or they could literally kill him and, planting his note in his dead hand, make the murder appear a suicide (WRITER DIES. COULD NOT SWIM IN THE DEEP LITERARY WATERS). Worse yet, they could send his note to some George P. Flack at *Rumoroid* magazine. "Just think of the best-selling headlines your suicide (note. J. K.) would make!" exclaims Marion Spitfire, recently promoted to the all-powerful position of Eidolon's publicity director.

But he that filches from me my good name robs me of that which not enriches him and makes me poor indeed. (Shakespeare, *Othello.*)

SS

Subsequently Kosky learns that in their finale tabulation the social scientists (SS) at the Thanatos Institute failed to figure out correctly which quasicide notes were real and which fictional, even though they used the latest methods of textual analysis. To Kosky, their fifty-fifty score (i.e. they correctly decoded only half of all the notes, J. K.) is a no-score-score (SS) which proves that reality and imagination are divided by a mere toss of a coin, such a toss being a

196

victory of the imagination, as well as chance.[16] **Chance is the pseudonym God uses when he'd rather not sign his own name.** [Anatole France]

Death is the sanction of everything that the storyteller can tell. He has borrowed his authority from death. (Walter Benjamin)

---

[16]A propos: do read the last two chapters of *Chance and Necessity*, by Jacques Monod (1971). (Once the spiritual pastor as well as director of the most innovating Pasteur Institute: in Paris. J. K.) Then proceed directly to *Origins of Molecular Biology*, A Tribute to Jacques Monod, edited by André Lwoff and Agnes Ullman (Academic Press, 1979).

11

These days our *waterchilde* splits infinitives while spawning his watery tales, most of which flow out of his life when, during World War II, it centered on fish of the Pripet—his literary Mare. Herodotis, as Pripet was named by the textbooks of Roman Antiquity.

"For almost two thousand years our era flows against Herod—and all for nothing." (Maria Kuncewicz, 1938)[1]

The Führer orders that German troops are to be empowered and ordered to recognize no restrictions in the methods they employ in this struggle, even against women and children, as long as they achieve success. (Field Marshal Wilhelm Keitel, 1940); hanged, Nuremberg, 1946.

Words are supposed to flow (as they do in Flaubert's Herodiada, (1877) but, do keep in mind, our "Pan Flobertsky"

---

[1]Maria Kuncewicz, (d. 1989) one of Poland's foremost Catholic writers, (*Tristan 1946*, *The Foreign Woman*, *Letters to Jerzy*) and a patroness of Poland's Jewish Presence Foundation, wrote *Herod's City:* Notes from Palestine, (1938), after she was invited there in 1938 by the Hebrew PEN Club—the precurso of PEN of Israel.

(Jay Kay) has always been troubled by the notion of flow, first, obviously, during the war, where Pripet means marshes as well as the flowing Pripet River. Then, he was troubled by the flow of desire, as well as by its often unintentional course. As an adolescent boy playing with his Self, with the flow of his semen, as well as with the flow of words which, let it be said here, have always flown out of him, as fast as water and as reluctantly as semen.[2]

The fear of falling into the water was the fear of falling into the vagina, which was perceived as dangerous because, once in the vagina, he would meet up with his father. . . . Hence, the adult symptom of the premature ejaculation was in part motivated by having to get out of the dangerous vagina as quickly as possible. (Michael H. Sacks, 1982)[3]

And now, after all these years of writing, our literary castration-feared narrator is still troubled by writing as one who, as a minor, had a fall resulting in a minor head injury and who, as a result, suffered from apraxia of speech muscles, his wartime speechlessness and his post-War aphasic symptoms.[4]

---

[2]"Everybody masturbates! From infancy to old age, both consciously and unconsciously, everybody masturbates. It is a universal practice indulged in by both sexes, in all societies, and even among certain subhuman mammals. It may be defined as every sexual act that is carried out alone," writes David Cole Gordon in Self Love and a Theory of Unification (1968).

[3]From "Psychopathology," by Michael H. Sacks, in *Introducing Psychoanalytic Theory,* ed. by Sander L. Gillman, Ph.D. (New York, 1982). "As you must know by now, psychoanalysis is obsessed with mental conflict," writes Lawrence Friedman in *Sublimation" (op. cit.), p. 69.*

[4]Aphasia: here, loss of speech resulting from head injury. "In

"Some of these most peculiar symptoms—their duration and manifestation—no doubt belong in your book number nine," Dustin Beach Bradley Borell, his editor at Eidolon, writes on the margin. Then, on the following day, he faxes Kosky a chapter from *Hughlings Jackson on Aphasia,* a classic statement on head injuries edited by—O irony!—Henry Head. There is a reason for this mailing: proposing a psychological approach to aphasia, Hughlings Jackson claims that "to locate the damage which destroys speech and to locate speech are two different things."

Now, Kosky is suffering from it again. This time as one engaged in WRITING (Literary): the muddy bilge that passes for prose; (Rodale)[5] as well as in WRITHING: (squirm) Mental gnarled; imaginative; ignominious; intertwisted. Epistolary. (Rodale)[6]

There are many ways for a stubborn writer's body to burst out of his creative persona and one of them is to burst out of it with the help of another body, preferably a body belonging

---

1906 Pierre Marie's paper on cortical function and localization caused considered discussion. To Marie, speech was an intellectual function for the adequate performance of which a particular portion of the brain was set aside. . . .The degree of defect, he believed, would vary according to the intensity of the lesion and the education of the individual," writes J. M. Wepman in his *Recovery from Aphasia* (1950).

[5]See *The Phrase Finder* (Rodale Press, 1958). "Name-calling is such a universal and ancient habit that one is tempted either to inquire into its original purpose and intrinsic value, or else to repeat critically, 'What's in a name?' " writes Edward J. Fluck, Ph.D.

[6]Remember that adjectives—like visitors—become a nuisance only when there are too many of them. The adjective is never the enemy of the noun until the adjective—like a drowning swimmer—drags down and strangles the noun. J. I. Rodale, (*The Word Finder,* 1947).

to a biological, i.e., non-transsexual woman, rather than to another quarrelsome writer (e.g., Conrad vs. Dostoyevsky, see "Joseph Conrad Today," *The Newsletter of the Joseph Conrad Society of America,* 1977, or Strindberg vs. Freud, or Ibsen vs. Kierkegaard; see *Ibsen,* by Michael Meyer, 1971).

What kind of woman? Jay Kay demands to know. Oh, I don't know, the omniscient author hesitates looking up to Emma Hamilton, Anna Karenina, and Mme de Stael. I guess any kind, he goes on all excited by the notion of a perfect *praczka* (dombi in Ruthenian, J. K.) providing she is just another shoestore slut, (SS) dramatic and tempting enough to do to me what countless women portrayed every month in *High Society Magazine* have done for their men and often for women either in the presence of their men or in their absence.

> I feel
> my "!"
> is a good bit too little for me
> A body stubbornly wants to burst out of me.
>
> (Mayakovsky)

A privately hired line editor readily comes to mind—one who, going through the text line by line, aligns the novel's narrative line pretty much the way a professional car mechanic aligns the front end of a car.

The compromise we worked out was that we would not put the clause in the contract, but that the book would be copyedited by an outside copy editor of the author's choice. It is a problem. Like most problems in author-publishing relationships, its solution depends on the amount of clout the author has. (Authors Guild Symposium, 1982)[7]

---

[7]Quoted from the transcript of the Authors Guild symposium on

Mobilizing all his existing as well as potential clout, Kosky asks Dustin to recommend a female Sexy Saxe—another double S! He describes her, as one who, *via his text* **"could enjoy my flesh through her flesh in order to compel her to feel herself flesh"** (Sartre). A few days later he receives a résumé of one Ann Pudeater Paterson, "a most dignified young line editor whose middle name pud means nursery, as well as child's hand or animal's fore-foot—does give you some idea of Anne's ability to nurse your text as well as you." Such are Dustin's words.

Well, literary comrades, the fact is that, by now, our tireless ghoul has hired, as well as gone out with (as his tax-deductions record shows most clearly) some sixty-eight different proofreaders, and line and copy editors—most of them females found to be most attractive by our omnipresent author's multiple personae.

Thou hast ascended on high. Thou hast led captivity captive. (Psalm 68) Or, in his native tongue, *pulap* (ceiling) is close to (*pulapka* (trap). J. K.)

While sixty-eight is a spiritually high number—consider the implication of being a captivity, captive,[8] the number sixty-nine is a one-of-a-kind number—a number so spiritually kind that it must not be treated as a mere consecutive

---

"Authors, Editors, and Editing" (held in February 1982 at the New School for Social Research in New York City: J.K.). The symposium covered the author-editor relationship in all its phases; among other topics the panelists discussed the all-too-common "assigning of authors to overworked editors to their equally overworked assistants, the plight of the author whose manuscript becomes an orphan when his or her editor moves to another company or when the author no longer benefits from his latest publishing company."

[8]Among the followers of Sabbatai Sevi, some believe that in the phrase "captivity captive," "the captive in question" means the inner Torah "forced to dwell in the prison cell of the material Torah." (Gershon Sholem, *The Messianic Idea in Judaism*, op. cit.)

one. His sixty-ninth in-line editor must be someone permissive, someone of high spiritual standing, as high as the standing of Saxe Commins[9] — the editor of such diverse authors as W. H. Auden and Eugene O'Neill, of Stephen Spender and Isak Dinesen, of Faulkner and Gertrude Stein.

His imagination responds by firing his consecutive SS-69 missile. Will he and Ann Paterson become AMERICA'S KINKIEST COUPLE — *(The Crier)* one who will make erotic history?

Only time will tell. "Time — that master storyteller and passion extinguisher." (Jay Kay) Time and Ann Pudeater Paterson — his most recent literary nurse. **Oh! Is that what I am? (Ann Pudeater Paterson, 1987)**

Only by the discernment of its individual features can we gain a true insight into the general nature and function of language. "He who does not know foreign languages does not know anything about his own language," says Goethe. We have to penetrate into foreign languages in order to convince ourselves that the true difference does not consist in the learning of a new vocabulary, that it does not consist in a formation of words, but in a formation of concepts. To learn a new language is, therefore, always a sort of spiritual adventure; it is like a journey of discovery in which we find a new world. (Ernst CaSSirer, 1942)

Ms. Paterson arrives in Kosky's apartment at 6:00 P.M. and she arrives dressed in, of all colors, a pink flannel suit, carrying in her narrow, long-fingered hand seminal *The Science of Folklore* by Alexander H. Krappe, 1964 and *Out of the Shadows:* Understanding Sexual Addiction, by Patrick

---

[9]*What Is an Editor? Saxe Commins at Work,* by Dorothy Commins. Chicago 60637 PN 149.9.C6 C6 (The PN number — so rich in numbers six and nine and letters CC tells it all: Jay Kay).

Carnes, (1988). Looking at her makes Kosky's innermost sexual shadow grow longer. She is tall. She is a natural redhead. She wears six-inch Stiletto Sneakers. Dustin is right: this woman is an ideal literary registered nurse who, most likely, delivers between sheets more than she promises. Since the color pink is said to be a diluted version of purple, this could also mean that this is her way of saying that, as an editor, she won't tolerate purple prose; that pink is what's left of purple when all the useless jizz is edited by her out of the narrative jazz.

Her wearing pink could also mean something else in her already steamy demeanor. For one, Dustin's letter also recommends her as "Hot literary cover girl who's no stranger to anything strange and certainly not to any literary stranger." The persona of *The Stranger,* in a novel by Camus, was the first literary being she was addicted to already in her Sorority House, she tells him at the outset. Camus, the so existentially-looking man, was the second, "though I am by no means a stranger to such strange sexual stratagems as the one demonstrated by Samuel Kramer in *La Fanfarlo,* the novel about a literary immitator written by that unimmitable Charles Baudelaire," she assures him, strutting serenely back and forth across the room, and occasionally quietly moaning, "O world! O time!" the Lament by Shelley "she has usurped as her own narrative Dreamin' and Creamin'." (Jay Kay).

For two, Dustin states that having once gone to the Beulah University School of Drama, "Ann has acquired a sense of tragedy—by being permanently perplexed as well as naturally complexed."

"My friends in the pub [here pub stands for publishing, as well as for public and a public pub: J. K.] tell me that you are an instinctive man, one subjugated by sex, that crudest of life's instincts. This alone makes you a practically extinct storytelling wimp." She treats him with **coldness humiliated. (Sartre)**

"I read somewhere that you're a professional water levitant. Was this another one of your original literary lies—or was it something you said into the woman reporter's microphone interviewing you for some silly sport newspaper or magazine?" She treats him with the contempt she clearly reserves for a man who, in her eyes, treats writing the way Sartre does women: as a sexual routine.

"I'm a Levi, not a levitant." He dismisses the issue of being profiled half-naked in the recent issue of *WaterSports* magazine.

"I like the color pink," she says without a trace of apology, just when, openly seen by her, by sheer speculation, he manages to catch sight of a small pink bird embroidered on the right leg of her seemingly seamless pale pink panties "which, crotch-revealing, are nevertheless called crotchless." (Jay Kay).

He serves her a cup of his special TeaPot® tea while she treats him to her résumé. Neatly typed on one-sixth of a page of a virginally pure bond paper, it mentions that even in high school (she went to the Simone de Beauvoir High School in Brookbridge, N.Y.) she was nicknamed Sexual Sophisticate[10] of her class. The résumé lists as her personal ideal Mrs. Jessie Conrad, that stigmatic wife of Joseph, and she mentions Thomas Wolfe (1900–1938) as a writer whose work—his enchanted work as much as disenchanted mind—she would not mind editing.

Between Conrad's life, then, and his fiction there exists much the same relation as between the two divisions (past

---

[10]See "The Sexual Sophisticate," in "The Struggle for Orgasm," (Chapter 6) of *The Sexually Responsive Woman,* by Phyllis and Eberhard Kronhousen; preface by Simone de Beauvoir (1964).

and present) of his life. (Edward W. Said) Enough said.

He peruses once more her résumé, then resumes his perusal of her as if she were about to join him body-to-body on the sex-sizzling pages of Bedlam, swinging scene (SS) magazine. This Jessie Conrad excites him, the way sharing certain textual descriptions borrowed by Conrad from Flaubert must have excited Conrad, but after all, Kosky's writing muse No. 69 reminds him, he was excited by almost every one of the in-line line-editing female editors who preceded Ms. Paterson—this Self-possessed literary predator.

The image of myself which I try to create in my own mind in order that I may love myself is different from the image which I try to create in the minds of others in order that they may love me. (W. H. Auden, 1956)

"Your face brings to my mind the portrait of an exquisite young Jewess drawn in pencil by William James while your body could be a centerfold in tomorrow's *Cavalier* adult man's magazine. The Jewess was the one with whom James is said to have been hopelessly in love, and he was the very first American to point out that 'in certain nauseated states the idea of vomiting will make us vomit.' "The idea—not just bad food or illness or half-swallowing one's index finger," says our master of the nauseated state. "The idea, meaning the power of words and of imagination. But then your résumé says you've spent six months working full-time as literary patient of Matthew Duke, working with him on *Underneath This Sacred Armor*, his latest tale 'Told by an idiot, full of sound and fury, Signifying nothing.' " [Macbeth]. Kosky goes on signaling her to respond.

"Indeed I did work with him. *With*, not just for," she corrects him sternly. "My résumé tells only the most obvious professional story. Matt and I spent so much time together that in his latest book the character called Marble Juno was drawn by him straight from me. To a shadow!" she whispers. Graciously, she leaves the length of the shadow to Duke's

207

biographers. "Normally I prefer to take a writer's manuscript—as well as the writer—to my home, where I can concentrate on the two of them better—and not necessarily at the same time." She laughs with throaty laughter perfected by those working in the world's second oldest profession. "Affections spring mostly from the mind," she says probably unaware she is literally quoting the words uttered to Jules Troubat by the dying Baudelaire, what, to Kosky, makes her even more dear. "Matthew, however, insisted that I work with him on the text, page after page and that I do it at his place every day—his wife was there most of the time—and so I did for over a year."

Ms. Paterson shifts position, and her shift, prurient as it is, could bring her in conflict with *United States of America* vs. *Sex*. "Why don't you write your sex-offending books either in your native Ruthenian or, better yet, in Esperanto, which I heard, was your second tongue?" asks Ms. Paterson. "Wouldn't it be easier?"

"Anything but. In Ruthenian, I would be rated against the Ruthenian best—while here, as a writer-in-exile, I carry no ratings, I knew some Esperanto as a kid. I forgot it all by now," modestly answers our vicarious literary vicar. **Esperanto has over a hundred years of practical use behind it and is not some items of linguistic theory, some project for a language, but the living and breathing idiom of a living and breathing speech community. (Humphrey Tonkin, 1990). I hold our Polish literature in too high esteem to spoil it with my unskilled work. For the English, my abilities are sufficient and they provide me with bread. (Conrad to Wincenty Lutosławski, 1899)**[11]

---

[11]Concluded Professor Lutosławski: "We are rich enough to give many such writers to all the nations of the earth, keeping for ourselves only the best who will express their souls in Polish."

"What's your current book about?"

"About *cosmic interior.*" (Karol Hiller)[12]

"What else?"

"About half-baked ideas. About mental action and novelistic reaction. About James Fenimore Cooper being thrown out of Yale for "too much pleasure seeking," he recites ogling her like an eagle.

"Novels are about action, not about ideas." She chills him.

"My novel attempts to turn ideas into action." Our alchemist is at it once more.

"Ideas are a motly crew. Most of them tend to be uptight, not tight. Idle not wild." She threatens him with her editorial pencil. Him, a man who back in 1957 landed at New York's airport then called Idlewild, carrying nothing but a writing pen, "which until then, was spiritually idle." (Jay Kay).

"Well, then, if a particular idea won't strike you in my novel as being particularly wild, mark it on the margin IDLE OR WILD! But don't strike it out: idle or not, it is *my* idea! You see, I believe that a true intellectual is a vendor of ideas. His kiosk must be open to everyone including the passersby as well as the owners of the kiosk and its suppliers. If he favors his buyers on the left more than those on the right or vice versa he is out of spiritual place."

"Ideas belong to everybody, but since I don't, how much will you pay me in U.S. dollars?" The New Nymph dismisses his apolitical stance, a stance our American Dream seeker has maintained for over thirty years.

"Somewhere—between sixteen and nineteen dollars per hour depending on how illegible my manuscript—or your

---

[12]Karol Hiller: born in Łodz, Poland, in 1891, Hiller invented heliographs—paintings painted by the painter as well as by their own inner light: (Jay Kay)

proofreading of it—will be." He watches her as if he were Deedee, a DD-cupper, whose bulbous boobs, densely packed, were spotlighted in an X-rated movie called *Chateau Soixante-Neuf*.

Neither financial need nor the entreaties of his publishers, who alternated between friendly reproaches and legal action, could dissuade Balzac from pursuing his expensive system. On numerous occasions he forfeited half his fee, and sometimes the whole of it, because he had to pay the cost of corrections and resetting out of his own pocket. But it was a matter of artistic integrity, and on this point he remained inexorable. (Zweig on Balzac)

"How would you want me to work? Under you, or away from you?" The lady starts a new paragraph while glancing at him with **sadistic attraction (Sartre)**, the very attraction Sartre betrays when writing about Baudelaire.

"How about working with me," says Kosky. "That means next to me—or, if you prefer, across from me. This means in my physical, as well as spiritual, presence."

"Where do we work? In my flat or in yours?"

"We'll work here at my place. *A world we invent cannot be false* (Ionesco)." Modestly, he drops his gaze only to recover it in triple size six by nine. "This will give me a chance to fool around with the text while you watch the fool in me." He catches a glimpse of her underarm which makes him long for a strong antiemetic called (a perfect combination of words of "drama" and "pantomine") Dramamine.

. . . from now on until they take the manuscript away from me finally and irrevocably, I have a tremendous job of work to do. . . . There is something final and terrifying about print, even about proof, and I want to pull myself together for this big effort and keep at it if need be until I drop. (Thomas Wolfe)

She glances around the apartment. "Is there, by the way, a voyeuristic Nietzsche niche hidden behind a false wall, where like that cocksure guy in your past cocky novel you too hide at night? From where like him, you too eavesdrop on your unsuspecting mistress and her unsuspecting lover?"

"There is—but only as a mental image," he reassures her promptly in case she would want to check it. His writing niche is his Innermost Inn.

Ms. Paterson shifts position again. Leaning back, she offers an unobstructed view of her armpit.

Tempted by the sight of it (to our *erotoman*, an armpit is a tempting orifice) in order to counteract his rising passion, Kosky, our master of part-time control, starts concentrating on Ms. Paterson's birthmark. Her birthmark is a single smudge which smirches the lower left side of her face, and smutches it all the way onto the neck and even part of her impeccably shaped chin.

"One day could you take me inside this niche?"

"I could, but I mustn't," says Kosky who *thinks out of self-indulgence*. (Brecht on Galileo). "This niche is my private annex. It reminds me of the niches where I used to hide as a boy during World War II, as much as it does about *The Diary of Anne Frank*, the most genuine diary there ever was, accused by some fools as not being genuine enough. Hence, it reminds me of my own survival." **In his little box of stage properties he kept six or eight cunning devices tricks and artifices for his savages and woodsmen to deceive and circumvent each other with, and he was never so happy as when he was working these innocent things and seeing them go. (Mark Twain about J. Fenimore Cooper)**

"You don't live anymore in Orwell's *1984*," says Ms. Paterson. "Now why would you—you, by now a relatively grown-up man—secretly spy on his own mistress, and police her lover, unless he is sick—or works for some sick private police?"

"Maybe because he loves her. Maybe because he needs her. Maybe because he can't help himself," volunteers Kosky.

For man has closed himself up, till he sees all things through the narrow chinks of his cavern. (William Blake)

Ms. Paterson edits again. "In your novel, Cocksure often uses his secret knowledge to emotionally punish and sexually humiliate his various lovers."

"I guess that's where I either part company with him or with your interpretation of what he does," says Kosky. In physical things a man may invent; in moral things he must obey—and take their laws with him into his invented world as well. (George MacDonald, 1893)

"Your reader never knows whether you were a model for your prime character or was he for you. Will I ever know this?" She looks at him with the look one finds on the Easy Rider—a young woman riding Buell, the state-of-the-art American motorcycle powered by a Harley Davidson power plant.

"What I mean is: for whom will I actually be working?" Her state-of-the-art sex stare (SS) rides all over him as if he were Sturgis, a comic strip character found in Easy Rider magazine or Sturgis, a Harley Davidson Black Hills motorcycle classic, or Sturgis, the name of a community in South Dakota, (near Deadwood and Spearfish home of the National Motorcycle Museum and Hall of Fame; J. K.) "When editing your texts am I to take your side or be on the side of your protagonist?"

"You'll decide as you go along," says Kosky. What is so sparkling, so fragrant, so intoxicating, as possibility? (Søren Kierkegaard)

He hands her an obviously freshly typed manuscript page. "A recent prose sample chosen by me as a sample for you to try your hand at," he says.

Biting the dull end of her pencil, Ms. Paterson starts reading. A critical smile—her other most attractive trademark—lights up her face. She says nothing. She keeps on reading. Finally she stops.

"For instance, like most American Sĺavs enslaved by their mother tongue, you slavishly abuse peculiarities and uses of the definite and indefinite articles 'a', 'an' or 'the'," she remarks offhandedly.

"What abuse?" He stares at her with his *waterchilde* four-S's starry-eyed slavishly sexual stare.[13]

"Well" — she hesitates — "in English, the definite and indefinite article are integral to the language, though I gather that the articles 'the', 'an' and 'a' just don't exist in your native Ruthenian."

"They don't," he agrees.

"Well," she goes on, "in English you can't just arbitrarily drop the articles and determinatives — as you have done in certain parts of this text!"

This book was a pleasure to write, and in itself this is a keen satisfaction to an author. (Cecil Hunt, *Word Origins: Romance of Language*, 1944.)

"Why not?" he inquires. **"A woman, *a* dog, and *a* walnut tree, The more you beat 'em, the better they be,"** he intones.

"Well — it has a lot to do with the 'countability' of nouns. In English, common nouns are usually (though not always) countable. For instance, one book, two books; one person, two persons; one bed, two persons — sorry, two beds," she corrects herself. "But then the material nouns — nouns describing a material from which something else is made — are usually, though not always, uncountable. For instance, flesh, bed, rubber. Since 'a' means 'one,' the indefinite article can appear in front of countable nouns when they are in the

---

[13]According to the *American Heritage Word Frequency Book*, the word *the* occurs three times as often as the word *of*, the second most common word. Among the other most frequently employed words are *and* (3), *in* (6) and *that* (9). The first most employable noun is *time* (60) followed by *people* (79) and *water* (90).

singular—a book, an hour, an ass—but not in front of uncountable nouns. You cannot put 'a' or 'an' in front of laughter, advice or blood."

"Nevertheless," Kosky argues, "they are used to give such nouns a sense of oneness, of singularity. For instance, a piece of ass; a pool of blood; a piece of advice about an item. A speck—or a spot—of blood."

"I understand," says Ms. Paterson. "But you've dropped the definite article 'the' from most of this page." She lifts the page—the offending article—in her fingers, then drops it on the table right next to a copy of *Assets*—another one of his favorite adult magazines. "This is unpardonable, since the definite article," she goes on "since the definite article in English language is not some sort of commemorative skull stud (SS) concho necklace. It is used to show that a noun, whether countable or uncountable, used in a definite and particular sense and not in a general sense. For instance, *the* bed, *the* ass, *the* rubbers." She looks at him with the saintly, yet so whorish, look of Pope's Heloise. **Oh happy state! To be my lover's whore,/And love in liberty, by nature's law. (Pope)**

"But then, whether with the rubbers or without them, don't we say in English: 'I feel like going to bed with you' rather than going to *the* bed?" says Kosky employing the verbal italics as matter-of-factly as he can make it.

"We certainly do," she agrees. "But only to indicate that we go there to sleep. After all, sleep, not sleeping around, is what a bed is for," she explains patiently. While ogling her smooth stomach (SS), he hopes that one day she will make up for him orally for what she misses verbally.

"To conclude"—she puts aside the pages he gave her—"without the article 'the' this piece reads like a telegram written by a foreigner. Someone to whom the English language is a foreign article."

"Let's see." He glances over her shoulder, sniffing her hair in the process. "I'm sorry," he exclaims. "It's my error. What you have read was not written by me—but by someone else." (He pauses.) "In fact, it is a quote from one Jeremy Bentham. Bentham was an Englishman who robbed the rich English language of most of its articles. Imagine that!"[14]

"Was Bentham Ruthenian?" she volunteers.

"He was not," says Kosky, handing her another page. **Advertisements, none. Bookseller did not, Author could not afford any. . . . (Jeremy Bentham, as quoted by F. L. Lucas, in *Style*, op cit., under "Brevity and Variety.")**

Ms. Paterson scans the next manuscript page.

"I read somewhere, or maybe I merely heard it from someone, that while teaching English prose at Beulah University you once asked some of your American students to analyze a fragment from a Joseph Conrad novel and to write a critical essay about it. When they did, and when, in their essays, they claimed to have discovered in it all kinds of Conradian word affinities and Conradian pitch, you admitted that some two hours before the seminar, you'd bashed out the piece yourself—a veritable caricature of Conradiana— and given to them by you in order to test them as textual critics."

"It's true," *I am obliged to write every book about six times.* (Conrad) Kosky laughs insincerely. "It was an unfair test of literary stereotyping. Unfair, 'cause **Nobody really knows**

---

[14]Jeremy Bentham (d. 1832): English philosopher and author of *Introduction to the Principles of Morals and Legislation* (1789) and John Stuart Mill (d. 1873) were proponents of utilitarian approaches to (situational, J. K.) ethics. Bentham identified happiness with pleasure and devised a system of moral arithmetic for measuring the relative value of pleasure or pain. In his brilliant prose, Bentham, the founder of utilitarianism and stylist par excellence, carried his motto "words as few as possible" to a truly utilitarian end starting with getting rid of the articles "the" and "a" in his prose.

215

what constitutes an ideal upbringing. (John F. O'Connor, M.D., 1984)." He makes his point.

Now, in order to give her a touch — a touch, mind you, not a sense — of his creative dependence upon her and of his need to be prompted to action by an image of a fallen woman, our *sopher* glances through the pages of *Sexual Compatibility*[15] at an angle which allows Ms. Paterson to catch sight of a narrative diagram of female genitalia in preexcitement state and the plateau phase.[16]

"May I ask how, in your text, does your philosophy of action — which, I take it, has a lot to do with circular live sex à la sixty-nine — performed in some literary circus — squares with safe sex?" this most modern woman asks him most directly.

"It does," answers our macho enigma. "I put the circle in the square."

Annoyed by the sight of him, Mrs. Paterson now reads aloud a text she assumes was originally written by Kosky though, in fact, written by the all-American F. Scott Fitzgerald, was retyped by Kosky word for word as Fitzgerald wrote it but without Fitzgerald's name attached to it. **"When I reached my wretched lovely house at West Egg I ran the car under its shed and, feeling wide awake, walked around the house and sat down on an abandoned grass roller on the lawn. It was a loud bright night with wings beating in the trees and a persistent organ sound as the full bellows of the earth blew the frogs full of life."**

"This is kind of messy. You can tell all this was written not by an American native but by a foreigner. And a recent one at that!" she strikes the page with her pencil. "You see" — she

---

[15] *Sexual Compatibility: A Practical Approach to Solving Problems,* by John F. O'Connor, M.D. (1984).
[16] Ibid., p. 69.

pauses tactfully—"no native American—writer or no writer, I don't care—would throw all this stuff—house, car, grass, roller, lawn, night, trees, frogs, even the organ sound, into one paragraph! All these material things mean too much to us to be easily thrown into a mere sentence. By the way, is the house lovely or wretched? You can't have both, you know! Also, whose wings are beating what—or whom—in the trees?"

Ms. Paterson shifts position on the sofa. As she does, so does her skirt. "I hope my criticism upsets you enough to rewrite the text, but that it doesn't offend you. I'm trying to be as open as I can," she says thoughtfully, while perhaps involuntarily, she opens up by spreading her legs with a fresh largesse. The result is a brand new vista in pink—and, this time, an unobstructed view of her upper thighs and lower belly. And here our prurient pleasure seeker is in for a spurious shock: there's no doubt that not only does Ms. Paterson wear custom-made pink panties—a slightly fuzzy'nd furry brand known as Swiss Tease, but that on top of them she wears—and this is the crotch of the matter—a leather corset fitted with—this is for him a moment of spurious suspense—an orgasm-inducing device known to the literary vice squad as a labia spreader—upon which our sexual Tantrist voluntarily opens his ejaculatory ducts.

He could, of course, assume that, knowing his books, and via them, voices'nd vices of his fantasy (to many people who don't know any better, know or can't imagine, fantasy is, by itself, a silent vice), she had put it on in order to put him on. Or that she had put on her corset and the spreader today the way she might have put them on every day or every other day, put them on for a reason (or a person) of her own.

"Sure you upset me but so what? You also excite me," he says openly. "If you're to become my privately hired, and paid entirely by me, line editor, I want you to be as open as you possibly can," he assures her with a firm skoal of his eyes.

217

"Please go on. Be as rough on my text as you wish: This is my ninth novel, and," he adds in galley proof No. 96, "it is also the fifty-seventh year of what I hope will be at least a sixty-nine-year-long life. I'm sure I can take it."

She reads from the text again: **"The shadow of a moving cat wavered across the moonlight and turning my head to watch it I saw that I was not alone—fifty feet away a figure had moved out from the long shadow of my neighbor's hedge and was standing with head thrown back, and eyes turned upward toward the silver pepper of the stars."** She stops and gives Kosky a thoughtfully reproachful look. "This is awkward step by step," she says. "One: Surely the cat's shadow wavered across the moonlit grass, not across moonlight. Two: The figure had moved out . . . and was standing. 'Had moved' and 'was standing' don't go well together. Why not just 'stood,' period? Three: If the figure's head was thrown back, your character couldn't see the figure's eyes, right? Four: 'The silver pepper of the stars' strikes me as another typically Ruthenian polka-dot—a heavy-handed metaphor. I recommend you cut this whole passage. Too many Ruthenian shadows!" She laughs, then locks her thighs, in what, speaking sexually, of course, he perceives as her resolution phase.

"Speaking of what you call 'typically Ruthenian', do you know Ruthenian?" our nit wit asks her off-handedly.

"Well, no. Of course not," she misses the polka dot.

"Then how come that to you my Ruthenian linguistics are evident in my English prose—prose supposedly as bad as this piece?" he asks.

Nobody can doubt that Conrad's works are haunted by the shades of his Polish past. (Gustav Morf)

"Ruthenian or not, it is certainly evident in the text," she says firmly.

As she moves about, her blouse pops out of her skirt, for a moment baring her belly, a visual drama which prompts our literary dramatist to tighten from within the cremasteric muscles helplessly lost in the loose skin pouch of his scrotal sac channeling the one and only *Kundalini* from the base of his spine right into the creative part of his brain: a process simply known as literary acclivity or the sexual Oli techniques.

She starts reading again. **"Something in his long scrutiny and his pocketed hands and the secure position of his feet on the lawn suggested that it was G himself—perhaps come out to determine what share was his of our local heavens.**

"I could not see his but I remembered that Miss Baker had asked me about him at dinner and I decided to speak to him. I got to my feet and was about to call out when suddenly I saw him stretch out both hands toward the sky in a curious way—as far as I was from him I could have sworn that he was trembling. Involuntarily I looked up. When I looked down again he was gone, and I was left to wonder whether it was really the sky he had come out to measure with the compass of those aspiring arms."

Lost in thought, she raises her pencil to her mouth, spreads her lips and sucks on its end. How she does it sends Kosky's inner stock market, pulsating, into a prostate gland Bedlam Exchange.

"This is a very, very raw text," she pronounces. "It's creatively uncooked—*saignant,* the French would call it. What's 'long scrutiny'? And why wouldn't G's feet not be secure upon the lawn unless he is drunk? Well, was he drunk or not? The text doesn't even suggest that he was."

When Kosky doesn't suggest it either, she goes on.

"A share of the local heavens? C'mon! Heavens! Also the reader might want to know what it means to stretch out one's hands in a curious way. What is 'curious way?' Don't you know that DESCRIBE—DON'T ANNOUNCE is the first rule of creative writing?" She laughs at him. "No, no, Norbert! Your text is too Ruthenian, though I'm sure a good American editor could easily fish out all that raw literary fish." A far cry from *The Almanac of American Letters*. (Randy F. Nelson, 1981).

"Then I guess I still have to work at it," says our Straight Face. "I didn't realize one could hear my Ruthenian accent in this particular text. In what I assumed to be particularly American prose."

"One certainly can. There's some charm in your rhythm, but it's a foreign charm. No American writer would write like that! Not in a **hundred years of solitude (Marquez)!**"

"I feel hurt, very hurt, though I appreciate your comments, I really do," says Kosky. **No passion in the world is equal to the passion to alter someone else's draft. (H. G. Wells)** "You make me realize the extent to which every native, American born editor must feel obliged to find such errors in my manuscript — not necessarily because my manuscript sounds foreign, but because I do. Now you know why I must rely only on myself — and take precautions against overpowering editors. They simply wouldn't dare to do to Fitzgerald[17] or any other U.S.-born-and-made-in-U.S.A. literary Fitz or Gerald what they feel free to do to the foreign-

---

[17]AUTHOR TO READER: Please compare this earlier draft of Fitzgerald's *Great Gatsby* with Fitzgerald's published text, which begins with: "I decided to call to him. Miss Baker had mentioned him at dinner, and that would do for an introduction. . . ." and ends with, "When I looked once more for Gatsby he had vanished, and I was alone again in the unquiet darkness." These and other fragments of the pencil draft of *The Great Gatsby* as well as its published version can be found in *Write and Rewrite: A Study of the Creative Process* by John Kuehl, New York, 1967.

PROOFREADER TO AUTHOR: Why didn't you tell Ms. Paterson you were testing her with the writings of Fitzgerald?

AUTHOR TO PROOFREADER: Because the purpose of the test was to encourage me to listen to my inner editor (rather than, say, to what she had to say) and not to discourage her from saying it.

accented Kosky."

But now he seemed sure of what he wanted to say as he walked up and down the room. He won't need to make any corrections, I thought; the style was simple and clear. Sentences like "Deprived of the right to say 'no,' man becomes a slave" stuck in my head. (Cynthia Koestler)

"What is it exactly that you want me to do?" asks Ms. Paterson, glancing at the new page.

"To pay attention," he tells her taking her briefly by her hand.

"Let's see." Under the pretext that he wants to look at the text from her point of view, Kosky moves from the chair to the sofa and sits down next to her. By now, even his *verumontanum*[18] is inflamed.

"Above all," says Kosky, "what I want most of myself is to be clear!" In a momentary act of creative surrender he spreads another page on the table in front of her. "Flag—or flog, if that's what turns you on—any word, any sentence, any description that doesn't make sense to you as a reader. I want my magneto in my all-American narrative bike to convert reader-kicking into high-voltage spiritual spark. (SS)" **The limits of my language means the limits of my world. (Ludwig Wittgenstein)**

"I see already. You spelled limpid as limpet and referred to Jews in your view, as seeing themselves, these days, unfortunately, as no longer fortunate, as fated by history but ill-fated. Surely, you meant feted by history; feted, not fated. A nasty error. Just think what a difference one vowel can make!"[19]

---

[18] *Verumontanum:* see schematic representation of the prostate gland in *Sexual Compatibility,* op. cit.

[19] "On this subject, the reader is referred to "The Second Holocaust" in Focus, *The Boston Sunday Globe,* November 4th, 1990," notes Jay Kay.

"Clearly, my minor typo. As one who majors in the Jewish narrative art, I make only major errors in sexual syntax," he admits modestly to another SS.

It must be said that Conrad was not always sure of his spelling. He made spelling mistakes in Polish, French, and English alike. In *Nostromo,* almost half of the numerous Spanish words are misspelled. A few are not even Spanish. . . . In French, he would often write *présant* for *présent, example* for *exemple,* and he was never sure about the endings -ance or -ence. In English, words like *although* gave him trouble, as Garnett reported in his introduction to *Letters from Joseph Conrad.* (Gustav Morf)

"I found another goody," says Ms. Paterson. "You say here 'Who will, may hear Bordello's story told,' and then again, 'Who would, has heard Bordello's story told.' " She mixes her smile with a sneer. "Both sentences make no sense — regardless of what happened in that bordello!"

"Oh, I'm so sorry. Another typing error!" Kosky looks over her shoulder. "It's not bordello — it's Sordello: It's from Robert Browning's 'Sordello'! Otherwise the quote is correct; that is, that's the way Browning wanted these two sentences to read. One begins his famous poem, the other one famously ends it."

"Robert Browning? *The* Robert Browning?" She looks at the text with horror she initially reserved for Kosky.

"Indeed." Triumphs quietly our hero over the narrative heroin. "George Eliot claimed that while reading Browning what we took for obscurity in him was superficiality in ourselves."

"Maybe so." Undefeated, she returns skeptically to the text. She reads for a moment, then says, "I just found a wrong quote. You say here *Women are men like us.*"

"It's a quote from Prudhomme." Sniffing her natural scent, he tries to distinguish it from her sweat, as well as from her equally natural Carnal perfume — both of which he finds most tempting—in women tending to their tender tendons in the Health'nd Swim Manhattan Club, where these days you can find our Male Literary Virgin just about every day.

"I know it's a quote. But quote or no quote, it just doesn't make sense. In your books, women are your icons of perversity. But no matter how perverse, women are *not* men and never will be. Your enlightened women readers would find this line most offensive."

"I must keep it for the sake of the story," says Kosky. "You see, that's Prudhomme's view, not mine. The quote demonstrates what and who comes to my protagonist's mind at a different time of literary creation; this is how he thinks."

"He could think of someone else. Why must he think of what's his name? Prudhomme?"

"Possibly because, being bilingual, he is attracted to anything or anyone who is bi—to a split between reason and dissent; and to anyone who bears a bilingual name. *Proud* is English, *homme* is French."

"Have it your way, then." Ms. Paterson glances at his manuscript again.

"Some of your quotes from other writers are all screwed up," she says, sucking sensually on the rubber-filled eraser end of her pencil.

"Screw them, or unscrew," he says.

"Stylistically, some of them don't make much sense." She snatches a page from the table. " **'Whoever has not himself been on the tentacles of this throttling viper will never know its fangs (H.),'** " she reads aloud. "To start with, a viper—a viper is a snake—doesn't have tentacles," she laughs. "Then, if the viper kills its victims with coils—coils are snake's body language—then the snake doesn't carry any venom either. Besides, a person throttled by a viper (here, I assume, the word *throttle* stands for Adam's apple strangulation, not for a hand job) can't feel the viper's fangs no matter how vituperative the snake or its victim is! By the way, who is H.?"

"Adolf Hitler," says Kosky. "Hitler was once a struggling writer — struggling with the German language as well as with the Jews: the most verbally, as well as orally — inclined people in history." **When I think of what our people have accumulated over the centuries that nobody will ever know about, it seems like a second holocaust, Hitler destroyed our people. Now we let their spirit die. We train rabbis for sisterhoods and men's clubs, but nobody knows our people's literature. You have a lifetime of work ahead of you. You have the mind and the depth to do it.** Abraham Joshua Heschel, (early fifties).[20]

"What else must I watch for?"

"Ordinary alchemical blunders." He remains vague on purpose.

"Anything else?"

I shot an arrow into the air,/it fell to earth, I knew not where. (Longfellow)

"Make sure I stay strong on verbs — in my text, verb stands for action and reaction. Also, keep strict count of all the attributive nouns."

"Wait a sec! Should I count their attributes as nouns or as pronouns?"

"Count pronouns and adjectives as nouns because, like nouns, they often beg to differ from verbs — even when they don't," Kosky rules. "You can hardly tell them apart." **Those who judge nominal style good do so implicitly, for the most part; nominal style is practiced more than preached. (Rulon Wells)**

"Now, when sexual all-out means a sickening fallout, I imagine your sex life must be Misery Unlimited." She

---

[20]As quoted by Richard L. Rubenstein in his *Power Struggle*, N.Y. 1974.

addresses him as if, favoring *The Obsession: Reflection on the Tyranny of Slenderness* by Kim Chernin (1981), he already sought her cruel literary favors.

"Must it?" he shoots back. "But what if I'll keep imagining that it isn't, and think for instance about you in my semi-sleep?" **Take them, Love, the book and me together: Where the heart lies, let the brain lie also. "One Word More" by Robert Drowning.**

"Any other things I must watch for?" She challenges him again.

"Keep my semi-Semitic (SS) influences intact. Also, please keep in mind that, as A. Q. Morton assures us, 'that structural linguistics has demonstrated the difficulty of formulating a completely satisfactory definition of 'sentence.' Whatever definition may be offered, exceptional and ambiguous sentences can be produced to challenge the definition.' "[21]

"If I were to follow your precepts, wouldn't your novel be at the same time too dressed up and overly bare—a bit like you?" she gives him the blank look of an **automatic sweetheart. (William James)**

"There's only one way to find out," says Kosky, still transfixed by the sight of her by now perspiring armpit. "Let me try to build a brand new, yet tested by, among others, Talmudic tales—a state-of-the art narrative drag bike—and drag race my innocent readers all the way to the Black Hill Classics."

Every punctuation mark has its own intonation. Treasure the spoken word. (Stanislavsky)

---

[21]A. Q. Morton, *Literary Detection* (1978), p. 99.

12

"The Hollywood Academy Awards is by far the biggest show on earth. And the slowest." Oswald Ortolan, a producer-director of the forthcoming fifty-first Hollywood Academy Awards, beams at Kosky, and he beams at him across a gold-plated table during their tête-à-tête luncheon in Monroe Stahr (PRINTER: not Star Monroe) restaurant—Manhattan's most notoriously exclusive place.

"This year, in order to boost Oscar's National Index Rate we've got to produce some surprises." He lifts his index finger at Kosky. "For one, we want you, you, Norbert Kosky, to be the only Oscar presenter who will present not one Oscar—but two! Two Oscars—to two different winners, of course! One Oscar for the most original screenplay and one for the most original adaptation of someone else's original novel or play or anything else made up of words: word is your schtick, isn't it? Now, isn't this neat? I mean, having you, a relatively unknown, never-heard-of literary somebody, presenting two of the best-known literary Oscars in town?"

He lifts a small finger. Instantly, the servile steward materializes with yet another bottle of wine.

"Six hundred million people will watch you, a writer awarding other writers at this year's Academy Awards. You couldn't buy publicity like this for six—make it nine—million dollars!"

"Too bad most of my novels are either all sold out and not reordered by the booksellers, or only available in the too expensive trade editions, or out of print," moans Kosky.

There is no prestige attached to being an author in Hollywood. An author (of standing) in London, in Paris, even in New York, enjoys a certain distinction. He is acceptable. He is even desirable. His opinion is worth something. But when he reaches Hollywood, he finds himself curiously, unexpectedly and completely anonymous. (Mildred Cram)

"Your novels? What novels? Who cares about your novels? I'm talking fame." Ortolan leans his lean torso all the way across the table. "More than half a century passed since Sam Goldwyn founded within his studio a writing collective he called the Eminent Authors [6/9/1919]. It's time to remind people that moving pictures must be written in words before they can start moving." He sips his wine. "Aren't you grateful to be chosen?"

"Of course I am," says Kosky casting a non-envious look at the latest edition of Movie Companion To Which Movies No Longer Move You. (1982) — a gift from Oswald Ortolan.

"Face it, Norbert." A gentile squire, Ortolan faces Kosky squarely. "How many obscure storytellers do you know who had instant fame delivered to them just like that — on a silver-screen platter in front of so many spectators watching you from all over the world?"

"I can't think of even one — except perhaps Moses." says Kosky.

"Good Lord!" exclaims Ortolan. "Even he had only a word-of-mouth for an audience — a Word, not the World. So what do you say: YES or NO?"

"I don't know. Not yet," Kosky mumbles, crossing knife with a fork in the form of a cross. "You see, my father taught me that happy life means living life unnoticed by others; according to him, only obscurity can feasibly lead to a happy life. Lead to it — not guarantee it. And what's more obscure than writing fiction — and writing it with the Word in mind.

A word—not even a reader—as I have done for over half of my life?"

"I can't see how obscurity can be happy, it's all too obscure for me!" Ortolan interrupts him noisily.

"Because, as my father did say," Kosky goes on, "obscurity stems from the obscure verb 'to obscure'—which means to dim the luster of life, and to dim it in order to take the glare away but only in order to be able to see life more clearly—and perhaps be able to find out what life is all about. Perhaps. That's why, while fame, reputation and notoriety derive from the presence of other people, only obscurity is original: one achieves obscurity quite by oneself."

"Your father obviously was not an American. Believe me, in this country fame is as good as a good reputation. Maybe better, and much tougher to lose. However," he goes on, "one bad headline, in even the smallest paper, can cost you your good reputation, however good, while no headline can kill fame which, made of headlines, means notoriety."

"I'm not convinced," mumbles Kosky, while Ortolan fixes upon him his crucifyingly tempting smile. "You see, in order to stay as obscure as possible, on the back cover of my books I used to list only my name and titles of my past books in lieu of a single biographical note."

"Those years are over," pronounces Ortolan. "I've just read 'On Kosky'—a special para-literary Life Support Program distributed by your publishers worldwide. C'mon, Norbert, say yes to my Video Crystal Display." Ortolan breathes out the scent of caviar dipped in champagne. "Besides, aren't you a writer who is obliged by his Jewish faith—his faith being a Jewish narrative tradition—to turn anyone or anything, be it himself or Hollywood Oscars, into a spiritually inspiring story?"

"Now I stand convinced," says Kosky, and as he says it, his tongue and lips, suddenly turn dry. "For how long will I be on live display on the Oscar stage?" asks our Medusa Man who is already suffering from early stage fright. **What was he up to, what was he doing, what did he want? That's rather** hard to tell, because he wanted so many things, but the thing he wanted most was Fame. Those were the years of his concentrated quest of that fair Medusa. (Thomas Wolfe)[1]

"For as long as it will take you to say a few catchy words plus catch the name of the nominees, plus 'May I have the envelope, please' — plus handing out the Oscars to the two — two, not one — this year Oscar catchers! And, go through it without a fault! And fast: every second of the The Oscars buys thousands of dollars worth of advertising, and thousands of advertisers all over the world buy every second of the show!"

The passage of mythological hero may be overground, incidentally: fundamentally it is inward — into depths where obscure resistances are overcome, and long lost, forgotten powers are revivified, to be made available for the transfiguration of the world. (Joseph Campbell)

The following week our storytelling bird hunter flies to Los Angeles for the Oscar ceremonies rehearsal.

He checks into a downtown Torquemada Inn where, trying to keep his stage fright in check, on an empty bladder he floats for hours in the bladder-shaped empty swimming pool. The stage fright is, of course, *angor animi,* an anguish of the spirit, as Anaïs Nin (his past literary colleague long since past,) knew only too well; it is an illness as damaging to one's creative psyche as is that dreadful Malison illness, or thanatophilia — a death wish. He attempts to calm his turbulent inner pond by looking at himself in the calm surface of the motel's swimming pool, an obligatory confrontation between

---

[1]Thomas Wolfe (who at one time starred in his own play) wrote about his manuscript *Of Time and the River,* stored in a giant wooden box: **There is an immense amount of it, millions of words, and although it might not be of any use to anyone else, it is, so far as I am concerned, the most valuable thing I have got.** *(The Letters of Thomas Wolfe)*

his literary habitat, his Self and the sudden bouts of palpitating heart.

Enough has been said about the BeShT[2] to show that his behavior as well as his relationship to nature and the supernatural was deeply influenced by his Gentile environment. It remains to add that in his appearance, too, he cultivated a resemblance to the Gentile holy men, many of whom were active in his days among the Raskol ("dissenting") peasantry of Ruthenia, Podolia, Volhynia, and the Ukraine. (Raphael Patai)

A day later he is picked up by an overly stretched limousine which, he is told by the youthful lad who is his driver, once drove Groucho, Harpo and Chico Marx Brothers but, happily for our anti-Marxist literary antihero, not Karl Marx. The limo car takes him to the Oscar rehearsals.

As they arrive at the *gigantesque* auditorium and stop at its back STAGE ONLY entrance, a sizable crowd of screaming kids and shouting grown-ups surrounds the car. "They all want your autograph or a picture, or both. They don't know you. But they know my limo. They guess you are — or soon will be — a somebody," says Lanky Aryan.

"What's this? I thought today was the rehearsal. Don't Oscars take place tomorrow?" Our Eminent Author panics.

"They do," says the driver. "Tomorrow is D-Day."

---

[2] Born in the super-magical year 1699, Israel Bael Shem Tov "usually referred to by the acrostic BeShT" (Raphael Patai) was the founder of the Hasidic movement.

Hasidism represents one of the most significant and most original phenomena not only in the history of Judaism, but also in the history of the development of religions in general. . . . By means of exerting a powerful psychological influence Hasidism succeeded in creating a type of believer who valued the ardor of feeling higher than the observance of rites, piety and religious fervor higher than speculation and Tora-study. (Simon Dubnow, as quoted by Raphael Patai, in *The Jewish Mind*, "Jewish Dionysians: The Hasidim." New York, 1977.)

"Then what are all these people here for today?"

"Today is the rehearsal for D-Day. Today they can see the celebs like yourself—a nobody suddenly turned into somebody—without paying top buck for the real thing," says the driver. "Tomorrow they can see the real thing on their TV. And after tomorrow they forget you and the whole thing."

Ready for extinction in the hands of the mob, Kosky extracts himself from the limo and, shaking with excitement, lets himself be photographed waving to the screaming kids as if he were an Oscar winner.

At the door to the auditorium, our *Le Juif Errant* (*The Wandering Jew*, by Eugene Sue, 1844. J. K.) is accosted by a oafish twenty-two-year-old American. Appropriately for our page-turning author, he introduces himself as Kosky's official page—"assigned to guide you, sir, without fail on your part or mine throughout the events of today and tomorrow."

They enter the auditorium. Here the sight of the stage filled with people and lights—and of the enormous auditorium filled to its last seat with screaming people—gives Kosky another massive dose of stage fright.

"Why are all these people here? This is an unfair publicity Fair. I thought this was a rehearsal." The author screams at his page.

"It is. That's why they're here," answers the gawky page. "Oscars are live, aren't they?" he goes on. "So is the rehearsal."

Stretching practically the length of a city block, the giant stage is crowded with anonymous stagehands and—imagine that!—some two dozen of movieland's biggest stars, young and old men and women who now face him face-to-face and whom, until now, he faced only on the screen of the street corner's Cinema 69, as well as from on the screen of his six-by-nine TV. Now, Kosky shakes hands with Mike Wordsmith, one of the show's directors, who then leads Kosky by a hand, to center stage. There, in front of everybody—and what a front that is!—he places Kosky behind a stationary pulpit equipped with a single microphone stand with a hand-held mike placed upon it. In a low voice he asks Kosky to start getting ready. From here and in this slot of time, rehearsing for the Oscars, Kosky will read aloud his Oscar remarks. Terrified and shaken, he is nevertheless pleased to notice that these remarks have been printed in giant block letters (so big he could read them from across a city block) on several cue cards as big as the biggest humanoid. The cards are stacked now one in front of another, next to the giant TV cameras which stand in the middle of the auditorium (as they will be during the actual Academy Awards ceremony) keeping pace with Kosky's speech, these cue cards one after another, will be removed.

"Now, don't you say anything bad to the audience. You can bad mouth yourself, but say nothing bad about the human race, America, or your Ma or Pa. Do you hear me loud and clear?" Mike warns Kosky in a whisper and sticks a mike into Kosky's mouth.

"Why not? The bastards can't hear us, right?" whispers Kosky. "The mikes are not plugged in yet."

"Oh yes, they are! The BASTARDS can hear us and they already heard, you called them Bastards. DIDN'T YOU?" Mike whispers in a stage whisper into the mike and as he says it the six thousand strong audience replies in unison, YES, WE HEARD YOU! Mike laughs at Kosky in unison with the loudest collective laugh of the audience.

Calm returns to the audience but not to our hero. On huge TV monitors facing the audience from under the ceiling, the collective eye of the audience can see our Trembling Bunting's hand trembling. Shaking silly, Kosky starts reading his text from the first cue card. "The Bible proves to us that in the beginning was the Word. . .," he recites firmly.

"Watch out, son!" says Mike.

"Watch out for what?"

"For how you say it. You pronounce *word* as *world*. It's not the same, you know! While to Gentiles, the beginning of the world was the Word, to Jews it was heaven and earth — the whole world." He pauses and the audience chuckles easily.

"That's like not knowing about the difference between a blue bird and The Bluebeard!" Mike goes on and gets another salvo of laughter.

Spiritually strained, Kosky now desperately attempts to temporarily censor his inner film director, his own nastiest critic. **I will return again to my place, until they acknowledge their guilt and seek my face, and in their distress they seek Me.** (Hosea 5:15) In order to achieve this, he starts thinking first about *The Secret Trial,* a little-known 1969 film about the Soviet leader Zinoviev,[3] who was tragically implicated in 1936 by Stalin, but this does not seem to help him. Then he turns his *videothoughts*® (a word he coined in an interview in the *Media Message* magazine) to a blond woman who, all clad in soft and pliant leather, in the very first row sits next to — wait a minute, next to whom is this blondie, this Satanella sitting? **Shimmering serpent bathed in light,/ Satanella, mill of mercury,/Satanella, cranked by heaven,/Is an undulating blur./Centrifuge of whirling hips/Satanella, dazzling moonbeam,/Silverflooded in** lamé Opera Ball, 1936, (Julian Tuwim).

In fact, Satanella sits next to — imagine that! — Beau Brummel, the American scene prime intellectual superstar! He is the one and only American Beau — the male Sex Seduction personified, who only the other day was portrayed half-naked on the cover of *DICK TRACY* magazine.

Kosky wets his lips. "In the beginning was the Word," he enunciates most clearly. **The director must die within an actor. (Vladimir I. Nemirovich-Danchenko)**

"Careful, baby!" says Mike. "Your Word keeps coming out of you as a ward. Ward means prison! You don't want all

---

[3] Zinoviev also founded the Zinoviev University in Leningrad which, in addition to courses in general education specialized in the until then much neglected studies of scientific technique for the investigation of criminal law, criminal offenses and techniques of criminology.

these decent folks in Montana, Mombasa and Kielbasa to think that in the beginning was a prison, do you?" His ethnically colored remarks get "prolonged applause," as such collective reactions are often called. "Try again!" he prompts our electronic village idiot.

"In the beginning was the Word. . .," Kosky strains. **A gesture is a movement not of a body but of a soul. (Feodor Chaliapin)**

"Careful, Norbie," Mike interrupts him. "This time it came out as wart. Wart is a skin tumor—a cancer. Now, how would you like to hear someone telling you from TV that in the beginning was a cancer, eh?" The audience roars and so does the slim'nd stacked Satanella (SSS).

"In the beginning was the Word—" Kosky begins.

"Stop right there! Szloma Szmul,"[4] screams Mike. "This time, your Word came out as *wort!* Wort—d'you hear? Wort as in walewort, wallwort, wartwort, willowwort, or whitlowwort," he says. "As every pothead knows, a wort is a pot herb," he says, and the audience roars once more.

"I thought I came closer to worth than to wort," says Kosky. "I thought I said worth. Worth as in worthless; as in the words airworthy, blameworthy, fameworthy, helpworthy, seaworthy. Worth, as in the nine worthies."

"Stop right there!" says Wordsmith. "You're practicing the wrong word, and you can't pronounce it either! You are not here 'cause you're worthy." He can't decide whether *wûr'th* is an eminent noun, a worthwhile adjective, or a worthy adverb. "You are here because you're a writer; a writer means being wordy, not just wordly, right? You're here because you're supposed to be a worthy writer—a worthy not wordy—otherwise why would they send me a painted birdy who can't say *word* in English?" **The experiences of the war**

[4]Szloma Szmul (from Szloma Szmulewicz): until 1939 more or less commonly found Ruthenian Jewish name. (J. K.)

years made him unable to conform to the patterns of thought and behavior demanded by collective society. Again he was the outsider, the Painted Bird. (J. K. 1965)

Kosky starts again. "In the beginning was the Word."

"It came out as *war*," Mike interrupts him. "Now, maybe *war* was at our beginning — war, not word — but we don't want you to be the first to word it worldwide on the Oscars, do we? Try again." He cracks up, and so does the audience.

"In the beginning was the Word. . . ." Kosky shifts his weight from one foot to the other. The only escape from such pressure and limitation was flight, a journey across an ocean and beyond the confines of a continent where no wings could be spread. In this flight the Painted Bird again become himself. (*Postscript* to *The Painted Bird*, Found only in the First print run of the first edition, 1965. J. K.)

"Try again," Mike cuts in.

"In the beginning was the Word," Kosky sweats out. Drop your voice an octave and don't lisp . . . count to six and look at that lamp as if you could no longer live without it. (Josef von Sternberg)

"Not bad, but now it sounds like *wourd*. What's *wourd?*" Mike roars and so does the audience.

"I don't know what's *wourd*. I've never heard that word before," says Kosky.

"Neither did we — until now!" says the director. "Give it another try, Norbert — I mean Robert."

Kosky tries again.

"Now it sounds like *worth*. Like in 'What's your worth?' I told you not to keep on saying *worth*."

"Maybe I should practice on Wordsworth, on a name?" says Kosky.

"Wordsworth? Who's he" Wordsmith rolls his hand to his ear.

"William Wordsworth." Kosky nods.

I do not ask pardon for what there is of untruth in such verses considered strictly as matters of fact. (Wordsworth)

"Go ahead. Try it again on your Wordsworth." Mike

Wordsmith seems offended.

Kosky mobilizes himself and in one long breath rushes the whole phrase straight through. **No feast, no performance. Our work is senseless if there is no holiday mood, if there is nothing to carry the spectators away. Let us carry them away with our youth, laughter, and improvisation. (Vakhtangov)**

"By George, he's got it!" Wordsmith triumphs. "Now let's go on with the rest of your speech. Take a deep breath. Here we go, Bert . . ."

After the rehearsals, on the way out, Kosky signs autographs and poses for pictures.

"Enjoy the last day of your privacy," says the lanky Aryan, gently escorting our Sweating Jew to the limo as gently as only an Aryan Gentile would. **The soul does not like to be without its body because without the body it cannot feel or do anything. Therefore build a figure in such a way that its pose tells what is in the soul of it. (Leonardo da Vinci)**

SS

Back at his hotel, Kosky rests by buoying up in the swimming pool, where he, a man who can't drown, is watched in silent wonder by two Arab children, their nannies and sand-shifting bodyguards. Tired, he goes to his room, and switching off, he switches on the TV. Finally, to prepare himself for what's ahead, his moving finger reluctantly guides him to another channel, on which a group of past-perfect Oscar winners debate the past Oscars imperfect. Then he falls asleep.

And by his side was that stern friend, the only one to whom he spoke what in his secret heart he most desired. To Loneliness he whispered, "Fame!" — and Loneliness replied, "Aye, brother, wait and see." (Thomas Wolfe)

He wakes up by midday. He is groggy, but not groggy enough. He knows this is his D-day. In order to rearm his defeatist soul for his D-day he soulfully watches on the Sex Orgy TV-channel the one-and-only Sandy Samples, a 21 year old Californian female rotunda with a 40 DDD bra size. And so his D-day countdown begins. In some six hours our Maverick Limerick from New York will enter the Planet Image.

A hermit once thought his oasis/The best of all possible places;/For it had a mirage/In the form of a large/And affectionate female curvaceous. (William S. Baring-Gould)

The limo picks him up on the dot, and on its way to the Oscars joins the stream of other limos.

At the CELEBS parking lot, past, present and future Oscar celebs park their cars. Here, our Jewfish[5] is spotted and picked up by Allan, his tuxedoed page. Walkie-talkie in hand, the ungainly page escorts our trembling bookman to his seat in the auditorium, which, he is told in no uncertain terms, he may not leave alone and from where, a few minutes before his Oscar presentation, he will be collected by his most faithful, and well-meaning though maladroit page. While his page hovers nearby, our trembling Pollack[6] introduces himself to the fish in the next seat (they are among other presenters)—a prime-time Broadway Stonefly Nymph on his left, and the Black Sea Bass, a leading Hollywood male star.

The finest trout fisherman in the world dare those who are expert with symphs. (Tom McNally)

Shortly before the Grand Mass is about to begin, Kosky's stomach begins to bulge from within. Stage fright turns into

---

[5]Jewfish: a large dark-colored saltwater fish which populates the shallows of the coral heads and caves of the South Atlantic and feeds on other fish.

[6]Pollack: a medium-sized, lightly colored saltwater fish which, feeding on shrimp, wanders in schools at medium depths of the North Atlantic.

stomach cramps. He is about to explode. Quick! He summons his page. He tells him he is about to blow up. His page leads him through the crowds, through the lobby, to the haven of a toilet. Thank heavens! Kosky locks himself in one of the stalls and, exploding in safety, suddenly sees Allan peeping at him through the crack in the door frame.

After a moment, Allan becomes aware that from within his stall, Kosky spies on him.

"I'm not allowed to leave you alone, sir! Not even for a most private moment!" he apologizes for being a spy. "If something awful happened to you, I'd have to alert the central stage—they would have to come up with a double real quick."

"What bad could possibly happen to me in a toilet?"

"You'd be surprised," Allan whispers to him through the door—while watching him through the crack. "People do funny things when they're as sick from bad nerves as you are now. Things that aren't funny."

"Like what?"

"Like taking the wrong pill. Like hitting the wrong vein with a needle. Like going through 'I want to go back home!' primal scream!"

Emptied of everything but fear, Kosky gets out of the stall and the lifeless page walks him over to his seat.

SS

No one has described fully the horror of this illness called anxiety. Worse than any physical illness, this is illness of the soul, for it is insidious, elusive and arouses no pity. (Anaïs Nin)

Back in his seat our Lion's Head resumes the posture of an ordinary U.S. literary lion who is suffering from ordinary hypotension and spiritual ischemia.

Just then the curtain goes up, baring the largest stage in the world. Suspended over the stage, a huge banner proclaims: **LIVE spells backward into EVIL, while EROS** reverses **SORE**. And, we should never forget the **SIN** in **SINCERE** or the **CON** in **CONFIDENCE**. Let's tighten up the slack sentimentality. (Marshall McLuhan) And remember that the word golf reverses to flog. (Flog as in flogging, printer! Flog not flag! comments Jay Kay.)

The auditorium quiets down. Oscars, the greatest show on earth begins, then proceeds in all its splendor.

"It's time!" says the listless page, motioning Kosky to follow him around on the double. Say goodbye to your Polish-Jewish Shtetl! whispers to Kosky his very soul.[7]

On the way to the big altar, they make a pit stop. At the pit, the lady makeup artist and her portable anti-perspiration powder kit neatly dispose of the heavily perspiring look of our literary man on the make. Too bad she can't do anything for a perspiring heart. After she is finished, the page escorts Kosky to the Green Box, the waiting room on the stage's right wing, assuring him that the stage's left side has its own Green Box. Our Green Box is full of journalists, other Oscar presenters, TV reporters and press photographers. These are the elders of the electronic village. TV is their sacristy.

The mass is in progress—the excitement builds. Everybody stares at the TV monitor. On it, Danny Boatman, the Oscar's least ceremonious master of ceremonies, announces the appearance of Beau Brummel, Hollywood's most secretive leading man. Beau Brummel will present an Oscar to the best director. In a moment, BB as he is fondly known all over the world strides out onto the right side of the stage.

Since, according to the minute-by-minute scripted program, Kosky must follow Brummel, with Brummel's appearance about to end, Pan Kosky panics.

---

[7]Shetl—a small town Jewish community found until 1939 in Eastern Europe from where most of today's Jewry originated. Read *Life Is With People:* The Culture of the Shtetl, by Mark Zborowski and Elizabeth Herzog, Introduction by Margaret Mead, 1967.

The nature of anxiety can be understood when we ask what is threatened in the experience which produces anxiety. The threat is to something in the "core of essence" of the personality. Anxiety is the apprehension cued off by a threat to some value which the individual holds essential to his existence as a personality. (Rollo May, 1950)

"I'm next, right?" Kosky asks his stock-still page for the ninth time. A rhetorical question. Everybody in this room knows Kosky is next. Why? Because next comes the Oscar for the best original screenplay, to be followed by an Oscar for the best screenplay adapted from another source — "both to be presented by Norbert Kosky, a little-known writer from the East who suddenly made it big in the West," in the words of the *Hollywood Purporter.*

"You are," says Allan, terribly excited but most polite. "Beau Brummel is now presenting the Oscar on the right wing. He is presenting it on the right wing — not to the right wing, right? That's why you follow him on the left. Left wing, that's where we are now, right? Good luck!"

"On the *left?* What left? But can't you see we are in the right wing!" screams Kosky, suffering a massive attack of instant sweat, but also a massive injection of world-wide awareness (world-wide, printer, not just word). Gripped by terror, but also by its drama, he can barely point out the sign above their heads. He is unable to move. Is he going to suddenly appear at the wrong end of the Hollywood Oscars stage in front of six thousand people in this auditorium and six hundred million people watching him from all over the world? The wrong end, meaning Kosky's cue cards happen to be stacked up in front of the lantern standing on the left side of the stage. And what about the two Oscar statuettes *and* the two envelopes containing the names of the lucky Oscar winners, which are also waiting for Kosky on the left side of the stage — where by now our unlucky Oscar presenter should have been long ago!

"We are on the right! That's WRONG!" The page becomes blank. Then, the blank page panics and blankly looks at everybody in the room. Everybody nods. This is the right side, kid, say their nods. This right happens to be the wrong one for Kosky.

"Oh, my God! It's my first job, and I got it all screwed up!" moans the blank page while our literary Ministrant goes through a massive attack of chest pain. Once again he sounds alarm no. 9. The pain, or perhaps only a spasm, takes place in the epigastric right upper quadrant of his chest; it radiates along his back and beneath the scapula all the way to the left precordial region and left shoulder.

The story of arrhythmias is particularly poignant because not only are they quietly devastating — attacking apparently healthy people with a blow that can kill in seconds — but often they are self-inflicted. More and more, it appears, our habits and emotions are deadlier than our diseases. *Heart Rhythms,* (1989) *op. cit.* p. 10

The pain becomes severe, and intensifies rapidly. It is accompanied by an instant belching, sudden bloating by abdominal cramp and sudden nausea. Discreetly Kosky reaches for a handkerchief and — discreetly — vomits into it. Equally discreetly he throws the offensive handkerchief into the garbage basket — or was it someone's shopping bag? His bloating and belching reassure his inner Dr. Kosky, M.D. that his one and only patient is going through not a terminal heart attack but, rather, an ordinary biliary spasm, precipitated, no doubt, by spiritual food fried in a spiritually disagreeable frying pan, a momentary illness most Oscar presenters probably go through. **All creative writers are hypochondriacs. (Harold Nicolson)**

"I got it all screwed up. There goes my next job, as an army recruiter — anything is better than an army recruit! The blank page keeps moaning, as he and Kosky start walking toward the left side. Just then Allan mindlessly, helplessly, activates his walkie-talkie.

"Where the fuck are you? WHERE IS KOSKY?" screams from it the voice of the stage manager.

"We're on the RIGHT. I mean we're on the wrong side,"

moans the blank page.

"Kosky is next! Get his ass here. Here, on the LEFT. NOW!" screams the walkie-talkie. Now the blank page and the scribe, "call him a torn-out page," (Jay Kay) start running through the back stage. The back stage is — easily — a mile long. It is, also, a labyrinth; a veritable marshland filled with stagehands, stage feet, stage toes, most of whom by now clearly suffer from stage fatigue.

"Get him here NOW!" the walkie-talkie screams again. Just then the blank page collides with a stage guard — and the shock of collision practically knocks him and his walkie-talkie down.

This time, Kosky doesn't wait for him. As if in a trance, he runs through entranceways marked FRONT EXIT and BACK ENTRY and DO NOT ENTER and EXIT ONLY and PRIVATE OFFICIALS ONLY, and STAY OUT OF MY ROOM, CHRIS! And anywhere he runs he hears the loud moans of the page and the page's walkie-talkie screaming: "We've got two minutes left! Where is Kosky? Kosky! Get here! Now!"

Kosky is running and he is running fast. This is no longer an ordinary run. This is a run for life. A save-your-face race. Already he sees the headlines: OSCAR PRESENTER FAILS TO PRESENT — NORBERT KOSKY CHICKENS OUT.

This is summer 1944. The simple one-way radio — the early-day walkie-talkie found by the village fishermen on the dead body of a German soldier — snaps the latest news. June 23: "On the Galician front the Red Army commences its last offensive against Germans on Russian soil." June 25: "The Red Army takes Vitebsk." June 28: "The Red Army takes Mogilev." July 3: "The Red Army takes Minsk." July 13: "THE RED ARMY APPROACHES PINSK."

The Germans retreat. Look at them all rushing home, this time ahead of their panzers who now protect their rears from the advancing Red Snappers, the Red partisans, and the suddenly invincible Red Army. The end of the war? Not quite, kid! You're on the home run, but not home free yet! The VLASOVITES ARE COMING. The Vlasovites are the deserters from the Red Army. They are big, strong, meaty. They ride horses bareback and barefooted. They eat meat raw, and they eat it *po Tatarsku (à la* Tartare), with their bare hands. Their pleasures are as raw as their meat or meatus. Raping men, women and children is their prime-time pleasure.

It was a terrible scene, one that will live in my memory until I die. After surrounding the villages, a command was given to burn it, together with all the inhabitants. The excited barbarians took firebrands to the houses and those who ran away were shot at or forced back to the flames. They grabbed small children from their mothers and threw them into the fire. And when the grief-stricken women ran to save their children, they would shoot them first in one leg and then in the other. Then, after such torments, they finished them off. . . . The fields behind the village were covered with the dead: here, a mother with a child in her arms, its brains splashed all over her face; there a ten-year-old boy with his *elementarz* (his schoolbook) in his hand. (witness, age 19, 1945)[8]

On the final stretch of his Oscar run, our Pan Kosky crosses another brook. It's full of panfish,[9] and every *pan* holds a walkie-talkie. "Hurry up, Kosky!" screams a Bluegill. "You've got about a minute left!" screeches the Green Sun-

---

[8]From "Experiences One Can't Forget," Chapter 6, page 266, in *Polish Children Accuse, 1939–45*. Part One: "Documents of Nazi Crimes," ed. and compiled by Jozef Wnuk; Part Two: "German Occupation Through Children's Eyes," ed. and compiled by Helena Radomska-Strzemecka. See also "Polesie Voivodeship," in *War Through Children's Eyes*, page 96, ed. and compiled by Irena Grudzinska-Gross and Jan Tomasz Gross, 1981.

[9]Ask the man battling a bluefin tuna off Cat Cay what the first fish he ever caught was. . . . To a man—or perhaps it would be more correct to say, to a boy—they will chorus that they grew up catching bluegills, sunnies and other panfish." (Tom McNally)

fish. "What's wrong with you? Don't you know you belong on the left side?" screeches a Crappie. "Run, buddy, run!" shouts a Yellow Perch. "Where is Kosky? WHERE IS NORBERT KOSKY?" shrills Rock Bass.

"My, my! You must be Norbert Kosky? You're the only Oscar presenter in history who disappeared at the Oscars. May I have your autograph?" squawks a Warmouth. Another eddy. Another dam. Don't fall over this dam. Imagine: OSCAR PRESENTER BLEEDS ON OSCAR STAGE: WAS HE SICK OR BEATEN UP?

He runs through a portable plastic forest just removed from the right side of the stage. Careful now! Don't run into a tree; watch out—too late: the plastic branch hits him in the eye. WAS OSCAR PRESENTER BLINDED BY AN OSCAR? An eye for an eye.

Another corridor, another village. Another inlet. Another sandy bank. "Hurry up, Kosky," squawks a friendly crawfish. "Slow down, buddy! You still have a minute!" bellows a spindly grasshopper.

His Inner Boy starts hyperventilating. Nice, sixteen, nineteen expirations per minutes! OSCAR PRESENTER HYPERVENTILATES TWO OSCARS. Instantly, his inner automatically programmed autodidact command takes over, ordering his body to start breathing at a slowed-down diaphragmatic rate. He obeys, with his glottis opened to full capacity. He is now exhaling six times per minute and is about to reach "the neutrality of the sense." (Tantra) Inhaling, he now directs the fresh air straight to the vagus (which causes an overproduction of aceteylcholine—the friendly enzyme responsible for arterial relaxation J. K.).[10]

---

[10]"Specifically, dream frequency, self-verbalizations, and certain forms of mental imagery seemed to differentiate the best gymnasts from those who failed to make the Olympic team." ("Psychology of the Elite Athlete: An Exploratory Study," by Michael J. Mahoney and Marshall Avener, in *Cognitive Therapy and Research*.

Running along, our Pan Marathonsky casts a quick glance at the TV monitor—one of the many placed along his run. On it, Arthur Atractor, the Oscar-winning director (who just had his Oscar handed to him by Beau Brummel) continues the litany of thanks to those without whom he believes his Oscar wouldn't be possible, without for once mentioning his own force of creation. In a few seconds Atractor will leave the stage, and Danny Boatman, the ultramundane master of ceremonies, will appear, crack a typical Danny Boatman joke ("Everybody in Hollywood knows the unimportance of being a writer. Have *you* ever heard of Norbert Kosky?"), upon which he will announce the imminent appearance of Norbert Kosky, "our literary present as well as presenter." But where is Kosky?

Run, kid, run. Thank God for the long breaks in the Oscar program offered by commercials. A final sprint over a spring hole, and—presto!—our Ministrant appears in the Green Box, without a drop of saliva or a breath of his own.

"Where the fuck were you?" yowls the stage manager. "You've got less than a minute left!" He guides Kosky to the stage. "Walk up the scaffold all the way to the top, but don't remain there. NOBODY STAYS ON THE TOP FOR TOO LONG." he instructs Kosky. "Turn around. Don't *look* at the audience. Rather face them. Face them with your true face. Your true face, do you hear? Face it, kid, this is no time for an acting lesson!" He instructs Kosky as if he were a boxing manager and Kosky his only hi-score boxer. "Now, keep facing the people, *the people*—not the TV cameras—until Danny ends his introduction of you. When he does, but not sooner, start walking down the second the cameras turn toward you. Walk down all the way to the lectern. Walk down naturally. The same way you walked all the way to the very top. Naturally means slowly. Go slowly! Slowly and naturally! And, for God's sake, don't fall!"

OSCAR PRESENTER FALLS ON STAGE, ALLEGEDLY UPSET BY THE CHOICE OF THE NOMINEES.

"Now don't try to improvise. Just read straight from your

cue cards as they appear and moving, replace one after another; they move not too fast but not too slow either," the manager goes on. "Where are your reading glasses?" The Manager panics.

"I'm farsighted," Kosky reassures him.

"When you finish reading the names of the nominees, get the envelopes. Once you say, 'And the winners are . . .' open the winner's envelope. Open it slowly. Peel up the flap ever so gently. Don't ever tear it with anger. Let the people get excited. Once you read the names of the winners, look ever so pleased—even if you hate their guts. Don't spit. Don't sneeze. Don't laugh. Don't wink. Don't do anything that could be construed as rejection."

"Anything else?" Kosky collects himself.

"Oh, yes!" The manager scratches his head. "Speak to them in English. Don't say anything in a foreign language— particularly not in a language which doesn't have a country of its own, like Desperanto."

"Esperanto," Kosky corrects him gently. "Esperanto is a lovely and facile language."

"Nothing in Willpuke—"

"Volapük," says Kosky.

"Nothing in Kliterlingua."

"Interlingua." Kosky straightens him out.

"Remember: once the Oscar winners walk up to the stage to pick up their Oscars, it's their show, not yours. Be naturally humble, but not overly servile. I said humble, that is, unpretending, not humbled, that is discomfited. Don't stand in their way. Don't do anything that might be construed as *obstructing* their path to glory. Remember that their glory starts the minute they pick up the statuette from you and lasts only until next year's Oscars. Now, please don't drop the Oscar. Would you drop a Bible?"

"I won't drop it. Not this time," Kosky swears. "I learned my lesson during the war when I dropped a missal (not missile) as an altar boy serving to the mass. I swear I'll hold onto each Oscar with all my strength."

Hearing this, the manager grabs him by the shoulder, then lets go with reluctance. "Now, forget your past. Hold each Oscar gently, and don't close your thumb over it. You might get a numb thumb cramp. The thumb is the most flexible of all digits, but it can get locked in its own saddle joint. It's happened before. Of course"—he winks at Kosky—"some presenters don't like letting the Oscar go. They enjoy standing up there, on the top of the world, in front of six hundred million people, being photographed with an Oscar in hand. Even with somebody else's Oscar."

"I'll be swift," Kosky promises. As swift as Jonathan Swift, that literary swifty who wrote a Modest Proposal: the harshest satire ever!"

"Don't be too swift. Be modest not harsh. Let Oscar out of your hand slowly—but without teasing! And don't turn your back on an Oscar winner. He or she just won an Oscar—and who are you? Also, don't encourage any mouth-to-mouth kissing. Give them your cheek to kiss, but not your hand or ass. Brace them but don't embrace them."

"I'll watch out," says Kosky. "Anything else?"

On the monitor, the Seneca Industries Hot Bath™ commercial ends; the TV zeroes in on Danny Boatman. It's time to go. The stage manager pushes Kosky out into the world-wide video ring, just as Boatman begins to introduce our literary boxer, who walks up the staircase of the scaffold. He stops on the top of the scaffold. He turns and faces the sea of faces. Ending his remarks, Danny Boatman surrenders the lectern to "AND NOW, LADIES AND GENTLEMEN, HERE IS NORBERT KOSKY."

Calmly, his heart even at sixty even beats per minute, the Survival Kid catches his breath as he slowly descends the grand staircase. At the lectern, with Boatman gone, Kosky takes over the boat. Another pause; another breath of time and air.

All composed, our altar boy starts reading from the cue cards: "The Bible tells us that in the beginning was the

Word," he begins. Another pause. Was it *wurth* or *ward?* Too late now!

Gatsby believed in the green light, the orgiastic future that year by year recedes before us. It eluded us then, but that's no matter—tomorrow we will run faster, stretch out our arms farther. . . . And one fine morning—So we beat on, boats against the current, borne back ceaselessly into the past. (F. Scott Fitzgerald)

SS

After the ceremonies a night letter from UG-TV in Dasein, Israel, reaches Kosky at his hotel.

I SAW YOU ON ISRAELI TV GIVING OSCARS IN HOLLYWOOD. STOP AS A WWII SURVIVOR I REMEMBER YOU FROM THE TIME AFTER THE WAR WHEN WE WERE BOTH KIDS. STOP WHEN OTHER KIDS CALLED YOU MUTE AND DUMB YOU USED TO CUT OUR BICYCLE TIRES IN REVENGE STOP I'M GLAD TO SEE YOU SPEAK AND SPEAK UP AGAIN. SHALOM RACHEL.

They had parted as children, or very little more than children. Years passed. Then something recalled to the woman the companion of her young days, and she wrote to him: "I have been hearing of you lately. I know where life has brought you. You certainly selected your own road. But to us, left behind, it always looked as if you had struck out into a pathless desert." (Conrad)

13

I love it here. . . . The point is once you've got it—
Screen Credit 1st, a Hit 2nd and the Academy award
3rd—you can count on it forever . . . and know there's
one place you'll be fed without being asked to even wash
the dishes. (F. Scott Fitzgerald)

A day like any other day—except that this one is a day
after the Oscars. Kosky's hotel room. The phone rings and
our instant yesterday's hero rushes to it instantly.

"Is this Mr. Kosky, Norbert Kosky? The author?" asks a
man, who speaks with the accent of King Edward, mixed
with the accent of Lord Mountbatten and Nehru. Mixed or
mixed up.

"Speaking," Kosky rings his Ruthenian *ing!*

"Oh, hello, Kosky," says the man. "My name is Gardiner.
Chauncey Gardiner. How are you?"

"I could be worse, as they say in Ruthenia!"

"Could you now?" Gardiner wonders. "Worse than you
were last night doing your poor-taste number at the Oscars."

"What did I do wrong?" Immediately Kosky's heart goes
into a paroxysm of ventricular tachycardia at a rate of 169
beats/min.

"In your hardly original opening, you said, 'The Bible tells
us that in the beginning was the War!' War instead of you
know what," says Gardiner. "Also, you dared to call the Ten
Commandments the world's first screenplay. What chutz-
pah!"

"That's not what I meant," Kosky objects. "I meant that it's time to 'restore spiritual order.' "

When the universe was in complete disorder, Moses was called to the mountain. A warning bolt of lightning, an overture of thunder, the skies parted, and a mighty hand reached down to give Moses the stone tablets. In a way, that was the first script. Some critics thought it was overproduced for just ten lines—but, by following it, mankind restored order out of chaos. (Academy Awards, 1982)

"I'm calling because, just by chance, you might say, I just read that old book of yours about a character called Chance, or Chauncey Gardiner and so I found out that in that very book you dared to invade my privacy." Gardiner's voice acquires a menacing tone.

"I—what?"

"You heard me: you invaded my privacy. Privacy meaning my spiritual inner flame."

"Nonsense. That book is a work of fiction. Fiction invades imagination, not privacy," Kosky intervenes firmly. "Besides, even though *John Doe vs. privacy* is not explicitly stated in the Constitution—in due respect, as an American, I perceive our American Constitution in its humanistic interpretation clearly pointing at a 'zone of rights' as Justice Douglas called it." **These story fragments come out of a lot of talk with friends or out of wandering around the streets, or sleeping . . . that's why it takes so long to write. You just have to let it go through you; you have to keep imagining. (Paddy Chayevsky)**[1]

"All I know is that you've portrayed me as your gardener. That's bloody unfair!"

"If indeed you recognize yourself in my character—in the

---

[1]Paddy Chayevsky: who thought of himself as "a writer of satire," and who wrote most of his satire (*Marty, Middle of the Night, Network*) for the stage and screen.

fictional character I created—such recognition belongs to you, not to me." Kosky raises his voice as a novelist. **Where a name is used, it, like a portrait or picture, must, upon meeting the eye or ear, be unequivocally identified as that of the complainant. If it is not, then, taken with the statement of the author that all characters portrayed are wholly fictional, the identity of name must be set down as a pure coincidence. (American Courts)**

"Not bloody likely! Would you prefer to talk about it in a court of law?" screams Gardiner.

"I would rather confront you face to face. Confront without a front, or affront." Kosky, a pacifist at heart, looks forward to testing his combat readiness.

"O.K. Why not?" Gardiner breathes. "Why don't we talk first? I'll send my car for you."

"But only as long as I'll pay for the gasoline." Kosky hangs up first.

SS

Gardiner's car is a Phantom Six, the silver screen's veritable ghost. Inside the "luxuriously appointed" *(Inside Car Magazine)* back compartment the six-screen TV set stares the passenger in his face from above the latest "let your voice do the dialing" memory mode telephone/Fax modular console.

"What does Mr. Chauncey Gardiner do these days?" Kosky asks the driver—a nondescript conscript from the Valley of Mexico.

"It's not for me to *decide* what he does, sir. I just drive. That's all I do," says the conscript, fearfully glancing into the car's rearview mirror as he guides his Phantom Six in utter silence.

Gardiner's house in Malibu is a fusion of sunscreen with skylight. It is a hybrid of love boat beached involuntarily on a sand dune and space ship which crashed on landing.

A Mexican manservant with the face of an Aztec Indian

wearing a feather cloak escorts *Señor* Kosky through a granite hallway, offering, along the way, a peek at a screening room, a health spa, a video-game room and a library while telling Kosky, in a smooth brand of English, why must he, a man, be a man servant to another. Outside, on a croquet lawn, Kosky faces a middle-aged, middle-sized man lounging in a hammock suspended high above the terrace built in the form of the base of a Mexican Zapotec pyramid. Bearded and mustached, dressed in a colorful toga first worn by Montezuma I, the man sports a sombrero with ultra-wide brim set low on his wide forehead, and dark glasses set high on his clearly Semitically shaped nose, which, depending on the point of view, is shaped not unlike number six or nine.

"Mr. Kosky! So happy to make your acquaintance," says the man. He clambers out of the hammock. The men shake hands, then sink into a pair of hospital beds disguised as sundeck chairs. "So you're the usurper of my life," says Gardiner.

"I usurped folklore, not life. I invaded fiction, not fact," says Kosky. **There was some suggestion that the defendant published the portrait by mistake, and without knowledge that it was the plaintiff's portrait, or was not what it purported to be. But the fact, if it was one, was no excuse. If the publication was libelous, the defendant took the risk. As was said of such matters by Lord Mansfield, "Whenever a man publishes, he publishes at his peril." (Justice Oliver Wendell Holmes)**

"Are you certain you haven't trampled on my family name, hence, on my family?" Gardiner exhibits his smile. His smile is his exhibit A, and Kosky panics: exhibit A seems familiar. Had Kosky, himself a survivor of a Nazi invasion, involuntarily invaded the life of another man? A man with a most familiar smile?

"Well—I almost did."

"*Almost?* That's not good enough for the British jury, sir! Didn't you know that we British love gardening?"

"Everybody knows that," says Kosky. "That's not an invasion."

"How about Chauncey—my first name?"

"An ordinary American name. First, or last. As ordinary as chance itself. Ask Tennessee Williams, who featured a man Chance in one of his plays," says Kosky.

"The fact is, your character, your Chauncey Gardiner, comes from life. From me. From property everybody in Yorkshire knows as Gardiner's Gardens."

Somberly, Gardiner jerks off his sombrero and he does it like a simple *hombre*, a Mexican lord of the prairie, fused with a *caballero* of New Mexico.

"My readers know just as much as the author about the State of Make-Believe. I believe my novel is a portrait. A moving portrait of a moving soul. It is a novel about the Media. The media which, God bless their free soul, are as free to interpret my Chance's conduct as I am free to interpet his soul." Kosky parades his narrative bill of rights.

"Please stop that abstract talk and stop it now." Gardiner gets up from his orthopedic stool, then turns around but the turn pains him; like Kosky he too suffers from a spinal pain.

"Unless you tell the public I'm your ideal character called Chauncey I'm going to have you"—he pauses, and just then says—"oh, what the hell!" and takes off his sunglasses. Then he peels off his beard and mustache and, one after another, his many other faces. Now, but only now, Kosky knows who this man is. He is Shaman Peters the one-and-only actor of the Satirical Movieland. There goes the face of Genghis Khan; there goes the police inspector—that closet queen!— who won't inspect his own closet. There goes the Onion Eater who, thanks to his Dionysian Hasidic upbringing, made the simple act of eating onion with lemon spiritually synonymous with great acting.

You can make an X-ray photograph of a face, but you cannot make a face from an X-ray photograph. (Arthur Koestler)

"I'm glad I fooled you. May I call you Norbert the Great?" Without leaving his orthopedic stool, Shaman Peters tries to embrace Kosky but his movement is cut short by his sore spine. "I'm glad I fooled you. Like most folks in the entertainment business I was born to a Jewish-Russian family which then went to Great Britain I guess. I was born as a voluntary fool. I have fooled everyone ever since, at the age of three, I was already declared to be an acting child prodigy, and a true three-year old *starets*," he declares, assuming a posture of a Russian *starets*.[2] "That's why, in your Chauncey, I recognize my inner *yurodivy*—a voluntary fool like me." No longer fooling, Peters orders via one of his many Mexican servants a bottle of Dönmeh 1969 semi-sparkling champagne.

"When did you first read my novel?" asks our Eminent Author.[3]

"I haven't read it!" Peters admits. "Like your Chance—or Chauncey—I like to watch. To watch not to read, remember? The Plug-in Drug." (Marie Winn, 1977)

"You haven't read my book?" Instantly, the eminent Author becomes less eminent. **Gradually there grew up within me a belief that the public was tiring of the star and a**

---

[2]Such was the *starets*, a man of the people who had attained the highest degree of wisdom complemented by divine grace, but one who still dwelt among the people, both in his inmost nature and in his actions. Official authorities, abbots and bishops, were often suspicious of the *starets*—he belonged to the people's religion, at once one of its highest manifestations and one of its wellsprings and luminaries. (Pierre Pascal, *The Religion of the Russian People*, 1976, p. 44). (this ISBN-0 66 2 99 7 tells you all!: Jay Kay)

[3]On 6/9/1919, "a day when High Brow Literature went to bed with until then Low-life Cinema, Samuel Goldwyn created within his film studio an intellectually select sect (SS) he called Eminent Authors." (Jay Kay).

corresponding conviction that the emphasis of production should be placed upon the story rather than upon the player. In the poverty of screen drama lay, so I felt, the weakness of our industry, and the one correction of this weakness which suggested itself to me was a closer cooperation between author and picture producer. (Samuel Goldwyn)

"I haven't read it not because I don't read, but because I can't read easily." His face becomes expressionless. "Letters and numbers bore me. They bore me visually, because visually they don't seem to drill into me—to bore into me easily, you might say. Still, as you can tell, I can tell stories and I'm hardly a bore."

"Then how do you know the story of my Chance?" Still perplexed, Kosky chances out.

"George Scarab—the son of Harris—my friend as well as yours first told me about it, then read it to me on the phone. I liked what I heard. And after I heard it, I knew I was your prototypical Chauncy Gardiner, and the story of Chance is SHAMAN PETERS'S OWN STORY," he headlines.

"I saw it in my head as a moving story, and I saw it first and last, last meaning for the sixty-ninth as well as ninety-sixth time, as a novel and not as a movie," says Kosky. The task I'm trying to achieve is above all to make you see. (D. W. Griffith)

My task which I am trying to achieve is, by the power of the written word, to make you hear, to make you feel— it, before all, to make you see. (Joseph Conrad)

The printed image is an old-fashioned mental camera obscura," says Peters. "It doesn't move images fast enough. It knows no special effects; it doesn't offer different angles. It talks of values, feelings, attitudes—things you can't show. Literature can't deliver sound of music. Only a movie can do all this—and so much more."

I see my novel as an inner hearing aid—not a concrete image projector," says our Verbalizer.

"Your gardener is a spiritual enigma. Nobody knows who he really is. All he needs is physical embodiment. Speaking of the cinema. All he now needs is a fine initial worldwide release and good theatrical distribution," says Peters.

"He knows who he is. Self-knowledge is all that matters to him. That's enough for me too," Kosky intervenes.

"It's not enough," Gardiner interrupts. "The minute he opens his mouth, everybody knows what he's talking about even if he doesn't. I don't want you to think that because he can't think straight neither can I." He starts perspiring.

When I say he did me the honor, I am not using empty words. It was a very real honor to be in the thoughts of so great a man as Captain Sellers, and I had wit enough to appreciate it and be proud of it. . . . He never printed another paragraph while he lived, and he never again signed "Mark Twain" to anything. . . . Mark Twain (pen name of Samuel L. Clemens) *The Almanach of American Letters.*

They are interrupted by the arrival of a youthful man, impeccably dressed in impeccable doctor's overalls, who shows up on the terrace unannounced and carrying under his arm *Quantum Healing:* Exploring The Frontiers of Mind/Body Medicine, (by Deepak Chopra, M.D. 1989.) also brings with him a bit of *Suspense* (Joseph Conrad, 1925).

"This is Dr. Daniel Chaucer. He is both a Ph.D. and an M.D. and this is Norbert Kosky, my new friend." Peters introduces both men. "Dr. Chaucer is the foremost specialist in Manual Medicine. He is to me what Ford Madox Ford was to that Slavic guru Joseph Conrad."[4] Peters goes on

---

[4]Wrote Dame Rebecca West: "The relationship began beautifully, with Ford as guru instructing the grateful Polish disciple in the refinements of English prose, and it ended with Conrad and Jessie (his wife) going frantic in their efforts to get the Djinn back into the bottle" *(Sunday Telegraph). Djinn* was Conrad's pronunciation of *gin* (a fluid, the substantial dose of which he needed everyday to be able to

excited.

The doctor takes one good look at Kosky. "I saw you on TV handing out the Oscars. You walked up and down the stairs like someone suffering from *Praise of Folly*.[5] I could tell, however, that you were not quite yourself when reading the text: that you were acting."

"How could you tell?" marvels our literary marvel.

"Tell him how, Doctor," Peters says to Chaucer.

"Acting is movement and movement comes from the vertebral column. From our spine," says Dr. Chaucer. He places himself behind Peters and asks the actor to sit up straight in the chair.

Peters takes off his shirt, displaying his firm body. A session of manual medicine is about to begin. Standing behind him, with one hand placed on Peters's shoulder and the other one holding onto his cheek, Dr. Chaucer starts rotating the actor's head as if it were an empty jug set on some static spire, a maneuver to which the actor submits with obvious relish.

"A necessary introductory procedure," explains the doctor, catching Kosky's surprised stare, "since this causes maximum flexion of the entire region of the cervical spine, and brings individual joints into their final, most extreme position." Dr. Chaucer keeps on palpating the actor's spinous spine.

The procedure is over. Dr. Chaucer is about to leave.

---

keep up his writing, his mind-settling spiritual routine: J. K.).

See William Amos, *The Originals. An A-Z of Fiction's Real-Life Characters* (1985).

[5]*In Praise of Folly* by Erasmus (1519). "A humanist who favored reform within the Church, Erasmus was classified by the Inquisition as an 'author of the second class,' which meant that his work could be read only if 'objectionable' parts were expurgated." (From *Censorship: 500 Years of Conflict*, The New York Public Library, 1984).

"Why don't you give Mr. Kosky a quick provocative test?" says Peters, putting on his shirt.

It's now Kosky's turn. He sits down on a stool while, standing beside him, Dr. Chaucer checks the working of his supposedly spiritually straight spine (SSS) and finds it, in his own words, "substantially crooked."

As its name suggests, provocative testing provokes pain. While Dr. Chaucer performs his medical tests called provocations, Kosky becomes testy.

"Why do I feel pain? Anything wrong?" asks Kosky who, a bit irate, begins to feel his irate joints.

"Indeed, your *vertebra prominens* is troubled," Dr. Chaucer nods.

"I wonder why," wonders Kosky.

"Is it perhaps because as a Jew I don't feel prominent enough after what was done to my people during World War II — and the anti-Semitism still prevailing today?"

"It's quite possible," says Dr. Chaucer. "Think of all the time devoted to the Holocaust and so many other *pogroms,* and not one prime-time TV program devoted to the spiritually most illustrious chapter of East European Jewish History," he says matter-of-factly.

"What else?" Kosky remains irritated by the obvious. In its traditional variant, Eastern Jewry had created a way of life that has been second to none in its ethical and moral standards. During the last century, it created modern Yiddish and Hebrew literature. It essentially contributed to the upbuilding of the American Jewish community and virtually alone built up the present-day Jewish community of Palestine. Within two generations, it gave the world at large many brilliant representatives of literature, art, and scholarship. It actively participated in the struggle for liberty in all countries of Eastern Europe. (Max Weinreich, YIVO, New York, 1946).

"Your Zones of Irritation of the Sacrum and the pelvis are irritated. Your sacroiliac joint is quite disturbed. Take care of your sacred sacrum without which you'll perish as a writer," says Dr. Chaucer as, ending his examination, he tactfully leaves the Actor vs. the Novelist.

"The fact is," says Peters, "that as long as Chance, your hero, lives inside your novel, most people don't know he exists. Let me play him on a big screen and your Mr. Arboretum will live forever."

"What if you or your film gets run over by the film critics who might not know who my character is, but who know only too well who you are? Who might, by now, think you're *too great to play my faceless Chance.* Too great, not too small. Forgive me for sorely testing your most sore point! Wouldn't an unknown actor—an unknown meaning 'spiritually pure'—be closer to my innocently unsinkable Fountainhead?"

"An unknown actor?" Peters grimaces. "Another John Doe? Another American version of the working class *Candide?*"

"Why not?" **If it was raining hundred-dollar bills, you'd be out looking for a dime you lost someplace. (Meet John Doe,** directed by Capra) 1941.[6]

Peters gets up from the the chair and paces around the terrace. "A John Doe would turn your Lotus man into Capra-corn. Besides, if your unknown Mr. Actor is, at his age, still unknown, it means he can't act. Worse yet, if he can't act or as an actor is not experienced enough to strip himself of all defences and appear innocent, he might overact in order to prove that, even though he's been unknown, he

---

[6]*Meet John Doe,* a film by Frank Capra, starring the utterly innocent Gary Cooper and the anything but innocent Barbara Stanwyck. In the first half of the film, everybody who meets John Doe wants to meet him again. In the second half of the film, after everybody reads what one newspaper had to say about him, nobody wants to meet him again. (George P. Flack, 1982)

sure can act. In this most innocent story, to act means to kill Chance's authentic simplicity. Simplicity which stems from his wisdom, not from ignorance."

"How then would you play him?" asks Kosky. **"The stage is a sacred object; . . . In theater, one does not listen; one receives."** Jean-Louis Barrault, *"Le Metier"* (craft, J. K.) *Espirit*, 1965.

"I would act actlessly. Also, I would *become* him. I would turn into him, into and in the role abandon being a pure *being"* — he points at himself — "a movie star." He gets up again from his chair and mindless of pain, walks around and through the garden, ready to milk milkwood and suckle the honeysuckle.

He is incapable of any of the defense mechanisms in which we have been trained, and expects everyone to respond to the simplicity with which he has learned to express himself. He stops a bewildered matron and says to her: "I am hungry" whereat she turns and flees. When he is accosted at knifepoint by a gang of teenagers he holds out his remote-control to turn off the ugly scene. (Dr. David H. C. Read, 1980)[7]

"Cut!" shouts Kosky, our literary offscreen director, just as a very young woman steps out from the half-opened door of the bedroom carrying in her hand *How to Give Yourself Relief From Pain, by the Simple Pressure of a Finger* (Dr. Roget Dalet, 1982). **The performance of an actor anchored to and built upon an object is one of cinema's most powerful constructions. (Pudovkin)**

---

[7]"Being There — In the Image of God": a sermon delivered by the Rev. Dr. David H. C. Read on January 13, 1980, at the Madison Avenue Presbyterian Church in New York.

14

"The swimming pool — a confined man-made environment — is a peculiarly late-20th-Century response to the Western ideal of freedom found in wide open spaces. It has become our place to dream . . . A vehicle for the descent into self, into that place where 'consciousness precedes being.' For it is in man's primordial connection to the essential element of water that sex and spirit co-exist — and memory mingles with dream. But it is also in man's nature for desire to exist." Nancy Jones, (1990).

Before leaving Los Angeles for New York, our past Oscar presenter presents himself at his motel's star-shaped swimming pool where, keeping his head above the water while craning his neck not unlike a Ruthenian crane, he hopes to present his floating act as a gift to the pool's lifeguard guarding him from the pool's edge. Clad in a mini-bikini, this blond donna, so spectacularly shaped, evokes in him the image of Donna de Varona,[1] the odalisque swimming queen who enslaves him in his wet dreams.

---

[1]See *Donna de Varona's Hydro-Aerobics* by Donna de Varona (the two-time Olympic gold-medal winner) and Barry Tarshis (1984).

Just then the phone rings at the pool's edge. The lovely donna answers it, then, reverently, brings it to him and tells him it is BEAU BRUMMEL HIMSELF WHO'S CALLING YOU. The way she hands him the phone and then discreetly walks away while looking him over by looking at him over her shoulder, tells him she has finally noticed in him a potential sexual marine.

"Hello, Norbert Kosky! You were great at the Oscars," Beau whispers on the phone in his Brummelian whisper.

"So were you," says Kosky modestly.

"With me it was not an accident," says Beau. **"Why don't you come up and see me sometime?" (Mae West)** he intones.

"When?" Our East Man can't wait to meet the male Mae West.

"Anytime you choose, but, if you don't mind, say, today, at six P.M.?"

The film studio of today is really the place of the sixteenth century. There one sees what Shakespeare saw: the absolute power of the tyrant, the courtiers, the flatterers, the jesters, the cunningly ambitious intriguers. There are fantastically beautiful women, there are incompetent favorites. There are great men who are suddenly disgraced. (Christopher Isherwood)

At six o'clock Kosky shows up at Brummel's own Brummel Annex at Parnassus Studios. Beau Brummel is not there. "He's been delayed by a young woman whom he had to see," says a secretary, a young woman whom he could have last seen naked, reaching out to him from pages 16–19 of the latest issue of the "for adults only" *Live!* magazine.

Will you accept three hundred per week to work for Paramount Pictures. All expenses paid. The three hundred is peanuts. Millions are to be grabbed out here and your only competition is idiots. Don't let this get around. (Herman J. Mankiewicz to Ben Hecht)

"I'm glad you could make it on such short notice," says

Brummel, injecting Kosky with a dose of Hollywood's instant ease. "The minute I saw you at the Oscars, I knew you were my man."

"I'm my own man, but I'm ready for a sacrifice," says Kosky. **The word does not express an idea, it creates it. (René Schwaeble)** He glances at the wall from where F. Scott Fitzgerald, Somerset Maugham, Maurice Maeterlinck and Faulkner look back at him from the photographs taken when they took to Hollywood and where most of them were taken.

"Not anymore," says Brummel, following Kosky's stare. "Hollywood wants you!"

"For a screen adaptation of my next novel?" Kosky reaches out.

"It's you I want, not your novel," exclaims Brummel. "I want you to be in *Total State,* a movie to be produced, written and directed by Beau Brummel and starring yours truly," says Brummel, modestly dropping his gaze.

"You want me to be what?"

"To be as visible as the verb to be. To be a full-line performer, not some dialogue-replacement artist. With your own credit line on the film's masthead, placed well above the name of the film makeup artist or even myself as this film's producer."

"Never mind the listing," says Kosky. "Tell me instead, how far below your name, as actor number one, my name will follow," asks Kosky.[2]

"Five lines below. How about being given number six? I want you to be a full-fledged American film actor, not another Ruthenian extra. When did you last act in the biggest Hollywood moral epic yet? Think what such experience

---

[2]Norbert Kosky, let it be said, was at that time already registered as a talk show "specialty act" with the American Federation of Television and Radio Artists (AFTRA), thanks to his book-promoting TV appearances. (Estate Editors).

might do for you as a man and as a writer."

"But I can't act. I can only instinctively react or act out."

"You certainly can reenact, can't you? That's all there is to acting."

"Reenact what?" Kosky becomes more eager to please.

"Something you've acted out many times."

"Reenact what?" Kosky persists.

"Something that would make the audience salivate. Create dramatic havoc regardless of whether you'll make a fool of yourself as an actor and me as your director or not."

"Reenact what?"

"Well — Brummel poses while pausing. "How about reenacting a scene, of, say, eating?"

"Eating whom?" ventures Kosky.

"Not whom, but what. Eating, say, onion and lemon. What my Studio Scouts (SS) tell me you eat with every meal and something every Russian revolutionary used to eat in order to fight not only the economic disease brought upon them by the Czar but also scurvy — a terrible gum disease."

"Done," says Kosky.

"O.K., then." Brummel settles the matter. "Be prepared to eat all the onion and lemon you can eat. A lot of it. Say, some twenty-five *takes* of it?"

"What's *Total State* about?" asks Kosky.

"The 1938 Moscow Purges: Doubletalk. Hypocrisy. Treason," Brummel whispers. "An epic film needs an epic budget. To make you look more epic, we'll pay your epic wages in Spanish pesetas accumulated in Spain by Parnassus Studios since the days of Lord Inquisitor Mendoza."

"Who are the film's other dramatic characters?" asks Kosky. **You don't have to keep making movies to remain a star. Once you become a star, you are always a star. (Mae Murray)**

"Andrew Delano Bullies, an American columnist covering these trials for the *Eastside Crier*. His wife, known as Red Flame. And Nikolai Bukharin. The Man on Trial." Nonchalantly, Brummel pulls from a folder a glossy black-and-white

266

photograph—a recent copy of an old photograph—and handing it to Kosky asks, "Does this picture ring a bell?"

"It does," says Kosky. The 1935 picture, well-known to those who at one time or another went to bed with history, shows TWO FRIENDS AT PLAY. The friends are Koba and Nicky, that is Stalin and Bukharin. Wearing only boxing shorts, socks, and semi-friendly smiles Stalin and Bukharin wrestle each other on a boxing mat in the Kremlin's own Gym. This wrestling match took place three years before Stalin had Bukharin executed and, by doing so had wrestled all the power from his Bukharinist opposition: (J. K.)

Kosky is about to ponder further the annals of modern hypocrisy disguised as history when a woman, as young and as pretty as was Anna Larina, Bukharin's wife (who, revolutionarily girlish was nineteen when he was fifty-two. J. K.), enters the room carrying a simple electronic steno pad in hand. Stunned by her beauty, Kosky calls her a stunning stenopad (SS) and wins another six hundred SS points. Silent, her eyes cast over her steno pad, she will remain for the rest of the time in the room.

"What about Bukharin? How much do you know about him?" Kosky retrieves the film-acting thread. **The literary man remains in essence an actor. (Nietzsche)**

"Not much. Except that, judging by his last 1938 photograph, you seem to resemble him strikingly," says Brummel. "What about you? How much do you know about him?"

"Enough!" says Kosky. . . . **Using a wide range of stylistic devices—irony, sarcasm, metaphor, hyperbole, similes, and rhetorical questions—Bukharin saturates his language with expressions borrowed from living folklore, salty words and phrases drawn from the depths of working-class conversation, or on other occasions, using strings of images borrowed from the finest literature (*Literary Encyclopedia*).** "To many members of my generation, Bukharin always has been an officially unmentionable hero."

"Quite right." Brummel nods, pulling out several other

photographs of Bukharin from his desk drawer. He hands them to Kosky. The pictures, once official party photos, show Bukharin as an editor of *Izvestia*, the State's main newspaper, addressing a Moscow workers' rally; Trotsky and Lenin embracing Bukharin; Bukharin reviewing a military parade; Bukharin in a Moscow park kissing his wife. Bukharin with an infant, his son, a picture taken in 1936, shortly before Bukharin's arrest, Bukharin leisurely walking with Maxim Gorky in a Moscow park; Bukharin with Boris Pasternak. Osip Mandelstam — all photographed at the First Congress of Soviet Writers. Finally Bukharin testifying in the Stalinist dock.

"My, my! Do you look like him!" says Brummel. "Now you can see why I think you should play him!"

"I was told I look more like Zinoviev,"[3] says Kosky looking into an oversized vanity mirror.

We shall be dealing in particular with the trial of Bukharin which took place from 2nd to 13th March 1938, (portrayed as Rubashov by Arthur Koestler in his novel *Darkness at Noon*). It is known that Rubashov has the physical traits of Zinoviev and the moral character of Bukharin. (Maurice Merleau-Ponty, 1947)

"You won't be the first writer to portray Bukharin, you know," says Brummel, "and I say it in order to encourage you, not to disillusion. Koestler did it in *Darkness at Noon*." He and the steno slut watch Kosky in silence. "I saw you at the Oscar Awards," says Brummel. "I knew something went wrong with your timing backstage — but whatever it was that

---

[3]Zinoviev: Lenin's "maid for all seasons," and, after Bukharin, Lenin's other closest associate. He was tried (with Kamenev) on charges of counterrevolutionary plotting in 1936 — two years ahead of Bukharin, Rykov and others — and executed, as were the others.

delayed you, you walked down those stairs and looked out at us with the arrogance of Bukharin. Wasn't that acting?"

"It was fear," says Kosky.

"If it was fear, then you mastered it. Master now the fear of acting. All you need to play Bukharin is to know the fear of Stalin, and the Stalinist State. All you need is to be yourself."

"I ran away from the total state out of fear. The fear of my Self becoming a collective," says Kosky. **This is just what this author has experienced: as suddenly it became clear that his acclimatization was relative and not absolute; that somewhere "in the well of his soul" lay, still alive, a desire for something other than could be supplied to him by that collectivized new world. (Joseph Novak, 1962)** "Why should I return to it—even if only in a movie?"

"If you're not free to act your fear out, you're still holding on to it," says Brummel. "In my movie, I want you to hold on to your very Self."

"To myself?" **I'm sure that sooner or later the filter of history will inevitably wash the dirt off my head. I've never been a traitor. [Bukharin]** Kosky gets up and paces the room. He is already acting. **You are going to be the first "natural" actress. (David O. Selznick to Ingrid Bergman)**

"In my script"—politely Brummel turns to his super-stenographer—"the movie opens with Bukharin being already aware he is No. 1 on the list of Stalin's enemies. He knows his days are numbered for him by Stalin, and he counts them, day by day. His account is made of fear."

"Who plays Bullies?" Kosky asks.

"I play him," says Brummel. "Think of all this as an adventure, a study in psycho-political contrast: Bullies can no more figure out Bukharin than I could figure you out."

"Will my scenes be filmed on location—in Russia?"

"Heavens no!" says Brummel. "You don't film a hanging in the hangman's house. All your scenes will be shot in Madrid."

"Madrid?" Kosky trembles. "Did you know that A. Lunacharsky, the man who published Dostoyevsky's *Notebooks*, one of Bukharin's closest associates, was assassinated en route to Madrid?"

Indeed he did. "So was André Amalrik, the Russian writer who wrote *Will Russia Survive Till 1984?*, who died in a mysterious car crash in Spain," says Brummel.

"Will I survive making your movie?" **Nothing can injure a man's writing if he's a first-rate writer. If a man is not a first-rate writer, there's not anything can help it much. (Faulkner)**

"Not only will you survive — you'll triumph," says Brummel.

"When do we start?" **Why do they want me to sign a contract for five years when I haven't even finished my first picture? (Garbo) I feel so sorry for you. (Garbo to her fans)**

"The sooner the better." Brummel glows.

15

I would give a hundred Hemingways for one Stendhal. (Camus)

In Madrid, Kosky is measured, fitted and clothed as Bukharin wearing replicas of Bukharin's original clothes made to measure by three Spanish tailors, who learn about the real life of Bukharin from the old photographs of Bukharin.

"The performance of an actor linked with an object and built upon it will be one of the most powerful methods of filmic construction." (Pudovkin). We have only to think of Chaplain to see the principle in operation. The dancing rolls in *The Gold Rush*, the supple cane, the globe dance in *The Great Dictator*, the feeding machine in *Modern Times*, . . . these are only isolated examples of Chaplin's endless facility for inventing new relationships with objects. (George Bluestone, *Novels into Film*, 1968).

PARNASSUS UNLIMITED Production OF TOTAL STATE
Director: Beau Brummel
Screenplay: Beau Brummel
Stand in: Mr. George Niskisko for Mr. Norbert Kosky.
Scene 96:

INTERIOR / DAY / NIKOLAI BUKHARIN'S EDITORIAL OFFICE IN *IZVESTIA* MOSCOW 1937

The room is large and impressive by Soviet standards, furnished with a mixture of pre-revolutionary furniture and Russian period pieces, modernistic by Soviet standards.

Sitting at the desk is NIKOLAI BUKHARIN. Fifty years old, of medium height, almost bald, he wears a mustache and beard and his favorite Revolutionary-style brown leather jacket.

Bukharin is in the process of correcting the latest galley proofs of *Izvestia,* (he does not know that, with his arrest imminent, this will be the last issue of this newspaper to be edited by him J. K.), which contains his own editorial, which will be the last published piece of writing to bear his name. (He does not know that either. J. K.) Bukharin rereads aloud the closing paragraph — "A network of deceit characteristic of fascist regimes" — and inserts a few corrections. The paragraph now reads, "A complicated network of decorative deceit in words and action is a highly essential characteristic of fascist regimes of all stamps and hues." Bukharin signs the galley proof, and with a sigh of anxiety pushes *Izvestia* aside.

He stares at his desk, cluttered with galleys, books, pamphlets, various documents and a stack of letters. On a platter, an omelet served peasant-style, with caviar, rests cold and untouched. Bukharin reviews the photographs. He glances at a mounted photograph of Anna, a stunning young woman who only four years earlier, at nineteen, had become Bukharin's common-law wife. Another picture shows her and Bukharin, the two of them holding a small boy, their only child.

Every revolution is paid for by certain attending evils, and it is only at that price that we can bring about the transition to higher forms of economic life of the revolutionary proletariat. . . . (Bukharin, 1921)

Stretching his back, Bukharin reaches for a German-Russian dictionary and opens it to a page.

BUKHARIN (murmuring to himself): The German words *Müssen, müssen* — in Russian, most clearly translate into *dolzhna,* in the sense of "should." But then the German language also has *sollen* — another word for "must," a must of a

272

different kind. Our new public is not yet ready for such fine and subtle moral distinctions. (He lifts his head and recites into the mirror.) And here I am, Comrades, ready to oppose Comrade Stalin — and to oppose him — him, as an enemy of the people. (He stops the public speech, then, no longer looking into the mirror, says as if speaking to someone else) And here I *ought to* — *ought* to or *must*? Should I substitute the word expose for oppose? But it is too late now. (Telephone rings. Jolted, Bukharin abruptly puts the dictionary aside and faces the phone. The phone rings again. Bukharin tenses, and remains still. Another ring. Bukharin rests his eyes on his revolver. The phone rings once more. Jerkily, Bukharin picks up the receiver.)

BUKHARIN: *Slyooshayou! Gavareet* Bukharin! Hello, Bukharin speaking . . . (He listens to the other voice and involuntarily stands up. Bukharin's lips turn dry and he keeps on licking them.)

BUKHARIN: Yes. (Pause) Yes, I understand. (Long pause) That can't be. Comrade Roginski must be wrong! (He loses his composure.) All three of them testified I had proposed it? Yakovleva too? But how could she? She knows it's a lie. It simply never happened! Are you sure she actually said it on her own — or was she perhaps coerced into saying it? (He listens to an answer.) Yes, of course. (He collects himself.) Tomorrow morning then: in your presence. (He replaces the receiver. Still rigid, Bukharin reluctantly lowers himself into the chair as if it were a bottomless well and as if the deep were about to claim him forever.)

For influence, in art, is always personal, seductive, perverse, imposing. . . . (Harold Bloom, 1975)

The telephone rings. Norbert Kosky, our American Nikolai Bukharin, interrupts his reading — he interrupts it both as he would, and hence, he assumes, as would Bukharin, a man of approximately Kosky's age — (and a writer, too. J. K.) He hesitates to answer it: there's always time for bad news. Finally, with finality obvious in his every movement, Bukharin picks up the receiver. "Hello? Bukharin speaking. . . ," says Bukharin. By now, to Kosky, the phone is as dead as Bukharin, but he must disregard such knowledge, and summon up his own brand of authentic apprehension, stemming from his own life in—and fear of—total state, this since, coming from Yezhov,[1] the head of the secret police, this telephone call must have been anything but dead to real-life Bukharin.

VYSHINSKY: That's what you claim. But Varvara Iakovleva says just the opposite. Does that mean she is telling a lie?

BUKHARIN: I don't agree with her, and I say that she is telling a lie.

VYSHINSKY: And is Mantsev also lying?

BUKHARIN: Yes, he too is lying. I am telling what I know, and it is up to them, their conscience, to tell what they know.

VYSHINSKY: But how do you explain the fact that three of your former accomplices are speaking against you?

BUKHARIN: See here, I don't have enough facts, either material or psychological, to shed light on that question.

VYSHINSKY: You cannot explain it.

BUKHARIN: It is not that I cannot, but simply that I refuse to explain it. (*Moscow Trials*)

After a few seconds of listening to the dead phone, our Bukharin—or is it Kosky? (only a movie director can tell.

---

[1]Newly appointed by Stalin as head of the NKVD, the all-powerful Soviet, Stalin-controlled, internal security agency, Yezhov "not only carried out Stalin's instructions but did so blindly and slavishly," writes Roy A. Medvedev in his *Nikolai Bukharin: The Last Years* (1980).

J. K.)—hangs up the receiver and sits down. Restless, he gets up, only to sit down again.

"CUT!" shouts Brummel. Instantly, the lights go off. Instantly, the cameras stop. Instantly Brummel leaves his directorial post and walks briskly toward Kosky. "Wow! This was good, Norbert, really good!" he says, patting Kosky on the shoulder. "Almost a classic. Almost. There was a definite apprehension in your picking up that receiver. Apprehension—yes, but not nervousness. Don't you think that, given what's been going on, after all, Bukharin knows he's being investigated—Bukharin would be nervous—and not merely anxious? He knows his whole life depends on what Yezhov is about to tell him. Doesn't he have a right to be worried?" he pauses and the instant he does, Kosky knowing what's at stake for Bukharin, Kosky knows his reenactment (reenactment, not acting. J. K.) requires another take. "Let's try again."

Brummel returns to his directorial seat. Another take. "CAMERA. ACTION!"

The phone rings. Bukharin won't pick it up. Not yet. He's too frightened. But wait a second—Kosky concentrates on the spiritual subtext of his acting—or is it now his acting out? He asks himeself: is Bukharin really frightened? Isn't Bukharin, by now, rather resigned to his fate? After all, by this time in his life he knows that he has been doomed. Either he must kill himself or be executed as a spy and saboteur on Stalin's orders. By now, he knows who the caller is. He knows it is Yezhov. The Soviet sub scoundrel (SSS), and Yezhov is synonymous with Stalin, not History. This call from Yezhov means death. Why must he talk to Yezhov? But then—why not? Isn't Yezhof, like everybody else, also subjected to death?

The phone rings again. And again. And again. You can almost hear Bukharin's wishful thinking: Maybe it is not Yezhov calling. Maybe it is Anna, Bukharin's wife? Or, better yet, a wrong number. Bukharin—but perhaps it was merely Kosky, not yet Bukharin?—picks up the receiver, but before he speaks into it, Brummel screams "CUT!" The action stops once more.

"That was good. I don't want to lose it and so, just in case, let's do it again, Norbert. Another take won't hurt!" Brummel speaks from behind the camera, while the makeup man powders Kosky's sweating face. Sweating, because, by now, Kosky knows that "I don't want to lose it!" Brummel's euphemism for "no good."

"But—" Kosky forgets about Bukharin. "Did I at least look upset? As upset—even sick to my stomach—as undoubtedly Bukharin must have been?"

"Upset—yes," says Brummel. "Restless—yes. Perhaps only upset, only restless—still not nervous enough. The issue is: Who is nervous? You, as an actor who's new to acting or is it that old Party hand Bukharin? Are you bothered, even worried, or concerned, about your performance in this or the next scene, or are you nervous as Bukharin, the man who now knows his life is over—but who doesn't know what to do with his knowledge. *Ought* he to kill himself, and save his reputation, or *must* he go on and face the farce of Stalinist trial? Must, or ought he—do it as a man or as an old revolutionary leader for the sake of the Party unity—even if this unity depends on sacrificing one's life for Stalin?" Brummel pauses. "Of course, should you choose to do it for me again, you might consider being even more nervous." He courts Kosky with all his "should" and "might." "By the time that phone rings," Brummel goes on, "Bukharin has already been interviewed many times by the NKVD. This is more than you've ever gone through. He knows that he's been caught in the NKVD's net of lies and denunciations—that his days are numbered—while all you worry about, Norbert, is your narrative numerology, your reviews, and your favorite number sixty-nine done with your latest sexual favorite in a sex club La Favorita." Brummel watches Kosky in silence, then says, "Never mind your own feelings: think of

Bukharin's actions; think the Magic If: What *if* that call were real? What *if* you *were* Bukharin? What *if* Bukharin had just received the most upsetting news? How would it affect him? How would he react? *Act* Bukharin, not Norbert Kosky. Think the Magic If."

"What if I can't forget what I already know about Bukharin's trial and execution, the knowledge Bukharin didn't have while answering that call from Yezhov. What if my Bukharin comes disguised as Rubashov from Arthur Koestler's *Darkness at Noon?* What if I can't forget the Magic If of history—of Bukharin's own magic?" **Who the hell am I supposed to be, anyhow? (Tallulah Bankhead)** asks Kosky, our magic man.

"You must forget what you know from History," Brummel cuts in from behind the camera. "When that phone rings again, know only what Bukharin did at the time. Think what you're about to do—don't think about what you feel. 'Act immediately,' says Stanislavsky. 'Proceed from yourself,' says Vakhtangov. You must transfer your temperament, as if it were blood, to Bukharin: you live within him, but the audience doesn't know it. All they see is Bukharin. You're not a method actor: in your acting, follow life, not the method. One more take then?" Brummel goes back to his post, and so does Kosky. **"It is not the consciousness of men that determines their existence, but . . . social existence (that) determines their consciousness."** (Karl Marx) **"Consciousness precedes being, and not the other way around . . ."** (Vaclav Havel, 1990.)

"Silence in the studio!" thunders Brummel. "Let my Tantric Bukharin concentrate! Are you ready, Comrade Bukharin? Remember: Yezhov's calling!" CAMERA—ACTION!"

16

Restless after ending his brief and mesmerizing film-acting stint, our stunt messiah keeps calling Voice Anonymous, his phone-answering service, at least twice a day, hoping for a message from a sexual messmate, a mute who would turn into a creative mess his suddenly overly orderly existence.

"You had several callers calling you, but only one of them left her name," says the anonymous answerette.

"Well?" Kosky pauses. *"Well — well — well?"* he intones.

"Well — what?" The answerette is impatient. "You had two anonymous male callers; one asked if you were in town, the other whether you were still alive. They did not seem friendly."

"Don't tell me anything without checking with me first," Kosky interrupts. "Voice Anonymous and I have legally agreed that you would pass on to me my messages only after you first asked me for a prearranged password. This, in order to verify that I — and not an imposter — will collect my messages. Didn't your supervisor tell you that the word *well* — repeated three times — is this week's password?"

I am made up of an intensest life — a principle of restlessness. Which would be all, have, see, know, taste, feel, all — This is myself. (Browning)

"I don't need to hear your password three times. Your

279

foreign accent is your best password." The answerette laughs.

"Who was the woman who called me?" asks Kosky.

"Emma Hart."

"Emma Hart? Are you sure?"

"Sure I'm sure. That's what she said."

"What else did Emma Hart say?"

"She said '**Ecstasy is a number. Baudelaire,**' but she left no number for it. Also she said she was coming down all the way to see her Leone Ebreo.[1] And she just hung up," says the answerette, as she herself hangs up on him.

. . . the relation between the forms we perceive and the soul itself is exactly the same as the relation between a book and its reader; when it perceives the letters, the soul recalls the denotation of those letters and their true significance. *The Fountain of Life,* Ibn Gabirol (Avicebron), 1069.

SS

With her telephone call, Cathy reenters his life as Shakti, the divine *dombi* of God Shiva, and brings with her the **permission of the prohibited.[2] (Judah Levi Toba) Shiva without Shakti is a corpse.[3] (Tantra)**

---

[1]Leone Ebreo (Judah Abranabel) a Spanish born Jew who, residing in Italy as a court physician, wrote in 1501 *Dialoghi D'Amore* (The Philosophy of Love)—the most comprehensive philosophical foot-teasing treatise on the nature of love, passion and desire. Written in vernacular Italian (though it is said the book could also have been written in Spanish, Ladino or Hebrew, the languages Ebreo was equally fluent in) the book became a worldwide sensation only in its Spanish-language translation in 1569. (English language edition, London, The Soncino Press, 1937).

[2]Judah Levi Toba (Dervish Effendi): a Jewish literary "dervish" who proclaimed "Freedom is the secret of the spiritual Torah."

[3]For the purpose of most secret tantric sex rites, women are

Emma Hart—her name is a literary code—is Mrs. Catherine ("Cathy") Hamilton Young, and on Kosky's mental slides, she appears portrayed as Goethe saw her first in his *Travels to Italy.* **Standing, kneeling, sitting, lying down, grave or sad, playful, exulting, repentant, wanton, menacing, anxious—all mental states follow rapidly one after another. . . . The old knight holds the light for her, and enters into the exhibition with his whole soul. This much at any rate is certain—the entertainment is unique. (Goethe)**[4]

Kosky places the phone in front of him on the desk. To call or not to call. Cathy is no longer a question: she is his spiritual sister (SS). **We think the act and it is done. (William James)** Cathy rules his will even from afar and after some nine hundred and sixty-nine days since he saw her last; this means he is not strong enough not to call her. She is both his *devidassi,* an ideal whore, and Devi, the goddess, either one capable of drinking **potions containing the semen of an enlightened master. (Philip Rawson)** He saw her first all base, on the bas-relief on the Devi Jagabamba Temple of Khajuraho, built—appropriately for this story—in the year 969. **How could an accumulation of adjectives or a rich-**

---

graded by men, and men by women, according to their spiritual, as well as ritual merit, each "spirit" sexually more advanced than the other.

[4]Johann Wolfgang von Goethe, author of *Faust,* "looked upon old age as something remote, frigid and disappointing. He was only twenty-five when he began *Faust* and forty-eight when he finished it in 1807." (Simone de Beauvoir, *The Coming of Age (La Vieillesse)* [1972]. See also Celebrating the Postwar Goethe, (in Aspen, Colo. in 1949. J. K.) "the greatest cultural festival of its kind ever held in our country." (Robert M. Hutchins, 1949) in Chapter 6 of *The Romance of Commerce and Culture,* by James Sloan Allen, Chicago, 1983.

ness of epithets help when one is faced with that splendiferous thing? For, under the imaginary table that separates me from my readers, don't we secretly clasp each other's hands? (Bruno Schulz, 1937, p. 1)[5] At another time he has been thinking about her—in the third person (and writing to her about their love making also in the third person) both in order to make such things easier to articulate—by seeing himself and her as protagonists who, depending on one another in life, exist independently of thinking which, like it or not, is always wishful. In such third person thinking he saw her as an Arab woman who wears *khimaar* and *thawb*—(and who is otherwise completely naked underneath). He then would see—in macro-photographic detail—lifting slowly her face veil, her *khimaar*, which actually falls well below her waist), and her long, loose-fitting dress—loose, yet fitting her better than any other dress he could think of—and lifting these domes of cloth with both hands, while making her stand immobile. She was his chosen Arabesque. And, undressing her in his thoughts, he kept recalling what The Penal Law of Islam (1988) has to say about (*Zinā*) "for an unmarried person punishment for fornication is one hundred stripes." (*zinā* also means adultery. J. K.)[6]

---

[5] From *Sanatorium Under the Sign of the Hourglass,* by Bruno Schulz (1937), translated by Celina Wieniewska, Introduction by John Updike, with 30 illustrations by the author, 1978. Also in *The Complete Fiction of Bruno Schulz,* op. cit. (1989) with never before published illustrations of Schulz. J.K.

[6] *The Penal Law of Islam*, by Muhammad Iqbal Siddiqi, New Delhi, 1988. Chapter 4: Adultery (Zina) Chapter 5: Fornication (Zina). See also, Stoning to Death of Non-Muslim in Case of Adultery: 'Abdullah b. 'Umar reported that a Jew and a Jewess were brought to Allah's Messenger (peace and blessings of Allah be upon him) who had committed adultery . . . ' Abdullah b. 'Umar said: I was one of those who stoned them, and I saw him (the Jew) protecting her (the Jewess with his body).

Cathy is his ideal sexual samovar (SS), with the word *sam* standing, let us recall again, for the Ruthenian self, and the word *ovar* for ovaries. She is the one who, an ideal sexual alchemist, for over a year has kept him on a steady diet of most perfect acclivity, generating in him, *day after day, night after night* the inner heat of the longest duration. She was an ideal *dombi*, one who, following his sexual free-floating with *evenly-hovering attention* (Freud, 1912), was faithful only to the drives of her own sexual self while belonging entirely to her lover; one who has gone through all he needs for his ideal sādhana,[7] and who has gone through it with zest'nd zeal, (ZZ) without a scream or a sleight. She is the one in whom, as in him, *orality as a sexual drive, not as a vital need, contains genitality* (Janine Chasseguet-Smirgel) Enough said though when he speaks of Cathy, nothing said about her seems to him to have been said enough. *Enough said:* (Jay Kay).

Not enough. Cathy transcends any fixed dimension. Her transcendentalist mother came from the bilingual Montreal, her father ("a bilingual bully," she calls him) from the bilingual New Orleans. "My mother wanted me to be Margaret Fuller,"[8] she told him once, "while my father opted for a new Adah Menken" — an "actress, dancer, poet and adventuress" (as described by Jeanette H. Foster).[9] Should he call her at

---

[7]"The most significant rituals of Tantrik sādhana are performed with women who have been specially initiated. What this initiation consists of has usually been kept secret and its reasoning hidden. There seems to be a variety of methods, perhaps used together." (*The Art of Tantra*, No. 68, p. 89)

[8]Margaret Fuller, "father-fixated" (Catherine Anthony), was the author of *Woman in the Nineteenth Century* and an intimate friend of Emerson, Carlyle and George Sand, the only woman she said she was in sexual love with.

[9]Adah Isaacs Menken was born either in Spain as Dolores Adios Fuertes, as her biographers claim, or in Louisiana as Adelaide

all? Should he call her and admit that his need of her still makes him uncontrolled as well as unfree—him, the royal yogi? That, since *"one can never know directly the contents of the 'unconscious'* (Freud) he has not resolved whether it was he who initially gave Cathy unlimited access to himself or Cathy who initated him up to no limit.

Busying himself consciously with various images of Cathy he dials her number and gets a busy signal.

He tries again and it is busy again. **Man being both bound and free, both limited and limitless, is anxious. Anxiety is the inevitable concomitant of the paradox of freedom and fitness in which man is involved. (Reinhold Niebuhr)** What if Cathy has taken the phone off the hook in order to hook herself to her little man in the kayak?"—her words for clitoris. What if she has taken it off the hook in order to hook her husband, or if her husband took it off in order to keep her in The Engorged State—uninterrupted— his way of taking her, or himself, off the sexual hook her words for love-making?

Kosky tries once again. This time the call goes through. On the ninth ring, "Hello, this is me. Who are you?" Cathy answers. Her voice finds Kosky voiceless. Subdued, Kosky apologizes for calling her so late but not for calling her.

Language is a skin; I knead my language against the other. It is as if I had words in place of fingers, or fingers at the tip of my words. My language vibrates with desire. (Roland Barthes)

McCord, as she does. A founder of the town newspaper in the town of Liberty, she contributed regularly to the *Cincinnati Israelite* and took liberties with a great number of great men of her time. She ended up her life at thirty-three—by then she was an intimate friend of Dumas, Swinburne, Gautier and Dickens. (Clement Wood)

"Oh, it's you! I hoped you would call me back," she says bit by bit sounding like a perfect Madame Salesmana — sounding him out.

"I saw you in *Total State*," says Cathy. "You looked good, Norbert. The voice of Bukharin suits you fine. So does his suit. You were always good at giving great phone. Will you act again — a bigger role, say, of a beggar — maybe also some better acting?" She sounds as if she and Kosky parted only the other day.

"I've got dozens of typecast offers. None exciting enough," he mocks. "In my next movie, I want to play either *The Wolf Man* (Freud) or de la Juan Cruz, a Latin lover."

"The Wolf Man, yes, I think of your W.W. II past, but a Latin lover? With your Esperanto looks?" She chuckles.

"Mind my mind, not my looks. Speaking of looks: have you retained your udderly splendid figure (udderly printer, as in woman's udders, not utterly)?" Kosky shifts small talk into another gear.

"Quite well. I bet I look better now than when you saw me last." Cathy does away with the passing of time. "What about you?"

"I'm getting bald. Time sags."

"Really?" She is not interested. "For some three years — or was it four? — I haven't read anything new about you — or by you. Are you by chance still writing?"

"By chance I am but no longer about chance or udder nonsense (udder, printer, not utter). What else but writing can I do from eight A.M. to five P.M. — and remain decent?"

"What is your opus going to be this time? Another cabaret of cruelty?"

"Another narrative bust, no doubt, but please don't knock the notion of the cabaret," says Kosky. "Where would literary entertainment be without burlesque, titter's titillation or vaudeville?"[10]

---

[10]"The doctrine of fair use allows the author to "take" — only

The work is in one movement. Six different timbres are used: flute-bassoon; clarinet-bass clarinet; trumpet-trombone; piano, harp; violin-cello (three different wind-instrument couples and three stringed instruments, struck, plucked and bowed). These six timbres merge into a single timbre: that of the piano (struck strings). (Karlheinz Stockhausen)

"Cabaret, burlesque, vaudeville? May I quote you?" she asks reminding him of her college days at Beulah where Cathy used to work as a free-lance reporter for the Scrubb's *Erostratus* magazine.

"You may. The literary work is not the mere reflection of a real, given collective consciousness, but the culmination at a very advanced level of coherence of tendencies peculiar to the consciousness of a particular group, a consciousness that must be conceived as a dynamic reality, orientated toward a certain state of equilibrium. (Lucien Goldmann, 1964)[11]

"In your faith, in the Jewish oral tradition, a quote is an extract and extract is poison. Isn't it?" she asks.

"It is, but not always. Not when the extract is used as a parable.[12] Not when it is used as a fictional footprint," he

---

for the purpose of burlesque — without fear of infringement, the locale, the theme, the plot as well as the character and dialogue of someone else's copyrighted work." (Courts)

[11] *Towards a Sociology of the Novel*, by Lucien Goldmann, 1964, translated from the French by Alan Sheridan, 1977, p. 9. Writes Goldmann: "The *social* character of the work resides above all in the fact that an individual can never establish by himself a coherent mental structure corresponding to what is called a 'world view.'

[12] "A scribe must provide a distinguishing mark for the section beginning *And it came to pass when the ark set forward*, both at its beginning and at its end, because it is a book on its own." *(Tractate Soferim)*

defends his *Fiction of Decomposition* (Kosky, in an interview, 1987).

"Oh, yes. Of course," she moans in jest. "I can already see your newest protagonist: a literary hitchhiker who like *Captain Wilder, T.N.* (Paul Horgan, 1990) gets all that intellectual mileage at no extra cost to the reader. Speaking of extra costs: are you still a triple-S: a single swinging swingle?" She puts stress on "still," not on "swingle."

"Terminally," he declares.

"Still living in that stateless 69th Street buoy?"

"Isn't my apartment stately enough?" he objects.

All he wanted was to get away as far as possible from Park Avenue, from the aesthetic jungles of the lion hunters, from the half-life of wealth and fashion. (Thomas Wolfe)

"It's a canoe, not an apartment. C'mon, Norbert! The war ended over fifty years ago, and you're over fifty-five. Men of your age routinely father children and grandchildren. They run governments and corporations. You've been listed in *LYP*[13] for years. Why don't you buy yourself a decent place somewhere in Boxbury or Martha's Graveyard, where other literary *Who's Whos* live?"

" 'Cause I've got other things to do and I'm late as it is," says our mini-Seneca. "By the time he was my age, Cagliostro was the best-known Freemason in the entire Free World."

"Careful now! You're well overdue. Balzac died at fifty-two. So did Cagliostro," Cathy interrupts him gently. Her mood shifts. "What are your plans?"

"To finish another novel, if there's enough spiritual spice (SS) in me! Spice as well as space!"

---

[13] *LYP: Literary Yellow Pages,* a directory of American poets, playwrights, essayists, editors and novelists published since 1960 by the American W.E.T. — the Association of Writers, Editors and Translators.

"And if there isn't?"

"I'll get a job selling the Book of Job in Salt Lake City. To be next to you." **You have rights regarding your wives and your wives have rights regarding you. (Termidhi and Ibn Majah)**[14]

"Are you kidding?" she says. "This is the Book of Mormon town. There are no witches in City Creek for you to go after!"[15]

"What about," he interrupts her gently. "You: my all-time Witch of Libido. The priestess of the Devi Temple of Oli, of womb fire."

"I'm married, remember? 'It's not good to be too free.' As a faithful wife, with no child to raise, I've been busy rewriting my past — and marriage." She sighs as if in pain. "By the way, the other day some people called asking me a couple of questions about you — and me."

"I'm glad there are people who still remember that you and I were a couple who once upon a time coupled. Who were they?"

"Two free-lance walkie-talkie reporters. They said they were doing a little piece about you (a literary 'floater par excellence,' they called you) for the *Crier* — or was it the *Courier* — or some newspaper like that."

"Good. My books could use some exposure. So could their author. What else?"

"They said they've chosen you for their split-profile of the year because of your star-quality; to them you are a typical Gemini," says Cathy.

---

[14]As quoted in *Handbook of Marriage in Islam,* by Dr. Abdullah Muhammad Khouj, Washington, 1987.

[15]The first Mormons were experts in using water from City Creek, and through irrigation, they initiated most agricultural enterprises in Utah. *(American History,* 1986)

"The stars impel, but not compel," our Gemini interrupts her, the typical Virgo.

"They said they singled you out because of your split astral background. They said that you can't be trusted!"

"Good for them. I'm a novelist, remember? Why should the Fourth Estate care whether Bovary was a Madame — or a madam in Flaubert's life?"

"And speaking of Madame Bovary," Cathy calmly goes on, "they said they believe I was portrayed in one of your novels as the girl called Nameless. They asked me whether I believe what you wrote about me was true. 'Don't believe a word he says,' I told them. 'His mind is a haunted tenement, stuffed with *Tailor's Dummies*, (Bruno Schulz) manikins and ballerinas, every one of whom is, I bet you, an 'autonomous phallus woman.' another version of Janine Chasseguet-Smirgel's 'the paternal penis woman.' ' "

"Good. Very good! I like that version or even vision of myself," says Kosky. "I hope they quote you in context."

Everything had been handed to him on a silver platter. I simply didn't like the man at all. Yet I didn't attack him; I simply quoted him. (A. J. Liebling)

"I'm sure they will. All they needed was my side of your story."

"What else did they say?"

"They said the Bible says that while a single witness won't do and can't do you in, three witnesses might. That they've already interviewed two other witnesses — numbers two and three. All they wanted to know is how you — a typical Gemini — work. Still and all, I was their witness number one." the earthy Virgo reassures the watery Gemini.

"What did you tell them?"

Once more: his own smithy is the only possible place for these developments — they cannot occur in the office of any editor whom Thomas Wolfe will ever know. (Bernard De Voto, 1936)

"Did I ever! I even told them" — she giggles — "how you and

289

I had first met. How, when I came to visit you—my professor—in your office, you said, with your European charm. 'It's quite warm in here. Why don't you take it all off, Miss Young?' "

" 'Take it off' meant your coat!" says Kosky.

Fictitious statements are examples of the courts' strong commitment to the principle that we should have unrestricted access to facts. If an author makes a fictitious statement or an erroneous statement, but *presents* it as factual, as the truth, the courts have ruled it must be treated as factual material, and that later authors have the right to use that material as if it really were factual. (Richard Danney, 1982)[16]

"It did not. You meant my clothes."

"I did not. When, hiding my geriatric crush on you," says Kosky, "I leave the room and return in less than a minute, a bottle of beer and two glasses in hand, I find you—" **Be in favor of bold beginnings. (Virgil)**

"You find your Lady of Shalott stripped and naked by the red'nd hot fire place and you don't so much as blink," she goes on, laughing. "You just hand me the glass and pour the beer, then practically burn my lips with yours—and set the rest of me and my bush, on fire."

It was marvellous to see Lord David dress a cock for the pit. Cocks lay hold of each other by the feathers, as men seize each other by the hair. Lord David, therefore, made his cock as bald as possible. With a pair of scissors he cut off all the tail feathers, and all the feathers on the head and shoulders as well as those on the neck. (Hugo)

"What are your plans now?" he intervenes on behalf of his

---

[16]See Authors League Symposium on Copyright, 1982, in the *Journal of the Copyright Bulletin*, 1982.

290

amrita. [17] **But there is also the clitorid, or sexual type of women. The whole matrix of their life is the physical and the lust for variety. (Maurice Chideckel)**

"First and foremost, to go after my divorce—my manuscript lost, so to speak. And then to finish *Manuscript Found,* my first novel—a sort of historical love story. [18] That is, if there's enough history or love in me," she says.

Kosky misses a heartbeat. "Divorce?"

"Well, yes, divorce! Rewriting of my marriage didn't work. The basic characters remain unchanged though their story is over. Over and out!" She sounds defeated.

"Divorce, then. But on what grounds?"

"Incompatibility. My husband has become overly orchitic. [19] The insecure bugger had our phone bugged and found out that I had a fling with a bartender. He couldn't take it and issued an ultimatum: either I get rid of my lover—or else. I've chosen 'or else.' I won't give up my sex life to rescue your pride, I said. Besides, good bartenders are hard to find." She laughs easily. "Who knows that better than you and I?" She livens up and goes on. "I'm separated from my husband, but I won't be free until after the divorce. Until I know where I stand—and on what."

"Do you stand alone now?" he asks tentatively.

"I live alone in the house, if that's what you mean, though I

---

[17] The head, the mystic moon, secretes *amrita,* which flows down in the body. As it reaches the abdomen, the fire of the mystic sun, situated near the navel, consumes it. The upturned tongue prevents the flow of *amrita.* (Tantra)

[18] "All one can do is to herd books into groups . . . and thus we get English literature into A B C; one, two, three; and lose all sense of what it's about." (Virginia Woolf)

[19] **The orchitic man corresponds to the uterine type of woman. . . . Normal coitus alone appeals to them. . . . The phallic type of man is exactly like the clitorid woman. In both**

know that what you mean is: do I have a lover? Yes, I do. By chance, he happens to be my divorce lawyer. Isn't it clever?" She is pleased with herself. "Who says the roles of advocate and witness are inconsistent?" She pauses. "It's good talking to you again, Norbert."

"Don't go—not yet!" He stresses "don't go."

"Would you want to see me?" she asks, stressing "want."

"I miss you," he bursts out. "I miss your company. You keep coming back to me through various back routes."

Love is the desire to prostitute oneself. There is, indeed, no exalted pleasure which cannot be related to prostitution. (Baudelaire)

"I miss you too, Norbert. You are my favorite sex misfit, and so I miss our fits. I miss my flood; I miss my *petit mort*. Though, in truth, I don't miss your tongue upturned, your para-epileptic *petit mal!*"

"And I thought my mal was *pas mal!* (not bad. J. K.) That it was *grand mal. Grand,* not *petit,*" Kosky moans in jest. **He was quite capable of deciding when the attack was over. These moments represented, down to the minute, an unusual speeding up of self-awareness—if the condition was to be named in one word—and at the same time of the direct sensation of life in the most condensed degree. (Dostoyevsky)**

"Let's say it was more mal than mort," she reassures him quickly.

"When will I see you, Cathy?"

Press the chin firmly against the chest, into the jugular notch as far as possible. Pull the spinal cord, work on the brain. (Tantra)

---

the greatest satisfaction in life is sexual congress with anyone to whom they are not married. How to prevent the mating of an orchitic man with a clitorid woman, or that of a uterine woman with a phallic man?" (Maurice Chideckel)

"I'm flying to New York for the weekend," she says. "I'll be at the Tarwater Hotel under the name Mrs. Flannery O'Connor.[20] Do you mind my impersonating one of your storytelling favorites?"

---

[20]Flannery O'Connor, "a storyteller of sexual water and fire (Niskisko)," is the author of, among other works, *The Violent Bear It Away.* "Water is a symbol of the kind of purification that God gives irrespective of our efforts or worthiness, and fire is the kind of purification we bring on ourselves." (Flannery O'Connor)

$$\boxed{17}$$

The Ruthenian-American Institute of Culture calls Kosky, with an urgent message. There has been a cultural mishap, they say. For reasons of health, or domestic politics, or both, Cardinal Gregor Starowyatr, the aged primate of Ruthenia, has canceled his forthcoming trip to North America, sending in his place a lesser-known, in the U.S., youthful cardinal, Viktor Essenes (pron. *Es-en-es)* who has been heading the Catholic church in Redore, Ruthenia's largest environment-poisoning, ore-manufacturing town. **As for the Old Testament, no Christian can read it consistently without subscribing to a recent pope's statement: "Spiritually we are all Semites." It is to the lasting glory of Judaism and Christianity that they have their roots in the Old and New Testament Scriptures, written so largely by Jews. No greater words have been penned than those of the Mosaic code and the Sermon on the Mount. (Billy Graham, 1985)[1]** Essenes has been nicknamed the Red Cardinal.

---

[1]From: *The Jesus Connection:* To Triumph Over Anti-Semitism, by Leonard C. Yasseen, with Introductions by Billy Graham, Theodore Hesburgh and Marc Tanenbaum, New York, 1985. (Indispensable Jewish cultural presence in America. J. K.)

Could Kosky meet with the Cardinal and, as his *cicerone*, either drive or walk him around mid-Manhattan, avoiding, at all costs, "going down on Gotham," an activity they know is so dear to the heart of our amoral Petronius.[2] (Gotham was the name by which Washington Irving writing in *Salmaguni Papers* first called Manhattan. J. K.) Our Petronius agrees, since, containing double SS, the Cardinal's name already suggests a spiritual sage as well as saga.[3] **I come as a pilgrim. (Pope John Paul II)**

The thought of meeting the Cardinal face to face unsettles his mind, then calmly sets it on *Nostra Aetate 1965* — the 1965 Declaration of the Vatican on the relationship of the Church to the Non-Christian Faiths — which states that "searching into its own mystery the Church comes upon the mystery of Israel." *(Nostra Aetate,* 1965)[4]

When I was a child, I sometimes wanted to be pope, but a military pope, and sometimes and actor. (Baudelaire).

A man of imposing youthful physique, Cardinal Essenes is a vegetarian and teetotaler; he is a spiritual descendant of Cardinal John Henry Newman, (d. 1890), that taleteller who authored *Apologia pro Vita Sua* and *Via Media*, his works about

---

[2]"Going Down on Gotham," Chapter 10 in *New York Unexpurgated*, by Petronius (1966), "an amoral guide for the jaded, tired, evil, non-conforming, corrupt, condemned and the curious."

[3]**The Essenes, a Jewish sect in the time of Christ, were vegetarians and teetotalers. Always dressed in white and devoted to contemplation and study, they took no part in public affairs. . . . These ascetics preached voluntary poverty, community of wealth and goods, and celibacy. (J. I. Rodale)**

[4]See *Stepping Stones to Further Jewish–Christian Relations,* an unabridged collection of Christian Documents; Stimulus Books, vol. 1: *Studies in Judaism and Christianity,* 1977. "The Road Ahead for Jews and Christians" by John Pawlikowski, in *The Priest,* 1987.

the necessity of mixing theology with the Self "mediated by media politics," (Jay Kay). Whether delivering a live sermon or a talk on a *Via Media,* the nation's newest TV talk show, Cardinal Essenes is a spellbinding storyteller who takes advantage of his poetic license.

We may call this speaker Pope, if we wish, but only if we remember that he always reveals himself as a character in a drama, not as a man confiding in us. (Maynard Mack)

An emotional man who understands the emotional role of the Church, Cardinal Essenes is quick to shake hands with an American union man, to kiss the forehead of a crying black child, to bless an old Hispanic woman, to console the sick and the dying. Each gesture shortens his distance from the common folks: by stepping down to them, he challenges his own spiritual charisma, and proves to himself—and others—that he is an ordinary mortal. Speaking to each other in Ruthenian, the Red Cardinal and Kosky walk through the steaming, teeming and so bilingually-Spanish-English streets of New York. To Kosky, a bilingual personality, each of the two languages, of his Ruthenian and English, is a time machine sending the mind back in time to a different spiritual storage. Hence, whenever Kosky, our *Water Witch* (J. F. Cooper) starts speaking Ruthenian, he instantly starts thinking in Ruthenian.

In the first place we are free to express our regret that Mr. James Fenimore Cooper has seen fit to make his novel (*Home As Found,* and *Homeward Bound,* both published in 1838 upon his return to the States from abroad. J. K.) **a vehicle for . . . promulgation of prejudice against his own country, her institutions, manners, customs, etc. (Knickbocker magazine)**

"I was told," says the Red Cardinal, "that soon after you arrived in America, you discarded the Ruthenian language, and have since written only in your own brand of Instant English. Haven't you been recently, at least tempted to write in Ruthenian your maternal tongue?"

"Tempted? yes. But a writer needs readers and for over thirty years I was kept away from visiting Ruthenia by the totalitarian Communists who totaled it. Meanwhile my parents, my last remaining blood relatives, died there — without me at their side or at their funeral and grave. For decades, the Ruthenian State owned publishing Party apparatus would not publish anything with my name on it other than anti-Jewish rumoroids."

The first amendment and similar provisions in state constitutions were apparently originally intended to embody the Blackstonian notion that freedom of the press means freedom from prior restraints, not freedom from liability for what has already been printed. (From L. Levy, *The Legacy of Suppression*, (1960). The correspondence between John Adams and Massachusetts Chief Justice William Cushing in 1789 as quoted by Dorothy J. Glancy, op. cit.)

"But now things changed! Ruthenia is again a free and democratic republic. And, once again, her Church triumphs with its primate as the country's prime mover!" the Cardinal opens his arms as if garnering between them the spiritual nobility of spouseless priesthood as espoused by Max Scheler, (d. 1928), then folds his arms piously. "Today, with you physically present at their publication in Ruthenia and appearing in person on Ruthenian television, your novels are appearing in Ruthenia one after another, translated into contemporary Ruthenian by Ruthenian writers who are masters of Ruthenian narrative, as well as the art of translation."

"Indeed, your Eminence," Kosky agrees tactfully. **Nothing could have been more flattering to Cagliostro than the welcome he received on his arrival in Warsaw in May 1780. Poland was one of the strongholds of Freemasonry and occultism.** (Trowbridge, 1910) "I am even lucky enough to attract in Ruthenia the attention of the newly opened Ruthenian Republic Club. One of its first public pronouncements was to declare me a National Calumniator and ask the

298

Ministry of Culture to ban me from entering Ruthenia for the length of my natural life! I guess for them this is a test for the newly won in Ruthenia freedom of expression!" He hides his conviction that in a truly free state nobody must be free to turn into a convict the free play of imagination.

"With Communists safely gone, call these pseudo-Republicans Ruthenian Khomeinists," (Khomeinists, not humanists, Printer!) the Cardinal laughs good naturedly, while our literary Sword Swallower (SS) swallows the argument with some difficulty.

This is of its kinds, a remarkable article, and should not be suffered to drift away unobserved on that foul current of republican abuse and calumny to which it belongs. It is worth while to catch hold of the vile thing — pulling it forth with a pitchfork — and exposing the intricate texture of its black web; — the materials being spite, envy, hatred of order, and of all deservedly exalted characters; hatred, too, of the best efforts of successful genius; and the whole production brought out for effect, under a pretended zeal for "principle." (*Fraser's Magazine*, XIX, 1839 about Cooper's article. J. K.)

"In spite of that, which one of the many spiritual and cultural currents currently flowing through Free Ruthenia matters to you most?" asks the Cardinal, as the two men pass by an imposing bronze statue of Sir Walter Scott.

"Freedom of expression. The ultimate feast and test of any democracy, your Eminence. Thus the American literary clerk in me rebels against a zealous clerical Ruthenian cloak: (Cloak, not choke, Printer!) For instance, as a naturalized American, I am naturally suspicious of introduction of religion, and of a country's dominant religion at that — into the public school system in all of Ruthenia as an obligatory subject. As if teaching religion on a voluntary basis in churches wasn't enough."

"You're speaking of Ruthenia. Ruthenia: a thousand-year-old country where religion is our historical clock as well as spiritual cloak." The Cardinal puts stress on the word Ruthenia, then goes on. "With Communists gone, this clock must no longer be hidden like the hidden clockwork on the Golden Globe calendar made for Nicolaus Copernicus in 1410 and now in the possession of Collegium Maius at the Jagiellonian University in Cracow, the oldest academic seat in Europe." (Like Copernicus, the Cardinal is an alumnus of the Jagellonian University. J. K.)

"I too am speaking of Ruthenia. Of pursuit of happiness there, your Eminence." In his own homily Kosky attempts to remain *homiletikos* (Gr. nice, social). "I am talking about Ruthenia where many religious minorities have resided for centuries — and many still are. Isn't Ruthenia universal and adept enough to fully adopt the Universal Declaration of Human Rights? Its Article 1 says: 'All human beings are born free and equal in dignity and rights.' What about 'Equal protection' of its Article 7? Its Article 17 stating clearly that 'Everyone has the right to own property'? Aren't one's beliefs private in Ruthenia? What of Article 18 protecting 'freedom of thought, conscience and religion.' What of 'freedom of opinion and expression' contained in Article 19? What about *The Right to Privacy*.[5] Why in Ruthenia, finally free of the deadly marxist dogma must religion *not* be private? In the very Ruthenia where the Government has only now privatized just about everything — and where churches are also private and belong to the Curia? Why *must* religion be taught for two hours a week in every public school — *must*, as not so long ago was the Marxist dogma — on Total Party's orders?" **Here he is, Comte de Cagliostro walking through the streets of French Strassburg. One fine day in September, 1780 . . . fresh from his triumphs in Poland where he established a number of his lodges of Egyptian Freema-**

---

[5] *The Right to Privacy*, by Samuel D. Warren and Louis D. Brandeis, [1890] (of both of Warren and Brandeis law firm in Boston, J. K.). Consult also *The Invention of the Right to Privacy*, by Dorothy J. Glancy, Arizona Law Review, 1979.

sonry, and had gained much fame as a necromancer and a medical empiric. And walking not alone, but with the most powerful man in France: Cardinal de Rohan. (Henry Ridgely Evans, Litt. D.).[6]

Cutting across another alley of Central Park, the Cardinal and our Cagliostro stop at the Central Park Zoo. There, like everyone else, they watch the baboons. Catching sight of the Cardinal's black soutane, one of the famous trio of black baboons begins to mimic him. While the Cardinal laughs his head off, the zookeeper reprimands the baboon by hitting him over the head with a stick. Understanding nothing, the black baboon begins to imitate the zookeeper — and promptly starts hitting on the head another baboon with a stick of his own.

On the street, an old beggar with a face of a conquered conquistador — conquered by some incurable disease — asks the Cardinal for an instant cure. Unable to cure him on the spot, the Cardinal blesses him instead; weeping, the beggar falls on his knees and kisses the Cardinal's hand.

Kosky and the Cardinal keep on walking. They stop on the corner of West 69th Street, at the newsstand where Kosky buys his newspaper and magazines.

Says Kosky, catching the Cardinal's troubled stare, a stare resting, momentarily, on varied and various adult magazines, the names of which, *Lady Bellaston, Harlot, Potiphar's*

---

[6]"Fantastic stories were circulated about him. The Cardinal de Rohan selected and furnished a house for him and visited him three or four times a week, arriving at dinner time and remaining until an advanced hour in the night. It was said that the great Cardinal assisted the sorcerer in his labors, and many persons spoke of the mysterious laboratory where gold bubbled and diamonds sparkled in crucibles brought to a white heat. But nobody except Cagliostro, and perhaps the Cardinal, ever entered that mysterious laboratory." Henry Ridgely Evans, Litt. D., in "The Conjurer and the Cardinal," in *Cagliostro, Sorcerer of the Eighteenth Century,* op. cit.

Wife, Sade'nd Masoch, Silkstocking, (do not confuse with Cooper's Leatherstocking. J. K.) *Roue, Rakish Tales* and *Philanderer.* All this involuntarily bring to mind Index Librorum Prohibitorum and the most imaginative torture inducing and crowd-pleasing unholy instruments of the Holy Inquisition. "Their presence is guaranteed to us by our First Amendment," says Kosky glancing off-handedly at the Sex'nd Shock stack, the portions of naked flesh portrayed on their hard core covers stare him face-to-face. (Say buttock-to-face, pleads Jay Kay—a plea hard to ignore. J. K.)

"Such is the troubled but free sex life of our Miss Liberty. I support wholeheartedly, The First Amendment even though, in my book, being first or number one stands for A, or Aleph, for a man seen as a collective unity—and by nature I'm most anti-collective."

Being is a mystery, being is concealment, but there is meaning beyond the mystery. The meaning beyond the mystery seeks to come to expression. The destiny of human beings is to articulate what is concealed. The divine seeks to be disclosed in the human. (Abraham Joshua Heschel, *Who Is Man,* **1965)**

The Cardinal and Kosky have just been noticed by the vendor. If looks matter, and they do, this man could not look more Jewish. In fact he looks like a bit younger Chairman Rumkowski[7] (the very Rumkowski who's been on Kosky's mind quite independently of what had been said or written about this most complex man by other luminaries of literary fiction and fictionalized history. The Vendor is a chubby

---

[7]Chaim Mordechai Rumkowski was the Jewish chairman of the Nazi ghetto in Łodz, Poland, a man charged with responsibility no other Jew was ever charged with. *The Chronicle of the Łódź Ghetto 1941–1944,* ed. by Lucjan Dobroszycki, Yale University Press, 1984.

"As his name alone indicates—how can you fail with "rum" in your name?—Rumkowski has been a subject of a great many rumors." (Jay Kay).

cherub with a round face and curly hair, always in control and a bit patronizing. He steps out from behind his stand to greet the two men as if he were a ruling Israeli monarch and they the Ruthenian-Jewish pilgrims. At the sight of the Ruthenian Cardinal and the sound of the Ruthenian language,[8] the vendor opens up like a Yiddish flower.

"My name is now Yankel Jacob, but in the old days when I lived on Gas Street in Łodz, and like every Jew there, spoke nothing but Yiddish, my name was Jakob Jankiel Levy. One of my ancestors—Yod, bless his soul! his name was Asser Levy—departed from Ruthenia for North America far ahead of me. So far ahead he became the very first Jew in the history of America who bought himself a brand new house in New Amsterdam, as Manhattan used to be called in 1661 when this Jewish record was set by him: Asser Levy—the very first American Jewish homeowner—Ashkenazi Jew, at that, not some Jewish Sephardim *hidalgo* from Spain![9] Not bad, not bad at all!" For a moment, he rejoices over Jewish victorious march through history. "Tell me, your Omenance, (Printer: he said omenance not I. J. K.) in your prayers, do you ever pray for us—the Jews who were forced to depart at one time or another from a place they called home—as I was in 1969—from the one and only Ruthenia?"

"Indeed I do. In every Mass for the Faithful Departed," says the Eminence. "And in my prayers I quote from the two books written about Judas Maccabaeus by the original ghost-writers of the Old Testament. They constitute the sacred evidence for the existence of Purgatory—and where would

---

[8]The primarily agricultural Ruthenians speak a dialect intermediate between Polish and Russian. "They are a sturdy people, well built and muscular." (Louise A. Boyd, op. cit., 1937)

[9]As verified by *New Amsterdam: The Last Stop*, Chapter 1. See *The Jews in America. Four Centuries of an Uneasy Encounter: A History*, by Arthur Hertzberg, 1989.

Thomas More be without it?"[10]

While Yankel lights his inner menorah, the Cardinal keeps on glancing at the newsstand's impressive array of tabloids and magazines. Kosky follows his glance. Their respective glances irrespectively stop at the shameless cover of *Fatican Flesh* magazine (Fatican as in fat, not Vatican), on which, a shamefully sexy Ava Maria Cardinale sprawls stark naked on top of some Health Spa bodyweight reducing rowboat like Rowing Machine.

"Even the sanctity of an altar won't stop these incorrigible porn makers," says the Cardinal. "Will they ever be stopped from growing such shameless harvests?"

"Let's hope never," says Kosky.

"It's smutty stuff (SS) read only by the sex-starved (SS) by people who have nothing better to do with their time than stare at pictures — rather than read books or play chess," says Yankel.

"Still, there ought to be a way of limiting its impact on the innocent at heart," wonders the Cardinal. "Perhaps some form of prior restraint?"

"Prior restraint is censorship à priori. Censorship is censorship, wherever it comes from. Today we ban the organs, tomorrow the organists,"[11] says Kosky.

Sexual modesty cannot then in any simple way be identified with the use of clothing. . . . The most we can say

---

[10]More's defense of the existence of Purgatory was taken by the reformers to be exactly on a level with his description of Utopia: one was as imaginary as the other, and More lied by claiming either existed. (Robert C. Elliott, *The Literary Persona*, op. cit.)

[11]"Organ: The introduction of the o. into the Sabbath synagogue service became a controversial issue between the Orthodox and the Reform movements in the nineteenth century. . . . The o. became usual in Reform and some Conservative services. It is also found in many Italian and French synagogues. In the West, it came to be used for wedding and other weekday services, even in Orthodox congregations." *The Concise Jewish Encyclopedia,* op. cit.

is that a tendency to cover the body and those parts of the body which declare it male or female goes together with sexual shame but is not an essential feature of it. (Karol Wojtyla)[12]

September 4
This is, for Kosky, the most troubling anniversary: a D-day marked forever in his Jewish history. This is the day when, back in 1942, turning his back on past and future history, Chairman Rumkowski, the famously infamous (or the other way around) Polish-Jewish chairman of the ghetto in Łodz,[13] addressed some two thousand of his fellow Jews over the German-made microphone. Speaking in Yiddish, Rumkowski asked his fellow inmates for a sacrifice which he considered essential to the preservation of life.

For: *Łodz Ghetto* (a film)
Sample Script: READER: NORBERT KOSKY[14]
Text: Word for word as Rumkowski spoke it. (Plus'nd minus the liberties of translation: J.K.)
PRINTER: Kindly set the following text in spiritually strong caps. Break the paragraphs as often as you can, in order to leave space'nd scene for tears and choked voice and sneezing

---

[12]*Love and Responsibility,* by Karol Wojtyla (Pope John Paul II).
[13]Łodz, (sp. Łódź, pron. woodz) (Poland's second largest city, one of the world's largest textile making centers, has also been a formidable center of arts, crafts and filmmaking. J. K.)
[14]ATTENTION: All but two members of Norbert Kosky's once numerous family perished in the ghetto of Łodz. (ESTATE EDITORS) "During a visit to Łodz, Eichmann witnessed the gassing of 1,000 Jews in sealed buses." From *The Nazis:* World War II, by Robert Edwin Herzstein and the Editors of Time-Life Books, 1980.
(Until 1939, next to Warsaw, some 120 km away Łodz was the seat of the largest Jewish community in the world. Today, some two hundred thousand Jewish tombs — with many conceived as lasting works of art — and the largest Jewish funeral house in the world testify to Jewish presence there. J. K.)

and coughing—the various, most dramatic acts of Chairman Rumkowski which break his speech. Since Chairman Rumkowski was a most effective public speaker, there is no way of assessing today whether these were either natural acts or an artificial display.

RUMKOWSKI (addressing the ghetto inmates in front of the ghetto fire station) Łodz.[15]

RUMKOWSKI:

THE GHETTO HAS BEEN AFFLICTED WITH A GREAT SORROW. WE ARE BEING ASKED TO GIVE UP THE BEST WE POSSESS — CHILDREN AND OLD PEOPLE. I WAS NOT PRIVILEGED TO HAVE A CHILD OF MY OWN AND SO I DEVOTED THE BEST YEARS OF MY LIFE FOR THE SAKE OF THE CHILD.

I NEVER WOULD HAVE IMAGINED THAT MY HANDS WOULD DELIVER THE SACRIFICE TO THE ALTAR.

IN MY OLD AGE I MUST STRETCH FORTH MY ARMS AND BEG: BROTHERS AND SISTERS, YIELD THEM TO ME! FATHERS AND MOTHERS, YIELD ME YOUR CHILDREN!

YESTERDAY AFTERNOON, I WAS GIVEN AN ORDER TO DEPORT SOME 20,000 JEWS FROM THE GHETTO. IF NOT, THEY WOULD DO IT.

THE QUESTION AROSE: SHOULD WE TAKE IT OVER, DO IT OURSELVES, OR LEAVE IT FOR OTHERS TO CARRY OUT? WE—THAT IS I AND MY CLOSEST COLLEAGUES—CONCLUDED THAT HOWEVER DIFFICULT IT WOULD BE FOR US, WE WOULD HAVE TO TAKE OVER THE RESPONSIBILITY.

I HAVE TO CARRY OUT THIS DIFFICULT AND BLOODY OPERATION.

I HAVE TO CUT OFF LIMBS IN ORDER TO SAVE THE BODY![16]

---

[15](EDITOR: Do not change. This is the REAL speech. J. K.)
[16]For further cannonade of Jewish legal arguments both for and against certain interpretation of the Jewish canon of never yielding to the requests for Jewish victims the delivery of whom would save further Jewish victims, the reader is referred to *Collaboration with*

I HAVE TO TAKE CHILDREN BECAUSE OTHERWISE — GOD FORBID — OTHERS WILL BE TAKEN.

I HAVE NOT COME TO COMFORT YOU, NOR HAVE I COME TO SET YOUR HEARTS AT EASE, BUT TO UNCOVER YOUR FULL GRIEF AND WOE.

I HAVE COME LIKE A THIEF TO TAKE YOUR DEAREST POSSESSIONS FROM YOUR HEARTS.

I LEFT NO STONE UNTURNED IN MY EFFORTS TO GET THE ORDER ANNULLED, BUT WHEN THIS WAS IMPOSSIBLE, I TRIED TO MITIGATE IT.

I SUCCEEDED IN ONE THING — SAVING ALL THE CHILDREN BEYOND THE AGE OF TEN.

LET THIS BE A COMFORT IN OUR GRAVE SORROW.

PERHAPS THIS PLAN IS DEVILISH, PERHAPS NOT, BUT I CANNOT HOLD BACK FROM UTTERING IT. "GIVE ME THE SICK AND IN THEIR PLACE, WE CAN RESCUE THE HEALTHY."

I COULD NOT MULL THE PROBLEM FOR LONG. I WAS FORCED TO DECIDE IN FAVOR OF THE WELL MAN.

I CAN UNDERSTAND YOU, MOTHERS, I SEE YOUR TEARS. I CAN ALSO FEEL YOUR HEARTS, FATHERS, WHO TOMORROW, AFTER YOUR CHILDREN HAVE BEEN TAKEN FROM YOU, WILL BE GOING TO WORK, WHEN JUST YESTERDAY YOU HAD BEEN PLAYING WITH YOUR DEAR LITTLE CHILDREN.

I KNOW ALL THIS AND I SYMPATHIZE WITH IT.

SINCE FOUR P.M. YESTERDAY, UPON HEARING THE DECREE, I HAVE UTTERLY COLLAPSED.

I LIVE WITH YOUR GRIEF AND YOUR SORROW TORMENTS ME.

I DON'T KNOW HOW AND WITH WHAT STRENGTH I CAN LIVE THROUGH IT.

I MUST TELL YOU A SECRET. THEY DEMANDED 24,000 VICTIMS. BUT I SUCCEEDED IN GETTING THEM TO REDUCE

Tyranny in Rabbinic Law by David Daube. Oxford University Press, 1965. Also, do read *Here Too As in Jerusalem*, Selected Poems of the Ghetto, Translated and Introduced by Adam Gillon, *The Polish Review*, New York, 1965.

THE NUMBER TO 20,000, AND PERHAPS EVEN FEWER THAN 20,000.

BUT ONLY ON CONDITION THAT THESE WILL BE CHILDREN UP TO THE AGE OF TEN.

CHILDREN OVER TEN ARE SAFE.

WE WILL HAVE TO MEET THE QUOTA BY ADDING THE SICK AS WELL.

YOU SEE BEFORE YOU A BROKEN MAN. DON'T ENVY ME. THIS IS THE MOST DIFFICULT ORDER THAT I HAVE EVER HAD TO CARRY OUT. I REACH OUT TO YOU MY BROKEN AND TREMBLING HANDS, AND I BEG YOU:

GIVE INTO MY HANDS THE VICTIMS.

HAND THEM OVER TO ME, SO THAT WE WILL AVOID HAVING FURTHER VICTIMS . . . AND A POPULATION OF A HUNDRED THOUSAND JEWS BE PRESERVED.

SO THEY PROMISED ME. IF WE DELIVER OUR VICTIMS BY OURSELVES, THERE WILL BE PEACE.

SHOUTS FROM THE CROWD:

WE WILL ALL GO! MISTER PRESIDENT, *ONLY* CHILDREN SHOULD NOT BE TAKEN. TAKE ONE CHILD FROM THOSE PARENTS WHO HAVE SEVERAL![17]

RUMKOWSKI:

THESE ARE EMPTY PHRASES. I DO NOT FEEL STRONG ENOUGH TO ARGUE WITH YOU. IF SOMEONE OF THE AUTHORITIES ARRIVES, NONE OF YOU WILL SHOUT.

I IMPLORED ON MY KNEES, BUT IT DID NOT WORK. FROM SMALL HAMLETS WITH A JEWISH POPULATION OF SEVEN AND EIGHT THOUSAND, BARELY A THOUSAND ARRIVED HERE, SO WHAT IS BETTER, THAT EIGHTY OR NINETY THOUSAND JEWS REMAIN, OR THAT, GOD FORBID, THE WHOLE POPULATION BE EXTINGUISHED?

---

[17]There are many fictional and nonfictional works written about Rumkowski. Whether exact or not they are all most exacting since they desperately try to account for his reign of warmth, "as well as for his pro-forma reign of terror." (Jay Kay)

ONE NEEDS TO HAVE THE HEART OF A BANDIT TO ASK FROM YOU WHAT I AM ASKING. BUT PUT YOURSELF IN MY PLACE, THINK LOGICALLY AND YOU WILL REACH THE CONCLUSION THAT I COULD NOT PROCEED OTHERWISE.

THE PART THAT CAN BE SAVED IS MUCH BIGGER THAN THE PART THAT MUST BE GIVEN AWAY.

Having finished with this most painful text—the reading as well as correcting in the galley proofs—which leaves him morally exhausted, Kosky annotates it with the following footnote:

Whenever Rumkowski spoke publicly in the ghetto—and he spoke publicly often—he always spoke with the authority of a feudal lord: the first Jewish feudal lord in history! **I will remove the troublemakers and agitators from the ghetto and not because I tremble for my life, but because I fear for you all. You have to be protected; as for me, my hair is white as snow, I walk with a stoop—my life is already behind me! (Rumkowski, 1943)**

In Norbert Kosky's manuscript of *"The Healer,"* (comments Jay Kay) in the text proper. (J. K.)

Rumkowski could proceed otherwise. Like any other regular ghetto-*dweller*, Rumkowski could have gotten rid of his job very easily. All he had to do was to improve on the example set for him on October 19, 1943, by a Jewish woman named Łaja.

Tuesday, October 19, 1943
SUICIDE ATTEMPT
On October 18, Łaja Krumholz, born in Łódź in 1920 and residing at 9 Wawelska Street, attempted suicide by swallowing a sleep-inducing drug. She was taken to the hospital by the Emergency Service. *(The Ghetto Chronicles)*

It is said that in his various speeches and remarks in the Łodz Ghetto—ironically and tragically, one of the largest Jewish communities—Chairman Rumkowski would occasionally refer to it as "My mini-Jewish State."

I have no faith in the political virtue of our people,

because we are no different from the rest of modern men and because freedom would at first make our heads swell. I consider government by referendum inadequate, for in politics there are no simple questions which can be answered merely by Yes or No. Also, the masses are more prone even than parliaments to be misled by fantastic ideas and to lend a willing ear to every ranting demogogue. Neither internal nor external policy can be formulated in popular assembly.

Politics must work from the top down. (*The Jewish State* [*Der Judenstaat*] by Theodor Herzl [1860–1904], with an Introduction by Joseph Adler, New York, 1970)[18]

---

[18]See *The Labyrinth of Exile:* A Life of Theodor Herzl by Ernst Pawel, New York, 1989. Also the review of the above book: "The Private Life of A National Builder, by Peter Loewenberg, *The New York Times Book Review,* Dec. 31, 1989.

18

This is the time Kosky reserves for the Other. This time the Other is Barza Omadi, a writer, playwright and essayist from Indostran whom Kosky invited for a meeting, their first, in Kosky's apartment.

Some six years earlier, Omadi, one of his country's intellectual ayatollahs, was arrested by PERSAUD, Indostran's secret service, on charges of ideological conspiracy and was kept in solitary confinement without trial. Once again, that is why in order to avoid similar fate, Kosky left Ruthenia, back in 1957. Now, asks the American Reader, why did he leave Ruthenia? Here, rather than answer it in his own words, that is fictionally, Kosky prefers to tell the truth (and nothing but the truth. J. K.) and to answer it with the words of Thomas Wolfe, who, also has always been a *Fugitive from Utopia*. (Stanislaw Baranczak, 1987)[1] "To love the earth you know, for greater knowing; to lose the life you have, for greater life; to

---

[1] *Fugitive From Utopia:* The Poetry of Zbigniew Herbert by Stanislaw Baranczak, Harvard, 1987. Zbigniew Herbert "a masterful Polish poet, masterfully translated into English by many masters of English language" (Jay Kay), was the first recipient of the Bruno Schulz Literary Prize awarded by the Jewish Presence Foundation and PEN-American Center. J. K.

leave the friends you loved, for greater loving; to find a land more kind than home more large than earth . . ." (*You Can't Go Home Again.*) In any case, while Kosky left Ruthenia on his own, Omadi was finally released from his prison. He too passed the imprisonment, the ultimate freedom test and was allowed to come to the United States at the invitation of Bakunin University in Kropotkin, Hawaii.

Santos, the doorman at the Manfred, rings Kosky on the house phone to announce the visitor.

"A most strange-looking stranger is here to see you, *Señor*," he whispers, "but he won't give me his name."

"Have you heard of the American Right to Privacy? It's *his* name," says Kosky. "Why should he give it to a stranger like you? Ask him to come up."

In a moment, the until now amorphous Omadi materializes at the door to Kosky's apartment, and enters it with some hesitation. He, who until now was known to Kosky only by his writing—his writing denoting, *nota bene,* the presence of the Islamic anarchic persona—becomes now a real-life person. The person is of middle height, middle age and wears nondescript looks of a most accomplished literary conscript. While Kosky and Omadi resemble one another a bit— Kosky's face could feasibly belong to Omadi (though not the other way around) they also could not be more different. Omadi is a writer *engagé* on the side of the politically predefined left or right—not merely on the side of the always individually defined RIGHT OR WRONG.

"Omadi is the Marxist Tolstoy fighting the Church of the Repressive State. Kosky is a Dostoyevskian version of Omadi. Enough said," (says Jay Kay.)[2] A climactic moment: confronting Kosky, (who, until now was an American abstraction to him. J. K.) Omadi bends his torso in a bow and,

---

[2]See *Tolstoy or Dostoyevsky: An Essay in Contrast,* by George Steiner, 1960.

suddenly, grabbing Kosky by his right hand, places on it with his parched lips a dry kiss. With effort, effort stemming from what total state and its smallest prison cell did to Omadi's biceps, triceps, anterior deltoids and other muscles, not just to his total life circuit, he walks to a chair. With effort, he sits down. With effort, he turns the table lamp toward Kosky. After so many years in solitary, he can't see well. "I want to see you better; you are my spiritual brother," he says. "I want to know you; you are the one to whom I owe the rest of my life though, I think I am about to die from the New York summer heat."

"You owe it to yourself," says Kosky. **To be free in the freedom of others — that is my whole faith, the aspiration of my whole life. I considered it my sacred duty to rebel against all oppression, no matter where it came from or on whom it fell. There was always a lot of quixotism in me, not only political but also private. I could not view injustice — to say nothing of actual oppression — with equanimity. I often interfered in the affairs of others without being asked, and with no right, and without having given myself time to think it over. . . . (Bakunin to Czar Nicholas I, 1851)**

"In prison, I thought of you each time when they gave me the 'ninety degrees': when they would lay me on the floor, legs up at ninety degrees, and beat my feet with a whip until either I broke, or the whip," says Omadi. He breathes deeper — "and what he now inhales so fully is American freedom." (Jay Kay). "I thought about you even when, for months, I had no news from my wife or children. When they gave me drugs. When they kept me without books, newspapers, without anything to read, not a piece of literature, not even The Koran!"[3]

---

[3] The Qur'an (or The Koran. J. K.) is the expression of the Revelation made to Muhammad by the Archangel Gabriel, which

"The main thing is that you're alive," says Kosky. "A dead rebel to the cause does no good to the cause, particularly when, as is the case in Industran, this cause is still very much alive."

Trumped-up charges of "anti-Royal-Court" both current and retroactive, had been leveled by PERSAUD against Barza Omadi and many prominent teachers, writers and clergy, who were sentenced without trial to spend years in PERSAUD prisons. To extract their confessions and denunciations, they were subjected to electric shocks and pushed into pits of human manure. PERSAUD had ordered public executions of several intellectuals; the deaths of many others were never made public, but it was established that Barza Omadi was not among them. He is said to be next in line. (George Levanter to Kosky)[4]

"Well, since I refused to starve or hang myself—how unoriginal to do by oneself what in any case will be done to all of us—they finally let me go." Omadi brightens. "One day the all-powerful prison director comes to see me. 'Who's Norbert Kosky?' he asks me.

" 'I don't know, sir,' I answer, for once truthfully.

" 'Don't lie,' says the director. 'That asshole Kosky has been for months turning the United States upside down for you. Is

---

was immediately taken down, and was learned by heart and recited by the faithful in their prayers, especially during the month of Ramadan. Muhammad himself arranged it into suras, and these were collected soon after the death of the Prophet, to form, under the rule of Calif Uthman (12 to 24 years after the Prophet's death), the text we know today. *The Bible, The Qur'an and Science* by Maurice Bucaille, Offset Printers, Delhi, 1988.

[4]George Levanter, the past president (1973–75) of the American Center of Investors International (and one of the partners in TRUSTAMER, the first foreign-majority American owned bank estblished in 1989 in Free Ruthenian since 1939. J. K.)

he an Armenian or a Ruthenian? A Jew, a Gentile or a Gypsy? Is he thoroughly insane or merely crazy? You must tell me who that man Kosky is and who he is to you.'

" 'I don't know, sir. I've never heard of him,' I say. 'If you don't believe me, give me another ninety degrees.'

"And so he does give me the ninety degrees, and after it's over, and even though I can barely breathe from pain, I still can't tell him who Kosky is. Only then he most reluctantly leaves me. But then, in a few days—or was it a few weeks or months?— then I lost the sense of time if not my senses—he is back in my cell, and he is most upset.

" 'This is important, Omadi,' he tells me. 'This can mean your end—and a painful one, I guarantee that,' he threatens. 'The other week, that man Kosky talked about you most urgently to the Indostran ambassador at the embassy dinner in New York. What he said to him gave our ambassador a serious case of indigestion. To willingly cause indigestion of our high court official is a crime synonymous with the desire to poison. Why did that man Kosky want to poison our ambassador over you?'

" 'I don't know, sir,' I say. 'But, tell me, sir,' I ask him humbly, 'why would our ambassador bother to have such a poisonous man to dinner? Can't our *Royal Cannibals* (Reza Baraheni, 1977)[5] take care of that man Kosky and give him ninety degrees?'

" 'We can't. Not now, anyhow,' the director says. 'He happens to be the president of W.E.T., an international association of the most elitist American intellectual elite. And, if that's not enough, he is a member of EON, the most exclu-

---

[5] *The Crowned Cannibals:* Writings on Repression in Iran, by Reza Baraheni, with an Introduction by E. L. Doctorow, 1977. "Reza Baraheni is the chronicler of his nation's torture industry, and poet of his nation's secret police force," (E. L. Doctorow) See also *Writer Says Ex-Premier on Trial Helped Free Iranian Intellectuals* (*The New York Times*, 1979).

sive American intellectual club. Once again, the prison director leaves me perturbed. In a few months, or may be in a year? (note that by then I no longer counted days), he's back in my cell again, this time with an official letter in hand.

" 'This is most serious, Omadi,' he tells me. 'I just heard on the official phone the other day that at an official New York reception given to honor Habeas Voyvoda, our prime minister, that man Kosky, who was among the guests, suddenly surfaced and in front of everyone he verbally attacked our prime minister for what we supposedly did to you — you, the intellectual nobody called Barza Omadi. Of course, our prime minister assured him he had never even heard of one called Omadi — and he was telling the truth. How could he hear about someone who formally didn't exist? Today the prime minister's office called me to find out if you were still alive — and I told them that you might or might not be. Life and Omadi are perhaps no longer synonymous, I said, and how's that phrase for someone as uneducated as me? Now if you intend to go on living you must tell me: who are you to Kosky?' the director barks.

" 'I swear I don't know,' I cry out.

" 'There's no way to know to what length that man Kosky might go to get you out of here,' says the director. 'The man is a yogi terrorist. They say he can float on water for hours like some sickening-to-look-at-crab.'

" 'If he's a floating terrorist, PERSAUD should drown him,' I propose, but this answer infuriates the director and so I get from him another ninety degrees. Afterward, the prison director leaves my cell all upset, only to come back a few weeks later. This time he is really shaken. He is unhappy. 'I was told,' he says, glancing at me harshly, 'that recently that man Kosky appealed on your behalf to all American media. Now, this is most serious. This could mean a boycott of our forthcoming International Horror Film Festival to be held in our new Nirvana Palace under the patronage of the Imperial Highnesses.' He leaves me in a fury — but forgets to give me the usual ninety degrees. In a few weeks he returns to my cell. This time he seems pensive and most concerned for my welfare.

" 'This is no longer possible.' He bites his lip. 'Yesterday, in New York, that man Kosky talked about you in person, to'—he swallows hard—'to the imperial highnesses. To the Imperator and the Imperatrice. Imagine that!' Tears well in his eyes.

" 'But that's impossible. How could he?' I say.

" 'He could, and he did. The many court witnesses say that he must have talked to them about you for over twenty minutes. Twenty minutes. Imagine that!'

" 'I can't,' I say. 'How could he even come close to the imperial highnesses—much less talk to them even for a second? Where was PERSAUD? Why wasn't he shot on the spot?'

" 'Don't be silly, Omadi!' says the director. 'This was at a black-tie reception: the highest security this side of the Koran. In fact, before talking to the imperial highnesses, that man Kosky was seen talking to the imperial highnesses in front of Henry Grandstand, the American Secretary of State, and Konrad Walenrodzky, the past American national security adviser.'

" 'But why would Kosky be invited to such a reception unless he has something to add to it?' I ask, for I still knew nothing about you.

" 'How do I know?' says the director. 'I run this prison, not an American Luny Park for the intellectual lunies.' He raises his hands to the imperial sky and leaves my cell in disgust." Omadi stretches in the chair, cools himself with a long sip of iced tea and goes on."

"A day later the director comes to see me once more, and his expression is as grave as prison.

" 'That's it,' he says without preliminaries. 'That's it, Omadi. It's over! The Imperatrice has just called Habeas Voyvoda, our prime minister, to find out how you are—and whether you still are. Now the prime minister called me in person. In person—' he repeats, 'and, in person, he ordered me to get rid of your person.' This time he did it quoting the *Elementary Teachings of Islam*. (Moulana Abdul-Aleem Siddiqui). 'This is the end.'

" 'I swear to you I had nothing to do with all these new provocations by that man, Kosky.' Now I plead for my life. 'Please give me another ninety degrees—make it a hundred! Anything! But let me live a bit longer.'

" 'What ninety degrees?' the director chokes. 'Can't you hear me right? It's over! This is the end! On your feet,' he commands—for the first time without using his whip.

" 'Where am I going?'

" 'You're going to the great beyond, to a place from where, I hope, you won't ever return.' says the director.

" 'I came from there when I was born some fifty years ago,' I say. 'I don't want to go back. Can't I stay here, in life, a bit longer?'

"You're going to America. The great beyond,' says the director. And then he hands me my passport and here I am today." All stirred up, Omadi catches his breath.

"It was a miracle," says Omadi. "A pure miracle. I feel like one who no longer fears drowning. But tell me, Kosky," he says, lowering his voice. "How did you manage to get me out? What methods did you use? Blackmail? Terror? Did you ever threaten to blow them up on a ski lift?"

"I can't tell you," says Kosky. "I must protect my fictional sources."

FOREIGN JOURNALISTS TOUR IMPERATOR'S PALACE. **From our Foreign Correspondent in Damar, Indostran. Following the sudden overthrow of the Imperator of Indostran by the Musmuh, the coalition of Muslim muhtis, the American journalists were offered a tour of the deposed monarch's Nirvana Palace, located high in the hills of the capital. On the night table beside the Imperator's bed were the books the monarch was reading before he escaped the ax of Musmuh. They were the memoirs of**

Gandhi and Ben-Gurion; Henry Miller's *Plexus, Nexus,* and *Sexus;* the Coldcut sisters' biography of Henry Grandstand, the U.S. Secretary of State; and the works of Norbert Kosky, the American-Ruthenian novelist known primarily for his anarchic literary characters. *(Centralia)*[6]

---

[6]*Centralia:* an elite literary magazine founded in 1919 in the small town of Centralia, (near CenterState — as Ruthenia is called in Jay Kay's newest novel. J. K.)

What once were vices are now manners.
(SENECA)

19

"Is there, in your new book, at least one love affair without sexual aggression?" aggresses upon Kosky a free-lance *reporteress* at the Convention of American Storytellers Association.

A perfect head-turning mixture of Cinderella and Conchita, she comes onto him strong—straight from the pages of the sexual Muay-Thai Siamese Sin magazine and not even Harry Houdini, the famous escapologist could escape her perfect aSSets. (Thank you, printer!)[1]

"There is. Call it loveless carnal carnage," he states solemnly, watching her nubile Siamese hips.

"Is there in it at least an old fashioned '69 B. J.? so commonly perfected in my country." Her purple lips deliver a final blow job to his latest Book-of-Job.

"There is galore," he assures her calmly while setting his kundalini on 69° sybaritic degrees fire by inhaling this woman's Soixante-Neuf perfume.

"And, in these days of Sexual Substitutes, how does your hero define oral pleasure?"

"He defines it as **tongue lashing (Cathy Young).** He defines it as sexually straight talk, meaning the right to use

---

[1]See: *Thai Boxing:* Muay-Thai; the Arts of Siamese Un-armed Combat by Hardy Stockmann, Bangkok, 1979.

and abuse a lover by using on him or her at bedtime very bad words—bad, meaning 'far more inventive than simply obscene' (Niskisko), and using them either as the right word at a bad time, or a bad one at the right time. These bedtime-bad-words rights are, though in some States its use is heavily restricted, even at half price after midnight, guaranteed to us by the First Amendment Today." He concludes, "These words are the prime carriers of OTT—of Orally Transmitted Tease. Tease, printer, not disease!

SS

"You're not divorced. In this country adultery is still punishable by law. Another sex law, no doubt drafted by ALF[2] lawyers," says Kosky, helping Cathy to unpack the neatly prehanged dresses in the hotel room. "Was it wise to come to New York for just one day?" Our Dionysian stares her straight in her lips.

Many of our present beliefs concerning average sex experiences and normal sex life have the status of surmise standing on foundations no more secure than general impressions and scattered personal histories. (Robert Latou Dickinson, M.D. 1933).[3]

This is her way of saying to him: Times became sexually insane. This time, times are *unsane*, this time not you and not I. For instance, fluid used to mean life just as ash meant death. Today, out of their fear of AIDS, people fear one another's fluid and, as a result, the corporate state sucks their

---

[2]ALF—the Anti-Libido Federation. "First of all it must be said that *libido*—to use the Latin word—is misunderstood if it is defined as the desire for pleasure." (Paul Tillich in *Love, Power, and Justice: Ontological Analyses and Ethical Applications*, Oxford University Press, 1954, 1982).

civil liberties dry! Corporate state, not corporeal! With the death of a routine kiss, how can you dare to write a full novel about 69? True, we all love sex — and we know this as well as we know one another, as well as Colette would know Marcel Proust. True, we are love addicts: addicts of life. "Yes, my faithful Lassie," she teases him now. "As of today you too are a member of LASA: a life-addicted-sex-addict — the past member of NASA, (National Association of Sex Addicts. J. K.[4] A new Sex-Love Code is needed," raves his Khazarina. "A brand new Sensuality Code and one not at all synonymous with the Anti-AIDS State Behavioral Code recently proposed by Senator Abraham Ronald Tamerlane, that smelly skunk of a politician from Carnalia."

She ends her case. What is he to do? Must he tell her about *Stream of Consciousness*,[5] the only state a fiction writer can comfortably inhabit, in the wise words of that publicity conscious Jay Kay?

Must he say more? Must he ask her point blank Do You Still Love WET? With the word *wet,* for once, openly standing for *fluid-transmitted disease called AIDS,* and, for once in this text, not for WET, his favorite Writers, Editors and Translators Association? He must not. *"Why not?"* (Jay Kay) Because Cathy is his spiritual source; she is simply his ideal fictional being, "the only one he dares to call his narrative call girl — always on call in order to promote writing: his only true calling." (Jay Kay).

---

[3]Quoted from a motto to *The G Spot and Other Recent Discoveries about Human Sexuality,* by Alice Kahn Ladas, Beverly Whipple, and John D. Perry, London, 1983.

[4]NASA: National Association of Sex Addicts (founded, not accidentally, at the 1969 San Francisco Counter Obscenity Convention).

[5]*Stream of Consciousness in the Modern Novel* by Robert Humphry 1954–1962.

"Well, was it worth it? Answer me!" and as he asks her this sex-oriented question, he recalls the nubile lips of the girls from the oral—oriented *Oriental Women* magazine.

Forms, colors, densities, odors—what is it in me that corresponds with them? (Walt Whitman)

"I came to be with you. You're my Mani: my 'Jewish Christian.' " (Gilles Quispel) She looks at him most meaningfully and her look brings to his mind the entire erotic art of Tantra found in the erotic temples of Nepal.[6]

I recognized him and understood that he was my Self from whom I had been separated. (*The Mani Codex*)[7]

He won't argue with her. Not now. This is the time for magic; for celebration of real-life illusion. This is the time when, in preparation for *congressus subtilis*,[8] for his spiritual *sā dhana*, he had set in motion the Breath Magic No. 6—an entirely different kind of breath. **In love every man starts from the beginning. (Søren Kierkegaard, 1855)**

This is the time for *samarasa*, that sublime moment in which the two arrests, the arrest of semen and the arrest of breath, lead to freedom of exaltation, when **One sees the lotus seed, pure by nature, in one's own body. (Kanha)**

This is the time when the mere thought of being with Cathy **brings him from the chill periphery of things to the radiant core. (William H. James)**

---

[6]See "Sex and Religious Art," in *The Art of Nepal*, by Lydia Aran (Kathmandu, Nepal, n.d.), pp. 60–69.

[7]See *Jewish and Gnostic Man*, in Eranos Lectures 3 (1986), p. 6; these lectures contain *The Birth of the Child: Some Gnostic and Jewish Aspects*, by Gilles Quispel (1971), and *Three Types of Jewish Piety*, by Gershon Sholem, originally presented at the 1969 Eranos Conference in Ascona, Switzerland (*Eranos Yearbook* 38-1969).

[8]*Congressus subtilis:* an intense Tantric carnal copulation carried out by a bodily present being with one whose body exists only on an astral plane.

Torn between restraint and arousal, our Tantric self-master calms himself by employing an old literary trick. He begins to watch Cathy—to watch her every move—in a carnal closeup, a closeup found usually in sex-oriented Narrative Art magazine.

> . . . unhurried, unobtrusive, not cold, but also not effusive, no haughty stare around the press, no proud pretentions to success, no mannerism, no affectation, no artifices of the vain. . . . No, all in her was calm and plain. She struck one as the incarnation—Shishkov, forgive me: I don't know the Russian for *le comme il faut.* (Pushkin)[9]

"Tell me again: what's your new literary orgy about?" Cathy asks offhandedly, hanging her various voluptuous Maithuna night dresses in the closet—already a secret part of their most secret Tantric voluptuary.

"About Verbal Video literary mix-up," he says offhandedly, loading film into his camera. Holding a camera motionlessly offers him a perfect breath-holding exercise.

The Orgy is not a novel, and I hate the non-word "nonfiction." I have written other works grounded in fact: poems, biographies, films. . . . The Orgy is a book—whatever happened to that category?—and it is a pity your reviewer did not read it as a book. (Muriel Rukeyser)[10] Music mixes. So does video and film. Why can't fiction mix?"

---

[9]*Eugene Onegin* by Alexander Pushkin. (was written with "the distance of a free novel." Pushkin.) Translated by Sir Charles Johnston (1977).

[10]Muriel Rukeyser: an American poet and essayist and past president of the American Center of P.E.N.

"Tell me more." Seemingly somnolent and detached, she is readying herself for coitus. She bounces around the room. She is his living erotic temple — full of "erotic representations. Toward the east, there are some erotic reliefs on both sides of the window on the ground floor. Some copulatory scenes are presented, while some can be found only in an embracing pose. In some cases, perverted sex or lower congress is shown." (lower congress, Printer, not lover!) *Erotic Themes of Nepal* (1980–81 edition.)

Camera in hand, snapping one picture of her after another, he hopes to capture a glimpse of her rebellious inner view. "Isn't Self an aperture opening caught in a brief moment of Self-exposure?" Cathy asks him while he follows her, one crayfish craving for the flesh of the other. Without answering her, our literary headhunter crawls backward photographing Cathy from the unique point of view reserved for one about to give head,[11] by one who is in a position to give it.

Her impact (impact = imp + pact: J. K.) upon our literary Imp of the Perverse (Poe) forces him to recall his pact with Seneca and with the Tantric Age.[12]

This is the time when, changing the zoom's focus, he

---

[11]Head giving: opposite of head hunting; a Tantric ritual in which the giver literally commits his thoughts to the other person almost to the point of excluding himself — or herself. Assigned number 69 on the spiritual index by *Western Tantric* magazine where, let it be repeated, number six stands for accord and nine for invention.

[12]The Tantric Age, which followed the lifting of the Puritan tendencies of orthodox Buddhism, became the age of abandon, in which erotic poetry . . . and frank references to sexual practices of great finesse began to flourish in literature and other forms of art. (Lydia Aran, op. cit., p. 61) "The erotic carvings are vivid. The wood has its natural color and is not painted. The workmanship is really excellent." See also *Erotic Themes of Nepal*, by T. C. Majupuria and Indra Majupuria, (Nepal, 1981), p. 69.

focuses on the outside lines of her outer thigh, as tempting and as suggestive as the inside of her inner thigh was only a few sensual frames ago.

"Will the book sell?" She changes her position.

"It will, I'm sure. The footnotes alone are worth the price of literary admission," says Kosky.

"Footnotes? In a work of fiction?"

"Autofiction," says Kosky. "Autofiction is a form of autofocus. *I am what I see* (Heschel, 1965)."

"Go on." She urges him with her subtle body.

"Think of it as written by an autolytus (a creature which reproduces by producing at the point near the posterior end numerous new segments of literary worms, which, attached for a time, then develop into new beings."

Slowly, Cathy begins to take off her boots. Slowly, she rolls down her lace stockings. She looks at him—and she looks at him slowly.

Quickly, he reloads his Neo-Realist 1990 camera (the equivalent of the old 1969 Icon 69 sold over the counter at Times Square at half the price after midnight) with Nepalese-made super speed film inside sets the camera to ME, a manual mode just in time for another snapshot of Cathy portrayed as a sexual sleazebag, a sexual sizzle sucker straight from the pages of PRIVACY, advertised as "the most sex explicit magazine for the homeless allowed by law."

"You still haven't changed," says Cathy. "You can't wait to fuck me right now—in the state of undressing—rather than wait for me."

"I don't have to wait for you, slut. You're my *dombi*, remember?" **This odious being whom I call Me. (Stendhal)**

"I'm your *dombi*, true—but unlike man's stalk which needs *space* to grow, female emotions need *time*. Think of them as leaves—leaves, not lips! Admit it: time is more complex than space."

Being candid about sex—sex as soma as well as spiritual matter—is as natural to Cathy as speaking a body language which, like body English, she—a full-time resident of the corporeal people's republic—speaks very well. Cathy learned her refined body language, her sexual Esperanto, sensual as well as Esperantido, already as a child, pretty much the way he learned his.

Cathy unsnaps the bra, freeing her breasts. She poses for him, carrying in one hand her dress and one of her marble breasts in the other, and under her calm stare he becomes a Simple Simon (the cretinous sex maniac from the 1969 adult movie called *Scum of Kilimanjaro*. J. K.)

She puts on a translucent nightdress with matching shawl and sits down on the bed, crossing her faultlessly muscular legs under her buttocks. He keeps staring at her, he, a Ruthenian *sroka*, a migrating magpie, as overwhelmed now by the sight of this American bird of paradise as he was each time he had seen her in the past.

"Don't look at me with such an obscene eye. When you do, you look like that fiendish Adamite, the sexually secretive sectarian (she knows Kosky's passion for multiplying the letter S), in Bosch's "Garden of Earthly Delights". says Cathy.

The remote island in which I found myself situated, in an almost unvisited sea . . . the rude uncultured savages who gathered round me . . . had their influence in determining the emotions with which I gazed upon this "thing of beauty." (Alfred Russell Wallace)

Cathy gets up. Thirsty, she inspects the contents of the room's bar. Meanwhile, full of melancholy, Kosky, not unlike Bosch's "The Wayfarer," walks to the window and looks out at Manhattan. This is still his triptych, his private town, his spiritual shop (SS). This is where he feels free to be anybody—while always remaining himself. **It was towards that buzzing hive that he now looked as if already anticipating the honey he'd suck out and, grandiosely, he said, "Now it's between the two of us." (Balzac)**

Cathy moves between him and the window, blocking his view.

"My lawyers tell me that in order to avoid score-settling litigation, my husband might prefer to settle our differences out of court. Soon I could be free. Meanwhile let's do something." She looks at him, reading his mental quotes.

Let no-one, least of all the author, complain about infamy. (Thomas Mann)

Under her watchful eyes he undresses, leaving his clothes in a heap on the floor. There goes the impeccable starch-guaranteed shape of his favorite ultra-white jeans. Next, naked and, appropriately for a Tantric, semi-Self carnally conscious, our sexy spider slips under the bed sheet. She snuggles next to him. **One of the most characteristic qualities of living matter, plant or animal, is its capacity to respond to touch. The normal, first reaction of an organism is to press against any object with which it may come into contact. . . . (Kinsey)** Marble Juno is cold. She is, she says, sexually stilled. She is, she says, a study of still life as exciting to him as anything written by the Marble Juno Trio: Henry James, Sacher Masoch and Mérimée who all wrote about the one and only Wanda Von Dunajew, the *Venus in Furs,* (Sacher Masoch), then disguised as the *Venus of Ille,* (Mérimée) and *The Marble Juno,* (Henry James). Now, our Tantric guide guides his concentration in the general direction of Cathy whom he now perceives as a Subtle Body, as his Venus Rediviva.

forehead	fingers
eyebrows and eyes	hands
nose[13]	lower arms
cheeks	upper arms

[13-16]"At these places, as you proceed from the head to the toes, you may pause for two or four breaths. There are no pauses for breathing as you proceed upward from toes to head." (Sri Swami Rama of the Himalayas, author of *Exercise Without Movement* [1984].)

mouth	shoulders
jaw	chest
chin	heart center[14]
neck	stomach
shoulders	navel region
upper arms	pelvic region
lower arms	upper legs
hands	lower legs
finger	feet
fingertips[15]	toes[16]

"I know what Rilke means when he says, 'Like an arrow enduring the string only to leap out, love frees us from the one we love,' " says Cathy. "Loving you," she pauses, uncertain, "loving you makes me aware of what I need."

"Loving me?" Hesitantly he picks up the thread while glancing at the book in Cathy's hand.[17]

"Loving you. What's wrong with it?" asks our Severin Von Kusiemski of his Wanda von Dunajew.

"The form *ing*. It weakens the verb. Why can't you simply say, 'I love you, I love you': not even 'I'm in love with you' — unless you'll correct it in the galley proofs to 'I'm in love with love, not you.' " He laughs in order to throw her off.

"I say it the way I feel it." She refuses to shift to another mood.

"The other day, after I called you and left the message with your answering service, I got frightened by my own feelings. Do you know why I felt I ought to come to New York?"

"Why?" He produces the shortest sentence of his oeuvre. **I said ought to, not must. (Bukharin, 1938)**

"Because you are the only floater I know who keeps his head above the water. Wisely so, since these days waters are polluted."

---

[17](Title not to be listed: J. K.)

For a moment she cuddles next to him the way, on his bookshelves, the slim *Bangkok by Night* (1981) a sixty-six-page-long photo-volume about sensuous Siam, cuddles next to *The Book of Letters (Ksiega Listow:* J. K.) of Bruno Schulz,[18] whose erotic drawings bring to mind the poetic images of Charles Baudelaire.[19]

She runs to her suitcase, retrieves from it a video cassette and inserts "this modern visual suppository" (Norbert Kosky) into the videola with electrifying ease or EE. In Kosky's vocabulary, electrifying ease also stands for the sexually electrifying Elisabeth Eve, his favorite modern *dombi*, who learns how to enjoy *watching her lover* while making love to herself. The screen brightens, as it projects, in Tantric color, *The Woman and the Tongue*, part six of *The Worship of Shakti*, an adult movie filmed entirely on location (Dasein Productions, 1969).

"Sex is my favorite wheel of life," says Cathy.

Slowly Cathy becomes consecrated on her altar as he performs his first and foremost sacrifice, "a fluidless optically induced perfect No. 69." (Jay Kay)

"In the good old days, could you ever generate that much

---

[18]Bruno Schulz, *Ksiega Listow*, (*The Book of Letters*) ed. by Jerzy Ficowski (in Polish) Krakow, 1975. In it, you must see drawing no. 6 entitled by Bruno Schulz *Autoportrait with Two Women* (pencil, circa 1934 J. K.)

The drawing shows the already balding Bruno naked, as he crawls out from under a table only to be embraced — or bracketed — by two voluptuously naked young women.

[19]*The Intimate Journals of Charles Baudelaire,* translated by Christopher Isherwood; introduction by W. H. Auden; illustrated by Charles Baudelaire (1957). "What kind of a man wrote this book? A deeply religious man, whose blasphemies horrified the orthodox. An ex-dandy, who dressed like a condemned convict. A philosopher of love, who was ill at ease with women. A revolutionary, who despised the masses. An aristocrat, who loathed the ruling class. A minority of one. A great lyric poet." (Christopher Isherwood)

kundalini without your visits to the sex clubs?" she challenges him openly, at the end of their first fluidless spiritual session.

"I could not. These clubs were my populas womb, Cathy." **Where else could you see a virgin twenty feet high, and learn how it works and looks? (U.S. Commission on Obscenity and Pornography, 1969).** "That's where I was free to go on for a very long time. Free to get hot. So hot I would reach my sexual *regha*.[20] Didn't you notice I just did?" He presses his body against her. **The more depraved the woman, the more debauched, the more fit she is for the rite. Dombi is the favorite of all Tantric writers. (Mircea Eliade)**

"You're not just hot; you've got a fever of at least ninety-six degrees on Lotus Scale." Having said this, excited by the experiment, she dips her handkerchief in cold sparkling water, then places it on his naked chest. Steaming hot, the handkerchief dries in an instant. She looks at him impressed. He tells her:

"I'm burning my inner flame at your temple. A mere transmutation of sex into heat, a mental state for which in Nepal I could receive the highest Vatsyayana watermark." His Royal Yogi dismisses his royal Self. **By the same acts that cause some men to burn in hell for thousands of years, the yogi gains his eternal salvation. (Tantra)**

---

[20]The shortest span of time, or, Hebraically expressed, the shortest perception of time, is *regha*, "a beat, or as von Orelli so suitably suggests, the pulse-beat of time. The word is not used with *ayin* (eye) either as a verb or as a noun, as is German *Augenblick* (twinkling of an eye). If, as von Orelli assumes, the movement of the eye formed the middle term of the conception, then certainly the conception is different from that in our notion, "twinkling of an eye." "In *regha* there is originally something violent." (From *Hebrew Thought Compared with Greek,* by Thorleif Boman, translated from German by Jules L. Moreau 1960).

"Take a shower! Oops!" She corrects herself. "I know you take baths, not showers. Showers remind you of the showers of gas the Nazis first lavished on those who, like you, were pronounced by them to be certifiably insane. Of course, I say this *in light italics*." She pacifies him.

"And what does taking of a shower remind you of?" Our *Count Valerio* (Henry James) is just about to enjoy himself in the act of watching her.

"These days your sexual salvation (SS) rests in writing your sickly sex (SS) novel, not in having sick sex (SS)." She kicks him, and with him every decent American male novelist, in his sore spot (SS). She lets him play with her wrists and elbows, a new sensual substitution for wet sex. "There's a pagan element in all of us . . . and the old gods have still their worshippers." (Henry James)

"So what is left for the two of us to do together other than looking for another right-on woman?" he asks her, reluctant to turn to another page.

When a woman falls in love with another woman, must she then be made to feel that her own womanliness is in question? (Sidney Abbott and Barbara Love, 1972)

"Reading. What's left of 69 sex is reading. Reading about sex. Today, we witness a *librarylization* of sex. Forget sexual liberalization." She too likes to play with words now, when words unite her with her bookish lover.

"You look troubled," says Cathy, somewhere in the midst of their verbally charged '69 lovemaking. "What troubles you? Is it the absence of voluminous sex in your newest sexual volume? Or is it the by now confirmed rumor that Kosky is said to be one of the few surviving East European Literary Khazars?[21]

"I keep ruminating about Rumkowski, the Chairman of

---

[21]The Kingdom of the Khazars "held its own for the best part of four centuries," says Arthur Koestler (op. cit.).

the Łodz Ghetto, known for his ruminating in public," says Kosky, drinking the rest of his Bermuda Shorts Rum.

"Are you talking just *pathos?*" Cathy interrupts him while examining his most intimate part for signs of his tantrically trained Khazar past.

"What about the knowledge? The knowledge that even the King of the Khazars could not save the life of his Rumkowski's kingdom? The pathos, yes, but the pathos of knowing that within a year or two, *maximum three,* every single Jewish man, woman and child is doomed to chemical extinction simply for being Jewish, or even for bearing a Jewish first or last name?" Cathy speaks to him like a converted Lady Khazar. "There's only one way left for you to go on living, and to forget about the Kingdom of the Khazars and Rumkowski's mini-State." She allows his right-hand fingers to have a free-for-all intercourse with her left hand — the new-sex substitute for the old 69. (Jay Kay)

"What's next in sex?" moans our sexual desperado.

"Sex defined as part of one's mental environment. Mental, not physical.

It is sex as a verb, a noun. Sex as **one of the nine reasons for reincarnation . . . the other eight are unimportant. (Henry Miller)**

"Go on," prompts her our so immature *Melmouth the Wanderer,* (Charles Maturin, 1820).

"Sex as **the warm beast. (Camus)** Sex as opposite of lyricism of the masses! Sex as defined by your good friend Charlie Baudelaire, the one preoccupied with one-on-one sex never sex *en masse.*"

"Enough about sex as 'celestial supremacy and repose.' (Henry James)." says our Gogol, the one for whom (like for Gogol) there never was enough sex; one to whom the words *sex* and *enough* simply don't go together. "Tell me about your own *roman* — is it going to be a *roman à cleft* or *à clé?*" he asks her. The question is a trap. **You must never ask the serious novelist what his novel is all about. (*TV-Talk Show Maga-***

334

zine, NoHo House, 1987. See also *The Guide to the American Art of Conversation Watching,* SoHo Press, 1988).

"It's about religion," she says, and her "about" tells him that even though once so imaginative in staged sex, she is not a literary writer who knows novels are about, **"persons ('personen') who are ends in themselves." (Kant)** not subject matters.

"Here." She reaches out to her traveling bag and hands him a gift she has brought him. It's *The Child in Polish Painting,*[22] a thoughtful gift indeed. "Take a look at painting Number sixty-five — *Autumn,* by Józef Chełmoński: In this village scene, one of the two boys making a bonfire reminds me of you! Now see *The Storm* painting Number sixty-six with a small village boy terrified by the storm and the lightning. He too could be you. Aren't you afraid of storms?" She puts down the book — and him.

"Only of sudden thunder." He licks her sweat, while she rotates her hips in order to set him on fire.[23] She glances at the muscle lovingly, and so does he, the man who still suffers (SS) from survival syndrome (SS).[24]

The deSSicated Husk (Dasein Productions, 1990) kisses the breasts of Nadine The Black Widow (Dasein Productions, 1990). Is he smelling her salts or are they smelling salts made by House of d'Oliva? Is it her artificial aroma or her natural body perfume? He sniffs again. A whiff of some-

---

[22] *The Child in Polish Painting* (a bilingual Polish-English edition, Warsaw, 1979).

[23] "The body produces an extraordinary heat that can, as you say, dry the sheets. There is extremely reputable written evidence concerning this 'mystical heat,' or rather this heat produced by what is termed the 'subtle physiology.' The experience of the icy wet sheets drying very quickly on a yogi's body — yes, that is certainly a reality." (Mircea Eliade)

[24] "Is There a Survivor Syndrome?" See *Encountering the Holocaust: An Interdisciplinary Survey* (op. cit.)

thing—but of what? Of a real emotion—or of another Dasein productions Video Flick?

"One day, when I am through with my book, but not through with you, will you read my book all the way through, and tell me what you think?" Cathy asks quietly.

"I'll peep through it," he says thinking about his own literary peeping Tom sex show (SS) of the moment. **The more distinct, sharp and wiry the boundary line, the more perfect the work of art. (William Blake)** "But frankly, I would rather be asked to review for the *National Sex* magazine having sex with you." **Once more I have even lost the precise understanding of what I look for and yet I keep on looking. (Sartre)**

"Our sex? Sex with you is like reading Milton," she arches her back. "It's nonpoetic. No foreplay. No rhyme."

"I'm prosaic, not poetic. Besides, rhyme restricts. Sex is a free outpetaling—not outpedaling of the lotus."

Significantly, there is no word for "Original Sin" in Yiddish, the language spoken by the majority of the Jewish people for nearly a thousand years. And the Hebrew term for it occurs as late as the thirteenth century, when it presumably appeared under the impact of medieval Christian-Jewish disputations. (Abraham Joshua Heschel)

"It seems I came to it rather early in my life of bondage. My mother told me that as a little boy I planted a pair of tailor's scissors in the breast of one Pani Teofila, my nurse."

"Never mind Teofila. Describe your mother to me," says his Emma Hart, reenacting for him in a live-sex show Sexual Skullcrushing straight from the Leggy Woman magazine.

"It's too much fiction to tell." **He takes in and leaves out according to his taste. He makes many a big thing small and small thing big. He has no compunction in putting into the background that which was to the fore, or bringing to the front that which was behind. In short he is painting pictures, and not writing history. (Rabindranath**

Tagore)[25]

"Only when I saw my mother sinuously stretched on her deathbed (since at the time I could not enter Ruthenia, and so she came to see me in cold November 1971, in Hotel Polonia in friendly Amsterdam) I realized that, until then, I always saw her not as her son but as a photographer who at least once photographed his mother naked. As one who photographed her as a persona called 'The Artist's Mother.' " **There is a constant return to sources. The portrait of Rodchenko's mother (1924) is the most striking example, for it has all the virtues of a symbol. (François Mathey, 1983)**

"You photographed your mother without clothes but with her face on? In your faith, isn't portraying a real face synonymous with defacing?" She lets him peek at her marble body's candid crack.

"It all depends on the nature of the act, not on the nature of faith or face. Since my faith — faith, being for me separate from religion — allows creative self expression. In any case," he goes on, buried between her thighs and examining her stocking's stain, "this is the time when, on my memory slide, my mother looks more like Catherine the Great, with Rasputin at her bedside." **Consequently, the Hebrew language formed no specific expressions for designating the outline or contour of objects and did not even need them. We shall first of all try to feel with the Israelites how they could experience the world visually and still get along without the notion of outline, form, or contour. (Thorleif, Bowman, op. cit.)**

"Were you really her Rasputin?" With her forefinger, Cathy makes a foray into his hollow and sexually uneventful knee hollow.

---

[25]From *Doubly Gifted: The Author as Visual Artist,* by Kathleen G. Hjerter; foreword by John Updike (1986).

"Was I? How am I to know? Already then I saw myself as a waif, my first fictional persona. Wait, I'll show you how I saw myself then." He picks up a copy of *The Child in Polish Painting* and guides her all the way to painting No. 6. It portrays Jan, the youngest son of King John III Sobieski. He then shows her the portrait of the handsome Dominik Radziwill, as shown on painting No. 9.

So it is not to be wondered at that this hysterical girl of nineteen, who had heard of the occurrence of such a method of sexual intercourse (sucking at the male organ), should have developed an unconscious phantasy of this sort and should have given it expression by an irritation in her throat and by coughing. Nor would it have been very extraordinary if she had arrived at such a phantasy even without having had any enlightenment from external sources. . . . (Freud)

Cathy wraps herself around him. Lazily, Cathy lays on her back. Lazily, she first parts her legs, then just as lazily braces him with her calves and feet. "Go on. Tell me what happened when you were twelve?"

"I fell in love defined as 'the poetry of the senses' (Balzac), not yet as a 'wine of existence' (Henry Ward Beecher)," says Kosky. "I fell in love with a girl—let's give her here the name Bożena[26]—a skinny creature who was either a year older or younger than me, but who, nevertheless, gave me my first premonition of 69. Premonition rather than ammunition." He keeps his sex record straight.

"Here, that's how I still see Bożena." With Cathy's head in his lap, and, regretfully, no longer between his thighs, he now guides her head headlong to painting No. 69. Called

---

[26]Bożena: a spirited Ruthenian female name. Boże is a declinable form of *Bog*, Ruthenian for God. (*Boże* drogi! means *Dear God!*) The name Bożena corresponds (but not often enough) with the Anglo-Saxon name Godetia.

Girl with Landscape in Background, it was painted by Kazimierz Alchimowicz, a painter whose last name alone brands him as an alchemist. The painting shows a sinuously slender young girl who, wearing a simple one-piece dress, dips her naked foot in the unruly stream of water.

"Such a cute cuticle cutter. Who was she?" says Cathy looking into "Women Do Look," a segment in *My Secret Garden* (Nancy Friday, 1974).

"She lived in a small house separated from the house in which my family lived by a small garden—so small it could be called secret—(he reads her sexual phantasies as well as did Nancy Friday. J. K.) and a rather fast mountain brook—or was it a man-made post-Freudism stream?" Here, teasing the reader, he pauses meaningfully.

In the body of every boy who has reached his teens, the Creator of the universe has sewn a very important fluid. This fluid is the sex fluid. . . . Any habit which a boy has that causes this fluid to be discharged from the body tends to weaken his strength, to make him less able to resist disease. (*The Boy Scout Handbook, U.S.A.,* 1934)

"Across that stream," Kosky goes on, "over and over again, I would eye her. So soft. So golden. So freshly stacked. Ready to be loved'nd laced." **When I lie tangled in her hair and fetter'd to her eye. (Lovelace)**

"You see? Think of hair. Hair as a modern fetish. This too is new sex: Isn't shampooing hair the Great American Fetish Number One?" She offers him yet another version of shampoo sex (SS).

"One day, after one more mute lesson in English taught to me by my erudite and infinitely patient father—I suffered from a bout of aphasia—I finally crossed that stream." Kosky goes on. "Hiding in a bush, I waited for her. And one day, the love I felt for her hair fused with a love I felt for her lips. By alchemically fusing hair with lips I got . . ."

"You got your sick love of hair." Cathy interrupts him rudely. "I can see how, right then and there, you turned your passion into a **malady without a cure (John Dryden)** only to become **the bright foreigner, the foreign self." (Emerson: _Journals_)**

"But" — Kosky goes on with his story — "when I stepped out and said nothing, Bożena thought I was too shy to talk. To put me at ease she talked to me, and talked and talked. Finally, I just went over to her, and kissed her hair. **Desire is portrayed by the caress as thought is by language. (Sartre)** Only when she didn't mind my kiss, and she embraced me with both arms, I kissed her on her lips. Her lips felt wet. Wet, not dry." He pauses and as if posing for a photographer from Hot Kisses adult magazine, he kisses Cathy's lips. Her lips, not the rest of Cathy.

CAN A LITERARY PERSONA ACQUIRE FROM THE AUTHOR THE ACQUIRED IMMUNE DEFICIENCY SYNDROME? TO WHAT DEGREE IS THE PERSONA IMMUNE TO THE DEFICIENT AUTHOR AND THE AUTHOR TO HIS DEFICIENT PERSONA? asks the reputable Byron Chillon in his "Literary Sex: Strategies for Fictional Survival," _Writer & His Work_ (1986), pp. 66–69.

"Kissing Bożena gave me a taste of a truly wet kiss," he says.

This episode will have lived for years in his memory and even in his wonder; it had the quality that fortune distills in a single drop at a time — the quality that lubricates many ensuing frictions. (Henry James)

"Go on," Cathy urges him with a slight kick of her feet delivered to his chin. "Tell me more about your first infantile urges — most of which seem to remain intact."

"All I knew was petting. A dry hand pushing up a dry hole, the village boys called it. I'd practiced it many times. But with Bożena, it was different. I wanted Bożena wet. Wetted from within. Pretending I was wrestling with her, I made her fall to the ground where, somehow, she found herself under me."

The old dragon straddled up to her, with her arms kimboed again, her eyebrows erect, like the bristles upon

a hog's back, and, scowling over her shortened nose, more than half hid her ferret eyes. Her mouth was distorted. She pouted out her blubber-lips, as if to bellow up wind and sputter into her horse-nostrils; and her chin was curdled, and more than usually prominent with passion. (Richardson, 1748)[27]

"And of course, involuntarily seeking voluntary intercourse, you moved on top of her," says Cathy. "You were Lovelace and she was Clarissa."

Kosky won't be distracted. **I am a machine at last, and no free agent. (Richardson)** "I kissed her, but between kisses, she wanted to talk and to be talked to. To keep her quiet, to make her think I was a kisser, not a talker, I kept on kissing her."

She struggled violently under his hands. Her feet battered on the hay and she writhed to be free; and from under Lennie's hand came a muffled screaming. (John Steinbeck) "And then I couldn't stop."

"Couldn't stop—what?" Cathy pulls away.

"Kissing her. Biting her lips. Sucking on her until I marked her until she bled."

"Biting her? With your incisors?" With her knee Cathy kicks him in the groin.

"Then she bit me too, and cut my lip open. We kept on kissing, her blood and my blood all mixed up. **The erotically excited kiss as well as the inward feeling of physical well-being, which is so difficult to describe, of a mother nursing her child at her breast, feeds on fare that is both coarse and infinitely fine and becoming finer; but all this in the sense of the primeval evolutionary fact that in the**

---

[27]Samuel Richardson, *Clarissa: Or The History of a Young Lady:* "a novel about deflowering of a flower child." (Jay Kay)

beginning the whole skin was the seat of sensual pleasure. (Wilhelm Bölsche)

For a moment, Kosky engages Cathy in a brief sequence of sixty-six, his favorite kiss, far less engaging than *soixante-neuf*, banned by so many States of the Union for being "dangerously premeditated and easily persuadable." (Courts, 1986)

"What happened to Bożena?" says Cathy, biting her lips.

"Finally, Bożena panicked, although not at the sight of blood. She began to hit me with her fists as well as words. Being literally speechless, making faces and gesturing at her were the only ways I could answer and appease her, but this convinced her she had been attacked by an idiot. At one moment, she pushed me into the stream and ran away. A few hours later Bożena came to our house accompanied by her parents who complained I'd forced myself upon their daughter. One minor vs. another.[28]

That in every large community there are certain abnormal individuals who participate in lewd and lascivious acts upon or with the body of a child is a matter of common knowledge (*People vs. Ash*)

"By chance, soon after, my father had his second heart attack. As a result I learned how to interpret both the Sex Crime Code and the electrocardiogram."

"Never mind the Sex Crime Code," says Cathy. "You clearly caused your father's heart attack."

"I couldn't prevent it," says Kosky. "He was my father. Fatherhood pains."

"Well," says Cathy, "the Bożena incident marred you for

---

[28]*Sex and the Statutory Law (in All 48 States)*, Volume 9A of the Legal Almanac Series by Robert Veit Sherwin, L. L. B. (Oceana Publications, 1949) was "the first American legal manual I read in English in Ruthenia on my father's advice before embarking upon my trip across the ocean, to Oceana, as I then called the New World." (Norbert Kosky)

life. It explains why you hate kissing me on the mouth — and why you don't mind my menstruation."[29]

"It explains why I love it," says Kosky. **By impersonating the aggressor, assuming his attributes or imitating his aggression, the child transforms himself from the person threatened into the person who makes the threat. (Anna Freud)**

"It explains why you love to hurt women's lips," she goes on.

"It explains why I love to kiss them."

"Do you now!" Cathy laughs his head off.[30]

Rejected, he retires to his corner. **A writer develops the muscles of his mind. This training leaves but little leisure for sport. (Cocteau)**

"Tell me about your current sexual stage coach," asking this of her he undergoes another sudden mood shift. "What happened to your multiple multipack lovers — all those college wrestlers, or wrestling coaches you used to use and be coached by during our days together?" He pauses in order to give her enough time to feel the hurt.

"Now, why would you remember them?"

"Will I ever forget all those guys!" Our mockingbird now mocks her openly. "All those amino-acid bodies, isolated biceps and crystalline tricepts. All those protein-filled abdominals and pectorals, molded by bodywork, coated in the body shop? And, of course, your herculean preoccupation with hamstrings, adductor flexibility, and

---

[29]Here, in order to understand Cathy better, and Kosky's fascination with her, the reader is referred to *Female Psychology:* Contemporary Psychoanalytic Views, An anthology of articles, Harold P. Blum, M.D. Editor, New York, 1977.

[30]PROOFREADER TO AUTHOR: You mean she is laughing *her* head off?

AUTHOR TO PROOFREADER: I mean she's laughing *his* head off. The reader knows what I mean.

groin muscle extension. Could I ever forget the hegemony of their pumping iron and oxygen over my Boy Scout's fluid?" **Those who believed in the buildup of the body were on the lookout for a man of muscle who, by eating, drinking, and exercising, added size to his limbs. A big body, they believed, contained more world and took more space. Once they found a country fit to build a body, they took residence in it. (Nachman of Bratslav)**

"Now don't be facetious." Cathy presses his face down on her fat-free stomach. "You are now in America, not in Pripet. What you fail to notice at your health club," she lectures, using his chest as her lectern, "is that body building is artistry. Bodybuilders are sculptors — sculptors who sculpt themselves the way poets sculpt their own words or good writers curb their language. And let me tell you something, *you cruel little Jew,*" she intones (clearly without any anti-Jewish overtones. J. K.) "In spite of all that power, as big as they are, these guys are never full of themselves. Never hard the way you skinny Jews so often are. These Gentiles let the woman be on top. And when she is on top of them they don't bite her, d'you hear?" Here, she bites his nipple so hard that, jerking in reflex, he almost throws her off.

"What will happen now? Will you continue seeing them?" Reluctantly he ventures into her sexually adventurous joint ventures.

"I will. Why not? I like to follow up in life on what's been going on inside my head." She smiles sweetly, while looking at the photographs of several handsome young men who sinuously stretch their bodies on satin sheets of *Hot Male Review,* several issues of which she keeps next to her bed. "By the way: did you know that other than having a fling with Baruch Spinoza whom I met in Amsterdam when visiting the Esnoga[31] and *Sephardim: the Spirit That Has With-*

---

[31]The Esnoga, the Portuguese Synagogue in Amsterdam, "was built in 1675 at the then astronomical cost of 186.000 guilders,

stood the Times (Piet Huisman, Amsterdam. 1986). You are the only Jew I've ever been close to? Like you, Baruch was a fusion of ostrich with peacock — or vulture with an eagle, whichever you prefer."

Reading disdain on his face, she asks. "Are you jealous, my dear Jewish Khazar?"

"Khazars were not jealous. Like Jews, they were chosen people — chosen to protect the Muslim conquest of Eastern Europe." he retorts. "Besides, why would one who's chosen to be Chosen be jealous? **'In Khazaria, sheep, hone, and Jews exist in large quantities.'** (Muquadassi, *Descriptio Imperii Moslemici* **[tenth century]),**"[32] says Kosky, quickly donning one of his Khazar spiritual disguises. "Jealous indeed! Didn't I drive you day after day to Horatio, the bartender at Consolazione — your favorite man of Marble? The very Horatio who today still is a Sex Safe (SSS) Wonder Boy at the very same Consolazione!" he delivers the tripple S punch to her.

"You drove me to Horatio, all right. Emotionally," she says. "The way you drive me to him now by telling me that Horatio, that handsome shit, is *still* working at Consolazione. If I went for Horatio, it was because of the need for sexual consolation. And why do you have to tell me again

---

because the Sefardim who worshipped there wanted it to be the finest in the world . . . In addition to its splendor, the Portuguese congregation also achieved a place in Jewish history when it excommunicated the Dutch-Jewish philosopher Baruch Spinoza in 1656." (from *The Jewish Traveler:* Hadassah Magazine's *Guide to the World's Jewish Communities and Sights,* ed. by Alan M. Tigay, 1987).

[32]"It can . . . scarcely be doubted that but for the existence of the Khazars in the region north of the Caucasus, Byzantium, the bulwark of European civilization in the east, would have found itself outflanked by the Arabs, and the history of Christendom and Islam might well have been very different from what we know." *The History of the Jewish Khazars* Princeton, 1954. Here, as in all matters concerning how much Civilization has mattered to the Jews (and vice versa, J. K.) the reader is referred to the indispensable *Heritage: Civilization and the Jews* by Abba Eban, 1984.

and again that you are not jealous? Is this your way of making sure that, as long as I keep more than one man afloat, you won't drown in me? That, as long as I remain your *dombi,* I am free to pick up any other man as you are to go after any other woman?"

"Possibly it is." He attempts to pacify her.

"Forget Horatio. Bodybuilding doesn't excite me anymore," she announces. "In any case"—Cathy consoles him with her tongue—"I'm into fencing now. I fence practically every day. Every third morning you can find me dueling like crazy with Romashov, my fencing coach, at the Rosencrantz and Guildenstern Beau Sabreur fencing studios, 906 Kuprin Avenue in Salt Lake City."

"Fencing?"

"Yes, fencing. A gentle sport. So gentle, it replaced painfully bleeding cut by a painless electric contact."

"Fencing is antiseptic, not gentle," says Kosky. "Face bleeds. Face guard doesn't. Neither does it betray emotion." Our Cyrano uncoils his foil.

"Why this constant preoccupation with emotions?" asks Cathy. "Do you believe emotions show only when one is showing them off? Can't they be safely hidden behind a face guard?" She pauses. "Fencing is reaching out to the other, with one's arm extended!"

"Fencing is keeping the other at arm's length," says Kosky.

"Fencing is a sport that won't tolerate Byzantine foul play," she retorts.

"But it glorifies a *faux pas,*" says Kosky.

"Fencing is face-to-face combat."

"It's an about-face duel. There's something unnatural about generating all that gravity, all that motion, without emotion."

"Look who says it," she mocks. "You're the original motion freak for whom G forces are everything." She lets him reach out to her belly. "The G-spot is all you believe in. No wonder," she puffs. "You like to ski, to polo and to float—all sports which carry you up or down by a force other than your own, but you watch true contact sports, football and boxing, basketball and wrestling on TV, not even in a real-life." Cathy sighs. "By the way, do you remember the names of those two reporters who once called me about you?" She is the first to sober up.

"I know who they are," he tells her. "They often write 'The Recurring Hoax' column for *The Crier.*"[33] She lets him do a happy-foot suck show, then.

She puts on fresh nylon crotchless pantyhose and crowns her feet with a pair of brand new shiny leather Patent Pedestals: high heelers that raise her by at least nine inches in his eyes, and sprays them with Fishnet Stocking lotion.

"Next thing you know, these two **wayward press pissants (A. J. Liebling)** will print all that piss that I and others told them about your sex life!" She submits to his exclusive touch.

"So what?" he says while her nipples enjoy his expert copulative touch the way hummingbirds enjoy Passion Flowers. "So what?" he goes on. "A claim that Hieronymus Bosch painted his copulating nude devil-queens, gluttons, wastrels, blasphemous urinators and other hell-bound incubi and succubi from life and not fantasy could upset a religious art dealer and even prompt Papal Bull *'contra sectam maleficiorum'* (1484). But what can be said about me that, one way or another, I haven't already spilled out as my own narrative sex spa? (Sex spa, not sex spy, printer) Besides, didn't I admit on *The Johnny Boatman TV Show* that 'I like to watch?' That I am an addict of live sex shows? That I even like to watch *Cable Sexvision* — the deathvision of sex without 69? Doesn't this penultimate Spectacle State (Roger Gerard Schwartzenberg)[34] still know the meaning of the word *voyeur?*" He laughs

---

[33] See "Hoaxes, Forgeries, Frauds, Theft," in *Almanac of American Letters* by Randy F. Nelson, op. cit.

[34] *L'État Spectacle: Essai sur et contre le Star System en politique,* by Roger-Gerard Schwartzenberg (Flammarion, 1977).

the whole matter off.

"They certainly can quote or misquote you a lot. And how!" says Cathy, offering him a full 69mm tele-lens closeup view of herself.

"So what? Let them quote or unquote me! This is the country of the free, and of all the entertainers a novelist is the freest!" exclaims our First Amendment Man, while his swirling tongue turns her goose bumps into a triple-S sexually swirly semicolon.

The conventional media position is that the threat of legal action and its attendant heavy costs could prevent the full exercise of First Amendment rights. Any libel win, to some, could result in censorship through intimidation. Query whether the cost of libel defense should be a trade-off for loss of reputation."[35] (Alan J. Harnick)

"Is it? Are you sure?" Cathy moans. "Isn't the story of Joseph K one of your favorite horror stories?"

"He certainly is," he agrees. **Someone must have been spreading lies about Joseph K, for without having done anything wrong he was arrested one morning. (Kafka)**

"These two reporters could be as mean in what they will write about you as you are when you write about your characters!" Cathy takes another tack.

"So what?" he mumbles, lost in her flesh. "Aren't most writers satirists? Aren't satirists mean? Is my autofiction — or for that matter my life — less or more autoerotic — or autoerratic — than any other domestic or foreign made narrative auto?"

"What do you intend to do to protect yourself against having your Self publicly slanted?" she asks.[36]

---

[35]First Amendment/Libel: Should There be Punitive Damages for Knowing or Reckless Falsity?," by Alan J. Harnick, *New York Law Journal*, 1987. *The Journalist's Handbook on Libel and Privacy* by Barbara Dill, New York, 1986.

[36]"Doubtless 'character' is an inadequate word here: we are not speaking of a coherent personality or intellectual position. Rawson,

"Not a thing! By virtue of what I do I am a public figure and as such my vices are as public as my virtues. This is my faith's central fact!"

"Are you talking about your faith or your about-face?"

"My faith: everybody's got a faith."

"Everybody's got a face!" she corrects him. "And if that's the way you feel, why don't you ask your Warren and Brandeis lawyers from Boston to put these guys on notice."

"C'mon, Cathy! We're talking about free opinion expressed about me—a writer, a free man, by two men who, writers like me are free to express it," says Kosky. "You can't restrict expression unless you intend to restrict everything else as well. To be free to write, the writers must be free to write their *libelli*, as well as libels. Already in 1890 Louis Brandeis wrote to Alice Goldmark (his future wife): "The most perhaps that we can accomplish is to start a backfire, as the woodsmen or the prairiemen do."

A defamatory act makes the plaintiff appear to other people to be worse than he really is — less trustworthy, less chaste, less competent, or merely more ridiculous. . . . There are few people whose sense of self is not affected by how others see and treat them. Reputation and self-respect are intimately related. (Emile Karafiol)

SS

At Consolazione, during their tender dinner *à deux*—this is Horatio's night off—Kosky and Cathy run into two middle-aged ladies, who, at the sight of Kosky, instantly peel off from the group of their postmenstrual peers and introduce themselves as Mrs. Pilgrim from St. Paul, Minn., and Mrs. Kohen from Zion, Miss.

---

who has a splendid way with language, speaks of the tale-teller as 'an amorphous mass of disreputable energies,' " writes Robert C. Elliott *in The Literary Persona,* (1982).

"We've enjoyed seeing you in *Total State* and at the Oscars," says Mrs. Pilgrim without a glance at Cathy. "Was Beau Brummel fun to be with?"

"Is it true that you and Shaman Peters first kind of hit it off together — but then hit each other off?" seconds Mrs. Kohen.

"In addition to acting and writing for the movies, aren't you also a writer of books?" asks Mrs. Pilgrim. "Didn't you write *The Confidence Man?*"

"Hello, ladies," says Cathy. "Am I a ghost?"

"Well, of course you're not, dearie," says Mrs. Pilgrim. "It's just that we saw Mr. Kosky on our TV — and we haven't seen you."

"Do you enjoy such accolades?" Cathy explodes the minute the ladies retreat. "Do you really need a spotlight?"

20

Returning to Salt Lake City, Cathy leaves Kosky with a catty remark she borrows from her favorite Petronius: New York is the toughest town in the world for a lady to get laid in. And you wonder why? In his "Gypsies" Hadn't Pushkin already described the big city inhabitants as Gypsies who **"Of love ashamed, of thought afraid,/Foul prejudices rule their brains./Their liberty they gladly trade/For money to procure them chains?** She leaves him, she says, whom she still loves, but "now my love for you walks on stilts." She is eager, she says, "to return to my half-empty conjugal twin bed and try to fill the other half with a spiritually straight guy to whom it would never ever occur that **To appear sublime or grotesque — such is the alternative to which we have reduced a desire. Shared, our love is sublime; but sleep in twin beds and yours will always be grotesque. The contradiction to which this semi-separation gives rise may result in either of two situations, which will reveal to us the causes of many conjugal catastrophes. (Balzac, 1899)**

What is our Rastignac to do now? How is he to prevent his inner media from headlining Cathy's departure as a proof of his creative failure — and from showing clips of her life with him? There is only one way. It is called distraction; for him it means driving back and forth through Times Square, and around it. "All alone in his Desperado V-6 convertible front/rear engine all wheel sexually super drive extended pick up truck ready to haul his mental cargo as well as from two to sixteen passengers. Name this sport/utility all purpose vehicle *The Reverberator* (Henry James)," comments the always automotively minded Jay Kay. Tonight, as every night, the place is filled with a lonely mass of human antonyms who have found no questions and just as many solitary though well-paired synonyms. Self **sexual dereliction is a way to an inner exile (Niskisko)** where such self most often resides.

The tableau of urban life which opens before him diminishes in his memory to the size of the painting called *The Boy in the Manure Pit.*[1] To the storyteller in him, this is lowlife at the low ebb. Every homeless bum is here, be it a simple stewbum or a serious stumblebum.[2] Times Square is a spiritual spiral (SS): every marquee proclaims in yellow neon IMAGE VS. WORD, or VIDEO VS. PRINT.

Paradoxically, the Waterman of Thames, the famous six-story structure which since 1869 has housed the old-fashioned editorial offices of the *Times Square Record,* is also located here. The prestigious TSR (pron. TSAR) is a newspaper sporting "all the words that make the news," with a journalistic record like no other. **My range is limited, I think. It embraces a half-dozen specialties like boxing, and the press, and the war, and French politics. (A. J. Liebling)**

Here, inside this building, every staff writer's immediate

---

[1]*The Manure Pit:* a painting by George Welkopfin portrays a small dark-haired boy crawling out of a steaming pit filled with manure while several festively dressed Bosch-like peasant men and boys, all laughing, watch him from a distance, covering their mouths and noses with hands and white handkerchiefs, as if guarding themselves against the stench.

[2]See *Without Shelter:* Homeless in the 1980's; a Twentieth Century Fund, 1990.) Also, *The Rights of the Poor* by Sylvia Law, New York, 1974.

description is instantly measured, weighed and verified many times over by a supportive staff of dozens upon dozens of other staff writers, proofreaders, editors, lawyers, word experts and other less-than-ordinary wordsmiths.

But this is also "the place where spiritual language of the sense often surrenders to the often senselessly sterile language of civil procedure, since by placing the burden of proof on the respective parties who no longer respect each other, and not on the judge or jury, the American civil procedure is senselessly the tensest. **"Burden of proof" often means what Wigmore has called "the risk of nonpersuasion." . . . What Wigmore has called the risk of nonpersuasion is more often called "the burden of persuasion," or "the persuasion burden." *(Civil Procedure,* op. cit.)**[3]

Here, at the *TSR,* the until now free language of free expression is being freely tested, becoming, in the process of *newspaperization* (Henry James)—and out of fear of costly litigations "not necessarily less free though, undoubtedly, more and more self-controlled and censored by the collective Self" and the remnants of prior restraint and the Sedition Act (which became constitutionally extinct only in 1964 after *The New York Times* vs. Sullivan." adds the legally minded Jay Kay.)

Words, groups of words, words standing alone, are symbols of life, have the power in their sound or their aspect to present the very thing you wish to hold up before the mental vision of your readers. The things "as they are" exist in words; therefore words should be handled with care lest the picture, the image of truth abiding in facts, should become distorted or blurred. (Conrad to Hugh Clifford, 8/9/1899).

To Kosky, Times Square offers easy enlightenment of sex-

---

[3]See "Some Basic Concepts in the Procedural System Developed Around the Institution of Jury Trial," in *Civil Procedure,* by Fleming James and Geoffrey C. Hazard (1977).

ual videorama mixed with societal video drama. This is his American Place Pigalle, with the native pigs and gals galore, the world of undressing, cross-dressing and overdressing. It is a world of its own, and very much on its own.

Our Solitary Singer (Walt Whitman) parks his all-American automobile at the waterfront of the Hudson River and starts walking east, toward the United Nations Plaza. Passing a Pornutopia, the basest of the city's adult video sexporiums, Kosky spots a *mamarazzo,* (a gay *paparazzo,* J. K.) who, dressed in fatigued army fatigues, untiredly takes one picture of Kosky after another — all capturing our Boy Scout standing in front of a most unwholesome sex shop. **You furnish the pictures and I'll furnish the war. (William Randolph Hearst)**

21

On an appointed day, at the appointed time, the two reporters appointed by the *Courier*[1] to interview him appear at the door of the apartment of our literary D.A., with D.A. standing for once for devil's advocate, and not for district attorney.

These are the two Writing Persons who have already talked about him to Cathy when they first called her on her phone, purposefully rigged by her husband.

He knows their names. One of them is Theo de Morande, the other Tom Carlyle. While Morande is wearing a *proletkult* pullover by Marx Brothers, Carlyle sports a *Kalvingrad*, Calvinist straight jacket. Let it be said at the outset that while Kosky loves the reporting profession, this reportorial duo makes him queasy. In their presence he becomes uneasy the

---

[1]Founded in 1823 by Stakhov and Khovanski in the small village of Velizh, in the Russian province of Vitebsk, *The Velizh Voice* was the first paper credited with starting The Velizh Affair, in which some forty-two people (all of them Jews: J. K.) "were seized, put in chains, and thrown into jail." (S. M. Dubnow, op. cit.) The paper changed its name to *Courier* when, in 1835, all those sentenced in 1826 were declared innocent and released — except several of those released during their imprisonment by merciful death. See *History of the Jews of Russia and Poland,* 3 vols. Philadelphia, 1946.

way an *unsane* person is. (PRINTER: unsane, not insane. For the origins of this word see the already quoted *Journal of the American Medical Association* [JAMA]). **Certain librarian claims in a certain paper that I write a novel about myself, that is a Career Handbook." (Maria Kuncewicz, *Letters to Jerzy,* [in Polish], 1988)**

They come equipped with paper and pencils and a tape recorder, but, just by looking at them and their attitude of emotionally low altitude, you know that what is missing is a will to be pleased by life and to please it.

Suspiciously, they look around and as they do, they themselves begin to look suspicious.

Now, granted some of his uneasiness stems from him, and not only from them; it stems from his spiritual solitary confinement first under the Nazis, then, after the war, in Ruthenia, under the yoke of Stalin's top Commissars for Ruthenia. Some of it stems from Jewish history. From a fellow writer Josephus, who, once a Roman commander in Galilee, wrote the famous *Bellum Judaicum,* in which Jews, with parabellum in hand, attempted, in their numerologically lucky year 66, to shake off the Roman yoke under which they had already spent sixty spiritually painful years. When the Jew failed to shake it by the numerologically even luckier year 69, the Romans finished them off. And the rest of it, at this moment in Kosky's life, (to make this short story a bit longer) stems from Polish-Jewish history. From the fate of Bruno Schulz, his Polish-Jewish literary idol No. 69, (and in whose honor and after whose name Kosky named The Bruno Schulz Literary Award. Ed. 1990).[2]

Of the two reporters who came to see him, Kosky particularly fears the one wearing the *proletkult* pullover. Why? Because he senses that the Pullover is a headline-eager para-literary beaver who feels he has been unjustly pulled

---

[2]In 1992 The Jewish Presence Fund will observe both the 100th

356

over and given an unjust traffic ticket by life's highway patrol while the Jacket seems merely resigned to his stutter-preventing speech. Keep in mind that Kosky's own headline-making career began early in life. It began with the catchy, headline-making headline: A BOY OF THREE IS ALREADY AN ASPIRING ESPERANTO PRINCE. Soon after, it was: AT FOUR HE SPEAKS ESPERANTO BETTER THAN ZAMENHOF. Zamenhof, the inventor of Esperanto, came from Bialystok,[3] a Polish textile town and one not unlike Kosky's Lodz.

From this, it was only one step to: IS NORBERT KOSKY, AGE FIVE, OUR BILLY SIDIS? an article which must have spiritually stirred Israel Kosky's otherwise happy life. This article was then followed by an interview with Elisabeth Kosky which, appearing in *The Jewish Piano* magazine, was headlined: I NAMED MY ONLY CHILD NORBERT AFTER NORBERT WIENER, WHO INVENTED CYBERNETICS — EVEN THOUGH MY HUSBAND WANTED TO NAME HIM JAMES AFTER THE AMERICAN GHOSTWRITER JAMES HENRY AND AFTER JAMES WILLIAM SIDIS — THE FAMOUS AMERICAN CHILD PRODIGY KNOWN HERE AS SIDIS BILLY. (This interview was published only a few days before September 1, 1939, when Germany invaded Poland. J. K.)

---

anniversary of Bruno Schulz's birth (1892) and his death in 1942 when he was shot by an annonymous SS officer.

[3]"My parents, I realize now, personified the two conflicting traits that had tugged at the history of Bialystok ever since the Polish Count Branitzky invited Jews to come to his seventeenth-century village on the Bialy river to build a prosperous city. . . . Today, in New York, London, Paris, Melbourne, Buenos Aires, Tel Aviv, and other cities, there are substantial communities that trace their lineage to the people who emigrated from Bialystok in the late nineteenth and early twentieth centuries. These people have made an internationally recognized contribution quite disproportionate to the city's size . . ." (*Of Blood and Hope* by Samuel Pisar, New York, 1977.)

"Like writing, interviewing is an art.[4] Let's have your sss-side of our sss-story," says the Jacket who, from now on will effectively multiply in various ways the letter S in his sss-stutter thus gathering many S-points for Kosky's inner verbal game.

"First tell me what's the gist of yours?" asks our anxious Sidis Billy.

"The gist of our story is that we keep asking ourselves why we are doing what we are doing." The pullover laughs with Stalinist charm. "Why are we writing this story about you?"

"Are you sure you're not writing it in order to sink me?" charmingly asks our Bukharin.

"We might call our story: HE SURE CAN TELL A FLOATING STORY — BUT CAN HE FLOAT?" clarifies the Jacket à la Yezhov. "Or we might call it: A FLOATER OR A SWIMMER? HE SURE CAN FLOAT BUT CAN HE SWIM? The Pullover, the Jacket and Kosky settle down around a coffee table covered with Kosky's old adult cinema magazines.

"Now why of all the chosen literary people have you chosen me?" asks Kosky.

What has preserved Jewish civilization in the Diaspora for two millennia is Judaism, and what has preserved and in fact defined Judaism during this period is not Hebrew but Halakhah, not land or language but a legal system transcending both. As long as at least a significant minority continues to adhere to that system — either in its pre-Enlightenment or in a modernized form — Judaism will continue to survive and renew itself. Roman A. Foxbrunne, *Commentary*, 1990.

"Because you've floated in our literary waters for over a

---

[4]See "The Art of Interviewing" (a symposium), *Authors Guild Bulletin*, 1982.

quarter of a century now," says the Pullover, stressing the word "floated," as well as "quarter of a century."

"Because you've been profiled swimming on the cover of *SwimLife,* magazine. This was already sss-suspect since, even in your own words, you are a floater, not a sss-swimmer," sneers the Jacket.

"Because, as a swimmer, you've never said a word about how, where, or under whom you learned to swim."[5] The Pullover stresses the word *swim,* and à la Yezhov, plants a poisonous lie into his next question.

"Because no one seems to know anything about the exact nature of the sss-secret devices which keep you — not even a good sss-swimmer — afloat," squints the Jacket.

"All this makes us question you," says the Jacket.

"To clarify this please tell us why you don't sss-sink in your own unedited words — words which we and our editors will then edit. Edit for you, since, *obviously* you're a man no more born into English language than CCC-Conrad was."[6] The Jacket keeps on insinuating.

---

[5]Swim, 1. Float on or at surface of liquid (sink or —; *vegetables -ming in butter; with bubbles -ming on it).* 2. Progress at or below surface of water by working legs, arms, tail, webbed feet, fins, flippers, wings, body, etc., traverse or accomplish (stream, distance, etc.) 3. Appear to undulate or reel or whirl, have dizzy effect of sensation *(everything swam before his eyes; my head -s; has a -ming in the head).* 4. Be flooded or overflow with or *with* or *in* moisture (eyes, *deck, -ming with tears, water; -ming eyes; floor -ming in blood).* 5. *-ming-bath,* large enough to — in; *-ming-bell,* bell-shaped *-ming* organ of jellyfish etc; *-ming-belt* to keep learner afloat; *-ming-bladder,* fish's sound; *-ming-stone,* kind of spongy quartz. 6. n. Spell of *-ming; -ming-bladder* (rare); deep pool frequented by fish in river; (fig.) main current of affairs (esp. *in the-* engaged in or acquainted with what is going on). *(COD)*

[6]"A man not born into the language but one consciously adapting

"Tell us in your own simple words, whether there is any truth to your claiming a unique—or shall we say spiritually sacred—relationship to water?" says the Pullover.

Instantly Svāmin Svātmarama, the commander of Kosky's Spiritually Strategic Advance Team also known as SVAT, sounds a yellow alert for Kosky's entire sacred reactor called the Writing Annex. Such alert is sounded anytime Kosky's narrative free expression is being threatened, be it from within or without. He doesn't want things to get out of hand, particularly when his hand holds Galilee narrative seawater.

"Quite a collection of certificates!" certifies the Jacket glancing at Kosky's many printed memorabilia hanging on the room's wall.

"Only your floating certificate is missing," says the Pullover.

"No, it is not. Here it is," says Kosky. **As an individual I discovered that I am a wave in the mysterious movement of Jewish history. Israel is the premiss, I am the conclusion. Without the premise, I am a fallacy. I had not known how deeply Jewish I was.** (Abraham Joshua Heschel) He stands up and, like a military commander, salutes his eight novels backing him up on a bookshelf in their hardcover and downright dirty paperback editions. Anything to keep the reporters at bay—at bay, yet far from the water. **"What good is it to learn Hebrew if we don't know who we are?"** Bernard Adelman, *Commentary*, 1990.

Now, our Heretic sits down behind the desk, facing the two para-inquisitors who settle at the table across from him, their drinks, writing pads and tape recorders separating them from him. Read *The Inquisition in Literature and Art,* in *Inquisition* by Edward Peters, 1989.

---

himself to it becomes more aware of its rules and curious irregularities; he does not have habit on which to rely. . . ." [*Joseph Conrad* by Martin Tucker, 1976. (the last paragraph of the book.)]

The Jacket begins the hearing. "Mary Terentyeva,[7] a certified Ruthenian-American sss-swimming coach, told us that over twenty-five years ago in New York she answered an anonymous ad in *MultiSports* for a swimming instructor to instruct someone how to act as a swimmer. When Mary answered the ad in person, she's almost sure she found you waiting for her, on the side of some abandoned sss-swimming pool."

"Mary, then, seems to recall your telling her that you are eminently unsinkable as a floater, but sinkable as a swimmer — and that to you this meant no contradiction," says the Pullover.

"In other words, if you can't sss-swim, how can you float unless your floating is some fancy almost sss-stunt?" says the Jacket.

"Given almost three decades which elapsed since, and lapses in her own memory, Mary can't — or won't — swear it was you. But she won't deny it either," says the Pullover.

"In fact for years I kept placing such ads all over the place," says our literary miser. "Misery loves company. Writing is misery. Why should misery be miserable alone? Only last week I advertised for a free-lance swimming coach — to teach me how to crawl in the Swinging Socrates swimming pool, one of my neighborhood's newly opening Safe Sex clubs. **I remain an "am-ha'aretz:" religiously untutored!** Leon Poliakov, *Commentary*, 1990.

"We have talked to other people who have come in touch with you," says the Pullover. "Every one of these rather com-

---

[7]For the unfolding of the manifold role played by Mary Terentyeva and at least two others in this period of "Compulsory Enlightenment and Increased Oppression," as it was called by S. M. Dubnov, the well-known historian of Jewish affairs, the reader is referred to "6. The Ritual Murder: Trial of Velizh." S. M. Dubnov, (op. cit.)

mon folks said that at one time or another he or she heard you boast about your rather uncommon Tantric yoga floating yoga."

"And while supposedly you're a less than average polo player, as a sss-swimmer you're not even good enough to be a water polo goalie," adds the Jacket. This brings to Kosky's mind Spinoza's (d. 1677) excommunication by the Amsterdam Jewish community (1656) as well as **"human power is extremely limited, and is infinitely surpassed by the power of external causes; we have not, therefore, an absolute power of shaping to our use those things which are without us." (Spinoza, *Ethics*).**

"When it comes to being assisted in the water—*in* the water, not *by* the water, 'assisted' can mean many different things, including *psychic breathing* (Robert Crookall, 1985) which, hardly crooked can be used by all," says Kosky, measuring his meaning carefully. **The conscription horrors of that period had bred the "informing" disease among the Jewish communities. They produced the type of professional informer or *moser*.[8] (S. M. Dubnow)** "It can mean having some cold water splashed on one's face when one's head is too hot! Now that's hardly a blasphemy!" he goes on. "It can mean being momentarily pushed under the water in order to cool one's head off say, by a total stranger. That's not blasphemy either! It can even mean giving a blowjob to a blowfish or getting it from it!"

"Do you mean to say that you can always float without any aSSistance—or aSSistants? Without some auxiliary outer bladder? Without some helpful transparent fin?" Again the Jacket assists him à la Yezhov.

"Look here," Kosky gets up from behind his desk, and like Bukharin, questioned by Yezhov, he nervously paces back

---

[8]*Moser:* The Hebrew and Yiddish equivalent of "informer" S. M. Dubnow, (op. cit.)

and forth across the room, then sits down again. Just look at these two, at the Jacket eminently ill at ease, and the even more ill-looking Pullover. Look at their postures. Look how misshapen and out of shape their bodies are. In spite of being already in their midfifties, both of them still suffer from simple scoliosis, a condition usually found in young girls and defined by a slightly S-shaped spine. And look how dull yet nervous their eyes are! Eyes, said to be a direct extension of the nervous system of the brain.

He is exasperated. How can he answer their questions? How can he explain in a few words what his spiritual stabilizer consists of—a stabilizer, not a fin! What do these sport-simpletons know of Yoga-type breathing in which the yogi may change *his* ordinary rate of six to nine respirations a minute (versus say, the ordinary 16–19) to 1.6 "and reduce his ventilation volume a great deal." (O.P. Jaggi)[9] Just look at them; they hardly breathe. "Hate to think about the state of their spinal fluid and their PCs! (pubococcygeus muscles. J. K.)"

At this time, unless Kosky can come up with some natural answers to these unnatural questions—and how can he?—he might either say nothing and stick to his floating craft, and with it to the No Rumor pact he signed with Israel Kosky, ("tell stories about the Self but name no names.") Otherwise, inadvertently he might say something misleading because instead of leading the reader to a living person or a real land, whatever he says could only lead everybody back to his fiction—the main theme of his *autothematical story*. (Sandauer)

"Any interview with you we come across picks up a different Norbert Kosky biographical story," says the Jacket, all buttoned up.

"I'm a writer of fiction. That's why I haven't written my

---

[9] See also S. Rao, "Oxygen Consumption During Yoga-Type Breathing at Altitudes of 520m and 3800m," *Ind. J. Med. Res.*, 1968.

biography. Meanwhile, **Do I contradict myself?/Very well then I contradict myself,/(I am large, I contain multitudes.) (Walt Whitman)**

"It's all *Either/Or.*" The tight-lipped Pullover evokes Kierkegaard.

"I could also be both—or neither. Ask Joseph Conrad," says Kosky.

> VYSHINSKY: **Was the material you contributed selected tendentiously?**
> RYKOV: **Of course.**
> VYSHINSKY: **Perhaps it was of a slanderous character?**
> RYKOV: **Tendentious and slanderous, the one easily passes into the other.**
> VYSHINSKY: **That is what I am asking. Did your material pass from the tendentious to the slanderous?**
> RYKOV: **It is difficult to draw a line between these concepts.**
> VYSHINSKY: **In a word, it was both.**
> RYKOV: **In an acute question like this, everything tendentious is slanderous. (*Moscow Trials*)**[10]

"Then there's the issue of your topskin." The Pullover hesitates.

"Do you or don't you have it?" asks the Jacket.

"Now that's the unkindest cut of all. Who do you think I am: Diego Alonso?"[11] says Kosky. "Of course I don't have it. My *brit* is my certificate."

---

[10]Andrei Vishinsky: "one of history's most corrupt statesmen" (Jay Kay) was chosen by Stalin to be chief prosecutor at the Moscow Purge Trials. Aleksey Rykov, a former revolutionary who opposed Stalin's forced collectivization and, on Stalin's orders was, like Bukharin, sentenced by Vishinsky to death—and executed.

[11]Diego Alonso, the young "blond, curly-haired bachelor lawyer of the lineage of converted Jews" (Holy Inquisition), was charged by

"In my dictionary *brit* stands for herring and sprats: the foodstuffs of our whalebone whales—or Brit, for British. I know next to nothing about the Jews or their bloody blood ordeals," says the Pullover.

"And we're certainly not trying to pin a yellow (SS) Star of David on you. But are you, or are you not, Jewish?" says the Jacket, who doesn't know that the Star of David is blue.

He is not even a Jew! He is a filthy pagan,/a renegade, the disgrace and outcast of the world,/A foul apostate, a crooked foreigner. . . ./Move on, wandering Jew. (Hugo)

"Speaking of the yellow star, where exactly were you during the War?" The Pullover pulls another fast one.

"In Ruthenia. My fictional Center State. In the place Romans used to call Mare Heroditis. Some Americans call it Marshes of Glynn. Why do you ask?"

"Because we have traced your pre-World War II real-life nanny, who told us you were always afraid of water," says the Jacket. "She says you dreaded taking a bath, even a sss-shower."

"We also found your onetime wartime governess!" triumphs the Pullover. "She told us she tried to teach you how to swim, but the instant she tried, you ran away."

"During the War, war was my only governess—not counting Governor General Reich Minister Frank,"[12] says Kosky.

"We also obtained an affidavit from one Pan Anton Kweil," says the Jacket with a mysterious smile. "As your contemporary, he was your closest post-wartime pal. He recalls most vividly your pushing him into a lake instead of jumping into

---

the Inquisition with admitting to being a witness to a gust of wind blowing a piece of Host off the altar, a sacred Host, then admitting to it being nibbled at by mice, a crime of Host desecration.

[12]General government: a part of Ruthenia incorporated into the Third Reich administered by Reichminster Frank, Governor Gen-

it yourself. He says in your high school everyone knew KOSKY WAS AFRAID OF WATER!" The Jacket headlines his words vividly.

This ends the interview, and judging by their kvetchy'nd sketchy expressions, Kosky can tell that the oppressive Jacket and the nonstretchable Pullover are most unhappy. They either have been had by Kosky, or they have had enough of him.

The reporters collect their electronic belongings — and with them all the inquisitorial words they need to report The Case of the Desecrated Host. Politely, our immaculate host escorts the two unhappy members of the Fourth Estate to the elevator.

"We really enjoyed this reportorial *ménage à trois* with you — such an infamously famous person,." says the Jacket, while the Pullover nods.

"So did I. We must go through it together. Must or ought to, it really doesn't matter, does it?" Kosky tempts them.

"We must! Let's hope all this is only the tip of the iceberg," says the Pullover.

"I'm sure it is. I love icebergs: they float high above the water. Besides, ice is merely another form of water, and now that I float water is my element!" Kosky rejoices.

The elevator is on the way.

And in general the "public figure" had to have occupied that status prior to and independent of the story in question before the public-figure came into play. In short, a public figure is "anyone who is famous or *infamous because of who he is or what he has done. (The Rights of Reporters,*

---

eral, *"der deutsche König von Polen"* — the German King of Poland — as, Frank described himself when talking to Malaparte. See Curzio Malaparte, *Kaputt,* (op. cit) pp. 66–69.

1974)[13]

The elevator opens, silently swallows Jacket and Pullover, closes its maw and starts its descent.

---

[13]Even false statements of a defamatory nature had to receive some protection so that people would not have to speak or write at the risk of being unable to prove the truth of their remarks in court. . . . It must be remembered that "actual malice" is a term of art which has absolutely nothing to do with bad motives, spite, ill-will, or any other attribute of malice in the popular sense of that term. Rather, it means actually knowing a statement is false or having a total disregard of whether or not it is false. (*The Rights of Reporters:* An American Civil Liberties Union Handbook, Guide to Reporters Rights, New York 1974.

22

On the following day, an anonymous telephone caller leaves with Kosky's Anonymous, Inc., answering service an anonymous message. The message says: "Tell him that an ugly rumor about him is floating all around literary New York."

"That's all," says the Answerette. "The rumormonger left neither the text of the rumor nor his name."

"No name? But was it a man or a woman?" asks Kosky, distraught.

"With your callers one never tell," she says, hanging up on him.

Why would an anonymous someone go to all the trouble of leaving a message about an anonymous rumor?

Our Sword Swallower (SS) is troubled. In his faith, rumor kills three people: the rumormonger, the rumor referee, and, most certainly, the rumoree, the rumor's main target. Now you know why his faith wisely rates spreading rumor on a par with murder. Now you know why in his faith, even commenting upon the rumor (even a rumor about oneself inadvertently spread by oneself) with a simple "no comment" already means spreading rumor.

R: There is something impish about the pleasure you take in slightly bewildering your questioner, isn't there?

E: Perhaps that is part of a certain educational method. One mustn't provide the reader with a perfectly transpar-

ent "story." (Claude-Henri Rocquet to Mircea Eliade, 1982)

The lower-back pain[1] of our Pan Kosky pains so much he can barely leave his cot—or put on his tight-sleeved trench coat. With every move, a massive pain radiates from, and into, every pore of his body.

"Your sauna offers the only—albeit temporary—relief from his terrible affliction," informs *On Your Back*—the latest guide to lower-back ills and cures. But Kosky doesn't own a sauna and today he is in no mood to visit his Health'nd Swim Manhattan Club.

In his neighborhood, the only hygienically safe sauna can be found in the Reading Gaol Silicone Spa—a men-only bathhouse with a reputation of attracting "the most discriminating gays in town." *(GayLife)*.

The spa is located, literally, across the street from the Manfred, from where our literary cross-dresser draws his body—crossing the street at the diagonal—one step at a time.

He finds the Reading Gaol Spa to be what its ad, routinely placed in the Crier, proclaims every week: THE MOST LITERARY ROMAN BATHS IN TOWN—VISIT OUR ROMAN READING ROOM, OUR BESTIARY AND THE S.S. GOAL. NO SICK SEX (SS) ALLOWED. This is indeed the kingdom of maleness where a drag queen is king.

"Boy oh boy!" exclaims our Old Boy as he enters the place through its only unmarked door. He had entered such Roman thermae—hot baths of ancient Rome—already at the

---

[1]"Although we often tease about the buttocks being nothing but fat, they do contain, as you may remember from your anatomy lesson, strong underlying muscles—especially the famous gluteus maximus. The tone of this muscle is important in telling me something about the condition of your back," says Leon Root, M.D., co-author with Thomas Kiernan of their first-person narrative book, *Oh, My Aching Back* (1973), in Chapter 6 ("The Doctor's Examination") and on p. 69.

age of four or five, by reading about them, and what went on inside, in a book full of graphic illustrations. The book in question was *From the Life and Culture of Antiquity*.[2] This was the first scholarly book Norbert read. Beaming with family pride, it was written in most elegant Ruthenian and published by the famous Ruthenian Filomata Publishers, a year after Norbert was born, by no one else but Uncle Stan, Ph.D., Israel Kosky's so-Ruthenian-Jewish looking professorial brother.

People used to say of me that I was too individualistic. I must be far more of an individualist than I ever was. I must get far more out of myself than I ever got, and ask far less of the world than I ever asked. . . . The one disgraceful, unpardonable, and to all time contemptible action of my life was my allowing myself to be forced into appealing to Society for help . . . To have made such an appeal . . . would have been from the individualist point of view bad enough. . . . (Oscar Wilde, *De Profundis*)

Drama is essentially revelation, wrote W. H. Auden. At Reading Gaol, revelation is drama. This is the kingdom, and queendom, of men with youthful faces and even younger looking bodies, and of old men, old enough to father — or dare he say it? even grandfather — most of these youthful looking youths. STAY COOL'ND CALM reads a sign above the square.

These courageous men come here (here being courageous is not necessarily synonymous with straight) straight from the pages of the Dandie Dinmont All-Male Review, as much as from manly, edited for men only, such magazines as *Manchild, Manscape* and *Mandate* magazines. He has seen some of them on the pages of *Stallion Weekly* (anything to do with

---

[2] *Z życia i kultury antyku (From the Life and Culture of Antiquity)* by Stanisław Lenkowski, Ph.D. (Filomata Editions, Lvov). Vol. 1, 1934; Vol. 2, 1935; Vol. 3, 1936.

riding attracts him no end) and in the newest safe-sex oriented *Hand to Hand Quarterly*. These males come here from many walks of life but, given the climate of *New Sexual Epidemics*, they come here in order to pursue the verb "to watch," rather than "to do" or "to have". Hence, they walk back and forth around and across the spa, in order to see and be seen — seldom to touch. Here, in every corner, be it in frigidarium, tepidarium and caldarium, the frigid, tepid or downright hot lads and laddies — though never ladies — enjoy not only the reading facilities, but also the company of each other, displaying in the act the American facility for — and freedom of — expression.

At this HALF-PRICE-AFTER-MIDNIGHT time, the Reading Gaol is teeming with the lovers of self-sauna (SS). At the Voluptuary, the guest room near the rear entrance, Kosky runs into Teleny Douster, the American slipper snail called *Crepidula fornicata*.

Overweight, "medically overburdened" (Niskisko), Teleny has enjoyed being spiritually schizoid. He is basically a very good man, one who by now benefits far more from the ordinary American sauna than he would from one of Oscar Wilde's wildest asanas. One who, being on a pill, has been a pill as well. Too bad. That's why for years he has been most effective in his free-lance part-time job as divination expert in search of witching water. Recently, however, due to unemployment, Teleny's loss of income has led to a gain in weight.[3] Frequenting the Reading Gaol is the only way our Teleny, a physical misfat, as our misfit Kosky calls him, can afford to join the fat-free world of muscle and fitness.

---

[3]"The shape of the belly can be quite variable, as can be seen in Figure 27, a series of male subjects. Of all the myriad, possible shapes, we have delineated four basic shapes: enlargement of the upper half; enlargement of the lower half; overall enlargement; and flat" (p. 69 in *The Body Reveals: What Your Body Says About You*, by Ron Kurtz and Hector Prestera, M.D., 1984).

Wearing only an extra-long towel wrapped around his sumptuous waist, Teleny throws his extra weight around. Too bad he can't throw all this extra flesh away. He wears it, he says, in order to protect his virtue'nd virginity, what he calls "the enamel of the soul" (Jeremy Taylor) as well as "politeness of the soul." (Balzac) The extra 169 lbs. of weight and some nine pounds of New Spiritual'nd Sexual Anxiety do him no good. As a result, the otherwise "Symbol, Myth, and Culture" (Ernst CaSSirer) oriented Teleny has turned into a brisk Merchant from Brisk,[4] who keeps on chewing six times a day his doctor-prescribed weight'nd anxiety reducing bitter Super Serene pill. "Too bad it's not a suppository," he tells Kosky, his expression fusing pride with sadness.

I cannot bear being alone, and while the literary people are charming when they meet me, we meet rarely. My companions are such as I can get, and I of course have to pay for such friendships. . . . To suggest I should have visitors of high social position is obvious, and the reason why I cannot have them is obvious also. (Oscar Wilde)

"It's been six years since I've worked for you as a narrative wine steward in your so Balzacian *literary cuisine,*" says Teleny, whose life accomplishment consists of his introduction to *Dowsing,* a slim tractate on the art of latter-day rhabdomancy, followed by a preface to *Witching Waters.* "What a miracle to see you here, my Little Lord Fauntleroysky," he whispers as he and Kosky walk along the corridors, of Reading Gaol.[5] Teleny giggles. "I heard your old lady Cathy Young, your

---

[4]A merchant from Brisk ordered a consignment of dry goods from Lodz. A week later he received the following letter: "We regret we cannot fill this order until full payment has been made on the last one." The merchant sent his reply: "Please cancel the new order. I cannot wait that long." (From *A Treasury of Jewish Folklore,* Nathan Ausubel, ed., 1948).

[5]A *form of life,* as I understand it, is partially defined by a set of moral rules that participants in that form hold as binding upon each

Madame Edwarda (Bataille), is coming out with a book about her form of sexual life, her *bataille* (battle. J. K.) with you. I've just had an intimate talk'nd tell session about you and her with two laddies."

"Two ladies? You and the ladies? How could you my dear lad?" Kosky exclaims.

"Two handsome *laddies*, not ladies, you silly-silly boy! One lad wearing a most handsome jacket, the other lad clad in a simple pullover." Teleny a spiritually confirmed bachelor, corrects him sternly. "I gather these two are doing a story on you." He says shining brightly.

"Ruthenia. Ruritania belongs in a novel, about a prisoner of Zenda. Zenda, not Zen or Zelda as one who often writes for journals of public opinion, like them, you too understand the need for journalistic Old Spice."

"I certainly do," Kosky agrees politely. **"I am as isolated as you could wish me to be: the word has been given out to abandon me, and a void is forming around me."** (Freud to Fliess)

"They called me with some spicy questions about you because they knew bloody well that, when it comes to spicy headline-making I am the best."

"So what did you tell these two?" Kosky asks Teleny.

"I told them about my editing for you the semi-inverted commas while in a comatose state." Teleny giggles. I told them I did for you what John Hall Wheelock did for Thomas Wolfe.[6] That one day I too might be stepped upon by History as a footnote in a story about you." Teleny giggles.

---

other and by a set of factual beliefs, some of which constitute application conditions for the former. Bindingness may be understood as the mechanism through which the form of life is internalized and, hence, as the will-to-power of the totality upon its members, says Arthur C. Danto in *Mysticism and Morality:* Oriental Thought and Moral Philosophy, New York, 1972.

[6]**John Hall Wheelock, the editor of Scribner's who had changed *Of Time and the River* from the first person, in which it**

"Be careful, for whom you put-in or take-out such *tele* (Greek for far, esp. far fetched. J. K.) John Hall Wheelock stories, Teleny," our Literary telamon admonishes him firmly. **Dreiser, to borrow Thomas Wolfe's distinction, was a putter-inner rather than a take-outer. The job of cleaning up after him, of cutting and pruning his swollen manuscripts, straightening out grammatical tangles, and correcting misspelled words, was left to friends, editors, wives, and mistresses. He welcomed their tinkerings and he increasingly depended on them, but neither the complaints nor the compliments of critics appeared to affect his literary practices. (Daniel Aaron, 1990)[7]** "Look what happened to Thomas Wolfe and Theodore Dreiser."

"Don't you worry about a thing," says Teleny. "Everything I told those two writing farts about you I qualified by 'that's impossible to say.' " He saddens. "Now why have you never responded to any of my now-or-never love letters? All written in my own unique Gaelic style? Gaelic Style—not a style readily found in Ruthenian Galicia! Now why not, my dear boy?" he moans. "After all, I delivered them practically under your door. No wonder that out of despair I gave in to being ambushed." He offers Kosky a couple of sour grapes.

----

was originally written, to the third person, would be awakened by the ringing of the phone at 2 or 3 A.M. to hear Wolfe's deep, sepulchral voice say, "Look at line 37 on page 487 of *Of Time and the River*. Do you see that 'I'? You should have changed that 'I' to 'he.' You betrayed me, and I thought you were my friend!" (Elizabeth Nowell. op. cit.)

[7]See also *Brother Theodore* by Daniel Aaron, the review (in *The New Republic*, 1990) of *Theodore Dreiser: An American Journey, 1908–1945*, Vol. II by Richard Lingeman, 1990. (*At the Gates of the City*, Vol. I appeared in 1986. J. K.)

23

Writing is creation. **The Hellenistic period saw the birth of the novel.** *The earliest complete specimen, that of Chariton, is not later than the second century of our era, and the genre is certainly earlier.* **(A.D. Nock)**[1] Kosky cannot write his own story telling story—a full length novel at that— without writing, one way or another, about the very length to which a storyteller must go in his various trials of the writing process. Here, don't confuse process with trial, particularly not the writing process with putting a writer's writing—worse yet, a writer!—on trial. And writing means to him, skoaling life in the sizzling Swedish fashion since it is the Swedes who,

---

[1]"It is an imaginary narrative based on romantic history: the specimens preserved have plots which conform closely to a type. A young married couple (in later forms a pair of lovers) are separated by circumstances, pass through a series of tragic and violent misfortunes, and are finally reunited. The misfortunes generally include some very close approximation to death, often something which to the one member of the pair appears to be in truth the other's death, and generally the flogging of one or both parties, sometimes other tortures. Throughout there is an accent of theatrical pose. One incident may suffice." (*Conversion: The Old and the New in Religion from Alexander the Great to Augustine of Hippo* by A. D. Nock, Oxford, 1933, p. 199)

awarding yearly the Nobel prize to a novel (not the other way around printer!) consider fiction—that is, a novel, or even a novella—more powerful than dynamite invented by Nobel.

Hence, a writer skoals life even if as a writer he or she is defined as no more than "an engineer of the human soul" (Joseph Stalin) and no less than "writer, *n.* 1. penman, penner. *Sl.* pen-pusher. 2. leg man, sob sister. 3. scribe, scrivener, *Judaism:* sopher. 4. script writer, playwright, paraphrast, satirist, mythmaker". (*Rodale* dictionary.)

For Kosky, the Swedish eye-to-eye skoal potentiates to the ninth degree the spiritual contents of such highly charged toasters as Polish/Ruthenian *na zdrowie,* the American chinchin, the Russian *na zdarovye!* the Germanic *prosit,* the French *Santé!* A properly executed spiritual skoal begins with the Tantric meeting of eyes—an optical opening line, to "a protracted ecstasy of mind and body" (Philip Rawson) which can take place anywhere people gather. The toaster sends his glance searching for a potential toastee. Searching anywhere since skoaling can be done across a dining table, king-size terrace, a drawing room, or even across a single bed for two people. Preferably double bed. Better yet, queen or king size bed.

To skoal or not to skoal means to see or not to see, since the sense of seeing constitutes 69 percent of a skoal, says the authoritative *Skoal!* magazine. Upon receiving the first glance of the forthcoming skoal, the toastee responds either by "looking blandly the other way: the Swedish way of showing the other cheek," says *Skoal!* magazine, or by voluntarily establishing eye contact, "the Swedish paving of the road for a meeting of transmigrating souls," according to the *Swedish-Jewish Arts and Letters Quarterly.*

Next comes the dramatically tense raising of the glasses to eye level, first by the skoal-seeking toaster, then by the toastee, "followed by the well-timed *yet* spontaneous act of abrupt follow-through of bottoms up! to be followed up again by raising of the empty glasses—and skoaling each other again. All decent skoaling is done with the eyes locked in eye-to-eye i.e., I-to-I position maintained throughout the duration of the skoal by the strictly observed Self. Observed, that is watching one's Self while, via eye-to-eye contact, watching the Self of the Other—the one who skoaling my Self is also skoaling a Self of his or her own. Preferably, true skoaling should be done without as much as a blink and absolutely without a wink. No wonder. Winking does to skoaling what hiccups do to speech: it interrupts the flow; it insinuates another meaning. In skoaling, winking is optical double-talk.

It is said that the skoal—a visual language commonly spoken by all culturally versatile Swedes—finds its origin in the ancient customs of the Vikings. The clever Vikings, who invented the skoal, defined manners as a "contrivance of wise men to keep fools at a distance" (Emerson), not their answer to manners seen as a "hypocrisy of a nation." (Balzac) Suspicious, anxious to avoid an eye for an eye, and mistrustful of any eye-to-eye, the Vikings devised a skoal as a way of one man keeping an anxious eye on the eye of another. Apparently, it was their way of arresting another's movements (such for instance, as sudden as reaching for a dagger) with a simple movement of one's eye. "However cruel, even brutal was their arresting stare it was, nevertheless, the most peaceful form of arrest ever known to modern man." (Jay Kay).

In a hurry to skoal life, and, as a result, make life less lifeless—(lifeless, meaning "dully; inactively; languidly; inertly; lazily; torpidly; quiescently; silently; actually; heavily; passively; sluggishly; unusually"; (*Rodale*) our "sex skoaler (SS) searching for the best *dish* (here, dish-chick, i.e. a tasty female. Ed.) gulps down the remnants of last week's *bigos* his very favorite and most economical, meal. **HUNTERS' STEW (*Bigos Mysliwski*) One of the oldest traditional Polish dishes. Famous in poetry and in novels, this stew was served at royal banquets and hunts, and still is the *piece de resistance* after a hunting party. Since this dish cannot be prepared in small quantities because of the numerous ingredients required, it is wisest to plan to serve it at a large party . . . *Bigos* is even better reheated, so it may be**

prepared in the morning for use at dinnertime. Will keep in the refrigerator a full week. (*Polish Cookery.* 1958).[*] Satiated, he then rushes out onto the street. In minutes, he can be seen entering the newly remodeled Hotel Khazar-Esplanade (Owner: Onogurs & Ostyak; architect Al-Masudi and David El-Roi-Disraeli). The Khazar-Esplanade is the only hotel which has issued its own traveler's checks which bear American-Polish inscription in Hebrew lettering.[3]

In the hotel Kosky runs straight to its swimming pool. At this time — it's well after 9:00 P.M. — there's no one in the water. Quickly, he changes into his swim suit, and in minutes our literary mini-messiah buoys happily in the calm waters. This is the start of his new Sufi-like tale.

His mood shifts when, thanks to the involuntary shift of his sight, he sees the full-grown form of a female locked inside the pool's Lunar ultraviolet solarium, a stall separated from the rest of the room by an ill-fitting curtain of purple rubber. Safe in his waterhole, our water snake swiftly lets his

----

[2]Among others, *Bigos* contains: roast beef or pot roast, roast lamb, roast pork, venison or hare, chicken or duck, ham, sausage, roast veal, sauerkraut, dried mushrooms, onions, flour, salt, pepper, sugar and wine. *Polish Cookery:* The Universal Cook Book by Marja Ochorowcz-Monatowa (Poland's Most Famous Cook Book Adapted for American Use (use, as well as muse. J. K.) New York, 1958.

[3]"From Khazaria the Hebrew script seemed to have spread into neighbouring countries. . . . Some Hebrew letters (*shin* and *tsadei*) also found their way into the Cyrillic alphabet, and furthermore, many Polish silver coins have been found, dating from the twelfth or thirteenth century, which bear Polish inscriptions in Hebrew lettering, side by side with coins inscribed in the Latin alphabet. Pliak comments: These coins are the final evidence for the spreading of the Hebrew script from Khazaria to the neighbouring Slavonic countries. . . . They were minted because many of the Polish people were more used to this type of script than to the Roman script, not considering it as specifically Jewish.' " (A. Koestler, op. cit.)

inner current carry him motionless to the pool's darkest (and deepest) corner. There the snake raises his head up and, skoaling life, safely peeks through the narrow opening under the curtain. Again our literary anti-misogynist has been uniquely favored. Inside, wearing high-heeled Roman-slave sandals and nothing else, a lunar woman calmly bathes under the man-made sun.

I liked to walk up Fifth Avenue and pick out romantic women from the crowd and imagine that in a few minutes I was going to enter into their lives, and no one would ever know or disapprove. (F. Scott Fitzgerald) It is an admiration such as "those who have devoted their thoughts to the creation of beauty feel toward those who possess beauty itself," in the words of Thomas Mann.

The lunar woman is in her most sexually potent mid-twenties; a naked mermaid who has stepped down to our Samael, from the left-panel side of Bosch's *The Hay Wagon*. The lunar woman is a creature of physical contradictions. She looks as curvy, cuddly'nd creamy as Kirsten, the green-eyed superb Swedish Sexpot Sensation from the pages of the recent *Billingsgate* magazine, but given her swarthy and dig-nified look, she could also—please forgive this sudden associ-ation—be Jewish. A true Jewish fishwife, often known for her inveterate temper and loudly expressed sexual idiom. One of many such beauties who, together with the 500,000 other Jews—forgive me for bringing this about!—perished, burned alive in the flames of the Warsaw Ghetto.[4]

"Let us hope she is Hungarian!" Jay Kay introduces her, "Imagine, a bi- or even tri-lingual Hungarian woman." (To

---

[4]"In order to overawe the Jews, the Nazis first tried to break the spirit of the Warsaw Ghetto by breaking into it in six tanks on the first night of Passover." From *The Battle of the Warsaw Ghetto*, pub-lished by the American Council of Warsaw Jews and American Friends of Polish Jews (New York, 1944).

J. K. Hungarian signifies one who knows all there is to know about life defined, in the absence of a better term, as Transylvanian Cuisine.)[5]

Her shiny olive skin seems smooth and shiny. Her cheekbones, so high and Oriental, suggest her ancestors could have been the sea Gypsies of Tantric Thailand.

Every fixation necessarily changes the hormonal status. (O. Fenichel)

His hormonal status changed, Kosky also changes his position in the water.

Promptly, his spine erect, Kosky places the right foot on the left thigh and the left foot on the right thigh; places the hands palms upward, in the lap. **Good for meditating, this Lotus pose subdues sexual arousal in men and exerts beneficial influence on the womb. (Tantra)**

Meanwhile, in the solarium, the self-timer buzzes and turns off the UV sun. The lunar woman takes off her sunglasses, flashes her all-shaved vulva,[6] wraps her golden frame in a sumptuous silk robe and walks out of the solarium like **the lady whose bulk and bloom struck him to the point of admiration. (John Galsworthy)**[7] Our starry-eyed staring Tom (for once staring, editor, not peeping!) allows her enough time to take a shower, dry her hair, sit down in the lounge and order a double-size Cuba Libre from the poolside bar. Only then does he get out of the water, wash off the chlorine under the shower, dry in the sauna, and—clad in his solopolo robe—take a seat at the table closest to hers.

---

[5]Paul Kovi's *Transylvanian Cuisine: History, Gastronomy, Legend, and Lore from Middle Europe's Most Remarkable Region* (1985).

[6]Woman's *yoni:* It is, like reputation, "the universal object and idol of men of letters." (John Adams) comments Jay Kay.

[7]*A Stoic,* Volume 1, p. 69 in *Caravan* by John Galsworthy, (The Grove Edition, 1928).

Galsworthy was Israel Kosky's favorite English-language writer and this was Israel Kosky's favorite edition of Galsworthy's collected works appropriately starting with the story called "a Stoic."

In slow motion, hiking her black silky robe high on her silky thighs, the lunar woman crosses one thigh over the other. This is the time for maximum realism. **At your age, and in your condition, I recommend a little prudence. Now just take my terms quietly, or you know what happens. (John Galsworthy)**[8] Quickly Kosky adapts a standard mental telephoto lens, which, offering minimum distortion, also offers a moderately accurate — and closeup — view of her exquisite posture and exquisitely posturing thighs. Simultaneously the outer writer in him sends her a sneaky side skoal. Again, she simply won't notice him. Dejected, but not rejected, he humbly drops his gaze and skoals her calves. **There was nothing remarkable in the costume, or in the countenance, but the eyes, John felt, were such as one feels they wish they had never seen, and feels they can never forget. (Charles Robert Maturin)**

If he could only catch her glance — a Tantric prerequisite to catching her "by her eyes: eyes are the hair of her soul." (Tantra) Our Tantric coughs and coughs again. This is a spontaneously nervous cough; and it is his most natural one as World War II and escaping capture by the Nazis with the remnants of European Jewry, was his kindergarten. Since his cough easily impersonates sonorous sneezing, it alerts her, and for a brief moment she looks at him, (then, momentarily, into him.) Her glance says: Are you, buddy, suffering from COPD or COLD?[9]

He seizes the moment, and literally sinks his gaze into hers, then skoals her, taking precaution — just in case! — against Psychomental Poison,[TM10] the curse of the evil eye.

---

[8]ibidem, p. 96.

[9]CIGARETTE AND PIPE SMOKERS BEWARE: chronic obstructive pulmonary disease (COPD) and Chronic Obstructive Lung Disease (COLD) are irrepressible, airways obstructions associated with varying "combinations of chronic bronchitis, asthma, and emphysema." (*Merck Manual*, 1982)

[10]Psychomental Poison (a curse): a product of decomposition

The child said, "I am not afraid of the evil eye,/for I am the son of a great and precious fish/and fish do not fear the evil eye,/as it is written:/"They shall multiply like fish in the midst of the earth." (Genesis) This blessing includes protection from the evil eye. (The Zohar)

The lunar woman skoals him with her eyes as well as with her drink. Encouraged, he leans toward her as naturally as he can. Careful now! Leaning forward is body language; since a proper skoal depends only on the talk of the eye, using body language is against skoal's spiritual rules.

"A man should not be tame," says the Spanish proverb, and I would say: An author is not a monk. (Joseph Conrad)

Kosky gets up and walks over to her. "I'm Norbert Kosky. I live next door, on West 69th Street." he says bowing to her most humbly. "I wouldn't be faithful to my faith — my faith is oral tradition — if I didn't at least try to know you." He pauses.

"Carmita Cardobas. From St. Petersburg, Florida," she greets him with an open smile the spiritual origins of which come, no doubt, from the nature of Latin-American Spanish soul (SS) and/or *From Spanish Court to Italian Ghetto* by Yasef Hayim Yerushalmi, (1981).

Now he skoals her and her famous city. It's all in the name! Even the florid, wet and hot Florida's St. Petersburg still evokes in him thoughts of that other St. Petersburg — the one which, as capital of the old Russian Empire, always cold on the surface, boiled like a virulent boil under its surface.

---

obtained by concentration. Can be intentionally projected over any distance as a curse in order to distract, interfere and, depending on its vitriolic strength, destroy the psychic mass of someone else. The strength of Psychomental Poison™ is measured in units of vitriol (from nine to one), each depressive unit containing a higher concentration. (*Materia Psychomatica*, 1966)

Visited by the famous Alessandro di Cagliostro, too bad it was the only city where during his tour of European capitals, he failed to establish a lodge of Egyptian Rite. He failed because of some unmentionable rumors circulated by Countess von der Rocke, that wreck of a *cuntess!* The rumorization of these rumors—read: their "Newspaperization" (Henry James) was supported by the guild of Russian doctors who, envying Cagliostro's popularity as an expert of *Yogic and Tantric Medicine* (O. P. Jaggi), feared the spread of his so eminently successful medical doctrine.

"Please sit down. Right there, across from me." With her shapely sandaled foot, she kicks the only other easy chair in his direction as easily as if it were a semicolon, and when, a bit uneasily, our *erotoman* sits down on it, teasing him, easily she tilts back the back of her own easy chair and with it she sensually stretches her own back. Her pose sets in motion the gears of his fantasy. Now he sees her in front of him as she remains sensually stretched, lying flat on her back in his bathroom in the Kundalini-evoking Yoga pose. With his standing above her, suddenly, in one swift motion, she lifts her arms and legs off the floor, and balancing on her buttocks—the seat of sensation—she tightens the muscles of her abdomen and diaphragm, then just as fast, manages to release them only to repeat the procedure again and again.[11]

Normally, I would ask a man whom I was meeting for the first time in my life, 'What line of biomechanics are you in?'

---

[11]"Women should suspend all Yoga practices except Savasana and Nadi Suddhi (nerve purification: J. K.) during their menstrual period and also for two or three days afterward. . . . Those women starting Yoga practices for the first time should not do so during pregnancy or until six months after childbirth," counsels Yogiraj Sri Swami Satchidananda (whose name, most appropriately, means Existence-Knowledge-Bliss Absolute) in his *Integral Yoga Hatha*.

but I won't ask you." She tilts her torso and lets her robe open to one side.

"Why not?"

"Because you're clearly out of line! I know who you are."

"Who am I?" He goes for *The Taming of Chance* (Ian Hacking, 1990).

"A private hotel guide? Guide not guard! You're too old to be a guard and not bold enough." She laughs in the face of our Magic Flute man, and her overly easy, abandoned laughter puts another face guard No. 6 on his already masked face. Only now he becomes aware he saw this woman before even if only on his inner screen—and found her, potentially, a superb source (SS) of Ruh. (Ruthenian for movement; Arabic for breath. J. K.).

Artemis is Freedom—wild, untrammelled, aloof from all entanglements. She is a huntress, a dancer, the goddess of nature and wildness, a virgin physically and, even more important, a virgin psychologically, inviolable, belonging to no one, defined by no relationship, confined by no bond. (Arianna Stassinopoulos, op. cit., p. 69)[12]

This cultural pose,[13] then brings to his head Bruno Schulz's drawing No. 13, an untitled *cliché-verre;* Kosky title: *A Middle-European Erotoman Worships a Foot of a Robe-Clad Woman.* Enough said.

"Please sit down!" she commands him firmly, and her manner brings to his fatigued mind *Undula Taking a Walk—* Bruno Schulz's drawing No. 1. "This exquisitely executed artwork shows Undula who, all dressed up, and accompa-

---

[12]See *The Gods of Greece,* by Arianna Stassinopoulos, text, and Roloff Beny, photographs (1983).

[13]In the integral Yoga (integral Yoga is a combination of all main branches of Yoga), the Cultural Poses are practiced "mainly as an aid to gaining perfect health, and only a minimum number of such poses is required to gain the maximum amount of benefit." (See their complete listing in "Cultural Poses," Part Four, op. cit.)

nied by another well-dressed young woman, leads on a leash our unduly Undula's foot-worshipping Bruno Schulz." (Jay Kay)

With her shipshaped calf, she now kicks in his direction the only other chair, and she does it with the contempt of a writer kicking an upstart semicolon or comma. When, a bit ill at ease, "he finds her simply sinsational" (Jay Kay) (*Sin*, not *sen* printer, since in Ruthenian, *sen* means both sleep and dream, and in Japan its lowest monetary currency. J. K.) our upstart writer sits down, she ogles him with another brand of contempt — the contempt any fully clothed woman feels at the sight of a half-man, half-beast led on a leash by sex. (See Bruno Schulz's drawing No. 69 simply entitled "A Portrait of an Incurable Erotoman." Enough shown. (Enough *shown*, not enough said, Printer!) We are talking *cliché-verre*, not literary cliché!

Judging just by the length and shape of her legs, this leggy Artemis could easily compete with such leggy super-sluts as Josephine Dietrich and Baker Marlene — the two leggy sluts who seem from time to time to be making it together on the pages of the *Stained Silk Stocking Super Sex* magazine.

'Normal' implies that there is something which sex ought to be. There is. It ought to be a wholly satisfying link between two affectionate people, from which both emerge unanxious, rewarded and ready for more. . . . Since sex is cooperative you can cater to one another alternately to bridge gaps. *The Joy of Sex:* A Gourmet Guide to Love Making by Alex Comfort, M.B., Ph.D. 1972.

His newest Artemis leans over his face like a palmist over a palm. "Your face isn't exactly an open book. Now, seriously, who are you? An American con man or a French can-can artist?"

"I'm both." **Suddenly there seemed to be something sweeping into me and inflating my entire being. (William James)** "I'm a writer," he exclaims while inhaling her John

Profumo perfumes. **Artist: one who practices one of the fine arts, also: master, virtuoso, genius, prodigy, wizard, trickster, deceiver, cheat, fraud, swindler, confidence man, shyster, flimflam man; fox, sly dog, sharpie, horse trader.** (*Writers' Directory*)

She brightens. "You a writer? Really? That's unreal! Now, what do you write, really, now?" Her intonation dismisses.

"I write novels. Real novels. Real, that is all made up, down to the smallest fictional detail. Fictional, that is based on most detailed research of anything to do with basic human drives: be it a sex drive, a drive-in, or Simplex—the most affordable all American designed motor car. All this made up by me no less than by the collective consciousness" says Kosky. **Neither a primary reality, nor an autonomous reality, it is elaborated implicitly in the overall behavior of individuals participating in the economic, social, political life, etc."** (Lucien Goldman, ibid. p. 9) **Writer: one who writes, also member of the fourth estate, pen-pusher, word painter; ink spiller, quill driver, wordsmith, hack, swindler, word-slinger, potboiler; gazeteer, leg man; stringer, sob sister, scandalmonger, dirt-dealer; scribe, scrivener, recorder; copyist, sopher; scenarist; prosaist; paraphraser; mythmaker, horse trader.** (Artists Guide)

"I've never heard of a writer named Kosky. You see, I read only in English or in Spanish, the two spiritually equal languages of these United Hispanic States. What quixotic language do you write in?" She bares her shoulder.

"In English, what else?"[14]

But I experience my first three tongues as perfectly equivalent centres of myself. I dream with equal verbal

---

[14]"Language is this country's spiritual monarch, not an elected official. Given the growing number of Hispanics, introducing Spanish as a ruler equal to English might one day lead to the formation of the United Hispanic States—with Spanish as the only official spiritual ruler." (George Brayerin, 1986)

density and linguistic-symbolic provocation in all three. The only difference is that the idiom of the dream follows, more often than not, on the language I have been using during the day. (George Steiner)

"What? You write in English? With that accent?" She recoils.

"I hide my accent when I write—and I write only in my American-Jewish English," says Kosky.[15]

"You must have been published only in the British Commonwealth!" she rejoices. "The English are so much more tolerant of those who can't speak or write English well."

"Britannia no longer rules the waves of my English. No matter where I write them first, whether in Buddhistan (J.K.'s euphemism for Thailand. Ed.) or Calvingrad, (Jay Kay's euphemism for Swiss Geneva. J. K.) my books are published first in America as I once pointed out most firmly in *America First* magazine," says Kosky.

"I admit I don't read books," pensively declares the lovely female *pensador*, who then offers him for a reward a deeper view of her inner thighs.

"Don't worry," says Kosky. *I like to watch.* (Chauncey Gardiner, 1971) "How could you? Thousand books are published in this country every year."

She stretches, tensing the muscles of her calves. In vain, he—a Yogi with almost perfect control of his Selfhood—tries to control his self-erection. Promptly, he puts to work upon it his mental sensual backhoe, his sexual Cherry picker, even his largest psychic earth-moving versalift thought excavator. He is out of control.

To break her spell over him, our *escritor* runs to his dressing room and returns with a copy of his latest novel—he called it his newly issued—his passport of spiritual redemption No. 8.

---

[15]"See *Seeing Ease in Exile* by Edward Alexander in *Judaism* (an issue devoted to "Being a Jew and an American—Do They Mesh?") No. 127, vol. 32, No. 3, Summer, 1983.

"It's for you. I'll inscribe it to you later—if you wish," he says humbly, he a humble writer already humbled by the power of the English verb and noun. After all, isn't the English language his most demanding mistress?

She takes the book from him. Aloud, she reads its title. She glances at his photograph on the back cover, then at his face, then at the face on the cover again.[16]

"Not bad. Not bad at all. Your picture, I mean. Why don't you wear it over your face?" She smiles sweetly, then goes through his book silently, reading a few random fragments. She first places the book on the table, then pushes the book away. Her gesture disqualifies him as a man far more than it disqualifies his fiction.

But so what? Here he becomes purposefully corruptible. Who cares about fiction anyhow? (Can you name one person who can't live without reading fiction? I can't, J. K.) At this time in his life this woman excites him like no other, "and in his head the expression *this woman* refers just about to every passing-by or by-passing woman." (Jay Kay) Still, there is no need to get overcorrupted. Corruption by one's Self is one thing; quite another is corruption by the Other, particularly when, these sick-sex-obscured days, the Other is a sex-dispensing woman.

"Storytelling is a commodities business. A writer is a banker. A banker of Self. Self is a rare commodity, as rare as

---

[16]Sex is, as any student of advertising and publishing knows, a highly intriguing phenomenon, charged with explosive possibilities and accompanied by an infinite number of strange, beautiful, and terrible ramifications. With it are involved the most intense of human emotions: love, hate, jealousy, treachery, betrayal, cruelty, sacrifice, devotion. Suicide and murder frequently take place because of it. Life is brought into being as its consequence. Lives are dramatically and drastically changed through its agency. (Gina Cerminara) in "Sex: Some Karmic Aspects of Sex," Chapter 10 in *The World Within*, 1957.

platinum. As rare as group sex," he says referring her to *A History of Orgies* by Burgo Partridge (1960), and saying this he wonders whether in this age of sexual plague a woman with legs as beautiful as hers "prefers walking by just by herself," in the cryptic language of the Tantric text which also says that a "dombi's legs must beg to be watched in the act of sexual walking." (Tantra)

"Storytelling is serious business." Our fictional bank teller now tells her about his American storytelling bank. **Creation seemed a mighty crack/To make me visible. (Emily Dickinson) I have no wife, no parent, child, allie,/To give my substance to. (Pope)** "As I have no family to hand things down to, I hand them down on paper. You might say, fiction is my family business."

"No family? Isn't that bad for a writer?"

"Not for this one," says our Lord of Misrule.

Hermes is appointed messenger of the gods because he promises never to lie, but adds that "it may be necessary for him not to tell the truth in order that he may not lie." . . . Language and speech which, according to Plato, were invented by Hermes belong to the world of form. (*The Gods of Greece,* op. cit., p. 196) "For one, my father would disapprove of my writing my kind of fiction — fiction so unkind to the reader — one brought up on reading. He wanted me to read Shakespeare, John Galsworthy and Somerset Maugham, all of whom were to him literary Lions."

"You sound deliberate!" She reprimands him.

"Plotting a narrative plot evolves in one's mind beforehand, long before the writing hand takes over. That's deliberate."

"You sound selfish." She pronounces.

"I am. Writing comes from Self as much as it does from fish. If that's not selfish, what is?" our Jonas mentors. **I am a camera with its shutter open, quite passive, recording, not thinking. (Christopher Isherwood)**

She gives him a fresh glance. "Every Spaniard's dream is to *tenar un hijo, plantar un arbol, escribir un libro* — have a son, plant a tree, write a book. And here you are: a real *escritor* planted next to me like a tree." She looks at him—and her look is a *regard*, one that stems from regard for life—life typified by the love of oneself as well as love of the Other.

Now it's Kosky's turn. He looks straight into her eyes. This is eye-to-eye, as well as I-to-I. This is what her eye (as well as her I) say to him: They say: cut this literary shit, *Señor*. I don't give a fuck about what you write or in what language or for whom, and even if I were to give you a fuck, I wouldn't do it because you are a writer but because when I saw you drifting aimlessly in that pool of water, you looked sad'nd smutty.

Without a word, without another look at her or her thighs, Kosky gets up. He steps one step away from her. Slowly he begins to take off his robe. The slowness of his disrobing is anything but a tease. He learned to disrobe like this, then to stand semi-rigid (here rigid does not necessarily imply erected J. K.) not from life and not from phantasy, but straight from *Liberalia,* a liberal adult photographic publication which, published bi-monthly in Manchilde Village, Eastern California, openly advocates the implicit beauty of the male animal, portraying man as "a pliable animal, a being who gets accustomed to everything" (Dostoyevsky) as well as "the arch machine." (Emerson)[17] The disrobing accomplished, barefooted, Kosky stands before her. Then he starts walking toward the pool.

In the train I was tormented by a need for intercourse, and I thought of everything that has been said, written and published about dirty old swine, those poor old swine whom the little spermatic beast still gnaws with all its might. Is it our fault if nature has implanted in us such an imperious, persistent and stubborn desire for coming

---

[17]As quoted, rated and numbered in Stein and Day's *Dictionary of Definitive Quotations,* collected by Michael McKenna (New York, 1983). In polo, rating No. 10 is top.

together with the other sex? (Edmond de Goncourt, 1888)

He shivers. If all this could only take place in St. Petersburg, Florida. If she could see him our Lord Fauntleroy, polo-playing, position Number One (and being so good at offside backhand shot in an all-celebrity filled and celebrity watched polo game, mounted on The Maltese Cat, a splendidly trained polo pony straight from the stables of Rudyard Kippling. If she could only see our narrative Dandy in the saddle, attired in his zebra-striped purple polo shirt by Zorro wearing his ultra white Burchell's polo britches, matched by his self-styled Fabian polo boots! Wouldn't all this gamesmanship add in her eyes at least sexual size to our *equus burchelli?*[18]

Meanwhile, Carmita watches him as he is. Her look signals spiritual surveillance, as well as surveillance of a potential sex club member. Make it a member candidate.

In the pool, facing the deep end, our **spermatic little beast (Goncourt, as above)** lowers himself vertically into the pool under her very eyes, his feet first, letting his bony toes, bony calves, bony thighs, and bony chest slice the surface without a ripple. Pushing off, he lets the water gently engulf him up to his bony neck — but under no condition would he allow water to reach any higher. Yod forbid that water should ever flood his nostrils which bring oxygen to his head. Head is the seat of the brain. One's cerebral seat. Enough said.

Don't ever let the waves of the mundane flood you from within. (Israel Kosky to Norbert)

With his entry into the physical world accomplished, his spiritual reentry into himself begins. Peacefully, he stretches. It is his Sincerely Yours look. **My voice, adorned/with the**

---

[18]Named after a British naturalist, Burchell's zebra *(equus burchelli)* is lighter boned than any other zebra, hence able to run at thirty-five miles per hour for a long time and distance — "not unlike any well-trained all-American polo pony." (Norbert Kosky)

marine insignia:/Above my heart an anchor,/And above the anchor a star,/And above the star the wind,/And above the wind the sail. (Rafael Alerti)

Carmita walks over to the edge of the pool. At first she looks down — down at him — but then the minute she sees what he does her *regard* becomes altogether different. She sees our Buddhist monk in the 9 foot deep end of the swimming pool, but just when she expects him to start swimming, he brings his feet together, places his hands along his thighs, and, with his head above the surface, begins to float upright — as if he were a Lotus sitting on a transparent shelf. She examines him closely for a minute, then, quite assured that several meters of water indeed separate him from the bottom — and clearly he does not wear any device that could keep him so totally motionless, so totally and peacefully afloat. She decides to interrupt his Lotus-like meditation.[19]

"I don't know anyone who floats quite the way you do. Why d'you suppose you won't sink?"

"Because I don't want to sink. Sinking would forever flood my nostrils through which my breath flows in and out," replies our monk.

"Why don't you offer courses in, say, creative floating?" She offers demurely.

"Floating can be learned only by oneself. Either one knows how to generate it from within or one doesn't. It's like lovemaking or writing," says Kosky. As he says it he lets his inner current take him away from her.

Carmita returns to her deck chair. There she starts to read and continues reading his book. **Anyone who practices yoga properly and sincerely becomes an *iddha* (accomplished); be he young, old or even very old, sickly or weak.** (Hatha Yoga Pradipika).

After a while he leaves the pool. Engrossed in reading she,

---

[19]See "On the Seductive Power of Floating in Pools," Modus Vivendi, Zurich, 1990. (J. K.)

his newest **Lady of Pain (Swinburne)** does not even notice our sex-smitten author. A spiritual score!

"Have the things you wrote about really happened? Did you, for instance, ever meet a man who floated into the world, 'buoyed by a force he did not see and could not name?' " (*Being There*, 1971). She asks when our Floatus sits down beside her.

"Well — Yes or no?" She nudges his thigh with hers: flesh skoaling flesh.

"I don't answer such questions," our Incubus admits openly. "Fiction is a fetish. You'll have to decide for yourself."

"Now, now, don't so be touchy, Mr. Phantom. So what if it happened to you! Who cares about what happens in a novel! And to whom?"

Carmita stands up. So does he. Standing next to her, he feels like a stand-up comic. "I've been running all over New York," she says. "And I'm getting tired of this Feast of Fools. Do you mind if we move what remains of this report-talk to rapport-talk to my hotel room?"

"I don't mind. Not at all," says Kosky. **This chapter, in which we shall undertake the explication of Being-in as such (that is to say of the Being of the "there") breaks up into two parts: A. the existential constitution of the "there"; B. the everyday being of the "there," and the falling of Dasein of Being There. (Heidegger)**

They part company, but they part with each other like friends about to form a company of their own. His book in hand, Carmita retires to her room in order to, in her words, make order in the room, and also in her own words, make herself presentable for him. The word presentable contains the word present! Immediately he stands at *Attention!*

Kosky dresses quickly, then, slowing himself down, takes the express elevator to her floor — what luck! It is floor six. He runs to her room. He is lucky again: it is suite No. 906. She opens the door. She is dressed in a diaphanous gown, a gown which produces *phainō* (Gr. show) of the fine outline of her body. In silence she leads him to an easy chair puts him at ease. She sits down across from him. They wear their masks in silence.

Silence. 1. "A heading for all ailments." (Babylonian Talmud) 9. "A conversation with an Englishman." (Heinrich Heine) 10. "Your highest female grace." (Ben Jonson)[20] This is the end of the eye-to-eye. "Look at me and trust me," he says looking her trustworthily in the eye. "When you look at me forget the stranger in me. Remember I am a novelist, a writer. This means that, reality matters to me only insofar as it becomes a source for a fictional story, you can tell me anything. Anything at all. Tell me about yourself, or others, particularly if you've got a zest for story-telling, not only a story-telling body. Make up a story about you and me; a hypothetical story about a narrative sex affair. A story about how it began — or begins; how it could last, and how it might end. Call it The Story of The Two.

"Start talking," he says. **There's nothing like desire to prevent the things one says from having any resemblance to the things in one's mind. (Proust)**

"Talking about what?"

"Sex. For an opening," he encourages her.

Spiritual freedom in its fullness is neither an abstraction or a transcendent flight. It is not to be conceived onesidedly as detached knowledge or supernatural devotion. (Haridas Chaudhuri)[21]

She looks at him. Her look says: let's kill the bull. Let's be true to life, even if not to each other.

"The other day, after a Broadway matinee of *Hamlet,* I ran into the guy who played him," she says impassively. "Boy! A boyish Ben Hur. Every muscle a string, every vein a snake. An American Health idol if I ever saw one!" She curls a lock

---

[20]As ranked by Michael McKenna, op. cit.

[21]See *Integral Yoga: A Concept of Harmonious and Creative Living,* by Haridas Chaudhuri (1965).

of her hair with her forefinger. "Somehow he took me for a drink at *his* place." She leaves her hair alone and folds her hands in her lap—between her thighs. "A good talker, too. But then in bed—fumbling with his Frisky-Not-Risky prophylactic"—she takes a deep breath—"he just fell apart. His part turned out to be—somehow—all soft. As soft as Hamlet was supposed to be."

"Perhaps you met in him the stage Hamlet, not the actor. Perhaps he wanted to be a Lord Hamlet with you: perhaps being a Hamlet was his best part." Saying this Kosky lifts a paper napkin and, as if in warning, squeezes it into a wad. "Now I wonder why," she disregards his insight.

"Why what?" **Nor the exterior or the inward man Resembles that it was (Hamlet)**

"Why I go after every actor who plays Hamlet. I wonder who's more real—or dear—to me, the dramatic persona or the person who fills it?" She lets her robe disrobe her calf, then her knee, then her thigh. Fixed upon her every move, he watches her, transfixed.

To Hamlet madness is a mere mask for the hiding of weakness. In the making of mows and jests he sees a chance of delay. He keeps playing with action, as an artist plays with a theory. He makes himself the spy of his proper actions, and listening to his own words knows them to be but "words, words, words." Instead of trying to be the hero of his own history, he seeks to be the spectator of his own tragedy. He disbelieves in everything, including himself, and yet his doubt helps him not, as it comes not from scepticism but from a divided will.

De Profundis, (Oscar Wilde).

"Once in bed," she goes on, "I wanted to feel my Hamlet deep within—but when I couldn't feel him," she hesitates, "what I could not feel suddenly became more essential than what I could."

"Why couldn't you feel yourself? Your own body?" With his erotic telesens (tele-sens, not tele-lens, Printer!) Kosky boldly ventures into her sexual hamlet.

A seduction theory. Praise everything; luring a woman away from her husband and persuading her that she is decent (though indulging her in appalling obscenity). That's the contrast I'm fond of. (Dostoyevsky)

"I couldn't because he couldn't make himself *feelable*."

"Why wouldn't he?"

"Because, like Hamlet, he suffered from a divided will. He was all new to that new Condom Etiquette. He found this whole contraceptive business, overly businesslike — as Hamlet would. That's why," she says contemptuously.

"Maybe he wasn't sure you really wanted him that hard?" Our Amleth (Saxo Grammaticus, 1250) tries again. What would he do,/Had he the motive and the cue for passion/That I have? (Shakespeare)

"He was quite sure," she says with the smile of Ophelia of Elsinore. "I made sure he did."

"Maybe he was too hard-pressed?" Amleth won't give up.

"He wasn't. He was soft. He was as coherent as Hamlet — and as incoherent. In any case, my sexual pupil had lovely eyes with pupils that stayed constantly enlarged. Too bad nothing else in him was large enough." She concludes cruelly.

"He is an actor," says Kosky. "Perhaps he wasn't sure he was big enough for his new role. For some of us, finding simultaneous happiness with both a woman and a contraceptive is a tough psychic task — a task not a play. Also," — he pauses in false grief — "he might have needed help." Psychologically, he would be given the usual psychological treatment indicated in such cases; better home relations, remedial reading, perhaps, special tutoring in school work; various techniques of getting along better with others. (Gina Cerminara, op. cit. p. 69)

"Perhaps you're right." Calmly, she assesses Kosky. "I can tell that you don't find his case uplifting enough," she says. Then lowering her eyes in the direction of Kosky's Lower Depths which, from her point of view, might seem to be momentarily depleted of anima, she declares him soft on arrival. This glance, this obvious lowering of her eyes and, with them, of his true sexual status, raises her spiritual status (SS) in his eyes by a full point. This brings her to No. 6 on his spiritually-straight scale from one to nine.

In Tantra, in strictly defined straight sexual terms (SS), all this means she is a *dombi*, a washerwoman: one who, having been washed over—and out many times by everything in life's water, can now afford to be truthful—"since being truthful is *all* she can still afford if she is to be faithful to her Second Body, which, stands for one's highest intellectual properties." Carmita has, by now, passed the elementary sexual tests and she passed them with floating colors—floating, not flying—"because this Artemis is a washerwoman and not a water-child!" (Jay Kay).

Her new rating qualifies her to enter a spiritually Solid State—one which will render her spiritually more mobile and more contained at the same time. She seems spontaneously animated. Her energy emanates from her as steam does from a steamship.[22] To him, a universal Zen Hasid at heart, as well as at the bottom of his spine, animated means hot as well as wet. **In the Hasidic story the symbolic character of the occurrence is emphasized, whereas in the Zen story it remains concealed, and in the literature the meaning of the saying is discussed; it remains however almost without doubt that the washing of the dishes is here also a symbol of a spiritual activity. (Martin Buber, 1958)[23]** Because she is hot, and animated, she makes him steamed up

---

[22]With so many sleepless sailors riding her top and bottom a steamship is, out of situational necessity, always a female, says the 1969 *Naval Dicktionary.* (PRINTER: a dicktionary, that's right: as in Dickens or dickens—colloq. for devil.)

[23]*Zen and Hasidism* by Martin Buber, in *Zen and Hasidism: The Similarities Between Two Spiritual Disciplines.* Compiled by Harold Heifetz, 1978, p. 169.

in his own *kundalini* (steam is the ideal mixture of air and water), which, after Cathy's departure, has lain dormant, "a water snake asleep upon stagnant water." (Jay Kay)

So far so good. Carmita might turn out to be Cathy's spiritual substitute, another Sadhaka, who, practicing Tantric discipline, advances, in his eyes from her status as a disciple to that of the aspirant — one, in whose presence he, Sizzling Sex Master, can aspire freely. She might turn out to be one with whom he can practice *swara sadhana* (he scores another SS on his already high score point system), the essential Tantric practice in which our self-buoyant yogi "causes the breath to flow through the left nostril from sunrise to sunset; and through the right nostril from sunset to sunrise." (Omar Garrison)

Kosky, our spiritual follower of Sabbatai Sevi, is now ready to administer to Carmita one more test which, if passed, might admit her to his inner sardonic sanctum.

He didn't even notice when and how he yielded to the dangerous sway of her eyes. . . . He was swept by an impulse so difficult to express . . . as if confronted by the sight of a sea, suddenly uncovered and naked, a desert, or a chain of snow-capped mountains. . . . Now his eye did not fail to notice the thickness of the braid of hair which, without doubt, he could not have clasped with his soldier's fist. . . . There was something stifling in this beauty, something which stopped one's breath and made one's head swim. (Stefan Żeromski)[24]

---

[24]To Stefan Żeromski, Poland's prime novelist, (*Story of Sin*) female beauty, was like water, always "swishing'nd shining, steaming'nd sparkling, shadowless'nd silvery, starlit'nd seething, sweltering'nd scalding, surging." Note also "Woman is so artistic" (Nietzsche) 9 as quoted on p. 69 of *Spurs: Nietzsche's Styles* by Jacques Derrida, 1978. For some other creative person's perception of womanhood,

His head swimming from the overflow of seminal thoughts ("the brain's semen" Jay Kay) Kosky takes out from his ever present shoulder-bag a bunch of Plot-Quote cards, "the portable table game of literary invention," in the words of the nameless inventor. Each card contains a short fragment from a certain novel. **The body then becomes, as it were, a Book of Revelation. In it is condensed much of our secret history. In it are latent the necessities of our future. (Gina Cerminara, op. cit., p. 69)**

"To start with, read about love in *The Complete Fiction of Bruno Schulz*,"[25] says Kosky, handing Carmita the cards. Now in order to assure that his objectivity—call it Sex Stilled

---

the reader is encouraged to become familiar (though not overly familiar. J. K.) with *Idols of Perversity: Fantasies of Feminine Evil in Fine-de-Siecle Culture* (abundantly illustrated) by Bram Dijkstra, Oxford University Press, 1986, also, *La Femmes au Temps des Cathedrales* (Woman during the Time of the Cathedral) by Regine pernoud, Paris 1980 (in French; also in Polish translation as *Kobieta w czasach katedr*, translated by Iwona Badowska, Warsaw 1990).

Through water, everything is ultimately brought back to the fulfillment of God's goal. . . . The main vehicle for this is the Torah, which, as our sages teach us, is also a spiritual counterpart of water. (Rabbi Aryeh Kaplan, op. cit.)

For an extensive discussion of the literary climate the Polish-reading reader is referred to (1) Arthur Sandauer: Rzeczywistość zdegradowana: Rzecz o Brunonie Schulzu (The degraded reality: A thing (rzecz) about Bruno Schulz) in his introduction to *Proza*, collected writing by Bruno Schulz; Krakow, 1964. (2) Dzieło literackie jako książka (literary work as a book) by Danuta Danek, Warszawa, 1980. (3) Problematyka symultanizmu w prozie (The question of simultaneity in prose) by Seweryna Wysłouch, Poznán, 1981.

[25]Unlike Żeromski, Bruno Schulz was master of the narrative dry dock, a sexually most evocative narrative style. See *Wetness vs. Dryness in the American Literary Style* (Oceanid Press, 1986). **[Bruno Schulz] was small, unattractive and sickly, with a thin angular body and brown, deep-set eyes in a pale triangular face. He**

(SS)—won't be soiled—or spoiled—by bodily touch, which, though corrupting, can lead to *furor divini,* a divine frenzy, he moves his chair a few inches away from her knees. From now on, it's strictly sexually safe literary touch and go. She collects herself, then collects the cards, glances at several of them, and then, seduced by *philia*—the soul-to-soul kinship which, of all arts, only fiction promotes on the highest plane, she starts reading one of them.

Suddenly these strange books broke down all the walls around me, and made me think and dream about things of which for a long time I had feared to think and dream. Suddenly I began to find strange meaning in old fairy tales; woods, rivers, mountains, became living beings; mysterious life filled the night; with new interest and new expectations. . . . (P. D. Ouspensky)

Meanwhile, our partner in this pro-tem literary joint venture thinks of Carmita as an aqueous beauty. Aqueous, not "2. sodden'nd soggy," according to the rating of the word *watery* found in his old Rodale Dictionary.

"Is this one of the word games you play with your reading star student studs?" she asks him, letting down her sensuous Sephardic Spanish jet-black hair.

---

taught art at a secondary school for boys at Drogobych in southeastern Poland, where he spent most of his life. He had few friends outside his native city. In his leisure hours—of which there were probably many—he made drawings and wrote endlessly, nobody quite knew what. (Celina Wieniewska) On November 19, 1942, on the streets of Drogobych, a small provincial town that belonged to Poland before World War II (and now is in the U.S.S.R.), there commenced a so-called action carried out by the local sections of the SS and the Gestapo against the Jewish population. . . . Among the murdered who lay until nightfall on the sidewalks of the little town—who lay where the bullets reached them—was Bruno Schulz. (Jerzy Ficowski)

He does not answer. Intrigued, she stretches on the bed. "It could be exciting," she says, letting her calves cross each other.

"Did you ever ask a woman to do for you a real-sex safe-sex skit?" She picks up another card: it is a fragment from Kuprin's *The Duel*. In a pleasant sonorous voice she reads aloud, then says, "If I were to act out for you Alexandra Nikolaev, would you respond to me as her secret lover, as Romashov does in the novel, or as yourself, as a man who by reading about Romashov has learned what Romashov didn't know: that she—a woman he adored—was, spiritually speaking, a most uncommonly common community whore?"

"Definitely as Romashov," says Kosky. "Romashov is infatuated with Alexandra. Whore or not, she is life to him."

"Who is she really?" asks Carmita.

"Really she is a fallen woman. One who failed to raise herself to the status of a spiritual whore," he answers without a blink. "She is at once one of the most desirable and most despicable women in all of literature." **They embraced and touched each other's faces. . . . But Romashov felt that something imperceptible, murky and repellent came between them and a tiny cold current ran through him."** **(Aleksandr Kuprin)**

"I wouldn't bed a guy who, when in bed with me, thinks something 'murky and repellent' is going on between us. Murky and repellent. That sounds like chewing on tobacco." Carmita then throws the card at Kosky's feet. She glances through the stack and picks up another card. It contains a fragment from *The Man Who Laughs*.[26] (Kosky's favorite para-

---

[26]Victor Hugo, France's greatest epic novelist, wrote *The Man Who Laughs* (1869) at the age of 67 during his exile to Guernsey. The novel "the greatest epic of historical grotesque." (Jay Kay) takes place in the sexual-fetish-oriented seventeenth-century England, "where the English patriciate is the patriciate in the absolute sense of the word." (Hugo)

historical novel. J. K.) Again, Carmita reads aloud: " ' "Why, it is Gwynplaine!" said Josiana, mingling pleasure and contempt. "I prefer the astounding, and you are enough to astound me. . . . The first day I saw you, I said to myself, 'It is he! I know him! He is the monster of my dreams. I'm going to have him.' That's why I wrote to you. Have you read my letter? Did you read it yourself, or did someone else read it to you?" Again Josiana fixed her gaze upon him, and continued: "I feel degraded by you, and I don't mind it! I love you. I go for you not just because you are deformed—but because you are low. A lover who is despised, mocked, grotesque, hideous, laughed at on that pillory called the stage, attracts me no end. You are probably a devil without knowing it yourself. You embody infernal mirth. You are not only ugly: you are hideous. Ugliness is insignificant; deformity is grand. You surpass everything. You are just what I want. You are the monster without; I am within. We were made for each other." ' "

Carmita stops reading. "I like this. I like it a lot. Isn't this just great?" she says. And her words change the setting of his Kundalini from No. 66 to 69. "What a perfect description of an ideal male lover. One so straight you could never find him profiled in *All-Male Jock* magazine." She loosens her belt, widening in the process the open space between the lapels of her robe. For a moment, her breasts show. The moment is long enough. Her breasts are perfectly ordinary, predictably sloopish and uneventful, without the sensual push or the obsessional pull. Her nipples are thin, but not thin enough to constitute for him the source of attraction. Her aureoles are pale, but not pale enough to disappear entirely from sight and render her fetishistically aureoleless. Somehow, he drops his gaze to her inner thighs; *somehow,* she shuts down her robe, and the way she does it headlines that *The Breast Show* is over; "the play is closed, stricken by a single bad review!" (*Times Square Record*) She gives Kosky an equivocal look. It says, unequivocally: Show yourself, buddy! Show your true Self—even if it hurts; even if it will kill you. Stop wearing the face of Romashov or the laughing mask of Gwynplaine. Read me as if I were a sacral text; read my lines but also in-between. Forget about reading between my thighs. "If somehow, now, I were to become for you your one and only Josiana," she says, "would you make love to me — right now, right here — as Gwynplaine would to her in your imagination, or would you fuck me as you — as Norbert Kosky — the fella who needs to be known as a writer before he can put a make on?"

"I would love you as myself. Myself, but disguised as Gwynplaine," says Kosky. He won't surrender to her his literary dogma.

" 'It is wrong to compare flesh with marble,' " Kosky reads another card with text from by Victor Hugo. " 'Flesh is beautiful because it is not marble. It is beautiful because it palpitates, trembles, blushes, bleeds; because it is firm without being hard, white without being cold. A degree of beauty gives flesh the right of nudity; its own beauty is a veil!' " Kosky stops. **A little acting won't hurt. (Haggadah)** Our Actor nonchalantly lifts her robe above her knees high enough — and for long enough — for him to examine her waist and hips. Then, without mental salivating, he continues to read from the card.

" 'Josiana personified flesh. No passion tempted her, but she knew all about passion. Instinctively, she loathed its fulfillment, but longed for it at the same time. She was a virgin stained with every kind of defilement. In her insolence, she was at once tempting and inaccessible. Nevertheless, she still found it amusing to plan a fall for herself.' "

Kosky raises his eyes from the card.

"Am I supposed to fall for you now?" asks Carmita.

"It's all in the cards," says our Horned God.

"But what's the trick?"

"Being oneself. That's the trick," he says shifting in his psychic water. Inside his mental pool, his thighs spread, his feet tucked under him, his hands clasping his shins, he became motionless again, gently bobbing with the movement of the water.

Carmita picks up another card. " 'Josiana was bored,' " she reads aloud from it. " 'She and Lord David carried on an affair of a peculiar kind. They did not love each other—they pleased each other. Josiana postponed the hour of submission for as long as she could; she appreciated David and showed him off. They had a tacit agreement neither to conclude nor to break off their engagement. They eluded each other. There was a method to their lovemaking—one step forward, two back.' " Carmita lifts her eyes to Kosky. "Now you know about me and my Lord David back home."

"Are you going to marry him?" asks Kosky.

"I don't know. There's no rush." She throws her silky hair over her shoulders. Half-sitting, half-lying, she leans her shoulder against the wall. Stretching her legs, she *advertently* lets her robe open again. A sight for *Ecce Homo* of Nietzsche as it was rendered in a painting by Marc Chagall!

Again she reads from *The Man Who Laughs:* " 'It's unbecoming to be married. Marriage fades one's ribbons; it makes one look old. How commonplace it is to be handed over by a notary! Marriage suppresses the will, kills the choice; turns love into dictation. Like grammar, marriage replaces inspiration by spelling; it disperses mystery; it diminishes the right of the strong or weak; destroys the charming balance of the sexes. To make love prosaically decent—how gross! To deprive lovemaking of any wrongdoing—how dull!' " She turns to Kosky, the innermost part of her inner thighs staring him in the face.

"Well?" she says. This is the frontal-body skoal. "Now you know why Lord David and I haven't wedded. Or—for that matter—even wetted each other."

"Perhaps that's not the real reason," says Kosky, transferring himself from his chair to the edge of her bed—and edging toward her in the process. He picks up another card and reads from it. " 'What cannot escape us, inspires us with no haste to obtain it. Josiana wanted to remain free; David to remain young; to remain without a tie for as long as possible seemed to him an extension of youth. In those crazy times, middle-aged young men abounded; they grew gray as young fops. . . .' "

He looks up at her. "I still don't see why I should fall for you and your narrative brand of sex," says Carmita. "I'm not into sex. Sexually speaking, I am a narrative *entrada en blanc*—a blank entry."

Kosky reads again. " 'All her instinct impelled Josiana to yield herself wantonly, rather than to give herself legally. Pleasure is to be measured by the astonishment it creates.' " He puts the card away. This is no longer acting. He, the past master of the "I like to watch" routine, is at it again. Sixteen years later he is ready to be caught in the literary sex act— the newest sexual routine.

At bottom, every human being knows very well that he is in this world just once, as something unique, and that no accident, however strange, will throw together a second time into a unity such a curious and diffuse plurality: he knows it, but hides it like a bad conscience—why? From fear of his neighbor who insists on convention and veils himself with it. . . . Only artists hate this slovenly life in borrowed manners and loosely fitting opinions and unveil the secret, everybody's bad conscience, the principle that every human being is a unique wonder . . . (Nietzsche)

Carmita fidgets. "Somehow—I want to know what Josiana and Gwynplaine did that night. Give me a cue—or another card. Give me a better *introduccio a lombre*, a guide to the shadow."

"There is no other card," he says. **Stolen waters are sweet, and bread eaten in secret is pleasant. (Haggadah)**

"But how did they make out?" Once again she lets her robe split open and she opens herself in the process.

"I won't tell you," says Kosky. "This is the time when our Romashov has other things on his mind. Call them thighs, not things."

Romashov was exhausted but pleasantly so. He had

hardly time to undress before he was overpowered by sleep. And his last conscious impression was the delightful smell of his pillow: the smell of Alex's hair, of her perfume, of her beautiful young body. (Alexander Kuprin, 1905)[27]

---

[27]From *The Duel*, by Aleksandr Ivanovich Kuprin (1905), translated by Andrew R. MacAndrew (1961). Alexander Kuprin (1870–1938) is the author of *Moloch, Olesya, Breaking Point, Captain Rybnikov, Sulamith, The Pit* and others. "But please tell him from me that he should never pay attention to anybody's advice but just keep writing in his own way" was Leo Tolstoy's advice to Kuprin.

24

I have always considered myself a rather hermetic poet, for a certain limited audience. And what happens when this sort of poet becomes a kind of Jan Kiepura, a tenor, or a football star? Naturally, there arises a fundamental misunderstanding. (Czeslaw Milosz, 1983)

"I knew I could finally corner you for a literary tête-à-tête, my dear Jehuda Halevi!"[1] says a little man who bluntly accosts Kosky when, one calm evening, our calm author walks out of the Aeon Club through the only nonrevolving door left in New York. **There is a word which, when understood, wipes out the sins of innumerable aeons. (Zen**

---

[1]Jehuda Halevi (b. circa 1076–1141): the greatest Hebrew poet of Spain; ("and one of the profoundest thinkers Judaism has had since the closing of the canon."—Henry Slonimsky) wrote his once-celebrated book *Kuzari* (*The Khazars*) in Arabic. *"Kuzari,* written a year before his death, is a philosophical tract propounding the view that the Jewish nation is the sole mediator between God and the rest of mankind. At the end of history, all other nations will be converted to Judaism; and the conversion of the Khazars appears as a symbol or token of that ultimate event." From *The Thirteenth Tribe: The Khazar Empire and Its Heritage,* by Arthur Koestler (Random House, 1976.) See also *The Kuzari, An Argument for the Faith of Israel,* Introduction by Henry Slonimsky, 1964.

saying as quoted by Martin Buber)[2] The two-hundred-year-old Aeon Club is an intellectual reserve reserved for men- and women-of-letters.

"I hate the word *corner*," says Kosky. **Homo duplex has, in my case, more than one meaning. (Conrad to K. Waliszewski)**

In his sixties and impeccably attired, his gray hair pushed neatly to one side, the little man hands Kosky an ultra thin calling card. The inscription reads "Simon Thomas Temple, Sr., Textual Context Special Investigator: CLIFFORD, ASHLEY, BUCKINGHAM, ARLINGTON & LAUDERDALE, New York, Chicago, Los Angeles."

Impatiently, Kosky takes a look at the man, then at his card.

"You probably wonder what made me ask you to meet me," says Temple tentatively.

"I do," says Kosky. "I'm a wonder kid."

"Frankly"—Temple disarms Kosky with a smile—"ever since the manure shit from your first novel hit the literary fan, my wife and kids—we were your instant fans—call you Giuseppe Balsamo. (The man who by impersonating Cagliostro got Cagliostro into deep trouble: J. K.) But to me you are what the small press says about you in capital letters: our one-and-only literary Cagliostro." By starting like that, Temple unmasks himself—**He is a centrifugal man (Buber)** to whom impulse becomes act.

"It's just another newspaper story. Since there's nothing I can do for you, is there anything that you as a special investigator can do for me which I can't do by investigating myself as I've already done in my fiction?" says Kosky. **Expect poison from the standing water. (Blake)**

---

[2]Martin Buber (died 1965): a formidable Jewish philosopher "who at twenty-six rediscovered Judaism while reading the Baal Shem Tov's testament. "It was then," he wrote in a memoir, that "something indigenously Jewish rose in me, blossoming, in the darkness of Exile, to a new conscious expression." *The Jewish Pres-*

"For you, I can do a lot. Why? 'Cause yours is a typical writer's lot," says Temple offhandedly. "You might have heard of our firm's record in helping, among others, to settle out of court the case of the estate of the late Henry James vs. the Downtown Hagiographers, Inc. who claimed that, if James indeed had written by himself *The Ambassadors,* a novel he published in 1903, he could not have written by himself *The American* (a novel published in 1877) given the formidable difference they claimed existed in the writing style of both works.

"That's patently nonsense. Any literary patent expert knows novelists are self-styled stylists (SSS) who change their colors with every song they sing and with every new mental or physical habitat!" our Black Partridge (black partridge is multi-colored. J. K.) explodes with laughter.

"What you might not know is that back in 1867 we also advised Turgenev to clarify in writing once and for all what went on during that 1838 fire on the steamship *Nicholas I* after Prince Dolgorukov resurrected that old rumor about Turgenev's allegedly spineless conduct when Turgenev was a passenger on a pleasure cruise ship which caught fire at sea. As a result, Turgenev first reprimanded Dolgorukov on the pages of St. Petersburg's *Vyedomosti* then, already mortally ill with cancer of the spine, weeks before his most painful death dictated in French (he, a Russian writer! writing in French on his deathbed) to his friend Pauline Viardot a fictional story called *'Un Incendie en Mer'* ('A Fire at Sea') which was to set straight that old account. Since this story was translated from French into Russian by yet another woman only three weeks before Turgenev's so untimely death, this started yet another spineless rumor that it was Pauline Viardot, not Turgenev, who really wrote *A Fire at Sea.* Needless to say, with Turgenev's death, the fire is still raging."[3]

---

ence, by Lucy Davidowicz (op. cit.)

[3] Bilingual in Russian and French, Turgenev wrote in French *"Monsieur François,"* a story then translated into Russian under the

"Now I recall who you are," says Kosky, pocketing the man's calling card as if it were a passport to the wrong kind of sexual desire. "I heard you give a talk on the radio about your Literary Indebtedness Theory."

"I used the word infringement, not indebtedness," the man corrects him sternly.

"Infringement? How defined?" Kosky won't surrender. "Was it as '1. Disobedience. Noncompliance. Violence. Infraction' [Rodale]?"

"It was infringement as '2. Encroachment. Intrusion. Inroad. Incursion,' [Rodale]" says Temple, who does not mind playing literary rodeo.

"Never mind," says Kosky. "Only the other day I saw on that flashing World Headline Making WHM-TV headline: 'SCANDAL! SCANDAL! SCANDAL! SIM THOMAS TEMPLE ALLEGES JAMES JOYCE IS NOT THE SOLE AUTHOR OF MANY PURPOSEFUL ERRORS IN SPELLING, PUNCTUATION AND SYNTAX FOUND IN HIS ACCLAIMED NOVEL ULYSSES, THE VERY ERRORS LITERARY CRITICS CONSIDERED ESSENTIAL TO THE UNDERSTANDING OF THE GREAT NOVEL EVER SINCE IT ATTRACTED THEIR ATTENTION BY ITS OBSCENITY TRIAL. TEMPLE SAYS MANY OF THESE ERRORS WERE CONTRIBUTED TO THE NOVEL NOT BY JOYCE BUT BY MANY OF HIS TYPISTS PRIVATELY HIRED BY THE AUTHOR WHEN HE LIVED IN PARIS. TEMPLE'S ALLEGATIONS STUN LITERARY COMMUNITY.'[4] Kosky recites from memory. "That's not a headline.

---

title "The Man in the Gray Spectacles." "A Fire at Sea" was published in English in *London Magazine* under the title "An Episode in the Life of Ivan Turgenev"—a title which, unlike "Fire at Sea," suggests an attempt at autobiography, "as such is obviously a far cry from Turgenev's creative intentions." (Niskisko)

[4]After several professional typists refused to type episodes of Joyce's novel that they considered bawdy, the author's friends as well as part-time acquaintances undertook the task of typing the mam-

That's a beheading!"[5]

"I'm glad you like it." Temple smiles in his own enigmatic style.

"From now on, you might say, my name will be an eternal footnote to Joyce, and, in my book, Joyce stands for the temple of eternal Irish Joy. That's my way of being linked to James Joyce," says Temple modestly. "You know, I could stir up quite a stink about any American or foreign writer by merely tracking him or her to their earlier typists. They are all quqs."

"What does the word *quq* stand for?" says Kosky quizzically.

"*Quq* means quote—unquote—quote. A creative association," says Temple. "By tracing what and how authors write to sources other than their own writing, to what and how other writers already have written, I can prove that any text (or any author), no matter how recent, new and original, is not original at all, and I can prove it beyond reasonable doubt," stresses the literary gangster.

"But, as any writer knows, writing is composition and, not unlike music, no matter how original must include some existing music. Besides, could you be less eternal and more specific? Where, for instance, do you trace such natural

----

moth manuscript on borrowed typewriters. In the process, they not only added their own punctuation, but they also misspelled some words and corrected the spelling of others that the author intended to be misspelled. (*Times Square Record*)

[5]To understand better the notion of "extra-literary reality," see "Balzac, James, and the Realistic Novel," by William W. Stowe, in *Literary 1987* (Princeton University Press, 1987).

specific? Where, for instance, do you trace such natural literary tracings to?"[6] asks Kosky.

. . . Although the narrative mind is working in a field of free association, there is really no such thing as a free association. Every story is consciously based upon some story already in existence; it adds little increments or manipulates it — reverses the situation of it and puts plus signs for minus signs. (Thornton Wilder)

"To some other equally derivative literary floats, you might say."

"Wouldn't you rather try to trace the writer's spiritual origins? Better yet, go to the very source of their narrative talent?"

"Other than '1. habitual facility of execution' (Emerson) and '4. the excitable gift' (Anne Sexton),[7] nobody knows what talent is. However, thanks to the new wave of literary litigation, searching for quqs has become as important as searching for old-fashioned literary clues used to be."

A young Aziyadé, a stowaway from the Topkapi, Manhattan's newest red-light district, her miniskirt barely covering her thighs, struts toward them on a red light, smiling as if to an invisible video camera.

"Want company?" She mumbles at the world at large.

"No, thank you. **We've got each other.**" Kosky quotes somebody.

She widens her stance. "I give a good time."

"So does my watch." Kosky smiles back as he and Temple

---

[6]The more one understands an era, the more convinced one becomes that the images a given poet employed, which one assumed to be his own, in fact, were taken almost unchanged from another poet. Images are given to poets; the talent to remember them is far more important than the talent of making them anew. (Victor Schlovsky)

[7]Number assigned according to the listing by Michael McKenna (op. cit.)

step around and pass her by as if she were a clumsily stuck quote.

"Scientists claim that Aristotle's works on marine zoology," Temple goes on, "contain detailed closeups, so detailed in fact that they can be seen only with the help of a microscope or with eyesight found in only one nearsighted person in five million. Yet, science confirms that the microscope didn't come into existence until some two thousand years after Aristotle. Ergo: was Aristotle, that pupil of Plato, that tutor to Alexander the Great, also lucky enough to possess such one-in-a trillion near sight—in his philosophical foresight eyesight? Most unlikely! Somebody else, somebody near-sighted, must have contributed these closeups. In this country I was the first to claim that"—he twists his face to give Kosky an impression of an oracle—"ARISTOTLE DID NOT WRITE HIS WORKS ON MARINE ZOOLOGY. SOMEBODY ELSE DID. BUT WHO?" he headlines loud enough for everyone to hear. Two passersby give him a stunned look, but, being nearsighted, he can't see them.

In order to see better, Temple takes off his glasses and, blind for a moment, breathes on the lenses and polishes them with his handkerchief. His handkerchief is oily and dirties the glasses. He doesn't notice it; not yet, "you see, he can't see without glasses" (Jay Kay).

"Aristotle knew how to concentrate, he was a Tantric who knew about 'mental breathing.' Concentration provided additional dioptric power to his eyesight," speculates Kosky. "Being physically nearsighted prompted him to become spiritually farsighted, to see in the water, underwater, and through the water better than the nearsighted Greek divers who did the marine research for him. With his own inner eyes he saw such strange, wondrous creatures as the black eel which is born spontaneously—spontaneously meaning no mother, no father, no fuck—and born from what Aristotle called a superfluous dung of the marshes, his euphemism for a pit of natural manure. Until Aristotle, nobody had ever

415

encountered such an 'earth gut' — or spotted one ever since!" **Eels are derived from the so-called earth's guts that grow spontaneously in mud and in humid ground. Such earth guts are found especially where there is decayed matter: where seaweed abounds, and in rivers and marshes near to the edge; for it is near to the water's edge that sun heat has its chief power and produces putrefaction. (Aristotle)**

Here Temple and Kosky are accosted by a stunning female, a faultless piece of natural human engineering.

"Two handsome men all alone? How about a suck'nd snooze sexy souffle?" She oozes one letter S after another, focusing on Temple, who won't blink. Undeterred, she unsnaps her shirt and displays a pair of state-of-natural-art cannonballs.

Kosky has seen this female Splendor in the Ass at least once before. Her name is Julia Jones Wadman. She is about twenty-six years old, and, in her line of work this super-*dombi* is known as Widow Wadman. She is the one who, under the spiffy headline FIRM FAVORITE, he had seen in Tristram Shandy, the British adult magazine, photographed at her office desk, next to her firm's phone, dressed in beige, his favorite color, undressing, then naked, save for her black stockings, red garter belt and black stiletto shoes. She keeps on supposedly hunting for a second husband — "while in reality looking for a willing partner in her sex-oriented paramarital adventure." (comments Jay Kay).

"Do you know," Kosky says to Temple loud enough for the lady to hear, "that these days hypnotism is used to enlarge women's tits? That, in one experiment, some sixty-nine British volunteers were ordered to fantasize about warm fluid, or a heat-lamp, warming their juggs up? That, at the end of some nine weeks, most of these women got the tits they wanted? And even more, bought a bigger bra? That's something, eh?" **Some women managed almost twice these gains. (Gordon Rattray Taylor)**[8]

His words do the job. Instantly British Julia Jones Wadman becomes Brunnhilde von Lorelei, the famous German super sex rocket seen so often on the pages of the German Der Stern magazine. She pulls her pullover down and lifts her skirt up, displaying an exquisite crack of natural design. "Was this made by a hypnotist too?" She screams hypnotizing them both. Then, dropping the curtain, she gets lost in the dark.

"Your claim that Aristotle was not the author of his zoological works attempts to turn what's natural in book writing into illegitimate bookkeeping. I'm sure, had he been around, Aristotle could prove you wrong," says Kosky. **But the natural weakness of a great author would be different from the artificial weakness of an imitator, whereas the forger would be unable to maintain this equality in the appearance of his writings. (B. J. Jowett)**[9]

Temple becomes exasperated. "Oh, yeah? How?" he challenges Kosky. "Would he rent the Hollywood Bowl, invite the public and start writing his books all over again? But what if nobody showed up? Or worse, if they did, would they watch him well enough or long enough to be convinced he got no help from anybody? That there was no hidden transmitter planted in his ear? That he didn't wear special contact lenses? Would they stay watching him for all the years he took to finish his book? And would Aristotle — even he! — survive the impact of such headlines as TELL THE TRUTH, ARISTO — WHERE DID THESE MARINE ZOO CLOSEUPS COME FROM?" Temple throws his hands in the air. "He could no more prove that he wrote his book than could any other writer!"

----

[8]From "How to Keep Abreast of Things" in *The Natural History of the Mind* by Gordan Rattray Taylor, 1981. "A magnificently readable book." (Colin Wilson).

[9]*The Dialogues of Plato,* translated into English with analyses and introductions by B. J. Jowett, M.A., in five volumes, Oxford MD CCC LXXV.

They stop at the Facsimile, Manhattan's largest bookshop, owned and operated by the Neo-Fictionist Writers Cooperative. In the brightly lighted window the 2001 laser beams at the first row of current and future best-sellers, while the classics of the past occupy only the far-out rear zone.

"It's all literary waste," says Temple, assessing the window. "There is no writer, dead or alive, who hasn't involuntarily copied, invaded, or infringed upon the preexisting literary folklore.

"This goes for Shakespeare, as well as for the *Book of the Khazars* and its author Yehudah Halevi."

"Please—don't touch Yehudah Halevi," moans Kosky. **Thus, Halevi begins by converting the Khazars to Judaism and ends by converting himself to personal Zionism. (Jacob B. Agus)**[10] "Halevi is my all-time favorite Jewish writer. Without his *Book of the Khazars* ("An argument for the Faith of Israel."—Henry Slonimsky) I would never attempt to write *The Healer*, much less visit the Zion."

"What's more when it comes to story-telling, I can prove or disprove anything I choose to depending on which side of the literary litigation I stand," barks Temple. "Hence, I can either prove that there was an infringement because the text originated in the folklore, or that there wasn't, since, as most

---

[10]Never was a book so utterly a part of its author as the *Book of the Kuzari* was of Yehudah Halevi. The argument of the book led the author to undertake his famed journey to Zion, which was in truth an act of self-sacrifice, unique in the annals of mankind. Halevi undertook to go to the land then occupied by the Crusaders who had murdered all the Jews in Jerusalem, in order that he might "see" the "glory of God" and then die. The one moment of divine revelation would more than compensate for the death that was sure to follow. . . . Of this preparation, no element was as important as that of a personal pilgrimage to Zion. (Jacob B. Agus) (op. cit.)

literary folks know, folklore is not original. As you can see, I can testify either for the plaintiff or for the defendant." Triumphantly, Temple, the literary crusader, looks at Kosky through his still unclean glasses.

"Indeed, I can see," says Kosky. "What's more I've seen it cooked up in the Marxist literary kettle many times before."

A rather sordid, commonplace, unedifying incident is somehow transformed — not made better but seen. (Arnold Kettle)[11]

"There he is!" Temple exclaims. "Teodor Jozef Konrad Korzeniowski listed as Joseph Conrad!"

"Where?" exclaims Kosky, his nose pressed against the window.

"There! Sixth row, right of center, under the big letter C, standing next to Dante whom, by the way, Conrad openly quoted, and next to Dostoyevsky, whom he also quoted, but never openly, and whom he certainly most often misquoted, more than willingly. Conrad, that clever Pole who wrote in English at a late age, and who knew better than to cling to his old Polish name of Korzeniowski — in the nineteenth row! — under the letter K, somewhere between Kos and Kosin and Kosinski. Besides, who can pronounce Jozef Korzeniowski? It's a tough name" — he scans the window all the way to the eighth row — "as tough as the name Jerzy Kosinski." He grins. "Now how many people can pronounce Jerzy Kosinski the way it ought to be correctly pronounced in his once native Polish?"

"I can, it is pronounced *Yerzhe Kosheesnkyii.*" Says Kosky

---

[11]*Man and the Arts: A Marxist Approach,* by A. Kettle and V. G. Hanes. American Institute of Marxist Studies, Occasional Paper.

modestly.

"Sure *you* can. You're Ruthenian-American. Ever since Poland was officially baptized back in year 966, wasn't Polish the chosen language of the Jewish-Ruthenian, as well as Jewish-Polish, middle class? Such Polish-Jewish literary giants as Julian Tuwim, Alexander Wat, Bruno Schulz, Janusz Korczak, Julian Slonimski, Jozef Wittlin and dozens of equally great others wrote *only* in Polish even though many of them could probably write without difficulty in Yiddish, Russian, German or at least one other European language. But it was Polish, and only Polish, which inflamed their inspiration. Too bad Conrad, who was not Jewish, abandoned his Polish but then, had he written in Polish, who would read him either in Poland, a country then partitioned by Russia, Prussia and Austria, or in his neo-native England? Nobody!" Temple smiles at his own conclusion. "If in this country you pronounce the name of Władyslaw Kosinski (Polish literary folklorist born in Jurkow in 1844, d. 1914. J. K.) as *Vlaydislow Kosheenskii*," Temple strains, "the way a Jersey-clad native American from New Jersey would." He steps away from the window.

"Speaking of Conrad, that Polish-British literary duplex. By the time Conrad said, 'I do not write history but fiction, and I am therefore entitled to choose as I please what is most suitable,' " says Kosky, "he must have realized that, in order to remain creative, choosing Conrad for his regular surname and the English language for his articulate and inventive, writing (he was also fluent in French and in Polish: J. K.) was not cultural trespaSSing." (Thanks, printer, for this double SS!)" **I had to make material from my own life's incidents arranged, combined, colored for artistic purposes. . . . I am a writer of fiction; and it is not what actually happened, but the manner of presenting it that settles the literary and even the moral value of my work. (Conrad)**

"But it sure was an ethnic error!" says Temple. "Look at the

Conrad Affair![12] Look at what one wrong interview in London did to his reputation! Look what Eliza Orzeszkowa,[13] the best-known Polish writer of the period, did with it at home. Single-handedly, Madame Orzeszkowa turned Joseph Conrad one of the least-known of the English writers—into the most popular Polish literary renegade—and all this furor *only* because Conrad chose the English language in order to best express in it his Polish soul!"

"There are no renegades in art," says Kosky, "and if fiction isn't art, what it?"

It is particularly true of the renegade that, because of his sharp awareness that he cannot go back, the old relationship, with which he has irrevocably broken, remains for him, who has a sort of heightened discriminatory sensitivity, the background of the relation now existing. It is as if he were repelled by the old relationship and pushed into the new one, over and over again. (Simmel)

Kosky and Temple are interrupted by an intruder—who, as if he were a ghost, insinuates himself between the two of them. The man, call him—in the absence of any better name call him Pilpul, is a swarthy Jew whose age, here, synonymous with excessive "achromatic pallor and wanness of his face, as well as with boundless wisdom" (Jay Kay), stretches from nineteen to sixty-nine years of *psychosomatic* (Franz Alexander) existence.

Standing in front of a bookstore window, Pilpul resembles Israel Kosky; and resembles him in some not yet *en vogue* vague and remote storytelling fashion. Norbert can almost

---

[12]For a dispassionate assessment of the Conrad Affair (1896–1910), see *The Polish Shades and Ghosts of Joseph Conrad*, by Gustav Morf (1976).

[13]Eliza Orzeszkowa: a Polish novelist known for her over-realistic and most sympathetic portrayal of Polish-Jewish economic misery in pre-World War I Poland.

hear his father saying to his son **In a time of dehaga (anxiety. J. K.) concern yourself with Haggadah. (R. Hayyim)**[14] Suddenly Kosky becomes aware of this Pilpul in quite another way. What if?—a thought hits him like a pupil's rod—what if this Pilpul is his father's *persona* personified just for him post factum? His learned father, after all, was *the* Loewenkopf from Łodz via Zamosc married to *the* Weinreich who arrived in Łodz from via (Vilna. J. K.)—"the Jerusalem of Europe" (Jay Kay). What if his bookish father has now returned as a Pilpul from beyond the spiritual Grand Canyon, in order to check on the conduct of his seed. To check on Norbert's outer conduct true, but above all, on his inner growth. And if that is the case—wait, don't say *if*—it must be! It *must* be, because look what happens! The instant Kosky looks Pilpul in the eye, the blinking of his eye automatically raises the curtain in Kosky's inner dream theater filled with a barely visible audience. On stage, Israel Kosky, age fifty-six, and Norbert, age twelve, stand in front of a bookstore window somewhere in Ruthenia, circa 1946. Over the bookstore window, a large sign proclaims in English: WE BUY AND SELL AMERICAN AND ENGLISH BOOKS. WE SPECIALIZE IN MOST RECENT ACCOUNTS OF JEWISH CALAMITOUS W.W. II HISTORY.

"The Tremendum has ended officially, but the *mysterium tremendum*[15] hasn't ended really!" says Israel Kosky to his seed

---

[14]Hagga (Heb): anxiety. Haggadah (Midrash): a collection of penultimately original Jewish narrative literature originating in the Palestinian and Babylonian Talmud as well as in independent collections of narrative Midrashim pedantically collected elsewhere.

[15]"Before the *tremendum,* Jews could not have imagined that people could produce high cultural achievement and surrender to a politics of monstrosity; Jews could not believe that, having effected the rites of passage from ethnic enclave to cultural universalism, their lineage would still be traced by blood to their discovery and murder."

who still can't utter a word. Can't, not won't. (Has Norbert Kosky become mute, during the war, or is this only his way of muting the words with which he could but would not describe the unspeakable? only Norbert could answer this question but he won't. J. K.) "You must get out of here. Get out the first chance you get!" As Israel Kosky says it, the theater audience must deduce from Norbert's expression (and since he is silent, only from his expression) what the boy thinks. He thinks: here is my father, a man whom I love with my innermost heart of hearts. Barely seven years after the War began when, in order to save my life he had thrown me to the dogs, he wants to send me, his only son, out again alone into the wilderness. **Mandelstam's blood was thick with the agglutinants of Jewish identity. His observations of his world, his abhorrence of violence, his almost physiological discomfort in the presence of the powerful and anger with manipulations of power he traced (Madame Mandlestam confirms it) to his Jewish rage for justice.** (Arthur A. Cohen on Osip E. Mandelstam, op. cit.)

"When do you want me to go?" Kosky writes on his blackboard, hiding tears, as the audience weeps with him.

"Go the minute your English is good enough to rely on it when everything else is gone. Good enough always means being able to write in it. Write, not talk," he stresses. "Any idiot can say something in basic words and in as many gestures, but how many people can shape words? Readers are people who don't need to hear you speak to know who you are. In America, you will find many such readers — men and women who don't care whether their favorite author was deaf, mute or even dumb!"[16]

---

writes Arthur A. Cohen in *The Tremendum:* A Theological Interpretation of the Holocaust. (1981).

[16]As a polyglot in his own right, Israel Kosky knew some six or nine foreign languages, Hebrew, Yiddish, and Sanskrit among

"Why don't they?" writes Norbert.

"Because they know that what finally matters is free expression is the voice with which you write—not the one with which you speak."

"By nature, writing is mute—too bad all writers are not," summarizes his father, facing the audience. "Writing speaks," he goes on, "even if the writer does not. And, ladies and gentlemen"—his father raises his voice a bit too high—"what matters is the spiritual accent of the book, not the writer's own accent. Look again at that man Conrad."[17]

At the end of this moving scene, Israel Kosky kisses his son on the forehead. "In any case, all six doctors who examined my son agree that there's nothing wrong with his head." He addresses the audience. "My son is definitely not suffering from ordinary mutism, and certainly not from a common aphasia.[18]

---

them, and knew them well enough to write. Write—but, in accordance with his own dictum, not talk: "I hate art of conversation, it is the least communicable of all the arts," Israel Kosky would often say to his seed. After the War, in his official rank as head of the Ruthenian Linguistic Norm Institute, Israel Kosky ranked English as much easier to learn well enough to write in well, than French, Italian, Spanish and German—not to mention Hungarian, Finnish, Polish and Russian. (Estate Editors)

[17](Conrad's English accent was so foreign that many in England could not understand what he was saying. After hearing him speak, most people who met him didn't believe for a moment that this square Polish squire could ever command *Nostromo*—a British literary vessel—in English, the only language which Conrad commanded as a writer!: J. K.)

[18]Aphasia: from the Greek word for speechlessness. (J. K.) "Agraphia denotes a similar inability to express thoughts (or oneself. J. K.) in writing." From Clinical Evaluation of the Nervous System by (J. F. Simpson, M.D., and K. R. Magee, M.D., 1970). "Jewish aphasia: and agraphia: having too much vocabulary to express the conditions usually found among victims of trauma—

424

"WHAT IS WRONG WITH ME?" says Norbert with his lips.

His father gives him a long look. "Nothing," he declares after a pause. "Like millions of other children, you were first wronged by the War. Millions of Jewish children, Polish children, Russian, Greek, Gypsy and even German children. Second, like thousands of other kids, you went *speakless* for a while.[19]

The major difficulty for the examiner is to distinguish between a true language disturbance (aphasia) *and other disorders such as dysarthria ('defects in articulation, enunciation, and rhythm of speech')* confusion *and* mutism. It is important to keep in mind that if a patient's speech can be transcribed into logical sentences, or if he can express himself normally in writing, he is probably not aphasic, even if his speech is markedly dysarthric and almost unintelligible. Similarly, if a patient appears totally mute but can express himself correctly in writing and gestures, he is not aphasic. (John F. Simpson, M.D. and Kenneth R. Magee, M.D. 1970).

'What if I don't want to write in America? What if I want to fish there?" writes Norbert on his blackboard.

---

and those Jewish survivors of WWII who barely survived it as children," (elaborates Jay Kay, 1965).

"Marked anxieties were established and even with intense therapy therafter, the so-called 'ghost of the past' was always present and had its inevitable bad effect upon therapy. Establishing future goals is always difficult with the aphasic patient, but if approached slowly and realistically they can be of great value in motivating the patient to continued effort . . ." *Recovery from Aphasia* by J. M. Wepman. (op. cit.)

[19]See, among others, *Polish Children Accuse* (2 Vol), in Polish (op. cit.) 1962, and *War Through Children's Eyes:* Foreword by Bruno Bettelheim, ex. and compiled by Irena G. Gross and Jan T. Gross, Stanford University, 1981.

"Fishing won't do," declares his father.

"What if I want to ride, not write, in America?" writes Norbert.

"Don't even mention riding," says his father. "Unless your name is Ben Hur, horses and Jews don't mix. Ask Rembrandt! — the painter who understood the Jews he painted better than just about any other non-Jewish painter! See his most original rendering of an Israelite about to fall off his horse, in Rembrandt's all-time classic called *Paysage,* then take a peek at his *Good Samaritain,* a painting about what happened to that Israelite who, only one painting earlier, had fallen off his horse. Then look at his painting called *Paysage!*"

"I love riding — riding, not necessarily loving the horses," says Norbert, keeping his inner eye on his riding past. Wasn't he, as a boy of nine used to transport back and forth across yet another marsh of Glynn — call it Gliniszcze — a notoriously kicking mare who once kicked him, the sole navigator, out of his narrow kayak?

"How can a village boy like you not love horses?" His father keeps on nagging him.

"It all depends on a boy's past, not on his horse," says Norbert.

Cossacks from Don told me that it was not the fact that the Jews had beaten them in an agricultural competition which had overcome their former mistrust, but that the Jews had proved themselves to be the better riders than the Cossacks. (Feuchtwanger, 1937)

"I grew up among horses, and so one day I too will be a polo player," says our prototypic Polish Rider.[20] **There are no**

------

[20] *The Polish Rider:* a painting by Rembrandt Harmensz van Rijn at the Frick Collection in New York. Rembrandt was born in the spiritually unique year of 1606, since, as the Hebrews knew all too well, the Creation took six days demanding trial and effort. This

problem horses, only problem riders. (Mary Twelveponies, 1982)

"Nothing to it," says his father.* "As Rabbi Hayyim has proved beyond any reasonable doubt, people like animals not only because people are good by nature and look a bit like animals; they like them because animals *are* the past or future rehabilitated people! This means that if you like horses, you like their riders, too. Enough said."

My team came off better at polo than I had hoped; . . . I made two goals myself. . . . I tell you, a corpulent middle-aged, literary man finds a stiff polo match rather good exercise. (Theodore Roosevelt)[21]

"I also like skiing. For instance, I could ski in Aspen, in America," writes Norbert.

"Even though I can't recall any work of art created by anyone while skiing down — or sliding down, for that matter, this, I grant you, is one activity you could do but only as a sport and only in Aspen, a place which was brave enough to salute the German Goethe with the 1949 Bicentennial — so soon after the War.[22] And why not? After all, snow is water

---

might explain why among Rembrandt's closest friends, many of whom he painted were so many accomplished Jews.

[21]In 1986, *Free Polo,* the official publication of the United States Underrated Polo Players Association, celebrated its ninth anniversary issue with the publication of an essay called "Norbert Kosky Solo Polo." And why not? As of this writing Kosky is "the only living author of the only full-size novel in the English language devoted entirely to solo-polo," as it was endorsed by *Free Polo* magazine. "This explains why, since 1978, our riding master, to whom playing polo means having a ball, is, theoretically, at least, entitled to the short-term use of a polo field, polo pony, a polo saddle, a mallet and obligatory attendance at every polo ball and every American polo-playing social station. (comments Jay Kay).

[22]See *The Romance of Commerce and Culture:* Capitalism, Modernism, and the Chicago-Aspen Crusade for Cultural Reform, by James Sloan Allen, 1983.

temporarily solidified. Skiing is floating down. And with so many Siberian-Stalinist gulag bound Jews, then frozen to death in the snowbound Siberia, snow and the Jews are spiritual satellites."

"I'm also on very good terms with water, as you know. How about floating, then?" Norbert now talks only with his lips. "Better yet, father I could learn to stay flat on top of the water in order to lower my drag co-efficient — and without dragging my torso in the water, swimming more efficiently, than just about anyone."

"Stop talking like Billy Sidis," says his father. "In any case, what do you need floating for?"

"To save myself again from say, drowning, in a pond of manure. A pit, really, not a pond in which I almost did."

"What pond of manure? What pit? What did you say?" his father recoils. "You are not clear enough. What do you mean by 'again' and 'I almost did'? What did you do in the pond of manure?"

"Nothing," says our twelve-year old Hippocampus.[23] "Let's say it was just my latest fairy tale."

"Then, enough said about this Cotard's Syndrome,"[24] says his father. The inner theater closes.

SS

---

[23]Hippocampus: an ordinary sea horse. Also a mythical composite with the head and forequarters of an ordinary horse and the tail of an ordinary fish. Like literature, mythology is a composite. See also Northrop Frye, *Fables of Identity* (1963).

[24]"8. COTARD'S SYNDROME, *Le Delire de Negation*. To be or not to be . . . Shakespeare, *Hamlet*" (from *Uncommon Psychiatric Syndromes,* op. cit.). Cotard's Syndrome is a rare condition in which, on the one hand, the patient professes an overriding desire to exit, i.e., "to not exist," but, on the other, believes that *unfortunately,* he or she might never cease to exist, to be able to die.

Back on the street, the Pilpul abruptly departs without casting a single glance at Kosky or Temple. Clearly, strangers are of no interest to him unless they look strange enough. He is right. Why waste time looking in the direction of people you don't want to direct or be directed by?

Temple gives the passing Pilpul a passing look. "A Yankiel! Another ex-Ruthenian-Jewish philosophically trained Hasid! I bet he was born in Poland. Did you know that's where most of them came from?" says Kosky.

Around 962, several Slavonic tribes formed an alliance under the leadership of the strongest among them, the Polans, which became the nucleus of the Polish state. Thus the Polish rise to eminence started about the same time as the Khazar decline (Sarkel was destroyed in 965). It is significant that Jews play an important role in one of the earliest Polish legends relating to the foundation of the Polish kingdom. (Koestler, op. cit.)[25]

"Ever since 966, Poland adopted Christianity it became Europe's ethnic and religious melting pot free enough to let everyone either melt and speak Polish or to speak their own language — as millions of Jews did — speaking Yiddish there continuously until W.W. II." Kosky triumphs easily. "That's where all of my ancestors resided during the last one thousand years!"[26]

"A lot of assimilated Khazar-Yankiels in your intellectual family, eh?" Temple brightens. "Did you know that Conrad's Yankiel came straight out of the Yankiel invented by Adam

---

[25]Other Khazar enclaves have survived in the Crimea, and no doubt elsewhere too in localities which once belonged to their empire. But these are now no more than historic curios compared to the mainstream of the Khazar migration into the Polish-Lithuanian regions — and the formidable problems it poses to historians and anthropologists. (Koestler, *The Thirteenth Tribe,* op. cit.)

[26]See also "Polish Jewish Relations in a Philosophical Perspective"

Mickiewicz (d. 1855) in *Pan Tadeusz,* Poland's greatest poetic epic? Just think of the potential embarrassment," Temple goes on. "Think of: CONRAD STEALS YANKIEL FROM ADAM MICKIEWICZ STOP THEFT REPORTED TO LITERARY POLICE BY SIM THOMAS TEMPLE," he recites dreamily, then ponders another literary cloak and dagger. "Conrad said, 'I don't know what Dostoyevsky stands for or reveals, but I do know that he is too Russian for me!' Not true!" Temple exclaims. "Not for a moment. I was first to unmask Conrad by pointing out that in Russian, *razum* means mind and *raskol* means dissent.[27] From then on everything became a simple headline: CON-RAD'S RAZUMOV IS DOSTOYEVSKY'S RASKOLNIKOV. Conrad said, 'The word *Razumov* was a mere label of a solitary individuality.' But was it derived by Conrad from Razumikhin, another invention of Dostoyevsky? Dostoyevsky has Raskolnikov say 'Oh, no, it is not the old hag I have destroyed. It is myself!' and Razumov justifies his crime by reasoning, 'It is myself whom I have delivered for destruction.' Now, how's that for a quq! Like Raskolnikov, his literary identical twin, Razumov, is at the same time plaintiff and defendant, prosecutor and defense attorney. Quq again!" He pauses to unquote.

Temple continues. "Remember that Thornton Wilder's joke, and I quote, 'Your Honor,' said the shoplifter to the

---

(*Dialectics and Humanism,* Special Issue, 1989.)

[27] *Raskol* (Russian for schism or dissent) once denoted the "dissenting peasantry of Ruthenia, Podolia, Volhynia and the Ukraine." (Raphael Patai)

Raskolniks: a Russian monastic sect of the Old Believers who believed Moscow was the Third Rome.

Raskolnikov: the hermit-like antagonist of Dostoyevsky's *Crime and Punishment* (1866), the creation of whom led Dostoyevsky to write *The Idiot* (1868–69), "his most personal *opus epilepticus.*" (Niskisko)

judge. 'I steal only from the best department stores, and they don't miss it!' " Temple pauses, pressing the double-space bar on his mental teletype. "Think THORNTON WILDER ENDORSES LITERARY SHOPLIFTING."[28]

"I do think about it," says Kosky. "Such literary thoughts give me the creeps!"

"Careful now! In English *creeps* also means *ghosts!*" Temple stops him by putting his hand on his shoulder: he is an arresting wapentake. "Just think about the potential headlines: GHOSTS GIVE KOSKY HIS LITERARY CREEPS!"

The two men stare at the store window in silence. Temple breaks in. "Only Kafka was clever enough to admit in public that his work was a quq; that all writers invade one another by means of, in his own self-incriminating words, 'boisterously or secretively or even masochistically appropriating foreign capital that they had not earned but—having hurriedly seized it—stolen.' " The change in stress indicates that Temple might be quoting Kafka rather than paraphrasing him on the spot. "Believe me, in the literary disco, Lord Jim is only one quq away from Lord Hamlet."

"The trouble is that the general public doesn't know enough about the making of a book to know that there's

---

[28]After Joseph Campbell and Henry Morton Robinson accused Wilder's play *The Skin of Our Teeth* of being "an Americanized re-creation, thinly disguised, of James Joyce's *Finnegans Wake*." (From The Fine Arts of Literary Mayhem: by Myrlick Land, 1983) "Wilder had arrived in Aspen, a discouraged man," writes James Sloan Allen (op. cit. 1986).

Following Lotus-Floatus L'Affaire, Kosky devoted one year to an uninterruptred stream of writing, among the mountainous streams of Icogne, in the Swiss Valais, from where Rilke wrote to his Polish translator of his *Duinco Elegies* "The Angel of the Elegies is terrible

nothing wrong with such proximity," says Kosky.[29]

"They sure don't," says Temple. "And that's where I come in. I was responsible for such headlines as A. J. LIEBLING SAYS LITERARY BOXING IS SANCTIONED RELEASE OF HOSTILITY. LITERARY WORLD STUNNED."

"I don't know what Liebling meant by literary boxing," says Kosky.

You've got to—and this is the hardest thing of all— you've got to draw people to you and make them "spill," which is what a detective does in a nastier way. But you've got to have this little trick; it's more than a trick: You've got to have the ability to draw people out. You're happy when you know you've got it, and you're afraid of losing it. (A. J. Liebling)

"Now you know!" Temple exclaims. "How about my other headlines? EUDORA WELTY DESCRIBES HER PROBLEM IN 'WHERE IS THE VOICE COMING FROM?' LITERARY WORLD STUNNED."

"When it comes to such narrative head turners as where the literary voice is coming from," says Kosky, "even the Master's Voice does not know."

Temple interrupts him. "Remember Joyce? Well, then listen to what my Press Release said about him! INTERNATIONAL TEAM OF LITERARY DETECTIVES FOUND THE NAMES OF NINETY-NINE ANONYMOUS FRIENDS JOYCE ROUTINELY HIRED, FIRED AND REHIRED AS HIS PERSONAL TYPISTS AND PROOFREADERS. LITERARY WORLD STUNNED."

"Did you know," he goes on in his loud voice, "that LEO ROSTEN ADMITS HE REWROTE 'CAPTAIN NEWMAN M.D.' TEN, TWENTY, FIFTY TIMES. LITERARY WORLD STUNNED."

"I myself have run into something like that—a headline made of one's very own literary line!" says Kosky. **If I were to**

---

for us because we . . . still cling to the Visible." Today, nearby, at the Church of Raron, Rilke is buried. Ed.

[29]"Writers are interested in folk tales for the same reason that painters are interested in still-life arrangements: because they illustrate essential principles of storytelling." (Northrop Frye)

tell you that chapters of *Captain Newman, M.D.* were rewritten ten, twenty, fifty times, would you believe me? But it's true. I don't mean that I changed a word of a phrase here and there—I mean totally rewritten. One chapter runs about 8,000 words and was rewritten at least fifty times, from first word to last, cut, expanded, reshaped, remolded. (Leo Rosten)

"I only wish I could interview one or two—ideally three— of those copy and line editors Stefan Zweig hired in order to help him at night in his literary bed to write about the life of Balzac.

"What for?" asks Kosky.

"For World-Headline-Making WHM-TV channel Six Literary News, what else? Just think," he says, raising his eyes to the sky, "CESAR BIROTTEAU (1838) GROSSES BALZAC TWENTY THOUSAND FRANCS FOR THE SERIAL RIGHTS ALONE, SAYS STEFAN ZWEIG, THE AUTHOR'S BIOGRAPHER."

"That's not fair. That's a lie!" says Kosky. "The year 1838 was in fact the year of Balzac's financial disaster. Says Zweig 'The years 1836 and 1837 were years of strain for Balzac; one disaster followed swiftly upon the heels of another. By normal hazards, if anything in Balzac's life could be judged by normal standards, the year 1838 should have brought the ultimate turning point.' We know it should, but it was not—and you, Temple, know it too!" In the momentary anger Kosky raises his index finger in the air.

"I do, but the reader does not! Then how about this one, then," says Temple. "ZWEIG CLAIMS THAT 'WHERE GOETHE AND VOLTAIRE ALWAYS EMPLOYED TWO LITERARY SECRETARIES WORKING FOR THEM AND CRITIC SAINTE-BEUVE USED A FULL-TIME LITERARY SPADE, BALZAC EMPLOYED SIX PRIVATELY HIRED LINE EDITORS.' "

"That's also not fair, since it is taken completely out of context,"[30] Kosky objects. On the same page Zweig says that

---

[30]See *Balzac*, by Stefan Zweig (1946), a biography which, after ten year's of work, Zweig still left incomplete. (J. K.)

'Balzac looked after his entire correspondence and conducted all business matters all alone.' This means without a literary agent, but since in addition to writing, he was engaged in various investment businesses — no wonder he needed all the proof readers he could find!"

"How about this, then," Temple excretes. "BALZAC BIOGRAPHER (1946) SAYS QUOTE 'BALZAC DID NOT KNOW AND COULD NOT TELL WHAT HE WAS WRITING OR WHAT HE HAD ALREADY WRITTEN.' "

"That's the lowest blow." Kosky throws his hands in the air instead of throwing them at Temple. "Says Zweig, and I quote *in good faith,* 'Everything that Balzac wrote had to be set up in print at once because Balzac in the trance-like state in which he worked did not know what he was writing or what he had already written. Even his keen eye could not survey the dense jungle of his manuscripts. Only when they were in print and he could review them paragraph by paragraph, like companies of soldiers marching past at an inspection, was the general in Balzac able to discern whether he had won the battle or whether he had to renew the assault.' End of quote!"

"Can I have one more shot at your Balzac?" Temple hopes he can make it one day to a literary ticker-tape parade. "I bet this headline would finish him off."

"One more time!" Kosky agrees reluctantly.

This is my work, the abyss, the crater which yawns before me. This is the raw material that I intend to shape. (Balzac)

"O.K. Here I go: MAT, PAT AND BAT, THE THREE PROOFREADERS BALZAC FOUND TO PROOF READ HIS BOOK 'LOST ILLUSIONS,' CLAIM THEY HAVE EACH FILLETED SOME ILLUSIONS IN EITHER THE AUTHOR'S LIFE OR IN HIS WORK. I'M DISILLUSIONED BY THEIR INSUPPORTABLE CLAIMS BUT NOT DISHONORED, SAYS HONORÉ DE BALZAC."

"Just as unfair," says Kosky. "Particularly when Matthew Natty, Patrick Fatty and Eleanore Batty, Balzac's most often quoted assistants, subsequently all publicly denied that they

434

had contributed one inch of original wax to Balzac's own. Particularly after Jacqueline Demimonde demolished the whole mini-affair by the longest article in defense of a writer ever published on this side of the infamous Dreyfus Affair."

"In this country, such headlines headline a success story," says Temple.

"What about Flaubert, that literary suffering supreme!" says Kosky. **I'd rather die like a dog than rush my sentence through, before it's ripe (1852). I only want to write three more pages and find four or five sentences that I've been searching for, nearly a month now (1853). My work is going very slowly; sometimes I suffer real tortures to write the simplest sentence (1852). I can't stop myself; even swimming, I test my sentences, despite myself (1876). (Flaubert)**

"I knew you'd come up with him," triumphs our literary Temple. "Years ago my dispatch from Paris became a headline: MADAME GOSSIP MENSONGE, FLAUBERT'S LAUNDRESS, DECLARED FLAUBERT USED HER AS A PROTOTYPE FOR MADAME BOVARY AFTER THE AUTHOR ADMITS HE HAS PORTRAYED HIS FATHER AS DR. LARIVIÈRE. SAYS FLAUBERT: THIS ACCUSATION PAINS ME MORE THAN BOILING WATER."[31]

"That's most unfair," Kosky protests. "You can tell that woman bears a bitter grudge. A grudge for being asked by Flaubert, or not being asked, to pose as a *statue vivante* in his bathroom either naked or dressed only in the furs of Madame Flaubert. Ask *mon ami* Roland Barthes.[32] He's the one who knows all there is to know about Flaubert."

---

[31]"Boiling water spilled by the surgeon on the writer's hand caused a permanent scar and partial paralysis. Traits of Dr. Flaubert have also been discerned in Charles Bovary," says William Amos (op. cit.).

[32]"Flaubert and the Sentence," in *New Critical Essays,* by Roland Barthes. Translated by Richard Howard, op. cit., p. 69.

For Flaubert. . . . writing is disproportionately slow ("four pages this week," "five days for a page," "two days to reach the end of two lines"; it requires an "irrevocable farewell to life." (Roland Barthes)[33]

"Barthes? I've killed him with his own words!" Temple jumps with joy. "When his book entitled *Roland Barthes by Roland Barthes* came out, with Barthes's preface saying, 'It must all be considered as though spoken by a character in a novel,' I headlined it EVEN THOUGH SUPPOSEDLY NONFICTION 'ROLAND BARTHES BY ROLAND BARTHES' MUST ALL BE CONSIDERED AS THOUGH SPOKEN BY A CHARACTER IN A NOVEL and finished Barthes in the eyes of his readers who found his words too confusing. I did the same thing to Lowell. I said LOWELL SAYS HIS 'LIFE STUDIES' WERE NOT ALWAYS FACTUALLY TRUE. THERE'S A GOOD DEAL OF TINKERING WITH FACT, HE SAID. YOU LEAVE OUT A LOT, EMPHASIZE THIS AND NOT THAT. YOUR ACTUAL EXPERIENCE IS A COMPLETE FLUX. I'VE INVENTED FACTS AND CHANGED THINGS. LOWELL'S ADMISSION STUNS LITERARY WORLD."

"All these made-up admissions stun only the nonliterary crowd, but never the Fourth Estate who knows all there is to know about **Fourth Prose** (Osip Mandelstam)." says Kosky. **"He tried to flee the craft of writer, to earn his keep by doing other things, but he was trapped by his incompetence to be anything but a poet. When even that dignity was humiliated and he (Osip Mandelstram. J. K.) was accused in 1928 of plagiarism in a case trumped up to humiliate him, he wrote in the enraged *Fourth Prose*"** I

---

[33]*New Critical Essays* arrives to remind us, as if in valediction, what a consummate literary critic Barthes could be. Ingenious, rigorous, epigrammatic, and genial, his essays on classic French texts are as startling and as fresh as any reconsideration since Hulme, Pound, and Eliot gave European literature their once-over." (John Updike, *The New Yorker*)

insist that writerdom, as it has developed in Europe and above all in Russia, is incompatible with the honorable title of Jew, of which I am proud." Osip Emilievich Mandelstam by Arthur A. Cohen, 1974.[34]

They have reached a Writerdom's Impasse. A dark street with no end and no view to speak of, dim lights, not a single double-parked car, and no police. Just as well. But here, here of all places, they've got a visitor who gives a sign of life. She is tall. She is statuesque that is, slim'nd stacked, (SS). She wears a low-cut dress, cut above her faultlessly carved thighs. She is also wearing confidence, femininity and Heart of Darkness perfume.

"Do you guys read me?" She stirs sensuously. **The Limits of our Sense of Hearing—We hear only the questions to which we are capable of finding an answer. (Nietzsche, Joyful Wisdom)**

"We read *Gaja Scienza*,"[35] says Kosky. "What about you Ms. Nietzsche? What do you read?"

She glances into space. "I see in front of me *Two Gentlemen of Verona*—and at my place I could read you both at the same time. "Are you game?" she asks, as her sculpted breast brushes Temple's arm. It's temple to Temple.

"I'm afraid I'm not," says Temple.

---

[34]Osip Emilievich Mandelstam, "the greatest and most difficult poet of modern Russia," from An Essay in Antiphon, by Arthur A. Choen, 1974

[35]Book Three, #108, *New Struggles:* "After Buddha was dead people showed his shadow for centuries afterward in a cave—an immense frightful shadow. God is dead: but as the human race is constituted, there will perhaps be caves for millenniums yet, in which people will show his shadow. And we—we have still to overcome his shadow!" (F. Nietzsche) In his "Buddha," Rilke writes about him: "For what tears us roughly to his feet/has circled in him for a million years./He, who forgets what we experience/and experiences what turns us away." From *New Poems* (1907) Rainer Maria Rilke, translated by Edward Snow, 1984.

"Then be afraid." She dismisses him and focuses the entire inner force of her androgynous being on Kosky. "What about you? Are you a gambler?"

"I play games; but I don't gamble," says Kosky. *Love is as strong as death* (Song of Songs [8:6])

"It's my gamble but your loss," she says, departing into the night.

"A lovely Platonida," says Temple. "What perky pontoons! that's what I call the original female form."

"Feminine, yes. Female not," declares Kosky. "You can change the literary genre, the appearance, but not nature's gender, not chromosomes. The lady is an Eone (from the word Eon, printer—not Aeon—so named after Chevalier d'Eon de Beaumont, who, himself a Queen of Studs[36] is said once to have courted the King Louis XV right at the court.

Expanding every possible care on their outward adornment, they are not ashamed even to employ every device to change artificially their nature. (Philo Judaeus)

They go back past the Jefferson Media Center, and the New Coliseum and, fatigued, sit down on a bench next to the monument of Byron, right in the center of—at this time abandoned—Byron Plaza.

The desire to see idols hurled violently from their pedestals is strong in all human beings. Byron had been one of the most successful literary men of all times. . . . He was too successful." From *Scandal!*, by Colin Wilson and Donald Seaman (1985).

---

[36]Queen of Studs: "a male who, created fatally effeminate by fate, as a result dresses and most often overdresses as a femme fatale." (Niskisko). See also *The Transsexual Phenomenon* by Harry Benjamin, M.D. New York, 1966.

"Those days I made a lot of headlines — and a lot of dough, thanks to Nikolai Leskov, (d. 1895) that Russian novelist, who as Gorky claimed, "was most deeply rooted in the people and is completely untouched by any foreign influence." says Temple, awkwardly facing Kosky. "And, speaking of gender-changing, how about Kotin the Provider and Platonida, Leskov's story? Soon after *glasnost* came around, my headline read: WALTER BENJAMIN DECLARES QUOTE THIS LESKOV'S FIGURE, A PEASANT NAMED PISONSKI, IS A HERMAPHRODITE. FOR TWELVE YEARS HIS MOTHER RAISED HIM AS A GIRL. HIS MALE AND FEMALE ORGANS MATURE SIMULTANEOUSLY UNQUOTE STOP LITERARY WORLD ILLUMINATED BY RUSSIAN LITERARY BISEXUALITY.[37]

25

Carmita, his penultimate Artemis, has passed the test. Too bad that so soon afterward she departed and departing is, for him, synonymous with passing away. (So begins another beginning of Jay Kay's book's mini-central Sufi-tale.)

In no time she would have qualified to become one of his best, and feasibly, most faithful proofreaders—faithful to him, as much as to his text, that is. **Proofreading is perhaps the most undervalued editorial specialty. I don't know of a publishing house that has staff proofreaders; instead proofs are sent out to freelancers who receive about ten dollars an hour for their expertise . . . A careless or hurried proofreader can ruin the best editing job in the world . . . (Laurie Stearns, "The Importance of Copy Editing,"** *Publishers Weekly,* **1987.)**

On June 1, alone and abandoned, Kosky returns from an extended no-phone, do-not-disturb Wednesday-through-Monday weekend in Killcats, the land, lake and sea Kosher-yoga spa for meditational sex swappers: an ecstatic experience not unlike the one described by Rupert Brooke.[1]

---

[1]Rupert Brooke's poem "The Voice" (published in 1918) speaks of an ecstatic experience in the woods.

There, surrounded by the parnassim—the elders and wardens of this "sexual synagogue" (SS), our Parnassus was brave enough to confront his newest preoccupation with Sabbatai Sevi.

Then days later, on May 10, Polizeipräsident Schäfer issued the order which closed off the ghetto population from the rest of the world. "Jews," he ordered, "must not leave the ghetto, as a matter of principle. This prohibition applies also to the Eldest of the Jews [Rumkowski] and to the chiefs of the Jewish police. . . . Even within the ghetto, Jews were not allowed freedom of movement; from 7 P.M. to 7 A.M. they were not permitted to be on the streets. (Raul Hilberg)[2]

Give this event a high SS mark and mark it for good. (Norbert Kosky, 1987) "This is how, where, and when, and thanks to whom I and my parents in 1939 left The Boat before it was too late. (Boat means Lodz in Ruthenian. Norbert Kosky was born and raised in the city of Lodz, the country's second largest: J. K.) But the weekend is over, and so our potential World War II Lodz ghetto dweller harnesses his historical memory—and he harnesses it by conveniently reverting to present-tense anxiety free Tantric Yoga breathing.

Our elegant Mr. Effingham[3] unpacks, then, at 9:00 P.M., calls his answering service. His suddenly-impressed-with-him answerette tells him that during his absence some nineteen people called. His public number is clearly up! But who were they? he asks her impatiently.

---

[2]"The creation of the ghetto is, of course, only a transition measure. I shall determine at what time and with what means the ghetto—and thereby also the city of Lodz—will be cleansed of Jews. In the end, at any rate, we must burn out this bubonic plague." (Uebelhoer, December 10, 1934)

[3]"Our elegant Mr. Effingham": The very first auto fictional hero created by James Fenimore Cooper in his two novels *Home as Found* and *Homeeward Bound*.

All, if not most of these calls, says the answerette, came by telephone, telegram and fax from newspapers, news and wire services, TV networks—and radio programs, both domestic and foreign.

"What happened? You must be the latest Sound'nd Video prince of Via Media," the answerette asks him impressed.

"I must be indeed. My fair Medusa must have finally arrived," he answers the answerette flippantly. **Beware of fame. Fame means being chosen. Being chosen could mean once again leading however obliquely, to "the deprivation of all Jewish rights some future SS."** (Israel Kosky to Norbert, circa 1946) *Enough said, Father!* Instantly, Norbert's mind becomes flooded by history of Lodz his native realm.

October 8, 1939: Propaganda Reichminister Dr. Goebbels, "an ideal father figure to several of his ideal German children" (Jay Kay), visits the city of Lodz, the setting for the soon-to-be constructed prototypical Nazi wartime Jewish ghetto. During his visit Dr. Goebbels is entertained by his subordinates with on-the-spot entertainment consisting of a mini-pogrom of local Jews during which several Jewish children are killed by being thrown out of the windows into the street. After his return, the Office for Racial Policy Affairs issues the following official recommendation: " . . . Both Poles and Jews are to be kept at an equally low standard of living, and *deprived of all rights* in the political as well as national and cultural fields." (November 25, 1939)

Still excited, and very babbly, the answerette says that when calling Kosky, his callers called him by all kinds of names, some of them—was it Mr. Wolfe or Sidis or Thurber?—said something about Mr. Cooper and about Mr. Effingham. Mr. Samuel Kramer (or Cramer) called in reference to a Mr. Cagliostro, and somebody else in reference to Mr. Bawdy Lair. Others—Mr. Edward Browne, among them—spoke about one Mr. Sabbatai Sevi, whom he also called Effendi. All his callers spoke English, she assures him, though however kind or unkind their inquiries about him were, most of them, spoke with one kind of accent or another.

May 3rd. The terrible uncertainty of my inner existence. (Kafka, Diaries)

Mindless of his hangover, Kosky hangs up in a state of excitement. *Mon cher ami*, this is recognition, he tells himself. Fame disguised as recognition. A quite tolerable form of fame because recognition does not demand fame's steady need for vanity ignition.

This is America of the free. Free and free-wheeling. Think fame, my friend. Think acting career. Slick Nirvana (Albert Van Nostrand) Think anything but SS.

Throughout the Second World War the Jewish people adopted the Allied cause as their own; they shut out many thoughts of their disaster and helped achieve the final victory. The Allied powers, however, did not think of the Jews. The Allied nations who were at war with Germany did not come to the aid of Germany's victims. The Jews of Europe had no allies. In its gravest hour Jewry stood alone, and the realization of that desertion came as a shock to Jewish leaders all over the world. (Raul Hilberg, op. cit., p. 671)

Wasn't it only last week that he saw on cable TV the movie he scripted: the one and only starring the one and only late Shaman Peters?

This is an important day. Remember, or learn again if you do not, that on May 3, 1791 (a Polish-American national holiday: J.K.), the Poles enacted the Polish May 3 Constitution which, following the example set by the American Constitution, was, democratically speaking, ahead of any other constitution in Europe; moreover, as the world's very first Constitution written down, it dared to impose a parliamentary responsibility on each king-appointed minister, abolished *liberum veto,* and confirmed the overall protection by the entire Polish State to everyone and all of the Polish Jews. "For the Jews, a historical first feast in their history." (Jay Kay).

No wonder then that there he is, about to march in this May 3 literary parade, so dashing in his custom-made literary uniform, his every move watched from the grandstands by Aleksander Wat, the man to whom already in Ruthenia of 1950 Kosky owed a firm conviction that as Wat had put it to him, a true democracy exists only in exercising one's right to self-invention, that is in writing fiction.[4]

By now, occupying, as Wat does, a very important place in Kosky's literary theory, every one of the literary grandees who defended the nature of literary work against every kind of literary attack will be watching over Kosky's shoulder.

For instance, consider the nonsensical attack against narrative originality which took place in 1966, when Pierre Macherey, started an all-out war against **the idea of the author as "creator." For him, too, the author is essentially a producer who works up certain given materials into a new product. The author does not make the materials with which he works; forms, values, myths, symbols, ideologies come to him already worked upon, as the worker in a car-assembly plant fashions his product from already-processed materials. (Terry Eagleton)**

However, since literature is folklore, and folklore is not an

---

[4]Alexander Wat, (born Chwat in 1900, suicide, 1969, J. K.) one of Poland's contemporarily timeless Polish-Jewish poets. In addition to his poetry (in Polish but also available in various translations, e.g. *With the Skin*, translated and edited by Czeslaw Milosz and Leonard Nathan, New York, 1989; the reader is encouraged to seek *My Century: The Odyssey of a Polish Intellectual,* by Aleksander Wat, edited and translated by Richard Lourie. Foreword by Czeslaw Milosz, Berkeley, 1988. Read also a "Masterpiece of Memory," (1988) a chapter devoted to Watt, in *Breathing Under Water and Other East European Essays* by Stanisław Baranczak, Harvard, 1990.

exact science,[5] the Macherey insurgency ended as quickly as it had begun, leaving in its wake one more title our gefilte sea lion can now safely wear: WRITER: 1. i.e., a maker of a book also defined as "6. the blessed chloroform of the mind" (Robert W. Chambers) and "10. spiritual repasts" (Charles Lamb).[6]

SS

After a Tantric bath which combines a few minutes of his intense no-motion locomotion exercises and change of clothes, our Second Lieutenant Kosky rushes out of his apartment and heads for the newsstand.

Now Romashov is by himself. Gracefully, dashingly, he approaches the enchanted line. His head is thrown back arrogantly and now his eyes turn left toward the general with a daring challenge. . . . And feeling himself the central object of admiration, the center of a glamorous new world, he says to himself in a sort of iridescent daydream: "Look, look, there's Romashov now!" . . . The eyes of the ladies shone differently when they looked at him. . . . One, two left. . . . At the end of the platoon, walking with supple grace, was a young second lieutenant. . . . Left, right, left. . . . (The Duel)

There Yankel, his old pal, greets him with a big smile, a handshake and a hug. "Congratulations!" Yankel repeats. "A small Razumikhin from Ruthenia makes it big in the

---

[5]"Macherey is indebted here to the work of Louis Althusser, who has provided a definition of what he means by 'practice.' 'By *practice* in general I shall mean any process of *transformation* of a determinate given raw material into a determinate *product*, a transformation effected by a determinate human labour, using determinate means (of production).' There is no reason why this particular transformation should be more miraculous than any other" (Terry Eagleton, op. cit., p. 69)

[6]As ranked by Michael McKenna, op. cit.

U.S.A., eh?"

He kisses Kosky on his forehead, then breathing onion, he pulls from a trashcan a copy of the *Courier*, thrusts the paper in Kosky's hand, the soot from the trash—or was it the smut of print—soiling Kosky's impeccably beige jacket.

"That's the paper with the bullshit about you," says Yankel. "What a story! It's a story every writer deserves. Too bad so many of them hear it only in their afterlife!"

"So where's the rest of **Steps Towards Heaven (Timothy Shay)**?" Kosky turns to Yankel. "To start with, give me the big news about me printed in red ink in the other newspapers."

"What other newspapers?" laughs Yankel. "So far, the *Courier* is the only one."

"Only the *Courier*?" Kosky can't hide his disappointment. "Only the *Courier*!" Yankel keeps on laughing.

Our literary Second Lieutenant now moves to the left side of the newsstand and, with martial music blasting from his inner speakers, unfolds the *Courier*. On the front page he faces a black-and-white picture of himself photographed leaning against a wooden statue. He has finally made it. Finally, he hits the front page. Rightly so, the front page hits him right in the face.

Written by Theveneau de Morande the fat-assed pullover with (*with* not *and*. J. K.) Thomas Carlyle, the straight jacket, who came to interview him in his apartment. the article occupies—invades rather—half of the front page, then goes on—and on—and on inside. The headline in Malison®—a bold typeface printed in Brickbat Red®—underlined with bold straight line printed on Obloquy yellow® literally spits one in the face. It reads: THE PUNCTURED BLADDER—DID NORBERT KOSKY EVER SWIM BY HIMSELF?

In the short preface to the main piece, Norbert Kosky is described by these two as "our literary Cagliostro" or "our American-Ruthenian waterpoloist." He is also named as "one of the American moral preservationists," "a literary conserva-

tive who advocates the takeover of America's collective soul."
Who are these kids kidding? He—a literary conserve—a
conservative? And since when is a human soul collective?

Their very names now bring to his vanity-filled mind the
unforgettable Thomas Carlyle, the British historian known
for his sexual histrionics, but also for his most obsessively
written History of the French Revolution, and his until this
very day not unexplained hate of Alessandro de Cagliostro.
". . . As a matter of fact," writes W. R. H. Trowbridge,
Carlyle's judgment of Cagliostro "is absolutely at sea; and the
modern biographers of Cagliostro do not even refer to it."

Theveneau de Morande was, on the other hand, as M.
Paul Robiquet says in *Theveneau de Morande*, "from the day of
his birth to the day of his death utterly without scruple."
Louis de Lomenie, another historian, writes: "There was
then in London an adventurer from Burgundy named
Theveneau de Morande, who, finding himself without resources, dealt in scandal, and composed gross libels, in which
he defamed, insulted, and calumniated, without distinction,
all names, if ever so little known, which came under his pen.
Among other works, he had published, under the impudent
title of *The Journalist in Armor* a collection of atrocities which
perfectly corresponded with the impudence of his title." (He
is the one and only spiritual food critic who gave the highest
Spiritual Service Award to the East Village joint called
Count de Cagliostro, owned by the one-and-only Giuseppe
Balsamo.) *This tells you! Enough said.*

So what does de Morande say? And why, as if afraid that
he alone won't be taken seriously, must he say it *with* Carlyle?

"This is an analysis of our para-literary Alger Hiss,"[7] says
de Morande with Carlyle. "This is a probe into the nature of
his floating, which we believe is a crude water act—acted out

---

[7]Alger Hiss: An American intellectual whose name became synonymous with an abrupt turn in one's career (*High School Annotator*).

with the help of a secretly worn, and by now worn-out, wet vest, not unlike one initially invented by Mr. McWaters[8] though perhaps invisible, or hidden inside his empty testicle sack or sore scrotum."

Writers speak a stench. (Kafka, *Diaries*)

Our fakir keeps on reading and as he swallows every word of their verbal icon — he swallows it the way a fakir swallows a knife or a burning torch — the stench of their seminal sleaze fills his lungs and begins to suffocate him, but only for a moment.

Having filled the lungs completely with air, the yogi floats upon the water like a lotus leaf. This is plavini kumbhaka. (Hatha Yoga Pradipika)

Nothing else is mentioned. Nothing about health or

---

[8]"THE MCWATERS METHOD: But water workouts aren't just for elite swimmers. New equipment and techniques make these soft workouts as accessible as a swimming pool. They can be ideal training for land-played sports, or can be toning and aerobics programs by themselves.

"One person who has given pool exercises some polish and sophistication is Glenn McWaters (yes, his real name), former director of Samford University's Sports Medicine and Fitness Institute in Birmingham Ala. . . . He began supplementing training programs with water workouts, having athletes cling to the side of the pool as they 'ran' like paddling ducks. The workouts were fine, but McWaters thought they could be better if the athletes were in deep water. He tried a variety of devices to position them: ski belts, life jackets, ski vests. 'There were problems with all of them,' said McWaters. 'Either they didn't offer enough flotation, or they didn't offer enough free arm movement.'

"McWaters finally designed his own 'Wet Vest,' a flotation device made of thick foam with Velcro straps to keep it closed and a Velcro crotch piece to keep it from floating up.

"Today, McWaters uses his Wet Vest to train elite athletes. . . ." (From "The Soft Solution: Weightless Workouts," by Paul Perry, *American Health,* 1986)

long life, only a rather extravagant-sounding promise. For we all know, regardless of how deeply we inhale, we will hardly float along like a lotus leaf, no more easily, in any case, than we are used to in swimming. (Hans-Ulrich Rieker)

As a result, within seconds Kosky's raging hypothalamus becomes free of humoral humors, as well as vanity and rumors.

Go on! Face other players, not yourself. Face the polo field. (Jabar Singh)[9] A veritable master of the Self, our Raja Yoga is now spiritually ready to stop reading and to throw the paper into the gutter, as well as to throw up. But he hesitates and this means he is not ready. Not yet, anyhow. This time he can't just float. This time — for the first time in years — his inner buoyancy act just doesn't work, and he is about to go under. Oh, yes, don't get me wrong, literary brothers! he sighs. I'm about to go under. To drown in their very words. But — wait — he already slows himself down. Aren't these guys writers like you? he asks himself. Yes they are. And now they have written a fiction about your public you, he answers himself. Still, why would they write it in the first place? Why not? Who knows why? Maybe because the *Courier* is a drag, not only a rag? It is a first-rate newspaper; first, if you recall, is lowest on Kosky's one-to-nine scale. What this means is that the *Courier* is not on the level of, say, such specialty publications as the highly technical *Swimming Pool* magazine — or the most respected *Journal of Toilet Water Safety*.

Then, as if this wasn't bad enough, these two urban swimming-pool rats, these literary bravados, chose to examine our

---

[9]Maharaja Jabar Singh (d. 1986): "an Indian-born aristocrat of the human spirit, Jabar Singh was, until the day he so prematurely passed away, one of international polo's most illustrious field masters." (Kosinski)

literary waterfowl only in terms of "his self-imposed ability to float, i.e., to *almost* walk on water," an act they call a "nautical fraud."

Having said this, they now examine his "questionable" (they call it) swimming career in terms of his "questionable" (they call it) past.

And suddenly
There was an uproar in my woods . . .
. . . a Voice profaning the solitudes . . .
You came and quacked beside me in the wood . . .
By God! I wish—I wish that you were dead.
(Rupert Brooke, 1918)

"Furthermore," they assume self-righteously, "he must have grown used to such a swimming mode at the outset of his 'pre-set' career when, he supposedly performed his water tricks in the swimming pools frequented by the agents of American Wildlife Agency—all of whom routinely wear secret flotation devices. If they must wear them—they, the ultra-professional swimmers—why mustn't he?" **A very good question. But why of all the people who swim, do you question me? (Norbert Kosky, 1982)**

Now these are hardly serious charges. Under normal conditions, how many normal people would believe that a man who can float can't swim? But these are not normal conditions. Our literary man is a public figure, first made public not by his books but by his public performances in the water. He was made particularly public by recently appearing stripped down to his navel on the very public cover of *MultiSports,* a magazine for which Carlyle once wrote and from which he was asked to resign.

Here, hitting Kosky with quq—the made-to-order quotes from Cathy and Teleny, strained and extracted like poison—

de Morande leads the reader to believe that Kosky's floating is spiritually suspect because, in de Morande's words, "in the already diluted world of swimmers and water freaks, one who floats so easily must be suspected of relying on someone else's wet vest, not an inner craft of one's own."

It is a hot day, some ninety-six degrees in the shade. It is also a hot story — it gives Kosky a sixty-nine-degree kick. The heat makes the print flow off the page, but not off Kosky. Although Kosky has read T. Carlyle — who hasn't? — he has read about Theveneau de Morande but never bothered to read him. Why bother? The man has established a definite reputation for himself.

As he keeps on reading, the contaminated print sweats, soiling Kosky's fingers. He begins to leave sweaty fingerprints on everything he touches — on his forehead, on his temples, on his cheeks. **The article is a nightmare — grotesque, circumstantial, eager, and untrue. (F. Scott Fitzgerald)**

The story continues on the back page (where, as if dropping his patron Carlyle, de Morande refers only to himself). Only now does Kosky notice that the venomous piece goes on for two more pages and that on the last page it is accompanied by a black-and-white six-by-nine photograph on which our literary floatus is photographed clearly sinking in some-one else's pool, next to a sculpture of a *Demon of Exile* by Lermontov: a demon who's simply laughing! Is he laughing at Kosky, or at Kosky's "sinking" picture?

Let us begin with one of many aspects of his novels that impress the reader, the frequent recurrence of material to which one must apply the adjective placental. . . . The symbolism of waters is obviously important to him, and the title of his latest novel is to be that of the series as a whole. (De Voto)

Kosky is not finished reading. Not yet.

What these two men write about his "literary yoga tantra

ways"[10] has certainly little to do with Shat Krijas, the all-too-well-known methods of body cleansing. By daring to question his mastery over his creative breathing, they automatically question the potential mastery of anyone, be it a man, a woman or a child, who might choose to follow in the footsteps of Jay Kay, his prime autofictional character, as well as follow his Tantric footnotes, and to realize—mark this, printer, in the biggest caps you've got—BREATHING DELIVERS OXYGEN TO THE BRAIN AS WELL AS TO THE BODY. BETTER BREATHING MEANS BETTER CONCENTRATION—AS WELL AS SURVIVAL IN A CONCENTRATION CAMP.

The Jews, on their part, sensed what the new arrangement had in store for them. There was no hope for anyone who could not work. Only the best and strongest workers, "the Maccabees," as Krüger called them, had a chance to live; all others had to die. There was not even room in the SS-army agreement for dependents. Survival had become synonymous with work. (Raul Hilberg, op. cit.)

Trust me. Here, Kosky addresses the invisible Public Self. I know what I'm talking about. I also know the difference between sitting on one's ass and drawing upon one's inner assets. To a writer writing means breathing and breathing means writing! It also means avoiding a sense of doom when you realized that something written about you, ABOUT YOU, NOT EVEN BY YOU, causes one of the loudest scandals yet in the wet vest'nd American swimming pool industry.

While thousands cheer, no one has yet pointed out that his exciting play is not an entirely original creation but an Americanized re-creation, thinly disguised, of James

---

[10]The term *yoga* has many meanings. . . . It is etymologically related to the English word *yoke*. It means to harness everything in us in order to gain more insight. Thus the situation, the tantra, in which this is the emphasis is called the Yogatantra. (Choyam Trungpa)

Joyce's "Finnegans Wake." Important plot elements, characters, devices of presentation, as well as major themes and many of the speeches, are directly and frankly imitated. (Campbell and Robinson on Thornton Wilder's Best Play of the Year.)

He is almost there. One more paragraph.

Finding that people would not buy his books. . . . which he (J. Fenimore Cooper: J. K.) put forth as outlets for his pent-up indignation — he resorted to his old trick of novel-making, and took advantage of those forms of literature, under which he had become popular with the American public, to asperse, vilify, and abuse that public. *(New World,* 1843)

Now, mind you, what he reads in their piece about NORBERT KOSKY'S IRREGULAR RELATION TO WATER, and reads it supposedly about himself, pains him the way *succés de scandale* once pained Byron. It pains him because, born in Ruthenia, he is only a naturalized American, naturalized, not a natural one.

The piece ends as it began: "the whole thing is not a piece of journalistic art, but a free-wheeling act of journalistic dispeller of boredom." (Jay Kay) The article is not the end of the world. Not even of his world — Old World or New. Says Dr. Steelheart, his inner-heart physician **"You must give up detesting everything appertaining to Oscar Wilde or to anyone else. The critic's first duty is to admit, with absolute respect, the right of every man to his own style."** (George Bernard Shaw to R. E. Golding Bright, 1894). **Suddenly I realized that something had happened to my voice: I tried to cry out, but my tongue flapped helplessly in my mouth. I had no voice.** (J. K. 1965)

He reads the article again. It is, after all, not an article of faith. It is rather an imitation of "Genius Is Not Enough." Reading it fast, Kosky might have missed a lot. Has he? Just then he hears the voice of the Demon of Exile. Speaking to him, the Demon of Exile always speaks of the nature of exile—never about the nature of self.

Now I had an overwhelming sense of shame greater than any I had felt before. I felt as if I had ruinously exposed myself as a pitiable fool who had no talent and who once and for all had completely vindicated the critics who had felt the first book was just a flash in the pan. (Thomas Wolfe)

He takes one more look at the article. *Read carefully and you realize it's just another high tale.* (Niskisko, 1982) He admits that from a purely narrative p.o.v., this is all well done: fusing the few elementary facts of his life with broken fragments of his public self, first so ineptly crystallized—crystallized as well as broken—by various members of the Amateur Swimmers Society. (ASS).

"What do you think about the implications of this sinking Lotus hullabaloo?" asks Yankel.

"I don't think about implications," says Kosky. "I take another lesson from history." As long as there are readers to be delighted with calumny, there will be found reviewers to calumniate. (Coleridge)

Don't be afraid to make mistakes; your readers might like it. (William Randolph Hearst)

I had been banished from society with one stroke. (Kafka) "But what do *you* make of it?" he asks Yankel point-blank.

"I can't say," says Yankel. "And if I can't say, who can?" he says in his openly amoral tone.

"It's bad enough I've got to sell such base rumor-based papers. But must I also talk about it and get all upset?" Yankel lifts his pale eyes to the sky, then dropping them all the way to a motto scribbled in permanent red ink on the wall of his one-man free-press enterprise.

We declare for a free press and oppose arbitrary censorship in time of peace. And since freedom implies voluntary restraint. . . . we pledge ourselves to oppose such evils of a free press as mendacious publication, deliberate falsehood and distortion of facts for political and personal ends. (Henry Gordon Leach)

"This is a rumor," says Yankel. "Don't touch rumor, not even with a fishing pole," he tells our literary Pole. "Let it starve. What do you think about it, Mr. Fenimor Kuperski?"

"I say: 'no comment'! and don't you dare quote me," says Kosky.

"Don't even say 'no comment,' " says Yankel. "Don't even allude to it. Saying 'no comment' to a slander is a comment — it is already spreading the slander. Do nothing, say nothing, show nothing. Look the other way, the Jewish way of show-ing — not showing off — the other cheek. Showing off is a comment."

Kosky ponders the alternatives.

After a few minutes, it was interrupted by a great tu-mult. Our hero had been quite aware that he was involv-ing himself in an action which, for the rest of his life, might be a subject of reproach or at least of slanderous imputations. (Stendhal)

"This piece is as phony as your own fiction — but funnier," says Yankel. "Why don't you laugh at it? Turning rumor into humor is the only way of making people laugh *at it* and not at yourself, providing, of course, that you've got a sense of humor."

"I write fiction, not humor," says Kosky. "Besides, I am not good at telling jokes."

An aged matron, aged only in terms of her parched skin, the depth and length and number of her facial wrinkles, approaches the newsstand and casts a starry eye at our liter-ary star.

"Don't I know you from somewhere? Aren't you the writer who played Bachaturian — a bad Red man in the *Oval State*, that six-and-a-half-hour-long movie?" she mumbles through her teeth, each one a knockout of dental repairs.

"Yes, I am," our literary exilechik admits politely.

"He sure was. He is the American literary hedgehog, who eats Spanish fly for breakfast — and you wouldn't want to know why. But if you would, then, here, madam, read all about him," says Yankel, pushing into her hand a copy of the *Courier.*

SS

26

At home, our waterfowl turns into a Blue Jay[1] turning bluer by the minute.

I am not trying to laugh it off, but it didn't hurt me, it doesn't rankle, I have no vengeful feelings; and in the end I may even get some good from it. (Thomas Wolfe)

He clips from the *Courier* the offensive article, then, always on the defensive, clips from other newspapers their various minuscule or maxiscule accounts of what the *Courier* wrote about him. Just look at these headlines! SWIMMER ACCUSED OF FLOATING: IS HE FLOATING OR SWIMMING? A FLOATER DENOUNCED BY HIS PEERS. WATER CHILD CHILLED. He spread the clips on the floor, then starts reading these assorted potshots.

The greater the truth, the greater the libel: If the language used were true, the person would suffer more than if it were false. (Lord Ellenborough)

The pieces grow less original with every one he reads, but, somewhere in between different "graspings" (Buddha) of his Self, a new spiritual aggregate is emerging. Jay Kay rounds

---

[1]Blue jay *(Cyanocitta crisata):* an eastern Nearctic species of race *bromia*. "Common to abundant migrant but resident as a species. Widespread breeder." (John Bull).

this thought out.[2]

I believe that art reflects morals and that one cannot renew oneself without living dangerously and attracting slander. (Cocteau)

Is it true, Carlyle and de Morande ask, that Norbert Kosky has said—or admitted—many times that he was a bad swimmer but a good floater? It is true, they admit, yet they call it a "grave contradiction." How can a "bad swimmer" admit to being a "good floater," unless he lost the very notion of water or, worse yet, of truth? Didn't Kosky himself once say in an interview published in PENTUP magazine that his water act was derived from being a dowser[3] more than it did from swimming as defined by *Swim Swim,* a complete handbook for fitness swimmers by Katherine Vaz and Chip Zempel, with the editors of *Swim Swim Magazine* (1986). This is, by the way, a book in which floating is not even listed in the index, while sunchristined swimmers (SS), swimming speed (SS), swimming stress and swimming strokes (SS) are all listed *en plein.* Isn't Kosky's water buoyancy act a trick Kosky

---

[2]"This is perhaps the most distinctive Buddhist teaching, that suffering is the product of 'the craving of the passions, the craving for existence, the craving for nonexistence.' It is, however, far from an obvious truth. Certain cases of suffering are plainly due to craving, namely, those that are due to frustrated desires. Desires may be eased by satisfaction or extirpation; and one may allow that if one stopped desiring, it would amount to preventing all the suffering due to frustration. But this does not prove the general case. . . . Body, feelings, perception, mentality, and consciousness are separate sets of graspings. There is nothing that *does* the grasping. *We* are the aggregate of the graspings, not something, apart from them, that does the grasping. This is an interesting and startling thought." (Proposed in *Mysticism and Morality: Oriental Thought and Moral Philosophy,* by Arthur C. Danto, 1972.)

[3]Dowser: "a water witch bewitched by the presence of water." (Norbert Kosky).

460

appropriated from some safe surf (SS) water-twister in the Oceanus Water Circus in Bumbledom, Florida? And so on. And so on, viewing him from now on as one more literary P.O.W. (—here, Prisoner of Water. J. K.) who allegedly once told "a New Yorker who refused to be named, that ever since he set foot on this Continent of the Free, Kosky set his mind on becoming as free in water as is that fellow Njord who, with his wife Skade and their daughters, Frey and Freya, do their weekly Water-Talks on WHM-TV—a talk show which often featured Kosky among its guests?

Lost in thought, at this moment—his thoughts are as dense as the Polesie forest and as murky as the Pripet Marshes—our *waterchilde* clearly hears an inner sound. **The only tyrant I accept in this world is the "still small voice" within. (Mahatma Gandhi)** The sound—it is a beam, not a moan—comes from the spiritual self-service center located at the center of his tower of strength.

A persona is the invoked being of the muse; a siren audible through a lifetime's wax in the ears; a translation of what we did not know that we knew ourselves; what we partly are. (R. P. Blackmur)

Instantly, Kosky eliminates all personal static. Now he can hear the beam, and he listens to it in silence. On his spiritual scale the language of silence is accorded the highest number, 96. And this time the scale is once again checked for authentic representation of his ZEN + JUDAISM + RUTHENIAN + AMERICAN UNIVERSAL CULTURE.

My time is nearly done. At fifty-seven the world is not apt to believe that a man can write fiction, and I have long known that the country is already tired of me. . . .

My clients, such as they are, are in Europe, and there is no great use in going out of my way to. . . . awaken a feeling in this country that has long gone out. (James Fenimore Cooper)

This is the time our "embattled persona" (Robert C. Elliott) must decide what binds him to life—whether it is his storytelling soul, or his psychosomatic soma.

Quickly, our wizard of literary Double SS turns his thoughts to Alessandro di Cagliostro, whom he had always considered, next to Rumkowski, the Chairman of the Lodz Ghetto: "**the most maligned free thinker in modern history. (Israel Kosky)**

Now, in order to escape from within the terror of his past World War II Self, he consciously turns his immediate present and past off, and turns to the *plus perfect* past — too old to be threatening. Now is an appropriate time for our maligned man of the hour to imagine himself as Cagliostro, that poor devil who only wanted fun and fame. Just think of the injustice: poor Cagliostro, sneaking out of London, his latest exile, after he was accused by Theveneau de Morande, writing in *Courier de l'Europe,* of being Giuseppe Balsamo, an Italian crook who owed money to a great number of people, and who conveniently disappeared from sight by the time de Morande wrote about Cagliostro. In such a way Kosky can view himself, but only through a metaphor, and one "through which the unconscious most naturally navigates. The locale and the setting are likewise metaphorical, for the whole journey could actually have taken place in the mind." (Kosinski, 1965)

Finally, if all this humiliation wasn't final enough for a man of letters — Cagliostro was, above all, a philosophical writer — imagine him and his wife arrested by the agents of the Holy Inquisition, then dumped into the dungeons of the Castle of St. Angelo. Charged with the crime of heresy, supposedly contained in *Egyptian Masonry,* his first, best-known and most stirring book, he was tried and sentenced to death by the Apostolic court. Did I hear you say "heresy" or did you say "hearsay?" asks Jay Kay. How could anybody charge Cagliostro with heresy? The man was a magician, a jack of all spiritual trades, not a heretic! "He was a literary alchemist — not a polemical chemist. He was a man who, masking his Jewishness with an Egyptian-made mask, made

462

himself the best-known self-made man in the eighteenth-century world," (Jay Kay).

According to the infamous Father Marcello, the Inquisition's official biographer-for-hire, when questioned by the Inquisitors, Cagliostro declared that he believed all religions to be equal, and that "providing one believed in the existence of a Creator and the immortality of the soul, it mattered not whether one was Catholic, Lutheran, Calvinist or Jew." As to his political opinions, he confessed to a "hatred of Tyranny, especially of all forms of religious intolerance."

When Cagliostro was in the hands of the Inquisition, his biography was written by one of its hirelings. Naturally, it portrays him simply as a scoundrel and cheat. The obvious question arises: If Cagliostro was such a contemptible rogue, how did he achieve such influence over so many people? Carlyle replies: Because he was one of the greatest cheats that ever lived. (Colin Wilson)

This statement, which Cagliostro made under oath to the Holy Inquisition, did not help him. By then the Holy Inquisition had bought at face value from Theveneau de Morande the claim that, in addition to being a crook, Cagliostro had also been a dangerous revolutionary.

Cagliostro a revolutionary? Nonsense! He is an artist, a fiction writer, an ordinary storyteller extraordinaire, a walking self-contradiction. His only revolutionary act was to write an open *Letter to the French People,* an open letter, mind you, not a project of a peace treaty or call to arms, an open letter in which, quite openly, he stated that, even if he were permitted by Louis XVI to return to France (after having already been banned by him), he would only do so "provided the Bastille had been destroyed and its site turned into a public promenade."

Was it Cagliostro's fault or the fault of his *Letter to the French People* that three years after he had published it, as mere wishful thinking forecast, the Bastille fell and, as if at his command, was, in fact, turned into *une promenade publique?*

Kosky gets up, kicks the clipping and, pacing back and forth across his room, evokes the past not in order to escape from the present, but in order to confront it—and to confront it spiritually armed.

Picture him, our wandering *Wunderkind,* facing his unholy Inquisition, and wondering: will the Inquisition buy de Morande's two-pennyworth charge that Cagliostro is actually Giuseppe Balsamo—in a new disguise?

Such claim was first advanced years earlier in Paris by one Sacchi, that little rumormonger, a scrupleless swine hired by some bitter French doctors in Paris in order to discredit Cagliostro—an Egyptian Jew they called him—whose medical practice took their practices from them—they had already lost to Cagliostro Cardinal de Rohan, the Catholic primate of Catholic France—the most important patient a French doctor could have. Now de Morande, the French spy working in London, borrows this long, discrediting claim practically intact from Sacchi, then in order to discredit Cagliostro in London, prints it intact in his *Courier,* as if it were his own discovery.[4] He knows only too well that by hanging on Cagliostro and Cagliostro's wife all the dirty linen that Giuseppe Balsamo and Balsamo's wife once wore in London, he would break Cagliostro by sending after him all the money-hungry, real and self-imagined debtors of Balsamo.

When de Morande kept on repeating his claim that Cagliostro equals Balsamo, Lord George Gordon[5] publicly came

---

[4]"Under the editorship of de Morande," says Brissot, "the *Courier* tore to pieces the most estimable people, spied on all the French who lived in or visited London, and manufactured, or caused to be manufactured, articles to ruin any one he feared."

[5]Lord George Gordon, past leader of the Protestant Association, who in 1780 once led one of the most violent Parliament-petition carrying demonstration in British history during which hundreds were killed and injured, and, as a result over twenty "Gordon

to the defense of Cagliostro by writing about him in an open letter published in the *London's Public Advertiser* for all England to read.

Now, would Lord Gordon, a convert to Judaism, risk his reputation among the British aristocracy and His Majesty's Government, by coming to the public defense of Cagliostro, had he not first verified the facts with the London police, the very police who, knowing the real Balsamo Duo only too well, could guarantee with every guarantee needed that Cagliostro and his wife were not the Balsamos? He would not!

But, argues Kosky's inner thumb-screwing inquisitor, to support his claim that Cagliostro was Balsamo, de Morande first quoted, then produced three witnesses who supposedly could finger the Cagliostros as being the Balsamos in disguise. When questioned by police—who knew the real Balsamo's!—as dishonest as they were, even these witnesses nevertheless refused to swear to it simply because, as they admitted in the court, *they had never seen Balsamo or Balsamo's wife in person! Never-ever.*

Still, who were these three witnesses, asks the inquisitor? And why would they so readily agree to confirm de Morande's story? They were, in order of appearance, the already mentioned Monsieur Sacchi, a hack writer who, a few years earlier, during the Diamond Necklace Affair, had published in Paris a libelous pamphlet against Cagliostro—so libelous that the Parliament of Paris ordered its suppression; a man called Mr. Aylette, a rascally British attorney convicted of perjury and exposed in the pillory; and one

---

rioters" executed. Defended by Thomas Erskine, (a renown jurist who among others, defended Thomas Paine's *The Rights of Man* against the charge of sedition). Lord Gordon was acquitted, though ever since he was nicknamed Lord Crop. Read *King Mob* (Gordon's biography by Christopher Hibbert (1958), and the account of the Gordon riots by Dickens in *Barnaby Rudge* (1841). (Originally conceived as a serial docu-drama. J. K.)

Signore Pergolezzi, a corrupt restaurant owner. Enough said? Not enough.

Listen to the verdict of the Apostolic Court:

Giuseppe Balsamo, also known as Cagliostro, attainted and convicted of many crimes, and of having incurred the censures and penalties pronounced against heretics, dogmatics, heresiarchs, and propagators of magic and superstition, has been found guilty and condemned to the said censures and penalties as decreed by the Apostolic laws.

Notwithstanding, by special grace and favor, the sentence of death by which this crime is expiated is hereby commuted into perpetual imprisonment in a fortress, where the culprit is to be strictly guarded without any hope of pardon whatever.

Likewise, the manuscript book which has for its title *Egyptian Masonry* is solemnly condemned as containing rites, propositions, doctrines, and a system which being superstitious, impious, heretical, and altogether blasphemous, open a road to sedition and the destruction of the Christian religion. This book, therefore, shall be burnt by the executioner. . . . (1791).

A shot of Bukharinskaya Vodka prepares Kosky for the rest of Cagliostro's sad story — a story of the first man "in pre-First Amendment literary history" sentenced to perpetual imprisonment by the yellow press for making free use of a bag of quaint essentially storytelling tricks and devises." (Jay Kay)

This is the rest of his story:

Cagliostro, who is then forty-eight years old, is locked in the Castle of San Leo, near Montefeltro. Situated on top of the monstrously high rock, almost hermetically sealed by nature, and once the site of the Temple of Jupiter, the ruins of which gave shelter to Saint Leo, the Christian hermit canonized for his ascetic virtues, San Leo became an impregnable maximum-security prison, reserved for the everlasting seclusion of the most dangerous enemies of the Church in

466

order to make certain that such everlasting seclusion was short-lasting.

Imagine Cagliostro, the past prisoner of the Bastille, now incarcerated in San Leo! Imagine him — him, the most exuberant man of the century — locked up for life in the solitary six-by-nine-foot cell of that maximum security prison as an enemy of God, of the Vatican and all Papal States! Now how do you deal with a deal like this?

Cagliostro's imprisonment is indeed short-lived. Fearing he might be liberated by advancing troops of the French Revolution, to whom Cagliostro was a hero, the Inquisition decides to get rid of him.

Shortly before the Polish legion (already the best-known due to its bravery as well as the best-dressed foreign legion of the French Revolution,) enters San Leo under the command of the Polish hero General Dombrowski, (and enters it expressly in order to free Alessandro di Cagliostro) Cagliostro is found dead. Dead, supposedly strangled by his jailer only hours before the arrival of the Polish legionnaires. How convenient for the Inquisition![6]

Just think: Cagliostro dead at fifty-two. **He was a pretender to genuine magic and occultism, and not a prestidigitator who exploited his wares for the amusement of the public. (Henry Ridgeley Evans)**

With another glass of Bukharinskaya Kosky skoals himself in the mirror. He just skoaled one who decided to leave to history the verdict about the Lotus Floatus Affair.

In the year 1910 a voluminous work was published in

---

[6]They thought of rescuing him," says Figuier, "and perhaps even of giving him an ovation similar to that which he had received in Paris after his acquittal by the Parliament in 1785. But they arrived too late."

Sentenced by the Inquisition to imprisonment for life, Countess Cagliostro remained confined in the convent of St. Appoloni, a penitentiary for women, in Rome, where she died in 1794, one year before of her husband of twenty-two years.

London which treats the subject of the arch-hierophant of the mysteries in an impartial manner. It is entitled *Cagliostro: the Splendour and Misery of a Master of Magic*, by W. R. H. Trowbridge. The author has, in my opinion, lifted the black pall of evil, which has rested upon the name of necromancer for a century and more, and has shown very clearly that Cagliostro was not guilty of the hundreds of crimes imputed to him, and, on the contrary, was in many respects a badly abused and slandered man. (Henry Ridgeley Evans)

27

In the aftermath of what was written about him, by de Morande *with* Carlyle, Kosky keeps on meditating while walking back and forth across Central Park.[1] No wonder: Nowadays there is always an anxious reporter or reporterette at his door. Meanwhile, in the McLuhanesque electronic village the headlines keep on flashing: POLISH-JEWISH CABALIST NEHEMIAH HA-KOHEN FROM LVOV ALLEGES SABBATAI SEVI IS NOT ORIGINAL JEWISH MESSIAH.[2] (Such headlines left Sabbatai's devoted friends from Jewish-Ruthenia stoned. Stoned, printer, not stunned.)[3]

---

[1]"Mindful walking is frequently used as a main exercise in *vipassanā* meditation, alternating with periods of sitting meditation . . ." See *"Vipassana"* ("Development of Insight"), in *Tranquility and Insight,* by Amadeo Solé-Leris (Boston, 1986).

[2]For the most complete account of the tumultuous, though brief, life of Sabbatai Sevi, the reader is once again encouraged to consult at this asexual Eastern Standard Time the already referred to earlier *Sabbatai Sevi: The Mystical Messiah,* (1626–1676) by Gershon Sholem translated by R. J. Zwi Werblosky, Princeton, 1973.

[3]Stoned, no doubt, on *kanabo (hemp* in Esperanto) which arrived in Eastern Ruthenia with the first Khazar settlers. See *Plants of the Gods: Origins of Hallucinogenic Use,* by Richard Evans and Albert Hoffman (1979).

Promptly Kosky kills the impact of the headline by firing at it his SS-65 and mind-blowing SS-69 inner rockets which, filled with his own unique brand of $C_{23}H_{30}I_7$, known as "Kosotoxin, a yellow physiologically inactive decomposition product" *(Webster's Second International)*, blow away the enemy's venom V-1 rocket filled with mere journalistic vitriol No. 1.

These days, after listening to what so many people, friends and no-friends, have to say about him — our floating Messiah imagines himself to be Sabbatai Sevi, Jr., a mini-replica of the senior Sabbatai, who was, as you may recall, the most day-by-day written-about man in the entire Jewish, (and possibly non-Jewish J. K.) written history. Written about day-by-day since, already at the age of six or nine, he displayed the unmistakable spiritual signs of being able to qualify one day — qualify in terms of the impact his appearances could make on the believers, non-believers and disbelievers — as a most potent potential Jewish Messiah. And if that is not enough, he was written about day by day, by full-time, part-time and certainly overtime professional Talmud-trained Jewish *sophers*. These grownup guys, mind you, whether Sephardim or Ashkenazim, whether indifferent to Sabbatai, friendly or unfriendly or down right skeptical and even hostile, watched him around the clock, and who recorded every shift of his spiritual mood by writing about his every doing, non-doing and undoing in their various private diaries and letters as well as in official, semi-official and nonofficial secret, semi-secret and candidly confidential accounts (all of which, one way or another, would almost instantly become public knowledge).

Meditating in his bathroom, for once with all his inner as well as outer lights on (his bathroom, like everybody else's, at times serves as his most private Kundalini Temple),[4] Kosky

---

[4] See "Temples of Three Goddesses," Chapter Six in *Erotic Themes of Nepal: An Analytical Study and Interpretation of Religion-Based Sex*

ponders the fate of Sabbatai Sevi—the very Sabbatai Sevi portrayed in the only known likeness ever made of him: he was sketched by an eyewitness in Smyrna 1666.

The sketch was first made available in print in Amsterdam in 1669, in which he was portrayed as a Jewish Keeper of the Book.[5] As the one who in 1665, in Gaza, "proclaimed himself the Messiah and swept with him the whole community" (Sholem)[6] and not as one who, in 1666, became a Turk, after an apostasy forced upon him as a result of denunciation by Nehemiah Ha-Kohen. In addition, this apostasy forced upon Sabbatai, a brand new name of Aziz Mehemed Effendi and a new honorary office, that of the Keeper of the Royal Palace Gate to be supported by a royal pension! And yet, in spite of such spiteful change in his career, during the spiritually seminal year of 1669 Sabbatai had "dictated a longer version of his doctrine (entitled *Mystery of the Godhead:* J. K.) to one of

---

Expressions Misconstrued as Pornography, by Trilok Chandra Majupuria, Ph.D. and Indra Majupuria, M.A. (Nepal, 1981), p. 69.

[5]An etching of Sabbatai Sevi as the Jewish Messiah occupying the heavenly throne wearing the Crown of Sevi with Ten Tribes duly studying the Torah with him, appeared first in Amsterdam, both in Hebrw and in Spanish in many editions of *Tiqqun* published in 1666, by Nathan, the personal prophet of Sabbatai.

From Amsterdam, the news of the New Messiah spread around the world. In America his arrival was heralded in 1665 in New England, by Increase Mother, a famous preacher in Boston. It was then confirmed in 1667 by John Davenport of New Haven (Conn.) in his Epistle to the Reader prefacing Mother's *The Mystery of Israel's Salvation Explained and Applied,* London 1669. (Parenthetically, in 1978 New Haven saw the creation of the very first in America Memorial to the Holocaust erected there by the city government at large.) Today, *Tikkun,* (Hebrew for "to mend, repair and transform the world," is a foremost Jewish cultural bimonthly published in English by the (nonprofit. J. K. Institute for Labor and Mental Health in Oakland, California.

[6]See also *The Messianic Idea in Judaism and Other Essays on Jewish Spirituality,* by Gershon Sholem (1971). A "spiritual *must.*"

his scholarly visitors, or a least induced him to write it down."
(Sholem)

Otherwise, our Judah Levi Toba[7] carries himself not unlike Sabbatai, who at a similar time in his life, according to
an Armenian poet, "was found to have relations with women,
and the prose account mentions accusations of lewdness, and
'debauches with women and with favorites.' These accusations, surprising and strange as they may seem, cannot be
dismissed lightly."[8]

Such a quote implies a lot—but says nothing! What
"women"? Which "favorite"? What kind of "lewd relations"?
Since such things make for a fascinating story, tell us more,
man, or shut up if you've got no lewd story to tell!

"Anything else worth mentioning here?" Dustin notes on
the margin. "Not much, really," Kosky writes on the margin
back-to-back. "Except that," he reluctantly quotes Sholem,
the spiritually shameless rumormaker, "More recently, important and weighty testimony has come to light, to the effect
that Sabbatai prided himself on his ability to have intercourse with virgin women without actually deflowering
them."[9]

SS

A special-delivery letter from Cathy (who first pedantically
faxed him she was sending it, brings not a letter but a

---

[7]Judah Levi Toba, also known by his Islamic name Dervish
Effendi, was a Jewish writer, poet and a great Kabbalist who lived
at the end of the eighteenth and beginning of the nineteenth century and "openly advocated the mystic doctrine of holding wives in
common." (Sholem, 1971).
[8]Gershon Sholem, *Sabbatai Sevi*, op. cit., p. 669.
[9]Ibid. At the time of Sabbatai it was (though mostly in England.
J. K.) a crime for a man to sexually enjoy union with a maiden
under ten years of age even when she consented. Ed.

Videomatic™ video cassette. No wonder: Cathy has become a video addict and a video camera buff as well. A fact which leaves him, **The Marble Fawn (Nathaniel Hawthorne)**, rather disappointed. Wasn't she once, like him, a storyteller?

"I'm so glad you've finally left your lair and agreed to serve as New York Library's only nonliterary Lion Fish.[10] Now, with your literary teeth pulled out by all this To Swim or Not to Swim *Affaire*,[11] you're like every other fish," says Cathy in her letter.

"These days, all arts end up as video, not as *roman*."[12] She goes on. "No wonder our literary lions are in trouble! And so is the entire literary jungle," she says, sounding like a book censor. "Any day now books will be written not in words but in predigested nonverbal images called up by a writer on a personal LIC—a literary image computer."

The impact of venereal disease is greater than it seems at first. Since some of Cupid's arrows are poisoned, the relations between men and women have become unwanted, belligerent, even sinister. (Schopenhauer).

Anything but eager to participate in the new sexual gadget nightmare, Kosky, our Eastern anti-gadget man, reluctantly plugs the tape—and with it his own Self—into his Videomatic™ TV set's own videotape. Starring Cathy as its only sex starved star (SSS) the video starts by showing her standing next to her bed in her bedroom. It shows her dressed in a Roman tunic made of rawhide, as she faces the self-focusing camera or—this too is a possibility—her unseen cameraman or camera woman.

"Norbert, my love," says Cathy, snapping open one button

---

[10]Lion fish (pterois volitans): A black-and-white "nightmare fish" which, most frightening in appearance, inhabits the Red Sea.

[11]Ironically, "in French, the word *l'affaire* usually means something one would rather not have." (Lewinkopf, 1982).

[12]Ironically, in French, *roman* means *novel*, while in Ruthenian (as well as in Polish: J.K.), as long as it is written *à la française,* and with the letter S at the end, the word means *a sexual affair.*

473

of her tunic. "This is the boldest moment of your adulthood. Defend yourself against the Ultimate Threat.⊛ By now, the Kosky Float Puzzle is no longer puzzling. **By now what you take for your vice others take for fiction, and vice versa."** (**Kosky to an interviewer, circa 1985**)

On the screen, she moves closer to him. "In one of your books you said that **When their nonsense reaches a level where it finally becomes apparent even to the undiscerning eye, one might as well say to them: the more reckless your statements the better. (Schopenhauer)**

"Plot a real-life potboiler. Plot it now in your inner boiler room," she says, starting her own Latex stocking tales (not Leather stocking printer! — she splits even higher her demi-split floor-length Latex skirt, and under it she lets him catch sight of her black fishnet Latex stockings and most of her black-and-white Latex garter belt, as if he were Suidas — her sexual Lexicographer.[13] "The more depraved and debauched the Kaulini (here, one who venerates Kundalini. J. K.) the more she is fit for the rite," writes Mircea Eliade.

"Plot this real-life potboiler anywhere you choose as long as you plot it alone — and for me alone. Aren't you a plot-master? In your book, doesn't plot mean complot? A cabal as well as a premeditated plan of action?" The sole selling sister (sole, printer, not soul) practically now presses her stark-naked breasts against the video camera. "You're Byzantine," the toe teaser says, excitedly slashing the air in front of the camera with her foot clad in a stiletto sex shoe. "Your books are full of sensual secrets, of coded sexual arrangements." She

---

[13]*Lexicographer:* A writer of dictionaries, a harmless drudge. . . . And there is the famous polysyllabic definition of *Network* (probably in reaction to Bailey's definition of *Net* — he did not attempt *Network* — as "a device for catching fish, birds, etc."): "Anything reticulated or decussated at equal distances with interstices between the intersections." (*Storming the Main Gate: the Dictionary, from Samuel Johnson* by Walter Jackson Bate, 1975.)

looks at him with suspicion. "Jerzy Andrzejewski[14] said that a writer's life is purgatory. That only after his death is it known whether his work went to the hell of oblivion or the heaven of remembrance. By turning yourself into the best-known literary profaner—the next best thing to being a certified prophet—you could be certain that the heaven of remembrance is yours for the taking! At your age, what else is there for you to take? By now, you've quite likely done at least twice over what most people wouldn't think of doing even once! And you haven't done once many things others routinely do—like bringing up kids, for instance. Aren't you about to turn sixty—and creatively turn yourself in? I love you." Cathy stops—and she keeps looking at him, eye to eye with that shrimping starlet look in the frozen shot, frozen purposefully almost until the tape ends, on a brief—all too brief—shot offering Kosky a quickie, a few-seconds-long glance at her a marble-like naked torso of *Salt Lake City Venus*.

Unsettled, Kosky walks away from his desk, and giving in to the urge, he leaves his apartment en route to ponder what to do with his Self, the central issue of his life, and to ponder it where else but in Central Park?

Outside his building, Kosky is accosted by a reporter, a young, baldish man, who promptly introduces himself as **GRIDE, ARTHUR: who has an air and attitude of "stealthy, cat-like obsequiousness" and an expression that is "concentrated in a wrinkled leer, compounded of cunning, lecherousness, slyness, and avarice." (Charles Dickens)**. The man says he is a free-lance attached to *The Ramblit* magazine, a new literary venture devoted to literary obscurity defined as "one of the most pernicious effects of haste." (Samuel Johnson, *The Rambler*, No. 169)

---

[14]Jerzy Andrzejewski: author of *Ashes and Diamonds*, "a marvelously gloomy novel about Poland's post-war doom, and a doomed political assassin." (Jay Kay).

"What do you say about the allegations that you can't swim all by yourself? That, in order to stay afloat, you used some secret floating devices filled with either helium or *ilium*," he mumbles. His tape recorder is already recording. Clearly, he is a jellyfish posing as a man-of-war.

"I say let *them* say it, particularly since I'm not the only Flotus alive," says Kosky most modestly. **Friends have been amazed at how I manage to stay afloat no matter what position I'm in. I also sleep while floating. . . . (Bunnie Ashley, *Life*, 1984)**

"Is that all? Under the First Amendment, you're free to tell the truth, you know!"

"The First Amendment guarantees freedom — not truth," says Kosky. "Free means exactly that — free. Free to plot your potboiler on the Upper West Side as much as free to starve to death writing your first novel in the **Trenchtown House, Impasse Row, East Village.** (*New York* **magazine**) about how The Homeless Sue For Toilets in New York (*The New York Times,* 1990). Writers must be as free to write reporting based on fiction as I am to think up or even to originate auto-fiction that reads like reporting. That's all. Read *Death in Cannes,* (*Esquire* magazine 1986)."

It was a random shot, and yet the reporter's instinct was right. Gatsby's notoriety, spread about by the hundreds who had accepted his hospitality and so become authorities upon his past, had increased all summer until he fell just short of being news. Contemporary legends such as the "underground pipe-line to Canada" attached themselves to him, and there was one persistent story that he didn't live in a house at all, but in a boat that looked like a house and was moved secretly up and down the Long Island shore. (F. Scott Fitzgerald)

"But" — the man hesitates — "if what is written about you is not true, hasn't someone abused the public's right to know?"

"Not really. Writers write and they publish what they write in public media. Hence, writing is public." With his empty hand he toasts the indifferent public sky.

But we are the sum of all the moments of our lives — all that is ours is in them: we cannot escape or conceal it. If the writer has used the clay of life to make his book, he has only used what all men must, what none can keep from using. Fiction is not fact, but fiction is fact selected and understood, fiction is fact arranged and charged with purpose. (Thomas Wolfe)

"Maybe, like so many other writers, I too can't tell the difference between swimming and floating. Between . . ." Caught in between, he breathes deeply and takes a sip of the oxygen hidden in the polluted air. "What happened to me could have happened to any floater floating in the Bazaar Spirit." publishing weekly, 1911." says Kosky.

Great writers did not invent anything . . . but merely poured their souls into traditional materials and reshaped them. (Thomas Mann)

"It could, but did it?" says the man talking like Sergeant Fury.

"Whatever was said about me by George P. Flack or Steadfast Dodge could also be said about any parrot fish or porkfish **Pushing to the Front (Orison S. Marden)** in the American counter culture literary aquarium," boasts Kosky.

"I doubt that," says the man. "It certainly couldn't be said about me. I know all there is to know about the composition of water."

"And I don't. I guess I'm still not mature enough," says our Ruthenian Melmoth the Wanderer. (Charles Robert Maturin) **Immature artists imitate. Mature artists steal. (Lionel Trilling)** I still can't tell the difference between the Castle of Otranto[15] and the Castle of San Leo."

---

[15]In his *Castle of Otranto* Horace Walpole, the inventor of the literary Gothic romance, introduced the haunted portrait — "the physical representation of a haunted human soul" [Jay Kay], and a castle patterned after the famous Castle of San Leo made infamous by the Inquisition.

"May I have your permission to quote you?"

"You don't need my permission. You don't even need my quote. You can make up a quote say, and freely attribute it to me. **The place to which we are going is not subject to any law, because all that is on the side of death; but we are going to life (Jacob Frank),**" says Kosky. "I'm a public figure. A public figure is a well of news. I'm a public phone number and numbers are **the only universal language (Nathanael West),** as any Miss Lonelyhearts knows. I'm a news bargain. Half price after midnight!" Waving good-bye, our Kosotoxin Man walks away from the toxin.

At the entrance to the park, a young Damsel Fish (Dascyllus trimaculatus) breezes by. Just look at her! She is mouthwatering! She sends him a sexually sleazy skoal which says to our embattled sex soldier SOLDIERS ARE RELEASED FROM THE COMMANDMENTS.[16]

Kosky examines the superior slum (SS) goddess. She is a perfect Princesse a l'Odeur de Poisson.[17] A classic *dombi*. Dressed in a yellow T-shirt which braces tightly her girlish tits, a yellow miniskirt which stresses and contrasts with her dusky Thai-like thighs and yellow shoes, she is **short, blunt-nosed, dusky in color, with a conspicuous white spot on the shoulder and another on the forehead. Small specimens do very well in the aquarium. (Axelrod and Vor-**

---

[16]"Soldiers are released from the commandments." This paradoxical slogan also recurs among the Polish sayings of Jacob Frank, who, born in Podole (Ruthenia), took it upon himself to "complete the mission of Sabbatai Sevi" and led his followers to Esau — a symbol of the unbridled flow of life. "The motto which Frank adopted here was *massa dumah* taken to mean 'the burden of silence'; that is, it was necesary to bear the heavy burden of the hidden faith in the abolition of all laws in utter silence, and it was forbidden to reveal anything to those outside the fold." (Sholem)

[17]Jean Przyluski: Princess with the Fishy Smell, *Etudes Asiatiques II,* 1925), op. cit., See also his *La Numération vigésimale dans l'Inde, Rocznik Orjentalistyczny (Oriental Yearbook),* IV, (Lwów, 1928).

derwinkler)

Suddenly it dawns on him. This Damsel Fish is Aileen Adamite, "the most exotic looking star of the American Adult Cinema since Hyapatia Lee splashed the screen in her *Canterbury Tales*,[18] in the words of Jay Kay.

"I'm Aileen Adamite. I come from Altamont, near Asheville, North Carolina," she says. "You must be Norbert Kosky, the guy who floats like nobody but won't swim like everybody. Am I right? Saw you handing out Oscars. Saw you in *Total State*, but read nothing by you. Only about you. Do you really float all by yourself, or is it only a newspaper story?" The Damsel Fish gives him a finger—either a sign of victory or an *up-yours!*, an American gestural skoal, and she signs off before our American Spectator has a chance to skoal her—gesturally, of course.

The questions, put to me frequently these days by others and by myself, can be summed up this way: If the press is increasingly insistent on knowing more and more about the private lives of people in public life, does it not have the ethical obligation to tell more and more about itself? (A. M. Rosenthal, 1987)[19]

---

[18] An American-Indian adult cinema superstar who starred in her own Hyapatia Lee's adaptation of Chaucer's *Canterbury Tales*. Do not confuse Hyapatia with "the world's most fascinating woman of letters. She lived in fifth century Alexandria, and died there at age 40, murdered by an unruly mob." (from "Egypt, Polo and The Perplexed I", by Jerzy Kosinski, in *Polo* magazine, 1989.

[19] "On My Mind: Sex, Money and the Press," by A. M. Rosenthal in *The New York Times*, June 7, 1987.

28

Journalism is literature in a hurry. (Matthew Arnold)
The sudden avalanche of print doesn't pass unnoticed, in a
town where, on every street, the First Amendment walks
hand in hand with the Sixth.[1]

The other day, at McCarthy's snack bar, he had run after
midnight into two reporters from the Liberty News Service
who want to interview him about Him on the spot. That's
bad enough. But then, a mere hour later, when, high on
Kundalini, he is visiting the editorial photo studios of the
newly started *RenaiSSance Sex* magazine, he is spotted by—of
all people—Thomas Oliver, who, nicknamed Twist, "has sin-
gularly twisted his *Six-Sixty A.M.* TV Talk Show into a prime
moneymaking World Headline Making TV machine" (Jay
Kay), a subsidiary of the All Media MegaCartel, Inc. He is

---

[1] The free press/fair trial issue is one of the most clear-cut media
controversies in America today—and therefore one of the most
difficult to resolve. The First Amendment to the Constitution guarantees freedom of the press, and the Sixth Amendment guarantees
the right of every defendant to a trial by an impartial jury. As many
observers have pointed out, the two amendments are very likely to
come into conflict during media coverage of a trial. (George Rodman, *Mass Media Issues,* op. cit., p. 269).

also editor-in-chief of *About Face,* a sexually slick widely looked at—looked at rather than read—TV-video magazine.

Oliver, whom Kosky has never met face-to-face, waves at our superstar as if the two men had known each other for years by virtue of having once appeared together on *Facing the Nation TV Journal* aired from somewhere in Emerson—or was it Heschelia—a small town in a state not unlike Montana or Nebraska.

Disgruntled, Kosky returns home. This tells you! he tells himself. This country is no longer the democracy-ville de Tocqueville saw. This land has become videocracy—a star system spectacle state. (Read "Television Democracy and the Politics of Charisma," by Tim Luke *(Telos,* 1986/87).

Lavratus Prodeo. I walk disguised. (Descartes) Easily said, Pa! But it is too late! Kosky's phone does not stop ringing. He is no longer WHO? in the news. He is news. News breeds news.

Soon after, the excited answerette tells him that during his momentary absence, while he was meditbackg in his bathroom, one Mr. Thomas Oliver, the producer of *Six-Sixty A.M.* TV Talk Show called him, and calling on Kosky person-to-person, he called on him, imagine—in person!

This is vanity calling!

Excited by the call, which might have something to do with Kosky's forthcoming yellowback,[2] our media midget calls Oliver back.

"You are news," says Oliver. "People want to know you. They want to know how you think and what you think about.

---

[2]Yellowback: A cheap novel so called in England because it was bound in cheap yellow board bindings. In France, the modern bestselling equivalent of it is called *roman de gare* (pron. *romain de gare:* J.K.), meaning in french a novel one reads between catching (or changing) trains (roman-novel, gare-railroad station) (a phrase from which Romain Gary coined his name in order to replace his Polish-Lithuanian-Jewish name).

I want you to be interviewed on my show by Bridget Bishop, who's as you know, a former Miss American Waters turned into a *Six-Sixty A.M.* newscasting star."

"People can find out how I think from my books. Preferably from *The Healer*—my literary catfish maximus," he brags happily.

Oliver isn't happy. "Well, yes." He pauses. "I trust that *The Healer*, your sum total, is just as good as was your performance in *L'État Total*. I saw you in *Total State* when I was briefly stationed in France. In French, you were dubbed by some silly Ruthenian sounding French actor."

"Are you sure it wasn't me?" Kosky bluffs.

"Well, no," Oliver laughs. "But I'm sure'm sure you're the man behind *The Healer*—and it's the man, not the healer, whom I want on my show." Again he breathes in and out heavily. "Now, keep in mind that our average wholesome U.S. TV viewer spends over one-half of his entire leisure time watching TV—that's over six hours every day! And only with a brief break for a commercial, and that's when it comes time to take a look at one's kids and wife. Six hours of TV per day, and—brace yourself, Kosky—six hours a year for reading books. [PRINTER: a year, not a day! J. K.] In this country TV is the healer." He concludes.

"Six hours would do to read *The Healer*," says Kosky. "Three hours to read it as fiction, and three as nonfiction. Add six minutes for those who in addition to reading it would want to reflect on the narrative nature of both while pondering, also, what, say, at the time of Hieronymus Bosch constituted, in the art of painting, a *narrative* invention."

Oliver laughs smoothly. "Our spectators would prefer to read you—not your book."

"Why would they?"

This is perhaps the most disturbing book in a fictional mode that thrives on reader disturbance. . . . Some readers cannot finish the book; others refuse to. Those who have read it are likely to express themselves somewhere

along a spectrum of reactions ranging from angry denial, a refusal to have our noses rubbed in one of the darknesses of twentieth-century existence, ..."(Ulrich Wicks, 1989).[3]

"Because you're a talking head turner. That's why." Oliver insists.

"That's no big deal," says Kosky. "It's so much easier to join a controversy than a country club. As I keep on repeating. In my faith spreading a rumor is a cardinal sin. A sin only a storyteller can avoid commiting for as long as he prefaces every story he writes by saying 'this is only narrative.' "

With the trials were our ancestors tried and in all of them their fate was not sealed except for the sin of slander. (Torah)

"Besides, each time I talk about my Self in an interview," Kosky goes on, "I take away what's mystic in my fictional mystification and each time I let my characters speak up—be it Jay Kay or anyone else—one way or another they seem to mystify **the quiet eminence of my being (Abraham Joshua Heschel)."**

"I see what you mean," Oliver agrees happily. "That's why I enjoy reading about you in Tongue Lashing—Herbert Lashon's syndicated tongue-in-cheek gossip column in *Rumorama* magazine."

"And so do I." Kosky sins easily.

"Whatever may be thought of the authenticity of its incidents, we hope this book will not be found to be totally without a moral." (Hames Fenimore Cooper—preface to *The Crater*, [1848].) **"The author sought to alleviate the instructive quality of the book, by casting it in the form of a romantic narrative." (Edward Bellamy**—preface to *Looking Backward*, [1886].)

"Do you have any other interests you'd be willing to con-

---

[3] *Picaresque Narrative, Picaresque Fictions*, a Theory and Research Guide by Ulrich Wicks. 1989.

verse about with Bridget Bishop? I mean other than your
writing career?"

"Downhill skiing, for one," says Kosky.

"Too seasonal."

"One-on-one polo for two," Kosky ventures.

"Too limited." Oliver recoils much too soon.

"I also play bowls.[4] The game of biased balls. Balls, not
testicles," he interjects quickly. "But I only played it once,
with a British lord, and, even though I hate competition, and
he and his guests loved it, *inadvertently,* I came in No. 2."

"Bowls? Too British. Wait! Weren't you once exposed half-
naked by *MultiSports* magazine?"

"I was. Meaning, I was shown levitating."

"You were what?"

"Levitating. I was levitating in a Harlem hotel swimming
pool."

"Levitating? You mean being suspended above the water?"

"I mean doing the dead man's float while being very much
alive with my head way up above the water. I mean napping
on top of the water, above the literary golden pond, without
even once, even in a dream, treading the water."

"How come?" asks Oliver.

"I'm a Jew and my floating coach—his name is Judah
Loew—speculates that certain Jewish bones might be filled
with special minerals—with *seikhel,* rather than ordinary *nefesh.*[5] And then on orders from my father, I filled my head
with the buoyant thoughts of R. Hayyim, the older brother

---

[4]Bowls: an ancient game of bias, played with wooden biased balls
on a plot of closely mowed greensward, with the purpose of matching the aim—and bias—of the player against that of an aimless but
heavily biased ball and then to roll each ball as near as possible to a
jack—a small white unbiased ball. (Ed.)

[5]Judah Loew believed the *nefesh*—a certain Gentile soul—originates in "being here," while *seikhel,* a soul commonly found among
the Jews, comes from "being there."

of Judah Loew who wrote such classics as *Well of Living Waters.*"

"All these materials might be of interest to our book readers, but not to our viewers," says Oliver. "Watching at *six-sixty A.M.* at seven o'clock in the morning most of our viewers are too sleepy to follow such immaterial stuff. All they want to know is what makes you so bodiless in water."

"Possibly the Word. I'm told that in Hebrew, a language I don't know, the word *teivah* stands for both ark and word. Otherwise, the proper way to breathe. Breathe in and breathe out."

"Go on. Keep on talking." Oliver prompts him.

"Floating exercises one's lung and heart while stretching the rest of the body. This benefits those who, always on the run, don't have time, say, for running. It greatly improves the stamina, and performance of swimmers, bicycle riders, tennis and polo players . . ."

"Go on. Keep stretching this a bit more," Oliver who never learned how to exercise patience, became impatient.

"Well — since floating depends upon mastering one's skeletal muscles while being in control of one's respiratory ones, this, by itself, is health promoting . . ."

"Go on. Anything to do with promoting health improves the rating of American TV." Oliver exhales loudly since, clearly, he is not in control of his respiratory muscles.

"By keeping one's head always above the surface, a floater's mouth, nose, eyes, ears and hair — or a hair do — avoid contact with polluted waters. Hence, one can safely float for hours in any water: be it in a swimming pool with too much chlorine in it, in a mud filled river, lake or seawater — so much of which these days was turned into a sewer. Parenthetically, levitating could be beneficial to those who can't swim because, say, they're afraid of drowning, as well as to the millions of *waterbabies*[6] [Charles Kingsley] who have had at

---

[6]Webster's 2nd Edition (1953) devotes some six of its densely filled 3194 pages to the word water. J. K.

least one bad experience with water," says Kosky.

Can you walk on water? You have done no better than a straw. Can you fly in the air? You have done no better than a bluebottle. Conquer your heart; then you may become somebody. (Ansari of Herat)

"Go on. Give me more," says Oliver.

"Floating makes you high. This calls for the release of the endorphines," Kosky proposes. "The very same endorphines released by a polo player, a swimmer, or a marathon runner."

"What kind of high is it?" Oliver coaches him.

"A most Self-absorbing high."

. . . If the yogin realizes this he need no long fear death by water. (Some sources add that, after this meditation, the yogin is able to float on water.) Mircea Eliade, in *Yoga*, (1958).

"By the way: after your float'nd swim expose how many letters did you receive from other levitationists? How many?" asks Oliver.

"Unfortunately not too many," says Kosky. "They came from Levin,[7] and Loew and even Lewinsky. Unfortunately, none of these men could levitate (like a true Lewinkopf. J. K.) **When one man considers the configuration of his body, he is able to reach an understanding of God. (Judah Loew).**

"Not a single one? Too bad! You see, while we would like to promote floating as a high-class form of physical cult, we can't promote it as a sport as long as you could be the only person in a class all by yourself. This means, dear Kosky, we can't put you on my show." He hangs up leaving Kosky floating in mid air.

SS

---

[7]Levin (archaic Engl.): to lighten, to emit flashes of light or insight.

Another telephone call. Since his answering service does not intercept it, unnerved, he does. The instant he picks up the receiver and says hello, our Mr. Trud *(trud* means *work* and *tough* in Ruthenian) knows he is in trouble.

"This is Dustin," says the overly familiar voice. "Are you already editing yourself out of — or into — this floating affair?"

"Good to hear you, Reverend Dan,"[8] says our Golden boy *triomphant.* By placing the receiver between his head and his shoulder, he frees his left hand and now trains his binoculars across the street, where, on the sixth floor of a modern co-op, lives Nana, the Zolaesque (See *Nana,* by Emile Zola, 1880. J. K.) the object of his most irrepressibly fervent interests. Nana, a twenty-some-year-old "pristinely debauched raun-chette" (Jay Kay) who, in white miniskirt, knee-high white leather boots, no blouse or bra, has posed for him from afar.

Nana knows that he is watching her: he has been watching her like this at least every other day for some time now. He is not the only one. "He knows it for a fact" (lingo meaning he merely assumes he knows. J. K.) that she's been watched like this by every male and some female tenants of the Manfred who's been staring at her with the sexual intent of "The Prisoners of Camus and Stendhal" *(French Review,* 1968).

Now, judging by the covers of the books Nana displays

---

[8]Rev. Dan Beach Bradley, M.D., "had an impressive number of accomplishments: He played a leading role in the introduction of printing to Siam; he was the first person to perform a surgical operation in that country, and, after years of futile experimentation, in 1840 he performed the first successful vaccinations for smallpox. His was the first newspaper to be published in Siam, and it was he who printed the first royal decree (against the sale of opium) that came off a press in Bangkok. Most of all, he was a respected friend of the Siamese people, and through his journalistic enterprises in particular, he looked after Siam's national interest in its relations with France and England." From William L. Bradley's *Siam Then: The Foreign Colony in Bangkok Before and After Anna* (1981).

next to her coverless body when she displays herself for him, (our Sex Videot reads their titles splashed across her book-shelves through his Vice Vision bi-sexual binoculars). Kosky judges her to be like good wine, **a good familiar creature if it be well used. (*Othello*)** She is no stranger to good books either. And, boy, does this turn him on. On the shelf next to her favorite water chair (the newest gadget which, stemming from water beds, resembles the French-made bidet) stand such classics as *Children of Gebelavi* by Naguib Mahfouz[9] and *Centered Riding*, by Sally Swift, next to novels of F. Scott Fitzgerald and—yes!—Emerson. He conjures up Nana or pictures her, here it just doesn't matter as being jazzed-up, rectally reared, intellectual jizz lover (jizz, not jazz, printer!). As one who knows about writing, defined by F. Scott Fitzgerald in his undated letter to his beloved Frances as— just listen to this, please!—"2. Swimming under water and holding your breath." Nana possibly knows the journals of Emerson, where—just think of another coincidence—good writing is defined and rated by the already quoted Michael McKenna as "1. a kind of skating which carries off the performer where he would not go."

"I get off by being stubbornly stared at by a stubborn scuz-scene scum like you," says Nana sensuously twitching her heavy lips, but since she is so far away, and the windows of her room are shut closed and seldom washed, our Buttman

---

[9]*Children of Gebelawi*, a novel by Naguib Mahfouz (1959), the Egyptian Nobel prize winner in Literature (1988) is set in a fictious Mukattam Desert, which Mahfouz dared to inhabit by, among others, Adam, Moses, Jesus and Mohammed. This and other of this novel's narrative devices made him in the eye of the Islamic laws, "offensive to the dignity of prophets" (Al Azhar), a decision Mahfouz refused to contest on the grounds that, as he said, "Fiction is more realistic than reality . . . The country already has many problems. I do not want to add a literary problem to them." (as quoted in *Cairo Today* magazine, 1989. J. K.)

can't tell whether—sexily supined on her black water bed—
the wad-lipper slut is merely silently moving her lips or
saying it out loud to our lip-reader. **"The world meanwhile,
its noise and stir,/Through a certain window facing the
East,/She could watch like a convent chronicler."** *The Essential Robert Browning,* New York, 1990, p. 69.

"Finally, I've got tantalizing news for you," says Dustin.
"You're invited to appear on *Controversy!*—television's hottest
literary program devoted to the illustrious literary dead. Did
you get that? Did you hear that word *dead?* You're the first
author to be so honored, and they don't want you to talk
about 'Euthanasia and Jacques Monod.'[10] Rather, they want
you to be entirely your own free Self," says Dustin, who for
once calls him not from another writer's home, but from his
own, from his beloved Brook Farm near Boston where he
lives with his never-to-be separated from wife of thirty years.

"Why do they want me? Am I already dead to them?
Already lost in *The Unbroken Chain* [Neil Rosenstein]? Already lost to the living in my writing delirium?"[11] says Kosky,
while watching Nana doing her *Myth of Sisyphus* dance.

"These guys say that in one month you got more multime-
dia attention than other writing fellows get in a lifetime.
They say that, to them, as a topic you are as good as Koestler.
As good as Romain Gary. As good as Kerouac. As good as
Capote—all of whom are, of course, whimsically most alive

---

[10]". . . to bring a merciful end to intolerable suffering to a patient
who has no longer any hope of recovery and his death is imminent,
is an act which may be considered lawful and ethical in Jewish law."
From *Mercy Death in Jewish Law,* by David Shohet, Conservative
Judaism, 1952. See also: "The 'Right' to Live and the 'Right' to Die:
A Protestant View to Euthanasia," by Joseph Fletcher; "A Catholic
View of Mercy Killing," by Daniel C. Maguire; and "Jewish Views
on Euthanasia," by Byron L. Sherwin. (Ethical Forum: Beneficent
Euthanasia. *The Humanist.*

[11]See "Postwriting Depression, False Stagnancy and Other Ills

even though, *physically,* quite dead."

"But I'm not dead. Hence, I won't go on the show," says Kosky, with the conviction stemming from Apter Rabbi.[12] **I had of late been much perplexed in touching the question of whether the Lord guided me in editing my newspapers. I have always asked God by much prayer to guide me, and I have believed much of the time that he would. But occasionally I have fallen into sad doubt about it, and I have felt that my labor was for naught. (Rev. Dan Beach Bradley, 1866)**[13]

As if hearing him, Nana gets up from the bed and, like a cordless human doll, she slowly unwinds by taking off her miniskirt. Soon, her body goes through many explicit Yoga-sanas postures, **practiced till the fruit — Raja Yoga — is obtained." (Hatha Yoga Pradipka)**

Ironically, she does them well. Damn well. She sits down, letting him, all gaping, gape at her gaping flesh, while with opera glasses in hand, she watches him, our modern day Tarzan being watched by his first truly sexual Tarzana.[14]

"Don't decide. Not yet," says Dustin. "I'll be taking the midday shuttle to New York. See you at your sunken ship,"

Caused by Writing Books," by Charles Salzberg in *The New York Times Book Review,* (1987).

[12]Apter Rabbi: the spiritual code name of R. Abraham Joshua Heschel from Apt, Poland (1749–1825), "one of the outstanding Hasidic leaders of his generation and a disciple of R. Elimelech of Lyzhansk. He is the ancestor of Abraham Joshua Heschel (1907–1972), one of the most outstanding Jewish thinkers and philosophers. . . . His concept of religion and philosophy found expression in his most popular works in English, *Man Is Not Alone* (1951) and *God in Search of Man* (1956)." See Neil Rosenstein's *The Unbroken Chain: Biographical Sketches and the Genealogy of Illustrious Jewish Families from the 15th to the 20th Century* (New York, 1976).

[13]From "Freedom of the Press," a chapter in *Siam Then (etc.),* by William L. Bradley, op. cit.

[14]"In a valuable study, Helmuth Plessner argues that I stand to

Dustin signs off. We have seen the gutter press in heat, making its money out of pathological curiosity, perverting the masses in order to sell its blackened paper. . . . Finally, we have seen the higher so-called serious and honest press witness all this with an impassiveness — I was going to say a serenity — that I declare stupefying. These honest newspapers have contented themselves with recording all with scrupulous care whether it be true or false. . . .(Zola)

my body in a relation that is at once instrumental and constitutive: I *have* my body but I also *am* my body. As a result I live in a state of tension with regard to my physical existence, while being at the same time wholly and completely bound to it." From *Sexual Desire: a Moral Philosophy of the Erotic,* by Roger Scruton (1986), p. 69.

29

In a worn-out fedora, Cranberry raincoat and three-piece Oxford tweed suit, Dustin enters Kosky's apartment **like a New England sailor long months outbound for China on a clipper ship. (Thomas Wolfe)**

In the apartment, Dustin carefully puts down his well-abused attaché case, no doubt a one-to-one latter-day replica of the one used by the Reverend Dan Beach Bradley, M.D. during his trip to Siam, then settles down behind Kosky's desk, and in front of Kosky's manual Zakhor portable typewriter, mindlessly usurping the place which belongs to the author — and only to him.

"You don't look too hot," he says, scanning the face of his author.

"Of course I don't," says Kosky. "I'm so stirred up. I can no longer tell a sea man from semen."

Then, quite at random, Dustin starts playing with Kosky's various ball point pens, picking them up one after another, from their wooden stand. Randomness is not one of Dustin's characteristics, even though he was at one time Kosky's editor at Random House in New York. It is unavoidable that to Kosky, the very name Random, however randomly, rings the narrative church bell of Radom a small provincial town in Poland, (as was Kielce, another town, J. K.) which was the

493

scene of an anti-Jewish riot, during which many Jewish World War II survivors who had just returned there from the Nazi concentration camps were killed wounded and brutalized. These riots were started by politically motivated Party thugs who freely distributing the Russian-made vodka Rumorova of double strength to the local thugs, often illiterate, crude and traditionally anti-Jewish, distributed it on the double to those among them who, no doubt, were experts in starting a riot.[1]

"You don't look too hot," he says, scanning his author's face as if it were the existentially static face of Camus.

Dustin then casts a glance at the loose mountain of press clippings, and the first headline.

----

[1] For an objective assessment of the events surrounding these two most tragic events, the reader must consult the various scholarly publications, among them, *The Jews in Poland*. (op. cit.) Read also, *A Christian Response to the Holocaust* by Harry James Cargas. Forward by Elie Wiesel, 1981.

"How have the Christians reacted to the plight of their Israelite co-citizens in German occupied Poland? The matter gave rise to many misunderstandings. I say: misunderstandings, because so few people know about the decree of Herr Frank, Hitler's proconsul in the General Government. Dated 15th October 1941, paragraph 4b reads: (1) Jews who leave without permission quarters allotted to them are subject to *the same* penalty. (2) Instigators and helpers are subject to the same penalty as the perpetrators of the crime. A crime planned will be punished in the same way as an act accomplished.

"Innumerable further decrees to the same effect signed by Frank and his henchmen reinforced the rule by promises of reward for everyone who denounced a stray Jew to the proper police organ. Also little known remains the fact that neither in Holland and Denmark, nor in France, help to Jews was *punishable by death*." Maria Kuncewicz, *The Jew in Polish Literature,* lecture in Chicago, 1969 reprinted in Dialectics and Humanism, 1990.

What sexy crystalizations are you taking against all these *head-aky* head lines?" he asks his sad'nd sole Stendhal.[2]

"Looking at myself with Proust's **"binocular vision" (Roger Shattuck)**[3] This, plus taking Emerson Syrup as a matter of course."

The last phrase unsettles Dustin, who promptly gets up from his settle.

"Emerson?" "What Emerson?" he repeats.

"Blotting Books. Numbers one, two, three and four,"[4] Kosky reassures him, curling up on his cot, his hands buried in his hair. **The first remedy of any victim of defamation is self-help — using available opportunities to contradict the lie or correct the error and thereby to minimize its adverse impact on reputation. (American Courts)**

"Don't you think that by now you have had enough? Shouldn't you pour some lie contradicting cold water on that silly stuff?" Dustin scores an easy SS.

"I should not. I'm a storyteller, whose unwritten mission — if any — is to start inner fires in my readers. Besides, trying to extinguish rumor, even with some Holy First Amendment

---

[2]"Sexy Stendhal," as he was called by his contemporaries, was, according to his many women lovers, so preoccupied with the sex act that he crystallized it in his fiction. In his *On Love* he called this process "crystalization Number 69." (J.K.)

[3]See Roger Shattuck, *Proust's Binoculars: A Study of Memory, Time and Recognition* in: *"A la Recherche du Temps Perdu"* (1967).

[4]Emerson's *Blotting Books* are part of Volume VI (1824–38) of *The Notebooks of Ralph Waldo Emerson* (Belknap Press, 1966). "The reasons given for Emerson's early interest in collecting quotations are many: personal inclination, the habit of the age, the ministerial tradition of the Emerson family ('the hereditary use of a text before a discourse,' as Oliver Wendell Holmes put it), the embryonic stirrings of that 'philosophy' of quotation which he later set forth in 'Quotation and Originality.' It is clear, certainly, that Emerson pursued the habit with great diligence." (Ralph H. Orth, 1966).

Wasser™ means *touching* rumor and in my faith, this means cardinal sin, morally so self-excommunicating in fact that even a storytelling cardinal such as myself can't afford it. That's all there is to it."

There are four acts that a man performs, the fruits of which he enjoys in this world, while the capital is laid up for him in the world to come. They are: honoring father and mother, deeds of loving kindness, making peace between a man and his fellow, and the study of the Torah which is equal to them all.

There are four things that a man performs, for which punishment is exacted from him in this world and also in the world to come. They are: idolatry, immorality, bloodshed, and slanderous talk which is the worst of them all. (Aboth D'Rabbi Nathan)

"Of course, you know, such reportorial canard has happened before," says Dustin. "After Thomas Wolfe so openly dedicated *Of Time and River* to Maxwell Perkins, his editor, 'without whose devotion given to each part of it . . . none of it could have been written,' one Bernard De Voto — a self-styled literary critic who wrote his own little thriller under the pen name of John August — went on to claim on the pages of a literary review, that in his fictional river Wolfe had not swum alone — but was assisted by Perky Marx, and by his own publisher's full-time editorial assembly line. As if an idiosyncratic, purely narrative literary work could indeed ever be 'assembled'!" Offhandedly, Dustin glances at the mountain of press clippings — all freshly clipped yet already yellow — spread on his author's rolled-down roll-top desk. Offhandedly, he glances at Kosky. His glance is a reprimand. For a spiritually split second he seems to reprimand Kosky, his literary adopted kid, for running too fast across the American literary uphill. For running too fast, and for being almost run over. As if this near-miss was Kosky's fault!

"Do you know that, by now, more poison-pen fiction has

been pentelled by others about you than penned by your own poison pen." Dustin says offhandedly.

"I don't mind," says Kosky. "Good poison-pen writing is hard to find and since I having once lived through Nazi's Zyklon B, I welcome such exercise in free journalistic breathing. Their exercise no less than my own." **Perkins was totally useless when it came to copy-editing or correcting a text. Such details meant very little to him. Consequently, the early editions of books like F. Scott Fitzgerald's novel "The Great Gatsby" were textually corrupt to a nauseating degree. One of my early tasks was to build a staff that could copy-edit with the accuracy that readers demand and authors deserve.** *In the Company of Writers:* A life in Publishing by Charles Scribner, Jr. New York, 1991.

"Surely you intend to take their floating argument apart?" Dustin is ruffled. "All you have to do is to give one press conference and, with all present, give a demonstration of your demonological float, not unlike Bruno Schulz who added to his own *cliché-verre* drawings in his *Book of Idolatry. The Drawings of Bruno Schulz,* (Northwestern University Press, 1990) his full of verve'nd nerve stories. As your prime-time publishers, we could easily arrange something visually informative about you. After all, as a duly dues-paying member of the Writers Guild of America you are entitled to the privileges accorded in this country to any Fourth Estate writing pro. For instance, we could release a video-cassette titled "Kosky Upon Water." Then, to be on the level with the press, we could ask other members of our Fourth Estate to question you, pretty much the way one adversary questions another during the American pretrial procedure known as discovery."

"I believe in creation, not in discovery," says Kosky.

S6.9 Privileged Matter

The discovery rules do not permit discovery of "privileged" matter, but they provide no definition of the applicable privileges. The definition must therefore be sought elsewhere. (Civil Procedure, 1965)[5]

"Look, Norbert!" Dustin settles back in the chair. "Unless you'll convince your readers that you can float the way they believe that you do, they might not sufficiently disbelieve what Comrade de Morande and Herr Carlyle said about you and your quasi-performance."

"I performed as an actor in *Total State* and that's enough," says Kosky. "I write fiction. I don't perform it. Fiction meaning invention, not convention. Fiction meaning making things up, not being made up of them. Fiction meaning a cock-and-bull story as well as a fishy-fish story. Fiction meaning canard, or a maggot. Fiction meaning a unit of spiritual SS or even an SS-run whodunit, not a mere Freudian *Who's Who* unit. Fiction meaning my own literary crotch. Fiction meaning my *Autoportrait with Women* (Bruno Schulz, pencil, circa 1934).

"I know what fiction means." Gently Dustin slams his fist on the table. "In case you didn't know, let me remind you that only last week we published the new annotated edition of Steinbeck's *Of Mice and Men* as well as Faulkner's *The Sound and the Fury.*"

"I read in *PPN (Publisher's Pub Newsletter)* that you turned down the new unabridged, author-anointed'nd annotated edition of Thomas Wolfe's *Of Time and the River.* How could you?" Kosky sounds furious.

"We simply couldn't afford to publish it. Nobody likes big books anymore. Big meaning heavy. Heavy meaning tough to swim through. This brings me to the point." Quickly Dustin blows his nose into a handkerchief as white and as pure as a wafer — and just as stiff.

---

[5]See p. 196 in the already-referred-to "Discovery and Other Pretrial Devices," Chapter Six in *Civil Procedure,* by James Fleming, Jr., and Geoffrey C. Hazard (1965).

"By charging that you can't float by yourself,—without being assisted by some hidden sea scooter or cryogenic lung,[6] de Morande and Carlyle strike at the very heart of your accomplishment. You must strike back. What are you going to do to this Hannah Arendt ideological elephant?"[7]

"Nothing," says Kosky. "Nothing. I'm a Jewish-Ruthenian frog. Frog, not a subversive quail. I live in a *nether* world of ether. To many Zenists (believers in Zen: J. K.), ether is, like semen, a form of one's inner water."

Behold the quail, the crow, the fly, the frog! They slew the elephant! Behold the hatred of the haters! (*Jataka Tales*)[8]

"This is no time for the Transcendental School.[9] This is fall-out time," says Dustin, who, like Kosky, has been progressively losing his already unnaturally grayish and worn-out hair.

"It's free speech brand of fall-out," says Kosky, loading his mental receptor with Mantraki Gold narrative glaucoma and

---

[6]Sea scooter: here, a well-known device which, propelled by electric motor, pulls the underwater driver at some 6.9 knots. Cryogenic lung: a device which, worn by the swimmer, converts him into an underwater gas-breathing sea creature.

[7]"One of the more outstanding signs, however, is the accuracy with which elephants are able to locate underground water in times of drought, thereby indirectly serving humanity." (Robert H. Leftwich). Hannah Arendt elephant: synonymous with her spiritually utterly untrue *Eichmann in Jerusalem*. (J.K.)

[8]In the Jataka tale called "Quail, Crow, Fly, Frog and Elephants," a small quail brings about the downfall of a mighty elephant who, seeking water, had trampled her offspring to death.

[9]Founded in 1836, New England's Transcendental School in Boston (Nathaniel Hawthorne, Ralph Waldo Emerson, and Margaret Fuller were among its illustrious students/teachers) once made Boston the spiritual capital "of this otherwise Profit-Oriented Republic.": Jay Kay.

seizure reliever. A receptor is a molecule on a cell surface where a substance attaches itself to create an effect, acting like a lock and key. The discovery of such a molecule occurring naturally in the body makes a substance like marijuana. (Philip J. Hilts, 1990).[10]

"It's a docu-slander, not a docu-drama," says Dustin. "Yet you've *steadfastly* refused *Steadfast Dodge* (Cooper) and *George P. Flack* (James) to *flack* your public. Instead, you keep referring everyone to the history of Lodz Ghetto where most of your family perished when the Nazis turned the anti-Jewish poison into Final Solution. That's O.K. with the public though it is not O.K. with me. But how will you justify for me your refusal to appear on *Controversy!?*"

"The same way I justify it for myself or for the public: by not justifying it," says Kosky. " 'Rumors are unavoidable in a society,' " he quotes Isaiah Kuperstein.[11] In a sense, the sin of one who gossips about something that is true is greater than that of one who tells false gossip. For when a man tells true things about another, people believe him and the victim remains contemptible in their eyes. . . .(Orhot

<hr>

[10]Writes Jay Kay: "Given the overwhelming need to counteract the often overly overwhelming impact of artificial stimulants upon so marvelously Self-stimulating human mind, the reader is referred to *The Drug Experience* (First person accounts of, among others, writers and scientists) Edited by David Ebin, (1961). See also *Findings Suggest Body Uses Natural Marijuana* by Philip J. Hilts, (*International Herald Tribune*, 1990).

[11]"Rumors: A socio-historical phenomenon in the Ghetto of Lodz," by Isaiah Kuperstein, *The Polish Review*, Vol. XVIII, 1973, No. 4. For better understanding of motivation of Norbert Kosky as well as of Jay Kay, the central protagonist of his novel, *The Healer* (1988, 1991) the reader is urged to read *The Chronicle of the Lodz Ghetto 1941–1944*, Yale University, 1984 and *Lodz Ghetto:* Inside Community under siege, New York, 1989.

Zaddikim)[12]

"But at least you could dismiss it by making fun of them. You were very dismissing in *Total State,* you know."

"My Hippocratic law[13] won't let me dismiss this issue either. I'm not Hannah Arendt, the writer who, usurping from Conrad the notion of banality of evil, went on to banalize the Nazis,"[14] says Kosky.

"Your Hippocratic law is an evil excuse," says Dustin.

"It's a remedy against evil—not an excuse for its banality."

"You are your own remedy, Norbert!" Dustin heats up, but, a true Brahmin, he instantly calms himself down by channeling his attention elsewhere.

Pedantically, with his thumb and two fingers, Dustin reaches into his tobacco *pochette,* removes a small pinch of tobacco, stuffs it under his lower lip and chews upon it like a polo pony. While, as befits a man named Dustin (who can't dust his anger—anger always disguised as anxiety), he dusts his fingers just as pedantically and just as angrily, as he would anxiety. Then, and only then, he closes his *pochette* and replaces it in his tweed jacket's lower pocket. In seconds, his

_____

[12]An anonymous Jewish medieval code of non-anonymous Jewish ethics.

[13]Hippocrates treated medicine as the most noble of all arts, and was the first to suggest that the noble artists whom we call physicians take his oath, in order to make sure their patients wouldn't be mistreated.

[14]"The banality of evil" (Conrad) was Hannah Arendt's excuse for those of the American Jews who during World War II tended to explain away Nazi extermination of the Polish and other East European Jews with a phrase "these Jews went to their death, like sheep." (And she dares to say it, as though not the Germans, but the Jews were sheep—by sheep she clearly implies the instinct of the horde: Jay Kay.) See *Eichmann in Jerusalem: a Report on the Banality of Evil* (1965).

eyes water and, not surprisingly for a tobacco chewer who was once a tobacco snorter, unable to hide his smoking habit, he habitually sneezes some six or nine times. His paroxysm over, he continues. "Go on *Controversy!* with me. Let's give the world a *Never Again!* lesson in creative floating."

"I no longer teach creative floating unless you call it Jewish Presence," says our Abraham Abulafia (d. 1296: J. K.) quietly.[15]

Finally, there is a need for a bold *new program whose importance cannot be overestimated. It is time that the Jew moved to establish close and regular contacts and dialogues with the people who, in the end, will have the most bearing on the future of the American Jews. These are the people who represent the American majority, the working class, the ethnic populations, the blue collar and the nonintellectual groups.* Never Again! A Program for Survival by Meir Kahane, 1972.

"If you'll allow me to quote Sophocles," says Dustin in a low voice, "you have 'too much pride for one drowned in ill fortune.' Think of the Effingham Libels.[16] Like Cooper, you too must state where you stand in this matter."

---

[15]With the exception of Abraham Abulafia (1240–after 1292), the Spanish Kabbalist, and his disciples, who developed a Judaized version of yoga in which breathing techniques and rules of body posture were stressed, the Jewish mystics for the most part did not place meditative techniques at the center of their system. (Judaism and the Gentile Faiths, op. cit.)

[16]"Mr. Cooper has libeled America, Americans, and every thing American, in a manner which should call forth the contempt and scorn of every man, woman, and child in the country possessed of the smallest portion of patriotic feeling. His libels on our people and her institutions are general; but he appears to have singled out Otsego, the county of his nativity, as the particular region of our

"My stand is fiction. Monodrama,[17] not melodrama," says Kosky. "Literally speaking I float upon water. For obvious reasons, please don't confuse my act of floating upon it with walking upon water. One Sabbatai Sevi was enough."

"I wish you'd reconsider your motives. It's all so wasteful."

"I won't. I don't recycle my motives. Nor do I waste them."

Zhivago is not merely a doctor, he is a poet. And to convince the reader that his poetry has true significance for mankind, you end your novel with a collection of your hero's poetry. In doing so you, Boris Pasternak, sacrifice the better part of your own poetic talent to this character you have created in order to exalt him in the reader's eyes and, at the same time, to identify him as closely with yourself as possible. Editors of *Novy Mir* to Pasternak (Long before *glasnost:* J. K.)

A long silence falls upon both with the force of spiritual Niagara Falls.

"At the time Thomas Wolfe was docu-slandered by De Voto," Dustin reflects after this overly long silent waterfall. "Maxwell Perkins wrote the following to him: 'One night in a nervous moment when the rumors were flying thick and fast, I wrote you by hand asking you if you would be willing to write a letter saying they were groundless. But then, in the end, I tore up my letter because **I thought it was only part**

---

whole country the most *boorish* and 'unprincipled,' and therefore meriting the infamous distinction of being held up in an especial manner to the contempt of Europe." (Park Benjamin, *New World*).

See also "The 'Effingham' Libels on Cooper," by Ethel R. Outland, University of Wisconsin Studies in Language and Literature (1929).

[17]Monodrama: the art of staging as well as acting out a dramatic monologue—"a monotone with plenty of change and no weariness," as Tennyson called his *Maud,* was initially introduced by Rousseau in his *Pygmalion.*

of the game that we should take our own medicine.' "
Dustin quotes Perkins from memory. "Maybe Perkins was
right after all." A troubled editor gives his troubled author
another troubled look. "This whole thing brings to mind
Conrad's *Nostromo*," he says. "Just because Ford Madox Ford
and Conrad worked together on some fragments of Conrad's
text, it made as much difference to Conrad's prose as would
three drops of water poured into the Conradian ocean."[18]

   With introspection over, time for literary inspection. Dustin puts on his glasses and eyes Kosky's manuscript. "How's
your work on *The Hermit?*" he asks.

   "I decided to call the novel *The Healer*," says Kosky.

   "*The Healer?*" Dustin concentrates, looking down. "That's
not bad," he exclaims, looking up. "After all, Christ was a
healer. But what made you change the title? What, or who. Is
it a new *dombi?*"

   "*The Healer* seems to better reflect the art of narrative
melampodium,[19] in the age of telephone, Fax, word proces-
sor and visual Video sex," says Kosky, "Besides, I learned
from W.E.T.'s Newsletter that another writer is soon coming
out with a novel called *The Hermit* and I'd hate to see it
confused (or, worse yet, fused by the readers) with my own
Working Papers."

   "No kidding! And who's that?"

---

   [18]Here, Kosky's editor clearly referred to *Conrad and Ford*, Chap-
ter III in Group Portrait: Joseph Conrad, Stephen Crane, Ford
Madox Ford, Henry James, and H. G. Wells, by Nicholas
Delbanco. London, 1982 [Estate Editors].

   [19]Melampodium—a herb meant to cure, cured the insanity of
women who, for one reason or another, could not, or would not, put
up any longer with the *sextazy* inducing cult of Dionysus, a herb
introduced to Greece and named after Melampus, ("Black Foot"),
the Greek physician who first taught the art of divination by Apollo,
then introduced the Apollonian worship of Dionysus to Greece.
(Jay Kay).

"Kosinski," says Kosky. "That other Kosotoxin Kid."

Dustin grins jovially. His grin ends the inevitably creative confrontation between the author and his editor. On the way to the door he picks up the abused by overuse pouch of his Skoal Bandits wintergreen-flavored tobacco, his fatigued hat, his worn-out attaché case and "his pre-World War II sexually suspect mackintosh," in the words of the always sexually suspicious Jay Kay.

$$30$$

Had Sabbatai Sevi remained in one place — say in Gaza! — instead of traveling from Smyrna, where he was born, to Patras, then Athens, then Salonika, Constantinople, Cairo, Jerusalem, Gaza, Aleppo and then — fatal error! — to Constantinople again throughout his **anecdotal life (M. Borowski as quoted by Henry Miller)** he would have written more and talked and be talked about less! All this exposure, all this public talking, did him no good! It only contributed to the ugly rumors spread about him and his wife, the Submissive Sarah.

For some six weeks now our *ba'al shem* had sat down every day for six or nine hours at a time in one place — at his desk, no less — yet our literary yeti has not added one meaningful phrase, not even a quote to his literary *collectanea*.[1]

Now, in the evening, out of boredom, washed my hands in the bathroom three times in succession. (Kafka, Diaries)[2] Is such stoppage a result of the permanent drying out

---

[1] Like his *The Universe* and *Blotting Books,* Emerson's *Collectanea* consists "largely of entries of some length, arranged however on a more formal plane." (*The Journals and Miscellaneous Notebooks of Ralph Waldo Emerson,* op. cit.)

[2] Says Henry Miller: "I must say, right at the start, that I haven't a

507

of the well of his star — or only the temporary emptiness of his creative well? Or, like so many other lesser writers before him (e.g., Baudelaire), has he too contracted the spiritually deadly Acedia Disease?[3] If not, is he, perish the thought, suffering from writer's block? A curse so grave that no creative writing course can lift it? **June 1. Wrote nothing. June 2. Wrote almost nothing. (Kafka, Diaries)**

Finally, the welcome Sabbath arrives (and in accordance with the Jewish calendar it arrives "sooner than in most non-Jewish calendars, that is, already on Friday." (Jay Kay) No wonder. The Sabbath is the *single most important day*. It is a day of rest — of obligatory pleasure, a Jew might say. In the Jewish faith, the penalty for desecrating the Sabbath — desecrating it by working, i.e. by not resting enough — is spiritual death.

Since this is the Sabbath, Kosky's all inner-working communication channels have been shut off for the day. All but one: the channel of meditation. **Further good evidence of authenticity in "annihilation" and divine delight in the above-mentioned concentration is the category of soul's**

---

thing to complain about. It's like being in a lunatic asylum, with permission to masturbate for the rest of your life. The world is brought right under my nose and all that is requested of me is to punctuate the calamities." (*Tropic of Cancer*).

[3]Acedia: a South American Atlantic flatfish. Acedia disease is manifested by chronic fatigue as well as stupor, torpor and sloth (one of the Seven Deadly Sins). "Like many lesser writers before and after him, Baudelaire suffered constantly from acedia, 'the malady of monks,' that deadly weakness of the will which is the root of all evil. He fought against it with fury and horror." (Christopher Isherwood).

This complaint (chronic fatigue) is encountered with outstanding frequency. (French's *Index of Differential Diagnosis,* ed. by Arthur H. Douthwaite, M.D., F.R.C.P. [Bristol, 1954], p. 299.) "Most colorfully written medical manual illustrated with the splendidly sickening color pictures." (J. K.)

attraction to the nearness of God during the whole day (i.e., the effect of his experience in prayer makes itself felt in the good deeds he carries out during the rest of the day—translator's note). . . . Further evidence of authenticity is that he partakes but little of the delights of the world, such as fame, clothes, good food and other coarse lusts. (Dov Baer)

"What should I meditate about?" Kosky asks Svāmin, his inner Buddhist monk whom he has recently appointed as a pro-tem head of his Department of Interior Judaism.

"Meditate about your favorite subject, as long as it does not deal with work in the ghetto. Not even in the ghetto of Lodz,[4] where most of your family perished." Comes a stern reply.

"My favorite subject is Desire vs. Death. Meaning: where did I come from? Meaning what kind of man am I? Am I a good being or only a fairly good one? Meaning: what is the meaning of goodness? Is this book No. 9 good or bad? Good 'cause I quote good people in it or bad 'cause I think Rumkowski was in principle a good man and—under such unheard of conditions an extraordinary leader," says Kosky.

"You must keep Rumkowski out of it. Rumkowski means *work*. Work even on Saturday. Work as a means of survival. Work meaning ALIVE! and *not* an armed rebellion. Work meaning *rescue through work*. (Rumkowski 1941; Israel Kosky, 1946) That the "rescue-through-work"—perhaps a melancholic illustration of the folk saying "respite of death is also life" *(Chaye shoo is oykh lebn)*—did not work in the long run does not by itself disqualify this policy. It is only

---

[4]"After the last resettlement there is (almost) no one in the Litzmannstadt ghetto over the age of sixty-five or under the age of ten. The hospitals have been liquidated—but does that mean there are no sick people left? September 25, 1942." From *The Chronicle of the Łodz Ghetto, 1941–1944*. (op. cit.)

by accident of military history that a considerable part of Lodz Jews did not survive. By the end of July 1944 the Red army had reached the Vistula and established a bridgehead on its western shore, south of Warsaw. The Red army did not continue its advance, but stopped some seventy miles from Lodz. Less than a month later, in August 1944, the 68,000 Jews still alive in Lodz were "resettled." (Isaiah Trunk, *Judenrat*, op. cit.) That's a nicely framed subject but the frame is not specific enough. It is a cliché. Clichés stem from too much work. It won't do."

"Then simply tell me what to meditate about." Kosky cuts his long story short, and in the process gains another point for "story-short," a brand new SS configuration.

"Meditate about numbers. Numbers one to five about the freeing of the Jewish soul from bondage of the Egyptian biblical soil. Then, devote all your spiritual strength to numbers six and nine: to 996 years of your soul's *unbroken physical presence* on the Ruthenian spiritually fertile soil."

"It's a tall order. In my book, Ruthenia is part of Poland." Kosky interjects.

"Meditate, if you wish, about being a spiritual being or even a nonbeing," proclaims Svāmin. "But under no condition must you meditate about human beings in general—that is spiritually most fatiguing. As your thousand-year-old Jewish-Ruthenian soul undoubtedly knows, Jewish spiritual fatigue does not stem from specific spiritual work, but from being, spiritually speaking, too general. Ask any Israeli general."

"Can I meditate, say, about a woman?" Kosky asks.

"Indeed you can, as long as in your thoughts this woman is not working since your thoughts must be at rest, and not actively thinking during the Sabbath," Svāmin declares.

"How about meditating about a Jewish woman who, in my novel is about to get married to one of the writers quoted in *Testimony:* Contemporary (American. J. K.) Writers Make The Holocaust Personal (1989) on June 13?"

510

"A woman's marriage seems to be a most appropriate subject on this week's Sabbath," says Svāmin, "particularly since the times of Isaac Luria, the sixteenth-century mystic of Safed, who believed the Sabbath was a queen. Here, *queen* means a bride."

From time to time Sabbatai Sevi's messianic fancies returned and it is probable that in one of these fits of illumination he decided to marry Sarah, an Ashkenazi girl of doubtful reputation who either had arrived by herself from Italy or was brought over on his initiative when he heard rumors about her from Italian visitors. She was an orphan of the 1648 massacres in Podole and used to tell curious stories about herself and her upbringing by a Polish nobleman. . . . Rumors that she was a woman of easy virtue preceded her and were current even later in the intimate circle of Sabbatai Sevi's admirers. (Gershon Sholem)

31

The Sabbath ends. The minute it ends Kosky goes back to work—that is, moves behind his writing desk and summons by phone Ann Pudeater Patterson: his sixty-ninth sexual proofreader disguised as a line editor. The instant she arrives—she refuses to fill his bathtub with hot water as well as with her succulent rack. For punishment, he asks her first to proofread, then, customarily, to retype a newly written part of his manuscript. This freshly written part, contains, he warns her, as an integral part of the text, a lewd letter written by Jay Kay, his often sexually disoriented protagonist.

"This is a sick letter, very, very, very sick letter, written by a sexually sick man," she declares after casting one glance at the letter. "This is offensive. I won't commit to it a single comma," says Ann. "I won't retype it for you either. My typewriter carriage just won't move one millimeter. My electric pencil stops here. Enough is enough."

"C'mon, Ann," pleads Kosky. "Of course it's an SS letter. It must be SS 'cause in my novel this letter comes from Jay Kay, who attempts to get healed by writing: by inventing a fresh Self in *The Healer*, his forthcoming novel. That's the only kind of SS letter this man can write. It is a good letter. No worse than any letter you find in the good book called *Great Letters*.[1] No worse than a letter written, say, by Bruno Schulz to Debora Vogel, a letter filled with rather extravagant sexual drawings Bruno routinely attached to his most *intellectual* letters. Still, it is his letter; *his* not mine."

In the course of that working day of eight hours I write three sentences which I erase before leaving the table in despair. . . . I would be thankful to be able to write anything, anything, any trash, any rotten thing—something to earn dishonestly and by false pretences the payment promised by a fool. (Conrad to Edward Garnett)[2]

"You wrote this letter. You not he. Jay Kay, that sick man (who often signs his letters with his J. K. initials, J. K.) is you. You not *him*," Ann screams. "In the last few years, I've edited some pretty sick stuff, published, unpublished and never-to-be published, but I've never read anything as filthy as this first draft. If published, I'm sure this letter will be listed in the *Literary Filth Dictionary*."

"I see this letter as being as open and *candid*. A ribald classic! says Kosky, then goes on.

"Listen, my dear Ann! In my novel, this letter was written by Jay Kay. By him, the novel's proto-protagonist." He ogles her splendid curves as if she were a lovely *kurwa* (whore in Ruthenian. J. K.) who dressed in a Pump-It-Up string bikini advertises her surprise sin strokes (SSS) in a Touch-phone/Touch Me Direct Contact magazine, but she does not respond in kind. And so, he goes on. "As one who authored Jay Kay's letter, I stand by him, true—but I merely tapped my

---

[1] See *A Second Treasury of the World's Great Letters*, selected and edited by Wallace Brockway and Barth Keith Winer (1941).

[2] See "Inspired by Despair," by Louis Menand, a review of *The Collected Letters of Joseph Conrad*, Vol. 2, 1898–1902, (ed. by Frederick R. Karl and Laurence Davies (New York, 1987), in *The New York Times Book Review*, 1987).

narrative shoe to the beast festering inside him. Inside him, not inside me. That's what narrative fantasy can do." He taps his shoe against the floor. Then he goes on. "In addition, Ann, this is a letter Jay Kay wrote to one Pauline Réage, who, in the text, is Jay Kay's privately hired part-time line line editor. She has been his *dombi* for at least half a galley page in the novel's current variant. Variant is a better word for this draft then version, given the sexual draft of the novel's current draft (draft or current? J. K.) Finally, Pauline is, as you know, a stand-in for you, Ann, and do you sincerely believe that it is I, not Jay Kay, who signs his letter to Pauline — *Sincerely yours on all fours?*" he asks her, his left *manu* placed upon the offending manuscript and his right upon Ann's "perfectly sassy-assy." (Jay Kay)

But the fact is, women today are writing erotic works, or works in which the erotic element figures much more prominently than ever before. . . . It's not that women ahven't written about love. There have been women poets through the ages, from the era of early Greece on down to today. And there have been some clandestine works of erotica written by women and circulated privately — not published — that I can think of, in my own experience. (*Confessions of O,* 1975 p. 69.)[3]

"This letter is as sick — maybe even sicker, sicker'nd slicker — than the letter Joan of Arc sent to the English.[4] As sick as the one Lord Nelson sent to Emma Lyon, alias Emma Hart, alias Mrs. Hamilton[5] just before his final battle. As sick as Paul Verlaine's 'Sonnet to the Asshole.'[6] This letter

---

[3]*Confessions of O:* Conversation with Pauline Réage, (*Story of O, Return to the Chateau,* et. J. K.) by Regine Deforges, translated from the french by Sabine d' Estree, 1979.

[4]See "Joan of Arc, before the battle of Orleans, commands the English to surrender," in *Great Letters,* op. cit., pp. 66–69.

[5]Ibid.

[6]"Sonnet to the Asshole" (*Le Sonnet du Trou de Cul*), in *Hombres XV,*

belongs in a manure pit. I won't touch it," she says, getting up from her desk. "For this kind of work you need an adult video film star. Why don't you call upon your sexually favorite — one so Chaucerian Hyapatia Lee!"

The very Ann who for the last few weeks used to, at least in his bathtub, exude provocative sexual slime (SS) now spews forth a useless venom.

"Editing, and sexual understanding not censorship, is what I pay you for," says Kosky calmly. The signal is clear. Ann Pudeater Paterson, his line editor No. 69, (who until now was his very best in the act of 69, J. K.) has just stepped out of her *editorial* hot-line. *Editorial*, not sexual. Enough italics.

Vanity often coexists with an experience that at first seems like its very opposite. This is the holding back we call pride. . . . The terms on which men and women can secure recognition as members of groups that allow for heightened (though unequal) vulnerability and for common allegiance enmesh them in power relations. Engagement in shared bondage. (*Passion: An Essay on Personality,* by Roberto Mangabeira Unger). op. cit.

SS

Without Ann, at hand and with no new Madam Edwarda (Bataille), a new proofreader proving to him the strength of his manly prowess, our monk's own creative hand begins to suffer. A despairing writer cures despair by visiting a book-

---

was written tongue-in-cheek by Paul Verlaine (d. 1896) with Rimbaud, Verlaine's friend at the time, who contributed the poem's last two stanzas. See *Men and Women,* Erotic Works (*Oeuvres Libres*) by paul Verlaine; a bi-lingual French-English edition, translated with an Introduction and Commentary by Alan Stone, London 1980, p. 96.

store. **Every man is more or less the sport of accident; nor do I know that authors are at all exempted from this humiliating influence. (J. Fenimore Cooper, Preface to** *The Pioneers***)** This time, our autofictional pioneer revisits the famous Astolfo Book Center on West 6th Street. This is where, in the book section devoted to *Spontaneous Recovery,* some of the city's best female proofreaders, copy editors, typesetters—and, from time to time, full-fledged literary *dombis*—hang out. **The aphasic adult is an individual exhibiting both internal and external needs with definable problems both in psyche and soma and others** *that are truly psychosomatic.* **(underline. J. K.) The aphasic adult is an individual exhibiting behavior which could only be the product of his biological inheritance, his early environmental conditioning (***thus his basic personality*** . . .** *Recovery From Aphasia,* op. cit. This is where only the other day, in the section of BOOKAMERICANA he almost ran into Sidney Lanier with whom, had it not been for Kosky's timidity, our Pripet man would love to talk about Lanier's "The Marshes of Glynn" and his study of music and experiment in language. Tonight, some six minutes to nine P.M., Kosky comes here disguised as one Monsieur Julien, who, judging by how our freak of letters talks and how he is dressed tonight, can be regarded as a well-educated bona fide bookish man of letters, who has just arrived in New York from New Haven the most bookish town in America."[7]

Tonight he has topped his disguise by also picking up a

---

[7]"After all, if we are dealing with maybes, the New Haven episode (being expelled from Yale University, J. K.) may have helped James Cooper's next enterprise. There by Thames and Sound the boy inland bred got his smell of saltwater and his glimpse of seagoing craft." See "Trial by Water," in *James Fenimore Cooper,* by Henry Walcott Boynton (American Classics, 1931, 1966).

new mustache as well as a new name—Julien Loti—which, he feels, will match his mustache best.

Like every word, every artifact comes with its own written and unwritten language. Example: the simple detachable mustache Kosky wears tonight is made of human hair. Now wouldn't he want to know who was its previous wearer? Was it a he or she? Then, even though he bought it in New York, the mustache was made in Hermit Islands.

But that's not all. A replica of a mustache worn in life by such dissimilar characters as Nikolai Bukharin, and the very Julien Viaud, who, once known as "The Magician," became known to the world at large as Pierre Loti,[8] the first French writer other than Victor Hugo to be given by his country a state funeral. (Kosky considered Hugo's *The Man Who Laughs* the single most imaginative novel of the XIXth century. J. K.) Loti, who wrote *Aziyadé*, "and the first writer who, speaking about himself, openly proclaimed in *Aziyadé*, (first true autofiction since J. Fenimore Cooper's *Homeward Bound* and *Home as Found*. J. K.) to the world in capital letters: I AM AND I AM NOT MY OWN LITERARY TYPE."

At this time—it's almost 9:00 P.M.—the bookstore is practically empty. In the fading background, three aging female proofreaders peruse the novels of Melville and Dos Passos.

---

[8] By 1892, when Pierre Loti was elected to the French Academy, he was still known to the public at large as the author of *Aziyadé*, "his first and his most personal work." (Personal as opposed to autobiographical: J. K.) "*Aziyadé* has always been surrounded by mystifications, scandals, polemics and theories as to its autobiographical verity. In 1892, referring to Loti's election to L' Académie Française, Goncourt wrote of 'this author, whose love, in his first book, was a Monsieur.' It had also been said that Loti made the transposition from feminine to masculine in the first manuscript, since he well knew the temper of Islam in any matter touching the inviolate harem," writes Lesley Blanch in her biography *Pierre Loti, the Legendary Romantic* (1983).

Next to them, in a brightly lit corner an aging Gay Gaius seems lost in the *Collected Works* by Adolf Dygasinski (d. 1902) another innovating autofiction in which well educated and in life professorial Dygasinski dared to write his own author's story in jargon borrowed from one of his own characters: a simple, brutal, uneducated peasants "for which Dygasinski was badly hit by Poland's top literary critics." (Jay Kay).

Some years earlier, Gay Gaius was Kosky's proofreader No. 77 whose part time proofreading ran its course, when, like Dygasinski he could no longer distinguish between the language of lullaby and a ditty, between a tongue twister and noodle story. **The correction of typos, the striking out of hyphens at the end of lines, the indication of em dashes, together with the assigning of point size to heads and subheads, can no longer be left to the judgment and taste of printers, because of the great variety of designs, the decline of artisanship, and the substitution of the typewriter and its offspring for the author's own hand."** (Jacques Barzun, 1984)[9]

Quickly, Kosky steps away and hides behind one particular bookshelf which disturbs him most. Dedicated to MAN, it contains books about only one man. His first name, Otto Adolf, like the first names of his father KARL ADOLF, are already menacing enough, even though when he was born Adolf was not yet the name which after Hitler, would menace us most. But it is his last name EICHMANN, and only his last which, since May 11, 1960, has menaced Kosky most.

Secretly caught by Israeli secret agents near Buenos Aires, in Argentina [Ed. to Author: Wasn't he kidnapped? Au. to Editor: He was caught: J. K.], Eichmann was then secretly

---

[9]See also "Behind the Blue Pencil: Censorship or Creeping Creativity," by Jacques Barzun, in *Publishers Weekly*, 1985 (the Essay originally appeared in the summer issue of *American Scholar*).

flown to Israel nine days later, and, almost a year after, openly tried in Jerusalem. Read *Justice in Jerusalem,* by Gideon Hausner (1966), the man who as attorney general of Israel calmly sat in judgment of Eichmann. Of Eichmann, not of the German people. Here, first, Kosky recalls Israel Kosky so fondly recalling the *Proclamation of the General Command of the Joint Armies of Germany and Austro-Hungary at the beginning of the First World War.* Which among other kind words, said in until then the boldest Yiddish language print yet: **Jews of Poland!** *We come to you as friends and saviors!* **Our flags herald justice and freedom for you:** *Equal and full civil rights, genuine freedom of religion, freedom to work in all economic and cultural fields.* **For too long you have suffered under Moscow's iron yoke. . . . The portals of life were shut in the face of the Jews, the portals of education were closed to Jewish children. Your sons and daughters have been chased out of Russian schools, Russian cities, and Russian villages. They were permitted to live in Russia only as prostitutes with yellow passports. . . . You have nothing to fear from our soldiers. They will not touch a hair on your heads. . . . Help in defeating the enemy and work toward the victory of freedom and justice!** (Translated from the original Yiddish into German, then English. *Germany Without Jews,* op. cit.)

Here Kosky asks the reader to pause and, kindly, attempt to perceive what Kosky sees. You see, Kosky perceives Eichmann as one who captured the sentiment of the pre-atomic German military long before he himself was captured. "German military" meaning all German World War II personnel, not merely the members of the Nazi party and SS, all so conveniently dismissed by all the computerized view of history "as the bunch of crazy Nazis." "This is a distinction too important to miss. This is not unlike missing the difference between a missile and a missal, or the difference between a child who misses at school a lesson in German history and one who is permanently missing due to German W.W. II. history lessons."

In short, if the case of the Jews (in various medieval German-speaking provinces. J. K.) is not viewed as distinct, as is common, but in the context of the social evolution and the situation of other groups, it is seen that they were not the most harshly persecuted, let alone the only victims of the arbitrary power exerted by medieval rulers. . . . Their faith, however, subjected them to vicious bloodbaths, the outcome of efforts at conversion, most of them unsuccessful; the worst butchery was perpetrated by the Crusaders moving to the Rhine from France. Many German Jews therefore migrated to the East, primarily to Poland, where the kings received them—like German Christian immigrants—with open arms. They were granted all rights and liberties because the emerging Polish towns needed tradesmen and artists. *Germany without Jews*, op cit.

He picks up a book and opens it at random on a chapter called, appropriately for him, our Concentration Man: "THE SECOND SOLUTION: Concentration." The "objective" attitude—talking about concentration camps in terms of "administration" and about extermination camps in terms of "economy"—was typical of the S.S. mentality, and something Eichmann, at the trial, was still very proud of. (Hannah Arendt, 1963)

But then, as he proceeds reading Hannah Arendt's account of Eichmann's proceedings all the way down, he comes across one passage which irks him most, and—wouldn't you know it?—he comes across it on the spiritually sacrosanct for him page ninety-six! Hence, he simply can't ignore it any longer.

. . . In an accompanying letter, addressed to "Dear Comrade Eichmann," the writer (an SS man stationed in the Warthegan) admitted that "these things sound sometimes fantastic, but they are quite feasible." (These things—meaning a quicker way to die than the one obtained by purposeful starvation: J. K.) . . . Eichmann never mentioned this letter and probably had not been in the least shocked by it. For this proposal concerned only *native* Jews, not Jews from the Reich or any of the Western countries. His conscience rebelled not at the idea of murder but at the idea of German Jews being murdered. ("I never denied that I knew that the *Einsatzgruppen* had orders to kill, but I did not know that Jews from the Reich evacuated to the East were subject to the same treatment. That is what I did not know.") It was the same with the conscience of a certain Wilhelm Kube, an old Party member and *General-kommissar* in Occupied Russia, who was outraged when German Jews with the Iron Cross arrived in Minsk for "special treatment." Since Kube was more articulate than Eichmann, his words may give us an idea of what went on in Eichmann's head during the time he was plagued by his conscience: "I am certainly tough and I am ready to help solve the Jewish question," Kube wrote to his superior in December 1941, "but people who come from our own cultural milieu are certainly something else than the native animalized hordes." This sort of conscience, which, if it rebelled at all, rebelled at murder of people "from our own cultural milieu," has survived the Hitler regime; among Germans today, there exists a stubborn "misinformation" to the effect that "only" *Ostjuden*, Eastern European Jews, were massacred. (*Eichmann in Jerusalem*, by Hannah Arendt, op. cit., p. 96.)

This is, in case you forgot, the same Hannah Arendt, who in purposefully obliterating Yiddish, went on to claim that *Yiddish is Hebrew in German letters.* (Hannah Arendt). "Further, the East European Jews created their own language, Yiddish, which was born out of a will to make intelligible, to explain and simplify the tremendous complexities of the sacred literature. Thus there arose, as though spontaneously, a mother tongue, a direct expression of feeling, a mode of speech without ceremony or artifice, a language that speaks itself without taking devious paths, a tongue that has a maternal intimacy and warmth. . . . The Jews have spoken many languages since they went into exile; this was the only one they called 'Jewish.'" Abraham Joshua Heschel, 1949).[10]

Since this is a novel of ideas, having been around since the beginning of oral tradition, like old invoices ideas are seldom original, let me state clearly my idea about this particular right of historical passage unsurped by Hannah Arendt. By quoting this passage supposedly in order to give us an idea "of what went on in Eichmann's head," Hannah Arendt gives us throughout her book an image of what goes on in hers. What is it? It is, simply "a contrast between university cultured German-Jewish scholars and university professors, whom Kube calls 'our own cultural milieu' and the milieu of the 'native animalized hordes' of *Ostjuden,* meaning particularly the Yiddishly inclined Jews of Poland!" (the very people even Nazi Governor Hans Frank saw as "the Jewish power reservoir." (1944).

Animalized hordes indeed! Take a look, reader, at *Polish Jewry:* ONE THOUSAND YEARS OF HISTORY AND CULTURE. At the unbroken chain of Polish-Jewish relations. Relations stemming from proximity, not distance.[11]

Enough said? Not enough!

Tell me this now, my *liebe* Hannah: WHO WERE THE ANIMALIZED HORDES OF TWENTIETH CENTURY EUROPE? The gas-dispensing Germans or the palm-reading Gypsies? How could you forget that half of all of the

---

[10] *The Earth Is the Lord's:* The Inner World of the Jew in Eastern Europe, 1949, 1977.

[11] See "Speaking for My Self," by Jerzy Kosinski in *Dialectics and Humanism: The Polish Philosophical Quarterly.*

world's Gypsies were gassed to death by your beloved Germans? HALF, HANNAH, IS MORE THAN ONE-THIRD. MUCH MORE. Enough said. NOT ENOUGH! And, while we are at it, what about the tragic fate of the almost 4.5 million to this day nameless Soviet soldiers who, initially kept in German prisoner-of-war camps by the German military[12] were either shot on the spot, starved to death or, most often, all gassed to death with the help of mobile gas ovens — which worked efficiently and did the extermination job in a remarkably short period of time. IS THE FIGURE FOUR AND A HALF MILLION SO INFERIOR TO THE JEWISH SACRED NUMBER SIX?

AND HOW ARE WE TO DISMISS THE MILLIONS UPON MILLIONS OF POLES, RUSSIANS AND OTHER SLAVES EXTERMINATED BY THE NAZI TOTAL-DEATH YIELDING MACHINE?

And, finally, Kosky goes on, since I survived the War among the Ruthenian peasants, *among them, as well as thanks to — their sheltering me* — let's talk about the East European peasants. Were these peasants, these Slavic folks more superstitious or less so than your CIVILIZED heel-clicking, oh-so-obedient GERMANS WHO BELIEVED IN A HIDDEN DEVIL — A DEVIL HIDDEN IN EVERY JEW? The fact is, my *liebe Professor Doktor Arendt*, that, given German behavior vs. the behavior of the Central European peasants, I would rather kiss every day the dirty feet of any Ruthenian peasant than ever again salute anything militaristically German and this goes for any Jewish intellectual Dragon Lady like you. Am I clear? Is it said enough? Not enough!

Surely, *Professor Hannah*, must know (must or ought to?)

---

[12]See also *The Stroop Report: The Jewish Quarter of Warsaw Is No More!* Translated from the German and annotated by Sybil Milton. Introduction by Andrzej Wirth. 1979.

that in America of her day, they, the spiritually inspired American East European Jews, show guts and exude creative juices, as well as, let's face it, decently earned big money. **In the course of their troubled and frustrated history during the last two centuries, the Jews have created works of lasting genius in almost every sphere of life. (Isaiah Berlin)** Each time she runs into one of them—and she runs into at least one of them on every American cultural street corner—she is first struck by awe, an awe a rhabdomancer feels when romancing the brackish water under the Negev Desert. But then, just as fast, she is struck by envy. By that old Iago complex: **"He hath a daily beauty in his life that makes me ugly"** (Othello).

Surely, you know that out of these "animalist hordes" of East European Jews came the largest spiritual and intellectual crowd in our Jewish history. That it was in Eastern Europe where in ten long centuries (ten is the magic number—the number suggesting past nine and the unlimited beyond) we built our cultural and worldly pyramids. Pyramids, Hannah, not tombs and barricades. Pyramids which spiritally sustained Jews of the entire world: and most of the world of Others; pyramids of art and science and technology.

Still elated by the atmosphere of the book shop, bypassing the shelf where in the past he had always found all his novels, he inspects it carefully only to discover that this time all Kosky's novels are gone. Are all his books sold out? **Where is human nature so weak as in the bookstore? (Henry Ward Beecher).**

After visiting Freud and Marx, he stops at the brand new stand named GERMANY 1990: SECOND COMING.

The 1990 reunification of Germany both reawakens and dispels Kosky's apprehension over the German germ, Order is Order (*Befehl ist Befehl*). Is the new Deluge[13] on the way?

---

[13]Read, by all means, *Before the Deluge:* A portrait of Berlin in the 1920's by Otto Friedrick, New York, 1972.

Still, since this is 1990, the year's double number nine gives Kosky a reason to be optimistic:

Nine The triangle of the ternary, and the triplication of the triple. It is therefore a complete image of the three worlds. It is the end-limit of the numerical series before its return to unity. For the Hebrews, it was the symbol of truth, being characterized by the fact that when multiplied it reproduces itself (in mystic addition). (J. E. Cirlot, 1962)[14]

Nevertheless, *El lobo pierde los dientes mas no las mientes,* a Mexican *dicho* warning that the wolf (make it German shepherd called Beowulf. J. K.) may lose his teeth but not his wolfish nature, and the British belief that a leopard can't ever change his spots, make our verbal German pointer point out that, after all, the creation of the Holy Roman Empire of the German Nation (962–1806) history's First Reich was already then unholy. Then, still back in time, he rushes forward to the year 1871.

There, he faces creation of the Second Reich by Bismarck's Prussia while looking at the emerging new Europe *Through The Looking Glass,* the book first published by Lewis Carroll in 1871, and views Bismarck's Reich not necessarily as a prelude to German Reich Number Three but rather as The Greatest Show on Earth — P. T. Barnum's circus which first opened in New York's Brooklyn also in 1871. He views all this as an inescapable chapter in The Descent of Man, a revolutionary look at evolution first published in 1871 by Charles Darwin.[15]

---

[14]A *Dictionary of Symbols* by J. E. Cirlot, translated from Spanish by Jack Sage, London, 1962.

[15]The Nazis adapted Darwin's notion of 'natural selection' for their Hitler-inspired 'social Darwinism' — the supposed right of the stronger race to destroy the weaker. "hitler himself held that 'in the search for self-preservation so-called humanitarian ideals melt away like snow in the March sunshine'. . . ." (*Anatomy of the SS-State,* op cit.)

Today, however, what foremostly matters to Kosky—after all, at fore he is mostly a writer—is the fertile German mind, (German, printer, not Herman!)[16] a mind about to be given a fresh expression by this so extraordinarily sudden and unexpected reunification. He recalls with awe the expressive German idiom through which for centuries so many divergent national and ethnic groups spoke their mind: Germans, Austrians, Swiss, Jews,[17] and so many others. He thinks of Swiss Wilhelm Tell, whose most telling story was so tellingly told by German Friedrich Schiller. He thinks of Robert Musil, the Austrian, whose novel *The Man Without Qualities*, "qualifies as one of mankind's most qualified novels." (Jay Kay). He thinks of Friedrich Dürrenmatt, whose theater thunders with the German Swiss mountaineering echoes. He thinks of Franz Kafka, that unforgettable Joseph K., from Prague, Czechoslovakia. Then, starting with Tacitus, whose treatise *Germania,* (completed circa A.D. 96, J.K.) "has given us after Caesar almost the only document of value concerning the barbarians" (*Medieval Myths,* 1961)[18] and *Beowulf,* "before 750 the greatest epic about heroic age of the earliest literate Germanic people" (ibidem), our Hero rejoices over *Simplicius Simplicissimus* by Hans Jakob von Grimmelshausen (1669), the very first novel written in German—and a precursor to the entire German narrative body—so opulent spiritually. From then on, Kosky embraces as a matter of natural narrative course the all-embracing literary German Storm'nd Stress (Sturm und Drang) period. Didn't it, he speculates, at least make up a bit for the Storm'nd Stress caused him and humankind by the death yielding WWII German SS Stormtroopers?

---

[16]Herman or Hermann, lit. a warrior. J. K.

[17]Read *Freud, Jews and Other Germans:* Masters and Victims in Modernist Culture by Peter Gay, New York, 1978.

[18]*Medieval Myths* by Norma Lorre Goodrich, 1961.

Finally, just for the fun of advancing the cause of verbal justice, he diminishes the impact of German-maniacal Nazi aviator Hermann Goering, the first name of whom connects to Hermes by recalling Hermann Hesse and Hermann Broch, the German giants of germinant narrative flight. Enough said? Not quite. From now on, evoking Goethe's idyllic *Hermann and Dorothea* (1797), he also evokes:

> **GERMANIUM (from Germany)** chemical element (first isolated in 1886 by Clemens Winkler, similar . . . to silicon ("think American Silicon Valley": Jay Kay). Important as a semiconductor (a good metaphor for Germany as one of united Europe's foremost cultural semi-conductors, J. K.) Germanium (not unlike German national character. J. K.) forms many compounds. . . . *Germane* (germanium tetrahydride) is a gas (Attention, reader: Do not automatically think of Zyklon Gas here. J. K.) Germanium is produced as a by-product of the refining of other metals; there is considerable recovery from flue dusts and from ashes. . . . (but not recovery from the eternal memory of dust and ashes of Auschwitz-Birkenau? J. K.) *The New Columbia Encyclopedia,* New York/London, 1975.

Rejoicing at the success of the reunited Germany, he is nevertheless suspicious. Maybe all his books are not only out of stock, but out of print? Quickly, but not anxiously, Kosky approaches the shop's mustached manager, a Proustian-looking Orlando Furioso.

"I do not *trouvé* or *retrouvé* anything by Norbert Kosky. Is Kosky all sold out?" says Kosky, with an exaggerated French accent.

"He's finished, not just sold out," says Orlando. "I doubt you'll find him—or his books—in any of our company's stores."

Our Tantric pretends to be stunned. *"Pourquois pas?"* he

asks. **A book is like a huge cemetery where on most tombs one can no longer read the blotted-out name. (Proust)**

"Because he is no more listed either under fiction or under nonfiction. That's why," says Orlando, furiously fingering the fingernails of his left-hand fingers with the fingernails of the other.

"What do you mean 'he is no more'? Is he dead?" says Kosky.

"Only as a writer. With that many exciting rumors floating about him in the press nobody finds in his real-life fiction exciting enough.

"I suggest, *monsieur,* that if you still intend to look for Kosky's books, look for them in a rare book shop, that is at the literary cemetery," concludes Orlando.

"A rare book shop *is* a literary cemetery," comments our Mr. Halloween quickly. Leaving the bookshop, he transfers his creative self wearing all his major disguises to the auditorium of the Reforming Arts Center. Going out in the guise of someone else is no joke, even if you don't know who that someone could be. Often, a disguise—a toupee—might fall off right in the middle of a conversation or lovemaking, say, and what do you do when in the middle of the most ticklish 69, a man suddenly loses the tickling power of his beard? Besides, wearing disguises irritates one's skin, and nothing makes your newly met friend, be it a man, a woman or a she-male, peel off faster than the sight of a man who had just let his mustache peel off.

During the intermission, Kosky, our anonymous face in the crowd, gets lost in a crowd, while suffering from a massive attack of stage fright. To him, stage fright is spontaneous Self alert. It alerts him to the dangers the novelist faces when facing the public. You always wanted to be a *sopher*, a storyteller, right? Isn't the written word public enough? Why do you also need a public? was Israel Kosky's first comment when, in the city of Łodz, he heard his twenty-four year old son's very first public lecture at the City's largest public hall.

529

What is music? What does it do? And why does it have the effect it has? They say music has the effect of elevating the soul—rubbish! Nonsense! It has its effect, it has a terrible effect—I am speaking about its effect on me—but not at all of elevating the soul. Its effect is neither to elevate nor to degrade but to excite. How can I explain to you? Music makes me forget myself, my real situation. It transports me into a state that is not my natural one. (Tolstoy).[19]

Suddenly, our Masked Man is accosted by a little man wearing a most unhappy expression.

"Hello, Mr. Kosky," the sick soul (William James) says cheerfully. "I hope you don't mind my barging in on you like this. Given your wartime past, you must hate people who chase you like the SS."

"I do, but it's too late to complain," says Kosky. "How did you recognize me?" he asks. "Who betrayed me?"

"You were betrayed by your walk," says the man. "You walk like Bukharin in *Total State*."

His cover broken, his disguises disqualified, dispirited by the invasion, Kosky leaves the concert hall and rushes to the underground garage where his wheels are. There, he accosts the garage attendant and hands him a claim ticket.

The attendant, a white young Viking, takes one look at our penguin and his long *peise*—another disguise legitimately falling out in strings from under Kosky's black hat.

"What sort of a *ghetto* car is it?" he asks.

---

[19] *The Kreutzer Sonata*, by Leo Tolstoy. "The appearance of this novel by the distinguished author of *War and Peace* and *Anna Karenina* precipitated one of the most violent controversies in literary history. Comparing it with other contemporary writers, Anton Chekhov said, 'It is hardly possible to find anything of equal importance in conception and beauty of execution.'" (Modern Library, 1957) Informs the book's American blurb.

"Electra Decapitado. Even though her Freud V6 (PRINTER: Freud, not Ford or fraud) knocks, don't knock it! It does no more, no less than a good car should do—'it gets you there and it brings you back.' (Ford)." says Kosky.

Hearing this, an old black woman garage-cleaner turns to him.

"You're Mr. Kosky, *the* writer, aren't you?" she says, her manner as worn out as her coat.

He gives up. "Yes, ma'am. Too bad my disguises won't work tonight."

"What disguises?" She is full of unaffected surprise.

"My hairpiece. My mustache. My beard!" he exclaims, pulling at his *peise* while scratching his nose "overly long but at least his own" (in the words of Jay Kay).

Puzzled, she scrutinizes him again. "You mean *the hairs* are not yours?"

"Of course they're not! When did you see me last?"

"See you? I've never seen you," she says, full of fervor. "No, sir! I only *heard* you. I heard you speak on my TV. You said "In the beginning was the War," and you said it with your very own foreign accent."

"Wait, wait!" says Kosky. "That was when I handed out Oscars one after another! But I was not disguised on that show. How could I be? I was there as myself, wearing my black tie, white shirt—without all this stuff." He pulls at what's left of his beard.

"I wouldn't know what you wore," she says wearily. "See, the tube on my TV is burned out. I look at it and see no picture. It's a blind telly. All I hear is the sound. Words are music to me. I listen to words with my eyes open," she says dreamily. "That's no different than watching a TV talk show with your eyes closed."

The attendant brings his car. Kosky drives out of the garage passing, on the way, an impeccably kept 1955 Dodge La Femme driven by a sexually spectacular (SS) femme fatale—a splendid Armenian *Thracophrygian* whom he would

531

love to frig. (frig, not phrig, printer!) Careful now, *piano piano* — this is neither the time nor place for verbal speeding or verbal slowing down. But once our RAFFI[20] drives onto the Eastway, he depresses the gas pedal, an action which, as most speed-exceeding Americans know, helps him to open himself up.

---

[20]"Raffi", the popular name of Hagop Melik-Agopian, a major Armenian storyteller. Originating in the ancient Thracian, a Balkan now extinct tongue, and Phrygian, an equally ancient tongue of Anatolia, modern Armenian is of Thraco-Phrygian origin.

32

His happily progressing work of fantasy is interrupted by an all too real event that nevertheless leaves him unperturbed.

On the following day Kosky the Scribe faces the following: The Manfred, a rent-stabilized apartment house, has suddenly turned into a destabilized cooperative. As a result Kosky must either buy his apartment at a royal price that would swallow most of his past, present and future royalties, two thirds of which have been recently recessed into nothingness due to the recession, or move out.

"What are you going to do about it, Norbert?" asks R. Judah Zevi Streitner, Kosky's dispassionate lawyer friend whose recent embrace of Kosher Yoga and Tantrism has helped Kosky save on many costly litigations.

"Moving out of an apartment in today's America is not the end of life, you know. Finding one is," Kosky writes to Streitner.

Do you know why I came to you? It is simply because there is no one anywhere in the whole great world I could go to. Do you understand what I say? No one to go to. Do you conceive the desolation of the thought — no-one-to-go-to? (Conrad)

But what if you've got no one to see and nowhere to go

to? A man needs to have a somewhere. He needs it at the time when he's got to go somewhere. (Dostoyevsky)

On Streitner's advice, Kosky returns a call from one Samson Brin, one of the six vice-presidents of Matthew Hopkins Incorporated ("the fastest growing personal computer company this side of a jury system"), who wants to talk business with him. Business which, in his words, will enrich Kosky in no time.

No sane man who's about to lose his shelter can disregard a message like this, and Kosky does not.

"I like the way you live. This place is full of *intellectual stench*," Brin says, looking around Kosky's flat when he arrives thirty minutes too early for their appointment. Brin is all fast sell. He is straight to the point. "This place is clean. It's functional. And it's simple. As simple as truth. I can see you living in this place as comfortably as a character in a novel called *Truthpit!*"

"A character occupies a novel forever. I've got to move out of this place and that's the sad truth."

"Truth cannot be sad," says Brin. "Truth simply *is*. I know what I'm talking about," he says. "I've been in the business of truth for over twenty-five years. Truth has been my calling! And that is why I've called on you!" sAVONarola.[1]

"I'm in the business of fable," says Kosky. "Now tell me the truth: why did you want to see me?" Kosky asks as he and Brin sit down and face each other across Kosky's desk.

What does "is true" mean? There are three fundamental answers to the question of a nature of truth: one we call the "semantic definition", the second, the "syntactic definition", and the third, the "pragmatic definition" . . .

---

[1]Fra. Girolamo Savonarola, the "Hermit of Florence," who, preaching a pure doctrine from the pulpit of the puritanical church of Santa Reparata in Florence, attempted to purify the sex-infested papacy of Alexander VI—the orgiastic Borgia—and who failed.

According to Aristotle, 'to say something which is true', is 'to say that which is, is, and that that which is not'. It is 'to hold that that which is separate, is separate, and that that which is connected is connected'; it is 'to speak consistently with the facts'. Jacek Jadacki, 1990.[2]

"Why?" Brin leans forward. "Because you need my company and because we need you. My company manufactures the most advanced line of the Time-Truth™ machines, and you've been one of this country's most talked about TV talkshow guests. Brin gives Kosky a pointed look. "We need you because we have followed your FLOAT-OR-SWIM controversy with utmost interest: it was a classic case of public drowning—which is exactly what in the good old days great public hangings used to be!" He pulls from his attaché case several worn-out press clippings and pedantically spreads them on the table, smoothing their rough edges.

"Like your characters, you too are a LAP: Literary Accident Prone." Brin cheers up. "According to our experts, a LAP is usually a writer who glorifies the incident, not the plot. Incident is in a novel what accident is in life. Many writers with the accident habit had very bad childhoods and bad experiences with authority. Such people invite accidents—the way the characters in your novels do. Maybe you have picked up their characteristics? In any case, your literary profile makes you an ideal LAP. Hence, you fall straight into my company's public relations lap."

"My literary profile?" Kosky wonders aloud. "Aren't you in the polygraph business?"

"We sure are. The word *polygraph* means 'multiwriting' and if multiwriting isn't literary, what is?" says Brin. "The truth is that, since the invention of polygraphs, writing—and, mind

---

[2]Truth, Its Definition and Criteria, by Jacek Jadacki, Dialectics and Humanism, 1990.

my words, the literary arts—will never be the same again."

"Neither will the truth," says Kosky. "Literary truth is a bit like *music concrete.*"

A quiet and spaciously composed continuity of sounds is disturbed six times by a short refrain. This refrain contains glissandi and clusters, trills, bass notes (in the piano) and brief snatches of melody, elements which are absent from the first form. . . . (Karlheinz Stockhausen)

"It is said that the accuracy rate of even the best polygraph, of the latest truth machine, is no better than fifty-fifty. That's no better than chance," Kosky goes on. "No better but—indeed—very bad when it comes to finding out who's telling the truth—and who's not."

"Wrong. Our truth machines are certainly more reliable than chance," says Brin.

"How much more?" asks Kosky.

"It's not our company's public policy to reveal such figures," says Brin.

"Why not?"

"Privileged information. This is the time of industrial spying. We've got competition, you know!"

"Would you reveal such information by answering questions posed to you by an Insight 900 Time-Truth™ machine?" asks Kosky.

Brin pulls back. "Now of all people why would I have to subject myself to taking a lie-detector test?"

"Say for the sake of a better-paid job with a better-paying company. Your potential new employer might request that you take the test as a condition for hiring you. What then?"

"Then I guess I would take it." Brin grins involuntarily.

"But what if, during the test, your privileged information about Insight 900 is detected by the examiner who, unbeknownst to you, might be working for one of your many competitors? Wouldn't that be disloyal to Matthew Hopkins?" asks Kosky.

"I guess it would, but such disloyalty is often the price for new loyalty," says Brin. "Believe me, Mr. Kosky, even though the laws of many of our States still prohibit employers from using any kind of lie detectors and polygraphs, soon, very soon, the whole American jury system will be replaced by mass-produced lie boxes—the American-made lie-detecting devices."

"Isn't the American jury system the original, and still the best, lie-detector?" asks Kosky.

"By now it's as original as the first Ford. And as obsolete as Thomas Jefferson's attacks on the king. Where is the king today?"

"Don't you dare to say this! Even in its draft, Jefferson's Declaration is, spiritually speaking, one of the nine purest spiritual documents ever written! Enough is enough!" Kosky raises his non-yogi voice. **I am . . . mortified to be told that, in the United States of America . . . a question about the sale of a book can be carried before the civil magistrate. . . . Are we to have a censor whose imprimatur shall say what books may be sold and what we may buy? Shall a layman, simple as ourselves, set up his reason as the rule for what we are to read? . . . It is an insult to our citizens to question whether they are rational beings or not. (Thomas Jefferson)**

"I meant Jefferson's autobiography,[3] not his Declaration." Brin grins.

"His autobiography was the very first nonfictional autofiction ever written, then rewritten," says Kosky. "That's why Jefferson mentions in it his brother and six sisters only by their number—NOT EVEN BY THEIR NAMES. That's why he barely mentions in it his marriage to Martha Skelton, and even her tragic death which followed ten years of his 'unche-

---

[3]The autobiography of Thomas Jefferson is the nonoriginal title of his narrative text Jefferson initially called *Memoranda*. Subsequently, this was first published as *Memoir* by Jefferson's grandson and literary estate executor—(Ed.)

quered happiness.' If that's not autofiction, what is?"

Whatever Jefferson is eliminating from his written account of his life — his personality, his inner feelings, his private relations — he is stating, affirming, and maintaining his original authorship of the Declaration. If, as author, he had to subject himself to the revision and censorship of a deliberative body, he is nonetheless — rather, all the more — the writer contending at the end of his life for his original text. (James M. Cox, 1978)[4]

"Now you see what I mean," beams Brin with another grin. "Even Jefferson, the greatest American who ever lived, did not tell the full truth, and if he lied, lied by not telling the whole truth and nothing but the truth, how could one trust an ordinary American — no matter how not ordinary he or she might be? Now you know why today, more and more juries rely on the use of the polygraph — and why so many of them, we hope, will use our one and only Time-Truth™ machine. They can no longer trust the assembly-line witnesses so difficult to assemble by the time the case comes before the court," Brin goes on. "In a society where nobody knows what the truth is, lying is a growth phenomenon. And so is the lie-detecting industry."

"Doesn't the outcome of your machine depend not on the truth but to a decisive degree on 'relevancy' — on the right questions asked of a witness at the right moment by one of your examiners? Examiners who, like the rest of us, could be prejudiced or arbitrary, originally sinful or just plain nasty 'cause of some undeserved unhappiness?" asks Kosky.

---

[4]*Recovering Literature's Lost Ground* by James M. Cox in *Autobiography: Essays Theoretical and Critical*, Princeton, 1980. See also *Autobiographical Acts: The Changing Situation of a Literary Genre* by Elizabeth W. Bruss, 1976, and above all, *Victims: Textual Strategies in Recent American Fiction*, "Kosinski: The Problem of Language," by Paul Bruss, Chapter 10, 1981. (Textual, printer, not sexual!)

I . . . pray you to remember, that when two lutes or two harps, near to one another, both set to the same tune, if you touch the string of the one, the other consonant harp will sound at the same time, though nobody touch it. (Sir Kenelm Digby)

"It does, but is the jury objective? The truth is that most people lie! Do you know of any better protection against uncertainty? Against human trickster?" Brian shoots back.

"Trust in faith. I can't think of anything else," says Kosky.

"Then have faith in our truth-manufacturing machine," says Brin. "Did you know that the Time-Truth™ Series 900 grew out of top-secret saboteur interrogation research conducted during the Vietnam War by the American military?"

"No, I didn't. But if the military research was top secret, how did your company ferret the top secrets from the top brass?"

"I knew you'd ask," says Brin. "We got it by being on top. By using an earlier version — an Insight 600 truth machine — on some of the top research people, who, while taking our top lie-detector test, told us straight from the top of their heads the truth about their top secrets."

"Wasn't that thievery?" asks Kosky.

"Absolutely not!" Brin raises his hand as if swearing to tell nothing but the truth. "We usurped the result of their research for the sake of truth and we've made some money on our contribution to justice and truth. And speaking of truth"—he glances at Kosky offhandedly—"we think we could help you answer *HOW MUCH OF REAL LIFE GOES INTO YOUR FICTION?* and *HOW MUCH OF YOUR FICTION GOES BACK INTO YOUR LIFE?* the questions so often asked of you."

"No writer could ever answer such a question except Cynthia Ozick," Kosky revolts. **Novelists invent, deceive, exaggerate and impersonate for several hours every day and frequently on the weekend. Through the creation of bad souls they enter the demonic as a matter of course. They** usurp emotions and appropriate lives. (Cynthia Ozick, 1987)

"We feel that answering such a question could be of great advantage to you — as it would be to any other Bruno Schulz-type novelist," says Brin.

"If any State agency — or an agent of the State — would even ask me such a creatively questionable question," Kosky declares solemnly, "I will refuse to answer it on the grounds that my answer might incriminate the entire field of imaginative literature — and with it the power of my imagination employed in the service of my Self."

"Once you answer this question and get the question of truth out of your way, the sky is the limit," says Brin. "You could even start a new Norbert Kosky Writers' School. You could again teach a Life vs. Art course at Beulah University or, you could open your own 'Church of Autofiction'."

"I would refuse to answer it first only as a writer," says Kosky. "As a simple believer I believe in the power of the imaginative workshop and in 'the Production of Desire' (Richard Lichtman)."

"But let's get to the point," Brin says. "Do you or don't you want to buy this apartment the minute your home-cum-office turns co-op?"

"Sure, I do," says Kosky. "I want it bad — but not bad enough to turn bad in order to get it. I'm into art, not a co-op."

"You don't have to get bad, in order to co-opt a bit of good life into your work. You don't even have to write another bad book or act in another silly movie," says Brin with a grin. "Didn't you, out of sheer need for money, play that red rascal Bukharin? All we want you to do is to play yourself in one of our Matthew Hopkins Incorporated TV commercials."

"What's the commercial about?"

"It's called a TRUTH DUEL. All you have to do is answer simple questions put to you face-to-face by an examiner — a professional literary critic working on the latest improved

540

Insight Series 960 Truth Computer."

"That's all?" Kosky marvels. "What kind of questions?"

"Simple. So simple that they all can be answered by a simple yes or no. I can already see the headlines," he goes on, obviously pleased with himself. "FICTION WRITER TELLS THE TRUTH ABOUT HIS FICTION. You'll be the first fiction writer taking an ultra-modern non-inquisitional public lie-detector test to guarantee that he told the truth in his fiction."

"Certainly not the first! Saint Augustine was probably the first," Kosky says. "He is the one who issued a moneyback guarantee truth of his book of most intimate confessions by openly dedicating them to God. That's why each time he was asked by the press whether he had told the truth he would raise his eyes and arms to His God and say, 'He knows I did. Would I dare to lie to Him?' The second writer best known for offering such a moral bargain was, surely, Jean-Jacques Rousseau. He is the one who improved on this guarantee by claiming in his *Confessions* that on Judgment Day he would stand before the Throne with a copy of his book personally inscribed to God and swear that in his book he had told the truth about himself and nothing but the truth. And, didn't Christopher Isherwood say in *Down There on a Visit* that his fictional character was in one sense his father and in another sense his son?"

"Those were all literary guarantees nobody took seriously in the first place," says Brin, chewing on an ice cube. "We are talking about you, a penultimate Self employed professional pen asked for the very first time, on commercial TV and in a TV commercial—this means in front of this whole country. DID YOU OR DID YOU NOT BASE YOUR NOVELS ON FACT? YES OR NO?"

"What I write is fancy, not fact. My autofiction is a vessel that floats on a natural suspension made of make-believe. Now fancy that if you can," Kosky says.

"That's why you're in trouble. Having dealt for so long in the make-believe you no longer know what to believe. You can no longer tell the difference between make up and making up; between forging ahead and forgery between gastronomy and astronomy. You go through life in order to write about it as fiction, or you write fiction so one day you can enact it in life. Let the Insight 960 sort it all out."

"Sort it all out—how? How do you sort out in me what I myself don't know?" Kosky despairs. **The mind is a kind of theatre, where several perceptions successively make their appearance; pass, repass, glide away, and mingle in an infinite variety of postures and situations. (David Hume)**

"Simple," says Brin. "Truth is an idea. An idea originates in the mind." He touches his head with his index finger. "Each time our examiner—think of him as an unbiased TV talk-show host—asks you a pertinent question, the Insight 960 translates your brain's inaudible discharges into graphic, and if need be audible, signals long before you respond to it with your YES or NO."

"I don't think your Insight 960 or any other past or future Truth Detective™ could ever truly detect what it is that my brain thinks, does, or says to me," says Kosky. **The conclusion now presents itself to us that there is indeed something innate lying behind the perversions but that it is something innate in *everyone,* though as a disposition it may vary in its intensity and may be increased by the influences of actual life. (Freud)**

"Because of their nature, words are ambivalent—their worth changes on the Verbal Stock Echange with each new word added to them—and so does the sentence we make of them—or the sentence pronounced upon it, say, by the Court," Kosky goes on. **The only thing that grieves me and makes me dance with rage is the cropping up of the legend set afloat by Hugh Clifford about my hesitation between English and French as a writing language. . . . When I wrote the first word of *Almayer's Folly,* I had already for years and years been thinking in English. I began to** think in English long before I mastered, I won't say the style (I haven't done that yet) but the mere uttered speech. (Conrad to Walpole, 1916)[5]

"That's why you've got nothing to lose," Brin exults. "If with the help of the Insight 960 our company will declare that your books are one big tall tale, that's O.K., because that's what fiction is supposed to be. And it's just as O.K. if we will pronounce them all true to life since that's what books are supposed to be one way or another. Either way, you'll get everybody off your literary back. What do you say?"

NOVELIST FAILS TO SHOW UP FOR TRUTH TEST

We have learned today that novelist Norbert Kosky has failed to take part in the Matthew Hopkins Time-Truth Insight 960 lie-detector commercial, in which he would have been asked, for the entire nation to hear, "Did you or did you not tell the truth about your life in your novels?" Also, Mr. Kosky failed to make himself available for comment, and all attempts to reach him by phone or fax failed. (*Times Square Record*)

---

[5]Published in 1916, Hugh Walpole's *Joseph Conrad* "literally drove the Pole up the wall" (Jay Kay). Says Conrad: "I have always felt myself looked upon somewhat in the light of a phenomenon, a position which outside the circus world cannot be regarded as desirable. It needs a special temperament for one to derive much gratification from the fact of being able to do freakish things intentionally, and, as it were, from mere vanity." (*A Personal Record*, by Joseph Conrad, 1919 [1982].)

33

I think I would have raised an outcry if I had believed my eyes. But I didn't believe them at first — the thing seemed so impossible. The fact is I was completely unnerved by a sheer blank fright, pure abstract terror, unconnected with any distinct shape of physical danger. What made this emotion so overpowering was — how shall I define it? — the moral shock I received, as if something altogether monstrous, intolerable to thought and odious to the soul, had been thrust upon me unexpectedly. (Joseph Conrad)

Odious to the soul or not, this is the time our fabled Hermes Thrice greatest (Trismegistus, J. K.) disguised as a Hermesian follower of Georg Hermes[1] rushes to the Eidolon Building — the imposing Literary Shrine which, appropriately imposed upon 969 Fifth Avenue, houses Eidolon Books, Ediolon Press and Eidolon Soft Hardware.

Once there, Kosky heads for the office of John Spellbound, Jr., the publicity director. As one of nine head-giving and head-receiving honchos John is said to be the sixth most

---

[1]Georg Hermes (1775–1831) a German religious brow-raising theologian.

important head man in the company, which somehow makes him the ninth most influential person in the entire publishing business—don't ask me why! **In the works of Dante and Saint Thomas Aquinas, nine is an angelic number. It is the holy trinity multiplied by itself. (Vartan Gregorian)**

Imagine John: a baldish booby in his forties. Think of Marion Spitfire, his fiery assistant as a twenty-six-year-old bookish buttman's dream.

John and Marion greet Kosky with sad skoals as our sad'nd saintly (SS) hermit crab[2] crawls in.

"Welcome to a Happy Media Twister!" says John shaking hands with Kosky, while Marion kisses Kosky's cheek.

John hands Kosky a mountain of press clippings, some of which Kosky—"our press martyr," Marion calls him—has already seen. "Our advertising department says you couldn't buy all this unsolicited adversity for six million bucks! As a result, you've been overexposed! And how!" he moans, noticing Kosky's semi-martyred glance.

"I never thought I'd hear any publicity director complain about his writer's media megaexposure," says Kosky. **What he had was not Fame at all, but only a moment's notoriety. He had been a seven-day wonder—that was all. (Thomas Wolfe)**

"Overexposure is one thing; notoriety is another. Overexposure expires; notoriety lasts," says Marion. "Just look at this!" She takes the press clippings and spreads them out in front of Kosky.

"You're Star Number One in a First Amendment Freak Show!" says John.

---

[2]Hermit crab: a decapod creature either marine or land oriented, which occupies the empty shell of a gastropod whenever it becomes available of its past owner, moving from smaller to bigger shells as it grows in size.

"Extend yourself!" comes Kosky's strictly coded Tantric reply.[3]

"Let's hope that what they said about you so far—so far we've got over six hundred worldwide articles—is only the tip of the iceberg," says Marion. "Let's hope there's more word flagellation on the way!"

"More *come* or more water from Funny, Nunny and Bunny?" John rejoices at the thought.

"More tongue-lashing from Batty, Nutty and Fatty?" Marion accompanies him joyfully.

"I say it's all Aziyadé.[4]. It's all a false alarm," says Kosky. "Somewhere one of the literary safety devices was inadvertently tripped by one of my sexual space intruders changing

---

[3]It is not easy to define Tantrism." (Mircea Eliade) In the word *Tantra,* the word *tan* means to extend oneself beyond one's Self. (Ed.)

[4]"Loti is *Aziyadé's* hero (even if he has other names and even if this novel presents itself as the narrative of a reality, not of a fiction): Loti is *in* the novel (the fictive creature Aziyadé constantly calls her lover Loti: 'Look Loti, and tell me . . .'); but he is also outside it, since the Loti who has written the book in no way coincides with the hero Loti: they do not have the same identity. . . ." *"Pierrre Loti: Aziyadé,"* by Roland Barthes (1970), in his *New Critical Essays,* translated by Richard Howard (1980). "Loti's unpublished journals reveal that there were, indeed, some dark secrets in his life at this time. Loti was in the habit of marking certain dates or entries in the journals with signs bearing sinister implications. A heavily scored cross, or a double triangle, crudely drawn, as if under stress, is found beside initials or cryptic entries. There is rarely any clue or details as to their significance. An entry for 28 March 1882 is more explicit. Under a heavily inked cross he writes: 'Beginning of *Le Souverain* affair. The Admiral has warned me officially that my honour has been attacked in the most odious manner from aboard the gunnery training ship (the *Souverain*) where he wished to appoint me. I was turned down by a vote of thirty *for having lost the esteem of my fellow officers.* I understand the accusations are terrible. I don't know of what I am accused, or yet, who accuses me.' " From *Pierre Loti,* by Lesley Blanch, op. cit.

my fiction to nonfiction. That's all!"

"Let's hope somebody drops another rumor about you on these two drips," says Marion, her thinking cap on fire.

"At best it's only a literary brainstorm; at worst, a critical cold water shower," says Kosky.

"Face it," says John. "These days, with the First Amendment for an umbrella, even *Nightfog*, that revisionist anti-Holocaust rag, doesn't need to worry about getting wet. The local rumor soil is so fertile that one quote from the Literary Local Union No. 69 is all you need to make your word-of-mouth garden grow!"

"I've nothing to say." **I have finally explained myself fully. (Romain Gary)** From a bookshelf Kosky picks up a big book called, simply, *Seneca*. **Come now, don't you know that dying is also one of life's duties? Besides, since there's no fixed number of duties laid down which you're supposed to complete, you're leaving no duty undone. Every life is, without exception, a short one. As it is with a play, so it is with life—what matters is not how long the acting lasts, but how good it is. It is not important at what point you end. End it wherever you will—only make sure that you end it up with a good ending. (Seneca)**

"Everywhere I turn, people have something to say about you, Norbert," says Marion, barely hiding her excitement while baring for him the upper region of her rather impressive chest.

"Too bad I've nothing new to add to all this mayhem. I've nothing to say that wasn't said much livelier in our land by Mayrick Land in his *The Fine Art of Literary Mayhem: a Lively Account of Famous Writers and their Feuds,* (1983)," says Kosky.

"The media want you," says John. "They've been calling us nonstop. Newspapers, magazines, the television and radio talks shows. They want you bad. They want you regardless of whether you're a swimmer or a floater. Good or bad. They all say that you can talk or float, or do both on their shows. Do I have to say what such megaexposure could do for the sale of your forthcoming past titles—not to mention your writing'nd healing[5] megaphone No. 9."

"Look, Norbert," Marion brainstorms again. "The media want justice done. Done, of course, by the media. They also want it to be seen on the media. What should we tell them?"

This is the time (time always means one's current moment) when he must decide whether he intends to be known to himself or to the world. "Headlines mean beheading." (Israel Kosky). This, of course, means being a guest on Channel Six, on the World-Headline-Making WHM-TV. To start with, as every bookish person knows, a new book is every writer's new start—and like any start, this could be a false one.

"Tell them that the First Amendment says a lot about freedom, but nothing about truth or justice. It says nothing about any Hippocratic writer's oath—the one I took voluntarily in front of the Statue of Liberty shortly after I arrived in this country," says our literary Hippo. **The newspapers never missed a chance to try and prove that he was insane, or psychotic, or simply a freak. In truth, Billy was a completely normal child in every respect. (Sarah Sidis, 1952)**

Marion gives Kosky a worried look. "It's always better to meet the media halfway than to be met by them in your hallway. Do what Gertrude Stein asked her pet dog to do: 'Play Hemingway. Be fierce!'"

"These stories about you have let all the water loose," says John. "Philistine Café crowd still can't figure out whether you're a liberal, a libertine or a libertarian." Says John.

"Am I not responsible for at least some of this rumor?"

---

[5]Recovering: *Writing and Healing*, ed. by Joan Rodman Goulianos (Writers at Work Series, Gallatin Division, N.Y.U. 1983). See also *Child and Tale:* The Origins of Interest by F. Andre Favat. National Council of Teachers of English, 1977.

Kosky does not sound apologetic.

But to make "assurance doubly sure," the author brings into the work the whole story of his grievances in relation to the "three mile Point," with which the public are familiar as a controversy between JAMES FENIMORE COOPER and the good people of the village of Cooperstown! Mr. Cooper's *Card* in regard to this matter is before the public — so also is the history of his libel suits against several editors for having dared to comment on the Point controversy. (New World, 1840).

"Sure you are!" says John. "For a man supposedly new to acting, you played Bukharin very convincingly! Too convincingly."

"How can I best enjoy my notoriety?" wonders our literary wonder-worker. **There is only one way of comprehending man's being-there, and that is by way of inspecting my own being. (Abraham Joshua Heschel)**

"Enjoy Being There[6] while it lasts. While fame brings you closer to other people, notoriety ostracizes," says Marion.

The phone buzzes. John answers it and listens for a minute. "The Opium Eater is ready for you with *his* confessions,"[7] he says, pointing downstairs. He doesn't look too happy. "See him and face some facts'nd figures."

Having heard this, our footnote lover, descends the staircase by foot all the way down to the sixth-floor office of Tom De Quincey, Eidolon's publisher as well as president, chairman of the board, and chief executive officer. **Hermit, ab-**

---

[6]*Being There:* Jerzy Kosinski's black-and-white novel and a Lorimar color movie (starring Peter Sellers, that shaman of the silver screen), about one Chauncy ("Chance") Gardiner, who becomes spiritually unsinkable in the book's beginning, and at the end of the movie based on the novel (and author's own screenplay. Ed.) ends up walking over a lake, the way an image is cast upon water.

[7]*Confessions of an English Opium Eater,* by Thomas De Quincey.

solve our sins which were never venal, / O you the pure and contrite whom we love, / Know our hearts, veil the games we delight in / And our kisses distilled to essence like honey. (*The Hermit* by Apollinaire.)[8] Furnished to resemble an opium eater's modern den, De Quincey's office offers our Comrade Bukharin a welcome Kremlin-like peace.

"*The Healer* is a setback which sets us back before it is published. A setback already, long before you have even finished your novel," says Tom, who has come a long way from selling antiaddiction books in a campus bookshop to running Eidolon Books. Once a dreamer too shy to succeed, today Tom has the body of a Tartar athlete capped with an Oriental face. He exudes corporeal, as well as corporate, confidence.

"A setback for you, Norbert—and for us!" he repeats.

"How far back am I set?" asks Kosky with pretended nonchalance.

It is that true literature can exist only where it is created, not by diligent, reliable officials, but by madmen, hermits, heretics, dreamers, rebels and skeptics. (Zamiatin)

Such is your reputation among your fellow-men that if you announce a revised edition of any of your works, even if you have added nothing new, they will think the old edition worthless. (Erasmus's publisher to Erasmus)

The publisher glances at a folder in front of him.

"For some reason, no less than a dozen foreign publishers have called to tell us that unless you state ahead of time whether the book is fiction or nonfiction, they are not interested in publishing *The Healer of 96 Degrees*."

---

[8]"The Hermit," a poem by Guillaume Apollinaire (assumed name of Wilhelm Kostrowicki, J. K.) See *Alcools* 1898–1913 Translated by William Meredith, New York, 1965.

De Quincey comes around from behind the desk and, facing Kosky, sits on the desktop. "Because the libel laws are more stringent abroad than in this country, the foreign publishers take what our press wrote about you very seriously. They hope you will clarify the situation the very minute you commence action."

"Action? What kind of action?" asks Kosky.

"A libel suit, of course!" says De Quincey. "Is there any better way to bury rumors?"

"Yes," says Kosky. "Doing nothing. **Whereupon true stasis without seed ensues. (O. P. Jaggi)**[9]

De Quincey stands up and leans against the desk. "What do you mean, nothing?" "Just look at this one." He shows Kosky THE BURIAL OF NORBERT KOSKY, AMERICA'S FIRST LITERARY FAKIR, the headline in the *Downtown Crier*.

"I won't do a thing about it. Not a thing. I won't say a word to it or about it. I won't even think about it. And I certainly will never write about it. I'll just ride it through." Kosky delivers his Oratory. **Just as a scab is a disease of the body, so is anger a disease of the soul.** (Solomon Ibn Gabirol)

"So what will you do instead?" De Quincey follows our literary Cubist around the room.

"I might cure my heart in the Sea of Sion,[10] my favorite

---

[9]"Since the yogi works on all levels of consciousness and of the subconscious (Mircea Eliade, op. cit., p. 99), stasis (Tantra) represents a spiritual stage in which, following concentration and meditation, a spiritual object of knowledge leads to a spiritual knowledge of the object." (J. K.)

[10]Sion, the lovely capital of the Swiss canton of Valais. The great period of the See of Sion began in 999 ("Three nines! How's that for a happy date?" J. K.) when the childless Rudolph II of Burgundy invested the Bishop of Sion with the revenues of Valais. In late 1069 (or early 1070) Ermenfroy, Bishop of Sion, visited England. As the Conqueror's coronation in 1066 (double six!) had been broken by riots, Ermenfroy crowned him again in 1070 (missing 1069 by one.).

topographical SS or move in again to Altos de Chavon, the writers colony in the Dominican Republic which decades ago I inaugurated as its first hermit-in-residence."

Resigned, De Quincey sits down. He folds and unfolds his eyebrows with obvious aversion. He folds and unfolds his fingers. "No wonder: this is not an easy book to read.[11] I think you're making a terrible mistake. Won't you reconsider?"

"I can't. It's a matter of conviction," says Kosky.

"Indeed!" says De Quincey. "You've been convicted in the press by one former swimming pool cleaner and one former critic of swimming style and now you don't care what everybody thinks about you or your relation to water."

"I don't know who 'everybody' is—nor do I care to know!" says Kosky.

"Everybody means your readers. Everybody means the media. Everybody means the public. Everybody means the nobodies who bother to buy your books and pay your bills. Face it: no public means no book." says De Quincey.

"Wrong!" Kosky sounds a moral gong. "At worst, no public means no sales. I can still write my next novel even without a public. Even without a publisher. I can have it published the Jankiel Wiernik[12] way."

"Sure you can," De Quincey mocks him. "You can also

---

[11]In the newspaper and printing offices laughing throngs gathered round to examine the astonishing scrawl. The most experienced compositors declared their inability to decipher it, and though they were offered double wages they refused to set up more than *une heure de Balzac* a day. It took months before a man learned the science of unraveling his hieroglyphics, and even then a special proofreader had to revise the compositor's often very hypothetical surmises. (Stefan Zweig).

[12]Jankiel Wiernik (b. 1890): deported to Treblinka in 1942. Wiernik, a socialist Jew who was a building contractor, played a

pass *The Healer* as a samizdat, and publish it on your mimeograph as your personal yellow sheet, a new version of *Affliction of Childhood*.[13] But where would you take it to sell — and where would it take you? Remember: a no-contest plea from you is an admission of guilt — the defendant's throwing himself on the mercy of the court."

"At best, a newspaper is a pool of public opinion — a pool, not even a court. It's buoyed up by the voice of its writers, not of its public," says Kosky. **When a Tantric Yogi reaches a very advanced stage of Enlightenment, he should practice the Tantric Madness or Act-of-Insanity by behaving like a lunatic, to completely emancipate himself from all conventional thoughts and habits and then reach final and perfect Enlightenment. (Garma C. C. Chang, 1977)**

"Is that your final stand?" De Quincey asks him, raising his eyes to the sky.

"As final as I can stand it," says Kosky.

---

decisive role in the Treblinka uprising. His report about the camp — one of the first — was published in a clandestine printshop in an edition of two thousand copies, all marked "Yellow Alert."

[13]In his *Affliction of Childhood* (*Suspiria de Profundis*), De Quincey points out that since we don't have exact recall of our childhood — not even exact recall of what afflicted us when we were young — our childhood memories are, at best, visualizations, not revisitations or re-creations of a childhood.

34

Pre-set to *ALARM!* the TV set in Kosky's room turns itself on at precisely six minutes to 6:00 P.M.—the time when under ordinary circumstances, Kosky makes a narrative pass at his Second State. **The Second State is the antithesis of dreaming, just as is the waking state. Recognition of "I am" consciousness is present. . . . Participation is as fundamental as it is in the waking physical state. Sensory input is not limited to one or two sources. Emotional patterns are present to a greater extent than in the physical consciousness, but can be directed and controlled to the same degree. (Robert A. Monroe)**[1]

In some six minutes, the case of Norbert Kosky will be discussed on *Controversy!*—a prime-time, high-rating TV program aired once every six days on Channel 69 prime-time cable TV.

---

[1] "Throughout the entire experimentation, evidence began to mount of a factor most vital to the Second State. Yet in all the esoteric literature of the underground, there is no mention of this, not so much as one word of consideration or explanation. This factor is sexuality and the physical sex drive." From "Sexuality in the Second State," in *Journeys Out of the Body*, by Robert A. Monroe (1977).

The whole thing came to pass so abruptly without his dealing with it or uttering a word, without his giving any opinion, acquiescing or denying; events had transpired so swiftly that he continued to be dazed and horror-struck without literally grasping what was happening. (Maupassant)

Meanwhile, on quite another channel, Kosky watches an American movie, a story of the first spiritual media man.

ABBAZ

"Dead, my ass! Now get this, honkie—you go tell Raphael that I ain't takin' no jive from anybody! You tell that asshole, if he got somethin' to tell me to get his ass down here himself!"

(edges closer to Chance)

"You got that, boy?"[2]

All this represents a perfect metaphor for what is about to take place on quite another TV channel, to which Kosky now reluctantly turns.

To our literary quail this will be a trying moment. To start with, *Controversy!* is watched "by some sixteen million North American viewers aged anywhere between the ages of sixteen and ninety years whose view of life, no longer dependent on reading books, has shifted to having them and their dead

---

[2]During this, as Abbaz becomes more hostile (Abbaz is black; Chance is white), Chance reaches into his pocket and takes from it his remote-control TV channel changer. He points the changer at Abbaz and clicks it three times as if trying to cancel the Outer Image which came to him involuntarily thanks to objective reality (no thanks!) and switch to another channel of his inner, and so much richer, life. Instead, Abbaz immediately pulls out a switchblade knife and holds it to Chance.

authors discussed live by two live'nd lively literati on the screen of their color TV," according to *Literary TV Cable*.

Like every other ghetto, the intellectual ghetto is a seat of poisonous snakes to whom concocting intrigues is the amateur's high art; among whom a fellow man's loss of reputation triggers solidarity of quiet joy — the commonest and most pleasurable of social sentiments. (Jozef Chałasinski)[3]

Sixteen million North Americans is a lot of people. Then, as if that number was not trying enough, a lot of new viewers might tune in to this segment of the show — the first one devoted to a living American. "Call all this either the Hunt of the Unicorn leading to his capture, or The Unicorn at the Fountain, that is his courtly love affair with the media." (Jay Kay)[4] On top of all this, a lot of non-TV viewers might like to see the program try out a new "living" format called, ironically, DEAD ON, and in the process see Norbert Kosky being tried on it and by it, as if he were already dead.

So what? Kosky says to himself again and again. Such are

---

[3]Jozef Chałasinski: One of the most distinguished Polish sociologists of culture, known for his works on the intellectual ghetto and *Kultura Amerykanska*, his magnum opus. (American Culture: *The Forming of National Culture in the United States of America*, written in Polish. Until 1957 Norbert Kosky studied sociology of culture — including the sociology of literary form — under the personal aegis of Jozef Chałasinski, whom he often called his "pedagogical father") (J. K.)

[4]"The Hunt of the Unicorn" and "The Unicorn at the Fountain" two of the seven Unicorn tapestries, hand woven in Brussels circa 1500 are today part of the permanent collection of The Cloisters, a branch of The Metropolitan Museum of Art devoted exclusively to art of European Middle Ages, "which, offering the most exciting monastic experience this side of afterlife." (Jay Kay). (See Jerzy Kosinski's Time Machine, in *New York Magazine* year-end double issue 1990. Ed.)

the spiritual **Advantages of Exile. (Cioran)** Kosky tells himself before committing his thoughts on this subject to Jay Kay. **What have I done to you, Lord? See I am a Unicorn . . .** ("The Hermit" by Apollinaire).

To the sound of "Barcarolle," Chopin's split-note nocturne, *Controversy!*'s theme song, the split-image face of Nocturnal Janus — the man who wears his straight face as if it were a crooked mask — fills the screen.

I'll have no scandal in my life . . . for a scandal amongst people of our position is disastrous for the morality. (Joseph Conrad)

Just as the music subsides, a *sotto voce* voice-over announces *Controversy!* as "a show of literary popcorn for the literary eye. Today, Dustin Beach Bradley Borell, perhaps the best known American Book Editor, is our special guest!"

PA-PAM! PA-PAM! PA-PAM! The show's triple electronic gong announces to the American electronic gang that *Controversy!,* "the worldwide TV show devoted to the worth of the word" (*Cable News*), is on the air.

Attired in a woolen cardigan and faded blue jeans, Watkins Tottle, the show's host, exudes hot air, mixed with an "unparalleled degree of anti-connubial timidity." (Charles Dickens) He first displays a bundle of books written by Isaac Deutscher, Mircea Eliade, Bronislaw Malinowski, as well as books by Conrad, Nabokov, Koestler, Apollinaire, Thomas Wolfe, F. Scott Fitzgerald and Thornton Wilder, the literary bigwigs Eidolon Press has published over the years as part of their DADI (Dead Authors Dead Issues) series. Then — and only then — he shows the world (and his small studio audience) eight hardcover novels by Norbert Kosky, while our gymnosophist trembles with vanity-induced tremor.

Let us say a man writes a novel which makes him, overnight, a celebrity. In it he recounts his sufferings. His compatriots in exile envy him: they too have suffered, perhaps more. And the man without a country becomes —

or aspires to become—a novelist. The consequence: an accumulation of confusions, an inflation of horrors, of *frissons* that date. (E. M. Cioran)

"Norbert Kosky, the author in question, is still alive," says Watkins Tottle, "even though, apparently, not alive enough to show up in person on our show and is reported by the press to "have been emotionally and spiritually stilled. Stilled, not spilled. THE ISSUE OF NORBERT KOSKY is nevertheless not a dead issue," he goes on. "Besides," he tries humor, "while on our show we routinely bring the dead issues to life; in this case"—he smiles sweetly—"we will bury Norbet Kosky alive! Well, not really," he protests mocking. "Let me assure you, our volatile author is very much alive and kicking—as evidenced by this"—here the host produces several life-size photographs showing "our volatile author" either half-naked on a polo horse, or skimming the surface of some reader-forsaken Golden Pond wearing nothing but his swimsuit. "Skinny *thing* that Kosky is," says Ms. Dombey Tox, the show's hostess.

She is a well-shaped, short-legged but not poorly bosomed, lick-it-clean petite brunette in a pale blue suit, who is the **very pink of general propitiation and politeness (Charles Dickens)**. It is she who, a *centrifuge of whirling hips* (Julian Tuwim) now introduces a video clip of Kosky clipped from a 1982 Oscar TV ceremonies. She then follows it up introducing a short scene from *Total State*. There is Kosky conducting his own defense at the Moscow Trials as Bukharin. The clip ends with Bukharin, by then to say the least, a very tired man, saying to the always well-rested Vyshinsky, "Isn't this at best hearsay evidence?" The host now turns to Dustin Borell. He introduces him as "an *eminence grise* of American book publishing, a man eminent enough to launch, single-handedly, his Counter Authors Series—which he started, quite àpropos, some thirty-three years earlier with the publication of a little-known first novel written by the then-little-known Norbert Kosky."

"How would you rate yourself as an editor, Mr. Borell?" the host asks with a rather silly smile.

"As an in-house editor who hassled and harassed is not often in the house," says Dustin. "The kind *NewsTime* recently profiled in their unkind cover piece appropriately headlined 'The Decline of Editing.' "

Now it is the hostess's turn. "And how would you rate Norbert Kosky, Mr. Borell?"

While Dustin, our impeccably attired Boston Brahmin, readies himself to answer her, a Sim Thomas Temple, Jr., Flash-Clash flashes in yellow letters which momentarily clash with the screen. LITERARY WATERGATE SERIES CONTINUES.

"I'd also rate him as the most difficult to work with," says Dustin, his face as grave as his purpose.

The hostess brightens; by easily confusing "bright" with "light" and light with heat, she thinks the controvsery might heat up. "Difficult? Why?" **For a brief moment she postures as a Satanella (Tuwim).**

"Because he's so damned serious about his writing business—yet he refuses to be businesslike and, for instance, hire like everybody else a literary or even a screen agent. Instead, he always complains **Oh, My Aching Back (Root and Kiernan),**" says Dustin. "Kosky acts as if one messed-up paragraph in his messed-up set of galleys could mess his life up—or put him on the gallows. He writes under pressure of **The Tremendum (Arthur E. Cohen, 1981).** And to make his point he hits you with his own idiosyncratic motivational nominal or verbal prose style. And, as if this were not enough, he then hits you over the head with his own *Vectors of Prose Style*[5] reinforced by someone else's quote—the quote is

---

[5]"The sample of objects studied here consisted of 150 passages from various sources and styles of English prose. Each passage was

his Talmudic moral weapon—and a kick in the groin with a nasty footnote."

The host glances at his notes. His notes are all messed up. "The general public would like you, Mr. Borell, to answer this question." He raises his eyes, as if the question in question came to him either from a single person called general public or from a publicly owned Wholly Ghost (wholly, not holy, since nothing so public can possibly be holy), a ghost called I AM THE MYTHMAKING CAMERA. "Isn't there something unethical about a book editor who's passing his or her creative wordy as well as worthy associations and wordy ideas on to an author? Any editor? Any author?" He pauses for effect. "Don't you think that writing credits on the books written by most of our major and certainly by minor writers and edited for them by some of this nation's foremost editors should be shared on the book's cover at least with the names of these very editors as a matter of ethics? For instance, *The Sun Also Rises,* by Ernest Hemingway sharing credits, so to speak, with Maxwell Perkins; *Look Homeward Angel,* a novel by Thomas Wolfe with Maxwell Perkins; *Courthouse Square,* a novel by Hamilton Basso with Maxwell Perkins; *Tender Is the Night,* a novel by F. Scott Fitzgerald with Maxwell Perkins?" he recites.

------

chosen so as to be more or less self-contained with a little more than 300 words. By selecting passages according to categories—novels (both British and American, both nineteenth and twentieth centuries), essays, newspaper features and editorials, biographies, scientific papers, textbooks, speeches, legal documents, personal letters, and sermons were among the categories used—we hoped to include the widest possible assortment of subject matters and styles. The sample even included several relatively low-grade high-school English compositions." From "Vectors of Prose Style," by John B. Carroll, in *Style in Language,* ed. by Thomas A. Sebeok (1960).

"I don't think so because I don't see any ethical credit violation here," says Dustin.[6] He reads aloud from his notes the following: **Writers constantly seek criticism from friends. And the question of editing was decided for all time in the collaboration between Wolfe and Maxwell Perkins, Scribner's "editor of genius," who pored over Wolfe's work, night after night, months to a book cutting, rearranging and pasting. Yet, Perkins would not have dreamed of being credited as a "writer." . . . An irony of American letters is that two of the figures who did the most to build the 20th-century American novel, namely Perkins and Edmund Wilson, critics of genius, could not themselves write a credible novel — and, in the case of Perkins, never considered trying. (Christopher Norwood)**

A commercial break devoted to Panacea™. During it the camera zooms over time and space to a chemical laboratory in Moscow, where, circa 1866–69, an aged Russian alchemist trots back and forth among his pots, vials and burners. A man's voice-over — the invisible American scientific authority — announces that Panacea™ (an American-made derivative of dimethyl sulfoxide,[7] a powerful penetrant, first synthesized by Aleksandr S. Saytzeff, a Russian alchemist. J. K.) "The clinical reports obtained during the 1960s from research by American scientists have proved Panacea™ to be the most important breakthrough since the discovery of peni-

---

[6]There's another tremendous problem: the revolving-door policy that many publishers have with their editors. In my personal experience, I have had to cope with the turnover of three editors during the editorial process for one book. (Authors Guild Bulletin, 1982).

[7]Dimethyl sulfoxide: also known as DMSO, is water's most serious competitor, since it is the only fluid other than water known to penetrate any living tissue — and, to penetrate it exactly the way water does.

cillin in our fight against vicious viruses and stubborn bacterias," says the V.O. "Panacea™ is a sure publicity-tested remedy for just about any infection, from herpes to poisonous bite." The commercial success story ends.

Leaning over, the hostess seeks self-reflection by glancing at her complexion reflected in the glass top of the center stage table.

"Will Kosky ever clear his face of all this float'nd swim editorial acne?" she reflects on the stage on Kosky's moral complexion.

"I'm sure he will, though not person-to-person and not on Facing the Nation," says Dustin who knows his literary iconoclast.

"Then how?" The host catches up.

"By writing a novel. By writing it in the third person. And why not? Writing is his icon."[8]

"I wonder what will he call it, Waterbed or Watershed?" wonders the host.

"He will narrate it entirely in metaphors. "A world ends when its metaphor has died," says Archibald MacLeish—and he is right." Dustin pauses thoughtfully.

The host exaggerates being perplexed. "It's a shame Kosky won't respond directly to what was said about him in the press.[9] And why not?"

---

[8]"The icon goes with a man for the whole of his life: he receives it at baptism, it is carried at the head of his wedding procession, and it goes before him at his burial. Parents use it in giving their blessing to those going on journeys, or to newlywed couples, and at the moment of departure from this life, to all those standing by," writes Pierre Pascal in *The Religion of the Russian People,* translated by Rowan Williams (1976).

[9]See *Victims: Textual Strategies in Recent American Fiction,* by Paul Bruss (Associated University Presses, Ltd., 69 Fleet Street, London, England, 1981), Part III, Chapter 10: "Early Fiction: The

"I guess he's ashamed to play a Victim." says Dustin. "Ashamed as himself, and as the twice-elected president of W.E.T. Besides, as Paul Valéry once stated, 'There is no true meaning of a text. The author has absolutely no authority. Whatever he may have wanted to say, he has written what one can use according to his ways and means: there is no certainty of its maker using it better than anyone else.' "

"Are you sure that's the reason?" asks the hostess. "We offered Mr. Kosky our show as a platform from which to rebut or rebuff his literary suitors, but, he turned us—and them—down, and he did so by not even returning our telephone call."

Another Flash-Clash: IN HER MEMOIRS CYNTHIA KOESTLER REVEALS ARTHUR OFTEN "HIRED" ENGLISH-SPEAKING SECRETARIES TO TAKE HIS DICTATION. FLUENT AS A CHID IN HUNGARIAN AND FRENCH BUT NOT IN ENGLISH, ARTHUR DID NOT BEGIN WRITING IN ENGLISH UNTIL HE MET CYNTHIA, WHO WAS ONE OF HIS ENGLISH SECRETARIES. QUERY: IN WHAT LANGUAGE DID ARTHUR DICTATE HIS ENGLISH-LANGUAGE BOOKS?

PA-PAM! PA-PAM! PA-PAM! The electronic gong summons the electronic gang back to *Controversy!*, "the program devoted tonight to Norbert Kosky—our absentee author hiding somewhere in his narrative village," the host unctuates.

"Are we in a program, or in a pogrom?" laughs Dustin, and his laughter is an easy mixture of a skoal with a smile.

"Hardly a pogrom!" The hostess laughs nervously. "Mr. Kosky's bizarre horseplay and foolery have been known in literary circles for as long as his love of polo, the rather silly, I must say, sport of the macro-macho."

Problem of Language," which, appropriately for Kosky's first work of fiction published in 1965, begins on p. 165. See also chapter 12, "Cockpit: Games and Expansion of Perception," which starts on p. 198.

"I beg your pardon, madam! Polo is anything but silly."
Dustin steams up the already steamy situation. "Ask anyone.
Ask Theodore Roosevelt, who played it and recommended
playing it to any middle-aged man of letters — and isn't Kosky
middle-aged? Of all mankind's early sports, polo is the most
literary, since already in the ninth century it produced the
poetic image of Syavoush as a polo player, not as a legendary
Persian ruler." Defending polo, Dustin defends Teddy
Roosevelt, as one of the authors published as part of his
company's Distinguished Literary Rough Riders Series.
"Like baseball and golf, polo is a stick-and-ball game; like
football and ice hockey, it draws its thrill from decontrolled
collision — an American fetish. Furthermore" — he turns toward her, his Kennedyesque profile — "polo can hardly be
called macho if the very sexily clad ladies of the T'ang dynasty played it on the T'ang dynasty seventh-century pot-
tery — the earliest surviving representations of polo. (*Chakkar*,
op. cit.) He pauses again. "As Virginia Woolf pointed out,
'Women have served all these centuries as looking-glasses
possessing the magic and delicious power of reflecting the
figure of man at twice its natural size.' Kosky admits that he
plays polo because it makes him look twice his size."

"For my part," says the host, clean, plump and rosy (Dickens), tightening his tie, "I find Kosky's floating half-naked on
the cover of *Watersports* magazine in rather poor taste. One
cannot quite imagine our serious writers — say, Matthew
Duke or Salome-Lou Moses — skinny-dipping in Walden
Pond for the sake of the press!"[10]

---

[10]In his *The Last Tycoon*, Fitzgerald is **perplexed** [Maimonides] by
the fact that "the Jews had taken over the worship of horses as a
symbol — for years it had been the Cossacks mounted and the Jews
on foot. Now the Jews had horses and it gave them a sense of
extraordinary well-being and power."

Dustin faces him squarely. "Yes, one can imagine: everyone of them! When it comes to Self-image-making, writers are shameless. Whitman used a quote from Emerson's shamelessly personal letters for a shamelessly positive blurb, shamelessly reviewed his own books, interviewed himself, and practically every day shamelessly planted controversial leaves of grass about himself in the daily newspapers."

"All Kosky writes about is evil; evil, never shame," hisses the hostess. "He is our—I admit I search our literary wax museum for a title perverse enough—our veritable *Imp of the Perverse.*" Her love for the perverse Edgar Allan Poe shows all over her literary skin.

"I agree he is." Dustin smiles wisely straight into the camera. "These days, having written his perverse opus number nine, our Ruthenian mocking bird turns out to be quite a Poeish raven!"

"A raven indeed!" The hostess clearly doesn't like Poeish jokes or Kosky. (PRINTER: Poeish, not Polish. Kosky, not Koski) "Even *Centers Review,* that bastion of male illegitimate intimacy, indirectly accused him of rape." She pauses for effect and gets it. "Of raping us in his novels that is. Of stripping us emotionally. What makes things so much worse is that everybody knows his novels embody his own life. He writes from life. Rape is all he writes about—and what he clearly cares for most.[11] He as a man—a man, never mind, as an author."

"Hate, not rape, is what Kosky writes about," says Dustin calmly. "He writes about it out of hate and because he hates

---

[11]A sudden blow: the great winds beating still/Above the staggering girl, her thighs caressed/By the dark webs, her nape caught in his bill,/He holds her helpless breast upon his breast./How can those terrified vague fingers push/The feathered glory from her loosening thighs? (Yeats)

anything to do with hate, including rape — rape, to him, is an act of hate — he writes about it hatefully." **"The public is a thick-skinned beast, and you have to keep whacking away on its hide to let it know you're there."** (W. Whitman).

"There are better ways to learn about hate than through violence and rape," she snaps. "There are lots of women in this country — and I hope men too! — who wouldn't as much as glance at Kosky's books."

"Don't judge him by an American yardstick only," Dustin intervenes peacefully. **"His life and art have been shaped by two of the most cataclysmic movements in the modern world: Nazism and Stalinist Communism. From the dual experience** [he: J. K.] **has survived with very few verities intact.'"** (Lawrence S. Cunningham).[12] "Isn't Kosky our Catastrophe Man?" again he asks the silent camera. "One who spent his formative years from the age of six to twelve surviving the most catastrophic period in the thousand-year-old European history?"

"Holocaustian he sure is." The hostess delivers her bit of World War II history.

"Don't cramp me with this crap, madam." Dustin, our Boston Brahmin, loses his cool. "He chronicles sin, isolation and fear. And he is not the only one. I strongly suggest that you read this, madam." In front of the camera he hands her the "Behavioral Study of Obedience."[13]

---

[12]*America*, Vol. II, 1978. (*America* is published by the Jesuits of the United States and Canada: J. K.)

[13]PRINTER: "The Behavioral Study of Obedience," by Stanley Milgram, describes a procedure for the study of destructive obedience in the laboratory. (as opposed to the obedience imposed in real life by the Nazi SS-State. J. K.) It consists of ordering a naive S to administer increasingly more severe punishment to a victim in the context of a learning experiment. Punishment is administered by

"His book covers might be gross"—the host swallows hard—"but I guess we all could profit from Kosky's literary douche."

"What douche?" snarls the hostess. "Kosky's art is as heavy as his accent."

"Joseh Conrad's accent was just as heavy," says Dustin. "Few who did not know him well could understand him at first—even his British publishers and particularly their secretaries didn't know what he was talking to them about even when he was talking about them."[14]

A station break. This is the time to get distracted. Quickly,

---

means of a shock generator with thirty graded switches ranging from Slight Shock (SS) to Danger: Severe Shock (SS). The victim is a confederate of the E. The primary dependent variable is the maximum shock the S is willing to administer before he refuses to continue further. Twenty-six Ss obeyed the experimental commands fully, and administered the highest shock on the generator. Fourteen Ss broke off the experiment at some point after the victim protested and refused to provide further answers. The procedure created extreme levels of nervous tension in some Ss. Profuse sweating, trembling and stuttering were typical expressions of this emotional disturbance. One unexpected sign of tension—yet to be explained—was the regular occurrence of nervous laughter, which in some Ss developed into uncontrollable seizures. The variety of interesting behavioral dynamics observed in the experiment, the reality of the situation for the S, and the possibility of parametric variation within the framework of the procedure point to the fruitfulness of further study. (*Journal of Abnormal and Social Psychology*, [1963].

[14]"The English critics—since I am in fact an English writer—when discussing me always note that there is something in me which cannot be understood, nor defined, nor expressed. Only you can grasp this undefinable factor, only you can understand the incomprehensible. It is *polskość* (*polonitas*), that *polskość* which I took into my work from Mickiewicz and Słowacki." (Conrad to Marian Dabrowski, 1914)

Kosky rushes to the cabinet from where he draws *Norbert Kosky Reads Himself* — a long-playing 33 rpm recording issued by Rockwell Records as record No. 96 in their 1969 Top 100 Spellbound Series. This is a recording made by him nearly twenty years ago, on the thirtieth anniversary of the beginning of World War II, and on it you can hear him reading, in his own brand of English, fragments of his first novel."

My style may be atrocious — but it produces its effect. . . . I shall make my own boots or perish. (Conrad)

Quickly, he puts the record on his predigital turntable. After the table reluctantly starts to turn, he listens to his own master's voice, to his foreign accent which he is sorry to say sounds now as heavy'nd strained by the presence of so many SS's in him as it did then, some twenty years ago.

Back to *Controversy!*

"Do you agree that in his novels Mr. Kosky constantly usurps Ruthenian folklore?" the hostess says with an inner **little squeaky voice (A. M. Rosenthal)** which, in her case, could have originated in a heavy-duty mare.

"He does and he does not. A novelist usurps folklore no less and no more than a weatherman usurps weather," storms Dustin. "In *The Financier* did Dreiser usurp the folklore of Chicago? Or the folklore of Yerkes, the magnate whose every step he followed by following press accounts in the local press? He did, yet he did not. In *The Peasants*, his Nobel prize winning novel, and *The Promised Land,* did W. S. Reymont usurp the folklore of both Polish peasants — some of the very peasants Kosky met during the war — and workers of Łodz, Kosky's native town?[15] He certainly did — and just as certainly he did not."

----

[15]See *Folklore On the American Land* by Duncan Emrich, Boston 1972. The chief touchstone to folklore is the manner in which it is

Another literary Flash-Clash clashes with his words: BRITISH JOURNALIST ARTHUR MEE DECLARES THAT CONRAD ADMITTED TO HIM HE DROPPED HIS POLISH SURNAME KORZENIOWSKI SIMPLY BECAUSE HE FELT THAT BY NOT BEING ABLE TO PRONOUNCE IT THE ENGLISH WOULD NOT BUY HIS BOOKS, AND THE IMPLICATION MEANING ALL CONRAD CARES FOR IS FAME AND MONEY.

QUOTE BY ARTHUR MEE CAUSES FURY OF ANTI-CONRAD QUOTES IN POLAND WHERE ELIZA ORZESZKOWA, POLAND'S FOREMOST LITERARY FIGURE, DECLARES CONRAD A LITERARY PERSONA NON GRATA. SAYS ELIZA: "WHEN IT COMES TO BOOKS THIS GENTLEMAN WHO WRITES NOVELS ONLY IN ENGLISH NEARLY GAVE ME A NERVOUS FIT WHEN READING ABOUT HIM." POLISH LITERATI STUNNED.

On the screen, the host confronts Dustin. "By the time you or any other editor is finished with a writer's manuscript, isn't the manuscript *different* from what it was before you all worked on it?" He makes quite a thing out of the word *different*.

"That's not a question: that's an ambush. Of course I don't deny the manuscript would be *different*, but so what? Even if in a writer's manuscript I would brake a paragraph, or cross out repetitions, the writer's manuscript, or printer's proofs, would be — technically speaking — *different* from what they were, wouldn't they? But only technically speaking!" Pensive, his eyebrows tightly drawn, Dustin looks at his notes, then goes on.

"What matters in literary matters is imagination; this belongs to the author, not to the author's editor. The story is

.

---

transmitted: One man tells another, one man shows another. Folklore circulates as easily as breathing, and as unselfconsciously. (Ibidem). Also, see *Dictionary of Polish Folklore*, ed. by Julian Krzyzanowski, (in Polish) Warsaw, 1965.

every inch of the way the author's story—and that's all there is to it. For proof, take a look at the writer's lot, at the preliminary drafts of any novel." *Write and Rewrite* **(John Kuehl)**[16]

Once more the host rises to his task, as he rises from his chair and clumsily walks toward the camera, forcing one cameraman to stop him with a gesture of his hand. "It's just that the public at large remains quite unaware of how a novelist works," he says in a conciliatory manner.

"Most people agree they could not easily play a piano concerto, but they believe that with the help of an editor anybody could write a novel," says the hostess, who, pencil in hand, all patently uncomfortable, remains seated behind her desk.

"A good point," Dustin agrees. **"Great editors do not discover or produce great authors; great authors create and produce great editors. (John Farrar)**

---

[16]Read *Write and Rewrite: a Study of the Creative Process,* by John Kuehl (1967). "With very few exceptions, the drafts and the authors' statements [represented here by Eudora Welty, Kay Boyle, James Jones, Bernard Malamud, Wright Morris, F. Scott Fitzgerald, Philip Roth, Robert Penn Warren, John Hawkes and William Styron: J. K.] have been transcribed as they were written, including typographical errors. Drafts incorporating revisions were printed instead of drafts exhibiting revisions for several reasons. Authorial changes often involve great mechanical difficulties in attempting to transcribe and reproduce them. Indeed, in a number of cases obliteration was so efficient that any earlier state or states were undecipherable. Besides, the writing problems treated here frequently transcend simple word or phrase changes." (John Kuehl)

Stiegler smiled deprecatingly. "Of course you can't. But who can nowadays? It's no problem. We can provide you with our best editors and research assistants." (*Being There*) (See also, "The Importance of Copy Editing," by Laurie Stearns, *Publishers Weekly,* August 10, 1987.

After another station break, *Controversy!* comes alive again. First, for the benefit of the camera, the host produces one more cliché of his supposedly still engaging smile as he confronts Dustin. "How often do you, as an editor, give a style to any of your writers?" He retrieves part of the old editorial thread.

"What?" Dustin snaps. "You're talking about a writer's style. Style, not a turnstile. Ask our good friend Joseph Conrad. He was the foremost exile of style."[17] He winks at someone beside the camera. "A novel is not a teapot and a writer's style not a tea bag. You can't just drop it into the pot and come up with a—you guessed it, a potboiler!"

"What about a writer's style?" persists the host.

"A writer's style is his spiritual stylus," declares Dustin. "It is as personally his as is his most idiosyncratic, often bilingual lovemaking. Ask Conrad. Ask Eliade. Ask Ayn Rand, or Koestler. Ask Ionesco. Ask Beckett. Ask Gronowicz, Nabokov, or Cioran. Ask any writer. But, please, don't ask me." With naming of these names, Dustin closes his attaché case—and with it the Case of Literature vs. Norbert Kosky.

A station break follows. Soon *Controversy!* is back on the air.

On the screen, the host blows his nose in a monogrammed handkerchief, folds it into a neat square, and replaces it in an inner pocket of his jacket. "In the Ruthenian language, *kos* means *mimus polyglottos,* the mockingbird, renowned for the quality of its own sound as well as for the faithful rendering

---

[17]In these circumstances you imagine I feel not much inclination to write letters. As a matter of fact I had a great difficulty in writing the most commonplace note. I seem to have lost all *sense* [italics by Conrad: J. K.] of style and yet I am haunted, mercilessly haunted by the *necessity* [italics by Conrad: J. K.] of style. And that story I can't write weaves itself into all I see, into all I speak, into all I think, into the lines of every book I try to read. I haven't read for days. (Conrad to Garnett).

of the notes of other songsters. Will the printed birds ever let our mocking polyglot go?" asks the hostess.

Just then, a heavy electronic curtain drops down over the electronic stage. "This is the end of our program but, not of the *Controversy!*" says the Voice Over. The show is finally over. **In the long list of controversies which the students of literature is under the necessity of examining, none seem so uncalled for and so discreditable to the assailants as this. (T. R. Lounsbury, about J. Fenimore Cooper, 1882)[18]**

---

[18]The most intense lover of his country, he became the most unpopular man of letters to whom it has ever given birth. For years a storm of abuse fell upon him, which for violence, for virulence, and even for malignity, surpassed anything in the history of American literature, if not in the history of literature itself. (Thomas R. Lounsbury about J. Fenimore Cooper) Enough said?

35

First, Cathy is gone. This means that, missing Cathy's spectral sex (SS), he also misses firing words of his literary missile No. 9 and without such firing, our literary missile carrier feels ready to join the firing squad. **Then as Gwynplaine, speechless, and with eyes downcast like a criminal, remained motionless, she added,— "You have no right to be here; it is my lover's place." Gwynplaine was like a man transfixed.**

"Very well," said she, "then I must go myself. Nothing could be better. I hate you!" (Victor Hugor, *Man Who Laughs*).

Our Gwynplaine is fatigued, and he finds writing fatiguing. Something is wrong. He must stop feeling being wronged by her.

Late evening. Time to meditate. This time by taking his custom-made meditative walk. He walks along Ninth Avenue, but then decides to walk all the way down Seventh, even though seven is not his lucky, i.e., spiritually stimulating, number. Why is it not? Simple. While he knows a great deal about the supposed conversion of the King of the Khazars to Judaism, the powerful Jewish Khazars, and about the hazards of the first Khazar princes and princesses, our literary American Khazar knows next to nothing about the Chaldeans who worshiped number seven. Unlike the Khazars, who once ruled a chunk of the non-Arab world, the Chaldeans kept on looking up from their unobstructed plains "from where, so they said, they could see a complete circle broken only by number seven." (Jay Kay)

He keeps on walking and, his inner meditative view obstructed more and more by the height of his inner American skyscrapers, he then crosses the avenue and walks into Whatever Street. There, he finds himself on the corner of a street called Gay, and a street called Christopher.

Then, suddenly, he notices he is now one of a multitude. Think of them as primarily, a mixed Friday night shrimp'nd steak-eating young Greenwich Village mixed multi-ethnic, mostly gay, lesbian, or bisexual crowd. **Homosexuals and those suspected of homosexuality were arrested by the Nazis and sent to penal colonies as slave laborers and to concentration camps. . . . Buchenwald in particular, where many died. As the War progressed, many more were transported to extermination camps. . . . One cannot even offer a viable estimate as to the number of homosexuals persecuted and murdered by the Nazis.** *Encountering the Holocaust: An Interdisciplinary Survey,* op. cit. 1979.

With six police cars and sirens and cops running all around, the crowd is looking up, still indifferent, still just looking. They, the young men and women of this after-midnight crowd, look at a young man "who, standing on the very top of an eight-floor building, with his arms outstretched like a man on a cross, obviously intends to jump and kill himself." (Jay Kay).

Since the young man is clearly about to choose jumping as a means of suicide, Kosky, an occasional jumper himself, first looks at him in terms of: WILL HE JUMP OR NOT? as someone just screamed in the crowd. In case you didn't notice, Kosky is also an athlete but only in a sense of **"a poor soul burdened with a corpse corpse"** (Epictetus, according to Marcus Aurelius). **"A little soul for a little bears up this corpse which is man."** (Swinburne).

While the young man waits, the crowd stands silent. Is

their silence ugly or banal? Jay Kay promptly detaches Kosky from "the reality of the more or less typical American urban scene where suicide is the No. 2 cause of death among those under twenty-six." (Herald Eastsquare) by asking him: ugly or banal? Correct it please: shouldn't you say evil? Evil of banality, not *Banality of Evil?*

Suddenly the young man leans forward. He then turns around, turns back again—and—wait, standing up, upright, looking first down, then up, then down again, he separates himself from the outline of the house and his body starts falling down, laid out in a perfect backward swallow dive. Now, most of the crowd moans with one loud moan: NO MAN, NO PLEASE! WHAT FOR MAN? WHAT DID YOU DO THAT FOR?

If then, the challenge is not unique, what have other generations of Jews, after previous Holocausts, made of Jewish martyrdom? Steven T. Katz, 1983.[1]

The body hits the street head on with a bang. A bang on the head. A bang, or a thud? Kosky will not think about it. Does his death really matter to him? Not now. Instead, he meditates about *The Cunning of History: The Holocaust and the American Future.* (Richard L. Rubenstein).

"Was the guy gay? Was his name Christopher?" asks someone aloud. "Why would he bother to kill himself on the corner of Gay and Christopher streets?"

Here, having read this, following in the footsteps—as well as footnotes—of this text, the reader is encouraged to meditate for at least six straight minutes about such current notions as WHAT'S ONE'S LIFE FOR? IS MEANING OF ONE'S LIFE DEFINED BY ONE'S OWN HISTORY OR FORCED UPON ONE BY OTHERS? IS ONE'S FALL AS INEVITABLE AS WAS THE FALL OF THAT YOUNG MAN?

In order to ventilate his spiritually soiled soul, which, this time, incorporates his Self, Kosky goes for a drink at Conso-

---

[1] *Jewish Faith After the Holocaust: Four Approaches in Post-Holocaust Dialogues,* by Steven T. Katz (1985). (Winner of the National Jewish Book Award.)

lazione, the "downtown's most notorious food'nd foot bust'nd leg worshiping speakeasy. Reservation a must." (City Guide).

At Consolazione, our sexual seeker seeks the *body's festival* (Mayakovsky, 1916). He pushes through the crowd, trying to reach the restaurant's private room without catching anyone's stare. He fails. He is caught by a quick and clever skoal of Horatio the bartender. The skoal stops Kosky at the bar. Horatio is one of the bartenders Cathy adored as much for being authentic as she adored *The Jargon of Authenticity* by Theodor W. Adorno.

Horatio moves along the bar like a swaying swan, a steroidal atlas fused with Bacchus the hormone-eater. He does so while remaining authentically oblivious of the adoring whispers his body elicits from those at the bar.

"Hey, Norbert! That stuff about you in the press — that's a mine field for my Ph.D. dissertation about the role of sex in your fictional mine-shaft!" says Horatio, flexing his biceps while salting the rim of a glass for Kosky's Esperandido. "On the house!" he says, putting the drink in front of Kosky.

"I thought your subject was 'Literary Lewdness in American Letters, In Letters, not authors,' " says Kosky, licking the salt off the rim of his glass the way he used to rim perspiration droplets off Cathy's back.

This story of how Balzac proposed to become a millionaire by one swift coup (by forming a silver mining joint venture in Sardinia. J. K.) **sounds so incredible that if it were incorporated into a novel it would be condemned as a poor invention wholly lacking in psychological plausibility. It was a piece of extravagant folly of truly Balzacian dimensions, and if it were not fully documented in every detail no biographer would have the courage to recount it as an example of the aberration of a genius.** (Zweig about Balzac)[2]

---

[2]"From the moment Balzac was obsessed by the illusion that his salvation would come from the silver mines of Sardinia and that they would not only defray the cost of his new house . . . but also

"Not anymore. From now on I must start asking you all kinds of questions. Also, one day soon I'll ask you for access to your past business notes about silver-mining in Ruthenia. Silver mining—or was it silver minting?"

"I guess you're lucky I'm still around." says Kosky. **As a matter of fact the Romans,** (Romans, printer, not Ruthenians. Not yet! J. K.) **with their undeveloped technique, had been able to extract only a small proportion of the silver from the lead ore, and the great slag heaps they had left there under the impression that they were entirely valueless contained a high percentage of silver which could be smelted out by modern refining process. Anyone who took the trouble to acquire the concession, which could no doubt be bought for a song, would very soon become a wealthy man.** (Zweig on Balzac).

"People writing their dissertations on Shakespeare's folio (folio, printer, not polio) are not as lucky. They will never know from Shakespeare's folio whether William suffered from polio or not." Horatio beams scholarly pride.

"Do you know her?" asks Kosky, interrupting Horatio by forcefully looking down the bar at a brazenly bleached blonde who seems ready to bare it all in a Squalor Motel.

"I don't, but I know she's your type." Horatio leans to Kosky confidentially. "Stay away from her, buddy. First, this kid is barely twenty-nine. Second, she is into reading magazines, not novels. She subscribes to *Fitness Magazine*—and *How to Combat Business Fatigue*. She won't go for you, a man

---

enable him to settle his outstanding debts and make him at last into a free man. . . . As soon as he had dashed off the last pages of *César Birotteau*, . . . and meanwhile Signor Pezzi would have sent him the specimen ores for which he had asked, he would fling himself with all his energies into the task of raising capital and providing the technical experts for his great new business venture." Balzac by Zweig (op. cit.)

who's been shown half-naked on the cover of *Open Fly Magazine!*"

"Excellent. I wish I could probe her mind. What else is there to probe in her?"

'She's into javelin and discuss throwing. She's the one who does her own warm-ups." Horatio explodes his final myth. "She's the one who—when nobody watches!—gulps down anabolic steroids, not cock-aine! She gets her dose of manliness sure, but only—via the male hormones, not via some Tantric Sexual Pantomime."

"Self-exercise is great for sex!" Kogky ogles the Scentful Blonde over Horatio's perspiring neck. "Stay away from her testosterone," says Horatio. "She could burn a pole like you with her lips alone not to mention her slugs'nd snail (SS) hernia-inducing scull-crushing positions! And à propos pole-burning: my dissertation will be titled 'Norbert Kosky: Controversy or Conviction.'"

"Too bad! I like your previous subtitle: **Denial in Fantasy (Anna Freud).**"[3] Kosky keeps on glancing at the "fat-free but undoubtedly sex-starved vixen." (Jay Kay)

From under the counter Horatio retrieves a small tape recorder, places it next to Kosky and turns it on, turning our hero off in the process.

"I want to have your spoken voice on tape," he says. "I need objective proof that you actually talked to me. Then, in my dissertation, I'll profile you as a failed businessman the way Zweig profiled Balzac." says Horatio.

"Zweig was a café idealist; he could not understand that had Balzac found a sound business partner in France—

---

[3]See "Denial in Fantasy," Chapter Six, starting on p. 69 in *The Ego and The Mechanisms of Defense*, by Anna Freud (New York, 1966). "As indicated in the title, this book deals exclusively with one particular problem, i.e., with the ways and means by which the ego wards off unpleasure and anxiety, and exercises control over impulsive behavior, affects, and instinctive urges," writes Anna Freud in her foreword to the 1966 edition.

France, not as he did in poor Sardinia, his eminently sound joint venture there would have been an astounding financial success."[4]

Among those with whom Balzac struck up an acquaintance on this occasion was a merchant named Giuseppe Pezzi, who told him quite casually, and certainly without the slightest intention of trying to dupe him or entice him into a venturesome speculation, of the treasures which could still be brought to light in his native land. In Sardinia, for example, the old silver mines had been abandoned because the opinion was held that they had been completely worked out by the Romans. (Romans, printer, not Russians, J. K.)

"I hope to have my dissertation about your work published about you. The more you say in it the better," says Horatio, hinting at writing NORBERT KOSKY: THE TRUE TO LIFE NON-AUTHORIZED BIOGRAPHY."

"Careful!" After your book is published I might blame your freedom to invent for what you say in it about my life. The very freedom to make things up as guaranteed to us

---

[4]Here Kosky quickly notes that Stefan Zweig, the author of, among other literary classics, *Joseph Fouché: The Portrait of a Politician*, a book swallowed up by his entire high school, also wrote *The Royal Game*, the most moving chess tale ever written. It was his final writing art — final, since shortly after he wrote it he and his wife committed suicide in 1942, in Petropolis, Brazil, his final exile, in an act of final protest against the however justified inaction of Jews of England, the United States and South America, unwilling or unable to seek a solution which could stop the mass slaughter of European Jewry during the Nazis Final Solution. To understand better — and to fully document the moral reasons for Zweig's suicide — the reader is most urgently referred to *WHO SPEAKS FOR THE VANQUISHED?* American Jewish Leaders and the Holocaust by Leon Weliczker Wells, New York, 1987. "An absolute must!" (Jay Kay), and see also, Rethinking the Holocaust: "On Sanctifying the Holocaust: An Anti-Theological Treatise," by Adi Ophir, *Tikkun*, (op. cit.)

both by the First Amendment." **The right against self-incrimination incorporated a protection against self-infamy. (Leonard Levy, 1968)[5]**

"And who would believe your story—however serious you could make it? Aren't you a professional story-maker?" Horatio laughs. "Look, Norbert, all I need from you is an interview about your views. A critical controversy over *my* thesis about your views—on sex, business, silver mining—you name it, could help get me a teaching job—even tenure!"

"Whatever I have to say, I've already said it in my novels. My fiction belongs to everybody; I don't," says Kosky.

"But don't you write with a business purpose in mind?"

"I write to express the essence of Selective Self. I'm a fictionist, not a propagandist."

"But aren't you responsible for the things you write about? Don't you want to steer your readers?"

"A fictional seer doesn't steer," Kosky muses, while sending the blonde Ms. Olympia another body-shaping sizzling skoal, (SSS) and one which, for the sake of his muscular readers, goes out to her by way of his optic muscle, as well as his optic nerve.

"If you won't steer me now, then don't blame me for putting things in your mouth," says Horatio. "For quoting you in the context of your being and out of context. Will you at least correct my errors in my spelling out of your various contradictory spells?"

"I will check only your spelling of my name, literary rank and narrative serial number as listed in the Talmud. I'm not a censor," says our literary footman.

For, you see, the issue then arises, where do we place the locus of value? Wherein is a human act right or wrong? Good or evil? Is the rightness or the wrongness of an act inherent and intrinsic in the act itself, so that it is

---

[5]Leonard Levy, *Origins of the Fifth Amendment* (1968). See also *Trauma and Affects*, by Henry Krystal, M.D. 1978.

right or wrong according to the context of the contingent circumstances? Joseph Fletcher, 1971.[6]

"Too bad. But never mind. At least, what you've said so far I've got it all on my tape. This should already give my work your *imprimatur,*" says Horatio. He turns off his tape recorder and hides it under the counter. Then he moistens the rim of a fresh glass with a wedge of lime, inverts the glass and dips it into the plate of kosher salt. He lifts the glass, shaking the excess salt off the rim. "How's Carnal Cathy giving head over heels these days?" he asks and pours Kosky another 'Ido.

"I don't know," says Kosky. "I'm no longer her Tantric mentor and she's not my dōmbi anymore."

"She sure is a salt-rimmed dame!" says Horatio.

"Being salty is not her fault," says Kosky. **Females do not emit as males do. (Auddalika)**

"She's sure too salty for me. I like a dame like that to be spicy, not stirred. Spoiled, yes. Soiled, no. All Cathy likes is to be shaken up from inside out. Anything to have her G-string, her G-spot and her G-men going. If I were you, I'd leave that G-cup gymnast to the womanizing pump it up—pump it in kind."

---

[6]See Situation Ethics: a debate (1971) between Joseph Fletcher and John Warwick, Minneapolis, 1972. Also, on the Writer's Relationship to Justice: an Essay on the Moral Responsibility of Being a Writer by Michael Blumenthal; in *Poets and Writers* magazine, 1991 (reprinted from *Tikkun*).

36

In Consolazione's private room, Kosky finds Cesare. Cesare owns the place. He also owns a great deal of real estate, some of it real, some of it only imagined. Cesare is the man Kosky is looking for. Cesare is his friend. Kosky, a man with no children, is the godfather of Polonius, Cesare's son and only child. At the sight of Kosky, Cesare puts aside his cognac and turns off the TV set.

"I was wondering what happened to you—the ultimate Polish wonder boy,[1] the night prowler turned into a wonder boy." He wraps his arms around Kosky. Some nine years younger than Kosky, a second-generation Italian-American, Cesare comes from a swarthy Italian family from Palermo. With not a drop of Jewish blood, as he often reminds Kosky, he nevertheless bears an uncommon resemblance to Kosky's father.

"How's all this press prostatis affecting your prostrate literary prostate?" asks Cesare, sitting down next to Kosky on a sofa.

-----

[1] Here, Cesare is most likely referring the reader to *Image Before My Eyes: A Photographic History of Jewish Life in Poland 1864–1939*, Museum of the Jewish Diaspora, Tel Aviv, 1979.

"Occasionally, it irritates my sacral sacroiliac joint. Irritates, but not inflames."

"You look broken to me."

"All they broke was news, not me," says Kosky, turning away in order to examine the room's new and sexy looking black leather upholstery.

Observation is a silent process; without the means of participation, the silent one must observe. Perhaps this silence is also a metaphor for dissociation from the community and from something greater. This feeling of alienation floats on the surface of the work and manifests the author's awareness, perhaps unconscious, of his break with the wholeness of self. ("Notes of the Author," 1965, as quoted in "Men into Beasts," a chapter in *The Holocaust and the Literary Imagination,* by Lawrence Langer, op. cit., p. 169)

"As we say in Mamadossola, *Se non è vero, è molto ben trovato.* Even if it's not true, it's well made up," says Cesare.

To start with, the reason Cesare has been invited to participate in this narrative is that he is an educated and reasonable man; hence, he is a non-prejudiced one.

"Face it." Cesare faces Kosky face to face. "By writing about you the way they did, de Morande and Carlyle buried you alive. Just as well that they left the coffin open enough for the rest of the media to peek at the fakir. To my mind, you are a literary Mt. Pompeii. Don't you think it's time for you to get up from that coffin? And when you do, what are you going to do to them?" Cesare nudges Kosky.

"Nothing," says Kosky. "They've got the green light."

"What green light? I'm not talking traffic. I'm talking face. I'm talking about being hit." Flushed, Cesare edges over to Kosky and with his right hand pats Kosky on Kosky's left cheek. His pat—pat, not slap—stings, but it's not painful. There is a common-law malaise in it, but no malice, no "wrongful intention generally" (*American Lawyer*), or "the desire to injure another person." (American Courts)

Cesare moves to the far end of the sofa; he is still breathing evenly. "You're not Mr. Little Guy," he says thoughtfully, and breathing normally, he is still able to collect his thoughts as if they were cash. "You're your own union boss. You are also my friend and the godfather of my kid! And you say you'll do nothing?" He loses a breath or two.

"I talk spiritual law, Cesare!" assumes a meditative posture. "In America this is the First Amendment."

"I'm talking honor and you are talking Amendment?" shouts Cesare. By shouting Cesare is no longer breathing correctly: no longer getting enough oxygen, the brain's bread. No wonder Cesare starts overheating: now his breathing is way off. He actually might go out of control.

"These two schmucks wrote that your swim or float was like Shakespeare's 'To be or not to be.'[2] They wrote all this in plain black-on-white basic English, for everybody to read again and again — and you say it's okay because of some First Amendment?" Cesare keeps on shouting.

"I say it's okay because I believe it's okay," says Kosky. "I believe in that, Cesare! To me, that law is basic oxygen, not basic English."

"That's crap. What comes first — being a man or a writer?" asks Cesare. "They spit at you in public again and again —

---

[2]CESARE GRIMWIG, THE OWNER OF CONSOLAZIONE, THE SIX-STAR ITALO-AMERICAN RESTAURANT SO POPULAR WITH THE JEWISH-AMERI-CAN LITERARY ITALIANS HE CALLED LITALIANS, CHARGES THAT SHAKE-SPEARE'S FAMOUS "TO BE OR NOT TO BE, THAT IS THE QUESTION" IS WITHOUT QUESTION AN UNACKNOWLEDGED WORD-FOR-WORD TRANSLA-TION FROM THE ITALIAN *"ESSERE O NON ESSERE, QUEST'E IL PROBLEMO'* FOUND IN "CONSOLAZIONE," A SIXTEENTH-CENTURY COLLECTION OF ITALIAN ESSAYS SHAKESPEARE "MUST HAVE CONSULTED WHEN WRITING HAMLET." ITALO-AMERICANS STUNNED.

and you do nothing!" Leaning forward, his elbows on his knees, he hides his face in his hands. After a moment he gets up and stands in front of Kosky. "They call you names, and you do nothing. This must not go unsettled." Cesare now chokes on his own inner respiration. "It must not—for your sake, for my sake, even for the sake of our little Polonius, who one day deserves to be proud of his godfather. If you do nothing, then I will make sure that they pay for what they've done to my son's godfather 'or **I'll eat my head**' (Dickens)."

"You'll do what?" asks Kosky, a calm Buddha calmly ogling the raging sea. **Writing is the most barren profession. (Leopardi)**

"I'll give them back what you owe them! By hitting you, these hit men hit me." Cesare raises his voice as well as his right hand.

"These people are writers, not hit men," Kosky goes on. "Freedom to write is *all they've got* and they have merely used that freedom to the hilt. That's all!"

"What are you—still a little war-kid?" Cesare walks Kosky to the door, a custom he too, like Kosky, learned from their mutual friend Dr. Salvarsan. "You're giving honor a brand new pen name: DISHONOR." By now Cesare has escorted Norbert Kosky all the way beyond the half-opened door.

$$37$$

"Face the music: as a Jew, you were born to hear 'Hear O Israel!' but also to talk music",[1] says Harold Rockwell, a man with absolute ear but who can, nevertheless, hear only himself. "A man's name is like his skin; it just fits him," says Goethe as quoted from Emerson in his *brudnopsis*, and he is right! Rockwell is into rock and, at fifty-two years of age, he rocks well. Unlike Kosky, who, lacking anything absolute, lacks also the absolute ear, Harold, the musical S.O.B., speaks English with a pure English accent, but the sly slob is anything but pure.

Rockwell is also (this too must be said) the spiritual descendant of Mordecai Gebirtig, a Polish-Jewish songster like

---

[1] For the unprecedented number of unprecedentally talented music-minded Jews, the reader is referred to "Music," by Marian Fuks, in *The Polish Jewry: History and Culture* (op. cit.), a chapter which, guides the reader along the extraordinary long and dense roots of centuries of Jewish music in Poland. See also "Significant Contributions to Polish Music Made by Jewish Composers and Composers of Jewish Descent" (ibid, p. 69). Also, see *Muzyka Ocalona:* Judaica Polskie (Music Rescued: Polish Judaica) by Marian Fuks, (in Polish) Warsaw, 1989.

no other, who carried his composer's task until the end, until he was shot and killed while being rounded up with other inhabitants of the ghetto of Cracow, on a railroad station in order to be deported to Belzec concentration camp while everybody sang his song, *"S'brent, undzer Shtetl brent"* ("Fire, Our Town Is on Fire!"). But what finally matters to the American non-Jewish reader unaware of the millennium of the Polish-Ruthenian-Jewish cultural past is that Harold Rockwell is a Jewish fiddler who, having fallen off the roof of yesterday's Ruthenia, now fiddles on an even higher American roof.

"Sure you're oral—so am I. Show me a Jew who isn't and I tell you he is not a Jew. We are all members of the Oral Tradition Club and we enjoy every minute of it. All I care about is music. So what if it is only rock?" says the old Rockwell Records Khazar.

"What is the essence of music if not lull'nd roll? Lull as in lullaby, roll like in rock," he goes on, rolling his eyes to the musically indifferent sky.

"I'm not commercially minded," protests Kosky. "I carve my prose out of my inner craving."

"In the beginning was the word, but the last word surely belongs to music. 'Music is Love in search of a word,' said Sidney Lanier[2] and he was right. These days only music brings the dough and fame. Write song lyrics for me! Such lyrics as:"

---

[2]Sidney Lanier, who for several years played first flute in Baltimore's Peabody Orchestra, wrote "The Symphony" and "The Marshes of Glynn," the poems "which alone would suffice to keep Lanier's name on the scroll of great American poets." (Reuben Post Halleck, 1934)

Were I a bird of domestic grove,
I would not sing in any stranger's clover,
Neither for water, nor for the forest,
But under your window and for you alone.

(Stefan Witwicki, 1829)

Rockwell intones Chopin's lightest mazurka, and even though he comes from Ruthenia, he does it in his heavy-duty Hannah Arendt German-Jewish baritone.

"I play on a different key," says Kosky, glancing through the window at Harold's own Rockwell Plaza, fifty stories below.

"So what's the big deal?" Rockwell shrugs. "Chopin once said that nothing is more odious than music without hidden meaning."

"Now that everybody knows you're your monastic Self hiding in your novels why don't you hide it in music? Write me a Scorching Song!"

"How does one write a pop song?" Kosky ponders aloud.

"First one picks a *leitmotif.*" Rockwell brightens. "Then, one polishes it, one dampens it, one plays with the drone bass, one sidesteps the sexually dominant sevenths, one sucks on the submissive triplets, one enjoys the feminine endings, and, again and again, one repeats one bar as often as you can! But, above all, if one is serious about art, about pure music, one remembers to preface all that by saying, as Chopin did in capital letters, "THAT'S MUSIC: IT'S NOT FOR DANCING." Rockwell is practically out of breath, but he knows how to make up for it and so he keeps on rocking well.

"Most of our top singles are two-strophe love songs which make up in intensity what they lose in length," he goes on, no longer breathlessly. "Today Chopin—even Paderewski and Aleksander Tansman would write rock—the music for the masses. It's simple. What else is left for you if not writing music after all that Floutus Lotus?"

"Silence," says Kosky. "I've been voiceless before." **Prose has no stage scenery to hide behind. It is spontaneous but must be fabricated by thought and painstaking. Prose is the ultimate flower of the art of words. Next to music, it is the finest of all the fine arts.** (H. L. Mencken)

"Your mother was a pianist and everyone knows you loved her—loved as your mother but also as a boob-bobbing lovely-to-look at woman. Now, as a result you love music. Music is your rallying cry. You were even able to write a novel about music disguised as a novel about *Le Sex Black*. That's the only one I really loved," the old goat goads him.

"Kosky's readers won't mind such admission from you," says Kosky. "And my publishers would love it!"

"Just think—" Rockwell muses. "Our spiritual origins are pretty much the same. You and I came to this country from Ruthenia more or less at the same time, and with no money and no connections, and look at us now! Today I'm a Big Boy record producer—and who are you?"

"I'm a novelist: a fabricant of tales about Carnal Confusion (CC). That's all."

"There's nothing wrong about being a fabricant," says Rockwell. "At one time wasn't your father a fabricant too?"

"He certainly was. Like most mortals, he needed breath as well as bread. He was engaged in a material enterprise only in order to pursue his reading. He saw himself as *kos,* a *Mimus polyglotos.*"

"He certainly was," Rockwell agrees. "But reading means you can only move your head only so much to the left or so much to the right. It's damn catatonic. You can listen to music in any position."

"One mustn't compare books with records," Kosky objects.

"Then compare your record with mine. Compare what your prose has earned you with what my *prosaics* have earned me! Did you know that just about every seventy seconds—make it sixty-nine—someone somewhere buys a Rockwell

592

record?" He points at a large wall poster which shows a young black woman, "photographed as a fusion of Socialist Realism with Capitalist Nirvana." (Jay Kay).

"I have never seen a black woman as good-looking as this one," Kosky declares. **What he needs is a woman. (Haggadah)**

"This one is sure not just another pretty sister," says Rockwell. "Call her Symphony in Black. Call her Black Spectacle."

"Could I possibly call on her?"

"Call on *her?* Are you kidding?" Rocking in his made-to-order easy chair Rockwell now sniffs oxygen from a custom-made oxygen bottle set in a gold container. "She is CARMELA LEROY—the lead singer of the Coybantes!" he headlines.

"Music is an important muse. I write to it as well as with it," muses our literary Muzak man. (Printer: Muzak, not music).

"Then keep on writing different songs for me and I'll have her spin it for you any time." Rockwell gives Kosky a calculating as well as cultivating look. "Would you like to have her?"

"I don't collect records," says Kosky.

"I mean, would you want to have her climb all over you?" Rockwell stops rocking in his chair.

"Sure I would. I'm her soul brother. Show me a soul brother who wouldn't want her for a soul sister?"

"You can be with her anytime," says Rockwell.

"How?" **Music is sounding form in motion. (D. Hanslick, 1904)**

"As a gift from me in exchange for a promissory music note." Rockwell smiles like Doctor Faustus. "Promise me that you'll give some thought to my prosaic offer."

"And if I promise but won't be able to deliver it?"

"It's my tax-deductible risk, not yours," says Rockwell, while our titubant titien titubates to the poster where, his nose between Carmela's ebony thighs, he examines her ebonesque body; a body without a trace of bone to it.

593

"I promise," Kosky dreams aloud.

"Then just tell me when you want the demo."

"The sooner the better," says Kosky. "I'm hard-pressed for creative time."

Once all this is firmly grasped, the mechanism of the sexual impulse becomes easier to understand. Don Juanism, for example, becomes immediately comprehensible. The easiest means of achieving an immediate broadening of consciousness is the sexual orgasm. (Colin Wilson, 1963)

38

At home Kosky pulls down the shades and turns the phone off. He makes up his cot, but he cannot make up his mind. To sleep or to write? **In the night which surrounds us only human creation traces the way. (Karol Hiller, 1933)**

Too bad that **We do not live in a void. We never suffer from a fear of roaming in the emptiness of Time. We remember where we came from. (Abraham Joshua Heschel, 1949)**

Too bad that **This freedom, which is an essential part of him and from which he cannot escape, carries with it the fact that he is radically threatened. (Paul Tillich)** Too bad that, when it comes to writing, **The damned stuff comes out only by a kind of mental convulsion lasting two, three or more days — up to a fortnight — which leaves me perfectly limp and not very happy, exhausted emotionally to all appearance, but secretly irritable to the point of savagery. (Conrad)** And, finally, isn't it great — great, not bad — that each time when Kosky went through one of his narrative fits, **The sense of life, the consciousness of self, were multiplied almost ten times at these moments which went on like a flash of lightning. (Dostoyevsky)**

Too bad that, in order to become able to come up with the

new associations of ideas a storyteller needs more than *A Stroll with William James,* (by Jacques Barzun, 1983). While human, and even humane, associations are easily found in any state, city or federal Directory of American Associations, new literary forms are not.

By now all ideas have been appropriated many times over by those eager to rest their foundations upon at least one lasting idea. Lasting, not last, and certainly not latest!

Moreover, when all the scenes have been completed and the narrative changed to a third-person point of view, I think there will be a much greater sense of unity than now seems possible. . . . (Thomas Wolfe to Max Perkins)[1]

His state of mind is in a state of insurgency. On one side quite united by now, a coalitionary force representing his inner government: the centrally ruling self-elected Self, the collective mind, and various other spiritual agencies all run by his Ruthenian-Jewish soul. At the other side rebelling against him, are the countless masses of arguments united under one blue star of David. These masses are kept at bay by his inner armed forces. His armed forces, in case you missed the *pointe morale,* comprise, above all, the SS-69 mis-

---

[1] "Moreover, since parts of the manuscript were written in the first person, [John Hall] Wheelock was obliged to change them to the third person all the way through. There was one 'I' which might have been intended to mean 'I, the author,' and which Wheelock therefore did not change to 'he.' Wolfe discovered it after the book was published, and brooded over it for years." (Elizabeth Nowell about Thomas Wolfe)

PROOFREADER TO AUTHOR: I hope Wheelock did not claim that as a result of making such changes he had given Thomas Wolfe his third-person style.

AUTHOR TO PROOFREADER: Of course not! As a talented poet who also became a legitimate book editor, Wheelock knew the difference between contribution and creation.

sile-armed narrative Navy: they protect the free passage of ideas and associations over his narrative waters. Then, there is the CC-96-equipped storytelling Air Force which, by guaranteeing the fresh and unobstructed supply of air to his lungs and oxygen to his brain, is in charge of the spiritually supreme Force Nine. Air—not Water!

Our sexual Don now dons a black'nd white pajama and, his inner alarm ringing, he goes to bed without setting his outer alarm clock. He has nowhere to go but into sleep.

A metaphor is an invitation to an activity, ending in an impossibility. (For you cannot _actually_ think of something in terms of something else: any metaphor must break down somewhere.) When one reads or hears 'Macbeth has murdered Sleep,' one tries to realize it in mental pictures but gives up baffled. (This, in fact, worried an eighteenth-century editor, who wanted to amend the line to read 'Macbeth has murdered a sleeper.' P.N. Furbank)

Kosky has barely fallen asleep when the sound of the house phone ringing in his kitchen wakes him up. So long, Macbeth! Groggy, he gropes his way to the kitchen and picks up the receiver.

"_Señor_ Kosky! _Señor_ Kosky!" Santos, the doorman, speaks to him in a high pitch. "There's a delivery for you, _señor._"

"What is it?"

"It's a lady."

"I don't expect a lady."

"Are you okay, _Señor_ Kosky?" Santos hisses. "Carmela Leroy is here and you don't expect her?"

"Carmela Leroy? Are you sure?" Kosky wakes up to his dream.

"Am I sure? Sure I'm sure."

"Tell Miss Leroy I expect her," says Kosky.

He rushes to the toilet where he sets a new record for fast self-service. Just when he is finished, his door bell rings six times.

Tripping over nothing, our Man of Conflict opens the door — and there, standing in front of him, is The Black Symphony.

"You must be Pamela Leroy, I mean *Carmela*," he says.

"I 'must' nothing. I am." The African Queen flashes her teeth.

"You look great. You are a living poster," our Khazar prince tells her. He then leads his queen to the black leather chair placed in the center of his living room.

"Had Freddie Chopin seen you looking like this" — Kosky intones, "what a black mazurka would he write!"

"Never mind Freddie. How about you?" She comes straight to the point sitting down.

"This is morally awkward," says Kosky.

"Awkward or wrong?" the pinup girl pins him down.

"It's morally ambiguous since I actually never expected to see you in person," he tells her the truth.

"You didn't believe I was serious?" she breathes.

"I didn't think Harold was. He's such a floating DOM."[2] Kosky inhales her buoyant aroma.

"Seriously. I like to play at any speed." Toying with him Carmela walks around the apartment.

"Jokes aside," says Kosky, "why are you here?"

"You know why. I'm here to convince you Harold means business. To convince you, not to corrupt."

---

[2]DOM (Ruth).): for House, but that's not what it means in New York. Says Petronious: "New York's *dirty old man* is the smartest, most elegant, best-dressed, most glamorous, cleanest, wittiest, most charming and sharpest D.O.M. in the world! And that includes London, Paris, Hong Kong and St. Petersburg. The New York D.O.M. must be fastidious, natty and stylish. Otherwise, he's just another dirty old man . . . always under suspicion and with a very limited range of operation." (1966)

She places her necklace and bracelet on top of the copier. Defiantly, our moralizing Fuddy Duddy tightens the belt of his fatherly robe while she slips out of her virginal Saharan wrap, leaving on her white-lace brassiere, white-lace panties and white-lace stockings for him to stare at.

To me inspiration and creativity come only when I have abstained from a woman for a longish period. When, with passion, I have emptied my fluid into a woman until I am pumped dry then inspiration shuns me and ideas won't crawl into my head. Consider how strange and wonderful it is that the same forces which go to fertilize a woman and create a human being should go to create a work of art! Yet a man wastes this life-giving precious fluid for a moment of ecstasy. (Chopin)

She unhooks her brassiere and, freeing her breasts, lets it fall to the floor. Her panties follow, then her stockings and shoes. A Venus of Bronze stretches on his cot.

"I'm ready," says the black mazurka.[3] "Put that needle on the record—but don't scratch it!" Needling him senselessly, she stretches sinuously while looking him in the eye.

"I am not. Not yet—and might never be," says Kosky.

Love, such as found in society, is no more but the exchange of two imaginations and two foreskins. (Chamfort)

---

[3]The Black Mazurka, Chopin's most exotic work, and the one least plotted along predictable ABABA, ABCA and ABAC lines, was written in 1849, a few months before Chopin died. It was published posthumously as his opus 68. (Too bad Chopin never made it to opus 69: J. K).

69

I was like a man who is drowning and who suddenly, at the last gasp of his dying effort, feels earth beneath his feet again. My spirit was borne upward by the greatest triumph it had ever known, and although my mind was tired, my body exhausted, from that moment on I felt equal to anything on earth.

(Thomas Wolfe, 1933)

"As *The Healer* was about to go to press, Dustin Beach Borell, the all-powerful chief editor quits Eidolon Press to become editor-in-chief of Flotilla Press — a large publishing concern concerning itself with the mass publication of para-literary easy-to-operate literary sloops and ketches rather than the more complex tall ships" in the headline-making words of Sim Thomas Temple, Jr., speaking on WHM-TV.

As a result, with no one in charge of Kosky, Kosky's manuscript went straight to the printing shop without having included in it the final text as it appeared in the author's final galley proofs. To Kosky, who spent all these years "mounting nonstop his narrative horse — all this amounted to his dishonorable dismount." (Jay Kay)

. . . what I feel is an immense discouragement, a sense
of unbearable isolation . . . a complete absence of desires,
an impossibility of finding any sort of amusement. The
strange success of my book and the hatred it aroused
interested me for a short time, but after that I sank back
into my usual mood. (Baudelaire)

At the Eidolon Press Office Building, Kosky, our raging
bantam, stands up to Marion and John, facing them both in
their newly appointed publicity suite.

"How many copies of the mutilated first printing of *The
Healer* have actually been sold?" asks Kosky. **A book is a
postponed suicide. (Cioran)**

"Not even ninety-six," Marion whispers.

"C'mon, tell me the truth." **He is pretty certain to come
back into favor. One of the surest signs of his genius is
that women dislike his books. (George Orwell)** (Books,
printer, not boots!)

"Not even sixty-nine," says John, swallowing one of Marion's Yoni'nd Linga Multipotency Vitamins.

"Please be serious," says Kosky.

"Do you really want to know?" Marion and John ask him
in Simultan™ — "a new tongue always spoken in unison in
the U.S. publishing business." (Jay Kay).

"How many?" our **wanton young Levite (Congreve)** goes
on, waving his own free copy of *The Healer*. **"What I have
written, I have written." (Pontius Pilate, John 19:22)**

"Frankly, as of this hour we haven't sold a single copy," says
Marion, and this time she says it with a glow of recognition.
"Not one copy sold," she repeats. "Not one copy in a nation of
some sixty-nine million potential book buyers! No other
book in recorded memory can claim such a no word-of-
mouth performance." She raises her tainted eyebrows and
almost forgets to drop them down.

"What do you make of it?" asks Kosky. Color his face

Alchemical Ash.

Gautier says: "In those days it was the prevailing fashion in the romantic school to have as pallid a complexion as possible, even greenish, almost cadaverous. This lent a man a fateful, Byronic appearance, testified that he was devoured by passion and remorse. It made him look interesting in the eyes of women." (G. Plekhanov, 1899)

"It's a publishing event! A publishing event like no other in the recorded or yet-to-be-recorded, history of the book business!" says John.

"It's a record-setting event with precedence set by *The Healer*. Pure literary magic," says Marion.

"This could be proof of your healing power: maybe you willed your past readers not to buy a single copy of *The Healer*—a book that could affect so many of their no longer innocent minds," says John, casting a soulful glance first at a single copy of *The Healer* held by Kosky in his hand, then at the trembling hand of Kosky.

"And all this happened in spite of a huge bag of mixed and mixed-up reviews." Hands down, Marion hands him a fat envelope.

"Wow! That's a lot of free ink!" moans John.

"Good." **A writer is an ink-spiller. Ink is a form of water. (Israel Kosky)**

"A lot of valid criticism too," cautions Marion.

"Good. **I like criticism but it must be my way. (Mark Twain)**

Time to go. The author and his publicity commanders embrace one another. It is an awkward parting, but so is the situation.

On the way out, Kosky runs into De Quincey. "Did you get the latest no-sales sales figures?" asks De Quincey.

Kosky nods that he did.

"I hope you are not upset by such upset," says De Quincey, walking Kosky out of the room, then escorting him the way a prison warden escorts a prisoner, all the way downstairs to the company's back door, the only nonrevolving door in the entire Eidolon Press Company. "Not an accident in the industry, known to be more revolving than evolving," (Jay Kay).

"I might be K.O.'d as an author but otherwise I feel quite O.K.," says our prototypical man-of-letters "whose latest narrative prototype never made it to the mass assembly line." (Jay Kay)

"Now why didn't your book instantly buoy up? Why didn't it buoy up to become at least number six or even nine on the *Times Square Record Bestsellers List?* Boy, it beats me!" says De Quincey.

"It also beats me," says our literary nameless Boy. "I've beaten my brains as well as my meat working on these Working Papers for 6.9 spirtually lean years," says Kosky. "Do you suppose the book failed because this autofiction is not a *sensu stricto* thriller? Because the time of it has not yet returned? Returned, from the *letterary* (letterary, printer, not literary. Thanks! J. K.) Grand Beyond."

"Why doesn't it sell?" De Quincey keeps wondering. "Is it because, for the first time in your assholistic fiction, you stayed away from female assets: your favorite obsession with aSS—with women's behind?"

"It's beyond me. Me and my behind." Kosky ends his new **Beyond sounds better than behind.** *(Safe Sex Dictionary,* 1988)

"Still and all, you've succeeded admirably," De Quincey says with a parting smile, as the author and his publisher are about to part company. "You've willed—I mean willed, not forced—your very publishers to publish *The Healer of 69 Degrees* at no moral cost to your readers, and, since we can deduct the total cost of its publication, at no financial loss to us," he stresses. They shake hands. Exits Norbert Kosky.

Isolated and withdrawn from the world, he is yet a light

and a beacon to others. *Yod* is the letter of the phallus, creative power, and in terms of sexual symbolism the Hermit means masturbation—the true self has reached puberty, as it were, the magician has found the Master in himself. Complete in himself, solitary and virgin, the Hermit's plants all have white flowers, emblems of purity, uninvolvement. He is a symbol of the fertility, of absolute self-reliance. (John Cowper Powys)

SS

These days, self-quarantined, our bitter and salty American storytelling PushHome™ pusher[1] has turned into an ultramarine hermit. He lives on *Nostromo,* an unassuming inboard-outboard American-Thai fishing junk of the Sea Robin class, which he has leased from the Muscovy Marina in Little Siam, the colorful part of New York with himself inside, he keeps it anchored on the Hudson River across from the Cloisters, "the New World's totally medieval museum." (Jay Kay). Simple living, like simple reading, comes to him most naturally. Isn't he, after all, the son of Israel Kosky and a grandson of Max Weinreich, whose namesake wrote in America the monumental History of the Yiddish Language? See Max Weinreich: Scholarship of Yiddish, in *The Jewish Presence, Essays on Identity and History,* by Lucy Davidowicz, 1977.

While—so the prospectus says—*Nostromo* can comfortably sleep six and feed nine, at this juncture in its sixty-nine years of service, the junk can comfortably sleep only one: Commander Norbert Kosky.

---

[1]PushHome,™ Kosky's name for Homeless Vehicle. (See Homeless Vehicle Project, in *October* magazine, MIT-press, Winter, 1988.)

These days, Commander Kosky does not complain. These days he believes a man is a spiritual island, even an archipelago—by this he means himself since as a good Jew he does not proselytize. At a time when most people must live a fixed existence and live it on fixed incomes and at a fixed address, his fluid income combined with an exclusively fluid address adds new spiritual substance to his already fluid character. **"I believe that the crowd, the herd, will always be detestable. Nothing is important but a small group of always the same minds who pass the torch to one another." (Flaubert to George Sand, 1910.)** To a writer, that is an advantage: it helps Kosky to concentrate, and to work, on his work No. 10, his next-in-line alchemical dramatical compost about Tristan and Isolda, the couple of about-town modern lovers.

The embarrassing difficulty is subsequently to return to my own self for, in truth, I no longer am very clear about who I am. Or, if one prefers, I never am; I become. (Gide)

When your house shakes in all its members and sways unsteadily on its keel, you fancy that you are a sailor cradled by gentle zephyrs. (Balzac)

"Life upon water comes as easily to me as it does to a Clown fish,"[2] Kosky writes to Dustin Beach Borell, who, with the word "beach" in his name, would surely not object to anyone floating full-time upon the water. "To start with," goes on our literary upstart, "this boat gives me freedom and comfort obtained at a third of the price I used to pay at the Manfred for my two-room writing cell." What he does not say is that the boat's limited space has forced him to edit out from his life "all the superfluous adverbs and adjectives and to stick to the verb and noun, to what really matters in good living as

---

[2]The Clown fish: "perhaps the best known of the marine aquarian

well as on a tightly written page," in Kosky's own words.

Leo has run away on the spur of the moment. Awful! He says in his letter that no one is to look for him — that he has left forever his peaceful life of an old man. As soon as I had read it I ran out in my anguish and threw myself into the pond next door. (Sophia Tolstoy).

Whether in life or in literature, the forces of life come wearing different disguises. Indifference is but one of them, and just think what a non-indifferent difference the letters *in* can make when added to the otherwise sexually exciting word *difference* to which the French routinely add the words VIVE LA. Suddenly, some of his friends, among them Cesare and Carmela, tell him on the phone (with no phone on his boat he calls them from a pay phone on the nearest dock) that his chartered *Nostromo* is not safe enough for them to visit. As if they could not see him on *terra firma* outside his *Nostromo!*

Alone on his boat, Kosky **circumambulates the city on a dreamy Sabbath afternoon** as Melville advises him to do, going **from Corlears Hook to Coenties Slip and from thence, by Whitehall, northward.** By now, he has discovered that **without fish, there is no Sabbath. (Haggadah)** and that there is more to water than fish: there is fishing — "though, since fishing is work, never on the Sabbath," (prudently advises Jay Kay.)

A million people — manners free and superb — open voices — hospitality — the most courageous and friendly young men.

City of hurried and sparkling waters! city of spires and masks!

City nested in bays! my city! (Walt Whitman)

To test *Nostromo,* as well as himself, Kosky takes her all the

---

fishes." (Herbert R. Axelrod and William Vorderwinkler, 1956) way up the Hudson River[3] and past Bear Mountain, then all the way down, past Wall Street—but no farther than Liberty Island, near Manhattan, the address of his beloved Statue of Liberty.

With *Nostromo*'s seaworthiness tested in the smooth, as well as rough, salty and sweet waters, our captain pronounces her spiritually safe. Otherwise, our angling author keeps one anxious eye on the sextant,[4] his favorite sexual-sounding instrument, and the other on the fat envelope he received from Marion, one which contains most of what the American Fourth Estate said about him and his *"free as a bird"* (Plekhanov) literary narrative master sheet piece.

Time to open Marion's envelope and feed his esoteric Self.

He reads review No. 1. **All one can say is that the novelist has mistaken his medium or fallen short of it. He is writing something that resembles Old Testament rhapsody but differs from it in not having the living core. He most certainly is not writing fiction. Perhaps his material might eventually prove to have the highest usefulness for fiction, but before it can become fiction. . . . it must stay longer in the tanning bath or the rising pan, it must be leavened—or whatever metaphor will suggest that a transformation must occur before it can acquire form. The essential thing has not yet been done to it. (De Voto)**

Imagine this! De Voto (alias John August) is the very man

---

[3]"The Hudson River moves in two directions. Twice daily 150 miles of the Hudson pulses with tides, first north from the Atlantic, then south as it drains from its merger with the Mohawk River." *Hudson River Villas* by John Zukovsky and Robbe Pierce Stimson, 1985.

[4]Sextant: sixth part of a circle; also an instrument used in navigation and surveying to measure angular distances; not to be confused with sextain (a stanza of six lines) or sextan, i.e., something recurring every fifth, or by inclusive reckoning sixth, day. Don't confuse with sexton, "officer charged with care of church" (COD).

who dared to declare that all American writers of the American twenties TURNED THEIR BACKS ON AMERICA.

Let's see, what else do we see here. Oh, yes, good old D. S. Merezhkovsky criticizes *The Healer* for its "moral format" which to him resembles the climate of the *Notebooks of Leonardo D.V.* How can a format resemble climate? C'mon Merezhkovsky, that's unfair. Enough said. Another review. This one is by A. A. Malinovsky (the pseudonym of the American critic Bogdanov, the guy who claims that new proletarian culture must break off all links binding it to bourgeois mankind: J. K.). He praises Kosky for "breaking away in *The Healer* even from the remotest notion of the novel," and has a few nice things to say about the novel's footnotes, which he calls "the indispensable tools of proletarian enlightenment." On the purely spiritual front, Yakov Frank, writing in the *Muslim & Christian Literary Magazine*, chastises Kosky for his use and abuse of Sabbatai Sevi but does not object to Kosky's use of Tantric Yoga as a means to "a veritable *kahal* of sensual ecstasy." He should know. He is the Polish-Jew who first connected to Islam via the Sexual Revolution, then converted to it only to become a Christian seduced by the freedom of Confession. What else? Oh, yes, a short review by Jerome Bentham, who has a few nice things to say about Kosky's abandonment of the article "the" as well as of his openness in matters of literary secrecy. **Bentham's pleas for publicity, and his claim that "without publicity, no good is permanent; under the auspices of publicity, no evil can continue," is, to my knowledge, the strongest challenge to administrative secrecy in print. (Sissela Bok, 1983)[5]**

---

[5]"Secrets of State," Chapter 12 in *Secrets: On the Ethics of Concealment and Revelation* (1983). See also her *Lying: Moral Choice in Public and Private Life* (1978). Above all, read "On Publicity," an essay on political tactics in *The Works of Jeremy Bentham*, ed. by John Bowring (Edinburgh, 1843).

Another clipping, another lost breath.

Mr. Conrad is words;. . . His style is like river-mist; for a space things are seen clearly, and then comes a great grey bank of printed matter. (H.G. Wells)

Just then, to the left of *Nostromo,* he spots a veritable high school of stripers, six or nine at one time, as these shamelessly nude fishes strip out of water and, arching into the air, seize their feed in a brief display of purple blotch against the green indigo. Meanwhile, a steady wind keeps pushing the unsteadily drifting *Nostromo* — drifting with the engine turned off — closer to the shore — while, resting comfortably on his cot, Commander Kosky keeps on reading one review after another.

One more? Why not. This one calls Kosky *a politically ultraconservative* 1969 literary sex invader. That's O.K. But then she also calls his character a renegade. His character, not him. Now what does this say about Jay Kay?

The *renegade* exhibits a characteristic loyalty to this new political, religious, or other party. The awareness and firmness of this loyalty (other things being equal) surpass those of persons who have belonged to the party all along. In sixteenth- and seventeenth-century Turkey, this went so far that very often born Turks were not allowed to occupy high government positions, which were filled only by Janizaries, that is, born Christians, either voluntarily converted to Islam or stolen from their parents as children and brought up as Turks. (Simmel) Enough of such ethnic reflections.

Another clip. This one from *Fictional Art* magazine. The headline: NORBERT KOSKY'S SELF-STYLED MONOFICTION. "Norbert Kosky stresses water, not air, as the main ingredient of his newest purofiction. A natural progression of a fiction writer who made a career of putting too much fiction into his life, but not enough life into his fiction."

Finally, at the bottom of the envelope, Kosky finds what he

has been waiting for: a major review written by no less than *the* R. H. W. Trowbridge, the British critic and biographer known for such classics as *Seven Splendid Sisters* and *A Beau Sabreur* and published in — *Sincerity and Authenticity Literary Monthly* (*SALM*), which, at the time of this writing, has been for years the country's most prestigious publication "devoted to literature viewed as confession — as well as to confessional literature." Entitled, simply, *Cagliostro,* the piece occupies — indeed invades, six full pages accompanied by a large, full-page caricature of our Count Alessandro di Cagliostro, shown on its front cover, the very way the already famous Cagliostro once appeared. Ironically, the caricature is an exact replica of Houdon's famous bust of Cagliostro made shortly before Cagliostro went bust. Houdon was then the most influential sculptor in the world.[6]

Kosky glances at the Trowbridge piece again maintaining within a posture no different from the one he reserves for reading the prestigious *Polo* magazine.[7] In choosing for his subject Kosky (whom he keeps on calling Cagliostro), R. H. W. Trowbridge says he was **guided at first, I admit, by the belief that he was the arch-imposter he is popularly**

---

[6]Jean-Antoine Houdon, French neo-claSSist — who influenced generations of European and American sculptors — visited the U.S. and made studies for a statue of Washington, as well as bust portraits of Jefferson and Franklin. See his *The Bather* at the Met. Museum. N.Y. (J. K.)

[7]See "The Florida Report," in *Polo* magazine, the official publication of the U.S. Polo Association. For the best and most inspired account of the most inspiring and exciting sport of polo, the reader is invited to read *The Endless Chukker: One Hundred and One Years of American Polo,* by Ami Shinitzky and Don Follmer (Polo Publications, Inc., 1978).

supposed to be. With his mystery, magic, and highly sensational career he seemed just the sort of picturesque personality I was in search of.

Kosky is disappointed but not upset by what he reads. Back to the critic.

The moment, however, I began to make my researches I was astonished to find how little foundation there was in point of fact for the popular conception. The deeper I went into the subject—how deep this has been the reader may gather from the Bibliography, which contains but a portion of the material I have sifted—the more convinced I became of the fallacy of this conception.

That's bad, very bad, Kosky complains aloud to the indifferent sky. How many readers read bibliographies? And how many bibliographies are complete? Besides, those who compile bibliographies are often as prejudiced by the subject matter as the biographers themselves: many of them probably hate books and authors and anything to do with print or maybe even with paper.

Kosky has now let his *Nostromo* take him all the way up to Harlem and the picturesque Harlem River. He slows down *Nostromo* to a negligible speed of 0.6 knots and, himself tense like a knot, keeps on drifting over the Harlem Straits.

Now, seriously, why is he here? Just imagine! Here is this serious man of serious letters, purposefully drifting alone, on a strangely shaped bark into the 69°-wide mouth of the Harlem River.

Look at the water here! At all this shit, all this floating phytoplankton and swimming zooplankton.

Here, our skipper skips the rest of Trowbridge's essay, and navigating *Nostromo* with one hand, with the other impatiently turns the pages of this spiritually burning literary magazine, all the way to Trowbridge's final conclusion. It says:

The mistrust that mystery and magic always inspire

made Cagliostro with his fantastic personality an easy target for calumny. After having been riddled with abuse till he was unrecognizable, prejudice, the foster-child of calumny, proceeded to lynch him, so to speak. For years his character has dangled on the gibbet of infamy, upon which the *sbirri* of tradition have inscribed a curse on any one who shall attempt to cut him down. (Trowbridge, 1910)

He takes the *Nostromo* up the Hudson River, and keeps watching from afar the shape of the city. Then he watches for an hour the wild birds of the Palisades. Enough of these images of natural beauty. He lets the boat drift all the way back toward Ocean City, as these days he calls Manhattan. Soon, you can catch him circling the *Oceania*, the seagoing crusader circling the Statue of Liberty, while our Intrepid ogles from below the calves and thighs of a whole school of pushy teenage Daughters of America who push each other against the boat's railing.

A skinny, miniskirted damsel screams at him, "Hey, Pa! Don't you like my little man in the kayak?" Another one, already in a swimsuit, shouts, "S'cuse me, sir, are you Captain Intrepid?"

Such is life on water.

A new generation of men came in—a more pushful set. I was one of them. (*The Book of Daniel Drew,* 1910)

On the way back to the East and Harlem rivers, he brushes elbows with boastful motorboats of de Tocqueville class, and their passengers too cocky for words. To attribute his rise to his talent or his virtues is unpleasant, for it is tacitly to acknowledge that they are themselves less virtuous or less talented than he was. (de Tocqueville) Too fast for shaking a hand. Then he shakes hands with an obnoxious ferryboat followed by overbearing tug boats, a slick cruise yacht, "and with some ordinary dozen oil barges full of merchant marine heavies vaporing fatigue from their spiritually overinflated dinghies." As seen by Jay Kay.

I am a hermit once again, and more than ever; and am — consequently — thinking out something new. It seems to me that only the state of pregnancy binds us to life ever anew. (Nietzsche)

Night is about to fall. Full moon! What kind of moody night will it be? Will Kosky, our incorrigible mood shifter, be in the mood to tell a tall story to a tall ship? To exchange a fast joke with a slow rowboat or a gross limerick with a delicate kayak? Will the water fowl in him offend a hydrofoil with an offer of a ride, for another fast narrative feast. A feast, not a quickie?

Night. He lets *Nostromo* list perilously close to an out-of-town galleon of the *Intrepid* class, then he, a class by himself, discreetly exchanges passing kisses with an outclassed local sloop, while a discreet cloud hangs over the indiscreet moon. He turns down the advances of that old boy windjammer, but then, before midnight, he accepts an invitation to hop abroad *Madame* — an all-madam-manned houseboat offering offshore sex at half the price after midnight. Later, at dawn, passing by the prison at Riker's Island, he momentarily surrenders to the searchlight of the Coast Guard boat surveying him — a writer on the loose. **Who I am/holds/on all sides/of me like glass/holds even/above me as if I were/a masked falcon held in a jar/I sing I beat/against the perimeter/of my madness/and still this thing leaves me here/with nowhere to go except alone. (Paul David Ashley)**

At dawn, the wind changes; waters calm down. A good reason to take off. In fact, anything could be the reason since, our Trappist monk feels spiritually restless yet physically trapped. The engines which propel *Nostromo* send shivers through the boat, but not through him. His inner waters are calm: for him, traveling no longer presupposes knowing one's destination. . . .**just one fishing boat, going slowly, and drawing the wind after it. (Oscar Wilde)** His destination is where he is.

Time for meditation again.

Speeding at 16.9 knots he puts *Nostromo* through a 69° turn, a clever maneuver called "sweeping swerve" (SS) in *marinese*.

It would be worth the while to ask ourselves weekly, Is our life innocent enough? Do we live *inhumanly*, toward man or beast, in thought or act? To be serene and successful we must be at one with the universe. . . . the least conscious and needless injury inflicted on any creature is to its extent a suicide. What peace — or life — can a murderer have? (Thoreau)

At times, when other boats and water gazers crowd the Manhattan waterways, our commodore takes his boat way out to sea, but not all the way out. He keeps it well within sight of the well-meaning Statue of Liberty from where once again he faces Manhattan: **a great don of the ocean. (Walt Whitman) A pink and white tapering pyramid cut slenderly out of the cardboard. (John Dos Passos)**

From his boat, our Ruthenian Sailfish looks the city straight in the face. For over thirty years this city has been his Fair Medusa, and, fair in its indifference, the city looks straight back at him. **The sense of being in an unfamiliar place deepened on me and as the moon rose higher the inessential houses seemed to melt away until I was aware of the old island here that flowered once for Dutch sailors' eyes — a fresh green breast of the new world. (F. Scott Fitzgerald)**

SS

One day, a most creative day full of authentic disquiet with his slowly deteriorating State of Self, Kosky takes his *Nostromo* all the way to Bistro Bay near Brighton Beach in Brooklyn. There, he docks the boat at the marina of the Hesperides Gardens.

Standing quietly at the bar, our heat-seeking SAM 69 missile seeks the heat-emitting priestess of High Times. "He seeks her, anxious to make up in still-life what he missed in his stilled literary sixty-nine narrative" (comments post-factum Jay Kay).

Here, in this bar, most of these young men and women are, ironically, writers. They are matured by life. None of them live any longer in the *Country of the Young* (John W. Aldridge, 1969.) Like him, everyone here is a dilettante, that is, **a sailor who sailed out searching for a new land but drowned on the way. (Stefan Szuman)** Mind you, Professor Szuman ranks dilettante artists on a par with great inventors, even discoverers. To him, a dilettante is one who, having been in love with Art for most of one's life, loves Art without reciprocity.

Here, at this bar, most of the writers are spiritually successful. They learned their art from life, and life from art. In fact, our Norbert Kosky is a typical example of such creative self-service (SS).

And now, so many years later, nearsighted and weary, paunchy and almost entirely bald, our Dilettante Writer is suffering from biliary spasm which he tends to confuse with an imminent angina pectoris coronary—or the other way around. This is an attack which must be stopped—and stopped by a young and preferably spectacular looking Tatyana, looking the way Onegin first saw her. First, not last.

But novels, which she early favored/Replaced for her all other treats;/With rapturous delight she savored/Rousseau's and Richardson's conceits. (*Eugene Onegin*)

Tatyana was her name . . . I grovel/That with such humble name I dare/To consecrate a tender novel.

The reason is that our Samotnik is here on a blind date with a woman. The woman in question, and a question she is, could be anyone: a Damsel Fish[9] or a Good Samaritan.[10] She can be a Tatyanesque Indian, Titanesque Black, or even Titianesque, i.e., a redhead painted by Tiziano Vecelli (also known as Titian, "the red-hair-fetish man." (Jay Kay)

She is the one who, replying to his purposefully odd newspaper ad advertising for "a spiritually sublime proofreader patterned after Pushkin's premarital Tatyana," replied by sending him a black'nd white blurry photograph of herself photographed naked while looking at a copy of *Good Writing*.

With her unclear photograph in hand, unclear on purpose, our Death Dreader wanders through the crowded room.

A gleeful Love Pawn, she stretches voluptuously in her chair, her hands hidden behind her back as if bound to an

---

[8]*Eugene Onegin:* a novel in verse, by Pushkin; a new translation of the *Onegin* stanza with an introduction and notes by Walter Arndt, 1963. Read also equally great translations of "this greatest novel in rhyme ever written" (Jay Kay) by, among others, Babette Deutsch (1964), and Charles Johnston (1977).

[9]For a color photograph of the Damsel Fish see *Saltwater Aquarium Fish,* by Herbert R. Axelrod and William Vorderwinkler (1956), p. 69.

[10]In his book *On Art and Esthetic Education,* commenting upon Rembrandt's painting *Paysage* (op. cit., p. 99) and *Good Samaritan* (op. cit., p. 100), Szuman analyzes a fragment in the painting's right corner. There, a wounded rider tilts to the side as he is about to fall off a barely walking horse (op. cit., p. 100), while in spite of his so obviously forthcoming downfall, the kin of the wounded happily ride away in the resplendent coach! Rembrandt himself must have considered this fragment of *Paysage* important enough to have it followed with *Good Samaritan,* a visual follow-up of the story.

invisible post. Says her stare: "Don't look at me like that. I'm chained to my own bed, by a despot whose name is FEAR OF AIDS."

He collects the last skoal from an Oriental beauty who feasibly in her past life was in Bangkok, where (he hopes) she modeled throughout the year Sexy Summer Swimwear. After all, the note from his blind date said, "Like you, I too am into Orient (into is not far from) and want to avoid another Holocaust—meaning the killing of one part of unkind mankind by another." Not bad for a girl who, judging by her handwriting, could still be writing for *Junior Cavalcade* magazine. Her skoal says, "I'm all sex. Watch me while I do it."

Each one wants the other to love him but does not take into account the fact that to love is to want to be loved and that thus by wanting the other to love him, he only wants the other to want to be loved in turn. (Sartre)

Finally, with the photograph of him in hand, an ordinary Sweetwater Nymph finds Kosky sitting alone near the bar. While wearing no bra under her semi-transparent blouse, she is nevertheless wearing a serious expression, as well as a leatherette miniskirt and high heels as high as his expectations. She is also wearing her stereo headphones listening to music coming to her from her pocket-size tape recorder hidden in her purse or pocket. At his sight she shakes the headphones off her head, and rising to her feet—she is almost as tall as he—she kisses him lip-to-lip. Then they both sit down at a table placed in the far corner. The kiss literally tilts him over, and no wonder.

His calendar was different from that of his contemporaries. Their day was his night, and their night was his day. (Stefan Zweig about Balzac) It is a dainty kiss, full of the contemporary safe sex, eye-to-eye as well as tit-to-tit. After the kiss, Kosky pulls away from her, not in order to disengage himself from her but—far from it—to become closer to her by seeing all of her better. She is "The Temptress,"[11] one he first saw at the 1969 Vienna Biennale or was it in Bâle? Imagine a watery-blue temptress no longer tempted by sex!

Breathless, she takes him by the hand. "Normally, I'm a square! I was too shy to talk to you when I first saw you at the Conlazio — Lasconsone — Zolocone — House Steak —" She seems lost for words.

"The Consolazione." He helps her out.

"At the Consolazione." She learns fast. "I'm basically a basic person. Basic not base. From what I saw of you in *Total State*, I thought that you didn't like basic people."

"I like Basic English," he says, consoling her quickly.

I even think that I think of it, and divide myself into an infinite retrogressive sequence of "I's" who consider each other. I do not know at which "I" to stop as the actual, and in the moment I stop at one, there is indeed again an "I" which stops at it. I become confused and feel a dizziness, as if I were looking down into a bottomless abyss, and my ponderings result finally in a terrible headache. (Niels Bohr)

She toasts him with a sensual skoal. Eager to touch life and be touched by it, our dilettante artist sits down at her side. He slides his hand along her perfect waist and hips all the way down to her own slide. This is life calling on life, as well as on Art. There is nothing wrong with it, ain't it so, Professor Stefan Szuman?

He looks at her and then via her stare fixed upon him, he looks into her as if she were a transparent slide. There is nothing wrong with such a look. Slides are life's reflection. His visual touch prompts her, and she rests her most perfectly formed thigh against him. Her thigh is a work of true

---

[11]"The Temptress": detail of the central panel of *The Last Judgment*, initially called by Bosch *The Ideal Fallen Woman*.

art. Her touch is spontaneous.

"Wow! Everyone is watching us—but talking only about you! What a pisser!" whispers the nymph.

"How do you know?" he asks her.

"Because I read lips. You probably think I'm a simple square."

"You're an original. First draft." He draws her closer.

"Now why is that?"

"Because words and numbers bother you and now they bother me too."

"I don't know much about books or writers. All I know is what I see on my TV." With her bare foot, she caresses his trousered calf. "Where do you work?"

"At home." He wraps his feet around her calves.

"What do you write?"

"Words. In my book words are numbers."

"Just words? Words like from the *Times Square Record* crossword puzzle?"

"Words as in a novel. A novel is a word puzzle. Word, not worth or war." The Oscar deliverer still struggles.

"Ever since I was a kid, words have been a real puzzle for me. I could never read a vonel. I mean, *velon*," she stammers a bit.

"You mean a novel," he corrects her quietly.

"A novel." She learns fast. "Long words are worse for me. I bet it would take me longer to read a short story than it took you to write a long book!"

The twenty-two-year-old human plant plants a wet kiss on his neck, another on his ear, licking off his aging nectar. Just then he sees her and himself reflected in a wall mirror. To see what he sees, see J. Baldun Green's *The Young Girl and Death,* if death attracts you, as it clearly attracts him. See also his *Death and the Ages* at the Prado Gallery, offering **the composition of disagreeable contrast. (Antonio J. Onieva)**[12]

---

[12]Antonio J. Onieva, *A New Complete Guide to the Prado Gallery* (Madrid, 1979).

"My shrink says that as a result of watching some eighteen thousand TV hours by my last birthday, my mind is too fatigued to come up with anything on its own. He says that eighteen thousand hours equal being for nine years on an eight-to-five job. Eight to five, or six to nine. What do you think?" She looks at him thoughtfully.

"I think *only* when I write. The word is my private-access cable TV," he says, unashamedly looking into her left eye, and no longer looking into her shamefully slutty decolletage. **The man who writes thinks differently when he writes than when he speaks. Among others, he writes slower than when he speaks. The written sentence has time to calmly mature in our mind. (Stefan Szuman)**

Orgasm is orgasm, however experienced. (Albert Ellis, Ph.D.)

"I once saw *Contra Versum,* a literary talk show on my TV." A perfect *dombi,* she reassures the nonwriter in him.

"Controversy! not *Contra Versum!"* He attempts to stay calm.

"It was about — wait — a dead famous writer whose name was — his name was Weroll! He was a foreigner but like you, he wrote in English. He was once shown in *Life* magazine as the literary person Number one."

"Weroll? Are you sure? I don't recall any *life*-size foreign writer Number 1."

"No, not Weroll. Wait! Revol? His name had something to do with revolver. He was also into *futures,* into science fiction." She sets a puzzle for him.

"Wait — I really don't know." He is embarrassed, but not for long. "Orwell," he exclaims. "You mean Orwell, even though ORWELL was not his real name. He was born as Eric Arthur Blair."

"Why would he call himself Orwell and not Blair?"

"Because Orwell is the name of a British river and he was awfully British. Also, because if you turn the letters around, you get *rewol.* As in *rewolver* and *rewolution.* Turn the letters around again and you get *lewo,* which in Russian means 'left.' It's all very Kafkaesque."

"Wasn't Kafka a writer who wrote about bugs and robots?"

"He was! He wrote *Amerika*—about this country, a country he had never been to."

"You mean he was a cheat? He wrote about something he never saw?"

"Not really. He wrote about Amerika as fiction—not factual America. Imagining can be as exact as the science of sight. A change of one letter, such as changing the letter C to the letter K, can often mean invoking a different Letter of the Literary Law. It's like the difference, say, between procreating and procurating."

"But you said he had not seen *Amerika?*" She lets him have it once more.

"He saw it only in his head." He kisses on the forehead his nonliterary sexual pet. "The way we see sex when we can't touch one another. When skoal replaces sex." He skoals her sex, while in fantasy he lets his Jay Kay show up again, and the knee jerk that he is fucks the brains out of her arabesque knee.

"I wish all words were just different colors. Colors, not numbers and letters. Just think how easy life would then be. Books make me sick." She squeezes her right hand under his right arm and she keeps it there for a moment. "I wish writers were painters—not writers."

"So do I. So do I," he says and he sighs inadvertently.

"So who is your favorite painter?" she asks him, wearing no expression.

"Lorenzo Costa," he replies without hesitation. "He is my favorite because his life was far more colorful than his paintings. Lorenzo is said to have once painted the "Last Supper"—the greatest painting that ever was—but then he destroyed it and left behind only a few uninspired works. He destroyed it after Mona Chiara, his mistress, who was the wife of Asdubale Tozzi, the local guard commander, was put to death by her jealous husband after he discovered she was

622

unfaithful to him—" Kosky hesitates, then goes on—"and she was put to death by a certain creature, a half-man, half-wolf, in the most cruel way."

"Don't tell me how," she moans. "I don't want to know. My father—he's a farmer in Fabyan, Connecticut—reads all kinds of books. And every book shakes him up. One day he believes in sex, the next he says sex doesn't agree with him. Then he reads some stupid book about woman's lib, about that thing called bilib—dolib," she ad-libs.

"Libido," says Kosky.

"And he blames his libido." She squares with him.

They keep drinking in silence. To the conversationalist in him, silence is not his favorite social pastime but it is hers.

New York is the only place where, no matter how cautious or wary a person is, both parties can come out a loser. Often in the same affair. . . . the more psychotic the arrangement, the better its chances of survival here. (Petronius, 1966)

Soon she seems lost and apprehensive. "What does that sign actually say?" she asks, pointing to a well-lighted wall sign reading MEDIC ALERT: DON'T EXCHANGE BODILY FLUIDS, and then adds, "I see the letters—but I can't put them together. What I've got is called word blindness. Word blindness is congentle and reditory," she recites.

"Congenital and hereditary." The writer corrects his ideal blind date.

Congenital word blindness, also known as dyslexia, is often accompanied by oral fantasies. (*Medicine Digest*, 1986)

"Congenital and hereditary." She struggles with the pronunciation. "The words maul me; I can never get them straight."

"Neither can I," he says, moving closer to her. **As in water face answereth to face. It is customary to have a master who desires to teach and a student who does not want to**

623

learn, or a student who desires to learn and a master who does not want to teach him; but in this case the master desires to teach and the student to learn. (*Tractate Soferim*)

Moving closer to him, lifting her blouse, she lets his hand glide over her back, then back and forth from one breast to the other, then all the way down to her waistline, and below, "to a territory begging to be subjected to drastic lip suction, but never to Liposuction Surgery." (quickly interprets Jay Kay.)[13]

Just then, as our nymph and picaro stare at each other inadvertently in the wall mirror, Kosky's stare falls upon two characters crossing the room. Passing by Kosky's table, they turn out to be nobody else but de Morande, who is walking arm-in-arm with De Voto, but this time several steps behind Carlyle.

Kosky watches them calmly. Kosky's recognition of these three now belongs to his past, a useless past best expressed in the French imperfect tense, wisely reserved by Balzac for mental states which seem to linger longer than they ought to.

Besides: that whole Float or Swim Affaire has been, for him, the literary supplicant, one great lesson in literary homeopathy,[14] and hasn't homeopathy been, for years, his (and

---

[13]Liposuction surgery: the removal of unsightly but only too well seen fat deposits by means of a special suction tube which, introduced through less than one-third-of-an-inch-long incision into the layer of fat, first dislodges then sucks out through its smooth nerve-and-vein serving end the useless fat lubules.

[14]In homeopathic medicine, "preparation of a potentized remedy is a detailed and complicated process. Briefly stated, the first stage is to prepare a tincture of the selected plant by soaking it in a solution of alcohol and water for a certain length of time. Then one part of the tincture is diluted in 99 parts of alcohol and water and shaken many times, resulting in a '1' potency. One part of this mixture is mixed with 99 more parts of alcohol and water and again shaken, producing a '2' potency. For home prescribing, remedies

once, his family's) most often prescribed remedy for just about every painful or otherwise intolerable condition? No wonder: the whole homepathic potency system depends on number six, number nine, a bit of alcohol, some minerals — and lots of water.

But one must rise by that by which one falls. (Tantra)

Meanwhile, exhaling into his ear, the sweet *waterchilde* unbuttons two more buttons of his shirt, her fingers exploring his severely sweating underarms. "When my man is a writer, what I like to read is this man's body, not his mind," she whispers, sliding her hand down his back between his pants and his shirt, well within the well of his behind. "By now everybody knows your mind's working papers. But how many of your readers know the working of your body. How many?"

"Not many. Not many at all," the fictionist in him agrees with her readily.

Just now, when I'm seventy, the napes of women's necks have a sexually arousing effect upon me, both the ones which are rounded as well as those which are fluted with that sinful little curl of hair against the glow of the skin. For the joy of looking at it, I find myself following a nape, the way other men go for a leg. (Edmond de Goncourt)

After the drinks, the dinner and the nonobligatory kisses exchanged defiantly, the nymph insists he take her to his home. She knows his home is *Nostromo*. He declines to take

---

made by repeating this process six to thirty times are used. The biochemics (tissue salts) are made by mixing and grinding the crude mineral in ten parts of milk sugar. Then, one part of this is mixed with ten parts of milk sugar again. A 6X potency is produced after six of these steps." From *Homeopathic Remedies for Physicians, Laymen and Therapists,* by David Anderson, M.D., Dale Buegel, M.D., and Dennis Chernin, M. D. (1979).

her there, claiming he has nothing more to show her of himself since, by staring at each other for so long, they have already exchanged all programs available on their inner-cable memory TV.

While his home is *Nostromo*, his address, keep in mind, is South Street Seaport, where, at an old and seldom-used pier, *Nostromo* is most safely anchored. On a clear night, the pier offers not only a view of the mouth of the East River, but also the mouths as well as other parts of the body of many Pierres and Pierrinnes who come to pet one another here.

But there is no one here tonight. The night is foggy. So foggy you can barely see the end of your outstretched hand — outstretched as in an act of a handshake, not in a military salute. Disoriented a bit — he is oozing booze — WAIT! NOT TRUE! PRINTER: he is oozing ozone, not booze! Isn't drinking air as if it were a water Yogi's spiritual trademark number nine?

The task of testing oneself, examining oneself, monitoring oneself in a series of clearly defined exercises, makes the question of truth — the truth concerning what one is, what one does, and what one is capable of doing — central to the formation of the ethical subject. (Michel Foucault)[15]

He knows exactly where he stands and he has not lost his sense of direction. To his left stands Bellevue, the hospital for those whose inner vue is no longer belle. A bit farther towers the *belle* United Nations.

He saw it all, he took it all in hungrily as part of his experience, he recorded much of it, and in the end he squeezed it dry as he tried to extract its hidden meanings.

---

[15]From *The Care of the Self,* by Michel Foucault (1986); see also *Self and Others,* p. 69.

(Thomas Wolfe)

The fog lifts. Across the river, the lights of Brooklyn flicker now, as they did when Vladimir Mayakovsky and Thomas Wolfe stood here. The beam from the Statue of Liberty pierces the clouds, as much now as it did then. Kosky is about to turn away from when somewhere behind he hears the vague sound of human footsteps. **For men are wise:/ They know that they are lost. (Thomas Wolfe)**

Involuntarily, he turns around. He listens. Again, he hears the steps of three or four men sneaking toward him in sneakers.

Their presence, their hiding at night, and in the fog, does not surprise him. He suspects that these men are like him, street-smart (SS) city souls momentarily lost at night in this dark and wet urban marsh. Still, they also could be after him. Just in case they are, he could try to escape. Escape is only one step away. But which step is it?

He hears their steps again, but this time he hears them more clearly. Is this the march of History? These men march with a goose step. This time the sound of it gives him goose-flesh. All said and done he is, after all, a child of World War II! *Never mind Childe Harold!*

Now does he at last realize that, like a Gypsy, he lives on the boundary of an alien world. A world that is deaf to his music, just as indifferent to his hopes as it is to his suffering or his crime. (Jacques Monod, 1969)[16]

The sound grows louder. This time as always, time spells out the inevitable. Inevitably, these somebodies march in his direction. Inevitably, there is no escape; life is final.

---

[16]See *Chance and Necessity*, by Jacques Monod (1971). "Monod was France's most accomplished Huguenot." (Jay Kay). See also "Death in Cannes," *Esquire*, March, 1986. See also *The Pariah Syndrome:* An Account of Gypsy Slavery and Persecution, Ann Arbor, 1987.

EICHMANN: With the Gypsies, as far as I remember, nobody

Motionless he waits. Sure, he could still run away from all of this and move his inner action from Diaspora to Israel or, for that matter, vice versa.[17] **Judaism is neither an experience nor a creed, neither the possession of psychic traits nor the acceptance of a theological doctrine, but the living in a holy dimension, in a spiritual order, living in the covenant with God. (Abraham Joshua Heschel)**

Does he, the Patient of World War II, wait for them so patiently, because he is lazy? Possibly, but only if by being lazy one means refusing to drag a fallen foot of a woman all the way up to bed (a fallen foot, not a fallen woman, Printer!) *(why not?:* Printer), or losing a footnote on the way down the page. To him, lazy means easy, and since he has been writing his opus No. 9 for over six years, clearly he must find his writer's life most easy going—easy, as much as sea-going.

He is lazy, yes, but only as one who is also a bit fatigued by all this mental travel and physical vagabondry. As one who

---

worried in the least about any specification whatever.
LESS: Why really did they exterminate all the Gypsies?
EICHMANN: Herr Hauptmann, that was one of those things, I think—Führer—Reichsführer—I don't know—there were—all of a sudden it happened and the order went out—I don't know.

Transcribed exactly as spoken: *Eichmann Interrogated,* transcript from the archives of the Israeli police.

[17]"For a 'mysterious relationship' obtained between the Jewish people and the Jewish land, the reader is advised to read Chapter 14: "Israel and Diaspora," in *The Insecurity of Freedom: Essays on Human Existence,* by Abraham Joshua Heschel (1966). When Conrad once said to a Pole that wherever he traveled over the seas he was never far away from his country, or when he declared to another Pole: "The leading principle of my life was to help Poland," he was of course falling into the typically Polish habit of exaggerating. *The Polish Shades and Ghosts of Joseph Conrad,* by Gustav Morf (op. cit.).

has gone by now through most of his Self's pastures and meadows, grasslands, steppes and savannahs. **Reputation, reputation, reputation! O I have lost my reputation! I have lost the immortal part of myself, and what remains is bestial.** (*Othello*)

He is not lazy, not really, he concludes. He is exhausted. That's it! He exhausted the resources of his very Self, and why not? Self is not inexhaustible.

"Mastership is exhausting." Our mini-Dalai Lama tells her. I have exhausted my own **lung power (Shari Miller Sims)**

I'm tired, writes Jay Kay, from the very holding of my breath when writing my Breathing Opus No. 9. Writing it by balancing most evenly the art of narrative inhalation and exhalation. I'm tired from having my lungs filled with **Kosin. 1. chem. A yellow physiologically inactive decomposition produce, $C_{23}H_{30}O_7$, of Kosotoxin.** (*Webster's Second International*) and not enough of my Polin Vintage 965.

Thereupon God took a piece of Eretz Yisroel, which he had hidden away in the heavens at the time when the Temple was destroyed, and sent it down upon the earth and said: "Be My resting place for My children in their exile." That is why it is called Poland (Polin), from the Hebrew poh lin, which means: "Here shalt thou lodge" in the exile. . . . "And what will happen in the great future when the Messiah will come? What are we going to do with the synagogues and the settlements which we shall have built up in Poland?" asked Mendel. . . . "How can you ask? In the great future, when the Messiah will come, God will certainly transport Poland with all its settlements, synagogues and Yeshivahs to Eretz Yisroel. How else could it be?" (Sholem Asch, *Kiddush Ha-Shem*)[18]

---

[18]*Polin, A Journal of Polish-Jewish Studies:* Institute for Polish-Jewish

Back to the dock.

Motionless, "our literary Hippocrates waits all alone on his literary island of Kos." (Jay Kay) Maybe these somebodies are, like him, harmless kosher fellow writers? And, with *kos* and *her* present in the word *kosher* maybe they are women? "Women? What kind of women?" (impromptu prompts him Jay Kay).

Motionless, our Kos waits for the other birds. Will they only mock him or peck him to death?

He could still get into his boat in time to cast off, but, for some reason, he does not rush and so he will not make it. Why not? Because, frankly, he feels fed up with this self-appointed novelistic investiture. Ever since the war ended, he had lived a tense life made of "a noncontinuous and continuous, active and passive condition perfect tense" (John Millington-Ward, 1953). By now, his once so distinguished World War II blaze is partly extinguished. Blaze, meaning, "1. Fire, flame, bonfire. *Obs.* Flagration, holocaust, wildfire" (Rodale, 1978). The fact is that already at the age of twenty or twenty-two, in the midst of his studies under the guru Chałasinski,[19] he did not expect to live long enough to be fifty-five years old. After all, his spiritual sob brothers were dead before reaching such an age: think of Cagliostro and Balzac, Pushkin and Thomas Wolfe, Sabbatai Sevi, Romain Gary and Marek Hlasko. Particularly Hlasko: the novelist

---

Studies, Oxford. *Vol. 1,* 1986; *Vol. II,* 1987; *Vol. III,* 1988. "The most scholarly assessment of the history of Jewry in the Polish Commonwealth. (J. K.)

[19]Jozef Chałasinski: "With Stefan Szum, Jozef Chałasinski ignited my longing for writing, for my inner *chalas*. After all, in Ruthenian *chalas* is as synonymous with *szum* (as *noise* is with *rumor.* (Norbert Kosky, 1960).

who in his *Eighth Day of the Week,* defined the loveless generation.[20] Loveless, because those in love could not find a space where, alone, they could make love. No apartment of their own. No place in which they could start a family — to name only those few.

Instead, he lived long enough. Long enough to regret that, given another chance to repeat himself, he would have remained at Beulah University. **He would have taught/He would have been teaching/He would have been taught/He would have been being taught (rarely used).**[21]

The steps near, their sound muffled by *Night and Fog* (Jean Cayrol, 1955). He can almost hear these marching men breathe — breathe in and breathe out.

Then from somewhere, from inside the fog, a single disembodied voice says: *We've got him!* Before he can confront its source, someone from behind hits him on the head with something hard. Stunned, but conscious, he falls to the dock. **A shapeless figure bent over him, he smelt the fresh leather of the revolver belt; but what insignia did the figure wear on the sleeves and shoulder-straps of its uniform — and in whose name did it raise the dark pistol barrel?**

A second, smashing blow hit him in the ear. Then all became quiet. There was the sea again with its sounds. A wave slowly lifted him up. It came from afar and traveled sedately on, a shrug of eternity. (Arthur Koestler, *Dark-*

---

[20]Marek Hlasko (b. June 14, 1934 — d. June 14, 1969) "a prototypical narrative Self-man killed by an overdose of loveless sex, enough fiction — but not enough love." (Jay Kay) Read: *Killing the Second Dog* by Marek Hlasko, originally published in 1965, translated by Tomasz Mirkowicz, New York, 1990. (Hlasko also wrote *The Eighth Day of the Week*).

[21]John Millington-Ward, *The Use of Tenses in English* (Orient Longmans, Ltd., Calcutta/Bombay/Madras, 1955), p. 69.

ness at Noon.)

Instead of hearing his head banging against the uneven cobblestones, Kosky wills himself to hear *Hear O'Israel* "Call this an act of imagination call upon it when confronting a Spartan State (SS)." (adds Jay Kay speaking for the last time from the pages of Kosky's novel about a Jewish/Gypsy Mini-Messiah.)

While his tormentors rasp with effort as they drag him on and on, he consults his diencephalon—his brain's nuclear reactor in charge of his Dreamy State. As his outer head suffers gravely, grinding into yet another stone, our Man of Tremendum effortlessly dreams about the Law of Gravity, the very law great Newton discovered in the very year 1665— the gravest year for the world's Jewry. This was the year which saw Sabbatai Sevi allowed to ride on a horse through Jerusalem (even though until then Muslim customs forbad a Jew to ride a horse) but far more gravely, a year in which Sabbatai proclaimed himself—and was proclaimed by Jews all over the world—as Jewish messiah: first such case in the Jewish Diaspora's own thousand-year old own laws of gravity. Just ponder the gravity of the consquences had Sabbatai indeed succeeded then to form such partnership with God![22] No wonder that, already in 1665, in Boston, Mass. Increase Mather, the well known preacher, warned that "the Israelites were upon their journey toward Jerusalem, from sundry foreign parts in great multitudes." As a result of such spiritual speculations (SS) Kosky's Self suggests: THIS CAN NEVER BE AS BAD AS . . . **As bad as "living through Nazi occupation of Ruthenia during World War II."** (J. K.)

He is impressed with their most even breathing, a sign of

---

[22]See *In Partnership with God; Contemporary Jewish Law and Ethics* by Byron L. Sherwin, Syracuse University Press, 1990.

their superior sense (SS) of control.

They keep on dragging him all the way to the end of the pier. Being dragged face up like this is no fun—unless, of course, one thinks of the alternative: of being dragged over these stones face down.

They drag him now behind the sign IMPASSE, all the way to the end of the dockyard. But what for? Does it matter, what for? What matters is life. Life is a state of reflection.

They stop at the sign marked DEAD END. So what? DEAD END does not mean death as long as he is alive and allowed to breathe more or less evenly.

Now, these faceless men pick him up as if he were a dead doll. First, they grab him by his arms, legs and torso; then they lift him high off the ground. They stretch him a bit— then swing him back and forth, forth and back as if he were a hammock suspended between them. Then they toss him, toss'nd throw him up in the air.

When I looked once more for Gatsby he had vanished, and I was alone again in the unquiet darkness (F. Scott Fitzgerald)[23] Him, Norbert Kosky, the unsinkable Lotus man disguised as the Unsinkable Molly Brown.

The end came suddenly. (Thomas Wolfe).

---

[23]"Involuntarily I looked up. When I looked down again he was gone, and I was left to wonder whether it was really the sky he had come out to measure with the compass of those aspiring arms." (F. Scott Fitzgerald)

I believe I understood among other things not to disclose any trade secrets. Well, I am not going to. (Joseph Conrad)

What makes all autobiographies worthless is, after all, their mendacity. (Freud)

Persons attempting to find a motive in this narrative will be prosecuted; persons attempting to find a moral in it will be banished; persons attempting to find a plot in it will be shot. (Mark Twain)

This book is a description of what is, so far as the Author is aware, a new kind of hobby. (William James Sidis)

THE ONLY ALTERNATIVE IS ANNIHILATION . . .
RICHARD P. HENRICK

SILENT WARRIORS   (3026, $4.50)
The Red Star, Russia's newest, most technologically advanced submarine, outclasses anything in the U.S. fleet. But when the captain opens his sealed orders 24 hours early, he's staggered to read that he's to spearhead a massive nuclear first strike against the Americans!

THE PHOENIX ODYSSEY   (2858, $4.50)
All communications to the USS *Phoenix* suddenly and mysteriously vanish. Even the urgent message from the president cancelling the War Alert is not received and in six short hours the *Phoenix* will unleash its nuclear arsenal against the Russian mainland. . . .

COUNTERFORCE   (3025, $4.50)
In the silent deep, the chase is on to save a world from destruction. A single Russian submarine moves on a silent and sinister course for American shores. The men aboard the U.S.S. *Triton* must search for and destroy the Soviet killer submarine as an unsuspecting world races for the apocalypse.

CRY OF THE DEEP   (3166, $4.50)
With the Supreme leader of the Soviet Union dead the Kremlin is pointing a collective accusing finger towards the United States. The motherland wants revenge and unless the USS *Swordfish* can stop the Russian *Caspian,* the salvoes of World War Three are a mere heartbeat away!

BENEATH THE SILENT SEA   (3167, $4.50)
The Red Dragon, Communist China's advanced ballistic missile-carrying submarine embarks on the most sinister mission in human history: to attack the U.S. and Soviet Union simultaneously. Soon, the Russian *Barkal,* with its planned attack on a single U.S. submarine is about unwittingly to aid in the destruction of all mankind!